Wrapped in Romance

12 NAUGHTY & NICE NOVELLAS

THE INDEPENDENT ROMANCE AUTHORS ASSOCIATION

Contents

Foreword

TIRAA, The Independent Romance Authors Association, is an online community of independently published romance authors from around the globe. After a few months of hanging out on our Mighty Networks platform, we decided to collaborate on an epic project–a Christmas Romance Anthology.

Wrapped in Romance is a collective collaboration of individual talents and expertise of all twelve authors. I am so incredibly proud to have worked with such smart and talented people who not only delivered sweet and spicy HEAs in their contributions, but also freely shared their knowledge and experience when it came to making some key decisions along the way. Finding and working alongside the rising stars of the romance world has been a privilege and a gift.

I know you're here to read and support the works of your favourite writers, but I hope you'll dip into the other stories and discover new authors to love (there are many!).

Thank you for supporting indie romance, we appreciate you.

May **Wrapped in Romance** bring you delightful escapism this holiday–
regardless whether you're on Santa's Naughty or Nice list.

Happy reading–and don't forget the mulled wine!
Cindi Page
Founder and facilitator of TIRAA.
www.independentromance.com

P.S.
Don't forget to leave a review on your favourite reading platform!

Odds in our Favor

BY PIPER LEE BURNS

Can a secret tackle the relationship between a hunky forest ranger and a sports radio host before it even begins?

About the Author

I was a sports reporter in a former life, but now I'm playing a different game.

I'm committed to writing passionate stories about strong men and even stronger women, many of whom are athletes, coaches, executives, reporters, and fans. I want my stories to be like an epic sporting event: full of highs and lows, excitement and drama, and complete with breathless, victorious endings.

When I'm not writing or at the day job, I'm busy with my own team at home, including the most amazing teammate anyone could ever have, whose love is an inspiration for these stories.

I love to hear from readers, so drop me a line on my Facebook page or on my website.

Facebook: www.facebook.com/piperleeburnsauthor
Website: https://www.piperleeburns.com/
Email: piperleeburns@gmail.com

Chapter One

Sarah

As the storm descends on downtown Seattle, the only thing louder than the heavy gusts of wind rattling the windows is my co-host's uncontrollable laughter into the microphone.

"Wait, wait, wait," he wheezes in between laughs. "You think Seattle's defense is...*underrated*?!"

Thank God it's Monday and it's a non-television taped version of our podcast because I give my co-host, John Starbuck, the finger.

"Sugi," he continues, pushing his thick, black-rimmed glasses further up his face. "Come on. You've got plenty of wild ideas, but this...is absurd."

I lean into the microphone and say in my calmest, most syrupy radio voice, "It's not absurd, you're a fuc-"

From under my desk, my phone chimes quietly in my purse, making my heart leap and pulling my attention from supporting the much-maligned Evergreen's defensive numbers with wins over expected averages.

I close my eyes and try to breathe through the brain fart.

"A fu-, a fu-," I stumble, wondering not what the quarterback sack average on third down was, but what amazing message awaited me on my phone. "A fu-, grrrrr, oh forget it! Stop! Stop!"

With a sigh, our producer, Brian, cuts the live switch on the recording and the light under my Evergreens helmet goes dark.

"I'm sorry," I mutter, yanking off the thick earphones, which knocks my backward baseball cap into my eyes. "It'll just be...I need to..." I tug my hat back into place, push back from the desk and dive under the wooden top for my purse.

Don't look. Don't look. Don't look.

Turn it off and finish the show.

I find the plastic brick and thumb the buttons on the sides of the phone resolute in recording the last bit of the big Christmas extravaganza and delaying, for just a few more hours, the giddiness bubbling around inside me like a hot spring.

Awww, man, I can't.

I mean, it is almost Christmas after all.

And what is Christmas without a little peeking?

I pull the phone out enough to read the screen:

Hunter: *Hard to believe I finally get to see you tonight. The waiting is absolute torture. Trying not to think of everything at once. Focused on taking my time and exploring...you.*

A surge of heat floods my cheeks and rushes through my body, igniting an electric thrum that has grown from the first message he sent to each long video conversation we've had over the last month.

A thrum that made me ache from the anticipation and delicious possibility.

"You okay there, Sarah?"

Next to me, Brian's quiet voice snaps me out of my super-heated thought box.

"Yep," I whisper, turning off the phone and shoving it back into my purse. "Totally okay." I straighten up, clear my throat, and roll back to the desk. Grabbing my headphones, I'm fully aware of the heat in my cheeks and the amused gaze of my co-host. "Let's do this."

Brian gives me an unsure glance but flips a few switches before putting on his headphones. "Let's start with the read again, shall we? In three..."

He counts the other two numbers silently and then points to me.

I take a breath and then say in an animated voice, "Hey, Evergreens fans! Sugi here with my friends from Rounders Sports Bar and Grill, the best place on the Sound to catch a game, host an event, or just hang out. And don't forget the Four for Four Friday nights, where everything is four dollars until midnight." I glance over at John, who's tapping at something on his phone. "And Starbuck and I broadcast live from three to seven. Rounders, Seattle's premier sports bar and grill."

Brian plays a clip of a baseball smacking a leather glove and a crowd cheering. I hesitate for a moment afterward and then settle into the microphone, elbows spread wide on the desk.

"Alright, welcome back to the Starbuck and Sugi Show. I'm Sarah Sugiyama. Next to me, watching porn on his phone, is John Starbuck."

"That's me," John says quickly into the mic before he goes back to his phone.

I roll my eyes and smile. "This is it, our final segment of the show. We've been teasing our prediction for the monstrous Christmas game between your Evergreens and those hated Los Angeles Missions. But, as you know, before we give our final predictions and lay down our double sawbuck, we like to play our favorite game, Head or Heart."

Brian presses the button and the intro to the segment plays over the headphones. As soon as it's done, I click my tongue and speak smoothly. "For those of you who are new, this is the part of the show where I destroy Starbuck's silly heart predictions with cold...hard...num-bers."

"Says the woman who thinks Seattle's defense is underrated," Starbuck jokes into the microphone.

"Okay, then, tell you what. If Seattle loses, which they won't-"

Starbuck cuts me off. "Wait, wait, does this mean I have to pick the Missions? Winners of ten straight? Best quarterback in the league?"

"If Seattle somehow loses this game, then I will not only double your winnings, I will, on-air, wear a Missions jersey."

Starbuck gasps, but not a fake radio gasp. I can see he's serious.

7

"That's how much I believe in this game. The numbers are screaming a course correction for the defense. They've been this close." I hold up a thumb and forefinger to my two co-workers. "Seattle will win this game. I won't have to wear the stupid red and gold. And Christmas will be ep-ic."

I press the button on crowd applause. After a few seconds, I let it fade and offer in my most sultry tone. "So, do we have a deal?"

Starbuck stares at me for a moment and then his eyes narrow playfully. "Before I take that deal, I want to raise the stakes."

"Okay," I say slowly, a small tremble in my chest.

"We all know how much you love Christmas, Sugi."

"Uh, yeah, best holiday ev-er."

Starbuck rubs his jaw and grins. "If the Missions win the game, you not only have to wear a Missions jersey during next year's Seattle-Los Angeles games, you also...can't decorate your condo next year."

"Starbuck." I gulp. "That's...*cruel*."

"I know. Now how much do you like that Seattle defense?"

Eyes narrowing into slits, I speak daggers into the microphone. "Even. More. Seattle wins. Straight up, no points."

Half an hour later, we're wrapped, Brian's in editing, and I'm rushing around the small office flat collecting my things.

Outside, the rain explodes against the windows like icy bullets. Despite it being early afternoon, the sky is black, and the city is lit up like it's midnight.

"So, you're finally meeting this guy?" Starbuck asks, arms resting against the back of his chair, hands wrapped around a coffee mug.

I stop briefly and look out at him from under my bright red rain slicker - helpful for Seattle drivers in spotting a small, half-Asian woman crossing sidewalks in the Pacific Northwest winter gloom - with a miffed expression. "For the thousandth time, yes. If I could just find my stupid bag I left here..."

"And you're not at all worried about driving two and half hours into the mountains? You know there's a blizzard up there. Snoqualmie Pass will shut down at any moment."

"I know," I say, looking behind the couch in the corner of the office. "I drive a Subaru."

"On top of all that, playing a road game with a strange dude..." Starbuck continues.

I open the tiny storage closet for the second time and yell out from behind the door. "He's not strange! I've been talking with him every day for a month!" Tucked behind the small vacuum is the shiny silver gift bag I've been keeping hidden from the nosy sneak that was my mother. I squeal in happiness, grab the bag, close the door, and storm over to Starbuck, trying to keep the slicker hood above my eyes. "And for crying out loud! I'm 33 years old! I don't need you or anyone worried about Who. I. Date. Understand?"

Starbuck holds his hands up in surrender. "Okay," he says, pushing his glasses up his nose. "No more."

The gift bag goes into the larger duffle bag, which holds half of what I need for the weekend. The rest waits patiently in my car a couple blocks away. My hand is on my purse when Starbuck coughs and says cautiously, "What town did you say you were going to?"

"None of your damn business. Population, you."

"What? I'm your friend, I'm making sure you're okay."

I raise an eyebrow and smile. "Don't."

"Oh, come on. You've seen what they say about online dating and the creepos. It's like a minefield."

"You watch too much Dateline, Starbuck, seriously."

"70 percent of people say they resent ever going on an online date."

I sling my purse over my shoulder and wrap my keys around my fingers. "And you miss 100 percent of the chances you don't take." I stick out my tongue. "My number's bigger, so I win. Again."

"Sugi..."

"Look, I'm sorry most of the world has had problems with online dating, okay? I'm trying to be good and not brag that the first time I did it, I found a great guy."

"Are you...sure?"

"Any guy willing to wait that long is amazing!"

"I'd wait that long," Starbuck says under his breath.

I ignore his muttering and zip up my rain slicker. "He also doesn't do that dismissive, chauvinistic, oh-God-here-goes-the-girl-talking-sports-again internal eye roll when I open my mouth!"

Starbuck says nothing, but his face looks as though his eyes are rolling internally.

"Finally, he gets me wet in *all* the right places," I say in my most lusty tone before flipping the switch and shrieking, "so, yeah, he's a great guy!"

I spin around on my heel and head for the elevator, knowing Starbuck's awkwardness over discussing my vagina.

Right before I hit the down button on the elevator though, I hear a sigh and a pleading voice.

"Sarah, please, why can't he come to you?"

"Augh, Starbuck!" A blistering response sits on my tongue. I open my mouth to let him have it but stop. Shoulders slumped, his face is loaded with concern. I let out a breath. "Look, I'll be fine. Okay? I'll text you when I get back to Seattle. How about that? You can buy me a beer after Christmas."

His chest lifts a little. "Deal."

Walking back, I fling my possessions around him and give him a friendly bro hug. "Thank you for being worried about me. You're like a brother I don't want."

Starbuck hisses. "Damn, that's mean!"

"Merry Christmas," I laugh, heading for the door. "Say hi to your mom for me!"

Starbuck's voice rings out as I punch the button to the elevator with my elbow.

"Dateline, Sugi! Dateline!"

Chapter Two

Hunter

Online dating.

Thank God my brothers didn't know about this.

Seriously. If they found out, I'd never hear the end of it. Lucky for me, they both live across the pond and can't see my computer through the phone.

Because if they did...oh boy.

I'd never been one to shun online dating, though I never sought it out. I still held onto a belief that you were destined to run into those meant to be in your life.

Except I never ran into anyone while out in the woods or sitting alone in my house. I did meet all the food delivery and Amazon drivers that came by, but none of them took the opportunity to stay and chat.

So, when my sister, Lindsey, suggested I try it before officially becoming the world's youngest hermit, I asked my favorite Amazon driver, Ricky, if I should.

With a planetary eye roll, he said, "For the love of God, dude, yes." Then he handed me my stuff and stalked back to the truck.

I never saw him again.

Which ended up being a good thing, because if I had seen him, I'd have punched him in the face.

For the very simple reason that, up until a month ago, online dating was a *disaster*.

Humiliation.

Disaster topped with humiliation and a side of head shaking to go with it.

Maybe it was the shallow dating pool of Meadow Valley that was the problem.

No, I was the problem.

I was better off as a reclusive, lonely troll in the woods.

Then I met Sarah.

And everything changed.

"What do you think of this one?"

I hold a t-shirt up to my chest. Zeus, my black and white English spaniel, lifts his head and cocks it to the side as if to say, 'Really? You're going on *theeeee* date and you're wearing *that*?'

"Yeah, you're right, good point."

I'd heard her on the radio a couple of times when I had to drive into Seattle to visit the field office and her voice and energy always put a smile on my face.

Then she landed in my inbox.

After a couple of days of deliberation and repeated smacks in the head from Lindsey, I texted her. She responded instantly and ever since, it was like the sun rising after a long winter.

I stuff the shirt back in the drawer and play eenie-meenie-miney-mo with the five dress shirts I have on hangers. Fortunately for me, my game lands on the one I want anyway. I hold it out to Zeus, who yaps his approval.

As I slip on the comfortable fabric, my phone lights up with a text on the dresser.

Sarah.

A grin spreads across my face as I read the message.

. . .

Sarah: *Just checked in. Unpacking like a maniac. Will be ready though. So, so, ready...*

"You going to be okay going to Aunt Lindsey's tonight?" I ask Zeus while buttoning my shirt. "I kinda want the house to myself."

Zeus jumps up and wags his tail.

"Figures. You and that border collie. Thick as thieves you are."

After looking out the window at the thickening snow, I grab my boots and snap at Zeus, who jumps off the bed and hightails it into the kitchen.

He sniffs out his leash sitting on the counter next to my keys. Black stringy tail wagging, he puts his front paws on the stool and whines excitedly.

"Alright, dude, hang on."

I check the time.

5:30 p.m.

The plan is to meet Sarah at 6:30 at her hotel - the only hotel in Meadow Valley - and go to dinner at Von Yum, then ice skate in the town square, which is what every travel magazine highlights as the must-do in our town.

After that...well, if our recent conversations were any indication...

I look around and make sure the fireplace is stocked and ready to go and wine - bottled and mulled - is at hand.

While Zeus paws at the door and looks at me expectantly, I wonder if I shouldn't have made my place more festive. Sarah had claimed to be the biggest Christmas nut in the Pacific Northwest, and while she understood my family's weird tradition of waiting to decorate until Christmas Eve, I can't help thinking she'd be disappointed.

Better keep her distracted then.

Taking a step towards the front door, I stop dead. A present for my niece sits on the buffet, half wrapped. Groaning, I quickly tape up the rest of the paper and grab the giant ribbon next to it. Unspooling the red glittery material and hacking through it with scissors, I realize I have no idea what to do with it.

I grit my teeth.

Time to go.

Leaving the ribbon on the buffet top, I grab the present - she's two, she won't care - and my jacket from the hook on the wall. Stomping into my boots, I open and close the front door, and tramp through the crisp powdery snow sparkling under the porch light to my truck. Zeus hops in the passenger seat, tongue lolling happily as the seat warmers heat his furry ass. I scrape the snow off the windshield, climb up into the truck, and a minute later, set off for my sister's house.

As the clock on the satellite navigation flicks to 6:25, I pull into the parking lot for the first date I've looked forward to since I was in college.

I don't want to be early, so I grab my phone, open the Relations app, and scroll through the hundreds of messages we've sent to each other.

Adjusting the tightness of my jeans at some of the, uh, hotter stuff we've sent, I scroll through, smiling and laughing at how well our personalities meshed, despite her being a chatterbox with no off switch (her words, not mine) and my decidedly quieter tone.

As my sister once told me, my chosen profession should have been a mime.

Shaking my head at my sister, I reread Sarah's claim she was the queen of Seattle football, which always gave me pause.

The one giant red flag.

The one thing that could topple everything we've built up.

I'd skirted around the issue every time she brought up football, choosing instead to talk about other things like her master's degree from Harvard in business, or her unquenchable thirst for books and television shows.

I know I should face the football issue, but Sarah was the first person I felt like I could be myself around in a long time.

Not who I once was.

And that right there was enormous, so much so I was willing to keep kicking the can down the road.

Since I brought the forestry truck, I make sure the compartment with the firearms is secure and my paperwork is hidden neatly in the back. Right at 6:30, I walk across the crunchy salt-strewn parking lot and through the front doors of the Bavarian Lodge and Spa.

"Hey Hunter!"

The bright voice from the lobby is not Sarah, which I hoped for, but Michelle, a girl I went to high school with and, for one very weird week last summer, tried to shed the "friends" label with.

Thank God we're able to laugh about it.

Because it was *awk-ward*.

"What are you doing here?" she asks, tapping her fingers against the keyboard, curly brown hair draped over a black business jacket.

"Uh," I hesitate, trying to figure out what to say.

While we'd been good sports with each other since the, uh, incident, there'd always been that hint of hurt and embarrassment hiding behind the jokes.

And I didn't want to hurt her feelings anymore.

But what was I supposed to come up with?

"I'm waiting for a date," I say, shrugging and shoving my hands into my pockets.

"Oh," she says. Though her voice stays bright and professional, her throat bobs and catches. "Well, awesome!"

I scratch at my freshly trimmed beard, feeling the dots of melted snow in the soft whiskers, and am about to try to talk about hockey when the elevator chimes.

When the golden doors open, my heart stops dead.

Sarah steps out, a radiant sight that steals the beauty from everything around her. Her silken black hair, falling in waves around her shoulders, glimmers and shines against the gold laced backdrop of the elevators.

A snug gray sweater dress shows off the womanly shape she teased in our late-night conversations, complete with knee-high black sable boots.

Even from across the lobby, her green eyes sparkle as they scan the empty couches and Christmas decorations before finding me.

In an instant, I'm transfixed.

A shy, yet confident smile flashes on her face as she looks down and tucks some hair behind her ear.

In my chest, a wildfire of nerves and excitement explodes, rushing heat to the very edges of me.

I lick my lips nervously and walk over, wiping my hands on my jeans before she can look up.

"Hi," I say in a quiet voice, my knees buckling at the gentle, delirious scent wafting into my nose. "You look astonishing."

She looks up at me and what little air I had to breathe is gone. "Thanks," she says, her glistening pink lips curling into a smile. "Have to say the same about you."

I look down at myself and laugh. "What, this? Clearly, one of us got the memo that this was a date."

She looks me over with a sharp eye. "You're doing just fine," she approves. "Now, are you going to feed me? I'm starving."

Chapter Three

Sarah

I f I could leave a million-star review for the Relations app, it still wouldn't be enough to capture how happy I am.

The app carries a warning, 'Caution: people appear better in person than on the computer. Schedule that date today.'

And holy shit, they were right.

Hunter Reed is So. Much. More in person.

Leaning forward in my chair, fingers caressing the stem of my wine glass, I listen with rapture as Hunter's husky voice tells me about last Thursday.

"So, we're at his house, serving a warrant for illegal poaching. Multiple neighbors had seen him hunting from his truck. Pretty easy case for the judge if we could just bring him in."

"Sounds like he won't be," I grin.

Hunter chuckles and runs a hand through his dirty-blond hair. As he does, a wave of jealousy washes through me. That should be my hand. He sips his beer and gives me a smile that warms me to my toes.

"We're at his front door and we hear cursing around back. He's trying to escape into the woods, but he runs into his own traps! Just before we get to him, he frees himself, leaps up and darts away."

Reflexively, I hold my hand over my chest. "Did you get him?"

"He was fast but had no stamina. Maybe thirty seconds before I caught up and tackled him."

"You didn't!"

Hunter nods his head.

I smile and raise my glass to him. Hunter Reed. Enforcer. Bambi protector. Tree hugger. A beard so perfect and delectable, I want to ride it and feel the fire in between my thighs.

"Cheers," I say warmly. "To you."

I take a sip and watch him over my glass. His eyes dart away for a moment, embarrassed, and then, with a breath, come right back to me, the embarrassment replaced by a dark heat that makes me sit straight up in my chair.

"Just doing my job. People think they can use the forest to get away with all kinds of crap."

Adding proud humility to the list.

Check.

Check, please.

"Well, I wasn't there," I offer, glancing around the dark wood and white Bavarian-themed restaurant for the waitstaff. Tucked next to the large tree with golden bows and white twinkling lights, they're busy looking out the windows at the falling snow. "But I'm sure your tackle would have impressed the Evergreens. I have a sense about these things."

Hunter laughs, a warm, rich sound that makes me smile. "I'm sure you do, but I'm also sure it looked awful."

"Oh, come on!" I exclaim, flipping some hair over my shoulder. "You had to have played some football! No?"

When I mention football, Hunter's face flinches and his excitement ebbs away like a wave pulling back from shore.

"Hunter? Is something the matter?"

He looks at me, opens his mouth for a second, closes it, and then pulls a false smile on his face. "No. Nothing's the matter. Yeah, I played some football. Small-town talent. Enough to earn a letter, but then I got an internship with the Forest Service and decided to focus on that." He takes a drink and exhales. "I, uh, I read your paper the other day, the one about advanced statistical metrics causing teams to overvalue offensive production. I thought it was really good."

For about two-tenths of a second, I wonder about the abrupt change of topic, but then I spend two whole seconds realizing he was being serious about my paper.

"You really read it?"

"Then I watched your TED Talk. But if you're asking me, the paper was better. Much more in depth."

Head cottony from the wine and warmth swirling in my belly, I playfully challenge him, "I think you're just saying that."

"Really?" He leans forward on the table, resting his elbows on the white tablecloth. At the cuffs of his shirt, some dark ink teases out and I have to do everything I can to focus on what he's saying and not the rest of what's waiting under that shirt. "Well, if I didn't read the paper, I wouldn't be able to say your use of the Hibbert tool for calculating usefulness rate was flawed. I would have used Manfred's pattern of repeating returns."

He sits back against his chair and takes a drink, a coy smile spreading across his lips. "I studied some statistical analysis while getting my forestry degree."

I sit there for a moment, frozen, a shocked smile creating a buzz that electrifies the warmth in all the best places. I trace my fingertips around the rim of my wine glass before asking in a breathy voice, "And you carry a gun every day?"

Hunter shrugs. "I wanted to do more than study trees."

Before my heart can even make its next beat, my head calculates the chances of ending dinner immediately.

"Can we get the che-" I start to say at the same moment Hunter asks, "Dessert?"

We both laugh awkwardly and then I give him a look that answers his question. The dark heat in those golden hazel eyes burns brighter.

"I'll get the check," he says.

Hunter's front door bursts open and we stumble through, covered in heavy snow, the heat from our frantic lips melting the flakes on our faces.

One of his hands leaves my waist to slam the door behind us. It returns a moment later, grabbing the soft fabric and bunching it in his fingers.

I pull him deeper into his house, backing up until we abruptly crash into a wall. I gasp as his weight shoves against me, feeling his need press against the damp jean material.

Teasing his tongue with mine, I slide my hand down from his neck, reaching for the cold, metal belt buckle. When I tug at the thick leather, Hunter pulls back and looks at me with burning eyes.

"Slow down, speedster," he growls, his voice thick and husky. "You got somewhere to be?"

"On top of you," I breathe, nipping at his lip and popping the belt buckle free.

Before I can do anything else, Hunter grabs my wrists and forces my hands above my head. With his strong grip, he easily pins them against the smooth wall. My breathing quickens as he looks at me, blond hair mussed and falling over one eye.

"I said I want to take my time," he says quietly.

He glances away from me for a second to a table next to us. Keeping me pinned, he reaches for a length of wide red Christmas ribbon. When he has it, he looks back at me. "So, I'm going to tie you up, then I'm going to unwrap you. Slowly."

My chest catches and I gasp at the words *tie up*. In my head, my idiot co-host pops up, his warning trying to douse the flames inside me like a squirt bottle in the middle of an inferno.

But those thoughts are extinguished when Hunter lays a gentle kiss on my forehead. "Unless you just *have* to be on top of me," he breathes.

"No," I whisper. "I'm right where I want to be."

A slow smile spreads across those sinfully delicious lips. He takes the ribbon, winds the coarse fabric tightly around my wrists, and makes a quick bow. My heart beats faster as he guides my hands along the wall until my fingers bump into something metal.

Coat hook?

He lifts my wrists and settles the ribbon over the metal. I gasp and look up. "That's convenient."

Hunter chuckles. "Totally not planned, but it will give me time to get a couple of things."

My brain scatters with a thousand images, none of them good.

I'm really going to kill Starbuck.

"Like what?"

He rakes his eyes down my body. I lift my chest, giving him as much to look at as I can, just praying he wasn't going to stick a knife into it.

"Well, unless you got something hidden under your dress, I'm thinking condoms, a glass of wine, start a fire?"

"Okay," I whisper, trembling with anticipation.

Hunter backs up and I moan at the sudden change in air pressure. He adjusts himself in his jeans, then turns and heads for the fireplace. Taking off his coat, he rolls up his sleeves, giving me another glance at the bright tattoos running up his arm. With practiced precision, a fire soon flickers to life.

When the flames seem strong enough, he stands and walks over to the Christmas tree next to the fireplace.

"I have a surprise for you," he says with a smoldering grin. "I know how you think it's weird I don't decorate for Christmas until the night before." He squats down, reaches behind the tree and a moment later, the tree lights up in warm, twinkling colored lights.

"Oh my gosh," I say in a wispy voice. "Hunter, it's beautiful."

"We can put ornaments on tomorrow," he says, standing. "Be right back."

He disappears down a hallway. I take a breath, feeling the pulsing electricity between my thighs and my heart hammering in my chest.

All the worrisome thoughts disappear, replaced by a desperate desire to know what he's going to do.

One thing he was right about.

Slowing down.

The whole month of video chatting had made me want to rush to the end instead of taking my time.

Hunter reappears, tosses a couple of foil packets on the table, and walks to the room behind me, which must be the kitchen.

There are clinks of glass, the rip of a screw cap, and then he reappears just as soft Christmas music spills out of unseen speakers.

He sets everything down and then locks his fiery gaze on me. The breath hitches in my throat as he undresses me with his eyes, and as they roam around my body, doing other things as well.

Walking slowly around the couch, he takes off his dress shirt, laying it gently over the back of the couch. The tattoos on both arms stretch up into the sleeves of his t-shirt, bright, colorful, and also mysterious.

But I'm not in the mood to ask because he stands in front of me and reaches for the ribbon. "Time to unwrap you," he says, voice rumbling like distant thunder.

As the ribbon falls from my wrists, I intertwine my fingers in his thick, silky hair and crush my lips against his. He responds by pressing his weight against me, pinning me to the wall.

His hands find the soft hem of my dress and I cry out into his mouth when his fingers graze my thighs.

"That exciting?" he mutters against my lips.

"I've sooooo wanted this," I breathe. "I'm more lit than that Christmas tree over there."

Hunter pulls back for a second and flashes a panty-melting smile.

Even though he melted them already.

Like an hour ago.

His fingertips run firm circles over my skin, gradually moving closer to the inside of my thigh. I part my legs an inch, inviting him closer. Locking eyes with me, his hand runs higher, the dress moving with his arm, until his fingertips graze my lace-covered underwear.

Even with this lightest of touches, I cry out, but then my brain short-circuits completely as his fingers move the flimsy fabric and slide over my pussy.

"God, you *are* soaked."

I lean my head back against the wall and close my eyes as he finds my opening, curling a finger inside me.

"I thought you were going to unwrap me," I mumble, my voice sounding a mile away.

When Hunter takes his hand away from me, I curse under my breath. Wrong fucking thing to say. I try to pull his hand back, but Hunter abides by my request. He grabs the hem of my dress and pulls up. I lift my arms without resistance and a second later, the dress hits the hardwood floor with a soft poof.

"Now yours," I whisper, drinking in the fire from those devastating hazel eyes.

Hunter leans back and takes off his t-shirt, tossing it on my dress. I reach out and run my fingers over his hard muscled chest, taking an extra moment to play with the soft covering of hair.

I trace the deep line between his pecs, following it down in between his abs, which flex quickly with each breath. My fingers curl around the button on his jeans. Not waiting for permission, I undo it and spread the fabric open.

"Sarah," he whispers.

"Yeah?" I work his jeans and boxers off his hips and over his bulge. A wicked smile spreads across my lips as his thick rod pops free, pulsing and pointing directly at me.

"You...I...," he fumbles, watching me slide down the wall, pushing his jeans to his feet. "I..."

I end his words when I take him in my mouth. I reach my hands around his hips and pull him toward me. Head resting against the wall, I let him slide gently in and out of my mouth, while my hands run up and down his thighs that feel like they're sculpted from granite.

Growling with appreciation, he pulls back a minute later. "Stand up," he orders in a voice that was losing control.

I do as he says, working my way to standing, releasing the hooks of my bra as I do. Hunter leans in and gently, passionately takes a nipple into his mouth, pulling on the puckered flesh until I cry out in surprise. He takes that as an invitation to do the same to the other. I thrust my chest toward him in response. Every swirl of his tongue releases zaps of electricity that travel to my core.

And just when I start to feel like I could come from nipple stimulation alone, his fingers find my hood and he pinches it gently. The pressure is so great, I bear down on his fingers, moving my hips back and forth, pushing the release closer. The coolness of the wall shocks my heated skin as the muscles in my legs start to shake and I grab his neck ready to, needing to...

"Oh, God!" I cry as the pressure snaps and releases, wave after enormous wave surging through me, obliterating the world around us.

Hunter holds me through my orgasm, pulling his hand away only after the waves have passed. As he licks away the small beads of sweat on my chest, my head falls back against the wall.

"Fuck m-" I whisper, heart hammering against my rib cage.

Hunter takes a breath and starts to pull us off the wall. "Condoms," he mutters.

I reach down and boldly grab his dick. "Don't go anywhere." Hunter hesitates, hot breath caressing the tender skin on my neck. "I'm on the pill. No STI's."

"Me too," Hunter whispers.

"Then nothing between us," I rasp. "I want this."

This was the last piece of the puzzle.

Everything else about Hunter felt right, everything...

I can't even finish my thought because Hunter grabs my ass, lifts me up, and just as I start to process the pressure of his dick against my opening, he thrusts in - hot, hard flesh into silky skin, recharging my body instantly. I shriek as he pushes all the way in and then settles for a moment, letting me adjust to him.

"Are you okay?" he whispers against my ear.

I nod and wrap my boots tight around his waist, allowing him just enough room to pull back and slam into me. I mewl and groan, every thrust sending jolts of electricity into my legs, building more pressure.

Completely suspended, I lace my fingers into his hair as he fucks me, his hot mouth nipping at my throat. Closing my eyes, I dive into the delicious tension between my legs. Hunter groans and growls, "You feel so fucking good, Sarah."

His rumbling tremble rushing to my brain flips the switch and my cries drown out the music on the radio, waves ragged and electric, torturing the same areas of my body in the best way, pulling the rest of the strength from my limbs.

Hunter hammers against me a few seconds more, tenses and then exclaims his own orgasm. After a moment, his body slackens, leaning further into mine. His heart hammers against his chest, mimicking my own.

I cradle his head in my hands, inhaling his manly scent, tinged with sweat. A quiet moment passes and then I whisper, "I'm so glad we didn't go ice skating."

Chapter Four

Sarah

Turns out, pinning me to the wall was only the start of things between us.

After a glass of wine, I demanded he show me his bedroom and did my best to pin that large hunk of man to the sheets.

I failed wonderfully.

Not one to give up though, I finally succeeded as the pale gray morning light crept into his bedroom.

Hunter's not the only one who knows their way around ribbon.

Or in my case, a pair of ties I found while going to the bathroom.

An hour later, my thighs still tingle from his beard.

Burrowing deeper into Hunter's warm, cozy bed, I smile and let out the most content of contented sighs. Under the covers, I can smell traces of Hunter, that wonderful warm woodsy smell, laced with just a hint of my dark flowery perfume.

I run my fingers over the indentions in the sheets next to me, listening to the muffled, distant sounds of Hunter moving around behind the closed bedroom door.

Wanting to stay where I'm at forever, ensconced in the heat and memory of Hunter, I realize I'm voraciously hungry. If I hadn't just ridden him until I was in a blissful coma, I'd be snarling like a velociraptor trying to become a vegetarian.

With extreme reluctance, I finally peel the covers back and roll out of bed. Stretching, I spot my dress and underwear lying neatly on the corner of the covers. Next to it was an enormous sweatshirt and pajama pants.

I laugh at the thought of trying to keep the pants on me and swoon at the thoughtfulness. In the end, I choose the blue-green Seattle sweatshirt that skims my thighs and nothing else.

You know, just in case things spontaneously happen.

Feet padding across the fluffy carpet, I open the bedroom door, walk down the short hallway, and forget how to breathe.

A deep green garland hangs above all the doors and archways. Outside the windows, snow falls thick and fluffy from the gray sky. Inside, candles flicker golden light from their holders on the windowsills.

Meanwhile, Hunter stands in front of the roaring fireplace, wearing nothing but a pair of gray joggers, his sizable bulge stretching the fabric of those sweats.

"Morning."

His deep syrupy voice cuts the tractor beam I'm in, which allows my other senses to join the party.

"Santa Baby" on the speakers.

Warm, sweet cinnamon. Orange and spice. Savory, salty bacon.

Best of all, rich, caramelized coffee.

Dear Santa, kindly forget everything I asked you for this year or ever again. Because nothing, I mean nothing, is better than this moment right here.

Hunter closes a cardboard box and starts moving toward the kitchen. "Are you ready for some coffee?"

Okay, Santa, maybe that moment.

As he walks by, Hunter squeezes my ass and plants a kiss on my cheek.

Nope! Definitely that moment!

Calculating the low probability of making it through another round with Hunter without passing out from low blood sugar, I run my hand through my hair and begrudgingly walk to the small, tidy kitchen.

"What are we having?" I ask. "I mean, besides coffee."

Hunters bends over, checking something in the oven. "Cinnamon rolls," he says with a glance. "Bacon. I can cut up some fruit if you want."

"That just gets in the way of bacon."

"Noted," he says, closing the oven door. "But first, coffee."

"God, yes."

Hunter turns and opens a cabinet, allowing me to ogle the thick muscles of his back. I spot thin red lines running down to those tempting divots just above his waist band. Flushing with embarrassment and proud savagery, I ask with a satisfied breath. "You're certainly talented in the bedroom. Is it too much to think you're talented in the kitchen as well?"

Filling a mug, Hunter laughs, then points to the garbage on the counter. "You'll just have to settle for the bedroom, I'm afraid," he says, walking my steaming mug of deliciousness to me and putting it on the counter. "I know enough to follow directions and not burn shit."

"Okay," I say in mock disgust. "I guess I can handle that."

"Also good to know," Hunter says, a smile spreading across his face. He leans down, resting his forearms on the counter. In the muted morning light, I see dimples form under his beard.

"How long have you had the crumb catcher?" I ask suddenly.

Hunter looks surprised.

"Sorry, you know that I pretty much say whatever pops into my head."

"You've mentioned that."

"It's just...I know we've been talking with each other for a month now, but I've never seen you without one and I've never asked, I don't think."

Hunter laughs and rubs his jaw self-consciously. "For a while. Why? You don't like it?"

"Like it?" I exclaim. "I love it!"

My thighs clench with the happy memory.

"Good," he says, standing up, heading for the oven. "Because it's going to stay for a while. I hope you like your bacon crispy."

"As long as the cinnamon rolls are soft," I say over the lip of the cup.

Hunter puts on an oven glove, pulls out the bacon and cinnamon rolls, and puts them on the stove top to cool. Throwing the glove on the counter, he takes a sip of coffee and walks up to me, filling my airspace with his electric presence.

If the kitchen already didn't smell good enough, I catch a hint of that fiery, woodsy scent on his chest and I'm instantly transported back to last night, face buried in his chest, hands raking down his back.

My nipples hard, I'm pulled from that memory by a gentle finger lifting my chin. "Before we eat," he says quietly. "I just want to say I'm so glad you're here. It's only Christmas Eve, but it's already one of the best holidays I've ever had."

His words make my chest tight and warm. "Oh, well," I stumble, making sure my grip is tight on the scalding hot beverage. "You're just saying that because I can do that thing with my jaw."

Hunter smirks. Without flinching, he shakes his head. "Not just that. Everything. The moment you stepped out of the elevator. How you looked standing outside the restaurant in the snow. You. Here. Now."

His brain must be suffering from a lack of blood flow because something grows against the cottony fabric.

I take the tiniest sip of coffee, thirsty for something else. "You make me wish I hadn't waited a month to meet you."

"Lucky we don't have to wait any longer."

Hunter gently takes the cup from my hands.

"Aren't we eating?"

He pulls me into his arms and lays a firm kiss on my lips. I don't protest as the sweatshirt is lifted off my body. He reaches down, lifts me up and sets me on the counter. The cold shock of tile against my butt ignites the heat between my legs.

"Thinking I can feed you and fuck you at the same time. You up for it?"

He reaches down and runs his fingers over the still sensitive skin of my pussy. I moan and wrap my legs around his waist.

"Starving," I pant.

Fresh cinnamon rolls from the oven?

Delicious.

Fresh cinnamon rolls being fed to you as a scorching hot man slow fucks you?

Fucking hea-ven-ly.

And that didn't include what he did with the frosting.

Belly full, legs still trembling, I hook a glassy red star and hang it from one of the tree branches. On the radio, Nat King Cole makes way for Kelly Clarkson.

"So why wouldn't your family decorate until Christmas Eve?" I ask, hanging a candy cane from one of the fresh pine branches. "I would have disowned them, frankly."

Hunter chuckles and takes a glass train engine from the box and hangs it close to my ornament. "It's something that came over with my great-great-great grandparents from Germany. I never understood it either, but you don't dare tell my mom that Christmas should be any other way."

"I hear that," I laugh. "Try having a Japanese mother whose idea of Christmas is buying a bucket of fried chicken and wondering why the hell people get presents and the day off."

"Is your dad Japanese as well?"

"Nope. Corn-fed as they come." I tuck a crystal snowman in front of a tree light so it sparkles and laugh at a memory. "My dad would try to take my mom to church for midnight mass on Christmas Eve. Now, in Japan, Christmas Eve is treated like Valentine's Day. So, the first time she went, she said out loud, standing directly below a bloody Jesus, 'This is the least romantic place I've ever been to!'"

Hunter laughs and checks his placement of a gold ball. Satisfied with it, he looks at me. "So, if we were at your place, the decorations would have been up since when? Thanksgiving?"

I blush a little.

"Before then?" Hunter asks, eyebrows lifting.

"The way I see it," I defend, "is if Costco can put out Christmas stock in October, then I can too!"

"Wow," Hunter says slowly, a smile creeping across his lips.

I throw a cotton snowball at him. "Last week you said it was cute!" I puff up my chest and do my best manly Hunter impression. "That's cute, Sarah. I love your passion for the holiday."

Hunter eyes me for a second, then says quickly, "Thanksgiving is a better holiday."

My jaw falls open. "Oh. No. You. *Didn't.*"

"I did," he says, eyes sparkling mischievously. "And I mean it."

I narrow my gaze, wishing my eyes could shoot dragon fire. "All those things I said in the kitchen? I take them all back."

Hunter laughs, rich and warm, and I have to do everything in my power to keep my angry facade. "Just because I love Thanksgiving more doesn't mean I wouldn't let you indulge in your obsession."

His words slip around my facade. It sounds like he's planning for future Christmases. Or am I crazy?

"Well, that's...good," I say, rummaging around the box ornaments for nothing in particular. "Getting back to parents, uh, are yours coming by?"

"No," he says after a sip of coffee. "They're taking care of my aunt in Florida. But you might meet my sister. She lives in town."

"Oh!"

"But I can tell her no if you just want it to be the two of us."

"No, I can meet her."

"Good. I promise she doesn't bite even though she's the stereotypical protective older sister. My brothers, on the other hand..."

"Ah, yes, the famous rugby stars. Right? For England?"

"Yeah," Hunter chuckles.

"Why didn't they just play football? Lot more money in it."

"They did play. Both were drafted, actually. But when one went over to London for a game, he fell in love with rugby, and a year later, recruited my brother to go with him."

"But not you?"

"I was already working for the Forestry Department. Didn't appeal to me."

A smile stays on Hunter's face, but there's definite sadness in his voice, the same sadness as at the restaurant.

Hunter swaps out a light bulb on the strand, making the rest turn on again. I open my mouth to ask but don't really know what I'm after.

"Where is..." Hunter grabs a box, lifts it up, looking for something that isn't there. He glances around the room.

"Whatcha looking for?"

"There's a box of ornaments that if I didn't have up, my sister would kill me."

I look around. "Oh, uh..."

Hunter grunts. "Office. That's where it is." He turns, starts to head down the hall, but stops when a phone chimes merrily from the kitchen. "Crap, I gotta get that. You think you could grab the box?"

"Sure."

As Hunter walks into the kitchen to grab his phone, I head down the hallway and into a small room across from the bedroom.

Inside, there's a desk with a computer, a sectional in front of a window, and a television mounted onto the wall. A dart board hangs on the back of the door, unused. Pictures of Mount Rainier and the Seattle skyline hang scattershot around the room.

A closet door sits ajar. I open it all the way and spot two file boxes on the top shelf. Not sure which one to grab, I pick one. Getting it down, I put it on the desk and open it up.

Balls of newspaper in various sizes fill the box. Picking one up and unwrapping it, an ornament comes tumbling out.

Jackpot.

"Got it!" I shout. I grab the box, start to turn, and then stop when something catches my eye.

A familiar face stares back at me from the unfurled newspaper. The color ink is faded, but those hazel eyes are unmistakable.

Those deep dimples, now hidden by a beard, on full display.

A younger version of Hunter smiles a thousand miles wide, body covered in a football jersey and pads, arm wrapped around some waifish thing wearing ribbons in her hair, wearing a crisp, pure white and blue cheerleading uniform.

The headline reads, *Leading the Way to the NFL?*

From the kitchen, Hunter grunts and mutters something into the phone. Hands trembling, I quickly scan through the article.

Hunter Reed. Star fullback for tiny Yakima College. Holds every scoring record in school history.

NFL scouts on campus for, like, the first time ever.

I put the newspaper back in the box, my breath ragged, head spinning.

Hunter did play ball. I knew it!

But why did he downplay playing so much? Every time I've mentioned football, it was like asking him to recall a prison sentence.

Gradually, the suspicion fades, replaced by a growing excitement.

Sweeping the box off the desk, I jog back into the room. Hunter's busy hanging a bushel of mistletoe over the entrance to the kitchen.

"Hey," I exclaim, putting the box on the table and grabbing the newspaper. "I knew you played football! I totally have a sixth sense about this! I can stand in the middle of Times Square and find every single person who's played! Why didn't you tell me, you goof? Forty-seven touchdowns your junior year? Holy crap! Okay, I know I'm going to get roasted for favoritism, but I totally want you to be on our show! It'd be amazing! Local Washington product, football star, complete sex god! Wait, I'd keep that part to myself. Hunt-"

Hunter slowly turns around. When I see his face, my babbling enthusiasm extinguishes like a flame running out of oxygen.

"Hunter? What's the matter?"

Chapter Five

Hunter

"Where did you get that?"

My voice is sharp and icy, but I don't care, because the only thing I'm focused on is trying to control the darkness flooding into my head.

"Uh, I..." Sarah looks down at the box. "Here?"

Without thinking, I storm over, grab the newspaper and snarl when I see the picture of myself looking happy. I crumple it into a ball and chuck it across the room. I grab another paper wrapped ornament, hardly able to read the words, eyes full of blurry rage.

Yakima Wins Conference Title: Reed Acts Right at Home Against Marshland, Scores 4 TDs.

"Hunter?"

My jaw is so tight, white spots explode in my vision.

Damn it! I thought I threw everything away!

I pull out another ball of paper. *Reed Carries Raiders to National*

34

Championship! Growling, I slam the ball down to the floor, smashing the glass within.

"What are you..."

Sarah's words disappear when I grab the box and hurl it across the room. It hits the door with a thud and ornaments scatter everywhere. Sarah yelps. I snap my head towards her. She jumps back and covers her mouth with her hands.

"I will *never* go on your show," I seethe, not knowing what else to say. "Understand?"

"Okay," she peeps, frozen in place, tears starting to flood her eyelids. "You don't have to..."

I look down to the floor, my chest lifting and falling quickly. I run a hand through my hair and start to say something else, but the words disappear when my mind brings up the image I spent years trying to pack away.

I close my eyes and grit my teeth. Even through the burning tears forming, I sense Sarah edging closer. Then the gentlest of touches is like an electric knife in my arm.

Recoiling, I back up as one terrible image turns into two. Two becomes four, four becomes a hundred, then a thousand, until my head is completely filled with pain and fury.

I stumble towards my bedroom. Numb, I pull on boots, my skin hot, forehead sweating. From what sounds like a million miles away, Sarah asks a question. I ignore it and swipe my keys from the dresser.

She stands her ground in front of the bedroom door and though my body courses with anger, I still feel my heart break at how beautiful she is, despite her looking scared and fearful.

I knew I shouldn't have done this.

Goddamn it, Hunter, way to fuck it up.

For a moment, I think I'm going to knock her over, but at the last moment, she backs away. As I reach the kitchen, she unleashes a torrent of language that would make a sailor blush.

I thought somehow we could ignore football, talk about the world and other shit.

But she's a football analyst, for crying out loud.

And I...hate football with every fiber of my being.

Football does nothing but destroy and take.

I kick the box from the front door and grab my keys off the floor.

And now it's taking Sarah away from me.

Fucking game.

I rip the door open and a rush of icy wind blows into the room.

"Hunter, where are you going?!"

But I don't answer her. Instead, I don't bother to look back until the engine of the truck roars to life.

Sarah stands in the doorway, still wearing my sweatshirt, shiny black hair spilling over her shoulders. Even through the snow I can see that she's crying.

Then she flips me the bird and slams my door shut.

Chapter Six

Sarah

Trembling from cold and fury, I stand in his living room, hands buried in my hair, eyes bugging out, looking around at everything and nothing at once.

Despite the warmth from the fire, my body chills as though I'm standing buck naked in a freezer.

Speaking of naked...

I look down at the enormous sweatshirt covering my body. Ten minutes ago, it was a source of comfort.

Now, it feels like a thousand tarantulas crawling across my skin.

Shrieking, I rip it off. When I do, I spot the coat hooks on the wall from last night. A wave of nausea rolls through me at the blisteringly fresh memories of Hunter pressed firm against me, his need against mine.

Then I remember Hunter's still on me from this morning.

Bile surges into the back of my mouth. As the image of his truck spinning out replays in my mind, I run into the kitchen and shakily turn on the hot water tap. Focusing desperately on the sink in front of me and not the mess we made next to it, I clean myself off and slam the kitchen towel onto the floor as the first tendrils of humiliation creep in.

How could I...?

No.

How could he...?

Tears sting the corners of my eyes. Trembling, I remember my phone in the bedroom and realize the generous view of my nakedness for the neighbors around his house, despite the swirling blanket of snow.

I race into the bedroom, make sure the blinds are shut tight, and look wildly around for my phone. Finding it on the dresser, I grab it with shaky fingers, find Hunter's text stream, and with embarrassed rage, hammer out a message.

Sarah: *You asshole! Where are you going! You fuck me and run away?!*

Growling, I hit send, knowing he deserves much more. So much more.

But I just want to get out and get as far away from Hunter Reed as possible.

I pause my phone activities to yank on my clothes and then pick it back up. Storming into the living room, I find the Lyft app.

I know I was distracted by Hunter last night, but I know he lives far enough from the hotel that I'd be an icicle by the time I get to my room.

Lyft is thirty minutes away though.

And if I stay in this house a moment longer...

Fuck it, I'd rather be an icicle.

I start for my purse on the floor when the knob jiggles and a key slides into the lock. My eyes grow wide as I spot an old baseball displayed on the small table behind the couch. I grab it, wind up, and get ready to deliver a strike to that bastard's head.

"Hunter?"

The female voice catches me off guard, then instantly sends me into apocalyptic rage.

Someone's *living with him*?!

A sharp bark though makes me pause. Moments later, the door shakes and bursts open as a dog tears into the room. I scream at the sight of it. The dog jumps backward and howls as though it was hurt, then the woman in the doorway spots me and screams as well.

"Who are you?" the woman shouts, hand flying to her chest. "What are you doing here? Where's Hunter?"

I start to say something, but the words dry up on my tongue. I blink rapidly, thinking my rage has boiled over into delusions because the woman standing in front of me looks just like Hunter.

You know, minus the beard, muscles, and penis.

"I..." I mumble, lowering the ball and spotting a picture of the woman standing next to Hunter on the mantle above to the fireplace. "I...I'm, um, I'm Sarah? You must be Lindsey, Hunter's sister."

For a moment, Lindsey looks stunned. "How do you...wait. Sarah? Sugiyama? Sugi from the Starbuck and Sugi show?"

I nod. Lindsey looks at me like an intruder a moment longer and then her body relaxes. "Oh my God," she exhales, coming in and closing the door. "I'm so sorry for acting like that." Stamping the snow from her boots, she unhooks the dog, who stays glued to her legs. "I don't blame you for defending yourself." She straightens up and sighs contentedly. "Sorry we had to meet like that. Hunter said come over anytime. I'm just so used to him being alone. I could have knocked."

"No problem," I say, under my breath, glancing around the room, trying to figure out what to do.

"Where's Hunter? I brought..."

My face flinches at his name. Lindsey stops cold, eyes narrowing. "Sarah? Everything okay?" She looks around the room suspiciously. "Where's Hunter?"

Her repeating his name is like a punch to my gut. I try to keep an even expression on my face, ready to walk the walk of shame back to Seattle.

But seeing Hunter in her is too much. A single tear falls onto my cheek.

"Oh no," Lindsey says, face falling. "What did that idiot do?"

I keep glancing into the kitchen, embarrassed as Lindsey obliviously works through our gourmet indiscretions, pulling a bottle of whiskey from the cabinet above the stove and filling two glasses with ice.

"Here," she says with a sad smile, putting the glass down on the small dining room table. "This will help."

Sheepishly, I take the glass, tip it back and let the fiery liquid burn the back of my throat. "Thank you," I wince.

Lindsey sits next to me, while what must be Hunter's dog pads to its bed by the fireplace and lies down, keeping a cautious eye at the table. "I'm going to be honest. When we're done with this glass, we're going to go find Hunter and kill him. Whatever you tell me here will only dictate what method I use, understand?"

Wrapping my hands around the glass, I nod. "Got it."

"Good." She tucks a chunk of long, blonde hair behind her ear and covers one of my hands with her own. A large diamond sparkles on her ring finger. "Spill it."

I finish spilling it as the room starts to darken and Christmas lights turn on in the windows. For a long time, Lindsey sits there quietly, staring at the table, tapping her bright red fingernails with little Christmas trees on the wood.

"Lindsey?"

She sighs and finally looks up at me. "Can I tell you something?"

"Sure..."

"I don't know how much Hunter has told you about me, but I like you."

"Oh," I say, eyebrows shooting up towards my hair. After an awkward moment, not knowing how to respond, I clear my throat and focus on the other part of what she said. "Well, he said you're pretty protective."

"Okay," she says, tilting her head, considering the idea. "Yeah. I will fully admit, I probably spend too much time meddling in his life."

"Uh..."

"I can't help it. I've been taking care of him since I was fourteen." She takes a sip and winces at the burn. "But that's a story for another day. Where I'm going with this is, I've been excited to meet you. Ever since you two matched last month, you've been good for him." She looks directly at me. "Seriously, he's been a different man. You have no idea how happy I've been. Therefore, I think you should know the truth."

Her words send a chill down my spine. "Truth? About what?"

Chewing on her lip, she hesitates and takes a deep breath. "Hunter's relationship with football."

"He made that quite clear," I sigh. My mind replays the anger in his face. I take a drink to get rid of it.

"Did he tell you anything?"

I shake my head.

"Well, at least if you know, it might explain some things."

After searching the table for answers that aren't there, I look at Lindsey. "I suppose."

Lindsey exhales, not looking entirely convinced I want to know. "It wasn't always this way. Hunter used to love football." She grabs the newspaper next to her and looks at the picture of a smiling Hunter and the brunette cheerleader wrapped in his arm. "From the time he could walk, he'd tag along with our dad and brothers and just throw himself around with them." She drops it on the table, her face conflicted. "He was never the fastest or biggest, but he played hard and smart. When our brothers stayed in London to play rugby, Hunter decided to carry on the football dream. Problem was, he had no college offers. Except one."

"Yakima," I say quietly.

"Hometown school. Well, nearby school anyway. They gave him a scholarship. Played fullback, defense, covered kicks. You couldn't take him off the field. He loved it."

Lindsey's voice wavers. She clasps her hands together, her already pale skin growing whiter. "Loved it even more when his little brother also went to Yakima to play football."

"He has another brother?" I ask, eyes growing wide. "He always said he only has two!"

"Had," Lindsey says quietly.

As Lindsey's eyes grow red, the realization dawns on me. "Oh."

"Corey was the runt of the five of us and he *worshiped* Hunter. Those two, my God, you'd think they were twins. While Hunter had some talent, Corey didn't. But that didn't stop him from making varsity in high school and walking on at Yakima, just to be with Hunter."

I take a drink and put the glass quietly on the table.

"It was a game against Grays Harbor and it was just a firehose. Rain sideways, wind making it hard to stand. Good ol' November Washington weather, you know? Anyway, Yakima was up big, and the coach decided to play Corey, who usually just stood on the sideline."

Lindsey flashes a sad smile.

"Sarah, I'm telling you, to be in a game with Hunter, you'd thought Corey won the freaking lottery. That feeling lasted all of about two minutes. On the first play, Corey...he got hurt. Lowered his head instead of protecting himself."

Lindsey gets up and turns on the light above the table. Sitting, she glances at the wall nearest her. I follow her gaze.

Family photo.

A younger Hunter, still maturing, flanked by his four siblings.

"Hunter saw it all. Corey lying motionless on the ground. The ambulance. The stretcher. His coach let Hunter go to the hospital. On the way, Hunter gave up the game."

Cold numbness seeps into my body and spreads to my chest.

"Hunter felt responsible for Corey's accident, even though it wasn't his fault. A year later, Corey committed suicide."

"Oh my God," I gasp.

"Hunter always tried to protect him and when he couldn't, he decided to take out his anger on the game. Threw all his jerseys, his trophies, anything football related, in the trash. If someone has football on at a party or a restaurant, he leaves."

"I don't get it," I say quietly, the stinging prick of tears in my eyes. "If he hates football so much, then why did he spend all that time with me? He knows who I am and what I do. There's no way in hell I could not bring up football!"

Lindsey taps her fingers on the glass for a minute before she says, "I asked the same question, and I never got an answer. If you want my guess? He likes you."

A couple of hours ago, that answer would have sent me to the moon. Now, it's a poisoned blade driven deep into my chest.

What do you know?

Starbuck was right.

"I'm not here to tell you what to do, or make a case for my idiot brother," Lindsey says flatly. "I just want you to know the truth. I know you love football. Hell, I listen to your show every week." Lindsey grabs the bottle and offers it to me.

"No," I say, waving her off.

She looks at it and then pushes it away. "Please don't think that it's you in any shape or form, okay?"

I let out a sad laugh. "Well, in a way, it is." I stand and take a deep breath, keeping the tears at bay. "Thank you. For everything. But I think it's time I go back to the hotel. I've...there's a lot to do back home."

"Do you want a ride?"

I shake my head. "I can order a Lyft." I take a step towards the front door and my phone, but then stop. "I do understand better, thank you."

"Of course."

"One more thing?"

"What's that?"

"You don't mind if I awkwardly wait around in the house, do you? It's freezing out there."

Chapter Seven

Hunter

Eight years ago.

"I can't do this anymore, Hunter."

Corey's voicemail chills me to the bone. I quickly dial his number, my heart leaping in my throat.

He left that message an hour ago.

How come I didn't get it until now?!

His phone rings distantly in my ear and then his voicemail connects. I slam the phone down and look wildly around the forestry office.

"Everything okay there, noob?" my supervisor asks lazily from across the room, feet up on the desk, phone cradled in their hands.

"I gotta go," I mutter, jumping up and grabbing my heavy jacket. Outside, the trees groan under the weight of the silver thaw, making patrols *dangerous and providing my boss ample time to beat his record in Treasure Runner.*

On cue, my boss fist pumps the stifling air. "I don't need to know about your poop habits, Reed."

"No, I'm leaving," I snap, making sure I have my keys.

That pulls his attention from the phone. "Leaving?! Where?! You've got an all-nighter with me, buddy!"

I yank open the door and close it without another word.

From behind the dirty windows, I hear my boss yell, "Reed!"

Slipping through the slush, I dial Corey's number again. Voicemail. Panicking, I clamber into the truck, turn on the engine, and lower the plow.

Where would he be?

I hope he's at Mom and Dad's, where he should be.

Driving as fast as the ice and snow covered roads will allow, I start working towards town while dialing Mom's number.

She picks up on the third ring, concern in her voice, not for Corey, but for me. "Hunter, everything okay?"

"Is Corey there?" I bark.

"Uh," my mom stumbles. "Yeah, why wouldn't he be?"

"Will you check, please?"

"Sure...why?"

Swerving around a downed branch, I debate telling her. But she was already so on edge with Corey, I didn't need to add this to her plate.

"Please, Mom, can you give him the phone?"

"Okay," she says suspiciously. There's a pause and then my mom calls out Corey's name into the house. A second time. Then a third. Finally, her voice fills my ear. "That's weird, he's not here, and I swear I didn't hear the garage door open."

The thought makes a ball of dread drop into my stomach.

"Why would he go out in this weather, anyway?" my mom wonders out loud. "He won't get very far. It's not like his wheelchair has snow tires."

In the background, I hear sirens pass by the house. After a half dozen go by, my mom comments, "Something's going on." She sighs. "Anyway, I'm sure Corey will be back in a minute. I'll tell him to call you. Bye, Hunter."

I don't say anything as the phone slips from my hand.

Oh, please, no.

Don't let it be.

Reaching some of the main roads in Meadow Valley, I'm able to lift the plow and drive faster, orange lights flashing against the black of the storm, putting horrible pieces together in my head, finishing a puzzle I hope isn't true.

My mom is right, Corey can't go very far.

But he can make it to the place I'd seen him at several times the past year.

It's only a couple blocks from the house and it used to be the soundtrack that put us to sleep in the summers.

I drive through the town center, running red lights and stop signs. As I near the old lumber section and the surrounding suburbs, a strobe of red and blue lights makes my heart leap in my throat.

Oh, shit, they got me for running the red light. Damn it!

I start to pull over and watch as the cop pulls around me and speeds past, heading in the same direction as me. He ignores my efforts to keep up and as I turn the corner to follow the berm the tracks are on, my heart stops dead.

A dozen emergency vehicles are stationed at the intersection a half-mile up the road. The road my parents live on.

The road Corey can access.

Even in the stormy darkness, I can make out the train idling further up the tracks.

Body resisting all efforts to inch closer, my mind wins out, and slowly, like I'm in some shadowy trance, I creep forward and get out of the truck.

The door slamming pulls the attention of an officer, who starts to yell at me but stops when they recognize who I am.

"Hunter? Oh, shit." He runs around his car and jogs up towards me, holding his hands out to get me to stop. "Hey man, you don't want to be here."

But I ignore him. My eyes focus on a piece of mangled black metal lying in the street, illuminated by flashing lights and red flares.

I can clearly see shreds of gray tires, the twisted wire basket, and then, as a paramedic moves out of the way, Corey's legs, still attached to the seat of the wheelchair, the entire upper half sheared off by the force of the train.

The only sound in the truck is the gentle tick of snowflakes landing on the windshield.

Pulled off to the side of the road, next to where Corey's wooden cross sits buried in snow, I read Sarah's text message over and over again.

I deserve every bit of it.

Frankly, I deserve even more.

I didn't tell her about Corey. Or how, in the rain and wind against Grays Harbor, I'd misheard the call and went right instead of left, leaving my little brother to run headfirst into an unblocked defender.

I didn't tell her I quit football in the ambulance or cursed the game after Corey committed suicide.

I just thought we could ignore it.

We talked about so many other things, I convinced myself we could make it work.

But who the fuck was I kidding?

She talks football every damn day.

How were we going to discuss our lives without mentioning football and how it destroyed me every time someone brought it up?

I was fooling myself and Sarah.

She deserves to be angry.

And I deserve to be alone.

It's better this way.

I toss the phone on the seat next to me and squeeze the steering wheel until my hand turns white.

Figures.

Sarah was the first woman I'd ever seen a real future with. The month we'd spent texting and emailing and video chatting was unlike anything I'd ever done and I craved every single conversation with her. She was smart and funny as hell in topics other than football, and after I'd pushed everybody away to keep them safe from my mopey, sad-sack act, she was the one I wanted to let in.

As we grew closer, I wanted her to know what was going on.

As the conversations grew more daring, more intimate, I needed and craved her in a way as elemental as breathing. I wanted to steal her from the rest of the world and devote myself to showering her with pleasure until there was no more to be had.

But I didn't want to scare her away.

So, I kept it hidden.

As my breath starts to appear in the truck cab, I finally open the door and stumble out into the snow. Sighing, I trod up to Corey's cross and squat down next to it. The wind and weight of the snow has pushed it to one side. I brush off the white powder and then clear a space around the base to recenter and anchor it.

Near the bottom, my fingers hit something plastic. I scrape off snow until I find a letter wrapped in a plastic baggie. 'Corey' is written in neat, flowing cursive on the envelope. I shove the package into my coat, fix Corey's cross, and then stumble back to the truck.

Turning on the engine, I hold my frozen hands to the heating vents long enough to regain feeling. As my skin tingles with painful electricity, I grab the baggie, open it up, tear off the envelope, and read the letter.

Corey,

It's been eight years and I am still so angry at you. I've cursed at you, I've screamed into pillows and I've broken every damn plate I could get my hands on.

What you did was so incredibly selfish. I told you I'd be there for you. No matter what the circumstances, I'd be right there, side by side, hand in hand. I even tattooed your name around my finger for Christ's sake!

I said it then and I'll say it again. I didn't care that you were in a wheelchair. You were still you. You still had your sense of humor. You still had that dimple in your cheek that turned me on every time I saw it. You still knew how to make your spaghetti bolognese.

You were still freaking alive.

I was ready, Corey. I could handle it.

You were the one who refused to give it a chance.
You were the one who couldn't see past the chair.
Not. Me.
And then you go and do this? Ignoring everything I said, ignoring all the sacrifices I so willingly made because you were still my Corey.
Fuck you.
I'm writing this to you to finally end things. I need to move on with my life. You could have been with me, and you chose the coward's end, so I need to stop pining for a dead asshole and go live the rest of my life.
The moment I seal this envelope, I will not give you another thought, Corey Reed. You will no longer cause me pain.

Vanessa

Tears run down my cheeks and onto the letter. It's been forever since I talked to his fiancée. We drifted apart, thanks to me mostly, and I assumed she'd long since moved on.

But the ink was still fresh, smudging under my trembling fingers, and the bag felt fresh out of the box.

I read the letter again, my mind swirling in thought.

I'm not the only one who had trouble moving on.

However, it looks like I'm now the *only* one who hasn't.

Vanessa was right. Like her, I still pined for a chance to fix the mistake I made, forcing myself to live in purgatory for it.

I can't change what happened, but I can stop punishing myself for it.

After all, Corey did tell me he was an idiot for leading with his head. Even if I had made the block, he still would have been injured at some point.

I need to forgive myself and live the rest of my life.

And I want Sarah to be a part of that life.

Because out of that month of conversations, I got the sense that she is the type of person who'd be there, side by side, hand in hand.

I'm willing to try if it means breaking free.

Reaching down, I start the pickup truck, hoping like hell Sarah isn't driving back to Seattle at a hundred miles an hour.

I need to apologize. And there's a twenty-minute drive back to my house to figure out what to say.

Letter tucked under my leg, I spin the truck around and, as quickly as I can, head for home.

Chapter Eight

Sarah

Tears blurring my vision, I pack away my dress and boots and close my suitcase with a frustrated grunt.

I pull the hotel towel off my wet hair and zip up my sweat-shirt, giving one last look around the place before heading downstairs.

I sigh when I spot my phone on the desk. Shit. Wouldn't want to forget that.

Walking over to the small desk in the corner, I pick it up, wondering with faint masochistic hope if Hunter has messaged me.

And when I see the gray message box pop up, I inhale sharply and then deflate just as fast.

Starbuck: *Hey! How's, uh, the weekend with the dude?*

· · ·

I ignore him, not really interested in a lecture, or an I-told-you-so. Instead, I scroll up to Hunter's text thread and with a galactic sigh, swipe left and tap the red garbage can button.

What a shame.

Gorgeous, well-read, could fuck like a god, but...couldn't be around football.

I didn't have a lot of must-haves in a relationship, though football was one of them.

So, while he might be 95 percent the perfect guy, if he couldn't be around football, then he couldn't be around me.

I glance at the time. Maybe I could get home for a late dinner with my parents. Yes, they'd be surprised and yes, I'd get the same line of questioning as from Starbuck, but at least it wouldn't be laced with that weird he-likes-me-I-don't-like-him awkwardness.

And I'd be there in the morning to open presents.

Christmas with Fred and Yua Sugiyama over a bucket of fried chicken.

I was winning at adulting.

So hard.

I throw my phone in my purse, praying my parents still keep their secret stash of Japanese whiskey, and grab my suitcase.

Clenching my hotel key between my teeth, I pull the handle to the door down, yank the door open, and scream.

A Christmas miracle stands at my door, ready to knock. Melting snowflakes sparkle like diamonds in his messy blond hair. Beard-covered cheeks red from the cold and the pain spread across the rest of his beautiful face.

Tear-stained hazel eyes.

Nearly every ounce of me cries out to hug him, to help ease his torture.

Fortunately, the rational bits left remind me that he freaked the fuck out over a simple question and proceeded to storm out.

Still, no better package can be left at my door.

"Hunter," I say breathlessly, hoping like hell there's some anger in my voice because my body is quickly melting at the tips of the tree tattoo over one side of his chest. "I'm leaving."

"Don't," he pleads in a low growl. "I need to talk to you."

"Now you need to talk?" I ask incredulously, my mind mixing with thoughts of rage and leg-clenching orgasms, not knowing which side to pick. "If you don't remember, we were talking. And then you stormed out." For a moment, the rage wins out and I start to push past Hunter. "Excuse me."

Hunter moves in front of me. "Please. Hear me out."

The sliding scale of rage and horniness moves further into the rage zone. "I *will* kick you in the nuts if you don't get out of the way. I don't like this hulking barrier act and I especially don't like being stormed out on. Not that it matters now, but I like to talk through shit." I clench my jaw and stare daggers at him. "Now, *move.*"

Not moving a muscle, he says in an annoyed voice, "I'm trying to talk to you. I just said that."

"You only get to talk to me if you don't storm out. Did I not make that clear?"

Breathing in, I shove my five-foot frame towards the hallway. To his credit, Hunter backs out of the way, hands held up in surrender. Plastic wheels clacking loudly over the wooden door, I nearly make it to the elevator before Hunter shouts from behind me, "I'm sorry!"

I freeze, finger halfway to the down button. The pain and sincerity in his voice bounces off the walls, thick as the snow piled up outside.

"You're right," he continues. "You don't deserve to be stormed out on. Ever. I know I screwed up. I'm just asking for a chance to explain."

By the time he's done, half of the doors in the hall click open. 'What's going on,' is the common refrain. From beyond the cranberry-colored door nearest me, an angry male voice screams at Hunter to shove his head up his ass and be quiet.

Without looking, I can feel his heated gaze on me. My chest trembles and my hand is unable to move closer to the button.

"It won't matter," I say quietly, the words directed more at my reflection in the golden doors than Hunter.

And the only reason I tell myself that is because Hunter had done the very simple thing he needed to do to be forgiven.

Apologize.

Because, good Lord, I'm not a monster. He had a very legitimate reason for hating football. To rage-hate him for real trauma is psychotic.

To rage-hate him for assuming I couldn't have a discussion about it was acceptable.

But then he went and apologized, and it was like air leaving a balloon. It gave my mind an opportunity to hold an emergency meeting with the goal of figuring out, in some way, some Hail Mary, that we could work something out.

A couple of doors click shut and before I know it, Hunter is standing there next to me, a rush of warm, manly air causing my eyes to close.

I feel his presence move towards the door and I hear the click of the elevator button. I open my eyes and look at him, confused.

"If those doors open and you get on, I'll understand," he breathes. Under his shirt, I can see his chest tremble. "But I hope you'll come back to the room."

"Hunter, I..."

The readout from the elevator displays the number two.

It's a three-story hotel.

"Just listen, please."

I shake my head. "Lindsey already told me. I'm sorry, Hunter. I'm sorry about Corey. It sounds truly awful."

Behind the golden doors of the elevator is a whirring of cables. The metal moves as the car lifts and starts to settle.

"Lindsey doesn't know everything," Hunter says quickly. "There are things I haven't told anybody, things I want...no, things I *need* to tell you." In a flash, Hunter reaches out and grabs my arm as the doors open. "When I'm done, feel free to slap me or storm out or whatever. Hell, I'll carry your luggage out to the car and then you can kick me in the nuts if you want, but please, just listen."

A small gasp escapes from inside the elevator. Standing in the back corner, a mother looks at Hunter with a shocked expression while her son looks at me with an idiotic grin.

Hunter grimaces, lets go of my arm, and we both clear the doors so they can walk down the hallway, their heads turned, hoping for more fireworks, and loathing us at the same time.

I hold an arm across the doors, staring at the metal and wood paneling of the elevator. A poster in a plastic holder advertises night skating in the square.

Closing my eyes, I let out a sigh.

Fried chicken and whiskey will have to wait.

"Okay," I say quietly. "I'll listen." I open my eyes and look at him. "But not here." I tilt my head towards the elevator. "Come on. Carry my luggage."

Chapter Nine

Hunter

The skating rink attendant, Julian, eyes us wearily, a mix of teenage indifference and the desire to shut down early for Christmas Eve.

Without a word, we loosen the laces on our skates, our breath curling into the cold, swirling flurries of snow that have started again. Sarah shivers under her thin sweatshirt, her damp dark hair collecting snowflakes like it was a competition. I'd offered my jacket, but she brushed off the gesture in defiance, content to stay silent, mind working on overdrive.

Which was fine because it meant she hadn't left.

When I'm done lacing up, I look over and grimace. Sarah's laces are a disaster. She yanks and pulls, hooks and unhooks, all the while growling under her breath. Finally, she gives up with an exasperated sigh and searches around for Julian, who's slunk away like a brooding, hormonal ghost.

I slide across the padded bench and then make my way toward her skates.

"I'm fine," she says, starting to pull her foot away from me.

But I reach out and grab her ankle tight. "Stop moving," I growl. "Otherwise, you're going to cut my leg off."

"I wouldn't aim for your leg," she snaps.

I look up and watch her as she resists and twists. But then, after looking around for help that isn't around, she ultimately relents. Lowering her foot, I start working, undoing the strings wrapped in the wrong direction.

"What did Lindsey tell you?" I ask her legging-covered calf. "About Corey."

Sarah's silent for a moment and then she says, "There was an accident on the football field. That you blame yourself, that Corey committed suicide."

After getting the laces untangled and down to the end, I glance up at Sarah, who's staring back at me, arms tucked across her chest for warmth. "That's everything?"

"Yeah," Sarah says, her voice guarded. "I totally understand, Hunter, and I'm so, so sorry that happened, but..."

"There's more," I say, trying to keep my voice even, though I can feel my throat start to tighten up. "What my sister doesn't know is I was there, on scene. I saw my brother...scattered across the train tracks. The cops handed me his suicide note. He didn't blame me. For the accident. For life. For anything. He said it was his fault but that he couldn't go on the way he was."

Tears start to burn in my eyelids as I work on the other skate.

"I know everyone says I shouldn't, but I do blame myself. I wasn't strong enough to tell him no. When we first started playing football, I saw how undisciplined he was, the lack of skill, but he didn't care. He just wanted to hang out with me. I wanted to keep him safe, but I couldn't bring myself to tell him he should do something else. And the coaches couldn't either because he was a warm body." I hesitate. "Small town football, you need everybody you can get."

I take a breath to steady my cold, shaking hands. Around us, the snow thickens. I look up and watch flakes land on Sarah's eyelashes, her face cast in a golden glow from the twenty-foot town tree in the corner of the rink.

She's still guarded but listening.

"As a result, I punished myself. I thought, if Corey had the world taken away from him, then I couldn't have anything either. I hid. I wouldn't allow myself to do anything because of my mistake."

"Hunter," Sarah breathes. "That's-"

"And then I met you."

Even through the shivering, I see her chest hitch.

I lace the shoestring through the first eyelet, this time in the correct direction. "I met you and for the first time since Corey's death, I allowed myself something. Sarah, you are so incredibly amazing. You're smart, hilarious, and the most beautiful thing I've ever laid eyes on. I allowed myself to get to know you, despite knowing how much you loved football. I told myself I'd figure something out. Some way of being able to mention the game and not have all those feelings come rushing back. But when I saw that picture, it hit me all at once, and I failed."

Gently hooking the laces around the eyelets, I tie things up in a bow and lean back on my haunches, snowflakes bouncing off my cheeks with an icy tick.

"I want a chance," I say, voice wavering. "I want a chance to figure out how I can be with you. Not just tonight, or this weekend, but forever. I'll do whatever I need to do because I don't want to ever risk losing you again."

I stand and grimace at the popping and stiffness in my legs. Flashing a quick smile, I hold out my hand.

"So, what do the odds say? Are they in my favor?"

Sarah sits there, unabashedly shaking from the cold, looking at my hand. Slowly, she reaches out and I wrap her icy fingers in mine. I give her a gentle tug and she stands shakily on her skates. I nestle her close to me for balance and warmth.

"It's 50-50," she says, looking up at me, teeth chattering. "But...I'm willing to take the risk."

A slow smile spreads across her face and my insides heat up. I lean down and gently plant a kiss on her lips.

"You won't be disappointed," I whisper.

"You're right," she whispers back. "Because I'll be frozen. One lap around the rink and then it's back to my room."

I grin from ear to ear.

"Cuddling only," Sarah warns. "Strictly for body warmth."

"No problem."

Her fingers wiggle out of mine and find their way into my hair. She pulls me down for a much deeper kiss. When she finishes, she leans back and looks at me. "Merry Christmas, Hunter Reed."

"Merry Christmas."

THE END

Letters to Santa

BY M. K. CONDRY

A coffee shop tease and a combustible attraction take Mr. and Mrs. Claus on a wild ride.

About the Author

M.K. Condry is a wife, mother, grandmother, and she may be one of the few authors who doesn't own a cat (she's allergic). After decades of reading all kinds of romance, she's trying her hand at writing them. If you like steamy contemporary romance, check out her other books on all good book platforms.

Follow mkcondry on Instagram and Facebook. Visit her website mkcondry.com to join her newsletter.

Chapter One

Malcolm

Monday, at seven a.m. sharp, I enter Superintendent Frost's reception area.

"Good morning, Principal Clausen," Helen, Frost's longtime secretary, greets me with her usual warm smile. A little faux Christmas tree sits on the corner of her desktop with miniature ornaments and LED lights. The big box on the floor beside her is filled with unwrapped gifts I know are for the toy drive next week. My attention returns to Helen, and I tell myself to think positive thoughts, but the sympathy in her eyes tells me my suspicions about this meeting are correct. "Go ahead and have a seat. I'll let him know you're here."

We both take in the new chairs in the waiting area. She seems to come to the same conclusion as me and makes a face. There's no way those chairs were made for a man my size. At six-four and two-hundred-plus pounds, not many are.

"I'll stand, thanks."

She smiles again before picking up her phone. How anyone can work this closely with a man like Frost and still smile as much as Helen does is beyond me.

Frost and I have a you-scratch-my-back-and-I'll-scratch-yours type of work relationship, but it's been seven years, and *my* back still itches.

After being the principal at three different elementary schools in Frost's district, I've learned a thing or two about the way the man thinks. This is how I know it's not a coincidence that the day after the scandal at Edgar Elementary School hit the fan, I received Frost's summons.

Because I have a person on the inside, I knew the whole story by school day's end. My best friend, Willa, who happens to be Edgar Elementary's PE teacher, couldn't wait to tell me their principal and a third-grade teacher were caught by a student in a compromising position. "The naked kind," she said with a laugh, and if the incident wasn't about to impact my plans to stay at the school I currently was at, I would've laughed too.

To make matters worse, it isn't just any student who found them, but none other than Superintendent Frost's grandson. No doubt my phone wasn't the only one ringing by four o'clock that same afternoon.

My guess is I'll be packing up my office and adding school number four to my resume.

Sighing, I grab a magazine and leaf through the pages.

Just once, I'd like to grow roots instead of being plucked out and planted somewhere else every few years. At forty-seven, my plan was to stay put until I retired.

Helen stands and gestures for me to follow her. "Frost will see you now."

Frost's door is slightly ajar, so Helen gives the opaque glass insert a courtesy rap before opening it for me. With a nod of thanks, I enter. To my right, the expanse of windows highlights a familiar stumpy silhouette. Even though my arrival is apparent, instead of greeting me right away, Frost remains where he is, hands clasped behind his back, lording over the cars in the lot. His signature cowboy hat sits tall on his head and a cloud of cigar smoke hangs in the air. I glance back at the no-smoking sign on the outer door and exchange a look with Helen before she turns and walks back to her desk.

I've always thought Frost was a hypocritical dick. But he's my boss, so I straighten my spine and address him with respect I don't feel. "Good morning, sir."

He turns to face me and takes a seat behind his desk without a word. I can see his gaze harden under the shade of his hat when I remain standing, towering over him.

I take great pleasure in the little things.

Frost nods towards the empty chair across from him with an impatient hand gesture. "No need to be so formal. Have a seat, Malcolm."

Once I sit, he taps his pencil on the desktop and wastes no time getting to the point.

"I need you to take over for Stewart as principal at Edgar."

Tap. Tap. Tap.

"I'd consider this a personal favor."

Tap. Tap. Tap.

"It's important to take immediate action and to adhere to stricter guidelines going forward."

Tap. Tap. Tap.

"I'm sure I don't have to tell you what a delicate situation yesterday's incident is."

Asshole.

The pencil pauses mid-tap. "What was that?"

Shit. "I said, 'No, sir.'"

"I've been fielding phone calls from concerned parents all day." I highly doubt that, but when he looks up, expecting a response, I nod anyway. "I've given them my word things will be handled promptly, of course." He stands and obnoxiously flicks the brim of his hat. For a moment, I picture crushing it—and him—under my foot.

I stand as well and head for the door.

"And Malcolm?" he adds. I pause and glance over my shoulder. "Do this for me, and we'll see about making this the last time."

"Thank you, sir."

I've dedicated myself to creating environments that would optimally meet Frost's vision for seven years. In all that time, I've clung to the assurance of a permanent location.

I close the door behind me, wondering if I should do the same on Frost's promises.

Frost's words play on repeat in my head as I drive to the coffee shop on Ninth and Sycamore. By the time I arrive, I'm back to feeling frustrated and used.

I'm later than usual and the lot is packed. I know I must look every bit as disturbed as I feel because as I walk towards the entrance, a group of loitering teens quickly steps aside. With their wide-eyed stares on me, I yank the door open with more force than necessary and promptly come to a halt at the line that backs to the door. *Perfect.* The festive holiday music and décor galore do nothing to improve my mood. Jesus, it looks like Party City threw up in here. Eager to bitch to someone, I whip out my phone and start pounding out a text to Willa while I wait.

ME: Ask me how it went.

WILLA: By your angry texting, I'm guessing not well?

Apparently, when you've known someone since childhood, they can tell your mood just from a text.

ME: Exactly.

It's oddly satisfying to add a series of angry emojis.

WILLA: Whoa. Maybe caffeine isn't a good idea right now.

My brows draw together.

ME: How'd you know I was getting coffee?

WILLA: I saw it on my Find Friends app.

ME: That's fucked up, Wil.

The dots start bouncing, but our understanding goes both ways, so I beat her to the punch.

ME: I'm getting your usual.

WILLA: Aww, you love me.

ME: Barely.

At first, the person's subtle movements are merely a blurry backdrop in front of me. But with each swish of her skirt, she stirs up her fruity scent, and now I'm having trouble focusing on anything else.

Back and forth.

Back and forth.

When the movement stops, I look up to discover a petite woman staring at me with scrutinizing blue eyes. Like her swaying, my texting is on pause while we stay locked in an intense staredown until someone behind me clears their throat and not-so-nicely informs us the line has moved forward.

The swaying woman's face turns a tempting blush shade, making the cinnamon dots on her nose and cheeks almost disappear. When she spins around, her russet-colored hair fans out, and I inhale another tantalizing hit of her scent. Drawn to it, I move closer than socially acceptable, and I'm rewarded when her whole body shivers.

Frost's dangling carrots are forgotten. The only thing on my mind now is that here's something that could be all mine.

MAGGIE

I shiver, but not from fear.

I should be intimidated by the sheer size of the man behind me, but instead, I love the way he towers over my barely five-foot height.

I lock my knees to keep from swaying again. God help me, if I accidentally brush up against him, I'd probably faint. Instead, I watch the expression of the barista's face go from friendly greeting to awe as her gaze rises high above my head.

The trace of cigar smoke and a subtle, more pleasing scent growing stronger are the only warnings I get before he utters his first words near my ear.

"What's your name?"

He barks out the command like I owe him. And I bite my lip to keep from groaning.

This non-jolly bearded giant must've cast a spell over me. That's the only excuse I can think of for why I don't tell him my name is none of his business. Luckily, before my name, rank, and serial number spill out of my mouth, a voice in my head reels me in. *Don't make it easy for him, Margaret.*

So, I decide to play a little game with that in mind, telling myself that if this massive growly man comes back each day for more, I'll reward him by marrying him and having his babies. Excited about the prospect, I lean forward and whisper my plan to the barista, who seems all too happy to be on my team.

I can still feel his gaze boring into my back as I make my mad dash from the coffee shop to my car. For a moment, I sit behind the steering wheel, feeling clever for leaving him the first letter of my name written on his cup and the promise of more to come. Giddy with anticipation, I pull out of the parking lot.

Chapter Two

Malcolm

It's been a long fucking week.

The only bright side has been seeing my Coffee Shop Girl every day. Now, it's Saturday, and I wake antsy as shit.

And the hot dream I had starring a blue-eyed redhead wearing nothing but a Christmas sweater has everything to do with it.

I down my coffee, staring out the glass slider leading to my back yard, wondering if my mystery girl goes to the coffee shop on the weekends.

The itch to get away from my quiet house has me reaching for my phone to call Willa only to remember the boys' basketball team she coaches has a tournament this weekend.

Which leaves me only one other choice.

Two hours later, I pull into my buddy Darren Granger's driveway with a bag full of gifts and a huge smile on my face when I see the whole gang outside. Five of his six kids play tag on their front lawn, while four-month-old number six rests in Darren's arms. A twinge of envy hits me at the sight.

I've been so focused on my career the last twenty years, kids weren't even in the back of my mind, and now I figure a family isn't in the cards for me. I'm okay with that, or at least I thought I was. Then I met Coffee Shop Girl, and I can't help but wonder if maybe there's still a chance.

I climb out of my car and I'm immediately accosted.

"Uncle Mal!"

"Pick me up!"

"What's in the bag?"

"Presents for you monsters," I say.

"Okay, kids, give Uncle Mal a chance to breathe," Georgie, Darren's young wife, says, then leans in for a hug. "Hey, you. Glad you could come by."

"Me too. You look gorgeous as always."

"Easy there, buddy," Darren scolds.

Ignoring him, Georgie turns to the kids. "Who wants cookies?"

My bag of gifts is all but forgotten as the kids run for the house.

"How quickly my appeal fades." I hold out my hands. "Hand over my girl." Once little Elizabeth is in my arms, I follow Darren into the modest ranch-style home.

"If she's yours, where's our child support?" Darren asks.

I barely have time to smell the powdery newborn smell before Georgie reaches for Elizabeth. I twist away. "Hey, I just got her."

"She needs to eat, and the last I checked, men don't lactate."

"Don't worry," Darren says. "She'll bring her right back. We don't get many volunteers these days." We enter the family room next to the kitchen, and the volume increases tenfold.

"I can't imagine why not," I deadpan.

Todd, their four-year-old, takes a cookie from his plate and holds it out to me.

"I wouldn't—"

"Thanks, Toddles," I say before taking a bite of the cookie. It's a little soggy, and I make a face.

"I tried to warn you." Darren laughs, then he lowers his voice. "Todd likes to lick his cookies. I think it's his way of marking his territory."

I gladly accept the water bottle he offers me, then sit on the couch.

"Tell me all about this new woman of yours," he says, and I raise a brow. "Willa called Georgie on Friday."

Shaking my head, I give him the CliffsNotes version of the past five days and hand him my phone. One day last week, I snuck a picture while my obsession wasn't looking. It's grainy, and you can't totally make out her face, but it's gotten me through the in-between moments.

He studies the image then blows out a breath. "Man, you're too calm. The waiting would be driving me crazy." If memory serves, he did go crazy when he met Georgie—especially when he learned she was still in high school. *Shit.* I really hope my girl is over twenty-one, at least. Darren tilts his head, and I fight the urge to fidget. "Hmmm, maybe you're not so calm after all, huh?"

"What are you two talking about?" Georgie asks, then lays a milk-drunk Elizabeth back in the crook of my elbow. She drapes a spit rag over my shoulder before sitting on the arm of the chair Darren is occupying. Immediately, he starts playing with the ends of her waist-length hair.

"I was just telling your husband the reason I haven't found someone to spend my life with is that you're already taken."

"Smooth," Darren says.

"What happened to the girl at the coffee shop?"

Darren pulls Georgie onto his lap and shows her the picture from my phone. "'Girl' is right," he says, and because I currently have one of his kids in my arms and the cookie-licker crawling all over me, I mouth, *Asshole.*

"She's not that young." *I hope.* "I'm guessing thirties, maybe."

He lifts a brow. "Maybe? Ow," he whines when Georgie pinches his arm.

"Don't listen to him," Georgie says. "Darren likes to forget that I'm fifteen years younger than him." Georgie zooms in and out on the picture. "She looks familiar; I just can't place where I've seen her before." She hands back my phone. "I'd kill to have her legs though."

Me too. I'd kill to have them wrapped around my waist. My face. Over my shoulders.

"Stop thinking dirty thoughts while holding my kid," Darren says.

I covertly flip him off.

"Seriously though, it's nice to see you focus on something other than work for once." I don't miss the way he gently caresses Georgie's stomach while he speaks. My mouth drops open, and Darren waggles his eyebrows. "What can I say? She can't keep her hands off me."

Georgie rolls her eyes.

"At this rate, your offspring will fill your district."

"Speaking of districts," Darren says, "how's it going with Frost?"

Being a superintendent for the school district south of Frost's and one of my best friends, Darren knows all about my struggles. Pausing, I shift Elizabeth to my shoulder. Then, with my free hand, I wrestle with Todd.

"According to plan. Just a little slower than I'd like."

Elizabeth starts to fuss, so I stand and walk around the room until she quiets.

Georgie smiles. "You're a natural, Malcolm. You'd make a great father someday."

An image of freckle-faced little girls running around calling me Daddy comes to mind.

As if reading my thoughts, Darren nods towards Elizabeth. "Maybe on Monday, when you get a name out of your girl, you can follow in our footsteps." Knowing marriage and kids weren't part of my plan, he holds up a hand when I open my mouth. "Sometimes plans change, man."

"I'll think about it."

And I do—all weekend.

Chapter Three

Maggie

I stop sorting laundry when there's a soft knock on my bedroom door. "Come in."

Donner Cringle, my seventy-five-year-old landlord, pokes his head around the partially open door. The late-morning light spilling in from my window makes his silver hair glow.

For the past five years, I've rented a room in his home. Sadly, last month, he fell off the ladder while trying to clean the leaves out of the rain gutter, and he's having trouble getting around, let alone maintaining the two-story home. Medical bills and a rundown house are taking their toll. I try to pitch in where I can, but we take two steps forward only to have life push us three steps back.

"Hello, dear. Got a minute?"

With a bad feeling in the pit of my stomach, I set my laundry hamper aside and wave him in. "Sure."

He hobbles to the middle of my tiny room, twisting a dish towel in his hands. "You know how I've been struggling lately?"

I do, and I know where this is going. I just wish it wasn't so soon. Fortunately, after two years of subbing for scraps and pinching pennies, I start my new full-time job Monday. *Un*fortunately, it will be two weeks before I get my first paycheck, and my last subbing job was a week ago.

My bank account isn't exactly flush.

"I'm so sorry, honey, but I put the house on the market this morning, and the real estate agent thinks it'll go quick."

"I understand." I do understand, and because he looks like he doesn't quite believe me, I give his frail body a gentle squeeze and add, "Don't worry. Things are turning around for me. I can feel it."

I'm hoping the more I say it, the more likely it'll come true.

Other than the two women inside, the laundromat is surprisingly empty for a Saturday.

After Mr. Cringle left my room, I scrounged around for as much money as I could find. I have a hamper full of Christmas sweaters and a new third-grade class to impress.

Don't forget Malcolm.

I couldn't if I tried. The man is impossible to forget. And on Monday, I'll give him the final letter of my name and see where we go from there— I'm hoping back to his place since I might not have one.

Choosing my machine, I drag my hamper over and begin shoving my first load in the washer. I'm pouring the off-brand soap in the designated cup when the hairs on the back of my neck stand at attention. I look up to find that both women are staring at me. A quick look behind me confirms that, yep, it is, in fact, me they're smiling at. A little uneasy and a lot unsure of the proper laundromat etiquette, I settle for a wave.

Apparently, that's all it takes to make friends in the laundromat because two hours later, Ellen, Candy, and I are sitting cross-legged on the machines devouring a bag of chips, a jar of salsa, and a couple of bottles of mulled wine that we bought from the liquor store next door. We pass the bottle around like a bunch of hobos, and I try not to think about how gross the combination is.

We're a bit tipsy by hour two, and I've told them all about my housing problem.

"Move in with me," Ellen blurts.

I drop my chip in the salsa. "What?"

"Yeah, I have a house with three empty rooms. You can even start paying after you get your first check." She shrugs like her offer is no big deal, when in fact it's huge.

"Ellen, are you serious?"

"I wouldn't have said it if I wasn't."

In the short time we've been here, I learned at least that much about her.

"If you have a house, why don't you have a washer and dryer?" Candy asks.

"I do."

Candy and I exchange a confused glance.

Ellen sighs. "Okay, here's the truth. I work all the time, and I have no social life. I get lonely."

"So, you come to the laundromat to, what... meet people?"

"Yes?"

Candy throws up her hands. "That's it. I'm moving in too."

Once we finish the laundry, we call for a ride so Candy and I can choose our new rooms. Afterward, I go home, tell Mr. Cringle my good news, and pack my stuff. He's so relieved he isn't leaving me homeless he doesn't charge me for this month's rent.

Maybe I was right, and things really are turning around for me.

Chapter Four

Maggie

"It's gonna be a good day, Maggie," I say, giving my reflection a little pep talk. Not only does my new job start today, but I get to see Malcolm after a two-day dry spell.

Because you had to string him along like an idiot.

I curse myself for the millionth time for not giving him my name and number on day one. Who knows how far we'd be if I had? My southern region tingles, having a few naughty ideas. I've never been one for hook-ups, but I'm feeling like it might be a good time to start.

With a bounce in my step, I open my door and make my way to the kitchen.

Thunder roars outside, shaking the patio doors. I flick on the porch light and watch as rain pours from the heavens. It seems that even Mother Nature is putting an end to her dry spell.

"You excited for your first day?" Candy asks, distracting me from my thoughts.

She shuffles barefoot into our kitchen, looking more like a college student than a professional in her sleep shorts, messy blonde bedhead, and an oversized sweatshirt. I smile as she makes a beeline for the fancy espresso machine. With her palms on the edge of the counter, she hoists her bottom onto the granite surface. Once a frothy foam tops her cup with a hiss and sputter of air, she lifts her gaze, scans my outfit, and smiles. "Let's see the sweater."

Self-consciously, I turn away and play with one of my Santa earrings. "It's just a simple sweater."

She tilts her head and raises her perfectly plucked eyebrows. When she hops off the counter suddenly to get an up-close-and-personal look, I yelp and spin away. We end up dancing in circles—with my arms protectively around my torso and her laughter filling the room.

"Stop it." I laugh too as she tugs on my sweater. "You're going to ruin it."

"Like you don't have fifty more just like it in your closet."

She's not wrong. As poor as I am, I have a couple of guilty pleasures. One is my morning coffee, and two is my many Christmas sweaters. If I could wear them year-round, I would.

Within seconds I admit defeat and let her admire the large Santa face on the front of my sweater. "Gonna play a little 'Malcolm sit on my lap' at the coffee shop today?" she teases, not realizing how close she's come to my earlier thoughts.

"Jesus, you two," Ellen grumbles when she walks into the kitchen. "It's five a.m., for Christ's sake."

Much like Candy did, Ellen walks to make a cappuccino for herself.

Candy digs her fingers into my side one last time before taking a step back and focusing all her attention on Ellen. "You look hot, El. Those barre classes are doing amazing things for your ass."

I join Candy in admiring Ellen's pinstripe-gray pantsuit and the generous curves it hugs.

Ellen poses, showcasing her rear, then turns to face us just as "BOSS" by Day1 plays from Candy's wrist. Candy springs into action with a squeal, forgetting all about my sweater and Ellen's rear.

Ellen and I exchange a look.

No matter how much Candy denies it, it's obvious the relationship between her and her boss is way more than employer and employee. Not gonna lie, I'm envious and a bit heart-eyed about the whole romance novel aspect, but Ellen is much more practical.

"That's gonna lead to trouble," she says, then grabs her black patent-leather bag from the counter and walks towards the door to the garage. Never one to sugarcoat things, she adds over her shoulder, "I give it a month."

The door closes behind her with a soft click, and I stand in the kitchen where minutes ago I was happy in my fantasy world where Candy could fall in love with her boss and live happily ever after.

But sadly, Ellen is probably right.

Good thing my new school has a strict policy where that stuff is concerned.

Chapter Five

Malcolm

Monday morning's forecast calls for dreary weather, and for once, they aren't wrong.

Thunder rumbles as I make a run for the coffee shop entrance. A gust of wind turns the fat raindrops sideways, making my umbrella all but useless. But come hell or high water, I'm not turning back to my truck. Because today I'm getting the final letter.

Since I have five of the six letters already, it doesn't take a genius to figure out her name is probably Maggie, but I'm having too much fun not to let this game of ours play out.

Our minimal-word flirting has become the most creative foreplay I've ever experienced. I'm so hungry for her at this point, any little morsel of attention makes me want to scoop her little body up and put her in my pocket.

The thought of her anywhere near my pants has me lengthening my strides.

Now under the awning, I run a hand over my beard, wringing the moisture from the short, coarse hair, but nothing could wipe the smile off my face when I see the familiar swaying of her hips where she stands in line. Anxious to get the first whiff of her sweet scent, I enter.

She turns her head to the side, giving me just a peek at her profile before she faces forward again.

Adrenaline rushes through my veins.

How has this woman worked her way so deep in just six days?

Her mother-with-a-phantom-baby swaying starts up again, and I clock the movement of her pleated skirt as I approach. *What would she do if I steadied her hips with my palms?* As if sensing my thoughts, the second I close the gap between us, her movements stop.

I hum low in my throat. "You smell like gumdrops."

She snorts but otherwise remains silent. She looks like a gumdrop, too, all colorful and sprinkled with glitter. If the last five days were anything to go by, today's sweater will be Christmas-themed as well.

"I'm oddly attracted to these sweaters of yours."

She turns her head slightly, giving me a glimpse of the freckles across her nose and a flash of her impish blue irises. With her lips so close, I can feel each one of her breaths on my face.

"After I give you the last letter," she whispers, "will you still come?"

Whether she means it to sound dirty or not, it doesn't matter because my body takes it that way, and my words run with it. "I'll come for you every day if you want." She stiffens at my double meaning but thankfully doesn't pull away. Encouraged, I move my body closer and wish we were somewhere more private.

The rest of our waiting carries on much the same way, and by the time her coffee is ready, her face is almost as red as her sweater, and I'm a mess of pent-up lust. With one last smirk over her shoulder, she rushes out the door.

I'm still staring after her, trying to decide if I should say 'fuck my coffee' and follow her, when the barista shoves my order under my nose. I look down at the large E written in the now-familiar print on my cup. Yep, it will take a lot more than bad weather to ruin my morning.

"Buckle up, Maggie mine," I murmur, then chase after her.

Chapter Six

Malcolm

I'm so focused on the message I'm typing to Candy, when there's a knock on my window, I jump. My phone slips from my hand and falls between the console and my seat.

With the little drummer boy beating in my chest, I glance to my left.

Malcolm bends, bringing his face even with the glass. His large umbrella shields him from the light rain. "Open up."

Logically, I know he didn't mean for his words to sound dirty, but I clench my thighs to keep them from spreading wide anyway.

I lower the window, and Malcolm instantly molds one of his big hands over the door as if to keep the window in place.

Faint crow's feet frame piercing green eyes, which seem to glow in the parking lot lights. I'm horrible at guessing ages, but I suspect Malcolm is older than me.

As if sensing my line of thought, he leans in closer and studies my face too. I squirm a little under his scrutiny. "How old are you?" he asks in that no-nonsense way of his.

"Thirty-two."

He curses, and suddenly I'm afraid he'll walk away.

I place my hand over his and feel his fingers twitch underneath. "Don't go." I cringe at how desperate I sound. But I *feel* desperate. Seeing him at coffee has been one of the best things that's happened to me lately, and I don't want that feeling to go away.

Before I can form a coherent thought, his large hands are framing my face. "Why would I go when what I want is right here?"

Oh.

"If you don't want my mouth on you, you need to say so now because I've waited days, and I'm not waiting another second."

I lick my lips and shift to my knees on the seat, never taking my eyes off his.

His gaze lowers to my mouth, and it may be wishful thinking on my part, but I swear he whispers, "Mine," right before he kisses me.

The kiss starts slow. Teasing. And all the while, his thumbs stroke back and forth across my cheekbones. I never would've guessed such a thing could send tingles of awareness to other places on my body, but I swear I can feel each pass like a phantom caress between my legs.

I lean back and stare at his face in wonder. He's so handsome and rugged, nothing like what I'm usually drawn to. *Is that why this thing between us is so powerful? So right?* Lightly, I trace his forehead where faint horizontal lines are visible. He closes his eyes and sighs when I reach his temples and apply more pressure. His skin is tan, on the reddish side, and I wonder if he works outdoors. When I first saw him, I remember thinking, *Holy moly, this guy looks like he belongs in the woods chopping down trees... probably with his bare hands.*

"What are you thinking?" His eyes are open again, and the green color swirls with emotions.

"I've never kissed anyone with a beard before."

"Me either." He winks, and I swat at him. Chuckling, he tickles along my jaw with his, until his lips are an inch from mine. "How was it?"

"Perfect."

"How about another, then?"

Before I can answer, he's leaning in for more. His learning bites and searching licks make me frantic—like him, for days I've wondered. Wanted. And I'd give anything to have hours to spend tasting each other. I moan at the thought, and he takes it as an invitation, sliding his tongue past my parted lips.

Things escalate quickly after that, and I have trouble forming a coherent thought. But oh, how I feel everything. The scratchiness of his beard. The dampness of my panties. The bite of pain when he fists my hair.

Goosebumps form on my skin when he toys with the waistband of my skirt.

A surprised squeak escapes me when his hands move lower and palm my bottom. All I can think about is if I'd known he'd be anywhere near my panties, I would've worn sexier ones.

"This ass of yours"—he hoists me up higher until I'm halfway out of the window—"has been tormenting me for days."

Later, I'll be grateful for the aches and bruises from his attention; otherwise, I'd think this eighties book cover thing we've got going on was all just another Malcolm dream. I'm so lost in all the feels I'm swimming in, I'm shocked to realize that we're both in my car now, and I'm sitting on Malcolm's lap.

"How did we get here?"

"Well, last week, I walked into the coffee shop in the worst mood," he says between kisses, "and then there you were, and I haven't been able to think about anything else ever since."

"Smartass."

He smirks. "Oh, you meant *here* here? That's easy... you let me in." The last part of his confession comes out low and sexy, and I want to hear it first thing every morning and last thing every night.

"We met eight days ago."

"We did," he agrees while sliding his big hands beneath my skirt, kneading and massaging as he works his way up my thighs. I shiver when his fingers sneak under the elastic of the practical white cotton, and a rush of moisture soaks the fabric. His growl is all kinds of pleased when he notices, and all worries of lacy panties go out the window.

"It's probably just sex... oh, my God." I groan when he continues exploring, uncovering secrets I had no clue existed. He works my dampness into my skin, like massage oil—painting the globes of my ass and everything in between with my own desire.

85

"What do you say we find out?"

"Right now?" I squeak when he spreads me open wide, dragging what feels like all his fingers from my pucker to my clit.

"Right. Fucking. Now."

"B-but we're in public," I say as I unbuckle his belt and start working his zipper down.

"I only see you, Maggie mine."

People hook up in nightclubs and bars all the time, right? What's wrong with a coffee shop parking lot? I mean, it's still dark out, and my windows are tinted. I bite my lip. *You did say it was gonna be a good day.*

"Second thoughts?" he asks. And right now, as I watch him roll a condom down his impressive length, I can't think of a thing other than *gimme.* "I should probably take you somewhere special," he adds as he drags his teeth down the side of my neck.

"This *is* our special place."

"Mmm. In that case..."

I sigh in relief when he moves aside my panties, and then the smooth head of his cock is right where I need it, rubbing circles around my opening. I wiggle and shift, lining us up like nature's puzzle pieces.

My head falls back, and my horn lets out a little honk of approval when my back hits the steering wheel. We laugh then groan when the move buries him between my folds. The urge to lower the rest of the way is so strong I begin to shake.

Malcolm is a big man, and it's clear now that he is evenly proportioned everywhere as I try to work my way down his shaft slowly. For a moment, I think I may have bitten off more than I can chew. Shaking that thought away, I double my efforts. It's a tight fit, but I'm nothing if not determined to make this work.

"That's so good." I rock my hips, shocked when I feel the beginnings of my orgasm already.

A whoosh of air leaves his parted lips. "Christ."

We're mid-grind when my long-forgotten phone starts the familiar ringtone of my alarm.

"Is it just me, or do you hear 'Jingle Bells' playing too?"

Panic sets in when I realize we only have minutes before the sun lights the sky, and worse, I might be late for my first day of work. "Hurry, I have to be at work in thirty minutes."

"Challenge accepted." Then, thankfully, he takes the baton and starts a slow roll of his hips. I feel a tug on my hair. "Give me that sassy mouth."

Christ, his voice rolls down my spine like warm honey. I shudder with pleasure when he grabs my hips, urging me to move faster.

The music plays on.

He nuzzles his face between my breasts. "I don't know what it is about these sweaters of yours, but they get me so fucking hard."

As if to prove his point, he seems to grow inside me. I moan and pump my hips faster. "I'm all for whatever gets you into the spirit of giving."

One touch of his thumb to my clit, and I see stars. I gasp as my body seems to turn to granite while white-hot pleasure ripples through me. The force of my orgasm surprises us both.

"God dammit." He bucks his hips so violently, chasing the waves and ripples, that the car rocks with the force. All I can do is hold on for dear life while he fills the condom.

Our breathing slowly calms until the rise and fall of our chests becomes in sync.

"It's official," he says into the crown of my head, "this sweater is now our lucky sweater."

Chapter Seven

Malcolm

Later, alone at my office, I line up all six cups like little toy soldiers. *Are you gonna be that guy now—the person who keeps everything?* Movie tickets. Glasses from our favorite restaurants. I finger the panties in my pocket—another keepsake—and stare at the cups.

MAGGIE.

We exchanged numbers before we parted, and I pull hers up now. It's been less than an hour, but I can't wait another minute to talk to her again.

ME: I miss your sweater.

MAGGIE MINE: Just my sweater?

My relief when she responds is beyond anything I've felt before.

ME: Your smile's nice too.

I hit send, and I quickly type out another text.

ME: But your freckles might be my favorite.

I wonder if her whole body is covered in them and vow to find out later.

MAGGIE MINE: "Coffee" in the morning?

God, this girl.

ME: You'd better bring an extra pair of panties.

Ten minutes later, I'm still smiling at the texts like a lovesick fool when Willa enters my office and lowers her tall frame into the chair on the other side of my desk.

"So, the vote was unanimous," she announces while pulling her long blonde hair into a weird knot thing on the back of her head. As usual, she has on her PE teacher gear—sweats and a t-shirt with the school logo on the front—and her whistle hangs from a lanyard around her neck.

I'm eighty-nine percent sure I don't want to hear the answer, but I ask for it anyway. "What vote?"

Ignoring me, she points to the extra coffee on my desk. "Is that mine?"

"Wil," I growl. "What vote?"

"The one where the staff decided you're playing Santa this year."

"Absolutely not."

Apparently, every year Edgar Elementary does this thing where the kids write letters to Santa, and some yahoo must read them all, then dress up as Santa and visit all the students on the Friday before the break. Because I didn't attend the meeting, I'm easy pickings.

Hoping Willa's too distracted rummaging through the bag of donuts I brought to notice, I gather up the cups and set them on my credenza behind me. Best not to give her any fodder.

"The only thing absolute is that it's been decided." She holds up her hand when I open my mouth. "You got the other guy fired. It's like that Santa Claus movie where the person who kills Santa steps in his suit."

Speaking of fodder, I get up and close the door before returning to my seat. These walls have ears that belong to Frost's spies.

"First of all, I didn't fire the last principal. He fired himself when he fucked a teacher on school grounds," I say, then add, "I'm not doing it."

Her smirk does not bode well for me. "What if I show everyone that picture of you in your Santa footie pajamas?"

I was ten! "That's playing dirty."

She shrugs. "I've been told to do whatever necessary to get you in that suit. So, have you met the new teacher yet?"

I narrow my eyes at her change of topic. "No. Why?"

With another annoying smirk, she crosses her ankles on top of my desk and rocks her sneakered feet back and forth. As the principal, I've earned a certain level of respect from the staff. Apparently, Willa didn't get that memo. "She's just super cute, that's all."

"Great. Just what I need." Since I've been principal at Edgar, the staff has been more than accommodating with the new rules. The last thing they need right now is a temptation. "What happened to all the old teachers like when we were kids?"

She stands to leave. "I don't know, but I have a feeling this one will be trouble."

Willa's prediction stays with me long after she's left my office. So, when the bell rings for morning recess, I figure there is no time like the present to meet the new teacher.

Ringing phones, the hum of copy machines, and the punching sound of the large paper-cutter in the work room fade as I make my way to the third-grade wing. I nod in greeting to a few teachers as I pass their rooms.

When I come to the new teacher's open door, it takes me a second to process what I see. She stands with her back to me, writing on the whiteboard. Soft Christmas music plays from the phone sitting next to a coffee cup that matches the six I have back in my office. I wish that's where the familiarity ended, but it's not.

The skirt.

The hair.

And everything else from this angle because I've stood behind this person for six days.

I must make a noise because she turns, and I watch as her expression goes from surprise to confusion at seeing me here at her work.

You and me both, babe.

An awkward silence follows while we stand frozen before she nervously straightens her skirt. *Now's not the time to think about her lack of panties.*

The sweater I'd dubbed our lucky one only hours ago now seems jinxed. I rub a hand down my face. *This can't be happening.*

She comes towards me, and I step back, self-preservation kicking in. The hurt on her face guts me.

"Please tell me you're not the new teacher, that you're not Miss Green." I know it's a stupid wish. I mean, Margaret Green. Maggie Green. *Jesus, you're an idiot, Malcolm.*

"I don't understand what's going on."

I stiffen my spine and harden my heart. "Miss Green. Welcome to Edgar Elementary." I hold out my hand, almost wishing I didn't have to admit what must be said next. "I'm Mr. Clausen. The principal."

Chapter Eight

Maggie

"I'm Mr. Clausen, the principal."

It's been less than twenty-four hours since my hopes of Malcolm and me having a future vanished in a puff of chalk dust. I can still see his pained expression when he held out his hand and introduced himself as my boss.

Now I frown at my home-brewed coffee and wonder if I'll ever have a decent cup again.

"They don't say 'it's a small world' for nothing," Ellen says as soon as I finish telling her and Candy about Malcolm.

"I've always hated that saying," Candy admits.

I have to agree. I try one more sip of my coffee before tossing the more-than-half-full cup down the sink.

Candy gasps and frantically grabs for my arm, but it's too late. We both watch as the liquid disappears down the drain.

"I think there's a place in hell for people like you," she mutters.

"Christ, Maggie," Ellen says when I sigh for the millionth time. "Just go get a damn coffee already."

"I can't go back there. What if Malcolm's there?" *Will he still go?* Or is he suffering a home-brew and a heartache too? My mind conjures up a sad-looking Malcolm, waiting for me, standing off to the side until it's obvious I'm not coming.

"Margaret Ester Green," Ellen says. I wince, regretting ever telling them my full name. "There have got to be at least fifty other coffee shops in town."

"I can't go to another shop. It would feel like cheating."

"Oh, good Lord." Candy throws up her hands and walks out of the kitchen.

"Maggie, wait up."

My newest friend and fellow faculty member, Izzy, hurries towards me with a gaudily decorated mailbox under her arm. Since my transfer was so last-minute, the assistant principal who hired me arranged for Izzy to help set up my classroom. While we worked, she filled me in on who's who around school and how shocked everyone was to discover the wildly talked about recent affair had actually been going on for a year before the culprits slipped up. In return, I told her all about my life. And I mean everything.

Almost everything.

Without thinking, I make a face.

"I know." She fingers one of the rhinestone embellishments. "Kara has interesting taste," she says about the school's librarian, then holds out the mailbox. "This beauty's all yours now. Once your class does their Santa letters, it's good to go. Congratulations, by the way."

"Thank you. I'm actually really excited to be Mrs. Claus this year."

"Oh, and here's the key to the supply closet where the costumes are," she adds, referring to the outfits the former principal and my predecessor wore last year. Of course, that was before they got caught *not* wearing them. Izzy clears her throat. "Um, they might need cleaning, if you know what I mean."

I wrinkle my nose.

"I'm just saying, I don't think anyone's been in there since Old Saint Dick's Day."

We're still laughing as we enter my classroom. I freeze mid-stride, and Izzy deftly sidesteps me. Without taking my eyes off the coffee cup sitting on my desk, I set the mailbox down.

Before I have a chance to, Izzy reaches for the cup, eyeing the writing on the side. "'Missed you this morning...'" If her eyebrows shoot up any higher, they'll disappear in her hairline.

I snatch the cup out of her hand. "Give me that."

"Did you skip out on morning car sex with Coffee Man this morning?" Suddenly the top of my desk becomes very interesting. "What? Did he do something?" She straightens and rolls up her sleeves like she's readying for a fight.

"Settle down, Rocky. He didn't do anything. Let's just say we discovered a conflict of interest." I shrug as if the whole thing isn't breaking my heart.

"Oh, sweetie. I'm sorry. Is he married?"

I shake my head.

"Girlfriend?"

Another shake.

Her eyes light up. "Boyfriend?"

Despite my misery, I laugh at her excitement over the prospect. "None of the above."

"What else could there be? It's too early to know if he has stinky feet."

Not known for having tight lips, I open my mouth and sink all the ships in the harbor.

"Oh, my God. You had sex with our principal?"

I rush to the door and close it. "Jesus, keep your voice down. Are you trying to get me fired?" Suddenly exhausted, I lower to my chair.

"Sorry. Lord, that's some small world you live in."

If one more person says that...

Izzy starts pacing in front of my desk. "Of course, *Malcolm*. Duh. Why didn't I connect those dots sooner? I mean, how many Malcolms the size of a mountain could there be? Not that it would've mattered. By then, you two were already like a Little Ceasars five-dollar pizza." When I don't react, she explains. "Ya know, hot and ready?" She waggles her eyebrows at me suggestively, and I roll my eyes. Her eyes go wide suddenly.

I look towards the door, expecting to see the man in question standing there, then blow out a breath when it's still just us.

"I guess this would be a bad time to tell you that after you left the staff meeting last night, we picked who would be Santa this year?"

Dread sinks like a brick in my stomach. "No."

"I'm afraid so."

There go my plans to stay away from Malcolm until after winter break. Because according to Izzy's intel earlier, he is the Santa to my Mrs. Claus.

Now we'll be forced to spend time together on Friday when we visit all the classes. If only we hadn't had sex, maybe I could think about him without wanting him inside me again. But there's no un-ringing that jingle bell.

"Mrs. Green!"

The papers in my hands go flying, making the students laugh. While I gather up the mess, I address Gracie. "It's *Miss* Green, Gracie, and please don't yell out in class." For some reason, Gracie has a hard time coming to terms with the fact that I'm not married. And not for the first time, I wonder if she's channeling my mother from the grave.

Gracie slides a paper on my desk. "You need to write a letter to Santa too."

"Oh." I'm about to say no when I catch the hopeful faces of the other students. *What's the harm in you writing to Santa?* Heck, it might even be fun. I'll just throw it away when I'm done with it. "Okay, sure. I'll write a letter too."

The classroom erupts into cheers, and I smile. "Okay, settle down. There are only twenty minutes left in class." The students lower their heads and begin to write, and I stare at the blank sheet of paper, chewing on the end of my pen.

After writing a few not-very-creative things down, I try to think of something I really want. Malcolm comes to mind, and my eyes sting. Blinking furiously, I write my last wish.

As usual, when the bell rings, loud chatter and screeching chairs fill the room. I take my place at the door and wait while the kids drop their letters into the mailbox before filing out.

With all the commotion, one of the kids knocks the box off my desk. Letters spill, like a paper avalanche, to the floor. Shouting that their wishes won't be fulfilled now, students start shoving letters back inside the box. Sighing, I do my best to soothe their worries and can't stop thinking about the glass of wine (or three) waiting for me at home.

Chapter Nine

Malcolm

It's Wednesday, December fifteenth. Only two more days until winter break. More importantly, it's been two days since Maggie last met me at the coffee shop. Not that I blame her. It's kind of hard to friend-zone someone after you've had sex with them in the front seat of a car.

I still go though, because I'm an idiot, hoping she'll be there, only to be greeted with a you're-so-pathetic stare from the barista.

The fact that Maggie obviously doesn't want to see me doesn't keep me from buying her favorite chestnut praline latte and putting it on her desk. This morning her scent is so strong it's like she ducked out right before I got there.

Now it's late afternoon, the last of the students have gone, and only a few teachers remain in their classrooms. I can't help but wonder if Maggie is one of them.

Friday will be the first time Maggie and I have been together since Monday, and I'm more than happy to put on the red monkey suit to make that happen. Sighing, I gather up the stack of letters on my desk and head home.

Two hours later, Willa sits on the opposite end of my couch.

"Thanks for helping me."

"No problem," she says. "It's not like I have a life." She holds up one of the letters. So far, they've been quite entertaining. "Get this one... 'Dear Santa, I think there would be more peace on earth if I got a puppy. Just saying.'" We laugh, and she picks up another letter. "'Dear Santa, a kid at recess said you weren't real, but after I punched him in the nose, he saw the error of his ways.'"

"That kid gets coal."

She clutches the letter to her chest. "What? No way. This kid was me when I was little."

I hold up my letter. "Okay, my turn. 'Dear blah blah, you get the drift.'"

"Wait. Are you saying that, or is that actually what the letter says?"

"It's what the letter says. This kid is probably friends with the nose-punching kid." I continue with the letter. "'I want my best friend to get out of detention for punching a kid in the nose.'" I raise my brows. "I rest my case. Where's the coal pile?"

Willa laughs. "Stop it. Give me that." I hand her the letter, and she picks up the next one. "This kid gets an A for penmanship if nothing else." She starts to read and then stops. "Huh, this must be from a teacher. 'I'd like donuts in the break room, and not the cheap kind. New white-board markers because someone keeps stealing mine—'"

"Probably the kid who punches people," I mutter.

Willa ignores me, then whistles. "Man, who did you piss off?"

"Me?"

"Yeah, this last part is about you."

"Well, read it already."

"Okay. It says 'I wish Principal Clausen didn't work here.'"

"Damn, that's harsh. Is there a signature?"

I don't miss her wince right before she sets the letter down. "I don't think they meant for anyone to see it, especially not you." I cross my arms over my chest. "Your principal glare doesn't work on me, remember?"

Willa is protecting me, but why? Then it hits me, and I fight the urge to rub the pain in my chest. "It's Maggie, isn't it?"

She nods, and I slump on the couch. "Wait now, let's think about this."

"What's there to think about? She stopped going to coffee"—I point to the letter—"and now this?"

"Malcolm," Willa says, "she had sex with her boss. She's probably worried she'll lose her job, not to mention embarrassed."

I'll give her that. "But to wish me gone?"

"If you weren't principal anymore, you could be together, right?"

I sit up straight again, seeing Maggie's wish in a whole new light. "You think that's what she means?"

"Why not? You said it was all good until she found out you were her boss, right?"

So good.

Chapter Ten

Maggie

"The scene of the crime," I whisper to the supply closet walls. The stale air still reeks of bad decisions, and I wonder if Izzy was right, and no one has been in here since the guilty parties.

I venture inside further. When I set my purse down, my new whiteboard markers rattle inside, reminding me to thank Izzy for the gift later. I found them on my desk this morning when I arrived with a note that said to keep them safe. I guess I wasn't the only teacher missing pens.

I take the last bite of my donut and dust off my hands. I was ridiculously excited when I saw donuts in the break room this morning. So much so, I may have overdone it by eating two and even taking an extra for later—a major perk of this new job, that's for sure. Of course, being able to pay Ellen rent is nice too.

I turn in a circle with my hands out wide, skimming the storage racks with my fingertips. I try to picture two adults going at it in here. I lift a leg and brace it on the opposite shelf. Huh, I guess it could be done, but you'd have to be pretty limber, and from what I've heard about the chubby old principal, it doesn't seem likely.

"Stop imagining other people having sex and find the costumes," I tell myself. The light that spills in from the hall is just enough to see what I wish I could unsee. Like a perfect bed for carnal delights, on the floor lies the Mr. and Mrs. Claus costumes. I can only guess what kind of bacteria has flourished after a year. I look to the ceiling for answers. "Now what?"

All at once, the room darkens as if the sun has fallen behind a mountain. "Miss Green?"

I don't need to turn to know the voice belongs to Malcolm. There is no mistaking the way my body reacts to him. My breathing becomes a little choppy, and muscle memory kicks in big time between my thighs. Embarrassed, I lower my leg and turn.

"Sorry to interrupt," he says, smirking. "I was making my rounds before leaving and heard something in here." And then, echoing my thoughts from earlier, he adds. "I'm not sure anyone's been in here since... well, you know."

"Old Saint Dick's Day?"

He takes a step closer. "Huh?"

"Never mind."

He gestures to the shelf where my leg was braced earlier. "So, what were you doing exactly?"

Suddenly, it's not the old principal and teacher I imagine on the floor, but Malcolm and me. My core tightens almost painfully, and my face burns. Instead of covering my cheeks like I want to, I gesture to the pile on the floor. "I came to get the costumes so I could take them to the dry cleaners, but even if they were dry-cleaned, they seem icky now."

The deep rumble of his laughter makes my stomach flutter. "Yeah, I can understand that." He crosses his arms, drawing my attention to the chunky cardigan he's wearing and how the light gray T-shirt underneath stretches tight over his barrel chest.

I swallow the puddle of drool that's gathering and pull my cell out of my pocket. I'm Googling costume places when Malcolm speaks again, startling me.

"You've been avoiding me."

Time to address the elephant, Maggie. "Look, what happened the other morning was a mistake..." I cringe, not liking the bitter taste the word leaves on my tongue. And the way he flinches as if struck makes me feel even worse. "What I mean to say is, I don't regret a second of it. It's just—"

"It can't happen again."

"Yeah." I sigh. "Honestly, I was this close to living in my car before, and this job is more important than..."

Us.

"I get it," he says. "Besides, with the dust still settling from the last principal's drama, it's not a good idea for us to, you know, so..."

He's moved within reach now, and I tilt my head to keep eye contact.

My hands twitch at my sides. If only I had pockets to give them somewhere to go, and if only Malcolm wasn't wearing a sweater that looks cozy and soft, then maybe I'd be able to keep my hands to myself.

But I don't.

And he is.

And it does.

So, I begin to finger the edge of the knit. "If things were—"

"Different," he finishes, running his thumb along my cheek.

"Yeah. Different."

Off in the distance, someone drops their keys. Malcolm comes to his senses first and steps away.

I clear my throat. "I found a costume place a little over an hour away with some replacements. I can be there and back before dinner."

"We." He takes a step towards me again, and I step back, hitting the metal rack next to me. *Jesus, get a grip, Margaret.* "*We* can be back before dinner," he says, then gestures for me to precede him down the hall.

"You want to come with me?"

"I should probably come and try it on, don't you think?"

That is a horrible idea. "That's a great idea."

Chapter Eleven

Malcolm

Being alone in a car for hours with Maggie Green is undoubtedly one of the worst ideas I've ever had. Having her only an arm's reach away? Yeah, such a bad idea.

I follow her to the mostly empty parking lot. She rummages through her purse, and I hear the unmistakable sound of keys.

"We can take my car," she offers and heads in that direction.

There's no way I'll be able to sit for over an hour in the car we had sex in and survive. I barely managed to not pounce on her in the closet a minute ago. I touch her arm, halting her steps. When her baby blues focus on me, I gesture to my truck. "I think I should drive."

I see the moment she understands. Her eyes go wide, and her lips form a cute little O. *Yeah, 'oh' is right.*

"That's probably best," she admits.

Side by side, we walk to my truck in silence. I gesture for her to climb in the open passenger door with a sweep of my arm. I stand for a second, taking in the sight of her.

I've dreamed of her in my truck, usually with fewer clothes on, but this is just as nice. No, better, I realize, almost like the restored bucket seat has been waiting for her this whole time.

Suddenly, I can see her clear as day, years from now, sitting just like this, streaks of gray in her hair. We'd have grown kids and grandkids on the way. She'd look up at me with... well, not confusion like she is now.

Feeling like a sentimental idiot, I close her door and round the hood to the driver's side.

The drive to the costume place is anything but quiet. By the time we hit the thirty-minute mark, I've learned many things while sitting next to my little Magpie. One thing that stands out above all others is that I understand now why the former principal couldn't wait before ravishing the teacher in the supply closet.

I'm ready to pull the truck over and drag Maggie onto my lap... again.

I groan.

"I'm sorry," she says sheepishly. "I know I talk too much."

Before I can think better of it, I reach over and cover her hand with mine. Hers is so tiny and fragile-feeling, I want to bring it to my thigh and cradle it there. I snatch my hand back and put it on the wheel where it's safe.

"Not at all. I like hearing you talk." I feel like a selfish dick for my dirty thoughts. I vow to turn it down a notch.

She turns her body sideways on the bench seat, and my gaze flits to her legs, and my mind remembers a whole lot of skin showing when she had her leg perched on the shelf earlier. My pants grow a little tighter in the zipper area. *Okay, I never said I wouldn't look.*

"Is your family large?" she asks, and I laugh. "I didn't mean size-wise, although you're quite large. How tall are you anyway? Your parents must be tall too, huh? They'd almost have to be to produce someone your size. Not that you're too big or anything..." I glance over at her with raised eyebrows, and she blushes. "I like your size, is all I mean."

I can't help but tease her. "Oh, yeah?"

She swats at my arm. "You know what I mean."

Cutting her some slack, I answer her questions. "I'm six-four." She whistles, and I laugh. "And both my parents and grandparents are gone."

"Oh. I'm sorry to hear that."

"My parents had me when they were older," I say. "I was an oops baby."

"You're an only child?"

"Yep. You?"

"We have that in common."

I glance over, and Maggie's staring at me with a soft smile. I fight the urge to rub the warm spot growing in my chest. She looks down at her hand resting on the diamond-stitched bench seat. She begins rubbing the leather, and I notice her nails have miniature Christmas trees painted on them.

She switches topics again, and I like that I'm starting to get used to her mind. "I like your truck."

"Thank you." Because I love it too, it pleases me she feels the same. Three years ago, Darren and I went to an auction, and I ended up going home with a fully restored 1950 Chevy. Thinking of Darren makes me curious about something, so I steer her back to the topic of family. "Do you want a big family... kids?"

"I'd like to find their father first, but yes, I'd like children someday."

What would you give up to be the one she finds?

According to my watch, it takes us an hour and twenty-two minutes to arrive at our destination. On the way, we stop at the store to grab some candy and water bottles to hand out to the kids on Friday.

Five cases of water and ten large candy bags later, we arrive at the Crazy Costume Corner. From there, everything goes smoothly until we get back on the road and come to a complete stop on the freeway. Ten minutes later, we still haven't moved an inch. Maggie pulls out her phone to check the traffic news.

"It seems there's been a major fuel spill ahead when a piece of a bridge collapsed on top of a truck." She looks up at me. "It's blocked all lanes."

Great. I check my watch, noting it's seven-thirty now. We'll be lucky to get home in time for school tomorrow. Both of us calling out, or worse, strolling in school in the same clothes we wore yesterday, looking like we slept in the truck, would not look good.

Maybe no one will notice.

Even I can hear the doubt in my thoughts. Our odds with Frost's spies everywhere are not good on that score. No matter. If I keep my hands to myself for the next however many hours, what could they say? And that shouldn't be a problem if we stay in our respective spots.

"Sorry," she says, scooting closer to me. "I get a little nervous in traffic."

Yeah, this is definitely bad.

Chapter Twelve

Maggie

For the fifth time, I check for updates on the cleanup. They estimate it will take another six hours before they have one lane clear for us to pass.

It's ten o'clock now, so if all goes according to plan, we'll be home by —*oh, my God, who freaking cares at this point*. I'm stuck in a truck that seems to shrink with every hour that goes by, with the most tempting man I've ever met.

We sit so close now I can feel the heat of his body all along my side. At some point, he rested his arm around the back of the seat. I want to grab that capable hand of his that dangles just over my shoulder and wrap it around me.

"I think I need to pee."

Malcolm chokes on the sip he's just taken from his drink. He reaches up and turns on the cab light. His gaze zeros in on the bottle in his hand.

I'm already shaking my head before he even says anything. "No."

"Well, I don't see another option, Maggie."

My tummy flutters like every time he says my first name. I'm happy we're back on a first-name basis, but does that mean we're at the stage of a relationship where peeing in a cup is acceptable?

"I can hold it."

"If you're sure."

I glance over when I feel his body shaking. "You're enjoying this, aren't you?"

"Very much."

"We'll see how funny you think it is when your bladder is screaming and you have to drop your pants in front of me and pee in a cup."

During my tirade, his body has gone still beside me. I look around to search for danger, but only see the same view that's been there for the last three hours. I don't know why, but I lower my voice to barely a whisper. "What's wrong?"

Slowly, he turns his head in my direction, and the only danger I see is the hot desire staring back at me. "I wouldn't have a problem dropping my pants in front of you."

Before I can think on that further, he turns back around, putting an end to the topic.

It's been three hours, eighteen minutes, and fifty-five seconds.

Headlights around us start to switch off. People step out of their vehicles to stretch their legs. And a motorhome just to our left opens its door and welcomes people who need to use the restroom. And bet your bloated bladder, I'm one of the first in line. Their simple act of kindness almost brings me to tears.

Back in the truck, I sigh in relief.

"Better?" Malcolm asks.

"Much."

It's obvious the children in the minivan next to us are getting restless. They've started climbing from seat to seat, rocking the whole vehicle. I make eye contact with the harried-looking mother, and she mouths, *Help me.* Malcolm chuckles beside me.

"That poor woman," I say and realize she probably isn't the only parent struggling right now. When Malcolm doesn't respond, I glance his way. He's looking at the motorhome with a thoughtful look on his face.

"Come on." He reaches behind the seat and grabs the bag from the costume store. "I have an idea."

Malcolm explains his idea on the walk over, and I want to hug him so badly my arms ache. Instead, I skip the rest of the way there with a laughing Malcolm trailing behind. Cathy and Lyle are more than happy to let us use their motorhome, especially once we tell them why.

Now, Malcolm and I have transformed into Santa and Mrs. Claus, and a giddy Cathy is busy taking pictures of us with her phone. "This is the best idea ever," she says. "Gosh, you guys make the cutest couple."

"Oh, we aren't a—"

"Thank you," Malcolm interrupts. "I think so too."

Malcolm looks down at me, and I can't help the smile that spreads on my face. His lips curl up at the corner before he whispers, "You ready to do this?"

I give in to my urge to squeeze him. He seems shocked at first, but then his arm wraps around my shoulder. It's not a full-body hug like I want, but it'll do. "You, Principal Clausen, are on the good list for sure."

He chuckles, and it makes his fake belly bounce. "Not with these thoughts going through my head, I'm not." I'm stunned when he presses a kiss to the top of my head. "Now, let's go make some parents happy."

Time flies by, all thanks to Malcolm.

Kids from a mile front and back come running to see Santa. We lower the tailgate, and Malcolm sits there while I hand out small bottles of water and candy. Before we know it, we have a line a mile long. It's the most amazing thing I've ever seen.

Malcolm leans over a little girl to hear her better. I snap a picture with my phone to catch the look of awe on her face. Her red hair is pulled back in two uneven pigtails, and I can see the freckles that dot her cheeks from where I stand. *She could be ours.* My heart flutters. Malcolm laughs at whatever she says, and the sound does something funny to my tummy.

I startle when my phone vibrates in my hand.

CANDY: Where are you?

I fill her in and send her a video of Malcolm and the long line of kids.

CANDY: WTF? That's nuts.

ME: I know. He's amazing.

CANDY: Mm-hmm.

ME: Don't you think it's cool?

CANDY: Of course I do, I'm not a total Scrooge, but you said HE was amazing, not IT.

Malcolm laughs again, and I can almost feel the deep masculine rumble against my skin. I forget all about Candy, the kids, the fuel spill. Everything fades away except Malcolm in that Santa suit or, better yet, Malcolm out of the Santa suit. I think back to when his arm was around me in the motorhome, how sturdy and powerful it felt to be held by him. Our gazes lock, and the smile on his face slips at whatever he reads from my expression. I can only imagine how I must look. I know how I feel, though.

Starved.

Like I could ravish him in a supply closet on a pile of St. Nick's coat and trousers.

Something passes between us, and suddenly, the need to touch him is overwhelming, and before I know what I'm doing, I'm moving closer. His gaze follows my approach. I don't stop until my body is pressing against his leg. I can feel the muscles of his thigh twitch, and the heat in his eyes nearly singes my panties right off. I'm seconds from climbing on his lap and making my wish come true when an excited shout from the next kid in line startles us apart.

"Oh, my God." I take a few steps back and try to calm my raging hormones. It takes Malcolm a minute longer before he breaks eye contact. Once he does, I feel relief and sorrow all at once.

Chapter Thirteen

Malcolm

Once the kids and parents disperse, Maggie and I head for the motorhome to change back into our street clothes. If I thought the sexual tension was thick before, it's nothing compared to now. The heated looks we exchanged are no doubt heavy on both our minds.

I glance to my left, trying to gauge her mood. The few headlights that are still on give me a clear view of her pink cheeks. Her bottom lip is swollen from where she keeps worrying it with her teeth, and I want to reach over and soothe it with my thumb.

After I help her up the motorhome steps, we make our way to the back where the bathroom is. It's surprisingly large for a motorhome. *Large enough for two,* my mind helpfully supplies. Cathy and her husband are still socializing with other drivers, leaving Maggie and me alone.

"Maggie," I whisper, and she freezes. I run my finger along her stiff spine, chasing the shivers that skate down her back. When I reach the white fur hem of her skirt, I pause, giving her a chance to stop me. "Tell me to stop."

"I... I don't want to."

Thank fuck. I remove one glove and drape it over her shoulder, so there's no doubt my bare hand is touching her next. With one ear to the door, I reach beneath her skirt until my fingers brush her bare thigh. We both groan as I draw tiny circles with my thumb. "You're so soft here." My mouth waters.

Gently, I push her further into the bathroom, pressing her against the sink. Cathy laughs outside, and we exchange a look of urgency in the mirror. I shut the door, lower to my knees, then lift her skirt. "Hold this."

Her nervous laugh ends in a moan when she looks over her shoulder. "What about—"

"Let me have one more taste," I plead. When she looks on the fence, I push. "When we get back to school, we can start over as friends, but for now, tonight, give us this."

Maggie nods and lifts her skirt, revealing white panties with tiny candy canes on them. *I fucking love candy canes.* To reward us both, I lightly bite one round cheek. She squeaks and starts to pull away, but I grab her hips and run my tongue along the seam of her ass through the cotton. Her moan is low and deep when I return to her wet center and suck.

Not wanting to make a mess of my pants, I reach down and grip myself with one hand while the fingers of my other have all the fun playing with her.

"Hold your panties aside for me. Let me get at you." As soon as she does, I slide three fingers, like a pledge, through her lips, spreading her wetness over the hood of her sex. When I tap her pulsing clit, she pushes her cute little ass in my face.

The voices outside the motorhome get louder, and I know we need to hurry. It's time to give her a little incentive. "If you come in the next sixty seconds, I'll give you three more orgasms in the truck later."

Her only answer is to grind down on my probing fingers. She fucks herself while I continue to bite and suck bruises into her flesh. Pre-cum dampens the fabric of my pants, and I know any second now I'm getting off with her. Frantically, I pull my dick out just as ribbons of come fill my cupped hand. I stroke her G-spot, and she curses, bearing down to my knuckle as her release rolls through her body.

Breathless, she collapses against the counter, and I sit back and take a minute to study her. I want to pull her into my lap, but I know we've already pushed our luck with time. So, I stand, gently nudge her away from the sink, and rinse my hand off. I watch her as she rights her clothes. When we're both done, I pull a blushing Maggie into my arms.

"I think we're both on the naughty list now," she says.

With a knuckle under her chin, I lift her face and lower my lips to hers. She sighs into the kiss, pressing more firmly against me. Needing more, I grip her bottom and lift her until her legs wrap around me. I tug my fake beard down, and we stare for a second before our mouths fuse again. The taste of her tongue and pussy mingles, and I wish I could go down on her once more. Breathing hard, we pull back, and I immediately press a line of kisses down her throat.

"Hey," she says, pulling off my Santa hat and wig to get her fingers in my hair. "We should get out of here." She tilts her head to give me better access.

"In a minute."

"We had our minute."

That reminds me. I lower Maggie to her feet and step out of the bathroom. "Hurry and get changed so we can get back to the truck." I wait for her to close the door before whispering through it, "Someone earned her three orgasms."

Chapter Fourteen

Malcolm

I made good on my promise, going down on Maggie the minute we returned to the truck, then using my fingers to make her come two more times on the drive home. Sated, she dozed the rest of the way while my mind spun around our options, coming up empty.

It's still dark when we finally make it back to school, and Maggie's car looks lonely in the lot. Later, when I walk into my home alone, I'll understand the feeling completely.

For now, I soak up Maggie's presence. Reluctantly, I remove my hand from hers. "I wish—"

"Don't speak." She rests her head against my arm. "Let me live in this fantasy for a few more seconds."

Placing a kiss on the top of her head, I inhale her scent, knowing it'll be the last time we're this close. She sniffles, and before I can speak again, she bolts out of my truck. I find it hard to swallow around the lump in my throat as I watch her drive away, taking a piece of my heart with her.

The solution hits me while I shower, and I can't believe how obvious it's been this whole time. But Darren knew, didn't he? He even planted the seed when I visited last.

Sometimes plans change.

So, by five a.m., I've already left a message on Darren's voicemail, and by six a.m. I'm walking out of the coffee shop with another chestnut praline latte, and if all goes well, it won't be the last.

When I arrive at school, Maggie's car's back in the lot, so I know she's here. I'm walking up the school steps, fighting the urge to go straight to her room. But I need to stick to the plan. I smile. *The new plan.*

My cell rings just as I'm opening my office door. I nearly drop it and all the coffees trying to answer it in my excitement. I juggle my coffees and laptop bag, reach inside my coat, and answer without looking at the caller ID.

"Five a.m., really?" Darren gripes.

"Good morning to you too, sunshine."

"Asshole," he says. "It's bad enough we've got the ankle-biters waking us up at all hours."

I kick the door shut and set my stuff down. A baby cries in the background. "Just think, you have another on the way."

"Ugh, don't remind me." There's a sound of a door shutting, and the noise quiets. "Well, I'm up now. Hit me."

"Okay, so—"

"Oh, wait," he interrupts, "before I forget, Georgie remembered where she'd seen your coffee lady before. It turns out she subbed at Brandon's school not too long ago," he says, referring to their eight-year-old. I don't have the heart to tell him his news is a little too late. "She's a teacher."

"Yeah—"

"Isn't that crazy? Small world, huh?"

"Darren."

"What? Oh." He laughs. "Sorry, go ahead."

"I have something I want to run by you. Do you think you could meet me for lunch today?"

I've never put much stock in fate before, but after my lunch with Darren, I can't deny the feeling of rightness that only grows stronger the more I think of the changes I'm about to make. It's not the future I had planned for me. It's better. I pull Maggie's letter to Santa out of my pocket and reread it for the millionth time.

What would you give to be the one?

Everything.

Willa pokes her head in my open door. "Knock, knock."

"Hey, come in." I nod towards the iced coffee I picked up for her on my way back to school.

"You're a god." Willa lunges for the cup. "How was your night?"

A speed reel of last night's events comes to mind, and I smile.

"You're scaring me. You don't normally smile that big."

"Shut up. Look at this." I slide my phone across my desk. On it is the offer Darren and I came up with at lunch.

She takes her sweet time, annoyingly slurping her coffee, making noises that could either be good or bad coming from her.

I lose my patience after the fourth grunt. "Dammit, Wil."

She laughs. *The brat.* "Sorry, I couldn't resist teasing you." She hands back my phone. Willa nods towards Maggie's letter, still open on my desk. "This wouldn't have something to do with a particular third-grade teacher, would it?"

"It might."

"I'll miss you. Hey, do you think the new school needs a PE teacher?"

I pick up the phone and dial Darren's number. "Let's find out."

It's showtime.

I secure the Santa hat on top of the white wig.

"You look—"

"Ridiculous, I know." I frown at my reflection in the mirror as I try to cover my beard with the fake one. "Come help me fix this in the back." I must admit, the costume is pretty great. Last night it was dark, and I was understandably preoccupied.

Now, in the light of day, it's easy to see why all the kids went nuts. I'm hoping Maggie doesn't think *I'm* nuts when I tell her my news. My stomach somersaults, and beads of sweat break out along my forehead.

"I was going to say awesome," Willa says while adjusting the collar of my coat. She grabs a napkin from my desk and dabs it on my face. "There. It's kind of cute that you're nervous."

"Yeah, real cute. I just want it over with."

"Ha. Just what every girl wants to hear from her soon-to-be husband."

My stomach drops a few inches. "Husband? Let's get the boyfriend role first."

Willa waves that away. "Whatever. You and I both know it's a done deal. I've already started shopping for the groomswoman dress."

"Stop it. You're making it worse."

"Don't be silly. Maggie's wishes are clear, and no one lies to Santa."

I take one last look in the mirror. "Okay. I'm ready."

Chapter Fifteen

Maggie

I f I didn't know better, I'd say Malcolm was nervous. We haven't had time to talk much with all the kids around, but the more classrooms we visit, the more agitated he seems to get. I side-eye him as we make our way to the final classroom, which happens to be mine.

It doesn't sit right with me, not clearing the air between us before we go on break.

I can hear the kids' excited voices the closer we get to my classroom. I put my hand on Malcolm's arm, and he stops immediately.

"Hey, are you okay? You seem a little tense." I worry my lip, and his gaze drops to my mouth.

His laugh is borderline manic. And coming from Santa, it's... odd. "I'm good. Let's do this."

While the last few students tell Santa their wishes, I sneak out to do a quick change back into my Miss Green attire, so I can help my kids prepare for the end of class. I make it back in time to see the final student resume their seat.

I'm so busy cleaning up, at first, when Malcolm clears his throat, I ignore it. But when he does it again a little louder, I glance up to find his intense focus on me. And just like last night, the urge to go to him is so overwhelming, by the time he summons me with a crook of his finger, I'm already walking towards him.

Smiling, he pats his inner thigh. "Come sit on Santa's lap, Miss Green."

The students start chanting encouragements. Slowly, I lower myself to his tree trunk of a leg. I squirm a little, trying to get comfortable, which isn't easy to do with my legs dangling a foot off the ground. When I bump and rub against his groin, I feel him harden underneath me.

With a low groan, Malcolm stills my wiggling with his large hand on my hip, then speaks for my ears only. "If you want this to remain G-rated, you'd better settle."

I can't help the giggle that escapes. "Sorry."

His brows draw together. "Something tells me you're not." Then, to my horror, he pulls out a very familiar-looking letter. The same one I thought I tossed in the trash. In his best Santa voice yet, he addresses the classroom. "I have here a letter from your very own Miss Green. Unfortunately, I cannot fulfill the final thing on her wishlist."

Oh, God.

The donuts.

The markers.

How did I not connect those things with my list? *You've been a little busy fucking your boss.* All the while, "Santa" has been fulfilling my wishes.

All except one.

The students gasp in horror, and I want to crawl under one of the desks until everyone leaves, maybe even stay until the custodian comes to lock up. I look at the clock and will it to tick faster. "I'm sure the students don't need to hear this."

Malcolm dismisses my attempt to end my humiliation with a flick of his wrist. The letter flutters in his hand, mocking me.

"What's her wish?" a little boy at the back shouts, and I make a mental note to assign him trash duty when we return from break.

"Well, you see, Miss Green wished Principal Clausen could love her." Giggles roll through the room. I scowl at Santa because we both know that's not what I wrote, but he only smiles out at the children like he isn't embarrassing the heck out of me.

"Malcolm, please," I beg.

But he speaks right over my plea. "What Miss Green doesn't realize is that Principal Clausen is already in love with her, so her wish isn't necessary."

Someone gasps, and I look out over the sea of shocked youths, sure that my expression mirrors theirs, then I notice other teachers and students have crowded in the room. Izzy stands with her hand over her mouth and tears sliding down her cheeks. My heart is pounding so hard it's hard to catch my breath.

I turn back to Malcolm. "You... I mean, he does?"

"He does."

"Do I get a new wish then?"

The fake white mustache curls up when he smirks. "Seems only fair."

I pretend to think about it. "I think I'd like to kiss Mr. Clausen."

Without taking his gaze from mine, he speaks to the room. "Santa and Miss Green will be right back."

And with that, he stands with me still in his arms and marches from the room. I catch Izzy's gaze on the way out, and she gives me a thumbs-up, and I know she'll watch over my class. The cheering and clapping fade as we make our way to Malcolm's office. Once we're behind the closed door, he wastes no time crushing his lips to mine.

Our teeth crash with an audible clack, and I don't even care if I chip a tooth. We use teeth and tongues, and it still isn't enough. Malcolm grabs my bottom and grinds my core against his abdomen.

"Holy cow," I breathe. "Do that again." He does, and then my eyes nearly roll back into my skull when he sneaks those large fingers of his under the elastic of my panties. I'm so wet already they slide easily through my folds.

"You feel so good." He tucks his face in my neck and sucks on the skin just below my ear. I shiver, and my moans compete with his. His fake beard tickles my neck, and I can't help but laugh. Malcolm leans back and pulls down the scratchy hair, revealing the real stuff beneath. Suddenly, I need my hands on him. I release his neck and set my palms on his cheeks, combing my fingers down his beard. He hums in pleasure.

Our gazes lock, and slowly he enters me with a single finger. My lids grow heavy, and I fight the urge to close my eyes.

"Stay with me," he says.

"I need more." My breath catches when he adds another finger. "Yes. God, so good." I shimmy my hips, trying to get him deeper. Frustrated with all the clothes between us, I start tugging on his coat. "Skin. Now."

He chuckles and spins us around, walking us to the desk with his fingers still inside me as if I weigh nothing at all—the perks to having a big man for a lover, I'm learning. I feel giddy with the thought of all the naked fun times we can have.

And then, like a bucket of cold water over my head, I remember something I can't believe I forgot. He's basically ended both our careers with his little announcement back in class.

I gasp when he bites my neck and decide to worry about it later. I mean, what's done is done, right?

"Pay attention, Miss Green. There may be a pop quiz later." He steps back and begins to remove his coat. The pants get left puddling around the boots, and he impatiently shuffles towards me. I stare in awe at the sheer mass of him.

"You are fantastically built, Principal Clausen."

"And you have too many clothes on."

Never taking my eyes off him, I begin to remove my clothing. His erection grows impossibly larger with each article I peel off. "The doo—"

"It's locked."

When I start to pull my sweater over my head, he stops me. "Leave the sweater."

Smiling, I shimmy out of my panties and watch his cheeks flush, making his eyes turn the brightest green I've ever seen. As seductively as I can, in nothing but a sweater with Santa on the front, I open my thighs like a book. He licks his lips then drops to his knees before me. His exhale bathes me in warmth, but I still shiver.

"You cold?"

"God, no. I've never been so hot in my life. Put your mouth on me."

He growls. "Have I told you how much I love when you tell me what to do?"

Encouraged, I grab the back of his head and pull him towards me. "It can't be as much as I love when you do what you're told."

The first brush of his lips hits just shy of where I need him.

I redirect him with a tug on his hair. "Stop teasing me. We only have so much time before someone comes."

"I'm guessing it'll be you first." His laughing mouth lands front and center, and I don't care if the whole school is standing outside the door. With one hand on the desk, bracing me, I use the other to comb my fingers through his hair. He moans into my pussy, and the vibration urges my hips towards the edge of the desk closer to his talented mouth. I want to scream. I want to bite. And when I think I'll burst, he inserts his thick finger inside me again. He does that crook-finger thing, and it's like he flips a switch that lights up my whole being. I shove my fist in my mouth to muffle my scream.

As I'm catching my breath, he bites down on my throbbing clit, and I fall back on the desk, arms outstretched, thankful I didn't just skewer myself with a letter opener. He licks over me, cleaning every last drop.

"I've never tasted anything like you." One more lick before he stands strong and tall, towering over my limp form.

I hold out my arms. "Come down here."

"I'll crush you."

"That sounds awesome."

"Hold that thought."

I watch as he hobbles around his desk to open a drawer. He rummages through it, cursing, then holds something up with a triumphant smile—a condom. Thank God one of us is thinking clearly.

Seemingly sick of the dancing steps he had to take before, he hops back to me. The whole thing should look ridiculous. Here's this mostly-naked, six-foot-four, two-hundred-plus man, with Santa pants around his ankles and his dick bouncing with each movement, but instead, I fall even more in love with him.

Standing over me, he gives his erection a firm stroke. "I'm taking the new principal position at Central Elementary."

"W-what?" It's hard to focus on what he's saying when his actions take up all my brainpower.

"My buddy is the super in that district and offered me the position this morning. If I stay here, at Edgar, we can't be together." He eases inside me. "I just want us to be together. I want to love you." He swivels his hips, and white spots dance in my vision.

"Oh, my God."

"I agree wholeheartedly." Pulling back his hips, he eases out, barely breaching me. I try to lift my hips and drive him further back inside me, but he places one large palm on my belly. "I want to love you just like this, without worry."

"No nooners in the supply closet?"

"Well, I wouldn't go that far." He enters me again with one hard thrust. "I could always visit you here." The hand on my stomach lowers until the pad of his thumb presses on the hood of my sex. I clench around him. "Ah... there it is." He presses more of his weight into me, adding pressure to my clit. I squeeze around him again. "Right there, huh, babe?" The pressure is building again. I can feel the familiar tingle start at my toes and work its way up my body.

Knowing he loves my words, I tell him what I need, and he gives it to me, pumping his hips hard and fast. I slam my hands to the desktop to ground me, knocking a container of pens to the floor. But it's no use because I'm soaring within seconds, and he follows soon after with a curse.

Moments later, we stand in front of each other, pulling our clothes on over the sweat cooling on our skin. "So, you love me?" I tease.

"You're okay, I guess." He leans down and licks a line across my bottom lip. "Now kiss me again. Santa needs to make good on your wish." He comes in for another kiss and groans when I pull out of reach.

"Malcolm?"

"Yes, Maggie mine?"

"I love you too."

THE END

All I want Forever Is You

BY K. L. COTTRELL

A sudden and disorienting falling-out has put Finn and Mallori at a tense distance, but forced proximity during a Christmas wedding weekend just might gift them a second chance at forever—if they can face and forgive one bottled-up truth.

About the Author

K. L. Cottrell loves to turn daydreams, real-life experiences, and unexpected moments of inspiration into romances that are as emotional and relatable as they are entertaining and spellbinding.

Instagram: @authork.l.cottrell
Facebook: Books by K. L. Cottrell
Website: https://www.klcottrell.com

Chapter One

Mallori

"There's no way." I blink tersely at the wildly familiar, gorgeous, unwelcome guy standing ten feet from me. "There's no way in hell I'm doing it."

"I said the same thing," Finn assures me. He crosses his strong arms and scrolls his blue gaze down my body. "But we don't seem to have a choice, do we, Sparkles?"

I roll my eyes at the nickname he stuck on me a couple years ago. Try not to blush about that incident all over again. *Refuse* to shiver from the chill bumps coming up over how he's looking at me now.

After what happened with us this fall, I swore I'd learn to be strong around him, no longer susceptible to the magnetic field he'd slowly, steadily drawn me into.

It's been a challenge—I won't lie about that.

However, our current situation is quite the distraction.

"There must be some way out." I swing my bag from my shoulder to the floor of this luxury cabin that, according to the lady at Guest Services, is housing both Finn and me this weekend, not just him. Same as when I received this news minutes ago, I insist, "There must be something that can be done to fix this, or somewhere else for one of us to go, or—"

"There isn't."

I blow out a dissatisfied breath.

He says, "The cabin you were gonna be in has an unworkable-until-Monday sewage issue. No other units are available because anyone who isn't here for the wedding is a random person you don't know. Nobody else you *do* know can take you in because everyone is already paired off and the max number of adults per cabin is two. And since your brother's fiancée's family sprang for this exclusive-ass venue, there isn't regular lodging nearby, only similar venues that also can't help you. Lavish Christmas weddings and individual getaways are popular around here."

Yeah, the receptionist told me all that.

So did the accommodations manager when he joined our conversation.

Even my older brother—Finn's longtime best friend—said he had no solutions when I called to beg for help.

Still, I grumbled my way over here, hoping a Christmas miracle would occur and fix the predicament we're in. The answer sure isn't in *my* hands. Finn isn't someone I'm afraid of, and I couldn't make him out to be because lying about something like that wouldn't be right. We do have a story, but it's private, so I didn't want to enlighten my family or confide in some stranger.

Finn tsks, then tilts his head of casually styled, ash-brown hair. "Short of one of us bailing on the wedding, there's nothing to be done."

"I'm not leaving Tanner's wedding to avoid you." I cross my own arms. "He's not just my brother. He's my friend."

"He's my *closest* friend, and I'm in the wedding party, so I'm not leaving either."

I hold his gaze. He holds mine.

As has happened every time I've seen him since our falling-out, his direct attention seems to weaken my knees.

I look away—and my eyes land on the huge bed nestled against the lefthand wall. It's the only one in the cabin; he hadn't needed another option back when booking took place.

Although I intend for one of us to sleep on the couch later, I can't help recalling this fall. Years of bickering and lingering looks and teasing and unexpected feelings led to a night that started out ordinary and ended with us sharing a bed...and our bodies...very much on purpose.

It's impossible not to miss those amazing memories.

But I also recall how he ruined them two days later by harshly stopping what my heart thought was just beginning.

It still hurts so much when I let myself think about it. He really had me fooled. I believed the earnest words he poured over me in whispers sweeter than any I'd heard before. I believed the passion was mutual because, God, no guy had ever reacted to me like he did. The depth of it all *had* to be as real for him as it was for me.

Well, it wasn't.

I slept with my brother's best friend, more than once, and got iced out right as I thought we were settling in to keep each other warm.

Now whatever distance I've managed to put between my pain and him is being reduced to nothing.

"*Fuck!*" I snap out.

I hear him clear his throat. "Yeah."

My foot starts up a flustered bounce. I wonder again how this is real. How are we supposed to share this cabin? We haven't been able to comfortably share space since early October.

Merry Christmas to us, huh?

Light rustling meets my ears. I look over and see Finn donning his coat.

"I'm gonna find some food," he says. "Make sure you close the curtains if you decide to change clothes. Don't want anyone else seeing your sparkly panties."

I scoff. He sends me a meaningful glance before opening the door and disappearing into the early afternoon.

No, he'll never let me forget him walking in on me changing while he was vacationing with me and my family. I loved my cute green panties and how the flecked glitter on them was the kind that doesn't end up all over everything; I hadn't realized I wanted him to love them, too, until his accidental interruption led to him smiling in the middle of his rushed apology.

'*I guess sparkles are my new favorite thing.*'

Later that day, he started using the nickname—our inside joke, which I only found funny half of the time over the next two years because the rest of the time, Finn was working my nerves as he's wont to do. Though he's never been mean to me, we often don't see eye-to-eye. He's sporty and popular and shining like my brother, and I'm artsy and introverted. He likes to relax and not be too serious about most things, and I'm big-hearted and easy to overwhelm.

Our differences worked in our favor for those few days this fall.

We were opposites, but it wasn't grating. We were counterparts that fit together, not extremes that clashed.

I don't know which is stupider: that I spent years developing feelings for a guy I should've known couldn't truly want me back, or that those feelings are still with me over two months after he turned me away.

I don't know how to let go of them when it felt like he did *truly want me.*

The thought rings in my mind.

I tune into how shallow and sharp my breaths have become in the quiet cabin.

Finally uncrossing my arms, I shake out my hands and try to compose myself.

I *have* to compose myself.

I'm flustered and frustrated, yes, and still hurt and angry. Still as attracted to him as I ever was, inside and out, because it's so damn hard not to be.

But...this weekend isn't about us. It's about Tanner and Nicole. They're in love and getting ready to celebrate their marriage. It'll be an intimate and beautiful event. And it really is a Christmas wedding; they're saying, *'I do,'* tomorrow, on Christmas Eve. I'm not a bridesmaid, but I've seen all the outfits and some of the decoration plans and enough of this stunning venue to know how magical everything will be.

I'm twenty-four, and Finn is twenty-six. We should act like the adults we are.

We have to get through today and tomorrow without our drama bleeding on everything else.

So I guess that *'no way in hell'* thing from before isn't true. There *is* a way to weather this, and it's called We Both Care About Tanner.

Sighing, I pick up my bag again.

I'm not changing out of these clothes just yet—I'll do that later for the rehearsal—but I do need to unpack and freshen up a little. The drive was long, and I spent much of it trying to prepare for seeing the breaker of my heart in closer quarters than I have in a while.

Ha.

Little ol' ignorant me.

I hadn't yet learned what close quarters are.

Chapter Two

Finn

Walking away from Mallori has been difficult for months, but it's especially hard right now, in light of this most unanticipated roommates-for-the-weekend thing.

I want so badly to turn and run back up the path, burst in the door, and confess to....

I've been telling myself for these months that I can't give into her pull again, that she's off-limits, out of my league. I've replayed Tanner's words in my head over and over, tried to hold onto the attitude I summoned the day he figured out what we'd done and flat-out told me I can't have her. Between certain parts of me agreeing with him and the rest of me not wanting to upset my best friend in the world, I closed myself off from her and have tried not to let those walls crumble.

Over time, they've crumbled anyway.

I've been unsure of what to do about it.

I didn't think it'd interfere with this weekend, though. Despite knowing that being around her wouldn't be easy, I didn't think my resolve would be tested like this.

It's like the universe is playing a cruel joke on me. *'Aw, you can't be with Mallori the way you wanna be? That sucks. But hey, here's a romantic weekend and a cabin you gotta share—go ahead and spend some quality time with her and her mocha-eyed resentment. That's technically still being with her, right?'*

"Fuck me," I mumble.

I break into a jog toward the main building, where the dining area is. Though it's freezing out here, the run comes easily, even feels good; playing football for years and now being a high school coach has left me in good shape.

As my frustration temporarily shifts to the back burner, I consider how beautiful this place is. The Skies at Devereaux is magazine-worthy, like a mini resort tucked away from ordinary civilization.

Unlike the two other Devereaux venues, the open sky is as much a part of the charm as the architecture—currently, it's a cloudy gray that promises snow. There are trees at the fenced edges of the property and walking paths dotted with benches. The buildings boast a sleek yet cottagey elegance, all built from inviting dark wood and stone and crystal-clear glass. The personal cabins are somewhat spread out from each other, and golf cart chauffeurs will take guests to or from them if they don't feel like walking. And near the main building is the all-important banquet hall, where the magic happens. It's called the Sky Hall because even the roof is made from glass so people can, say, get married under the stars regardless of how cold it is outside.

I'm sure everything will be that much more picturesque when the snow arrives. We'll get just enough for Mallori's winter-loving self to gasp over, not enough to cause problems.

She undoubtedly gasped over the venue when she arrived. Swear I've never known anyone who's as easy to move as she is. I often don't under-stand it, like how she can cry about pretty much anything, but some-times I do understand. I'll bet the look and feel of this place enveloped her right away, probably sparked a need to do some sketching this weekend.

I'd love to see her work. Always do. The clients at her new graphic design job are going to obsess over her talents.

My grumbling stomach interrupts my thoughts. Thankfully, I'm jogging up onto the low stone porch that wraps around the main building.

I hope food will help me know how to handle what I left behind in my cabin.

"There he is! Finn! So glad to see you, dude!"

I look up from the sandwich I've been savoring for the last half-hour. Tanner is across the way and heading for my table. He's a walking smile, a picture of true excitement.

I smile with him though my brain was just full of his months-old words about Mallori...again. As heavy as they've felt, he's been a solid friend to me overall. Seeing him happy should make *me* happy.

Plus, I should remember he was right when he said that stuff in October. Should remember he's a good guy who was trying to protect his sister. Can I blame him for protecting her even from me, his most treasured friend? We both know how I've always been with girls—casual to a fault—and that Mallori deserves better. Maybe it's because of how my parents were, but I've never been good at love.

'Love.'

I don't have time to dwell on what the word does to my thoughts of Mallori before her brother is at my table.

I reach out, and we grasp hands in a firm shake. "Hey, Mr. Almost Married. You guys get settled in?"

"Yeah!" He sits across from me. "Was hard to leave the cabin. I wanna spend the entire weekend in there. So freaking nice."

"I feel you. Where's Nicole?"

"Her bridesmaids were pulling up just as we were walking in here. She stopped off with them."

"Ah."

Tanner nods. As he drums his fingers on the table, he gives me a look I can't read.

Then he takes a breath and seems to force a smile. "So you and Mallori are stuck together this weekend, huh? She was mad earlier on the phone."

My heart does something funny in my chest.

"Yeah." After a beat, I feel like I should assure him, "But don't worry about us. I still respect what you said this fall."

He nods more slowly than before. Again, his look is one I can't decipher.

"I know you'll do the right thing for her," he replies. "You're the best dude I know."

Instead of lingering on the first part, I smile about the second. "I'm all right."

"Nah, Finn, you're the best. That's why you're my best friend *and* my best man!"

We laugh at the corny words.

He means them, though.

Heaviness aside, I mean mine too. "I'm honored to be both, Tan. Thanks for all these years of good times, doing stupid shit, letting me crash with you when things got overwhelming at home...."

He reaches across the table and claps a hand onto my shoulder. "I've got your back anytime."

Although he means that as well—for the most part, anyway—I say, "Thanks, but I know it's about to be you and Nicole against the world. She'll officially be priority number one, ahead of all the rest of us."

He sits back again. "Ah, yeah, you're right about that. Still, you'll always be big to me. She's just on a level nobody else can reach." He puts a dramatic hand to his chest. "The heart must come first!"

We laugh again.

And something about those sentiments whispers at me.

Tanner looks away and up. "Oh, hey!" he says with a fresh smile.

I follow his gaze, ready to greet Nicole—and my stomach leaps when I see it's Mallori who's walked up.

As she and Tanner hug, I try to listen to their excited exchange of words, but my brain is having a hard time. All it can focus on is how soft her rich brown hair looks and how sweet her smile is for her brother.

Her smile was sweet for me, too, this fall, in a completely different way.

A way I'll never get over no matter how hard I try.

"Finn, I'm gonna go find my woman. I'll catch you later, okay?"

Tanner's direct voice shakes me from my thoughts. I blink and find he's settling another unusual look on me.

I nod. "Yeah, man. Sure thing."

He tips a nod back to me, pats Mallori's arm, and leaves.

She and I lock gazes.

She's still sweet and soft and...

...then her expression shutters.

It pains me. I despise getting cold stares and bitterness from her because I know what they hide. I've seen the beautiful things that lie underneath, and *they're* what I want. Not distance.

Distance is what I always wanted with other girls—the girls to whom I didn't matter and about whom I didn't care.

Clearing her throat, she clasps her hands together. "Look, I've decided that although I pretty much hate you, we need..."

You don't hate me. You love me.

The knowledge startles me despite that my own brain unearthed it.

She didn't tell me so this fall, but I saw.... Even not having understood love before, I *felt*....

I'm as breathless as I'd be if I were shouting these things at her.

"...sure you're aware, Tanner doesn't deserve to have his special weekend with Nicole ruined by us. It's not his fault we're in this mess."

Yes, it is.

I'm more breathless yet.

No, it's not his fault Mallori has to bunk with me, and no, he doesn't deserve to have his wedding ruined. But regardless of how I shouldn't be mad at him, it *is* his fault that this time with her feels strained instead of fun, romantic, relaxing, normal.

She doesn't even know it.

She doesn't know we'd be a normal couple right now if he hadn't—

"Hello?" She waves a hand in front of my face. "Earth to Finn. Please give me some sign that you hear me and you agree not to openly display your distaste for me this weekend."

Trying to get my lungs to work, I absorb the impatience on her pretty face.

Indeed, she prompts, "Finn?"

"I don't have an ounce of distaste for you," is what falls out of my mouth.

Disbelief spikes through her expression—followed by stark sadness.

I clench my fists on the table because I can't believe I let that slip either. I'm supposed to be shutting her out, not letting her in.

Her spine straightens. Her eyes grow tense.

"Just agree to it," she whispers now. "There's no need to lie to me."

I try not to fucking say it, but it refuses to stay inside me: "I'm not lying."

She doesn't trust that, though. It's obvious.

Makes sense. She thinks I think we were a mistake because I told her so after Tanner found out about us. The truth of me not feeling that way at all may be slowly dismantling those walls I put up, but it doesn't change what I said. I still earned her hostility.

Her new whisper comes. "After you cut me off like you did, how can you say...? God, do you care at all about what you've been doing to me?"

It's the most perfect, most dangerous invitation to tell the truth.

The urge to confess myself to her swells up again.

But she turns and strides away, believing she already knows what my answer is.

Tanner's angry voice echoes in my mind: *'She's the one girl you can't do your usual thing with, Finn! I forbid it! She has a heart and you're gonna shatter it because the two of you don't want the same things! Fuck, man, how could you do something like this? Don't you know better?'*

Frowning deeply, I lower my gaze to the table.

Yeah, more and more all the time, I find myself unsure of what my next move is supposed to be.

My thoughts are a mess of facts, lies, misunderstandings. A tangle of things I didn't realize until it was too late.

Like how stopping myself with Mallori is what hurt her, not what saved her from being hurt.

And how much it hurt *me* to have found something truly meaningful with the most amazing person, only to have my closest friend shoot it down.

At the time, I did rush to agree with him. He was upset, and it scared me. Then my parents' critical voices were in my head, popping up to kick me while I was down, like usual.

Okay, I can't do this right now, I tell myself. *Just because the weekend is going this way doesn't mean I have to confront what happened. I need to do what's right for Mallori, as Tanner said, and close back up so everything can go as smoothly as possible.*

Except I can't even nod along with that before something in me strongly disagrees.

I've tried to shake it off, but even after almost another hour, it hasn't budged.

I've been at this table for way longer than my lunch necessitated, but that inner disagreement hasn't faded.

This fall, when I took Mallori's perfect face in my hands so I could kiss her for the first time, I felt sure she had changed me. Here and now, I'm starting to feel deeply *unsure* that closing off is what either of us needs me to do.

That prior certainty had been right. Is this uncertainty right too?

'Do you care at all about what you've been doing to me?'

I inhale slowly.

I care more than she has any idea of. Her pain hurts me more than she knows.

She deserves to know.

The moments keep ticking by.

Another minute passes.

And....

Sure, maybe the sudden drama of this weekend isn't fate's way of bringing me close enough to Mallori to fix what's broken. Maybe it isn't a sign that staying away from her has been the wrong move. Maybe it isn't anything more than a poorly timed coincidence.

But as I look at where she stood with that sadness on her face, I can't help wondering...well, what if it *is?*

Chapter Three

Mallori

Why would he say that stuff to me? Why would he bother?

I'm still wondering it an hour after finding Finn to ask him to be civil this weekend. The questions have become less aggravated, though, thanks to the fresh air; I swiftly returned to our cabin, bundled up, and grabbed a sketchbook to take to a distant bench. I felt inspiration stirring the moment I arrived at The Skies at Devereaux, and my schedule will only get busier as the weekend unfolds, so this was the perfect time to clear my head.

I've been somewhat successful. I have a pleasant sketch of the trees lining the fence across the way. And, yes, I'm less fired-up than I was in the dining room.

But now, more than anything, I feel sorrow.

'I don't have an ounce of distaste for you.'

Those words had sorrow slamming me before I could stop it. Summoning anger had been easy, of course, but it didn't erase the....

The sorrow and hope. Sorrow and longing. Sorrow and exhaustion.

Breathing deeply, I close my eyes and rub at them with one hand, careful not to stab myself with my graphite pencil.

In the brief darkness, I see his face. See how he looked at me while I stood by his table.

It was like...

...like he felt longing and exhaustion too.

And regret.

I take a sharper breath, reopen my eyes, drop my hand back to my sketchbook. But I don't keep drawing on the paper. The pencil hovers in the air just above some shading on a tree trunk—I move it back and forth, trying to convince it to lower into place, but it resists.

My brain isn't ready to switch back into creative mode, nor is my heart.

They're stuck on Finn's words and expression and what they could mean.

They don't mean anything special, my anger insists. *They don't even make sense! After how he ended things, it doesn't make sense for him to feel anything sweet toward you. He's an asshole who never matured out of junior high and thus never learned he can't play with people's emotions.*

That last part isn't true, though. And because it isn't, I can't forget the way we've always been.

Yes, there were many times over the years when we triggered the other's pet peeves, sometimes intentionally. Times when we mocked each other's dates because I found his vapid and he found mine pretentious. Times when his and Tanner's love for playing football made their love of *watching* football messy and disruptive, same as when I blasted my music with drawings or paints or crafts spread out in places that inconvenienced the boys somehow.

But then there were all those other times. Ones that brought looks of deep and playful and unshakable attraction. There were the quiet times, like when he'd stay at our house to escape his parents and both of us would end up sitting on the front porch to watch the rain, or like when he'd help me with chores despite not being asked to. Times when something would upset one of us and the other would instantly stand up straighter—like when I was sixteen and left the homecoming dance early after finding my boyfriend cheating on me. Finn was hanging out in our driveway, waiting for my brother to arrive, and he got me to talk about what happened. His eyes turned *so* hard...but not on me. He was soft toward me. He convinced me to dance with him right there with no music, only the sound of his voice and my calming sniffles.

He said my boyfriend was a fool for doing what he did. Well, *'a fool and a little bitch,'* to be precise.

I don't dive in any deeper; remembering it all makes this current situation sting worse.

An ache grips my throat. My body feels heavy. I realize my eyes are filling with hot, world-blurring tears.

I miss him.

The thought is as unstoppable as the frigid wind.

Fighting a sob, I hold down the pages of my sketchbook so they won't get ruffled.

Why do I still miss him, cry over him, care about him more than I've ever cared about any other guy? Why do I still feel so much when he feels nothing for me?

But the way he looked at me earlier wasn't nothing. It was more than he's given me in months. It was something, and it was big.

The wind settles, so I lift a hand to wipe away my tears. Then I stare at my sketchbook. The graphite on the paper stands out more intensely than before, somehow.

White paper, black lines...and lighter lines, smudges, textures, shadows. A scale from light to dark, with so much in between.

Everything works together to make the picture whole. It's flat with only the bold black lines on white paper; the in-between gives it depth, fills it out, makes it feel complete.

There are still so many familiar things twisted up in me—heartache, confusion, affection, bitterness, embarrassment, yearning—but something new is coming up. A comprehension.

Could it be that my and Finn's picture isn't finished yet?

I thought it was because he said what we did was a mistake that couldn't happen again, said we were over. What's unclear about those words, you know? And any time I saw him afterward, he appeared to be holding fast to them.

But maybe the reason I haven't been able to let go is that our picture is still mostly black and white, not filled out all the way.

Maybe the reason I haven't moved on from how we were is because it *was* real, *not* a mistake—

Or maybe I'm grasping at straws because I'm too stupid to accept reality.

My embarrassment heightens.

Momentarily, so does the bitterness.

Damn him for the way he affects me. How can two sentences and an earnest expression unravel me so quickly? Am I that pathetic?

My interest in sketching trees shifts into a need to leave something of myself on the page. I flip to the next blank sheet and take a moment to decide what to do.

"God," I whisper, the word a white puff in the air.

Then, because I need to although I don't understand why, I put pencil to paper and start outlining Finn's face.

With the wedding happening in such an expensive location, the attendee list isn't long. The core party consists of Tanner and Nicole, Finn and the maid of honor, two groomsmen, and two bridesmaids. My parents and I, Nicole's parents and stepparents, and her grandmother are honored guests. Then there are half a dozen other guests, all of whom are on Nicole's side because her world consists of rich people who can visit places like The Skies without issue.

I love her parents. They're kind and generous, the sort of wealthy people who give to charity and do good things with their money. If they hadn't insisted on splitting costs with those of us who are here to support Tanner, we wouldn't *be* here to support Tanner.

I've thanked them many times, but I'll also show respect by not looking shabby this weekend. The ceremony rehearsal is in fifteen minutes, so I'll start there.

"Okay," I sigh in front of the ornate full-length mirror in the cabin bathroom. My deep red velvet dress is long-sleeved, fitted up top, and flowy from waist to knee. It works with my black tights and heels. My hair is wavy and hanging loose, and I have a simple reindeer headband tucked in up top—I couldn't resist since holiday accessories won't be appropriate tomorrow. All in all, this ensemble is cute, cozy, and considerate of the occasion.

My bit of eye makeup looks good, so all I need is lipstick.

I'm deciding between matching it to the dress or going with my best nude pink when noise in the main room startles me.

It was the door opening. And now it's shutting. And now there are footsteps.

Finn is here.

Heart thumping, I blink at the lipsticks I'm holding and try to catch my shortened breath.

Earlier, the rest of my alone time did turn out to help me. I spent it sketching Finn's face from the dining room, and the shape of him sleeping beside me after our first night together, and the way he stood against a wall last month at Tanner's birthday party, regarding me with a closed expression before staring down into his drink for two entire minutes. And when I was done doing all that, I felt better. Didn't have to scream into a pillow or punch something to alleviate the pressure inside me.

I came back to the cabin knowing I could face him again. I wasn't free of the complicated things I felt, but they weren't overwhelming anymore. I knew that if it's up to me, we can endure each other.

Still, I feel tight-chested and shaky and warm because I hear him approaching the open bathroom door, and it's the first time I've been near him in a couple hours.

I realize I'm staring at the doorway only when he appears in it.

Everything is so quiet that as his eyes soak me up, I hear his soft intake of air.

I silently beg him, *Don't say I look beautiful.*

But don't not *say it either.*

His eyes do—they say it. And that's the truth, not something I'm imagining. He constantly looked at me like this back in October and so many different times in the past. I couldn't dream up that expression on my own.

The breath he takes now is of the pre-speaking kind.

I speak first. "Do you remember dancing with me in the driveway?"

His mouth closes on his words. That gaze goes all over me again. His fingertips ripple at his thighs.

He's still in jeans, I note—and sneakers and a thermal shirt. He needs to get ready for the rehearsal too.

"Yes," he answers lowly.

I look back up to his face.

"And the number of fake jewels on your hair pin, and how your makeup looked from your crying, and how big you smiled when I offered to go piss in that guy's convertible as payback."

Fresh amusement fires through me—I clap a hand over my mouth to silence it, but not quickly enough. My burst of traitorous laughter sits on the air, undeniable proof that I don't know how to hate him.

"Jesus Christ," he breathes out. "I love making you laugh."

Just like that, I'm sobered.

Not steadied, though, as my suddenly trembly hand drifts to one of my flushed cheeks.

He loves...? Then why did he start acting like I don't mean anything to him at all?

My voice comes out weaker than before. "What are you doing, Finn? Why are you different today?"

He shakes his head. "I...."

His expression shifts into one so chaotic I can't begin to try to read it.

"Answer me," I whisper.

"I don't know," he whispers back. "But—but I'm not even as different as you think—I mean, from when.... Since then, I've just...."

I tilt my head, curious and dismayed and, God help me, almost hope—

We jump as a hearty knock comes at the front door.

Shoving a hand back through his hair, he mutters and looks over his shoulder. His name comes through the door from a groomsman, I think.

I remember the lipsticks I'm holding. Just as he turns his eyes back to me, I turn away to the mirror.

"Mallori," he starts.

"Door's for you. Get it and then get dressed for the rehearsal. Don't wanna be late."

In the mirror, I catch him entering the bathroom, not walking away from it. My heart leaps. He looks straight at me, preparing to keep talking.

Then more knocking comes.

This time, he spins on his heel and leaves. "Son of a bitch!"

Breathless, I watch him go, then uncap the first tube of lipstick I can get situated in my fingers. Nice, it's the nude pink one—hard to mess up even while rushing.

In short moments, I'm ready to go. I exit the bathroom and see Finn standing at the front door with Stephen, one of his and Tanner's friends. I catch pieces of cologne talk while I make a beeline for my coat and wristlet.

On one hand, I wonder why Stephen dropped by for this. Aren't all the guys about to be together at the rehearsal? Couldn't he have asked to borrow cologne later?

But I'm also glad for the interruption. As much as I want Finn's attention and answers, I was dumb to start an important conversation when we have somewhere to be. We can't fit a talk about our unfinished picture into a couple minutes.

When I approach the door, Stephen steps aside, unlike Finn's former-quarterback ass.

"Hey, you!" he greets me. "Gotta say the antlers are cheesy, but you still look nice. Ready for the fun?"

"She looks perfect," Finn disagrees, making my pulse skip.

I've started inching past him despite that touching him is unavoidable and it sets my nerve endings on fire—and I almost explode when his hand goes down my arm, urging me to pause. Even through my coat and the sleeve of my dress, I swear his hand is on my skin, *and I almost explode.*

"Mallori," he begins again.

But he releases me, so I escape into the fading sunlight. "See you guys over there."

Stephen hums. "Yeah, so anyway...."

I lose his voice as my heels clomp rhythmically down the path, but I feel a certain pair of eyes following me as I go.

What was it Finn said a minute ago? *'I'm not even as different as you think.'*

What the hell could that mean?

"Oh, honey!" My mom and I step into a happy hug in the foyer of the Sky Hall. "You look so pretty!"

"Aw, thanks, Mama. *You* look pretty." I pull back and smile, trying not to give away that I'm in a weird mood. "I'm glad you and Daddy finally got here!"

While we hang up our coats, we whisper about the magnificent Skies at Devereaux and the upcoming wedding. I try my hardest not to get distracted when an appropriately dressed Finn arrives with Stephen and gathers with the other guys. Then my dad comes over to Mom and me; we hug big just before the wedding planner jubilantly calls for everyone to follow her.

Nicole and her girls hurry forward, followed by her mother and step-mother. Squeals of delight fill the air. Then Tanner, his guys, and the rest of Nicole's family go. I bring up the rear behind my parents.

"Holy shit," I say beneath everyone's excitement.

The large room feels both cozy and open. Warm lights line the walls, the windows on the far wall are huge, and the ceiling is made of glass that shows off the darkening sky above us. There's the perfect number of back-less benches angled toward the windows, where a slight platform waits to show off the wedding party. The wedding colors are elegant gold, soft white, and splashes of romantic red—whoever decorated used them with flawless class.

My eyes catch on where Finn and Tanner stand. Even from here, I can make out Finn echoing my, "Holy shit," to my brother.

"The reception room on our left is equally stunning!" the wedding planner promises. "For now, let's enjoy some complimentary champagne and begin our rehearsal!"

Complimentary champagne? Don't mind if I do.

On cue, a smiling lady comes up and offers me a flute from her tray. I gratefully accept, and as I watch her go, I spot Finn again.

This time, he spots me too.

He looks good in his light gray slacks and white button-down shirt.

I'm sure he hates those dress shoes, though they're nice on him; he's so comfortable in sneakers that I've literally seen him fall asleep wearing them.

Resolving to focus on what's happening around us, I pull my eyes from him.

I want to act respectable this evening, not just look it. Although I'm not really a social butterfly, I don't want to be zoned out when the time comes for us honored guests to practice walking to our reserved seats.

So I sip my champagne, stifle a moan about how delicious it is, and look for a bench to sit on.

Chapter Four

Finn

Weird how an evening can drag and speed by simultaneously.

Weird how I've felt Mallori's eyes on me even with everyone's attention flying around. Over the last hour and forty minutes, I've done an excellent job of keeping up with timing, positioning, and what to do as best man, yet part of my brain has stayed aware of her.

And I always love how she looks, but she's wonderfully herself tonight. The reindeer antlers are cute. The heels and tights are unassuming and unique; no other women are wearing tights with their dresses. God, and her dress is so good—it doesn't matter that it isn't form-fitting or revealing, because it's the color of honest adoration and sweet temptation, and she's the angel for whom I'm not supposed to reach because I'm just some human who doesn't deserve her.

It's not fair.

The rehearsal just ended, so everyone is moving to the next room. It's where the reception will be held tomorrow and where we're all about to eat and mingle to our hearts' content. I slow my pace quite a way back not just because Nicole and her friends are shrieking with new excitement and it's putting my hairs on end, but because Mallori is also lingering. Not for me, I don't think; she's just the kind of person who lets others walk ahead of her rather than elbowing her way forward.

I watch her shuffle along several steps behind a couple people, hands clasped low in front of her, and I think about how unfair it is that things had to end between us.

Also think about her mentioning her homecoming night when that dipshit cheated on her. I told her he was a fool for doing that. Then here I am, years later, having hurt her in my own way. I'm the fool now.

It's taken me so long to let that in. To realize I did the wrong thing by not standing up to Tanner.

He *wasn't* right when he said I'd break her heart by being my usual self. Yes, she's hurt right now, but it's because I listened to him. When I was with her, I wasn't still the old me. *Better* is what I was. Not even simply ready to change—I was already different.

I did deserve her.

And if idiocy hadn't gotten in the way, I would've given everything to her and never stopped.

But back then, I couldn't set Tanner straight since I suddenly couldn't think straight myself. There was so much on my mind so abruptly; I didn't expect him to appear at my place, and he was so mad and disappointed, which made me second-guess myself, which weakened me like crazy. So I tucked my tail between my legs and ran.

I've been realizing over time that the thing about running is you can't do it forever.

However, this morning is what really forced my perspective, harsh like a broken bone that needed attention: I learned Mallori and I would be sharing space after months of not being alone with each other. There was nowhere else to run.

It jarred me into sense. It was the snowball of change rolling down the hill—I haven't stopped gathering snow for a single minute all fucking day, and I've only been at The Skies since, what, noon?

...Wow, I've only been here since *noon*, and it's just past six in the evening now.

That thing I said about time both dragging and speeding by is real.

I've wasted so much time isolating from her.

Mallori has stopped near the wide doorway to the other room. I'm still hanging back. She slowly turns her head, looks over her shoulder; her gaze starts out on the floor, but it scrolls up until it reaches my face.

She asked why I'm different today.

Wish I'd responded better. I just didn't know how to explain it when it surprised me too.

But I'm getting a tighter grip on it, and I'll get another chance.

It's inevitable on my part—this is all suddenly enormous on my shoulders, and I'm an Atlas imposter who can't carry the weight for long—but also, Mallori cares enough to give me that chance. She may be upset about us and committed to Tanner's special weekend, but she still cares about whatever's wrong with me.

Except...

...as those eyes of hers soften, giving me the impression that she's recalling one of our best times, not one of our worst...

...I have to believe I'm snowballing not because something's *wrong* with me, but because something's trying to become right.

I'll admit that unlike earlier when he and I spoke in the dining room, I can't help feeling bitter about Tanner's part in my and Mallori's falling-out.

I keep it in, of course. Don't act out, glare, or ignore. Don't abandon the round table the wedding party claimed. But quietly, beneath my support of him and his happiness, beneath my appreciation for all the ways in which I am fortunate now and have been in the past, I let myself fully acknowledge how much he hurt me in October.

The more I watch him with Nicole, the more I want a happy ending of my own.

Never have I told him he wasn't good enough for something he wanted. It stung like hell that he said it to me about one of the *only* things

I've ever felt good enough for—and maybe the only thing I've ever truly wanted in the first place.

He didn't try to talk to me about her, didn't ask about my feelings. He just told me to walk away before I fucked things up.

I feel bitter, yes. Right here at his side on the night before his wedding.

And I still feel Mallori's eyes on me.

I wonder if she feels mine when they're on her while she's enjoying her salad, admiring the cluster of red roses on her table, looking at whoever she's talking to.

In my peripheral vision, I notice Tanner leaning to his other side, where Nicole sits. I glance over and see her whispering in his ear. She seems gently serious rather than flirty.

She blinks her eyes straight up to me, catching me watching them.

We both rush to smile at each other. Feeling rude, I look away.

Now I snag the gaze of a bridesmaid. The smile she gives me *is* flirty.

No, thanks, Little Black Dress. I want Sparkles.

Looking away again, I grin about Mallori's face being on fire that day I walked in on her changing.

I belatedly realize the bridesmaid might think I'm flirting in my own way. But hey, if she approaches me at some point, I'll just tell her the truth: I'm unavailable.

I fell for someone else a long time ago.

And I'm tiring of pretending I didn't.

Sitting, eating, and sipping drinks turns into people mingling at other tables. Instrumental versions of recognizable songs start playing, encouraging dancing in the open area at the center of the room.

Nicole's mom and stepdad are the first out. Tanner's parents go next. He and Nicole decide they want to dance, too, on their last night of being engaged.

He catches my eye. "Hey, why don't *you* ask someone to dance? I know at least one girl in here will say yes."

"Yeah, I'd love to," that bridesmaid confirms. I blink over and see another flirty smile.

A little way behind her, I also see Mallori standing at a window, talking with Nicole's grandmother.

Some throat-clearing has me looking back at Tanner. He smiles. "Do it, dude."

As he and Nicole walk away, the bridesmaid stands.

"Come on!" she says brightly. "I must admit I've been interested in you."

My attention returns to Mallori, whose sweet laughter is ringing out just enough for me to hear.

I stand, too, but I don't take the hand this other girl extends.

"I'm quite attached to someone else," I tell her. "Sorry."

"Wait, what?"

I leave her and go to the window. Mallori's eyes shift to me from the grandmother—she's still smiling, but my appearance has her breath catching.

I nod courteously at the older woman. "Please excuse my interruption."

"Of course!"

I look back to Mallori, swallow hard, hold out a hand. "Will you dance with me again?"

Tanner wasn't talking about her when he told me to dance with someone, but I'm choosing her anyway. I loved our driveway time all those years ago. It's something I truly haven't forgotten anything about.

And I want—no, *need*—to tell her something else that's real. A few things have slipped out by accident today, but now I have purposeful words on the tip of my tongue that I can't ignore.

Her smile has faded. A light crease has formed in her brow.

But her eyes are tender.

She sends light words to the grandmother: "Talking to you has been great." Then, for the first time since October, her hand is in mine.

The contact brings chaos to my insides.

I pull her away, weave us through tables, lead her around the other couples on the dance floor. Not once do I bother checking if Tanner has spotted us.

After we're on the far edge of the others, I face her, and...Christ, she drifts into place with me *so* effortlessly, her hand still in mine, her other finding my shoulder. Pulse wild, I draw her close because I can't stop myself, and she doesn't stop me either, just breathes with me. Like we dance all the time. Like I never shattered us.

But where my free hand has settled into the curve of her back, I feel her trembling, and I know it isn't an entirely good thing. She's rattled by how I've been acting today, on top of the last two and a half months.

Because I did shatter us.

Those words I need to say climb up my throat, past the knot there. As I look into her eyes, I feel steady, though my murmur doesn't come out that way.

"I'm sorry for breaking your heart."

Her fingers clench my shoulder and around my hand. Her new breath stumbles. And her eyes...beneath the frown now carving deeply through her lovely features, her eyes burn in ways that give me hope and in ways that hurt me as much as I deserve.

We'd barely begun to dance, yet we're already halting.

I'm a strong guy, yet my hand is starting to feel uncomfortable in her grip.

I do nothing about either fact. I just wait for her. God knows she's waited forever for me.

"Is that it?" she whispers at length. "Is that all you have to say?"

I hold her gorgeous, gutting gaze. "Not by a long shot."

Her exhalation is so sharp it makes it all the way to my lips.

I wet them and keep my voice low. "I need to tell you what happened after we slept together. Now isn't the right minute.... Tonight might not be the right night, this weekend might not even be the right weekend 'cause—'cause, baby, this is bigger than you know and I don't want it to ruin anything else. But today has shoved so much into my face, and you asked if I care about what I've done to you, and the answer is yes. Mallori, even if I don't get a good chance to be completely honest this weekend, I need to at least take this chance to say I care about every fucking *second* of pain I've caused you, because you have my heart, and I'm *sorry* for breaking yours."

My spilled words hang on the air.

While she absorbs them, I absorb her.

I live in these moments of her fingertips digging into my shoulder and her eyes digging into the rest of me.

I'm reminded of how she sometimes held onto me...*before*. It didn't matter if I was kissing her or touching her or rocking into her, didn't matter if we were in my bed, on my couch, or against the wall by my living room window after we looked out at that thunderstorm. Sometimes she was tender, but sometimes she held me like this. Like she couldn't be calm on the outside because she wasn't calm on the inside.

I miss her so much, in those ways and in all the other ways we belong together.

Part of me does want to keep talking right now. The truth has gotten so big in my mind that withholding it feels like torture by suffocation.

But I believe what I've said is enough for now. It's something she can trust so she knows I'm still in this body I tried to turn to stone—I'm still the someone *she* fell for a long time ago. I just got a little lost.

Tingles spread through my hand as her tight hold relaxes.

Her fingertips ease up on my shoulder.

I feel the tension leave the rest of her body.

Not all of the intensity leaves her eyes, but that's perfect. Those eyes don't belong to Mallori if they don't hold some kind of emotion meant just for me.

It's something I've always loved about her. Whether she looks my way with exasperation, sweetness, desire, amusement, or anything else, she always sees *me*. I'm never nothing to her.

Her breaths are a bit steadier now. They go a bit deeper.

"Okay," she murmurs.

I see glinting tears gathering in her eyes. This is one of those times when I understand why.

"Thank you," comes more quietly yet, but I still notice it.

I squeeze her hand and nod—it's all I know to do.

She squeezes back.

And actually, it's *more* than enough for now.

Chapter Five

Mallori

"Aw, are you sure?" Nicole asks me. We stand in the frigid night, the romantic lights around the area illuminating her happy face. "My friends and I would love to visit with you, almost-sister! It'll be a great time for girl talk, right?"

That's true, and I adore Nicole, but my general socializing energy has been sapped. The group part of tonight is wrapping up at just the right time for me.

There's only one person I want to talk to now.

I heard Finn when he said it might be better to wait, but I can't wait. His apology and touch and sincere words—*him saying I have his heart*—cracked me open. My own heart cannot wait for another day. These months have been hell already; lasting the rest of this evening was the best I could do.

"But you know," Nicole adds, "I understand being tired. It's okay if you don't wanna come over. People need rest!"

People also need answers.

I smile and beckon her into a hug. "Thank you, almost-sister. I'm gonna go off on my own, but tonight was fun, and tomorrow will be fantastic! Text me if I can help, okay?"

She hugs me back, giggling. "Okay!"

Two golf carts pull up to us, having already chauffeured a few people away, including her bridal party. We each claim one, and after checking that nobody else is coming, the staff take us our separate ways.

My gentleman is courteous. He asks how my evening has been, and we talk about the snow that's late coming; I've been looking forward to it. We're at my cabin in no time, and I try to tip him, but he refuses and wishes me a Merry Christmas. Touched, I wish him one too.

Then I head indoors so I can prepare to talk to Finn when he returns.

He said he was sorry back when it happened. You know: *'I'm sorry, but this was a mistake. We can't do this ever again. We're over. I'm sorry.'*

His apology tonight was different.

Part of me always feared we weren't on the same level and that he couldn't love me the way I'd started loving him. I dared to think I was wrong about that when we ended up giving into each other so fully, but then...he seemed to prove me right after all. He said those hurtful words, and that already-insecure part of me believed them.

What was different about tonight is *all* of me believed what he said. Sure, I was still upset, but there wasn't a little spot in my chest that worried he couldn't be serious. He looked straight at me and put his words out there, and they resonated with me. He felt as genuine as he did in every heated, quiet, goofy, normal moment we shared this fall.

That was the real Finn. And the guy who has been showing up in flickers today—calling me Sparkles, blurting out confessions, regarding me with deep affection, dancing with me without a second thought—that's the real Finn.

He was someone else between my last minute in his apartment and earlier today in the dining room. I'm dying to find out where the Finn I've always known went for so long.

When I left the Sky Hall, his eyes were on me, but he was conversing with the guys. I'm not sure if he plans to hang out with them, like Nicole invited me to do with the girls. Official bachelor and bachelorette parties were last weekend, but excitement is so high around here that I know the bride and groom want some last-minute fun with their friends.

Whatever Finn's plan is, mine is to be alone until he comes back.

I settled in a few minutes ago. Got my headband and heels and tights off, traded overhead lights for the fancy electric fireplace. Gathered my sketching stuff, wrapped up in a soft throw blanket, plopped down in this overstuffed chair.

I'm interested in doodling, but I haven't made it out of my head yet.

For the first time since October, it's not a bad place to be.

'I've never felt anything like you.'

Every part of me that his rushing whisper touched back then is hit all over again now. It drifts into my ear again, over my jaw, just down my neck, leaving me with chill bumps. It wraps around my heart again.

A moment I'll never forget.

I knew he'd been with other girls before, but I stood out to him. He said it and I felt it.

Same as how he stood out to me from other guys.

Although it's been months, he's still with me. His kisses, hands, embrace. His strong body over and under mine, so damn warm and satisfying—I swear, in those days, whether he was making me come or being silly or looking at me with unguarded eyes, I'd never known such satisfaction before.

But yes, as indelible as all that is, more than anything, his honest words of affection remain in my chest.

Now he says I have his heart. He says there's a side to our sudden ending that I don't know about. Does that mean we aren't over after all?

The possibility stays in my mind, as steady as the flames in the fireplace.

I yearn for it to be true.

It settles on me over moments that turn into minutes...that turn into...more minutes....

I'm tired.

It's been a long day. I got up early, drove for hours, got here and....

Now I'm so comfy. The cabin is so quiet.
My eyes are heavy.
And I....

Chapter Six

Finn

I didn't spend too long on groomsmen talk—maybe forty-five minutes—but Mallori is asleep when I return to the cabin.

I'm disappointed not to be able to talk with her, though I *was* a little worried she'd want to specifically talk about us. I already know she'll be upset when we get around to it.

Will it stand in our way? Despite how deeply I know she cares for me, what if she tells me to fuck off because I messed up too badly?

Well, I can't dwell on that. It does no good. My hope that she still wants to be with me is strong, but I'll just have to see what happens.

So I smile about how she's snoring in the big chair not far from the fake fireplace, all wrapped up in her blanket. After this day and how cozy the cabin is, I really don't blame her for dozing off.

The chair seems better for lounging than sleeping, and I already planned on letting her have the bed tonight while I take the couch. I strategize for a second, then lift her into my arms. "Okay, my girl. Let's move you to a better spot."

She snorts in her sleep, but she doesn't wake up. I try not to chuckle too much.

The comforter and sheets on the bed are luxurious. I'm sure she'd like to be tucked in among them. However, I think it's best if I settle her on top of everything and leave her in the blanket she already has. I put her on the side of the bed I remember she likes.

In a linen closet, I find a blanket for my own use. Once I'm ready to turn in, I shut off the fireplace and stretch out on the couch.

It promptly feels too short and too soft.

"Don't give me any trouble," I request of it.

Hoping I'll adjust, I close my eyes.

Mallori's soft snores meet my ears.

Funny though it seems, they help me relax.

"*Fuck,*" I groan, annoyed and uncomfortable. For probably the eighth time, I toss around to lie a different way.

The couch is a pain in my ass.

And back.

And shoulders.

I heave a sigh and open my eyes to stare tiredly toward the dark ceiling.

Also for the eighth or twelfth or twentieth time, I remember how big the bed is. I could fit on it without bothering Mallori.

I've been assuring myself I don't need to relocate, but you know what? I'm done with that.

I lumber my ass up off the couch and carefully step through the deep shadows. I can just make out that she's still in her own space on the bed. Chilled from being free of my blanket, I get under the comforter as quickly as possible without jostling her.

And I haven't been lying still for five whole seconds before I know this was the right call.

A pleased hum barely makes it out of me.

Drifting off is easier than ever.

Chapter Seven

Mallori

I stir into consciousness blinking blearily and feeling chilly.

Dimmest daylight helps my hazy brain remember the cabin, the wedding weekend, and Finn...but not falling asleep on the bed, nor him lying next to me.

I do recall using this throw blanket and wearing this dress. My bare legs are sticking out into the open air; that's why I'm chilly.

Finn must've carried me over here since I didn't mean to pass out in that chair.

The realization warms me on the inside.

Not so much the outside.

I examine the shape of him in the feeble morning light. He's facing away from me, snuggled under the half of the comforter I'm not lying on.

I want to be under there too.

Shortly, my blanket is at the end of the bed and I'm beneath the comforter, daring to inch closer to Finn's heat, and...mmm.

I'm more comfortable than I've been in a long time.

My eyes fall shut in relief.

The next time I wake, it's to the smell of coffee.

The sun is up. A light is on across the room. Finn is gazing out a window.

It's unfair how good he looks in his hoodie and pair of sweats. He wore that exact outfit one day this fall; after we had our fun with him out of it, I wore the hoodie myself while we cooked lunch.

Oh, those days.

Everything started with me craving orange-cranberry muffins. Tanner had my muffin pan—except when I asked to collect it on my way home from the grocery store, he admitted to letting Finn use it. Tanner wasn't in town and couldn't grab the pan for me, so with a fluttery pulse, I called Finn.

He was happy to see me when I got to his apartment. He was also watching *Chopped*, a show I love but hadn't caught in forever. I couldn't resist offering to share the muffins if he'd let me stay and watch. Smiling, he said that sounded awesome. Between his pantry and my groceries, we had all the ingredients, so we launched our spontaneous plan.

Baking and watching became talking and relaxing. We caught up and reminisced, bickered and laughed, had a glass of the cheap wine I'd bought, shared those significant looks we'd always shared...though they felt stronger than usual. I wasn't sure why that alone time was different from any other, even with the wine, but it was—*he* felt different. A deeper level of heart was showing, matching mine. We ate, complimented, grew serious. Our closeness felt even more welcome and buzzing; when he found reasons to touch me and I did the same to him, it felt more important.

A perfect unfolding.

Then my face was in his hands, and I was pulling him to me, and breathing was hard, and his whisper was on my lips: *'Can I kiss you?'*

And everything changed.

Thinking back on those times and on all that happened yesterday...

...now that I'm rested and not so overwhelmed...

...I let myself freely want what I've been too hurt and angry to hope for since October: reconciliation.

If I've truly had him colored wrong all this time—

"Hey, you're awake." I refocus and find him smiling at me. "You'll be happy to see what I see out this window."

Surging excitement yanks a gasp from me.

I escape the bed, grab the throw blanket, and tug it around me as I rush away. "It's snowing?"

"Yeah, but wait, you're barefoot!"

I'm already opening the door. I hurry outside, gasping again at how cold and beautiful....

We go so quiet, as quiet as the snowfall, that I can hear the shuffle of him coming up behind me.

I can hear his murmur: "It's below freezing out here, Sparkles."

My eyes are suddenly stinging over the nickname. And how badly I want us to heal. And his closeness. And how it feels to slip a hand from the blanket and watch snowflakes drift onto it.

I whisper, "Yeah, but I love this."

I sense him coming even closer. Then his hand extends, too, from behind my arm—he catches snowflakes with me.

"I know you do," he says.

My eyes sting worse. I blink a few times, then pull my hand back to myself and turn around.

He's right there, inches away—I knew he would be. He doesn't move, so I study the snowflakes building on his hoodie. Then I look up to his lips, his blue eyes, his increasingly snowy hair. And back down to his gentle expression.

He trades catching snowflakes for cautiously resting his palm between my shoulder blades. I feel his heat through the blanket and my dress, all the way into my spine.

We take a breath together.

He's sorry for breaking my heart.

He turns and nudges me out of the cold. My feet are happy to go.

"How'd you sleep?" he asks.

I clear my throat. "Much better than I would've if you hadn't moved me. Thank you." I wish I'd woken up and felt him carrying me.

He shuts us into the cabin. "No problem at all."

We look at each other again...and the curve of his smile is gentle too.

I'm melting.

He says, "Coffee should be done now. Want some?"

I nod.

"I'll make it for you." Already knowing how I like my coffee, he walks away.

And I find a clock.

Perfect—we have enough time for a conversation before wedding stuff begins.

I go brush my hair, rinse my mouth, and clean up a few makeup smudges. Then I head back toward him; he meets me halfway, bearing mugs.

He gives mine to me. "If you want, we can go for a walk in the snow and take pic—"

"No, I wanna stay here and talk. I want you to tell me what you have to tell me."

His expression shifts all over the place.

Momentarily, he regards me with uncertainty.

I don't waver.

"As badly as I wanna explain," he says, "I don't wanna tell you what happened and watch it wreck how you feel about this weekend. The wedding is today, and Christmas is...."

He sighs at how I'm shaking my head.

I try not to let my swelling emotions choke my voice away. "I don't know what any of that matters, but the truth costs what it costs, okay?"

"I...."

"You said yesterday that you're not different this weekend, but you've *seemed* different, so what does that mean?" I swallow hard. "And—and why were we happy before and then you suddenly didn't wanna be anywhere near me? *Please* tell me."

His gaze doesn't waver any more than mine, but he gulps too.

He says precisely nothing.

For many moments.

For half a minute.

For even longer.

I ache over how close and far away he is right now.

"Near you is the *only* place I wanted to be," he finally says.

My heartbeat utterly soars.

He gestures to the couch, soft resolve on his face. "Let's sit down."

Chapter Eight

Finn

Beside me on the couch, with her brow pinched and that blanket loose around her body, Mallori stares at me.

I feel trembly yet so damn freed up now that the truth is on the air between us. It wasn't easy to say, and I'm still afraid of how she might react, but we'd grown desperate for her to hear it sooner or later. I couldn't refuse her plea for the former.

I relive what I just let out after so long. We spent those few incredible days together, and on the last, a knock came at my front door. She was showering, so I answered—I thought our pizza guy had arrived, but it was Tanner. He'd been out of town and I didn't think he was back yet, definitely didn't think he'd stop by without texting. And *he* didn't expect to hear his younger sister singing in my shower. God, he knew it was her, and his expression went *so*....

Everything escaped me then, under the force of his glare.

I couldn't lie, couldn't explain, couldn't do anything but fear the way he was suddenly looking at me. The conclusion he'd jumped to was accurate—she and I hadn't been doing friends-only things—and it was like he didn't know me and also like he knew me painfully well, and—

"I don't understand," Mallori whispers.

I leave my thoughts and study her eyes. They're full of so much, like last night during our dance.

"My brother...." Her frown deepens. "He said you couldn't have me, and you just...accepted it? Without saying a word?"

I work on breathing as I nod.

"You're an adult, Finn."

"I know."

"And we weren't his business."

"Sure, but he cares about you. He thought I was being careless with you—but it wasn't even true. You weren't casual or trivial or forgettable to me, but he didn't ask—"

"Christ." She stands, tosses the blanket aside, lays a blazing look on me. "Holy *Christ*, Finn. After everything we—after *everything*, you dropped me without putting up a fight just so you wouldn't be in trouble with Tanner? He said, *'Throw her away,'* and you said, *'How far?'* like it was that simple? Like I meant nothing?"

I throb with shame. "Yes, because he caught me off-guard and scared me, but it wasn't what I really wanted. I figured that out too late—figured out how *not* simple it really was. You...." I look her in the eyes and finally confess, "Mallori, you mean *everything* to me."

Her exhalation is scoff-like.

My stomach clenches.

"I just panicked," I say like I did a minute ago. "He'd never been so angry with me, and I didn't expect it, and it's still hard to shake how a situation like that affects me. I've largely gotten away from how my parents were, but it still crops up, you know? My reaction to someone looking like they wanna hit me?"

Her frustration falters, softens. "Yeah, I remember how they were. I know they...."

She doesn't have to continue. I know she knows my parents were hard on me and unhappy together.

When she looks to my right arm, I recall being seventeen with a bruise there from my dad—and just below it, her touch, the softest thing I'd ever felt. He didn't often leave a mark, but he was forever harsh and hellbent on me being a football star, and my slipping math grades were jeopardizing my place on the team. He exploded at the thought of me being lazy, but I really just couldn't keep up with pre-calculus. My mom didn't do anything except tell me to try harder.

Abruptly, Mallori's face darkens. Clenching her fists, she swings her gaze away from me. Then she strides off.

"Where are you going?" I ask.

"To find my fucking overbearing brother and—"

"Oh no! No!" I jump up and fly toward her. "Don't do that!"

"I'm doing it!" She's already by the bed, snatching her high heels up from where she left them.

"This is what I didn't want! I didn't wanna piss you off and make you blow up at him!"

"Of course I'm pissed off!" She turns widened eyes on me. "He literally forbade you from being with me! Why does he get to do that and then be with who he wants and have a fairytale wedding while we're expected to attend and be excited for him? Happy holidays and a happy life to him and Nicole, right? But the rest of us can't do what we want?"

I block her as she tries to pass me. "I agree, but please don't go confront him right now!"

"Move out of my way, Finn!"

She tries again, and I step with her to that side, then to the other. Huffing, she attempts to fake me out, but I see it coming and catch her around the waist.

She wrenches away, then stomps her foot. "*Finn!*"

"This isn't the time! If you run over there and lay his ass out his wedding day—"

"*Why did you keep the truth from me?*"

My words die away as her shout ricochets around us.

I hold her gaze, which is shifting again, this time into heartache.

"You didn't even tell me Tanner came by!" Her voice is still loud but starting to wobble, along with her chin. "You didn't say anything except that we were a mistake. Do you know how that felt? Do you know how it made me feel to be blindsided when I thought we were solid?"

Her eyes are filling with tears, and my chest is filling with so many overwhelming things that I have trouble drawing a breath.

I manage, "I'm sorry."

She shakes her head. Her eyes overflow and send tears skipping down her cheeks. "You should've told me."

"Yes, and I'm ashamed I didn't. I'm sorry it took me so long. I'm sorry you've been so hurt. It's hurt me too."

Her gasp is jagged as I step up to her and slip my hands around her face.

"So I'm telling you now that I know I was wrong. I thought being distant was what I had to do, but it wasn't. From my actual soul, I'm *sorry*. And Mallori, I miss you—God, I'm not far from thirty years old and I've only *recently* learned what truly missing something feels like."

A breath and a sob get tangled up in her, sending a frail noise cracking out.

My throat constricts, but I make my voice keep working. "If you can ever forgive me—if you can give me another chance—I won't fuck up again. The way it felt to hurt you is something I never wanna experience again."

"And what about your best friend in the world?" she tries to snap. "Am I really worth—?"

"Yes, you are."

Her brow creases with the sweetest, most earnest frown.

And it's there again: unmistakable love.

It leaves me winded in the best way.

I thumb at her teardrops. "I don't care what he thinks anymore. I care about us. Yesterday, he said he's gonna put his wife before everyone else because the heart must come first—we laughed about it, but I *felt* it, and since then I haven't just felt it, I've *known* it. And I know now that I'll let go of him if it means holding onto you. I'll put you first. If you somehow still wanna be with me, then please know for certain that I still wanna be with you too. *That's* what I meant when I said I'm not different. I won't pull away from you again because I can't. I'm my entire self when I'm with you."

I try to decipher her mood as she takes all this in. Try to discern where I stand. Try to prepare for her shaking me off and—

"Yes," she chokes out.

My heartbeat stalls.

Then it goes *wild*.

"What?" I ask.

Her expression is...*gentling*. It takes me some blinking to make sure that's real, but it is.

Two thumps startle me. She's dropped her shoes to the floor.

Just as I'm surging with hope that she'll touch me, she does it—her hands find my waist and fist my hoodie.

"I wanna be with you so..." she shakes me lightly, "...*so* badly, Finn."

It feels like she's shaking me to my core.

"Really?" My voice trembles. "Really?"

She nods. Her watery eyes shine. "I never stopped wanting it. And I've only just realized something myself: I never even *tried* to talk to you about what happened. You didn't tell me, but I didn't even *ask*. I just withdrew. This—this is my fault just as much as Tanner's and yours."

I shake my head, not wanting her to blame herself, but she shakes hers harder.

"It's true and stupid and I'm only just now seeing it and I'm—I'm so sorry. Whether I was mad or missing you, I didn't do anything about it, and that was..." she grimaces, "...*immature*. How can I stand here and be upset when I didn't try to fix it either? When I pulled away from you as much as you did from me?"

Sincerity pours from her eyes and floods me like rain soothing a drought.

She says, "But what else is true is I don't want anybody to know me like you do. I don't want anybody's heart but yours. You said I have it, so please let me keep it. I won't act so stupid again either. Won't go cry in a corner without talking to you. I don't wanna do that. I want you back because I've never felt anything like you either."

God.

She remembers what I said to her this fall, when there was us and only us in so many ways.

I can't describe what it does to me.

I can only promise her, "Yeah, you have my heart. I swear it feels like your hands are around it right here and now."

Even after what she's said, I don't expect to see a smile, but a tiny one comes.

It completes me.

She completes me.

Her expressive, wet-lashed eyes are all over my face. I swipe a thumb over her damp cheek—then over her lips because I can't resist.

Her breath hitches. Those eyes spend a long moment on my mouth, then reconnect with mine.

"I forgive you," she says. "Will you forgive me too?"

Chapter Nine

Mallori

The words are like a lock being broken, a chain being loosened. Finn's eyes simultaneously light up in a way I've never seen before and in a way I've seen and missed like crazy.

"*Yes*," he whispers. He rubs at my cheek again, again. "Yes, but I'm not even mad at you, and I swear I'll never—I swear I've learned—"

"I believe you." I release his hoodie from one fist and find his pounding heart. "It's okay. Thank you, and it's okay."

Before yesterday, I didn't think this would be so easy to say.

Before yesterday, I didn't think there was much left of us to salvage. Thought I was dumb to still be hung up on him.

But somehow, the universe gave us what we weren't willing to give ourselves: a chance. He was too caught up in Tanner's reaction, and I was too caught up in resentment. He spent these months thinking he shouldn't make a move, and I spent them being too stubborn to make one myself.

If we'd faced this thing the right way, we wouldn't have wasted so much time.

I repeat, "It's okay," for both of us, because I see what matters most is that we're taking the chance now.

Breathing deeply, he drops a hand from my face and presses it over the one I have on his chest. His other notches under my chin, and he shuffles in, slants in as a soft noise leaves me.

"Can I kiss you?" grazes my lips like it did on our first night together.

That time, I nodded. This time, I answer with the push of my mouth up against his.

And it's like arriving home after being lost.

The kiss ends quickly with low gasps from both of us, and then my face is back in his hands and his mouth is claiming mine. I can't keep from whimpering or wrapping my arms around him or arching my body against his.

Or from confessing, "I love you. I love you."

His exhalation carries a groan, a moan, a noise of weakness and strength at once. "Mallori.... Look at me." Warm is his voice on my lips.

I meet his eyes. They're warm too.

Stroking my hair back, he nods.

"I love you, I love you," he echoes me.

I'm hit *so* hard by it, not just because his reciprocity means the world to me, but also because—

"I've never said that to anyone before," he whispers now.

I stand out to him.

Nodding hard and knowing my voice is too thin to bother with, I wind my hands up through his arms and take hold of *his* face. As I move in for another kiss, he closes me into a possessive embrace that makes me feel breathless, hot, steady. Our lips sink together.

Home.

Forgiveness.

Honesty.

Love.

His mouth makes love to mine, and I wish the rest of him would do that to the rest of me. He's so good at it.

But I can wait for a better time for that, because at long last, we're together again.

I have to pull my tongue from his and smile about that fact. I feel his smile right away and see it when he edges back from me.

My world is brighter.

We stand here and just...*be.*

I never forgot how good it feels to simply exist with him, but it's even better now.

Until we're interrupted by his phone dinging somewhere in his clothes.

We sigh and let go of each other. Reluctantly, I acknowledge, "We should get ready for the day."

"Yeah." He checks his phone. "Seems Tanner wants me to meet him in a few minutes."

"Best man duties start early, hm?"

"Guess so."

After a moment, I whisper, "Are you mad at him?"

He shakes his head. "I was, but now I'm calm."

I chew on my bottom lip. "I'm on the way to calmness. He's not the only person who reacted poorly, but I still...."

"That's okay. Just 'cause you and I faltered on our own responsibilities doesn't mean we can't feel upset by what he said. We weren't ready for that."

Yeah. He's right.

We grip hands and exchange smiles.

"Well," I say, "guess I'll go clean up and stop looking crazy." I gesture at my face, which can't be great after my crying.

But Finn plants a firm kiss on my cheek. "You're as gorgeous as ever."

Then he scrolls a downright mischievous look over me, so I go from feeling sweetly complimented to feeling amused and enticed.

"Need help getting out of this dress before I go?"

Chapter Ten

Finn

I enter the dining room in the main building and find Tanner at a far table, staring out a huge window. He looks...sad?

Uh oh. Has something gone wrong with Nicole on their wedding day?

My instant urge to help him drives home that my bitterness has truly faded. No part of me wants to see him with girl troubles right now.

I take the seat across from him. "Hey, everything okay?"

He turns his attention to me, looking troubled, indeed.

"I'm getting married today," he says.

"That's right." I study him. "How do you feel?"

His sadness stays, but he smiles. "I feel fantastic. Certain and excited. Blessed."

Strangely, I think he means that, which is confu—

"But one thing is poison in my mind, and it's that I got in the way of *you* being happy."

...*What?*

Astonished, I stare at him.

He's nodding. "I haven't known how to man up about it. I just waited to see if you'd realize I was out of line back in October—if you'd decide to ignore me and go be happy with Mallori. But you never did, and I know it's my fault. I'm putting it out there now 'cause I'm getting married today and I won't feel completely right about it when I know I hurt you."

My mouth has fallen open.

"From the bottom of my heart, I'm sorry I told you to stay away from her, and for your best man gift, I wanna say it's okay with me if you love her."

Holy shit.

"It—it is?" I ask.

"Yeah. Took me a while to get past the shock of you being together, but once Nicole helped me do it...Finn, I knew I'd fucked up. For the first time, I saw how you and Mallori look at each other, especially when one of you isn't paying attention. And I noticed how wrong you both suddenly seemed, which meant things were right before I interfered." He frowns. "Nicole and I would've been that broken if *we* couldn't be together."

"Oh," I breathe out. "Wow. I...."

I don't know what to say.

Is this actually happening? He understands?

The longer we look at each other, the more real it feels. I know Tanner. I know when he's being honest.

He says, "It's fine if you're mad at me. I just wanted to officially give you my blessing."

The words relieve me even though I really was okay without them. I don't *want* to cross him—keeping Mallori just matters most.

At length, I say, "Thanks, Tan. I did have some resentment, but not anymore, and I...."

He nods. So do I.

"Thank you," I repeat.

He seems relieved too. "No need for thanks. I was an asshole." Shifting forward, he points a finger at me. "But dude, I swear, if you—"

"I'm not gonna hurt her," I promise quickly.

"No, I know that." His eyebrows lift. "Nicole had the idea for you to dance with Mallori last night, and I was worried you weren't gonna take my hint and do it, so I'm glad you did. But don't waste any more time not being with her. I get she's been pissed off and your cabin is likely a warzone, but I don't think she knows this was all my fault, so if you tell her and put yourself out there again, she'll take you back. *However,* if you keep being distant 'cause you're too scared to speak up, like I was, I swear I'll—"

My laughter cuts him off.

He's surprised, but momentarily, he laughs too.

"I'll smack you," he threatens.

"You don't have to. Believe it or not, we made up not even an hour ago."

"What! Are you for real?"

"Yeah!" I point back at him. "But what's this about you hinting for me to dance with her? 'Cause that bridesmaid and I both got the wrong idea, and she was confused when I went rogue and asked Mallori anyway."

"Oh, God." Tanner laughs anew. "Yeah, Riley was *not* who I was talking about!"

Now I'm thinking about it, maybe I should've noticed his change of heart sooner. He didn't freak out when he learned Mallori and I were cabinmates...or even half-ass offer to switch things up so he and I could be in the same cabin and Mallori and Nicole in the other.

He just said, *'I know you'll do the right thing for her.'*

Was that a hint too? A hint that I should go for it with her because it would make her happy, not just me?

He holds out a fist. Smiling, I bump it and say, "Well, I'm glad you're not upset anymore."

"Nah, I've gotten my mind right." He sighs. "And I need to talk to Mallori next. Think she's gonna give me a black eye to show off at the altar?"

"I don't *think* so."

Briefly, he ponders that. Then he chuckles. "Either way, you chose well. She's a little star. As fiery as she is pretty."

"Yeah." My smile grows. "Yeah, you're right about that."

Chapter Eleven

Mallori

"So..." my brother takes a hesitant breath, "...you don't wanna kill me?"

It's been a long time since he last appeared to be afraid of me. But I *am* calm now.

Fresh tears spring to my eyes—from this and from the line he crossed in October and from how much I know he cares.

I reach out to pat his arm. He flinches, clearly recalling how I shoved him in only partly playful incredulity after letting him into the cabin. We share a light laugh.

Then I admit, "When Finn told me the truth, I was *really* mad. At both of you."

Regret flares in his eyes. "We let you down."

"Yeah, but your hearts were in the right place. I can see that now." I shrug. "All three of us should've done things differently. Better late than never, though."

He nods, and I can tell he's growing emotional too. "I'm sorry, sis. I already said that a bunch, but.... Since I love you to pieces and I'm your big brother, I jumped into protecting you. Reacted too fast. Didn't take time to see you weren't a plaything to Finn, you were the *real* thing, and you didn't need protection from him."

That touches my heart something fierce.

"Aw, Tanner," I say much more weakly than I squeeze his arm. "I love *you* to pieces." After a moment of settling perspective: "Thank you for caring what happens to me."

He gives me a watery smile. "I always will, though I know he'll take care of you too."

Finn would confirm if he weren't in the shower.

Decidedly in my feelings now, I let go of Tanner's arm to move in for a hug. He throws it around me.

"You're absolved," I wobble out.

He sniffles. "Thank you."

We step back and trade smiles.

"I'm so happy you two are happy," he says.

"So are we. And we're happy you and Nicole are happy."

His smile becomes a grin. "*God*, I'm getting married today."

"Yep!" I ruffle his hair. "It's gonna be a great day, Tan-Tan."

We aren't even outside in the open, yet the air feels so much clearer; we fill our lungs with contented breaths.

"Yeah," he agrees. "A great day for all kinds of love."

He's so right.

Finn and I prepare for brunch, attend brunch, and go for the final inspection of the Sky Hall and reception room.

Next, we get dressed to perfection for pictures. I take my time making sure his khaki-colored suit is in great shape. He zips me into my dress, then slowly runs his fingertips over the skin exposed by the off-both-shoulders top.

I thought the dress was beautiful when I bought it. It's dark brown and long with a fit-to-flare style and sleeves that hit my elbows. But I *feel* truly beautiful with Finn's murmurs of awe surrounding me.

Pictures take a while. Guys and girls are mostly separated for surprise's sake, plus there are different locations and special groupings to work around. Afterward, it's time for final touches to appearances. Finn goes with the guys and I sit in the bridesmaids' cabin, drinking mulled wine with the ladies of note, watching the photographer capture these last minutes while Nicole shines with excitement.

Then, at last, the ceremony is nigh.

Those of us who are honored guests part ways with the bridal party. My mom hugs my arm out in the frigid afternoon, and we giggle together.

Over near my and Finn's cabin, I can see his familiar form acting silly with my brother's. Their laughter is so loud it reaches Mom and me.

It makes my heart happy.

And I recall something from yesterday: me trudging to that cabin, aggravated about having to share it with Finn, wishing some Christmas magic would get us out of the predicament we'd found ourselves in.

The magic was already in motion, though. I didn't realize being forced together was the answer we needed, but it was.

Our problem wasn't us having to be near each other—it was that we'd been too far apart.

Never again.

Merry Christmas to us, indeed.

Love, the universe.

Chapter Twelve

Finn

There were many times over my twenty-six years of existence when I didn't feel my life was good. Times when I felt pressured, shallow, lacking, worn thin, betrayed, downright stupid.

Not anymore.

Life *is* good.

I stand by my best friend and watch him ecstatically, tearfully marry his soulmate.

I look to a nearby bench and find *my* soulmate radiating joy for her beloved brother.

The two best people I've ever known.

I wasn't always aware of exactly what Mallori meant to me. I just knew she was different from other girls—I knew she held significance I hadn't encountered before. She got under my skin in particular ways, but it wasn't always bad. She could snap at me like a viper attacking, but she could also be so gentle. All in all, she seemed matchless.

Now I know she is.

She meets my eyes. We smile widely at each other before looking back to Tanner and Nicole.

And we're the first to cheer when they're pronounced husband and wife.

So much celebration, laughter, elation.

So much champagne, amazing food, dancing.

So many tears, hugs, compliments.

When it's time to give my little speech, I stand from where I've been sitting with Mallori and look upon Tanner, who's at a special table with Nicole.

"You and I aren't just friends," I tell him. "We're brothers. We're stupid together, but we also improve each other. We're there for each other through thick, thin, up, down. We make messes, then we make them right. And that's how I know you're gonna be everything Nicole needs: because I know *you*. You won't just be married to her. You'll be *committed* to her."

The room loves that—especially our girls. He and I grin, but we're not afraid to let our own emotion show.

I lift my drink to him and Nicole.

"Congratulations, you two," I say. "You've been together for a while, but in a way, your love story is just beginning. Here's to it!"

Applause and cheers rise up. Tanner and I fist-bump through the air. Then he turns a kiss onto his first priority's lips.

I do the same to mine once I'm sitting again. I appreciate the hell out of the smile it puts on her face. And since her dress is such a deep brown that it makes her eyes seem light, the look we share glows that much more.

Yeah.

Life is good.

The last song to play at the reception is "Lover" by Taylor Swift. I know this because Mallori turned it on at my apartment one day this fall. She sang along with every word then; tonight, she just rests her head on my shoulder and lets me hold her close while we slowly sway.

As much as I enjoyed her singing those lyrics, I enjoy this so much more.

I relish every moment of our final dance of the evening.

That's not to say I don't want the wedding to end—my feet hurt and I'm tired, and I'm *so* looking forward to going back to our cabin together. I want to catch up with her, bury myself inside her, snuggle her in front of the fireplace, take a hot shower with her. I want to be in our own little world doing whatever feels satisfying to us.

On the part of the song that sounds particularly wedding-appropriate, she starts singing along, only loudly enough for me to hear. It makes me smile.

Think I've always loved this girl.

I definitely always will.

A single minute after the song ends, Tanner and Nicole are ready to escape the crowd. We all send them off into the snowfall with cheers and lit sparklers. Then goodbyes swirl between the rest of us. Mallori's parents hug her and me equally big, still the best mom and dad ever.

After making sure we have our essentials, including an unopened bottle of champagne, she and I claim a chauffeur and leave.

"Christmas is so magical," the driver remarks. "My favorite holiday."

"It is magical, isn't it?" Mallori muses.

I didn't know she thought that. It's kind of silly to me. But hey, she's *my* silly girl.

In the warmth of the cabin, we take a minute to chat about the festivities while settling in a bit. Then we meet in the middle of the room. She's shorter than before with her high heels off.

I smile at that and at her words from outside. "You think Christmas is magical?"

Smiling, too, she shrugs. "Only this one, really." Her eyes soften. "I didn't know I wanted us for Christmas...didn't dare to even hope...until this weekend."

And that isn't silly to me whatsoever.

I curve a hand to her cheek. "I know exactly what you mean."

"Yeah?"

"Yeah."

She tugs me toward her. I shuffle in and give her the kiss she's lifting her chin for—then another, slower now.

Swear it makes her melt just like it does me.

As her arms encircle me, I slip a hand into her hair, then find her lower back with the other and pull her even closer. Her mouth owns mine in the sweetest way. I'm happy to surrender to it; in my weaker moments during the last couple months, sometimes I'd let myself recall how this felt, and my mouth would water. Kissing her through smiles, moans, words, gasps for air...there's nothing like it.

There's nothing like Mallori, period.

Doesn't matter if our time together is cute or sexy or chill or anything else—she truly is matchless.

Which is why I murmur away from her lips, "You're all I want for Christmas, but not *just* for Christmas. I'm aiming for forever."

Though she bursts into a grin, I can feel how deep my words go. It's in her inhalation, her grip on me, the way she tilts back to look at me.

"Agreed," she replies. "You're the best Christmas present, but all I want *forever* is you."

I grin with her, and we chuckle together.

Then, as we hold each other's gaze, the truth of our feelings settles on us in earnest.

"Forever," I reiterate in a whisper.

"Yes," comes so softly that I feel the drift of it on my lips more than I hear it.

We're in another kiss, firm and unwavering. And one, two more.

My name touches my lips now. Our breaths are growing short. Desire is entering our fingertips, so familiar and yet so fresh; we let it lead us into pulling my suit jacket off, unzipping her dress, loosening my tie. Soon, the rush of air over exposed skin puts chill bumps on us, but mouths going down necks and fingers dipping below hips have us burning in the best way.

Then the only light in the cabin is from the fireplace, and we're undressed and burrowed in the bed, and her hands are pleading on my waist as I cover her body with mine. I thrust us together exactly like we want me to—our moans collide just before our mouths do.

I remember how overwhelming it was to be pulled into her for the very first time. Remember thinking I'd never have another first time with another girl. That one with her was it for me.

This surpasses that.

It isn't just us giving in. It's us being unbreakable.

We do let the passion have us, though. We'll be patient and relearn every inch of each other later, tomorrow, onward. Right now, our hips refuse to go slow. Our hands urge each other closer, as if we aren't already as close as we can get. Our mouths sear greedy kisses onto lips, jaws, collarbones.

Minutes we don't even try to hold onto.

"Oh my God, Finn." An utterly feminine sound fires out of her. Her lips stumble over my throat. "I missed us. Please don't stop."

"Baby, you know I...."

But I catch her up in a full kiss, my words not mattering, only the tension overtaking her body. I recognize it, recognize the press of her fingertips into my back. So I just keep giving what she needs, and she starts unraveling.

"Yeah, I've got you," I exhale from our kiss. "Come for me, Mallori. I missed us too."

Amid gasps and grasps, she does—and no, not even my first time thrusting her over the edge was as fulfilling or intoxicating as now.

She wraps me in her arms and legs and sweet breathlessness; she's got me too.

So I'm as gone as she is. I don't want to even try to hang on.

My days of trying to resist this girl are over.

We lie side-by-side, our hands tangled between us, her head on my shoulder and my head resting on hers.

"How many fake jewels were on my hair pin after homecoming?" Her murmur carries the warmth of a smile.

I'm warm, too, as I see sixteen-year-old Mallori in my memory. Her hair was gathered behind her neck in a mass of soft-looking curls. On the left side of it, she'd tucked that straight, glitzy pin into place. I counted the stones while she stood by my car with me and cried about her date.

"Seven," I answer. "All in a row. The first was the size of a dime, maybe. They got smaller from there."

Now I *feel* her smiling.

It's contagious.

"I love you," I whisper to her, so easily.

We squeeze hands. "And I love you. Seems like I have for forever."

"Mmm. Me too."

She's grinning now. "Hey, wanna drink the champagne and see some sketches I did of you?"

I perk up. "You drew *me?* Hell yeah, I wanna see!" What a gift.

Plus, we have a toast of our own to make.

Although we've been significant to each other for years, what I said at the reception is as true for us as it is for the newlyweds.

In a way, our love story is just beginning.

ONE YEAR LATER

Mallori

I lick the last bit of cookie-flavored sugar scrub from my lips, pleased with their smoothness. Finn will appreciate it, too, as well as how tasty this stuff is.

He'll *super* appreciate what I'm wearing.

I giggle and make one last adjustment of the sheer, deep red, glitter-touched bustier and matching panties. Then I leave the bathroom.

And on my way out of our bedroom, I trip over something that sends me stumbling. Pulse jumping, I burst out, "Holy—!"

"You okay?" Finn calls as I loudly catch myself against the wall. He's in the living room, waiting for me so we can open Christmas gifts.

I roll my eyes at what my feet got tangled in. He is forever leaving clothing on the floor by our closet, like the laundry hamper isn't *right there*.

I call back, "When are you gonna quit leaving clothes in the middle of the floor? I was hurrying through the room just now and almost busted my ass tripping on your jeans!"

His chuckles reach me. "What are *you* doing running indoors?"

If this were any other day, I'd accuse him of changing the subject.

However, it's snowy Christmas Day, and I'd rather give him his biggest gift —me in this lingerie—than squabble about his special brand of laziness again.

So I clasp my hands behind me and finally enter the living room, returning to the sweet and sultry way I've felt since waking up. "I was running 'cause I'm excited to show you your present."

From the couch, he looks at me over the top of his mug—and chokes on his coffee. He's suddenly in a coughing fit.

"Oh no!" Gasping, I hurry over. "Babe, I'm sorry!"

He sets the mug on the end table, waving his other hand. Then he catches his breath, stands, and reaches for me. "Don't you dare apologize. This is all for me?"

I let him take hold of my hips before I do a slow spin so he can see the lingerie in all its glory.

"I heard you like sparkles," I say with a grin.

He grins, too, though desire is radiating from him. He pulls me closer, runs his eyes over the chest-flattering top and his hands over the panties.

"I *love* sparkles," he replies. "But only on you."

As he shuffles back toward the couch, he takes me with him.

"And I love you on me," he adds.

I'm well aware of how true it is, but I still blush, same as how his obvious approval makes me blush even though I was sure he'd give it.

The way he feels beneath me when I straddle him confirms that he truly doesn't *like*. He *loves*.

A hot kiss comes and goes, then becomes another. I press myself down on his lap, and we moan over so many things—his arousal and mine, his strong hands spreading over me and moving me against him with promise, his teeth and tongue on my bottom lip.

"I just love *you*, Mallori," he groans as I tug his shirt up.

"Perfect, 'cause I love you too."

"Perfect. And you taste good."

I smile and start to explain the lip scrub, but then his shirt is gone and his fingers are in my panties, seeking me out. Through my gasps, he huskily begs me to keep the lingerie on.

I refuse to refuse.

After we've thoroughly given ourselves to each other, leaving kiss-swollen lips and pleasure-rocked muscles in our wake, he wraps me in his arms. I slump here where I am. We're warm and slightly sweaty, but hugs are important.

A minute passes before he murmurs, "You know, the dress you wore to the wedding rehearsal last year wasn't sparkly, but it was this exact shade of red. I loved it on you."

I hum in pleasant surprise. "Really?"

"Yeah." He chuckles. "Put that on for me sometime, eh?"

I chuckle too. "For your birthday, eh?"

"It's not ruining the surprise if I ask for it myself, eh?"

We laugh more. He loosens his embrace, then nudges at me. I take the cue and sit back enough to look at him.

His blue eyes are sated, tender, calm. Happy. Swirling with honest affection that mirrors what I feel for him. He strokes my hair back with one hand, tucks it behind my ear.

Nuzzling his touch, I whisper, "Merry Christmas. I love you, I love you."

His smile brightens those eyes. "I love you, I love you. Merry Christmas." He winks at me. "I'll even give you the bonus gift of putting my laundry in the hamper."

I burst out laughing. "Wow! I knew you could do it!"

He laughs, too, and we get to moving.

We reconvene at the Christmas tree after a minute. I start to sit on the floor, but he stops me, then hands me a small, red-bow-topped gift I didn't notice he was holding.

"Open this first," he requests.

Just as I register that it's a jewelry-type box, he sinks down onto one knee in front of me.

And everything around us slows.

Well, except for the quick swell of my heart in my chest.

"Finn?" I ask softly.

His gaze is tender again, his cheeks going pink.

Gorgeous.

Taking a weak breath, I ease open the top of the box.

We're quiet for a few moments while the ring sparkles up at me. His gentle hands find my wrists.

Then he says, "All I want forever is you. Let me keep proving it to you?"

Our watering eyes meet.

I nod so hard it makes me dizzy.

Yet my promise is as steady as his: "I'll keep proving it to you right back."

I've loved Finn's smile for many years, but the one he breaks into now is *unparalleled.*

So is the new level of adoring joy I feel over him—it's so strong that I drop to my knees and kiss him before he can even get the ring out of the box.

Last year, Christmas magic seemed to bring us together, but this year, we don't need its nudge to help us along. We're taking the steps on our own. We *are* the magic.

We're each other's magic every day.

And as he slips the ring onto my finger and dissolves into happy laughter with me, I know that'll be true forever, indeed.

THE END

It Started One Christmas

BY ELLE FIELDING

At Christmastime, even enemies fall in love.
Breanna Webber and Lawson St. James have been enemies since Christmas
Day fifteen years
ago. Sure, they spent one hot night together not too long ago, but that was
a mistake. Or was
it? When the pair are forced to work together over the Christmas break,
they must decide
whether a repeat is in order. Is there more to their antagonistic
relationship than either of
them has dared to admit, like love?

About the Author

Elle Fielding is an Aussie gal obsessed with love and romance. As a teenager, she read Dolly Fiction, Love Stories, Loveswept and Harlequin Mills & Boon, and she journaled prolifically about the boys she fell in love with.

Since none of her journal entries had happy endings, she decided she needed to write those sought after HEAs herself. Mostly, those first attempts at the genre were terrible. Then she stopped writing about herself and they got much better.

Eventually Mr. Perfect stopped ignoring Elle, and now Elle lives out her happy ending on Australia's Mornington Peninsula. But that hasn't stopped her from reading or writing (or listening to) romance.

Find more of her books on popular reading platforms, Substack and Vocal.

Happy reading!

Chapter One

The summer sun burns my back through my pink cotton tee as I speed towards the dirt park on my new bike. I've only just managed to convince my father to let me out for an hour, and I think that's because he'd had too much of my aunt's mulled wine. I've never been more grateful for her tradition of making that stuff. Every night for the past six months, I've gone to sleep thinking about and wishing for the Pink Nitro BMX I laid eyes on at Whitby's Bike Store back in June. Today is Christmas Day, and it's finally mine.

The scents of roast turkey and meat on the barbecue and the sound of people shouting and laughing fill the air. Everyone in our neighbourhood has their Christmas lights on. I wave to some of the families I know. The Allens are playing street cricket. The Bourke kids are skateboarding. Jilly Bourke looks to have a new board and her brother Jamie is putting a ramp together out the front of their place. They have my favourite decorations up: a giant inflatable Santa surrounded by snow and reindeer. Normally, I would stop to admire it and talk to Jilly and Jamie, but not today.

After months of imagining myself racing up the dirt hills at the bottom of my street, I'm going to experience the rush and the thrill for myself. I've walked past the bike park so many times on my way home from school, and every day I watch the same boy performing the most awe-inspiring jumps. Today, I get to watch him up close. If he's not away for Christmas, that is.

I spot him as soon as I walk through the gates. He thrusts his bike up the hill right in front of me, somersaulting in the air before he hits the ground. After landing gracefully, his gaze flicks to me briefly before he rides off.

"Whoa," I whisper.

He could be a movie star—or, even better, a stuntman. I want to do jumps like that. Will he teach me if I ask him nicely?

I'm so busy being impressed by his speed and agility that I don't even register there's someone standing beside me until they tap me on the shoulder. Momentarily, I forget my idol as I turn around.

I find myself staring into the face of the most gorgeous boy I've ever seen. His shaggy long brown hair is bleached by the sun, one lock nearly covering his eye. He's tanned with green eyes the colour of moss.

"Hi, I'm Jax. Don't see a lot of girls here at the bike park."

I check out his wheels. His bike is a really good one. "I've been begging my dad to buy me this bike for months so I could ride it here."

I don't want to tell him I even wrote a letter to Father Christmas even though no one in class thinks he's real.

Jax looks down at my pride and joy. "Your dad caved."

I shrug, as if talking to a cute boy isn't anything particularly out of the ordinary. "Yeah."

"Cool," he says. "So, what's your name? You know, so I don't have to call you Nitro."

The idea of being named after my bike makes me grin, and I tuck a lock of my light brown hair behind my ear. "Breanna. Bree for short."

"Nice to meet you, Bree. Where do you go to school?"

"Rosebud East Primary."

"Saint and I go to Rosebud Heights Primary, so I guess that explains why I haven't seen you before."

"Saint?" I ask.

Jax motions to the superstar currently performing another somersault in the air. 'Saint' lands on the ground fifty meters from where I'm talking to Jax, pausing to watch the two of us.

"That's Lawson, my brother," Jax says. "People call him Saint."

That's his brother? Wow, I'm in the midst of bike royalty. "Why do they call him Saint?"

"Our last name is St. James."

I don't ask why Lawson is known as Saint while Jax is known as Jax. What I really want to know is whether Lawson is as nice as Jax, and whether he'll teach me to ride the way he does.

"Saint's really good," I tell Jax as I watch his brother pedal towards where we sit astride our bikes.

Jax chuckles. "Don't tell him that. He already thinks he's the best."

Saint might be right about being the best, but I keep my mouth closed and my opinion to myself as he brakes hard in front of me, causing dirt to fly out from underneath his wheels. When he takes his helmet off, I stare into a face identical to Jax's. Saint and Jax aren't just brothers, they're twins.

Fortunately, there are a couple of notable differences. Jax has a sprinkling of freckles across the bridge of his nose while Lawson's skin is freckle-free. And while Jax's eyes are a bright, untainted green, Saint's have flecks of brown in them.

"Hi," I say while Saint stands there quietly taking me in.

Jax jerks his thumb in my direction and says to his brother, "This is Breanna. She got a new bike today and she wants to ride."

Saint's eyes flick between me and Jax before falling on my bike. "The girly tracks are on the other side of the park."

It isn't the first time a boy has implied I can't do something he can, and I know it won't be the last, but there's something about *this* boy implying it that makes me so steamed I want to punch him in his gorgeous face—right after I prove him wrong.

I narrow my eyes at him. "I want to do *this* track."

Saint sits back on his bike, arms crossed. "Bet you ten bucks you fall on your arse coming over the first hill."

"When I nail it, I don't want your money; I want you to teach me how to do some of your tricks."

Nerves make my stomach feel as if it's trying to take flight as his hazel eyes hold mine. Then he smirks, as if the idea of me winning this bet is ridiculous. His attitude makes me even more determined to prove him wrong.

"Deal," he says.

Jax grins. "Shake on it."

I don't give a second thought to shuffling forward on my bike and extending my hand. Saint reaches out, taking my hand and shaking it. My hand and my entire right arm tingle as if I've just touched the electric fence on Nan's farm. My heart beats extra hard, and my stomach does a somersault as I put my bike into gear and ride towards the first hill.

It isn't the biggest hill in the park, but it's still pretty steep. I race up it easily enough, then quickly lose control coming down the other side.

When my front tyre hits a rock, I don't even have time to think. One moment I'm on my bike, the next I'm kissing the dirt.

Tears prick at my eyes as my knees and hands sting, but I blink rapidly to make them go away. I refuse to cry in front of Saint and Jax.

Jax races over to me. "Are you okay, Breanna?"

I sit up and nod, looking over at Saint once I know I'm not in any danger of letting my tears spill. Anger boils up inside me as I take in his smug expression.

"Told you so," he declares easily.

"That was my first time. I just need some practice."

He shrugs. "You owe me ten bucks. Come on, Jax. Let's get out of here."

Jax doesn't seem to be in the same rush as his brother, and he offers me his hand, helping me up. "Where do you live, Breanna?"

"Banksia Street." I rub the dirt off my knees. They sting and my entire body aches from the fall. Thank God my bike is okay. I can only imagine the look on my dad's face if I went home with my bike mangled.

"We live on Gumnut Drive. We'll walk with you."

"I'm not walking with that loser," Saint spits.

"Fine," Jax says. "I'll meet you at home."

The look Saint shoots me is filled with resentment, like he hates me, even though I don't know how he could when we just met.

Well, when he rides off without looking back, I decide I hate him just as much.

How can anyone call him Saint? There's absolutely nothing saintly about Lawson St. James.

Chapter Two

As I pull into the long driveway leading into Point Heaven Holiday Park, my stomach is in knots. How am I going to spend the next month working alongside my nemesis? A nemesis I know *intimately*, thanks to my stupid night drinking at my best friend's wedding a fortnight ago.

Taking a deep breath, I loosen my grip on the steering wheel and push away the memory of the hottest night of my life. Why is it that the guy I hate the most can turn me inside out and make me orgasm harder than anyone else?

Nope, not going there.

For Jax. I'm doing this for Jax.

If I hadn't gotten over my love for Jaxon St. James years ago, watching him get married two weeks ago would have been heartbreaking. But he'd told me in no uncertain terms on my eighteenth birthday that he loved me as a friend and nothing more. It shattered me at the time, but now I see it as the gift it was. No one wants to be in unrequited love with their best friend for ever and a day.

Now he's currently on his way to Europe, where he'll be honeymooning for the next month and a half with his British bride. He always wanted to experience a white Christmas. Lucky bastard. Meanwhile, I'm stuck with the arsehole Saint.

Carefully, I navigate the speed bump and park in one of the spots reserved for guests checking in. Saint is going to complain, but I only need to pick up my keys to the cabin where I'll be staying and then I'll move.

Alarmingly, there are no Christmas decorations up in the park yet. We're going to have to talk about that. Saint is one of the clichéd grinch-types, and normally I'd let it go because arguing with him seems to give him a sick sense of satisfaction. But this place is Jax's baby. He's here all year round, and he's all about the Christmas decorations. This is the biggest time of the year for the park, and it's the holiday season. Coming here means absorbing the Christmas spirit.

Once I'm out of my car, I walk inside the simple log hut that is the reception building, only to find the place empty and the phone ringing. Sighing, I bend over the long reception desk and answer the call.

"Point Heaven Holiday Park. How can I help you?"

Thanks to my career as a freelance sports and nature photographer, I've had the time to help Jax out during a few holiday seasons. I'm sure that was one of the contributing factors to his decision to leave his beloved business in my hands during peak time. That and the fact his brother is part owner. Saint isn't a freelancer like me, but he has a huge social media following because of the frequent adventures and extreme sports videos he posts. Most of the year, he's on the road, but when he isn't, he's working here. Between the two of us, I'm sure we'll be able to take care of the place.

Providing we don't kill each other.

"Good afternoon. This is Doris Gupman calling from UPD Unlim-ited. Am I speaking with the manager?"

The nature of the call is suddenly obvious, and I have no problem letting the lie roll off my tongue. "Uh-huh."

"How are you today?"

"Fine, thank you. What can I do for you, Doris?"

"You've been selected for a free hour-long appraisal of your energy options—"

"I'm going to stop you right there. We're not interested. Thank you and have a wonderful day."

Saint walks into the cabin just in time to hear me tell Doris we're not interested. As I hang up, I worry he's going to assume the worst and snap at me for being rude to a customer, but he just raises a brow. "Solar panels or insurance?"

"Neither. We just turned down a free one-hour appraisal of our energy options."

He rolls his eyes and then drags his hazel gaze over me. "Long drive?"

I'm suddenly aware of my crinkled t-shirt and shorts. "I take it that's your way of telling me I look like something the cat threw up."

He smirks and doesn't bother denying it. Meanwhile, Saint looks perfectly put together in his shorts and t-shirt stretched over his muscular frame. I try not to drink him in, but I can't help myself. His sun-streaked chestnut hair curls over his forehead, looking so much like his brother's. He's so big and tough, and even though I'm fit and healthy and tall, Saint towers over me, making me feel small and delicate, and not in a good way.

While Jax has been my soft place to fall for the past fifteen years, my confidant and my biggest supporter, Saint has brought out the worst in me. In fact, I'm pretty sure we bring out the worst in each other.

So when he'd turned up to my hotel room the night of Jax's wedding with a bottle of bourbon, looking a little lost, I have no idea why I invited him in. Even more puzzling, when he leaned in and kissed me, I didn't push him away. Rather, I held on for dear life, spreading my legs for him and letting that heat and anger that's always simmered between us explode in an entirely different way for once.

Despite the fact I'd imbibed enough liquor to drown an elephant, the memories of Lawson St. James and our hookup have stuck in my memory on repeat. Trying not to relive them when I'm in bed has been hell. The memory of the way he held himself over me, the way he looked at me—not as his enemy but as something... more—is there every time I close my eyes.

The mere reminder leaves my cheeks hot, my body flushed and wet, my breath coming out a little strangled.

Tearing my gaze away from his, I glance through the lodge window. "I need to move my car."

He grabs a set of keys from one of the hooks on the wall and tosses them to me.

I catch them one-handed just as he says, "You're in 101."

"Where are you staying?"

He smirks. "In 101."

I narrow my eyes at him. "Just so we're clear, Saint, I'm not sleeping with you again."

Not after the way he left me last time. He was gone before I woke up. No explanation. No follow-up call. Our night together meant nothing to him. The hurt I felt when I didn't hear from him was unexpected and unwelcome.

He scoffs. "Cool your jets, Breanna. I only need to make a mistake once to learn."

"And sleeping with me was a mistake?" I bite out, ignoring the way my heart feels as though it's being squeezed in a vice.

I don't even know why I'm asking. He made it clear he regrets our night, or at least doesn't care to ever repeat it. Even if I once stupidly hoped our time together meant something to him, that it was the start of something, I won't make *that* mistake again.

He cocks an eyebrow. "Wasn't it?"

"Of course. I was drunk."

"There you go." He paints an imaginary cross over his heart. "Promise you I won't touch you."

"Good."

"We're booked solid—that's the only reason we'll be sharing Jax's quarters. I honestly didn't think you'd have a problem with it. Jax made it sound like you're aware of how crazy the holiday seasons are here."

"Of course. It's fine."

I walk out and try not to think about the horrible way he told me he didn't want to sleep with me again. Sometimes, I swear the two of us inter-acting causes him to devolve into that twelve-year-old boy I met fifteen years ago.

Without thinking it through, I walk back into the reception office, finding him in the same spot. He quirks an eyebrow in question.

"Are we going to be able to work together?" I ask.

"Why wouldn't we?"

I try not to laugh. "Maybe because you've always been a dick to me."

"You have a high opinion of yourself, Bree. I'm a dick to everyone." His dark eyes lock with mine. "You're not special."

His words make me flinch as they lash at my heart, but I don't give him the satisfaction of seeing that. Never will I admit I have secretly wondered if there's another reason he's always been an arse to me. Oftentimes when boys pull pigtails, it's their way of getting a girl's attention. For a short time, I thought maybe Saint was mean to me because he wanted mine. But the way he's just spoken to me reminds me that sometimes when boys pull pigtails, they're just being arseholes.

I make a hasty exit and climb into my car.

I drive past the beach entry, the boat ramps, the bike and walking tracks, all the way to the last cabin—101—my home for the next month.

Walking through the place littered with clothes and take-away containers, the scent of Saint's aftershave everywhere, I sigh.

One month.

Living with Saint for a month.

How hard can it be?

Chapter Three

My first afternoon, I do a bit of a clean-up of my new lodgings. Sure, it's not my mess, but I refuse to live in a pigsty just to stand on principle. Plus, I know how busy it gets here. Saint has been running the place on his own for about a week, and that has probably contributed to the mess more than anything. Jax has had Adrienne—his fiancée-now-wife—by his side, helping him manage the place, so it's really a two-person job.

Once the cabin looks respectable, I change, tidy myself up, and then go back to the reception office to check the calendar and operations manual Jax left for me. The fact I've worked for him before means he knows I'm able to follow his directions without needing extra details a newbie might need. I don't need a heck of a lot of supervision. The holiday park has a combination of powered sites, unpowered sites, caravans, and cabins. My main role will be manning the reception office and liaising with campers. Meaning, hopefully I won't have to interact with Saint too much.

I spend the rest of the day talking with some of the staff I already know and answering the never-ending stream of phone calls and emails, stopping only to order a dinner delivery. Despite wanting to avoid Saint, I still look for him to ask if he wants anything, but he tells me he's busy and he'll grab something later.

All in all, the day goes off without a hitch, to the point where it lulls me into a false sense of security.

Believing Saint is only too happy to avoid/ignore me, and assuming he's already up and at it when I wake up the next morning, I get up and drag myself into the shower. Thus, when the bathroom door flies open right as I'm in the middle of showering, I screech in a very unladylike manner.

"Get out!"

"Just need to grab something."

Saint probably can't see much more than my silhouette through the white shower curtain, but I spin around anyway. "You have no business—"

"I've seen it all before. Really wasn't that impressed."

"God, you're such a jerk."

"She cuts me so deep with her original insults."

"You don't deserve my original insults."

"Ooh, sick burn."

As if it isn't bad enough that he gets the last word in, he walks out and turns the hot water on, so my water runs cold. "I hate you," I shout, shivering and turning off the shower.

It's going to be a long freaking month.

"How are things?" Jax asks me via FaceTime several days later.

"Great."

I can barely hide my yawn. It feels like I haven't stopped working since I got here, running around like a turkey with its head cut off. While I try to spend as much time as I can in the reception office, the campers keep me busy with their requests. With facilities such as a large community kitchen, laundry room, tennis courts, and boat and bike hire, there's always something to attend to. Then there are the requests for extra linen, baby seats, cots, et cetera. Keeping busy isn't so bad, though. It keeps me out of Saint's way as much as possible.

"Is Saint behaving himself?" Jax presses.

"Sure."

"Bree," he chides, looking half exasperated and half amused. "How bad is it? Do I need to talk to him?"

"No, you need to enjoy your honeymoon. Everything is fine here."

By that, I mean Saint and I are still alive, but I don't need to elaborate on that definition for Jax. He has a strong preference to stay out of my relationship with his brother. They're as close as any twins would be, and I know it hasn't been easy on Jax having his best friend and brother at each other's throats. I'm only thankful he has no idea Saint and I slept together.

Jax starts laughing. "Say, now I know you're lying; things are never fine between you two."

"Our love for you means we've set our differences aside."

He sighs, and I can tell he's not buying it.

I say, "Don't worry. When you return, I'm sure we'll go back to trying to kill each other."

"Good to know."

"Isn't it?" I tease. "Now, enough about work. I'm trying to live vicariously here. How's Adrienne?"

His voice gets this soft and dreamy quality as he talks about his new wife. He tells me about the play they saw in London and how her family is so pleased they'll be there for the holidays.

We talk for longer than we should, but since he's the boss and the one paying my wages, I let him chatter. Eventually, he runs out of things to tell me, or at least he's ready to end our call, but I stop him before he can.

"One last question. Where do you keep all your Christmas decorations?"

He frowns. "Saint hasn't put them up?" When I shake my head, he sighs. "He's never liked Christmas as much as I have."

"That's because we became best friends on Christmas Day."

It's supposed to be a joke, but the way Jax winces makes me believe I've actually hit a lot closer to the mark than I intended.

"Oh my God, tell me that's not actually why he dislikes Christmas?"

I can't quite keep the hurt out of my voice, and my best friend knows me well enough to hear it. Maybe I shouldn't feel hurt; I know Saint and I have never been friends, but to think he hates the holidays just because it's the day I met him and the day I met Jax and befriended him? Well...

I remind myself of how he said I'm not special. He is an arsehole to everybody—that's what he said.

"Of course not," Jax answers after his long pause, his voice tight.

"Uh huh," I say, letting him see my disbelief. "I can't believe I didn't know."

"Bree—"

"It's fine. It's not like I care."

"Breanna."

I ignore his gentle command. "You're OK with me putting the decorations up?" When he gives up and nods, it's my turn to offer him a too-bright smile. "I have to go now. I'll talk to you soon."

I end the call before he can say anything else, trying to swallow past the lump of hurt in my throat.

I am here for Jax, not for Saint. Saint might hate Christmas, but Jax doesn't. I am going to decorate the hell out of this place and too bad if Saint hates it.

Except I hung up before Jax could tell me where he stores the decorations.

My phone vibrates when I pull it out to text him.

Jax: It's not what you think. Call me back when you're ready.

Jax: Christmas stuff is in shed 3. Keys are on the hook on the back of my office door.

Jax: We always have a Christmas party on the 24th.

Me: I'm going to make sure it's the best party ever.

And if Saint hates it, even better.

Chapter Four

"What are you doing?"

Saint storms towards me, 6'3" of hard muscle toned from all his extreme sports, barrelling towards me, his eyes spitting fire. Damn it, I might hate the guy, but even I can appreciate how toe-curling the entire package is, especially when it's pissed off and looking hella broody. It doesn't help that I know how good he is in bed, how he can bring me to climax faster than any man before him.

Perhaps that's the reason I feel like pissing him off further. It's bad enough to know I slept with him. But knowing how good it was and the fact I already know I'm going to compare every future lover to him just pisses *me* off further.

Better to focus on the anger than on the hurt.

I reply, "What does it look like I'm doing? Skiing, of course."

He takes me by the hand and pulls me down from the ladder. I'm half expecting to fall on my face, but he catches me against him, sliding me down the front of his body until my feet hit the ground. His glare punches the breath out of me, but that's not the only reason I'm breathless. The last time we were this close, I was spread wide open beneath him, and he was pressing into me.

I glare back up at him but can't for the life of me come up with a witty retort when the warm and spicy notes of his aftershave give me another playback of the one night we had together.

Pushing away from him, I focus on the memory of waking up to find him gone, and I try to harden my glare. "You shouldn't drag someone off a ladder. It's dangerous, Saint."

"It was the only way I was going to get a proper answer."

"And what did you need a proper answer to? Your ridiculous question about what I'm doing? C'mon, Saint. You can see I'm hanging up Christmas decorations."

He scowls. "Fine, maybe you could answer the question of why, then?"

I pop my hip out. "Maybe you haven't looked at the calendar recently, but it's—"

"Quit trying to be funny, Bree. You're not."

"Damn. And here I was hoping to start a career in stand-up."

"Don't quit your day job."

I motion to the decorations I was putting up. "This is my day job, and I'm doing what Jax asked me to, which is hanging the decorations."

His scowl deepens. "You told him they weren't up."

"Yup."

He shakes his head and looks at me with disgust. "So, you went over my head to my brother. Real nice, Breanna. I know we can't stand each other, but maybe you could show just the smallest modicum of respect for my title and the fact I'm part owner. I don't get to take charge often here because Jax is competent and I have other obligations, but I was looking forward to giving him a proper break from responsibilities for once."

His glare is full of heat and anger, and even though I don't want to feel bad, his words make me feel stupidly petty. I would hate it if someone went over my head, and clearly, I've pissed off Saint. While that was my intention when I started decorating, I'm now regretting how I went about it.

I step back and try to offer him a placating look. "Okay, I hear you, and I'm sorry for going over your head. It's just that I know you're not the biggest fan of Christmas, but Jax always celebrates it and the people who come here year after year expect it. Got to give the customers what they want, you know..." I trail off.

"And so you see it as your job to take the decision out of my hands, go to my brother in an effort to give the customers what they want?"

I feel a lot like I'm being told off by him, and I don't like it. Nor do I like the way Saint is looking at me, as though I've *hurt* him. Which is ridiculous. This man doesn't have feelings when it comes to me.

"I'm sorry," I find myself repeating anyway. "I know Christmas isn't your favourite time of year."

I'm not going to bring up why that might be just now, not when I'm still feeling my heart squeeze at the thought.

"I was trying to help. I thought it would be easier if I just took... ownership and—"

"Bullshit. Try to spin it any way you want to; we both know you went over my head and reached for the decorations to piss me off."

I wish he was one hundred percent off the mark, but he's not. So, I reach for the only truth I can give him. "I really was worried that you wouldn't put the decorations up for the holidays, and Jax wouldn't like that. As much as you dislike the holiday season, it's part of the reason people come here. Take Chase Lindley and his daughter in Cabin 14. They lost Mrs Lindley a few years back and have no other family to celebrate with. They come here because this is a community, and they like to celebrate with—"

Saint laughs, cutting me off. "You think I don't know that? You think I don't know the customers? *My* customers."

Suddenly second-guessing myself, I look between him and the decorations. "Were you going to put the decorations up?" I ask tentatively.

"Well, you know, you could have asked me that yourself instead of going straight to Jax." His glare holds me captive. "You know what your problem is, Bree? You go to Jax about everything. *Everything*."

"I don't."

"You do. Do you even get that he's married now? You're not his number one anymore. Maybe you could just let him be for a bit, let him enjoy the honeymoon without you sticking your big fat oar in there and disrupting—"

"Hey!" I cut him off, any guilt I felt for going to his brother disappearing as he lights my fuse. "That's not fair, and you know it. He called me—"

"And I bet you answered straight away, just like you always do."

I put my hands on my hips. "This isn't about the decorations at all, is it? This is about your problem with Jax's and my relationship. It's only been, what, like, fifteen years?"

He scoffs at me. "Fifteen years of him telling you he's not interested, and you're still chasing after him."

"Okay, I'm done now."

He can go screw himself and finish putting up the decorations without my help. Or he can put them away. I don't care. I'm not hanging around to listen to any more of his vitriol.

Turning on my heel, I go to leave, but his hand on my arm stops me. "What's your problem, Bree? Can't bear to hear the truth?"

"The truth?" It's my turn to scoff. "The truth is that you've disliked me from the start, even though I never gave you any reason to."

I hold up my finger to cut him off before he can deny it.

"The very first time I met you, you hated me simply because I wanted to ride over the same hills as you. I rode up to that bike park with my pink Nitro, the one I'd begged my dad to buy for months. I couldn't wait to speak with the boy who I'd stopped to watch so many times on my way home from school."

I was so nervous to meet him, so excited.

"Yeah, yeah," he rolls his eyes. "We all know Jax is amazing."

"No!" I slap the palm of my hand against his chest with no real force. "You, Saint! I went there to ride my new bike, but I wanted to meet *you*."

He narrows his eyes. "You went there to talk to Jax, not me."

"I spoke to Jax because he spoke to me first! You were the one I'd watched on my way home from school so many times. I thought Jax was related to bike royalty when he told me he was your brother. Months—I'd been watching you for *months* and then your brother started talking to me and I was fangirling over how I was talking to *your* brother."

For the first time since we started this conversation, Saint looks unsure.

I pull my arm from his grasp. "You might want to think about that sometime, Lawson St. James. I went there because I wanted to be like you. You were the reason I even wanted that damn bike in the first place. But you made me your enemy. So, now you don't get to complain when you were an arsehole and Jax wanted to be my friend."

My god, I think I've shocked him. His eyes cling to mine, searching for any hint of deception. When he doesn't find it, he looks at me like he's never really seen me before.

Now that I've stunned him speechless, I should take my leave.

Except I can't just let what Jax said earlier slide.

I add, "Which is why I'm just going to tell you straight out that it's ridiculous you hate Christmas because it's the day Jax made me his friend."

He shakes his head, his smile mocking. "You sure are full of yourself, thinking I feel any way about the day because—"

"I know, I know. I'm not special. Except I can't think of another reason you'd hate Christmas."

"I don't hate Christmas. I just think it's an over-commercialised—"

"No, you can't fool me. You're a grinch. No two ways about it."

"A grinch?"

"If the shoe fits..."

He starts walking backwards until he reaches the boxes I hauled out of the shed earlier. They now sit atop the folding tables I dragged out at the same time. Reaching into the box closest to him, he takes out a giant green and red elf hat with bells.

"If I was a grinch, I wouldn't put on this..." he studies the item, lips pulling down at the corner, "...hat."

The way he says 'hat', as if the title offends him, is nearly as amusing as the hard look he shoots me before he puts it on his head. I cover my mouth, barely smothering a laugh as he makes the bells jingle by moving his head from side to side.

"Fine," I say, holding my hands up in an act of surrender and taking a step back. "You're not a grinch. Happy?"

"No." He surveys the boxes full of decorations before looking at the ladder propped against the reception cabin, where I decided I'd focus my efforts first. "I'm going to need your help putting all this stuff up."

When he looks at me, I see the question there, and maybe... uncertainty?

"Unless you have something better to do," he adds.

I shake my head.

"Good, better get a move on, then. I have stuff I need to do. Can't be here all night."

I roll my eyes, but when he starts rummaging through the boxes, I join him.

Chapter Five

W e work tirelessly through the late afternoon and early evening, stringing up Christmas lights in the large rotunda in the middle of the park, putting up multiple Christmas trees complete with ornaments, and attaching giant Christmas characters to the lampposts that illuminate all the roads and paths in the place. As the hours tick by, we maintain an unspoken truce.

That doesn't mean I don't stir him. He teases me back, of course, but he's not being an arse. For once. He's almost being... playful.

After we've done as much as we can in the daylight, Saint tells me he has other stuff to get to.

I offer, "I'll help."

It's not like I want to spend the extra time with him, but I do feel a bit guilty that I sort of hijacked his afternoon. I know he didn't put aside a chunk of time for decorating today.

"Nah, all good. Take the night off."

He smirks when he sees the look I throw him. I would have knocked off at least an hour ago if I hadn't been helping him, and he knows it. But it probably would have taken me the better part of three afternoons to get all the decorations up by myself, between answering phones and dealing with customers, so in that way Saint has saved me time.

When I get back to the cabin, I jump in the shower. It's not until the scorching water hits me that I realise I'm sunburnt. I was wearing a hat and sunscreen while I was working outside, but my t-shirt was pretty low-cut the whole way around, and I didn't apply enough sunscreen below the neckline at the back. With the water stinging my back and part of my shoulders, I hurry through my routine, getting out quicker than I would have normally.

Once I'm dressed, the scent of chips, chicken salt, and fish tickle my nose, making me realise just how hungry I am. I pop my head out of my room just in time to see Saint walk over to the smallish table opposite the kitchenette, dropping a bundle wrapped in white paper.

"There's enough for you if you want some."

I raise an eyebrow and decide I'm not going to complain; I hadn't planned what I was going to do for dinner but knew I'd probably end up having to drive into town to grab something to eat. And after my active afternoon and shower, I'm starving. My stomach rumbles just as I conclude this, making Saint grin.

"I'll take that as a yes."

I nod and move towards the kitchenette, reaching into one of the cupboards for plates and cutlery.

Saint opens the fridge. "Beer?"

I nod, and we take our haul over to the table. I don't even give a crap over how greasy the food is as Saint opens the package and my eyes feast on the plentiful fried food.

"You're salivating," he says.

My mouth is too full with the chips I've just crammed in to respond.

He shakes his head and pops the cap off his beer with a bottle opener before doing the same to mine and handing it to me.

Taking it from him, I finish my mouthful and sit opposite him. "Thanks." I hold the bottle out. "Cheers."

Saint clinks his bottle against mine, even as he raises an eyebrow. "What are we toasting?"

It's more habit than anything for me, toasting a good meal, so I shrug. "How about us working together and not killing each other?"

"There's always time."

"True."

We lapse into silence, which isn't uncomfortable. My attention is on my food and not making a fool of myself by moaning out loud. The fish and chips might be super fatty but have been cooked to perfection, and I think it was exactly what I needed.

"So." Saint swigs his beer then puts the bottle down, leaning his forearms on the table as he studies me. "You were impressed by my riding skills?"

Sure enough, he's wearing a smirk, but I can also see the genuine question in his eyes. Clearly, he's not letting my earlier confession slide so easily.

I shrug. "I was eleven. You were the boy at the park performing tricks I could only dream about. You looked like someone in a stunt film. I wanted to do what you could do."

"You got a bike because of me?"

"I wanted to be like you, sure," I agree, refusing to be embarrassed by the actions of my younger self.

"I was showing off for you, you know. There was a cute girl watching me and I wanted to impress her. I wanted to impress *you*."

My stomach hollows as his words hit me. I swallow my food and set down my fork, staring at him. "You acted like you hated me and told me I wasn't good enough."

He nods, picking up his beer again, but not drinking. "When I saw you talking to Jax, I assumed you were just there to talk to him. All the girls who came to the bike park seemed to want to talk to him." He looks down at his plate. "I got mad because I'd hoped you were there for me."

There's the smallest bit of vulnerability in his voice, but then he clears his throat and I decide I imagined it.

"So, you acted like an arsehole."

He shrugs. "I was twelve. I'm not claiming I was mature or that it was the appropriate response."

"Well, that explains your behaviour that day. What's your excuse for every day since then?"

He gives me a slightly feral grin. "Told you; I'm an arsehole to everyone."

"Does your dislike of Christmas have to do with the fact I met Jax that day?"

Bringing this up again does sound stupid and conceited, and I wish I could pull it back the moment the words leave me to hang in the air between us, but I can't. Besides, I need to hear him say Jax and I aren't part of his resentment for Christmas, because Jax seemed to think the two were related and even though I'd never admit it out loud, the thought stings.

"I told you, I don't dislike it, per se," he says. "I just think the holiday revolves around getting people to spend as much money as possible. Instead of spreading Christmas spirit and joy, or focusing on giving, people end up miserable, yelling at shop staff, overspending, and overeating. People shouldn't need a specific time of year to give to charity or donate, or whatever. As you said... it's not my favourite time of the year."

"I see."

I can see the logic in his reasoning, but I don't fully believe it because it doesn't fully fit him. Holding a grudge fits him. Why wouldn't he admit he's been holding one, though? He has no reason to lie to me. This is Saint, after all, so it's not like he'd ever purposefully spare my feelings. But Jax indicated it was more than that—that it was something to do with me.

"You see?" he prompts.

I nod, refusing to ruin the dinner by calling him out. "You're a cynic; it's not a crime."

His lips twist up. "True." He gives me a pointed look. "Just as I guess it isn't a crime to enjoy Christmas."

I can't help but smile back at him. "I have always loved Christmas."

"Tell me, what is it you like so much about it?"

I shrug. "Christmas takes me back to feeling like a child. The excitement, the anticipation... the feeling that absolutely anything is possible. It's as if a Christmas miracle lingers around the corner."

Saint nods. "You get to be a kid again. For someone who had to grow up really young because her mum walked out, that's an appealing thought."

The fact he's put that together about me stuns me into silence, and my stomach swoops as he studies me, dark hazel eyes reading the emotions that are probably playing across my face.

Forcing a smile even though I feel see-through, I say, "You might be right about that." Wanting to move on from the sudden knowledge he's read me so well, I change the subject. "Jax said he always throws a party on the twenty-fourth. Can I take point on organising the party?"

He raises an eyebrow. "You're asking me this time?"

I sit back and copy his posture. "Yes, I am. You're right; I shouldn't have gone to Jax first."

He nods, seemingly placated. "It would help a lot if you could."

"Okay then."

I think we just had an entire conversation that didn't devolve into war. There might be hope for us yet.

I told Jax that Saint and I would go back to trying to kill each other when he returned, but this might just be a new way of being for us, and even—dare I say it?—the start of something we can one day call friendship.

Chapter Six

The next morning, the sunburn feels even worse after my shower. After trying unsuccessfully to apply aloe vera while in a towel, I dry off and put on a clean pair of panties before giving it another go, straining to slather the lotion on my back.

That's how Saint finds me when he walks into the bathroom without knocking.

"Hey!" I snap. Bending over and picking up my discarded t-shirt from the tiled floor, I cover myself the best I can.

"I didn't realise you were in here."

"There's this thing you can do nowadays; it's called knocking."

"I'm sorry."

He sounds genuine, but he doesn't retreat, his hand remaining on the doorknob as he stares at me. And the way he's staring? The pure heat in his eyes caresses me between my legs and hits me low in the belly. I know that look. I *remember* that look. It's how he looked at me as we undressed each other after Jax's wedding. Back then, it was as if he couldn't get inside me quickly enough. Just the memory has my skin flushing, my nipples pebbling, and a throb igniting between my legs.

"You can look away now," I say, my voice soft and husky. "You know, since you've seen it all before and weren't that impressed the first time."

I throw the statement at him for both our sakes, but more than anything, I want it to be a reminder to myself. For one night, he made me feel cared about. Prized. Then he left me to wonder what the hell happened, never calling or explaining why he came to me that night. He made me feel like it never mattered. Like *I* never mattered.

Remorse flickers across his features. "I lied."

His voice is just as husky and full of gravel, causing more wet heat to gather between my thighs as my breathing shallows.

He takes a step toward me, his gaze full of an intensity and heat that turns me inside out and makes my legs tremble. "I was very impressed." When he reaches me, he runs a finger over my shoulders and back. "You're burnt."

His touch should hurt, but he's being so soft and gentle, it makes goosebumps break out across my shoulders instead. I suck in a giant gulp of air as my nipples tighten, my sex contracting.

"I was putting on aloe."

In fact, I'm still clutching the t-shirt to my chest with one hand while the other clutches the aloe.

"Let me," he says, taking the tube from me. "Turn around."

"I don't—"

Gently, he turns me so that my back is to him. The moment he smooths the cold lotion over my red skin, I moan softly and let my head fall forward. He pauses, but before I can look up and ask why he's stopped, he continues. Long fingers massage the lotion into my skin, sending a rush of pleasure through me.

It isn't until the sting dissipates that I realise he probably should have stopped by now. A tremor runs through me when I look up and meet his eyes in the mirror, aware that not only is he watching me, but he's still touching me. He drops his hand, but his beautiful green-brown stare remains on me, hot and heavy. And when he lifts his hand again and brushes the backs of his knuckles along my cheekbone in an affectionate and intimate gesture, I'm left reeling.

Stunned, I watch that same hand trail down my neck, his touch feather-light, before he brushes the tips of his fingers over my shoulder. When I shiver, he dips his head, letting his lips follow the same path his fingers just took. My nipples are so hard now, the need to have his hands on them out of this world. I'm clutching the t-shirt to my chest still, but when he tries to tug it away, I let him so that I'm standing there with my chest bared to both of us in the mirror.

This man played me expertly during our night together. Despite the fact we'd barely spoken a kind word to one another in fifteen years, he showed me he knows exactly what I like and how hard I like it. I've been trying desperately to forget that night, but as I stare at myself in the mirror, there's no pretending he doesn't affect me. My lips are full and soft and pouty and undoubtedly pinker than usual. There's a high flush on my cheeks, and my eyes are large and darker than their normal honey colour.

He takes a step forward so he's pressed against me, and I can tell I'm not the only one affected. He's hard against my back. My breathing comes out short and shallow as I wait to see what he'll do next. The moment he finally puts me out of my misery and swipes the pad of his thumb over one of my painfully hard nipples, I'm pulsing between my legs. I chase the contact, arching into his palm, my arse pushing against his front, wantonly demanding all of him.

He chuckles at my reaction, but even I can feel the dark edge to it, the needy undertone, and perhaps that's why I don't stop him. That, and the fact my mirror image gives my desire away. *Undeniable.* My eyes close as he finally takes the weight of my breast in one hand, cupping me, his fingers squeezing and gently tugging my nipple in a way that sends tingles straight to my sex. I'm a needy and moaning mess when he finally cups my other breast.

He slides the other down my side, burning my skin with his touch until he gets to my panties. It's almost too much to bear when he starts kissing my neck and shoulder, one hand working my breast and the other tracing the lace trim of my panties before dipping inside. I spread my legs and he lets out a guttural noise when he finds me wet and ready for him.

"Saint," I beg.

The sensation building deep inside me, so hot and heady as he slicks my wetness over the bundle of nerves between my legs and toys with me, is volatile and too exciting. Clutching at the sink in front of me, I whimper as he takes me so high there's nowhere to go but over, the fever breaking.

He turns me around, and even though I'm sure he saw it all in the mirror when I was coming, I feel far more exposed this way.

How quickly did I come for him? The moment he put his hands on me... was it even a minute? It feels like it took him barely any time to get me off. My body is still humming from his ministrations, my sex aching and empty. And there's a buzz beneath my skin as if I've been sipping coffee all morning. A feeling that's not at all helped by the way he's looking at me.

"Stop staring," I chide, my voice still unmistakably husky.

A wicked grin curves his lips. "Can't help it." Leisurely, he strokes every part of me with his heated stare, causing need to tighten low in my belly. But it's the way he's leaning into me, caressing my face, that truly takes my breath away. "You're too beautiful to look away from, and you have the best body I've ever seen."

I'm fit and healthy, and I regularly cycle, jog, ski, and do anything else I can outdoors. I likely weigh more than some of the waifs I've seen him with over the years.

"I have more muscle than the girls you usually date."

Shock flits across his features. "You're perfect. You remind me of one of the surfer girls I used to have tacked on my wall."

"I do?"

"Oh, yeah."

He moves in closer, and when he kisses me, I don't push him away.

The way his lips move on mine, nipping at me, drinking from me, teasing me with his tongue and teeth, is intoxicating. And when his tongue sweeps into my mouth and strokes mine, lust rockets through me. Need builds between my legs until I'm aching too badly to ignore it, my body demanding his. I run my hand over the hard length of him, savouring the way he moans into my mouth. When I reach for his t-shirt, he lets me take it off him.

As a stuntman with more athletic prowess than anyone I've ever known, he's built to perfection. The night we spent together, I allowed myself to explore him thoroughly, but I don't want to hold back or take my time this morning.

As if the past few days we've lived together have been foreplay, I can't undress him fast enough. He chuckles darkly as he helps me out of my panties. I divest him of the rest of his clothes between kisses, until his hands grab my butt and he lifts me, perching me on the sink. His hips spread my thighs in the best way, his eyes feasting on my slick centre as he helps me balance with one hand and uses the other to guide himself to my entrance. Then his eyes never leave mine as he thrusts forward, burying himself inside me in one long, hot glide that sends pleasure shooting through every nerve in my body.

I cry out at how good it feels, how good *he* feels inside me. I reach for him, needing to hold on to him, but he picks me up and backs me against the closest wall, showing his strength and power with how easily he holds me as he moves, thrusting into me. As he gives me what I need, I wrap myself around him. I arch, I beg, and I plead as each stroke of his body in mine drives me higher, until I'm a sobbing mess. The angles he uses help him hit every spot I need him to. Only when he makes me come so hard I see fireworks does he give into the same pleasure, shuddering and emptying himself inside me.

My head falls forward, resting on his shoulder as I try to catch my breath. I think he just wrecked me.

God. Why is it always so good with this man?

Saint lowers me onto legs that feel as shaky as every other part of me. He keeps one hand on my hip, holding on to me as he grabs my t-shirt from the floor next to the basin. Then he motions for me to put my arms up. When I do, he slips the shirt over my arms, tugging it over my head.

"Thanks." My voice is also shakier than I'd like it to be.

Touching my face, he lifts my eyes to meet his. "Do you ever wonder if we're looking at this situation the wrong way?" he asks, his voice like gravel once more.

"What do you mean?"

"You're here, I'm here."

I smirk. "Great observation."

"We already know we have chemistry between the sheets."

His words hit me in the belly, causing another wave of heat to rush through me.

"What are you suggesting?"

His lips tip up. "Do you really need me to spell it out?"

"Saint, we're living together."

"Exactly. Why not make the most of it?"

"We're also working together."

My protest is pretty weak, all things considered.

He leans in, smug as all hell. "Technically, I'm your boss."

"Jax is my boss," I say before I can think better of it.

His jaw clenches and he takes a step back from me, ice replacing the heat that was there in his eyes a moment ago, sending a shiver through me.

"Not because you don't own the place, too, but because..." I trail off, suddenly sure that anything I say to Saint about being here for Jax won't go over the way I intend it. I don't want to upset Saint, especially when we actually proved yesterday that we can get along. And, for some reason, he's overly sensitive about my deference to Jax. "I mean, yes, technically you are my boss, too. Isn't that more reason to not... make things messy?"

"They don't have to be messy, Bree. We're here. We're both single, I presume?"

I glare when he raises an eyebrow. As if I would have slept with him if I was in a relationship.

"Exactly," he continues. "Why not enjoy our time together while it lasts? Then when Jax comes back, we go our separate ways."

I don't doubt Saint is serious. I've seen him enjoy spending time with plenty of women over the years. He always seems to walk away unscathed when it ends. I've never seen him fall for any of them.

"Can I think about it?"

He studies me, giving me a slight tip of his chin. "Sure, take your time."

Pressing a kiss to my lips that's softer than I would have thought him capable of, Saint causes my heart to flutter in my chest. Then he walks out, leaving me alone with my thoughts.

Chapter Seven

Saint is performing maintenance on one of the park fences when I hunt him down later that evening. His shirt is off, and he's bent over, hammering something into the ground, giving me the perfect view of his tanned muscular back and round, perfect arse.

"Hey," I say, letting him know I'm there. "Are you coming home for dinner?"

Turning from his crouched position, Saint raises an eyebrow. "Home for dinner? What are we, married?"

I ignore the way my cheeks flush at the implication. I've spent the better part of the day trying to work out what to say to Saint, how to tell him I might be interested in this arrangement he suggested this morning after all.

I tuck my hair behind my ear. "Of course not. I just thought... well, I bought food and I cooked. I thought you might be hungry."

I've been asking myself all day what's the worst that could happen. I ignored the part of my conscience telling me that agreeing to Saint's proposal would be insane and wouldn't end well for me. This time, I'm not expecting him to call me the morning after. He's not promising anything. Both of us have careers that aren't exactly conducive to commitment and relationships.

Besides, resisting him for the next few weeks seems impossible after the way I caved to lust this morning. If sleeping together means our relationship is less of a battleground and we spend more time together like we did yesterday, talking and joking, that would make it easier to work together. Right?

His face gives away nothing as he says, "I ate not that long ago."

"Oh." I take a step back, trying to hide my disappointment. "Okay." Clearly his talk about enjoying each other was limited to sex, not involving company and conversation. So much for thinking that acting on the crazy chemistry we have could bring us closer to being friends.

Seeing my face fall, Saint stands up. "Actually, maybe I am kind of hungry."

"I'll make sure there are leftovers you can heat up later, then."

"Bree—"

"It's okay, really. You're busy."

Ignoring me, he starts collecting his tools. "I'm just going to put this stuff away and I'll be there for dinner."

I nod and head back to the cabin. Even though my first instinct is to tell him to forget about it, that will only lead to more arguing. Something I'd prefer to avoid.

By the time Saint walks in the front door, I have dinner served. It's just simple salads and grilled chicken with roast potatoes. I can't look at him as he walks into the kitchen because my heart is racing, adrenaline peaking as I rehearse the conversation I want to have with him in my head.

He meets me in the kitchen, and I wordlessly pass him a plate.

After we've taken a seat at the small dining table, he asks, "Wine or beer?"

"Beer, please."

Saint gets up and returns with two beers. Unlike last night, I don't clink his glass with mine or go to toast anything. I have too much going through my head and I want to get this over with first.

"Thanks for cooking," Saint says.

I shrug. "I had to eat, figured you did too. You bought dinner last night. Not a big deal."

Except it is. I made sure I bought groceries and wanted to surprise him with a home-cooked meal. And with the way he initially reacted to my suggestion to eat, he knows, because he changed his mind.

We eat in silence, and I use the time to drink my beer and gather my courage. Once the meal is finished, the silence is beyond uncomfortable; it's also hot as hell in the cabin. Or is it just me? I'm practically squirming in my chair with a combination of desire and nerves.

I've overthought the whole arrangement idea. Time to bite the bullet.

"I… don't think your suggestion this morning was a bad one," I say finally.

He sits back in his chair. "What changed your mind?"

A little bit of honesty here is necessary. "It might be nice to do something else instead of fighting all the time."

"Something like…?"

He knows. And I'm so edgy right now, so turned on and flustered, I want to snap at him. Only the dare in Saint's eyes stops me. He's baiting me, knowing I can't turn down a challenge—not when it's from him.

With some reluctance, I put down the beer bottle and let him look at me, really see me, see the desire and the need I feel for him.

His eyes burn, the almost fierce and possessive expression he's wearing turning me inside out as he leans forward, his gaze never leaving mine.

"Say it, Breanna," he commands.

There's no smirk, no arrogant gloating or anything like that. My need is his and his is mine as he sits there, staring, watching, waiting.

"I want you," I say. "I want you in my bed, and I want to be in yours."

And I don't know that I'll ever stop wanting you.

As soon as I've thought it, a shiver runs through me. God, I hope it isn't true. I can't imagine what it would be like to not stop wanting him. But no man has ever made me feel like he does. Maybe it's how long we've known each other. Maybe it's just that it's Saint. Something about the man threatens to bring me to my knees. The hard and hot and demanding way he is with me in bed makes him irresistible to me.

"C'mere."

I don't hesitate. Standing on wobbly legs, I go to him. He pulls me down on his lap. His forehead rests against mine for just a moment, and then he kisses me, shattering any last reservations I had. He feeds me kisses so hot and wet and needy they make me beg.

"Saint."

I won't come out of this unscathed. I know it, even as I push the thought to the back of my mind.

"Love it when you say my name like that, babe." He picks me up. "We need a bed this time."

Then Saint carries me to my room, closes the door behind us, and gives us both exactly what we need.

Chapter Eight

"Oh my God, what time is it?" I bolt upright, scrambling to get out of Saint's bed.

I guess this is what happens when you spend night after night having mind-blowing orgasms. When Saint's phone alarm went off this morning, I opened my eyes and thought about getting up. Then he wrapped me in his arms, and I snuggled back into him and went straight back to sleep. Apparently, he did too.

A quick glance at the bedside clock sends my heart into overdrive and gives me a hit of adrenaline. It's nine o'clock, meaning we should have started work thirty minutes ago. Saint sits up, and I go to grab the sleep singlet sitting on the bed—the same one he tore off me last night—but he grabs it before I can put it on.

"Saint," I protest.

He holds the singlet out for me to grab, but the moment I reach for it, he moves it.

"Really? What are you? Twelve?"

His wide grin only makes him all the more handsome, and my heart flutters. "I wouldn't know how to make you come six ways from Sunday if I was twelve," he says in a sleep-roughened voice.

My sex clenches at the reminder of how capable he is of bringing me pleasure. Of course, the way he's watching me does nothing to dissipate the tension coiling low in my belly.

He pats the bed next to him. "Give me ten minutes. I'll make it worth your while."

"I don't doubt that, Saint, but the Christmas party is this afternoon, and I still have so much to do. We both have work to do."

Even as I say it, I'm contemplating whether I can spare ten minutes.

No, absolutely not. I have to get to work.

He sighs and holds the singlet out to me again. When I reach for it this time, Saint hooks his other arm around my waist, pulling me onto the bed on top of him. Then he rolls us, grinning down at me.

"I do have work to do, but doing you is so much more fun."

I laugh. "You are so corny."

This playful side of Saint is irresistible. I've laughed and smiled more in the past couple of weeks than I have in years.

His grin widens. "You love it."

My heart stutters and trips over itself, my breath rushing out of me as his words hit so much closer to the truth than I'm comfortable with. Saint and I have been 'making the most of it' for two weeks now. We eat together every night, often work side by side to get things done more quickly, and we haven't spent a night apart in the past fortnight.

His expression turns serious as he searches my face. "We're running out of time."

"I know," I murmur.

Lately, any reminder that our time together is coming to an end makes me feel like I can't breathe, or like my chest is splitting open, or both. As crazy as it sounds, I'm dreading Jax's return because it means Saint and I will be going our separate ways.

He dips his head, kissing me so softly and gently my heart flutters, my stomach flip-flops, and every part of me burns and tingles in response.

Insatiable. That's what I am when it comes to this man. I'm ready for him already, the emptiness between my legs growing into a full-blown ache as his tongue sweeps into my mouth.

I hold him tighter as he rocks against me, building me up with his kiss and his body. I've never experienced this desperate need with anyone before. The reason why is one I can't acknowledge when he's still planning to walk away from me in the end without a second thought. Stroking my hands over his broad back, I let my fingers dig into his firm arse as if I can hold him there and never let him go.

When Saint's phone begins vibrating and ringing on his bedside table, I groan from frustration. The insistent throb between my legs protests the very idea of leaving his bed without another earth-shattering orgasm, but our workday should have started already. Technically, we're both on the clock.

"Don't you need to answer that?" I ask.

"Probably."

Instead of stopping, however, he trails kisses along my jaw and down my neck before sucking on one taut nipple and overloading me with sensations and emotions. I shudder, the walls of my sex contracting as he turns me to putty beneath him.

"Saint," I protest weakly.

His mouth comes back to mine. Sometimes the intensity in the way he kisses me makes me wonder if this is more to him than just a holiday fling. Is he finally starting to see me as someone other than Jax's best friend and person he's been at odds with for over half his life?

The caller hangs up and calls again. It isn't until the third time this occurs that Saint rolls off me. Letting out a frustrated sigh, he reaches for his phone on the bedside table before slamming it back down again.

I frown. "Who was it?"

"Doesn't matter."

"Saint—"

"It was Jax."

Guilt squeezes me, motivating me to get moving. Maybe it's also motivating Saint, because he's finally up and getting dressed.

"Maybe he's calling to find out why we're not at work," I say.

"I'll call him in a minute."

"You should call him now. Something could be wrong."

He glares at me. "Then I'll find out what it is in a minute."

I want to argue with Saint, but his mood has taken a turn, his eyes glacial now instead of warm, and tension has crept into his shoulders. Our conversations about Jax tend to do this to him, and I can't figure out why. If this was anything more than just a holiday fling, I'd want him to help me understand, but it isn't, and I don't have time to push him right now.

Resigned, I head for the bathroom, apply some dry shampoo, brush my teeth, and use shower-in-a-can deodorant. I'll shower properly later this afternoon, before the party. Once I'm done, I head for my room and grab the first t-shirt I find in my drawer, pulling it over my head, covering myself just in time for my phone to start ringing.

Of course it's Jax. Saint appears in my bedroom doorway dressed in his shorts, t-shirt, and work boots, and shakes his head as if he wants me to ignore the call. I'm torn. I don't want to piss off Saint, but this is Jax, my best friend and also my employer.

I press Answer, not realising until too late that it's a video call.

"Hi, Jax. What's up?"

"Finally," Jax grinds out. "Where are you?"

"Um, I overslept and I'm still at the cabin. Sorry, I—"

"Do you know where Saint is?"

My gaze flickers to where Saint still stands, shaking his head at me.

"Um, he slept in, too."

It comes out as more of a question, and Jax knows me well enough to realise I'm covering.

"Put him on."

"But—"

"I know he's there, so cut the shit, Bree. Also, why the hell are you wearing his shirt?"

I look down and see that, sure enough, I'm wearing Saint's favourite AC/DC t-shirt. Crap!

"Ah, it must have fallen in with my washing."

"You always have been a terrible liar, Bree." Jax looks at me, studying me, and I'm afraid he sees the truth all over my face. "Oh, Jesus."

He hangs up. Less than a minute later, Saint's pocket starts ringing.

"Told you not to say anything," Saint says, taking his phone out. This time, he accepts the call. "Jax," he grunts.

"Are you fucking kidding me?"

My stomach knots when I hear Jax's roar down the phone. And the knot only gets bigger when Saint turns his back on me and storms out of the cabin. Without thinking, I follow, desperate to make sure things don't get too out of hand between the brothers. I always knew if Jax found out we were sleeping together, there would be trouble. He's had to put up with our bickering and arguing for fifteen years and he's probably terrified it's going to get much worse now.

When Saint heads for the back property line, his long legs eat up the distance much faster than mine do, leaving me to fall farther behind. Still, I can hear Jax talking. I can't quite make out what he's saying, but he sounds just as angry as he did when Saint picked up.

"We're just having fun," Saint says in response to whatever Jax has said.

More yelling from my friend.

"There are no feelings involved."

Agony rips through me, but Saint isn't done yet.

"I don't feel that way about her, so I wish you'd stop talking about it. I don't know why you ever thought I did. We're simply making the most out of a bad situation. It's convenient, Jaxon."

The crack of dried leaves and twigs underneath my feet alert Saint to the fact I'm behind him. Or perhaps he heard my heart cracking inside my chest? He spins around, takes one look at my face, and swears.

"I have to go, Jax," he clips out, taking a step towards me.

The wide-eyed, slightly desperate look in his eyes when I take a step away from him cuts through me, but I can't do this with him right now. I turn on my heel and take off, doing my best to hold back the sob trying to wrench free when he calls after me.

I knew what this was, and I'm not supposed to have feelings for him. This isn't his fault, but I can't lie to either of us anymore. Feeling my heart rip in two when I heard Saint tell his brother he doesn't feel any way about me drove it home that I did the unthinkable—I fell for my best friend's insufferable brother.

Chapter Nine

J ax: *Pick up your damn phone, Bree.*
Me: Don't worry about me and Saint. It's over.

Jax keeps calling me, but I can't talk to him right now. Not when my heart feels as though it's starring in a 'will it blend?' video. The moment I stop working, I'll let the tears fall, but I don't have time to fall apart right now. I've thrown myself into the last-minute preparations for the Christmas party and my giant to-do list is the perfect excuse not to talk to Saint every time he tries to get me alone.

We're over and I don't know that we need to have a conversation about it. If we do, we can have it later. We have a week left until Jax gets back, and that week will be more bearable if we can just ignore or avoid each other. That's what I'll be proposing, anyway.

I ignore the tears pricking at my eyes as I think about waking up on Christmas morning without Saint. I'm used to waking up on Christmas morning alone.

"Is it okay to put this here, Bree?"

I nod to my assistant for the day, Mina Lindley, who puts the large platter of gingerbread down on one of the last remaining bench spaces in the community kitchen. Around an hour ago, I received my food delivery, and now the kitchen is full of the many platters of food I ordered from the local stores in Point Heaven. We have salads, roast meats, pudding, pavlova, fruit salad, and ripple cake. I also ordered copious amounts of wine and beer, and even made some of my aunt's famous mulled wine. Though I don't know if anyone will be drinking that with the temperature well over thirty degrees Celsius in the shade.

When Chase, Mina's dad, asks me if he can help with anything, I accept his offer since I have less than thirty minutes until the party is set to kick off.

Barrelling into cabin 101, I shower, blow out my long hair, apply makeup, and put on perfume, all the while trying to ignore the way every room and surface of the cabin reminds me of my time with Saint.

One more week.

I just have to get through one more week.

With a final glance in the mirror, I make sure I look put together and not like my heart is breaking. My red dress is short and sequined, and my strappy sandals are gold. The cherry on top? My earrings are little Santas holding Santa-sacks.

I head out to the gazebo in the centre of the park, where some campers are already gathering.

"You look so pretty," Mina tells me when she sees me.

"Thank you," I say, doing a little spin and curtsy. "And so do you, Mina. I love that dress."

She copies me, spinning and letting her dress fly up, giggling. Her laughter is infectious, and I can't help but join her; it's the first time I've laughed since this morning with Saint, and it feels good.

Taking a deep breath, I head into reception and hit Play on the playlist I set up earlier. I've mixed Mariah Carey, Michael Bublé, Human Nature, Bing Crosby, Frank Sinatra, and a range of my go-to artists when I want Christmas carols. So many of the songs mention snow, and it's the wrong time of the year for snow in Australia, but that never stops me from singing about a white Christmas.

Can't say I feel like singing today, but the smile I've forced all day whenever dealing with people feels a lot less forced when 'White Christmas' plays over the speakers on top of the rotunda. I've been looking forward to this party for weeks while planning it, and now it's time to do my job, the job Jax is paying me to do: make sure the campers have a good time.

I help myself to a chilled glass of Sauvignon Blanc in the kitchen, take a large sip, then step out and throw myself into the role of hostess, ignoring the way my chest aches. Saint is supposed to be here with me, mingling and helping me host the event, but I tell myself it's a relief he isn't here. Then I top up my glass, accept people's compliments, take pride in their enjoyment, and get them talking about themselves.

Even with the crowd as thick as it is, I see Saint the moment he shows up. Despite the fact he's all the way over on the other side of the grassy area the rotunda backs onto, he has my complete attention. I don't think he's ever looked more heart-stopping than he does now in a pair of navy linen shorts and white button-down. His hair is mussed under the ridiculous elf hat he put on weeks ago. He jiggles his head, making the bells on the hat ring, and when he offers me the smallest of smiles, I can't help but return it. I'm surrounded by happy people, and even though my chest still aches, I don't want to fight with him. Not tonight. Not at Christmas.

My heart skips several beats as he starts in my direction, and I realise I can't ignore him any longer.

"Hey," he says when he gets to me, dipping his head and brushing a kiss over my cheek. "Sorry I'm late. I needed to speak with Jax about something."

I motion around me. "I handled it."

"I see that." Instead of looking around, his intense gaze stays on me.

Momentarily, he slants down again and whispers in my ear, "You look amazing." His hot breath causes me to shiver. "You took my breath away when I saw you, but then you always have."

My eyes fly to his. "What?" I breathe out.

"I know you heard me tell Jax I don't—"

"That you don't feel anything for me?"

He nods. "But that couldn't be any further from the truth." He closes his eyes, and when he opens them again, he looks lost for a moment and more vulnerable than I've ever seen before. "I have... always been jealous of my brother, Bree."

"What?" I whisper. "Why?"

"Because you talked to him first. You liked him first. At least, I

238

thought you did." He pauses, taking a deep breath and letting me see everything he's feeling. "But mostly because you loved him."

The raw anguish in his voice punches me in the gut.

He hurt me so badly this morning. Still, I want to soothe *his* hurt. "He didn't love me back," I remind him.

"Yes, but he insisted things stay platonic because of me."

"What are you talking about?"

He takes me gently by the arm, guiding me away from the Christmas party so we're standing under one of the trees a little farther away from everyone else.

"Jax told me he always thought we'd end up together. He never saw you that way because in his mind, it was always supposed to be you and me."

"Why would he think that?"

"He saw right through my act. I just... I knew you loved him. It's why I walked away after our night together after the wedding. I didn't want to be a substitute for him."

"You weren't a substitute, Saint."

You rocked my freaking world and I wanted more than just one night.

He whispers, "All I could remember as I held you was your shattered expression when he told you he didn't love you."

"Yes, he broke my heart, but that was years ago. I got over it."

"He kept his distance because of me. Don't you hate me for that?"

God, it explains so much if he pushed me away because he thought I would hate him when I found out the truth. It doesn't excuse some of his behaviour, but it does explain it.

I shake my head. "I've seen him with Adrienne. He was never like that with me. And if he loved me like that, he would have told you he loved me and gone for it."

"You're not still harbouring feelings for him?"

"No."

"You always go to him whenever you need anything."

"Because he's my best friend, not because I'm still in love with him."

He plucks my glass from my fingers and puts it on one of the two-seater tables near us before coming back to me and pulling me to him. "I messed up fifteen years ago. I should have smiled at you that first Christmas. I should have walked you home, after I encouraged you to ride with me. Instead, I pushed you away for fear you would like Jax better than me no matter how much I tried to make you like me. I didn't want to get hurt."

"That was a long time ago," I murmur.

"I know. I've messed up every day since then as well, afraid of never being enough, of not being the one you truly wanted."

"Saint..."

"For years I've stood back, waiting for a sign you were over Jax, a sign I wouldn't be your second choice. A sign that maybe you wouldn't hate me for coming between the two of you if you still loved him. Now I'm scared I've left it too late to tell you all of this. I didn't mean any of the things I said to Jax this morning. When I called him earlier, I told him he was always right about how I felt about you. I told him I love you."

He takes my breath away with those three last words.

This time the tears pricking my eyes aren't there because of the pain he's inflicted. I reach up and touch his face.

"Tell me I'm not too late," he whispers down to me. "Tell me I haven't screwed up everything we've been building these past weeks. Can you forgive me, or am I too late?"

"You're not too late," I murmur.

I pull him down into a fervent kiss that threatens to melt my brain.

It isn't until we hear clapping and whistling that I remember we aren't alone. When Saint pulls away, I see we're surrounded by the campers. The entire staff and all of our customers are watching us, grinning, and looking thrilled for us.

Mina bounds up to me and beams, pointing to the branch Saint and I are standing under. "It's a real Christmas kiss," she says as I look up at the fake mistletoe she and I hung earlier.

"Maybe even a Christmas miracle," Saint whispers in my ear.

Chapter Ten

"Merry Christmas, Jax!"

Jax's green eyes twinkle as he takes in the way Saint and I sit side by side on Saint's bed during our video call.

"A very merry Christmas, by the looks of it. I'd say this is unexpected, but it's really not. Glad to see you got your head out of your arse, bro."

Saint tries to scowl, but he can't quite pull it off; the smile tugging at his full lips is too strong. Eventually he gives up trying and reaches for me, pulling me against his side.

"I did have my head up my arse, but it's out now." He nuzzles my neck, kissing me and nipping me there, liquefying my insides until I'm at risk of melting into the bed.

Jax raises an eyebrow at me in response to his brother's obvious affection. "You made him grovel, I hope, Bree."

"Uh huh," I breathe out, squeezing my thighs together. "He made a decent start at an apology."

"I have plenty more apology in me," Saint says huskily, dragging me onto his lap, nearly knocking the iPad out of my hands.

Jax grimaces. "That's more than I need to hear or know."

"Sorry, brother."

"You aren't."

Adrienne joins us, sitting next to Jax, holding a steaming mug of cocoa, and the conversation turns to their Christmas. It's morning there and evening here. Saint and I have spent the day eating leftovers from the party, sleeping, and wishing our campers Merry Christmas.

"Is it a white Christmas?" I ask Jax.

He turns his iPad camera around, showing me the view through the window.

"Stunning," I murmur.

"We'd like to come back again next year," Adrienne says with a small smile, the question in her eyes.

Saint nods. "We'd be happy to look after the place for you."

I turn to look at Saint. "We would?"

"Well, I would," he says, gaze still locked firmly on mine. "I'd love it if you joined me."

I nod, liking his answer.

Then I look back at Jax and see his eyebrow is raised. "What's next for the two of you? How are you going to make this work once we're back?"

Saint says, "I figure we're both on the road a lot of the time. Maybe we can... travel together."

When he looks to me, I grin. "That's... kinda perfect."

It would be easy to take my work to the locations Saint visits. Life on the road can be lonely sometimes, so when I'm not shooting a campaign, I make a habit of going home to be around friends and family. I'd love to travel with Saint.

Saint nods. "You can record me, take videos."

Despite the fact I've just been imagining how much I'd like to do that, I mock-glare at him. "I'll have my own work. If you want me to work for you, you'll have to pay me."

"Of course, babe. I have so many ways I can pay you."

I smile as he rolls me underneath him, causing me to drop the iPad.

"Saint!" I reprimand.

"Gross," Jax says. "We're going now. Merry Christmas!"

Jax hangs up, and I really should tell Saint off, but I can't stop grinning up at him as he presses his lower body into mine.

I wrap my legs around his waist. "Does this mean you like Christmas now?" I whisper.

"You've convinced me Christmas miracles can occur."

My heart swells in my chest, thumping madly. This—Saint and I being together—feels right. This newfound feeling, this happiness I feel with him, our ease together does feel a heck of a lot like a Christmas miracle.

And as he presses his lips to mine and I pull him closer, I can't help but think about how we first met on Christmas, and how we found love exactly fifteen years later.

We were a little slow on the uptake, but oh, what fun we'll have catching up.

THE END

Rocking Around the Holidays

BY LILI GROUSE

Escaping Australian summer for Swedish winter, Emma expected to be freezing. She did not expect reconnecting with a childhood crush that would warm her up like mulled wine.

About the Author

Lili Grouse writes American small-town romance from her apartment in Sweden's second largest city. For TIRAA's anthology, however, the author is venturing into unknown territory: writing about a semi-fictional part of Sweden *and* in Australian English.

Website: grousehillpublishing.com
Instagram: @grousehillpublishing
Bookbub: https://www.bookbub.com/profile/lili-grouse
Goodreads: https://www.goodreads.com/author/show/12105161.
Lili_Grouse

Chapter One

"Would you like the seasonal cake for dessert, Mrs. Anderson?" The flight attendant offers me a plate with a Victoria sponge sandwich topped with candy cane shavings and I simply nod, resigned. Christmas cheer is all around me, and no matter how many times I've corrected the attendants that it is, in fact, 'Miss', no one seems to be getting the message. The business class cabin is quiet except for the clattering of dishes, and with a second serving of mulled wine I am ready to fall asleep after the rich three-course meal (not including the cheese and fruit platter and the pralines scheduled to be served after dessert).

I jab at the sponge cake half-heartedly and reach into my handbag for the gift my best friend handed me before I passed through Security. Knowing Rhi, I'm lucky to have gotten through Security without issue.

I peel away the crimson wrapping paper to find a box of condoms and a note. I stuff the former back into my handbag before I read the latter.

Dear Em,
Wishing you a merry Xmas and an explosive New Year's. Remember,

the best way to avoid frostbite is to share body heat ;) See you in the new year, babe.

    Love always,
    Rhi.

I roll my eyes, but a smile rests on my lips. I love Rhiannon. We met in uni. In a way, I think my Nordic frost was drawn to her Aussie fire so she could thaw me out. When I first came to Australia over two decades ago, I was very much a product of my upbringing. My dad had returned to his home country shortly after I was born, and my mum had raised me on her own in Sweden.

Now, I'm going back for the first time since graduating from upper secondary school—or '*gymnasiet*', as we would call it. My student cap hangs on the wall in my flat now. My ex-fiancé would always suggest throwing out the old white cap with the black brim, but I could never part with it. Unbeknown to him, one of the reasons why was the message scribbled inside, on the blue and yellow fabric there. A message I didn't notice until it was too late. A message from someone who didn't sign their name. Part of me will probably always wonder 'what if?'. I know that has more to do with me than with my secret admirer. If I had been truly happy with Mick, I probably would have gotten rid of the old cap. Maybe he did me a favour, breaking our engagement last year.

I shake my head and take a sip of my wine. It's time to move on. The first step is putting some space between myself and Mick and his eight-month pregnant girlfriend. Visiting Sweden and my old schoolmates over the holidays should give me some new perspective. If nothing else, the girls' weekend at a ski resort should provide a distraction.

The cold is bracing as I trod from the taxi to the timber cottage the girls have rented. I really should have dressed warmer coming up here.

It's afternoon on Christmas Day and fairy lights are wrapped around the porch railing, lighting the way. From inside, a warm glow beckons, and I hurry to climb the porch steps and rap on the heavy wood door.

"Emma!"

The door flies open and my old friend Emilia beams back at me. Twenty years have passed, yet she looks the same as I remember. How is that even possible?

"Hi," I say, my voice muffled against her over-sized red wool sweater as she hugs me close.

"Close the door!" someone calls from inside, and I am quickly ushered into the warmth of the cottage.

"You're here," Emilia says, stepping back to look me up and down. "And looking smoking hot, I might add."

I laugh and rub my hands together for warmth. "I think I still have some warming up to do."

"Is she here?" another familiar voice says, and I look over to see my friend Karin approaching. "Hi!"

I open my arms for a hug, and we hold on tight for several seconds.

"I've missed you," she says softly, pulling back slowly. "It's so good to see you again."

I open my mouth to respond, but then all the other girls come rushing up to greet me.

"You look so different!"

"Can't believe you made it!"

"What time is it in Australia now?"

"Do you surf? You look like you surf."

"What was the weather like when you left?"

"Are there really surfing Santas down under?"

The barrage of questions is overwhelming, but also... fun. Clearly, we won't struggle to make conversation.

"Okay, okay, maybe let Emma breathe for a few minutes," Karin says, shooing off the other girls.

I smile my thanks and look around the room properly—the fireplace, the wide couches, the hardwood floors, the bar... the people.

We've all aged, obviously, but I can't say my friends have changed all that much. Some are skinnier, some have fuller faces, some have crow's feet or laugh lines, but they all look healthy and happy. And it feels like we're all teenagers again. Maybe reconnecting with my teenage self will help me figure out who I want my future self to be.

Chapter Two

The Lodge is a sprawling compound with all the amenities you could possibly want for a ski holiday or spa weekend. Tonight, it's party central, and as we head into the After-Ski lounge, the beat of the music pulses in my veins.

"Screwdrivers all around, right?" my friend Susanne says as we find a table that seats all eight of us.

There's some groaning and chuckling, but we all agree on toasting to the good old days with our old beverage of choice. These days, I prefer a chilled Moscato to vodka drinks, but when in Sweden...

"I still can't get over that you're actually here," Karin says, shaking her head as she leans back in her chair. "And this is the first time you've been back in twenty years? Did your mum move to Australia, too?"

I pick up a laminated menu and sit back. "No, she remarried right before I went off to uni in Sydney. They honeymooned in Europe, but they had an accident on the Autobahn on their way home. Neither of them made it."

I press my lips together to keep the tears at bay. It's been two decades since I lost Mum, but talking about it has me getting emotional. I reach for one of the pitchers of water on our table and pour myself a glass.

"Oh, Emma, I'm so sorry," Karin says, her pale blue eyes glassy.

I drop my head and focus on my water, the sympathy only making it harder to cover the sudden emotions. I take a deep breath and paste a smile on my face.

"Thank you. Let's talk about something less depressing, yeah? What is your life like these days?"

Karin chuckles and nods. "Well, my twins keep me busy—they just turned four."

"Girls or boys?"

"Girls," she says and pulls a face. "My mum says they're exactly like me and my brother at that age. It's not a compliment," she adds with a wry smile.

We both laugh at that. Karin, Emilia, and I often played together as kids as we lived on the same street. Karin would think up all kinds of mischief, and Emilia would remind us of the rules. Meanwhile, I just tagged along. In fact, I never took much initiative until I decided to move to Australia to study. Well, Dad wanted me to join him there, so maybe I was just tagging along back then, too...

"Eight Screwdrivers," Susanne announces as she and Emilia set down two small, round trays on our table. "Get 'em while they're cold."

I shake off the memories and reach for one of the highball glasses.

"Absolut?" I ask, stirring the drink.

"*Absolut!*" she answers, making us all chuckle. While I can enjoy drinks based on other brands, there's something about traditional Swedish vodka that just *feels* right.

We raise our glasses in a toast just as a band takes to the half-moon stage. The first bars of a rock song on a bass guitar play over the speakers and the audience cheers.

Craning my neck to see if I recognise the band—unlikely, given that I've not been outside Australia for the past twenty years—I make out a couple of older faces with longish hair. But then a bald singer steps up to the mic stand, wrapping his hands around the mic as he leans in.

The spark of recollection nearly kicks me out of my seat. I know that voice. I scramble to stand, and that's when I see him—Liam Holm. His old, curly, dark hair is gone, and he's definitely packed on a few pounds of pure muscle mass, but that's him. The guy I had a crush on for most of my school years. We were friends back then. I felt so lucky that he paid attention to me, even though he always seemed to have a girlfriend in another grade. None of his girlfriends looked like me, so I was pretty sure I was not his type. The fear of embarrassment and losing his friendship kept me from making a move on him, and so I didn't date anyone until I moved to Australia. No one in Sweden could compete with the fantasy of Liam Holm.

His voice is deeper, mature like an aged wine, and raspy—not from smoking, but from singing at full volume. The sound makes my uterus contract and I fight the urge to fan myself. Am I going into early menopause? Is this one of those hot flashes Mum mentioned?

The song finishes and the applause snaps me out of my trance. I hazard a look at my friends, but they're on their feet and applauding, too.

I clap my hands until the band starts up another song. I take the opportunity to sit down with the rest of my friends. Emilia shoots me a look across the table, no doubt remembering how I was always drawing hearts around Liam's name on the inside jacket of my notebook. I mouth the words "so hot" to her and she grins and nods in agreement, fanning herself theatrically. I laugh and raise my glass to her.

A few drinks later (yes, I stick with the vodka drinks), the DJ has taken over from the band and I've finished my beer-battered fish and chips—nothing like the ones back home. We're just about to hit the dance floor when one of the girls, Sandra, stands up and waves to someone. Within seconds, I see a tall, broad-shouldered man weave his way towards our table, grinning broadly as other patrons clap him on the shoulder, winking at a few of the girls nearby as he passes. Liam.

"Hey there!" he greets our table. "Glad you could make it."

"Wouldn't miss it," Sandra gushes. "Our own little Liam, killing it on stage."

He smiles, but there's no way of knowing if the compliment makes him blush or not. He's tan, a light sheen covering his sculpted face and neck like he's just been sprayed with gold and not just sweating from the heat of the lights on stage and the cram of bodies on the dance floor he just had to cross.

Liam's brown eyes—I know they're brown with little golden flecks around the pupils because I spent years studying his beautiful face when I should have been studying math—sweep around the table until they land on me. His forehead creases as he no doubt tries to place me.

"Emma's visiting from Australia," Karin supplies, and his grin widens.

"Emma? Wow, I didn't recognise you," he says and strides over. "It's been forever."

I almost topple my chair over as I scramble to stand for him to wrap me in a crushing hug.

"Good to see you," I mumble against his broad, warm chest.

It's not a brief embrace, but it still feels like it's over far too soon when he steps back.

"Pull up a chair," Emilia says, and my stomach flutters as he grabs one from a nearby table and straddles it right next to me. His cologne mixed with his sweat makes for a heady potion and my head swims.

"How've you been? What are you up to these days?" he asks, focusing entirely on me, his eyes glittering in the flickering light of the tealights on our table.

"Oh, not much. I've been living in Sydney since after graduation. Right now, I'm a partner at a law firm."

"Impressive."

"Not really," I say with a shrug. "But you... you're doing what you always wanted to do. Talk about impressive. How long have you been in the band? You sounded great, by the way."

He smiles and grabs an empty glass, pouring himself some water. "We've been together for about five years now. Before then, I was a music teacher at our old school."

"Wow. Has it changed much since we went there?"

He chuckles. "Well, they have *slightly* newer computers, and the ceiling in the dining hall has a fresh coat of paint."

I feign shock. "No way! You're telling me the remnants of mash and beans are finally gone?"

Liam shakes his head in regret. "No respect for history."

In my peripheral, I notice the girls are heading for the dance floor.

Apparently, the DJ has switched to ABBA. A wave of disappointment hits me when I look over at the empty seats. I don't want to stop talking to Liam.

"I guess I should—" I start, turning my head back to focus on him, and the words fall away.

Liam's not moving. He's crossed his arms over the back of the chair and is resting his chin there.

"I can't get over it," he says, his dark eyes studying me.

My cheeks heat and I take a swig of water to offset the alcohol coursing through my veins.

"What?"

"How gorgeous you still are."

I'm pretty sure my jaw drops. It's definitely time to guzzle water if I'm hearing things.

I shake my head. "I'm sorry. I think I blanked for a moment. What did you just say?"

Liam sits up straighter and clears his throat. "Sorry, I had a few beers before going on stage. It seems the alcohol washed away my manners."

His gaze drops to my hand, where I am clutching my glass of water tightly.

"How long have you been married?"

I look down and spot the ring. On my right hand.

"Um... wedding rings are worn on the left hand in Australia, too, you know."

"Oh. I thought it was one of those upside-down things—like the water in toilets going in the opposite direction."

I laugh, breaking the tension building inside me. "You're not too far off, though. I was engaged at one point."

"What happened?" Liam asks, studying me. "I mean, unless you'd rather not..."

I shrug and sip my drink. "He decided he wanted something else. *Someone* else. A younger woman who could give him the children he decided he wanted all of a sudden. His girlfriend is actually pregnant now, so good on him, I suppose."

Liam's eyes go wide, and I set down my drink and pick up my glass of water instead. Maybe I've had one too many, as the memory of Mick's surprise announcement doesn't hurt nearly as much as it did a few weeks ago.

"That sucks, Em."

"Pretty much." I lean back in my chair and look him over. "What about you? I imagine the girls are lining up at your door, you being a rockstar now and everything..."

Liam shakes his head and takes a swig of water. "I've been focusing on writing music, working on my vocals and all that. We're getting a bit too old for groupies, I think."

Sure, the other guys in the band look to have been around in the heyday of glam metal, but Liam's only 40. And smoking hot.

"Besides, I had my fun back in college," he adds. "I have a teenage son, if you can believe it."

"Wow."

My stomach twists up a bit at the idea. Not that I ever really wanted kids, but now the possibility of starting my own family is minimal at best. Meanwhile, the people I grew up with could be becoming grandparents soon. Scary thought.

"Yeah... it's crazy how time just..." He shakes his head. "Anyway... How long are you here for?"

"Over New Year's. Then I'm headed back to work."

"You start work right after New Year's?"

"Well, no, but with the flights and the time difference... you know. Time flies."

"We're playing a set at the Lodge every night until New Year's, but I have most of the days off. Do you want to meet up for lunch sometime? Tomorrow, maybe?"

I nod, only because I can't seem to form words. Is Liam Holm asking me out on a date? A lunch date, sure, but... even so. Inwardly, I shake my head to rid it of these nonsense thoughts. It's just an old classmate wanting to catch up as he doesn't have other plans.

"Yes? No?" he prods, and I clear my throat.

"Yes. I'd like that. Where do you want to meet?"

"Reception? We'll go from there."

"Okay, sure."

One of his bandmates walks up, tapping him on the shoulder. Liam looks up and nods, then he stands and flips the chair around to push it under the table.

"Twelve o'clock, yeah?" he says, backing away from the table.

"See you then," I respond right before he is swallowed up by the crowd.

I have a lunch date. With Liam Holm. I need to go shopping.

Chapter Three

T hankfully, the girls were sufficiently sloshed by the time we all headed back to our cottage, and only a few teasing comments were thrown my way.

Also, the booze kept them sleeping late, so I was able to duck out for breakfast without facing an inquisition.

Maybe I dreamt it all? Or maybe just imagined parts of our conversation last night. Maybe I'll be waiting at Reception for hours because Liam never actually told me to meet him there...

I shake my head. Focus. First stop—find some fine yet functional outfits. And warmer shoes.

The streets don't have pavements here; we share the snow-covered road with any cars or snowmobiles that pass through the town centre— and the snowploughs, of course. I stop outside a shop advertising boots next to sparkly high heels for New Year's. The entrance has been cleared of snow and two pitch torches are burning on either side of the door. The heat is a welcome warming breath on my jean-clad legs.

An old cowbell on the door announces my arrival, and the shopkeeper looks up with a bright smile.

"Welcome!" she says, her blonde, wispy hair sticking out under her

Santa's hat just like on the little wooden, bearded figurines on the counter. "How can I help you today?"

I glance around the shop, taking stock of the familiar traditional decorations—the straw goat by the door with its red sash, the pyramid-shaped electric candle holders in every window, the tiny flags wrapping around the fir tree like tinsel, straw stars hanging from individual branches next to shiny red baubles.

"I'm looking for some warm shoes," I say, glancing down at my stylish, heeled leather boots. "Something sturdy."

"For hiking?" the girl asks, walking around the counter towards me.

"Not really, maybe just for walking around."

"Well, then I'm thinking wool lined boots. Do you want a heeled boot or flat? We have both ankle boots and snow boots, or—"

I walk out of the shoe shop with several pairs of warm socks—both for wearing with my new ankle boots and with my new snow boots—and for sitting curled up on the couch by the fireplace. You'd think I was staying up here for the whole winter and not just for a week.

After a visit to the sporting goods store for a proper winter jacket, gloves, a hat, and scarf, as well as insulated leggings and ski pants, I head over to the Lodge.

There is a fire going in the massive fireplace across from the check-in counter and I head over to sit on one of the couches facing it. I need to go back to our cottage soon to freshen up, but I just need a few moments of quiet first.

Instrumental Christmas music is playing over the speakers on a low volume, and I close my eyes as I sink back against the soft leather. I'm exhausted. Maybe jetlag is finally catching up with me.

"Late night?"

I sit up with a snort at the sound of a familiar voice. Did I fall asleep? Was I snoring?

Liam smiles as he drops down right beside me on the couch. He smells like pine and soap and is wearing a white cable-knit sweater with dark jeans. He looks warm and casual. Meanwhile, my armpits are at risk of staining my long-sleeved shirt underneath my jacket.

"Is it noon already?" I say, reaching for my handbag.

"A few minutes past, but you're all right. I'm not in any rush."

I check my phone. 12:15. "Wow, I can't believe I fell asleep. I'm so sorry."

"No worries. I'm just glad I spotted you over here. I was starting to worry you'd stood me up."

The playful smile on his lips suggests he wasn't worried one bit about me not showing up.

"I'm sure that never happens to you," I tell him, rolling my eyes.

He shrugs. "I don't go on many dates these days."

Does that mean he considers this a date?

"Well, if this *had* been a date, I'd have made a terrible first impression," I quip. "Going straight from shopping for sensible winter clothes to falling asleep and almost standing my date up."

Liam shifts on the couch, slinging his arm across the back of it and angling his body towards me.

"Shopping for winter clothes, hm? Are you considering staying past New Year's, then?"

"No. I just didn't have much in the way of winter clothes to begin with. Winters in Sydney don't exactly require snow boots and ski pants."

"Yeah, I get that. Besides, you guys are in the height of summer right now, aren't you? Can't imagine it was easy to pack for much cooler weather."

"Very true."

"What made you decide to come? Not that I'm complaining, but you didn't show up until Christmas Day, so you've missed out on the whole Swedish Christmas Eve experience."

"I know. Can you believe I missed out on *From All of Us to All of You* again?" I say with a laugh. It's been twenty years since I last watched the Disney special from the 1950s.

"And the jumping around the Christmas tree like little frogs," Liam points out.

I chuckle. "You didn't actually do that, though, did you?"

Liam grins. "Nah. That's for the tourists. They hand out little pamphlets here to describe a traditional Swedish Christmas, and they've included the frog dance in it."

"But isn't it more for Midsummer? My family never danced around the Christmas tree, as far as I can remember."

He shrugs. "My grandparents did, but not my parents. Besides, your dad probably brought his own traditions with him, right? What is a proper Aussie Christmas, anyway? Surfing Santas?"

"You mock, but our surfing Santas are way hotter than the old guy trudging through snow up here."

"Sounds like something I need to see for myself," Liam says, winking.

I shrug. "Well, if you're touring Australia next year, come up to Bondi on Chrissie and join the festivities."

Liam laughs and heaves himself up from the couch. "I'll pencil that in. For now, what do you say to a traditional buffet in the main dining room? They've got meatballs and prince sausages," he adds in a sing-song voice.

I take his proffered hand and let him pull me up, landing me inches away from his broad chest. He holds on to my hand as I look up at him, and my heart skips a beat. Liam looked sexy on stage, tantalizing in the low light at the table last night, but he's completely mesmerizing this close up.

I suck in a breath and get a proper sniff of him—pine, soap, musky undertones... all male. All intoxicating.

"Ready?" he asks, his voice slightly huskier than before. It sends shivers down to my belly, curling there with blossoming heat.

I manage a nod. "Mm-hm."

Keeping hold of my hand, Liam heads for the main dining room at the Lodge and I follow, grasping for my sanity that I seem to have lost along the way.

Lunch with Liam was great, and when I got back to our cottage, the girls were all out on the slopes, so I could take a nice, long, luxurious bath in the hot tub out back, surrounded by snow-covered fir trees and bushes.

The crisp winter air—easily below zero—was a stark contrast to the heated water in the tub, and I relished the feeling of breathing clean, cold air. Not that the air up in the Blue Mountains is anything to scoff at, but there is something special about the Swedish Mountains. Something unique.

I am wrapping myself up in a robe when I hear the front door open and close. I hurry across the wooden patio floor in my bath slippers and go inside before I freeze.

"There you are!" Emilia exclaims. "We were starting to think you'd packed up and left. Or shacked up with Liam," she adds with a grin.

My skin is on fire—likely from the sharp contrast between the cold air outside and the blazing heat of the fireplace in our cottage—and I shake my head.

"You're bonkers. I just needed to pick up some clothes; it's colder here than I remembered."

"Ooh, what'd you get?" Karin says, taking off her ski pants by the door.

"Just practical stuff—boots and outerwear. At least I remembered to pack layers, and my dancing shoes."

"Well, slip those on because we're headed to the After-Ski again tonight. It's 80s night, so you know the dance floor is going to be packed," Emilia says, sashaying off to her room.

"Nice." And Liam's band is going to be playing cover songs—some Bon Jovi, he mentioned at lunch.

"Liam's going to be there," Karin says with a wink as she passes me on the way to her room. "It looked like you two really hit it off last night."

And today...

If the Lodge was hopping last night, it's nothing compared to the frenzy we walk into tonight. There are no tables for dining, only tall, round tables for talking over drinks. The actual bar is chockers; people calling out orders to the bartenders, desperately trying to make themselves heard over the music.

The DJ is mixing Christmas songs with techno music and there doesn't seem to be much room to do anything but jump up and down in place on the actual dance floor.

"Let's get our drink on," Sandra yells, pointing to the crowded bar section.

I'm trying to make eye contact with one of the bartenders when two hands are planted on my hips. I'm about to push the overeager patron off when I hear his deep voice in my ear. "What's your pleasure?"

Liam. Liam Holm is my pleasure.

I look up to find him smiling at me. "Your choice of drink, I should say."

"Oh... um... a bottle of Smirnoff Ice?" Unless I'm being served at a table or I know my drink hasn't been left unattended at any point, I prefer to drink straight from the bottle. And see it uncapped.

"Got it," Liam says, signalling one of the bartenders.

I assume he's mouthing out the drink order, because I don't hear him speak and yet the bartender appears to note the order.

"Join me backstage?" Liam says to me, his breath tickling my neck. "They'll send someone back with our orders."

I glance around at my friends, still trying to get their orders in, and catch Emilia's eye.

"Go. Have fun," she mouths to me, and makes a shooing gesture.

My face is in flames, but I push the embarrassment aside and turn to let Liam guide me backstage.

His hand enveloping mine feels all too right, and I try to push any romantic notions aside. He's just making sure I'm following him. It's a dense crowd, after all.

Backstage is literally the back of the stage; cables and other equipment I couldn't possibly name take up most of the space, but there are a couple of couches and a few tables for the performers to sit. They're all vacant.

"Where's the band?" I ask Liam as he directs me to one of the couches, his hand regretfully no longer encasing mine.

"They should be getting here in a couple of hours. I'm early," he explains. "We don't go on until around midnight."

"Oh."

"Were you hoping to meet the band?" he asks, frowning.

"No... I mean, I just expected they'd be here, that's all."

"Do you want to go back to the bar? I just thought we'd get a moment to talk in normal voices back here, but if it makes you uncomfortable..."

"What? No, of course not."

"Good."

Just then, a bartender walks in with a round tray. "Smirnoff Ice and a Norrlands Guld," she says, setting the drinks down on the small table in front of us.

"Thanks, Katti," Liam says with a wink and the bartender scurries off, her cheeks tinged pink.

I chuckle.

"What?" Liam asks, grinning as he picks up the bottle opener provided and uncaps my drink.

"It's just... you always could turn girls' heads, and now it's even more obvious."

"Oh, really?" he says, raising his eyebrows. "And did I turn your head, too?"

I reach over to grab my bottle from him and our fingers touch around the sweating glass. I look up to find Liam looking at me intently.

"You know you did," I croak out, not breaking eye contact.

"I was a blind fool back then," he says, his voice low and hoarse. "Do I get a do-over?"

I'm not a hundred percent sure what he means, but on the off chance that things might head in a new direction between us, I nod.

Liam is wearing the sweetest smile as he cups my cheek and leans in to kiss me.

"Uh... what's going on?"

We pull apart as if scolded by the unfamiliar voice of a young man. As I turn my head, I see a carbon copy of the boy I had a crush on all through compulsory school and suck in a breath.

"Tommy," Liam says, sitting up straight and clearing his throat. "I thought you weren't coming up until New Year's."

The kid—late teens, I'm estimating—shuffles over to the other couch and flops down. "Well, Mum and Rolf decided to ditch me early—they got a last-minute deal on a flight to the Canary Islands."

"They drove you up here, though, right?"

266

Tommy shrugs. "Nah, just to the bus station. It's fine, though. What's going on here?" he asks, repeating his unanswered question from moments ago. "Who's this?"

"This is Emma. We went to school together," Liam says. "She lives in Australia now."

"Cool," Tommy says, giving me a nod of approval before reaching for Liam's beer.

"Yeah, I don't think so, buddy," Liam says, snatching it up.

"Oh, come on, Rolf lets me have beer."

Liam's face hardens. "Yeah, well, someone should remind him you're not 18 for another year."

Tommy rolls his eyes, sinking back into the couch. "Man, for someone who's supposed to be a rocker, you seriously lack chill."

Liam laughs. "Being a dad to a teenager will do that to you—sucks all the chill out. Be sure to remember that when you go off to college."

"I always use a rubber, Dad," Tommy says, sighing. "Like, seriously."

Liam's cheeks grow slightly redder, and I hide my smile behind my bottle.

Liam clears his throat. "Anyway... do you want me to take you up to my room to drop off your bag?"

"No sweat," Tommy says, picking up his phone to tap away at it. "Mum booked me my own room; she said you might be 'entertaining' in yours, seeing as you weren't expecting me yet."

Now it's my turn to go all red in the face. Was that where tonight was heading before Liam's son showed up? Was our kiss going to lead up the stairs to his hotel room?

"Your mum—" Liam breaks off and clears his throat. "I don't have anyone else staying in my room, so you crashing there won't be a problem."

"Yeah, well, if it's all the same to you, I'd rather have my own space."

Liam looks momentarily taken aback but recovers quickly. "Sure, whatever you prefer, buddy."

Tommy looks up from his smartphone and looks between me and his father. "I'll head on up to my room; give you guys some privacy."

"Oh, no, that's not—" I start to say, but Tommy is already on his feet.

"See you later, Dad," he says and nods our way before going back through the door he must have entered through.

"Wow," I say, leaning back against the sofa back. "I can't believe you have a teenage son. I mean, I know you said you did, but I guess I couldn't really picture it until now. He looks just like you."

Liam sighs and sinks back into the seat right next to me. "I know. I hardly believe it myself."

"So, you met his mother in college?" I ask, turning my head towards him.

"First week of initiation," he says, mirroring me. "We hit it off straight away, hit the student pub a few times too many, and, well..."

"You 'hit that'?" I say, making air quotes.

Liam chuckles. "Yeah, you could say that. Anyway, I was careless, and she ended up pregnant. She wanted to keep the baby, so we made it work. Until it didn't."

"When did you guys break up?"

"Tommy was around two when we officially split. But it wasn't an ugly breakup or anything. We were just too young. We co-parented Tommy, though, and our parents helped a lot. Somehow, we made it work."

"You're still on good terms?" I ask, given the tension I picked up on when Tommy mentioned his mother and stepfather.

He nods. "Most of the time. She married Rolf a few years back, and it's not exactly been smooth sailing between us since then. Tommy is living with them full-time now, so he can finish school. I travel a lot with the band and that doesn't exactly afford him the stability he needs."

"Why do I get the feeling that's a direct quote?" I say softly, studying him.

"You're very perceptive," Liam says, matching my tone before he clears his throat. "Rolf pushed for Lina to request full custody, even drafted an application for a summons. I talked to Tommy about what he wanted to do, and when he said he'd like to stay with his class and graduate with them, I told Lina I would sign an agreement between the two of us, without the court's involvement, as long as Tommy would be free to visit me whenever he liked."

"And that's the arrangement you have now?"

"Yeah. But next year, Tommy will turn 18 and the custody issue will be a moot point. He'll finish up his senior year, then head off to college."

"Does it make you feel old?" I ask, smiling.

"You know, I've heard people say that having kids makes you feel younger, because you look at the world through their eyes, but having a teenage son when you're only 40... it puts a whole new spin on that midlife-crisis."

I laugh. "What, you've got a red Corvette waiting for you outside? A busty blonde waiting for you in your suite?"

Liam grins and leans in. "Just a beautiful brunette with sun-streaked hair waiting for me to kiss her."

"Is that so?" I say, leaning towards him.

"Mm-hm."

His lips brush against mine and I open for him, eager for a proper taste. What does it feel like to be kissed by your unrequited crush more than twenty years later?

Heaven.

Chapter Four

"Hey, you. Where did you run off to?" Karin yells over the music when I join her and the other girls on the dance floor.

I just shrug and keep on dancing. Emilia catches my eye and raises her eyebrows in a silent question, to which I cannot help smiling in response. She gives me two thumbs up and I laugh.

I glance around the room for Liam even though I know he's probably upstairs by now, hanging out with Tommy. The After-Ski is 18 and over, so Tommy can't be in the bar unsupervised, which I can imagine isn't going over too well.

I can't help wondering if Liam will tell Tommy about the stranger his son almost caught him kissing earlier—and if he'll tell him we did, in fact, do a lot of kissing after he left.

If I wasn't completely sober—well, with one bottle of Smirnoff Ice in my system, but still—I would have been sure I'd dreamt it. It's such a cliché—the jilted woman, homecoming, the old crush who's all grown up, single dad, a holiday-themed setting—my goodness, I might have hit my head and fallen into one of my favourite romance novels.

I discreetly check the back of my head for lumps. Nope. No obvious head injury. Then again, if I were dreaming, would I really have a head injury in my dream? Okay, maybe I'm a little buzzed, after all.

An old song starts playing, and of course the DJ works his magic with it, upping the tempo of the sultry track to make it more dance floor friendly. Laughing, I join my friends in attempting the old moves, including the exaggerated painting of a figure-eight with my butt.

My laugh gets stuck in my throat when hands land on my hips and follow the movement. I look up over my shoulder to make sure it's Liam —it is—before relaxing into his grip. Well, relaxing is a bit of a stretch, but at least his are welcome hands on my body.

The girls catch sight of him in our midst and, by the widening of their eyes, they can definitely tell something is going on between us.

It's a rebound thing, right? It must be. Don't they say women are at their sexual peak around 40? I think I read that somewhere. That's probably it. Hormones. And a childhood fantasy carrying over into real life.

But so what? I'm not looking for a steady relationship right now. And I'm especially not looking for one here in Sweden. Australia is my home now. I have no ties here anymore.

Bolstered by my internal pep talk, I lean into Liam, effectively rubbing myself up against his front as I dance. His grip on my hips tightens, and I can feel his hard body come alive behind me.

Definitely hormones.

Liam makes me promise to wait for him after his midnight set, and I am only too happy to oblige. When I duck into the bathroom before his band is set to come on stage, Karin and Emilia are hot on my heels.

"Oooo-kay, what was that?" Karin asks as soon as we're alone. "Did you hook up with Liam?"

In the back-lit mirror, I can see myself blushing. "No."

"Not yet," Emilia supplies, winking.

"We just... we hung out today, and backstage, and... I don't know. I just feel like going with it for a change, you know? Whatever happens, happens."

Emilia grins while Karin frowns, looking me up and down.

"You've changed."

I shrug. "It's been twenty years. Haven't we all?"

Karin mutters something and ducks into one of the empty stalls.

I raise my eyebrows at Emilia, silently asking what's up with Karin. She shrugs her shoulders in response.

I duck into a stall myself and finish what I came in here to do, then rejoin the girls at the sinks.

"Okay, am I missing something?" I ask Karin, who is diligently scrubbing her hands.

She shrugs. "It's just... I was looking forward to spending time with you, but you seem more interested in Liam."

Oh. I'm a total jerk. "I'm sorry. I guess I just got caught up in... it doesn't matter. I came up here to spend time with all of you, and I've been selfish. That's going to change, I promise. Tomorrow, I'm all yours. Well, unless you're out on the slopes—you know I never learned to ski," I add with a smile.

"We'll hang out by the fireplace and drink all the hot chocolate," Karin says and gives me a side hug.

"Oh, that reminds me—I brought Tim-Tams," I say, brightening.

"What's that?"

"Oh, you'll see. They'll go great with the hot chocolate."

"I like the sound of that," Emilia says, wrapping her arms around me and Karin. "Hot chocolate tomorrow afternoon, dancing our asses off tonight."

We are all laughing as we leave the Ladies'.

With Liam's raspy voice belting out the lyrics, you could almost believe it really is Jon Bon Jovi on that stage. The crowd is eating it up. It's as if I've been transported back in time, watching him on stage with a couple of the other guys from our grade at one of those school concerts in the assembly hall. I was so in love with him back then. Unrequited, of course. And now...

Liam catches me watching him and winks, shooting arrows of heat straight down to my core.

All around me, people are dancing—or at least jumping up and down —but the only person I can make out clearly is him. Everything else is white noise.

The band finishes their set and I find Karin, telling her I'll see her by the fireplace tomorrow afternoon. She gives me a puzzled look, but then looks behind me and nods.

Liam wraps his big hand around mine and gestures for the exit with his head. I blindly follow. Wherever he's taking me is fine by me as long as he's right there beside me.

"I have a surprise for you," he says as soon as we're away from the ear-splitting music and the crowd. My ears are ringing, making his words appear distant, but I can still hear them.

As he leads me towards the elevators, I'm thinking I'm probably going to enjoy his surprise.

He doesn't pounce on me in the elevator like the romance heroes I read about tend to do once they get their love interest alone. Instead, he holds onto my hand and smiles, saying nothing.

The elevator dings and we step out onto his floor, but he doesn't drag me to the room. He simply strolls along, in no hurry to get me alone. Hm. This is not going the way I expected it to.

"Come in for a bit," he says, unlocking his room door.

For a bit?

Inside, there is a clothes rack in the middle of the room, full of winter clothes.

"Um..."

"I'm just going to grab a quick shower. Pick out something to wear while I'm gone. Layer up," he says with a wink, heading for the bathroom.

We're going outside? Past midnight? In the cold?

I shake my head as I start looking through the selection, revising my earlier sentiment that wherever he's taking me is fine by me. I did not sign up for blistering cold and frostbite.

Chapter Five

The only thing I can make out of my surroundings is the snow in the headlights of the snowmobile practically flying across the vast nothingness. I'm holding on tight to Liam, who is driving, but I'm not experiencing the swooniness of a girl wrapped around her man on a motorcycle going on an adventure. I'm bloody terrified.

I've got goggles, a ski mask to protect my face from the biting cold, thermal clothing, and I'm convinced I'll freeze to death before anyone finds me if I fall off the back of this thing.

Finally, Liam slows down and I dare to look up at the night sky, bright with stars. Wow. It's like the starlit sky above the desert lands in Central Australia, yet clearer somehow. More... crisp. Or maybe that's the cold.

The snowmobile comes to a stop, and I have the irrational thought that we've run out of petrol—or diesel. Liam doesn't seem worried, though. Instead, he's opening the trunk and grabbing a couple of wool blankets, along with some sort of aluminium sheet.

"Come on, it's right around this bend," he says, clicking on a headlamp to light up the snow in front of us.

"How do you know?" I ask, puzzled.

"GPS," he says, and I can hear the grin in his voice even though I can't see his face properly.

His gloved hand wraps around mine and he leads me into the abyss. Figuratively speaking, of course. I hope.

As we approach his destination, it's as if I can see better in the darkness. Is that the sunrise? No, the sun won't rise until much later, and it'll only stay up for a short while this time of year.

Then, as he lays out the aluminium sheet and the wool blankets, turning off his headlamp, I see it.

The Northern Lights.

Flames of green dancing across the night sky. Sweeping brushstrokes of aqua and magenta painting the dark canvas laid out before us. It's magical, nothing short of it.

"Wow," I whisper, sitting down beside Liam, who drapes another blanket over the both of us.

"Did you ever come up here to see them before you moved?" he asks softly.

"No. We never went skiing, and I didn't even know you could see them this far south. I thought you had to go up to the arctic circle, or at least Kiruna, to be able to see the lights properly."

"I saw online that we would be able to see them here after midnight for most of this week. A rare treat."

"Definitely," I say softly and rest my head on Liam's shoulder.

We sit in silence, watching the spectacle before us with reverence, until the cold seeps in and I'm feeling the urge to move around. The lights fade away and Liam seems to know what I'm feeling. He gets on his feet and pulls me up to stand pressed up against him. I look into his eyes, the last flashes of light dancing across his face, and start to wet my lips when I realise that's a bad idea in these temperatures. Instead, I tuck my lips in and pull my hood tighter around my face.

"Come on," Liam says, still holding on to my hand. "Let's go back to the Lodge and warm up."

Yes, please.

Liam's room is devoid of the clothes rack from before, and the bed has been turned down, a couple of individually wrapped chocolate hearts on the pillows.

A giggle escapes me, and I wonder, not for the first time since being back here, if I'm really 40 years old.

"What?" Liam asks, amused.

"It's just... do they always leave you those little chocolates?" I nod towards the bed.

Liam grins and picks up a box sitting on the dresser, showing me its contents. Chocolate hearts.

"Every night. I've been putting them in here, saving them for Tommy."

"Or a ski-bunny you've invited upstairs to your room," I tease him.

He puts down the box and reaches for me instead. "The only ski-bunny I'm interested in is right here, wearing far too many clothes."

I laugh. "Well, you're the one who made me put all this on."

"Does that mean I get to take it all off?" he asks, a wicked gleam in his eyes.

Instead of answering him, I hold out my arms, silently inviting him to undress me.

He makes quick work of my jacket, the fleece vest underneath, and the long-sleeved thermal shirt, leaving me in a tank top. Next, he undoes my ski pants, my thermal leggings, and, after my nod of acquiescence, my second pair of leggings.

Then, he steps back, his gaze so heated on my bare legs that I don't think I'll ever need thermal leggings again.

"My turn," I say, my voice unrecognizable to my own ears.

He mimics my earlier pose, and my fingers shake as I peel back the layers until he's in a tight T-shirt and black boxers.

"Wow," I say, swallowing hard.

"Better view than the Northern Lights?" he asks, teasing me.

I laugh and shake my head. "Different kind of wow."

Liam grins and reaches for me. I go willingly and tilt my head back for his most scorching kiss yet.

I'm definitely not going to need clothes to keep warm tonight...

The room is pitch black when I start to wake up and I reach for my phone to check the time. I feel around the bedside table, but my phone's not there. Where did I last have it?

A slight movement in the bed startles me, and the memories flood in. Liam. Cover songs. Dancing. Northern Lights. His hotel room...

I'm afraid to turn on a light in case it's still the middle of the night—though it shouldn't be, as it was well past midnight when we got back to the Lodge. But I really need the bathroom...

As my eyes slowly adapt to the dark, I can make out the contours of the room, including the path to the bathroom. I slip out of the bed as quietly as possible and pad over there.

The brightness of the bathroom lights burns my eyes, and I squint my way over to the seat. Once relieved, I wash up in front of the mirror, taking stock of my appearance. Yikes. If anyone saw me like this leaving Liam's room, it would be a clear walk of shame. My hair is messier than ever, my lips swollen, my face blotchy with old makeup, and there's a mark on my neck eerily similar to a hickey. Do people my age still get those?

I shake my head and wash my face the best I can, considering I don't have my makeup remover wipes here. I'm left with clean but sensitive skin —I've never worn much makeup as my eyes tend to swell up the next day, but I wanted to look my best for last night... Maybe I could sneak off now, leave Liam to believe I always look like I did then...

No such luck. When I inch open the bathroom door, there is a soft light in the room. The lamp on Liam's side is on.

I instinctively cover myself the best I can—considering I'm stark naked—but Liam simply smiles, beckoning me back into bed with a curled finger.

I quickly duck under the warm covers, and he scoots closer.

"Morning," he says, his voice gravelly.

I resist the urge to pull the covers all the way up over my head. Barely.

"Hi," I squeak.

"It's still early," he says, his fingertips dancing across my bare shoulder.

"How early?" I ask, biting my lip.

"Ten-thirty."

"What? How is that early?"

"When you're a musician, it's basically the break of dawn," he says with a low chuckle. "Especially when you're up in the north in wintertime."

Oh, I really need to find my phone. Karin and Emilia must be worried sick. I promised I'd spend time with them today and look at me now.

"What's wrong?" he asks as I look around the room hoping to see my clothes strewn about somewhere.

"Uh... nothing. I just... I should get going."

I clutch the covers to my naked body as I start to climb out of bed, but his voice stops me.

"Don't go."

I turn my head to look at him, his broad and muscled chest on full display as he sits up against the headboard. I can't believe I had a one-night stand with an old classmate. With Liam freaking Holm, no less.

"Emma," he says softly. "Please stay."

I shake my head, turning away from him, yet I can't seem to leave the bed.

There is a rustle of sheets behind me and then his hands are on my shoulders, rubbing soothing circles there.

"You're so tense," he comments, kneading the knots I hadn't realised were there before. "You need a proper massage."

"I'm okay. Really."

"You want me to stop?"

One of his thumbs finds a particularly sensitive spot behind my shoulder-blades and a moan escapes me. "Definitely not."

Later that afternoon, I'm cuddled up on the couch in our cottage with a blanket, a generous cup of hot cocoa, and a fire roaring in the fireplace. I am feeling nice and toasty until the topic of conversation turns to Liam. I put aside my cup and pull at the collar of my "ugly Christmas sweater" that Emilia foisted upon me.

"So, what's the next step?" Emilia asks. "Are you moving back to Sweden?"

"I need to get back to Sydney," I say, shaking my head. "I have my job there, my friends, my dad, my whole life, really."

"And Liam's got his whole life here," Karin points out.

"Yeah."

"So, is this just like a holiday fling, or...?" Emilia asks.

I complete her question in my mind, the whispers of 'what if' reverberating throughout my body. *Is this something more?*

I sigh deeply and shrug. "I guess that's all it is. Our lives are too different. Last night... it was like I finally got to live out my adolescent fantasies."

"And?" Emilia prods. "Was it everything you imagined?"

I shake my head and pick up my cup again to hide behind the steam still rising from it. "Better."

Emilia's practically bubbling with glee, while Karin is focusing on her own hot cuppa.

Growing up, Emilia was the responsible one and Karin the wild child. It seems like the roles have reversed over the years. Or I'm just not seeing through the surface appearance.

"Anyway, enough about me. Tell me more about your lives. Karin, you said you have twin girls now. Did your husband take them somewhere for the holidays?"

"They're with my mum and dad," she says, stirring her cup. "Carl met someone new a few years ago and started a new family."

"Oh, I'm so sorry," I say, reaching out to touch her shoulder. Guilt rushes through my veins. I've been so insensitive, focusing far too much on Liam, who is also a divorced man with a child. Granted, Tommy is almost an adult, but still. I would never want to take Liam away from his flesh and blood. I remember how much it hurt when I was younger, and my dad met someone new and didn't have time for me. He never had any children by any of the women he shacked up with, but it still hurt that he preferred to live on the other side of the world from me.

As the conversation turns to Emilia's life—disgustingly happily married (her words)—and more of the girls come back to the cabin from their outings, my mind keeps circling back to Liam.

We can never be more than a holiday fling between two consenting adults. There is no future for us. It's best to just have a clean break after this weekend. No regrets. No second guessing. No 'what ifs'.

Chapter Six

The next morning, I wake to a scream. Well, more like a squeal, I realise as I come fully awake.

I pad out into the common room and find Emilia, Susanne, and Sandra huddled over a piece of paper.

"What's going on?" I ask them, still bleary-eyed from a restless night's sleep.

"We're going to the spa!" Emilia exclaims, waving the paper around.

"What?"

"It says the spa has been reserved for our group this afternoon and we get our choice of treatments, free of charge, for three whole hours."

"But why?" I ask, taking the paper from her to study it. There must be some sort of caveat—these types of facilities don't give away their services, especially not on a big holiday week such as this.

"Who cares?" Emilia says, snatching the paper back. "Maybe the Christmas guests are leaving today, and the New Year's guests aren't coming until tomorrow or the day after that. Either way, it's a free spa day."

The girls hurry off to share the news with the others and I shuffle over to the kitchen area to pour myself some coffee. I didn't see Liam last night, as we ordered in dinner and skipped the After-Ski, and we did have quite a lot of mulled wine, *glögg,* as we sat and talked. Later, Susanne made us all special holiday drinks—shots with Absolut and melted *skumtomtar.* Or 'foam gnomes' as I would probably translate it to my friends back in Australia. Safe to say, I'm not in the best shape this morning. Hopefully I won't fall asleep in a spa tub and drown.

"Emma Anderson?" one of the spa attendants says, appearing from behind a curtain to the right of the reception desk where we've just checked in.

"That's me," I say, lifting a hand to identify myself.

"Right this way, please," the attendant says, and I look over my shoulder at my friends, who are getting Mimosas from a table off to the left side of the reception desk. I catch Karin's eye, and she nods. I guess that's my go-ahead.

The treatment room is bathed in soft lighting and smells vaguely of lavender and cinnamon. I'm handed a towel and directed to step behind a screen to change, then lay down on the massage bench face down.

The other girls were handed a menu of treatments and were still deciding when the attendant came to collect me. How do they know what type of treatment to give me?

There is a light knock on the door just before a woman asks if I'm ready. I quickly arrange myself on the table and let her know I'm decent.

There is a stirring in the air as the door opens and the whiff of musk blends with the essential oils already diffusing in the room.

A male massage therapist? I shift slightly on the bench, feeling more exposed now.

The door clicks shut and I'm about to ask for another towel when the man steps closer.

"Emma."

I snap my head up when I hear Liam's voice. "What are you doing here?"

"I was thinking I'd give you a proper massage," he says, walking over to a table to gather some oils. That's when I notice he's wearing the same type of uniform as the other spa attendants.

"You work here?"

He turns his head and smiles. "As a matter of fact, yes. At least I used to. Back in the early days when we were coming up here for gigs, I needed to pick up some extra work. I guess I didn't mention I worked both as a music teacher and PE teacher at our old school?"

"No, you did not. So, you arranged all this?"

"I hope that's okay," he says, frowning now. "You were so tense the other day, and I had this idea that you might enjoy some pampering. I can get a different massage therapist in here, though, if I make you uncomfortable."

I shake my head. "No. You don't make me uncomfortable. I was just surprised, that's all. This was very sweet of you."

Liam pours some oil into his hand and rubs his palms together. "So, it's okay if I put my hands on you now?"

A laugh bubbles up and I nod. "Yes, please do."

Liam's hands are warm and firm on my back, and I soon melt against the bench. The scent of lavender fills my senses and I start to doze off. I can't remember the last time I felt this relaxed, this...

"Emma?"

I blink myself awake and realise a warm towel is covering my entire body. When did that happen?

"Oh... did I fall asleep?"

"Just for a little bit," Liam says with a slight chuckle.

"Did I snore?" I ask, horrified.

"Just a little bit." He's smiling as I sit up, holding up a robe in front of me.

"Oh no..."

"I thought it was cute," he says, helping me into the robe. "And I was happy to see you relaxed."

"Well, I guess I have you to thank for that." I turn around after tying the belt.

Liam shrugs. "I missed you last night. This was my selfish way of getting some alone-time with you today."

I look up at him and my heart fills with warmth. "How are you this perfect?"

Liam chuckles and I realise I've spoken my thoughts out loud.

"I added some jasmine to the oil blend; it may be clouding your mind. The essential oil version of rose-coloured glasses."

I shake my head and lift onto my toes to offer him my lips. "I have a feeling it's all you."

His hands are warm and fragrant as they tangle in my hair, and I drink in his kiss like a sweet Moscato.

It's a holiday romance, that's all. I'm letting myself get swept up in the fantasy of it all. Only a couple more days of this time-out from reality. I had better make the best of it.

Chapter Seven

"Have breakfast with Tommy and me tomorrow," Liam says as we're lying in bed the night before New Year's Eve. "I want him to get to know you."

I roll onto my back and stare up at the ceiling. "Do you really think that's such a great idea? I mean, won't that confuse him?"

"What is he supposed to be confused about?" Liam asks, propping himself up on his elbow so he can look down at me. "He's not a toddler anymore. His mother remarried years ago."

"I'm leaving the day after tomorrow, Liam," I say with a sigh, looking up into his warm, gold-speckled brown eyes.

"Does that have to be the end of us, though?" he asks softly.

"Liam... we just met, for the first time in two decades."

"I know that. I'm not proposing marriage here, Em."

I roll back onto my side, facing him. "What *are* you proposing, then?"

"We could start by staying in touch. There's this thing called email, and Skype, and WhatsApp... we could get to know each other better, and I could come visit..."

I squeeze my eyes shut to hide the burgeoning tears from spilling out. Liam reaches out and smooths what I'm expecting are frown lines on my face.

"What's the point?" I croak. "We both know it's going to end badly. Why suffer the heartbreak when there's no hope?"

"I don't know that," he says, cupping my cheek. "Emma, look at me."

I reluctantly open my eyes again, blinking away the moisture on my lashes.

"All I'm asking is for a chance to get to know you better. Not the person you were, but the one you are today. We have a connection; you can't deny that."

"Maybe," I mumble.

"We do. And I for one am not about to let something good go without a fight."

I don't argue with him. I don't have the heart to. Instead, I cup the back of his head and pull him into a kiss to stop the words from pouring out from either one of us.

As his weight settles between my legs, I am relieved to have distracted him from the discussion. My heart, however, is anything but.

I sneak out before Liam wakes up. Like a coward. Having breakfast with him and his son is just too much too soon. We're in a holiday bubble right now. Once I leave, he'll realise that's all it was, and he'll be happy that his son was kept out of it.

I get back to our cabin before any of the girls are up and I get started on breakfast. I take out two loaves of wort bread—something I've not had in years but have become addicted to once again while I've been back—liver pâté and low-fat margarine, pickled cucumber, and the small jar of Vegemite that I brought with me and have yet to succeed in getting anyone else to try. I arrange the spread on the kitchen island and get started on the fried eggs. The girls will thank me for this hearty breakfast later tonight when the champagne is flowing.

"Ugh. I need coffee," Emilia groans as she pads into the kitchen in fuzzy slippers and pyjamas with a blanket wrapped around her. "How are you up so early?"

I focus on flipping the eggs in the pan. "Just getting an early start, I guess."

"Hmm," she mutters as she pours herself a cup of coffee. "What really happened?"

I sigh and turn off the stove, leaving the eggs to finish cooking on the after-heat. "I snuck out," I admit, turning to face her.

"Why?"

"He wanted me to have breakfast with him and his son. For us to start something real."

"And you don't want that?" Emilia asks, leaning against the kitchen island as she studies me.

"I'm going back to Australia," I remind her. "There's no future here."

"But what if this is the one?"

I chuckle. "I know you're 'disgustingly happy', but I have no illusions about there being someone out there who is my perfect match. People hook up and break up all the time. Mum and Dad couldn't make it work, coming from opposite sides of the world, why would I?"

Emilia nods. "I get that. But what's the harm in staying in touch? As friends, if nothing else."

"Because I'm so good at keeping in touch with old friends," I mutter under my breath.

Emilia sets aside her now-finished coffee mug and puts her arms around me.

"We've all been busy living our lives in the past decade or two, but we can start over from here."

I hug her back tightly before we break apart, tears forming behind my eyes. "I'd like that."

"Good. Because I've been dying for a second honeymoon, and now I can convince Daniel that it makes sense to visit Sydney as I have an old friend living there."

I laugh. "You're welcome any time. I'll take you guys bushwalking in the Blue Mountains, round up some funnel-webs for you to look at."

Emilia beams. "Ooh, funnel-webs, is that like fairy floss?"

I grin. "Deadliest spiders around."

She pulls a face. "Um... maybe we'll stick to the city limits, then."

I laugh and shake my head. "I'm kidding. Funnel-webs tend to live in residential gardens. Just don't go digging around someone's back yard and you should be fine."

She punches my arm and pours herself another cup of coffee while I plate the eggs. In the reflection from the window, I catch myself smiling. Maybe it's time to reconnect with old friends, after all. We've all changed, but there's shared history between us. Something to build on. Maybe it *is* possible to be looking back while moving forward.

"You snuck out," Liam says, filling up the doorway to my bedroom at the cabin.

I set down my makeup brush and turn in my seat by the mirror. "I know. I'm sorry."

"Listen," he starts, stepping over the threshold and closing the door behind him. "I understand that you're reluctant to get involved so soon after your break-up, and maybe I pushed you too far with Tommy, but I meant what I said the other night. I want to get to know you better."

I stand, securing the corner of my bath towel firmly between my breasts. "I'd like to get to know you better, too. As friends," I add, stepping closer to him.

"Friends?" he says, frowning slightly as his gaze travels down to my cleavage.

"Yes, friends corresponding and getting to know each other again," I say, reaching up to toy with the strings on his hoodie.

"And this whole 'friends-only' thing, when does that kick in?" he asks, sliding his hand in between the folds of my towel.

"When I get on that plane," I say, reaching up on my tiptoes to offer my lips to him.

"Oh, thank goodness," he says with a groan, yanking off my towel completely as he captures my mouth with his and presses me against his hard body.

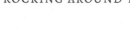

Liam leaves to rehearse with the band and I take another shower and start the beautification process all over again. By the time I'm ready—in a short black sequined dress paired with knee-high, stiletto-heeled leather boots—the girls have already started on the pre-party drinks. Karin thrusts a champagne flute at me, and I gulp it down in one go. The bubbles tickle my throat on the way down, then dance their way down to my stomach.

"From the sound of things, you are probably going to need something to replenish all the calories you've been burning," Emilia says, handing me a tray of cheese-topped snacks.

My face burns—either from the drink warming me from the inside, or from the embarrassment of my friends hearing me and Liam. Probably a bit of both.

"I don't know," Susanne says, snatching up a canapé, "sounded like our girl here already had a mouthful of meat today."

My jaw drops. I am mortified by the snickering all around me.

"Definitely got something in her," another one of the girls calls out from one of the bathrooms.

"Hilarious," Karin says drily, scowling at them. "Don't mind them, they never left puberty," she says to me, making me laugh.

I do need some food, though, so I make myself a sandwich before we head out for the Lodge. There should be finger foods and a buffet set up in the main dining hall, but I don't want to be drinking on an empty stomach. I intend to enjoy my last night in Sweden. Who knows when I'll be back?

The massive Christmas tree is all lit up in the corner of the dining hall and the buffet tables are set with white tablecloths, sprinkled with confetti, and decorated with flower arrangements—orchids, white hyacinths, and red amaryllis. One table is piled high with party hats, tiaras, and feather boas, along with bowls of little noisemakers and party horns for people to blow at midnight. Another table offers champagne flutes, a sommelier manning it. Several bottles are chilling in wide silver bowls filled with ice. One section of the dining hall is clearly dedicated to families, with a soda station for the kids and coffee for the adults, a buffet offering burgers and chips, pizza slices, veggies cut in fun shapes, and hot dogs with all the condiments.

I spot a familiar face at the sommelier's station, clearly displeased. Despite the knot quickly forming in the pit of my stomach, I head over there to say hello.

"Tommy?"

Liam's son looks up at me, his face twisted in a scowl.

"I'm Emma, an old classmate of your dad's," I say quickly, as if we've never met before. As if he didn't walk in on me almost kissing his dad backstage a couple of nights ago.

He gives me a curt nod, then looks back at the sommelier.

"Come on, mate, it's New Year's. I'm turning 18 next year, which is really just a couple of hours away now."

"Sorry, there's nothing I can do," the sommelier says, sighing. "I'll lose my job and the Lodge could lose their liquor license if I serve you."

Tommy looks over at me. "What if *she* gives me a glass?"

Uh... "I'm sorry, Tommy, but that's not up to me. You should ask your dad. Is he with the band?"

"Mum called. He sent me downstairs to grab him a plate."

"Oh."

Tommy studies me. "You're from Australia, right?"

"Well, my dad is Australian, my mum was Swedish, so I grew up here, but I've been living in Sydney for the past twenty years."

"Your parents are divorced, too?"

We drift away from the sommelier's table as more people try to grab their drinks.

"Yes. When I was really young. Dad moved back to Australia, and I stayed here with my mum."

"He didn't want you?" Tommy asks, quickly glancing down at the floor when I try to study him.

"I guess he wasn't ready to be a father. My parents were both fairly young when they had me."

"Mine too," Tommy says.

I gesture to a pair of empty chairs, and I'm surprised when Tommy actually accepts the invitation and sits down with me.

"You know what's weird?" he asks after a moment of silence.

I shake my head.

"I live with my mum and her husband, you know?"

I nod.

"But it's like... Dad's the one who actually wants me around."

My heart squeezes in my chest. I should probably say something like 'I'm sure that's not true', but that will just close this door he's cracked open. Just another adult not hearing what a teenager is trying to tell them.

"You know, when I was around your age, my mum remarried. I had already planned to go to Sydney for uni, but I remember thinking that she was relieved to see me go so she could focus on her own life."

Tommy nods. "Exactly."

"But now that I'm older, even though I don't have kids of my own, I think I understand it better. I was practically an adult, and I was leaving the country for at least four years, and she would have been alone for the first time in almost two decades. Finding someone else to share her life with would have been almost essential to her well-being. At least that's what I like to tell myself," I add with a shrug.

"You haven't asked her?"

I shake my head. "She and her new husband died in a car accident while I was abroad."

The colour drains from Tommy's face, and I inwardly curse myself. Mortality has a way of bringing you down.

"I'm sorry, I didn't mean to upset you," I say softly.

He shakes his head. "I'm fine."

He's clearly not, but it's not my place to argue.

"Hey, what's going on over here?"

The sound of Liam's voice sends tingles down my spine and fills my stomach with dread as I realise he's walked over just as I've almost made his son cry.

I'm afraid to look up and meet his eyes, but as I told Tommy moments ago, I'm an adult. So, I do it anyway.

Liam's not looking at me, though. He's looking at his son, frowning.

"What's up, mate?" he says, worry lacing his every word.

"Nothing. Sorry, I was going to grab you some food."

"Don't worry about it," Liam says. Then his gaze finds me, and it's not warm.

"We were just talking about life stuff," I say, getting to my feet. "I'm afraid I put a damper on the evening with my own walk down memory lane. Sorry again, Tommy."

"No worries," he says, standing as well. "Sorry about your mum, Emma."

"Thank you," I say softly.

Tommy heads over to the main buffet table—presumably to get Liam the plate he promised—and I can feel Liam's presence behind me. This time, it's an ominous one.

"What did you say to him, Emma?" Liam asks, his voice low and cold.

I take a deep breath, steeling myself, and turn to face him.

"We were talking about our parents, and I told him about leaving Sweden and about my mum being in a car accident."

"Why?"

"Because I was trying to connect with him. He shared something with me, and I wanted to reciprocate. I'm sorry I made him sad, but isn't this what you wanted? For the two of us to talk?"

"I haven't even told him about us yet," Liam says, his voice barely controlled.

"Yes, well, maybe that was a good thing," I say, hugging myself. "He doesn't need his dad going off to another country chasing a piece of tail."

Wasn't that exactly what *my* dad did, after all? At least I kept that part of the story to myself...

"Is that what you think this is?" Liam says between clenched teeth. "That I'm having some sort of midlife crisis and all I can think about is some woman?"

"Well, technically, if you want to go with the stereotype, that woman should be a blonde twenty-something, not someone your own age. But yes, that might very well be what this is."

"Then I guess it's a good thing you skipped on breakfast this morning," he says, biting out the words.

"I guess so."

All the excitement of tonight has fizzled out and left nothing but a sour taste behind. I glance around the room to see if my friends are around, and Liam sighs.

"I need to get backstage," he says, dejected. "I might see you later."

"Yeah."

He stalks off, and I press my lips together to hold back my tears. Maybe this is for the best, but I didn't expect it to hurt this much.

Chapter Eight

Liam is on stage with his band as we get ready to ring in the new year, belting out "Final Countdown" as the clock strikes twelve. The sound of party horns inside almost rivals the sound of fireworks outside. The crush of people on the dance floor moves as one towards the outdoor patio to watch the sky light up with artificial explosions of colour, making me long for the magic of the Northern Lights shared only with Liam. I look over at the stage, which is now empty. He's likely outside with Tommy, enjoying the fireworks show.

Whatever energy I had left in my body is quickly draining and I start moving in the opposite direction of everyone else. I need to get back to the cabin and pack the rest of my things. By this time tomorrow, I'll be on the plane back home.

I'm out in the reception area, waiting for my coat, when I hear my name being called. I look up as Liam reaches me.

"Don't go."

His words are like shards of glass digging into my heart.

"Why not? We both know it's better this way. A clean break and all that."

"I talked to Tommy. He told me what you talked about."

"Okay."

"I'm sorry, Em. I saw my son in pain, and I lashed out. It wasn't fair to you."

I shrug one shoulder, my eyes on the floor. "You were being a good dad. No need to apologise for that."

"I was being a jerk," he says, and I look up at him. "Please, Em. Stay with me tonight. We'll have breakfast with Tommy in the morning."

The pleading tone in his voice draws me in, the temptation too great to resist.

I place my hand in his and let him guide me to the elevators.

We don't start off the new year with a bang, though.

We start it off making love.

Liam takes me to the airport the following day and hugs me tight as I prepare to go through Security. He passes me an envelope and gives me strict instructions to not read it until I'm on the last leg of my flight back home. I have only just been served the complimentary champagne on the Singapore—Sydney flight when I rip open the envelope. As I unfold what appears to be sheet music, a second sheet of paper falls into my lap. It's a hand-written note on the Lodge's seasonal-style stationery paper.

Emma,

When you are reading this, you will be halfway home already. If you followed my instructions, that is. I know that wasn't always your strong suit.

I frown. What is that supposed to mean?

I am so grateful that I got to spend this time with you - that you came back into my life after all these years. I can't wait to come and visit you, but for now, I wanted to share something with you that I never got up the courage to say all those years ago. It was actually Tommy who found my first attempt at song writing - an original cover song, if you will - when he was looking through my old notebooks. I wrote the first verse back when we were still in school together. I wrote the last ones while you were still asleep in my bed in the early hours of this new year. You were my muse before I knew what that meant.

I miss you already.

Yours,

Liam

"Is everything all right, Ms. Anderson?" the flight attendant asks me, and I swipe at my cheek to wipe off the tears lingering there.

"Yes. I'm fine, thank you."

"We are preparing the cabin for take-off. May I clear your glass for you?"

I blink and realise I'm still holding the champagne glass. "Um, yes, please."

"We will be serving drinks and warm nuts as soon as the seatbelt sign is turned off."

"Okay. Thank you."

I settle in, making sure my seatbelt is as tight across my lap as it can be with the built-in airbag. Then I turn on the reading lamp to see the sheet music properly.

I woke up Monday mornin'
    Dreams fillin' up my head
    My pillow's old and lumpy
    Alone here in my bed
    I can't wait to get goin'
    So I can see your face again
    I'm a rebel on a leash
    The day is coming
    To tell you how I feel

. . .

When you came back in my life
    You had starlight in your eyes
    Your voice like soothing honey
    Like a balm upon my soul
    It tells me that I'm wanted
    Yeah, I'm a wanted man
    You came back for something
    Yet I gave you nothing
    No reason you should stay

I'm begging now
    For you to see me
    Take me how
    Ever you choose
    I'm begging now
    For you to love me
    You know I never did say
    What I felt for you
    As I planned back then
    Under the Sun

I'm no music expert, but even I can hear Jon Bon Jovi belting out the chorus. The original was one of my favourite songs back then. And the message scribbled in my student cap, "Meet me under the Sun at six", referring to a well-known sculpture in our town square... It was Liam who wrote it.

I hug the sheet music to my breast, squeezing my eyes closed to hold the tears back from running down my face. I can't believe it. The guy I had the biggest crush on—the guy I thought only saw me as a friend back then—actually had feelings for me. And I was too afraid to find out.

Just like I'm afraid to get hurt now by embarking on a long-distance romance. Maybe it's time I stop being afraid. Maybe it's time I start living again.

Epilogue

One year later...

I tear my eyes away from the surfing Santas as a new band takes the stage set up for the Christmas celebration on Bondi Beach. All my friends are here, even Mick and his girlfriend with their almost-one-year-old baby boy, safely tucked inside a tent for protection against the sun.

The days I spent in Sweden a year ago had indeed given me a new perspective. I realised Mick hadn't been the right man for me—as evident from the fact that he felt the need to date other people while we were engaged—and I had been wrong about my priorities. I thought I needed a husband and children of my own to have a full life. Maybe that had to do with my parents, both seeking companionship in different ways, but I wasn't them. Reconnecting with Liam taught me that life has a way of sneaking up on you, of surprising you. After realising how fear had stopped me from taking chances in the past, I knew I couldn't keep letting my fears control me. So, I gave Liam a chance. A real chance this time around.

We emailed each other and Skyped every week, making up for lost time. Even Tommy emailed me from time to time, asking questions about Australia and about the university I went to. And now, one year on...

"Merry Christmas, Bondi! Are you ready to rock?"

The crowd cheers and Rhi bumps my hip as Liam booms into the mic.

"My great-grandparents came to Australia for the gold rush, but it looks like they should have given Sweden a try," she half-yells into my ear as Liam's band starts to play a rock version of a traditional Christmas song.

I roll my eyes at her. "You've always told me your great-grandparents were convicts."

She shrugs. "Either way, they loved their gold. My point is, you struck gold, Em. He's a good egg."

I laugh. "Please make sure I'm there when you tell him that. I can't wait to see his reaction."

"What?"

"After twenty years, I understand most Australianisms, but Liam's new to the country. To us Swedes, good eggs come from healthy, free-range chickens."

"No worries, mate. My dad will catch on soon enough."

I look over to see that Tommy's joined us and I laugh. He's got the words down, but his accent is not quite there yet.

"You don't call a sheila a mate, mate," Rhi chides him, poking his side. "I'd better take you under my wing and teach you a thing or two."

Tommy's eyes are wide, and he nods eagerly, his gaze not quite staying on Rhiannon's face.

I roll my eyes and pull her to my opposite side, acting as a human shield between the 18-year-old boy and my 30-plus bestie.

"I'm sure Tommy will have no problem finding someone at uni to help him navigate Aussie society," I say. "Someone his own age," I add under my breath as I glare at Rhi.

She just laughs.

"So, are we going to throw some shrimp on the barbie?" Tommy says after a few moments of watching his dad on stage.

Rhi groans. "First of all, it's prawns, yeah? And we barbecue steak over here."

"The Aussies do love their meat," I tell Tommy, and quickly shoot Rhiannon a warning look before she can make a lewd comment about me and Liam in front of his teenage son.

The crowd applauds and I realise Liam's band has finished their set already. But then he steps up to the mic as his bandmates clear out.

"Thank you for the warm welcome, Bondi," he says. "The guys from Remarkable Rockers will be up here shortly, but I was hoping you would indulge me for a few more minutes. You see, I recently came to Australia to see my girl, and my son is starting at UNSW in the beginning of next year, so I'm hoping to spend some more time here in the future."

The sound of the crowd's cheers rivals that of the surf breaking.

"Around this time last year, I was up in the north of Sweden, performing with my band, when this vision of a woman walked in. As it turned out, she was not just a gorgeous sheila," he drawls the slang word like an American would imitate an Aussie, making me cringe, "she was also a childhood friend."

His tale earns him scattered 'awws' from the crowd, a whoop from Rhi, and a pained groan from Tommy. Me? I'm too stunned to speak, and afraid to move as my heart is beating out of control.

"So, I'd like to sing another song for her in front of you all, if that's all right?"

The response from the audience is unanimously affirmative.

As he picks up a guitar and starts thrumming the first few bars of a famous song, the crowd quiets, and when he sings in his raspy voice, my heart stops and I clutch at my chest.

What song is he singing, you ask?

Well, let's just say that my answer to Bruno Mars' question is a resounding yes.

Yes, Liam, I think I wanna marry you, too...

THE END

Comfort & Joyce

BY BARBARA KELLYN

When Grumpy meets Sunshine, the snuggle is real.

About the Author

Canadian romcom author Barbara Kellyn is tickled that readers have crowned her "the Queen of Banter." With four romantic comedy novels now available as ebooks, including *Morning Man* and *Forever Endeavor*, Barbara's MO is writing funny, steamy stories about likeable heroines worth rooting for and alluring heroes worth the trouble of falling for.

Learn more at BarbaraKellyn.com or on Instagram @barbarakellynauthor.

Chapter One

"This is crazy. I'm going to cancel," Marcus grumbled, stabbing at the glowing screen.

"Put down your phone this instant!" Fiona demanded. "You know how hard it was to nail down a meeting with this girl? She has amazing ratings. So don't you dare waste the best Christmas gift I ever gave to you by flaking out now."

"But Fee, hiring a paid cuddler? It's all so... so..." He shivered with disgust.

"What? Good for you? Actually, it'll be good for us both. I can't keep shouldering the burden of you all by myself. It's very draining."

He scowled. "Gee, thanks a lot."

"Darling, you're quite needy, and I say that with the utmost affection." She sniffed. "Not only will this meeting benefit your personal growth, but it'll get you out of this dismal dump."

He took exception to the industrial-style loft being called a dump, as stark and sparsely furnished as it may have been, but Fiona wasn't wrong about him needing to leave it more often. After two years of working at home, Marcus had grown accustomed to going days, sometimes even letting a week slip by, without encountering another soul. Thanks to doorstep delivery of every conceivable convenience being a few keystrokes away, it was far easier to stay inside to write his column or listen to music from dawn until dusk than it was to face the agonizing process of dragging himself from point A to point B. Except for physiotherapy and the required maintenance for possessing natural hair and teeth, if Marcus had to venture out, it had better be for a damn good reason. "Obviously you like it, or you wouldn't hang around here so much."

"I would love to challenge you to a battle of wits, but clearly, you're unarmed." She tossed her shiny blonde hair over her shoulder. "This cuddling thing is supposed to be a positive therapeutic experience, so why not give it a try? You have nothing to lose."

"Other than my dignity." Miffed that Fiona was once again getting her way, Marcus angrily screwed down the black cashmere beanie over his ears. "Okay, I'll go, but only to get you off my back," he groused. "You know how much I hate going out."

"Translation... you hate trying new things and meeting new people, you ol' crank."

He pulled on his coat. "And I especially hate them both at this time of year, remember?"

"I've been the recipient of far too many of your lame, last-minute Christmas gifts to ever forget how much you detest the holidays. The all-time low was that gas station trifecta of a pine-scented air freshener, trail mix, and a double pack of batteries. Toy not included."

"I thought it was rather practical, and as they say, it's the thought that counts." He reached for his crutch, slipping his forearm into the cuff and grasping the hand grip for support. Shifting his weight, he snapped to attention for final inspection. "Well? How do I look?"

Fiona nodded her approval. "Like a nimrod in desperate need of a hug. In other words, perfect."

A nearby coffee shop served as neutral territory for the introductory meeting with his cuddler-for-hire, ensuring a quick escape if things went south. Not that Marcus would be able to hightail it anywhere in a hurry. If the limp didn't signal how easy he'd be to catch, the mobility aid was a dead giveaway. When his ride pulled up to the address, he pushed open the door and unfolded his cramped legs from the back seat like a twisted flamingo. Securing the brace around his forearm, he leaned on the crutch and found unsure footing on the ice crud-covered curb. The driver called out, "Merry Christmas," forcing Marcus to turn around, unclench, and mutter a half-hearted, "Same to you."

As he'd dreaded, the hipster café had decked the halls with a tinsel-tangle of holidazzle overload, from the marshmallowy globs of snow-flocking that made his fillings ache, to the yuletide crooning that could flock off too. Hell, avoiding seasonal influenza was easier than dodging Michael Bublé in December. Hefty holly boughs decorated the counter, where customers sipped or waited to sip their orders while others staked out tables, immersed on phones and laptops. Marcus scanned the faces in the crowd. What did a professional cuddler look like anyway? Probably some New Age bohemian decked out in vegan hemp slippers and hippie-dippie rags made from organic cotton and recycled pop bottles.

He, on the other hand, had been coerced into completing an online application with a physical description for easy identification. He went with the basics: six-two, hair and beard the color of rust, and walks assisted. (Fiona made him change it from "gimp," claiming people found the term offensive. Whatever.) After picking a pseudonym for anonymity, Marcus hit *submit*, complaining to all within earshot (well, Fiona at least) that he was doing so under duress.

Seated alone at a corner table was a cute brunette cradling a cereal bowl-sized coffee mug. The twinkle lights above her blinked to the beat of *pah-rum-pah-pum-pumming*. Could that be her? It had to be her. He kind of wanted it to be her. With short hair falling just below her chin and framing her heart-shaped face, she looked like the nurturing type, what-ever that meant. Welcoming. Warm. Soft, maybe. Probably smelled like cookies. No, wait... that was actually the scent of freshly-baked shortbread wafting past.

They made eye contact, and hers smiled and sparkled hello. She raised her hand, signaling to him that it was safe to approach. "Alexander Nevermind?"

"Uh, yeah. Hi. That's me." Marcus waved back before clumsily maneuvering between the tightly spaced tables.

She extended a handshake. It was indeed welcoming, warm and soft, pleasantly pliant but not doughy. "Nice to meet you. I'm Joyce."

"Sorry to have kept you waiting," he apologized.

"No worries, you're not late. I only arrived a few minutes ago myself."

Quite certain that was untrue, Marcus appreciated the grace period extended in his favor. He rested his crutch against the wall and proceeded to unfasten his coat before Joyce uttered a halting, "Uh oh."

He froze. "What's wrong?"

"I'm sorry, Alexander. I don't think this is going to work out," she said with a frown.

"But I just got here." He hadn't even had the chance to sit down, let alone say or do anything to screw things up. Yet. He followed her gaze aimed at his shirt. "What?"

"You're a Radiohead fan?"

"What's wrong with Radiohead?"

"Nothing, if you're into the most overrated band of all time."

He guffawed at the audacity. "Care to back up your absurdly misguided theory?"

"I mean, they're not bad, I just wouldn't say they're all that good. Sure, 'Creep' was a huge hit, but their songs are so dark and morose. Not exactly a party bus playlist. And what the heck's up with the glockenspiel?"

He pulled out a chair and planted his butt in it. "Artists from Mozart to Jimi Hendrix have used the glockenspiel, you know, including Springsteen and a little quartet you might've heard of called... The Beatles?"

Joyce sneered. "Ah, now I get why you're into Radiohead. You're a pompous music snob."

"Actually, I'm a *professional* music snob," said Marcus self-righteously. "I'm a critic."

She rolled her eyes. "Everyone's a critic."

"No, I mean, I'm a music critic. People actually pay me for my pompous opinion."

"That doesn't make it better than anyone else's. I mean, people pay me for cuddling, but my hugs are probably no better than that guy's." She pointed out the jacked barista behind the counter with arms the size of honey-glazed hams and a bushel of facial hair that resembled those bee beard wackos who wear live swarms from nose to neck.

"I'll take my chances." Marcus turned back as a server approached the table to ask if he'd also like a peppermint mocha latte. He sized up the frappa-mocha-choca-lata-ya-ya-whatever in Joyce's ridiculously enormous mug and shook his head. Definitely not. He ordered a regular coffee, black. "Are you always like this with new clients?"

"Like this? No," she admitted. "But I could tell that you were skittish and ready to bolt. I wanted you to engage with me so that you'd sit down and stay."

He chuckled as he shook his head. "Ahh, so that ruse was your idea of an icebreaker."

"Once you get to know me, I think you'll see I'm actually a pretty nice person. And, full disclosure, I appreciate all types of music – even Radiohead." Joyce continued with a sly smile. "So, Alexander, what made you decide to give cuddling a try and hire me?"

"Actually, I didn't. A... uh, friend of mine heard about your agency and insisted on buying me this session as a Christmas gift. I really didn't think it was legit." He cleared his throat, hoping to dislodge the size-twelve boot he just crammed into it. "Sorry, no offense."

"None taken, and yes, it's definitely legit." Joyce smiled. "We're hardwired to be touched and hugged, and when that need is denied or we don't have a way to satisfy it, we suffer. The way I see it, I'm providing a safe space for people to get what they've been missing." She used both hands to hoist the hefty mug to her lips. "Are you comfortable with me coming to your place on Christmas Eve? I prefer outcalls."

With Fiona constantly hanging around the loft, it would not only be awkward, but it'd also be downright impossible to relax. Maybe she'd be willing to bugger off for a few hours. After all, she had a stake in making sure this thing wasn't a total disaster. "Should be okay. I have a roommate, but they'll make themselves scarce. Do you mind if I ask how your sessions work? I mean, do I have to talk? I'm not a big talker."

"Some clients like a little conversation, some enjoy the silence, most do a little of both and we just go with the flow."

"Can we put on music?"

"Of course. Music, TV. We can even watch a movie or play cards if you'd like."

He slowly sipped his coffee, wondering why such a perfectly lovely, seemingly normal person would want to be a professional cuddler. Why would anyone choose to hug total strangers for a living? Then again, what kind of loser had to rent someone to hug?

"So, how long have you been doing this?" he asked.

"Just over a year," she replied.

"And snuggling with strangers was merely a side gig for you before that?"

Her laugh twinkled like the lights surrounding them. "You're funny, Alexander. No, I didn't become trained and certified in the ways of the Cuddle Sutra until I got laid off at my old job."

"Sorry to hear. What kind of work did you do?"

"Remember Tandy's department store? I worked in the grand old dame's mail-order business until it finally fell to the online juggernauts." She heaved a melancholy sigh. "Tandy's was such a magical place during the holidays. Spectacular window displays filled with toys and candy, giant tinsel-covered trees glittering at the foot of the escalators. My favorite part was that my grandfather played the best and most beloved Santa that the store ever had. Adoring children would crowd the aisles waiting to catch a glimpse of him. Of course, it took me years before I figured out that it wasn't the real McCoy under that red suit. That's how good he--" Joyce clapped a hand over her mouth, interrupting the flow of sugar-sprinkled nostalgia. "Sorry, I got carried away, didn't I?"

"I hadn't noticed." He'd been surprisingly enthralled by her sentimental story. "Alas, I don't have the same fondness for the holidays as you do."

"I should've guessed by your grimace when you walked in that you're not a Christmas person."

He smirked. "That obvious?"

"Just a tad Grinchy," she said, pinching her thumb and forefinger together.

"That's me, a tad Grinchy. Will that be a deal breaker?"

"Not at all, I love a good challenge. Did you read the rules the agency sent over?"

"I did. Rule number one, when it comes to touch, ask first or simply don't do it."

Joyce nodded. "Consent and respect are essential, so let's agree to communicate if anything makes us uncomfortable," she said, hugging her mug. "Oh, and one more thing. For both our protection, the agency will know precisely when and where we meet, so if I don't check in and clock out on time, the police will politely bust down your door with a battering ram."

His hand shot up in scout's honor. "I swear, I'm not a creep. Or a weirdo."

She mirrored the gesture, giggling at his Radiohead reference. "I swear, I'm not a creep either. And I'm only a weirdo on weekends."

Their hands dropped on the table at the same time. "So that's it? You don't need to know anything more about me?" Marcus asked, hoping she wouldn't pry further.

"Nothing beyond what you want to disclose, Mr. Alexander Nevermind. Or do you like Alex instead? Or maybe you prefer I call you the Artist Formerly Known as Alexander?"

He was impressed as hell. "You know who Alexander Nevermind is?"

"Of course." She smiled. "It's one of the aliases Prince used when he wrote songs for other artists. You could've also picked Jamie Starr or Joey Coco for that matter."

Now he was gobsmacked and grinning like a fool. This girl knew her stuff. "Alex is fine."

He instantly regretted the snap decision to continue under false pretenses. Admittedly, this unusual girl had piqued his interest. Joyce had a sparkle to her – perky without being utterly nauseating. She'd instantly put him at ease and had even caused him to crack a smile or two. Maybe allowing this stranger to spoon him wasn't completely ludicrous.

"Actually," he said, lowering his guard a bit more, "I guess it's okay if you want to call me Marcus."

Chapter Two

Like a Volkswagen trapped beneath a snapped tree limb, Joyce lay motionless under the weighty forearm draped across her body. Graeme's breathing had deepened to a slow, steady rhythm before falling into the telltale buzz of his throaty snore. He'd drifted off. After watching the wall clock's second hand complete three more sweeps, she raked her fingertips through his coarse arm hair and reached down to give his plump fingers a gentle squeeze.

"I'm afraid that's our time," she whispered.

"Huh?" Graeme startled, his heavy eyelids blinking away the last remnants of his cat nap. "Already? That went by so fast." Drowsily, he pried his head off her shoulder and rolled away, a rush of coolness filling the warm, damp void where their bodies were pressed together. He yawned and stretched. "Marvelous, Joyce. That was exactly what I needed."

She smiled with satisfaction. "Glad to hear it. It's important that you take care of yourself this season. A lot of people are counting on you."

"You're preaching to the choir," he said, his shiny eyes crinkling at the corners. "If you'll pardon the expression."

Still chuckling, she swung her legs over the side of the bed. "Good one, Father."

The opposite side of the mattress dipped and then sprang up as he planted his feet on the floor. "Could I book another session with you before Epiphany?"

Joyce instinctively reached for her phone to check her schedule before being hit with a sobering reminder why her calendar was wide open. "I'm sorry, Father... I forgot," she said, trying to keep her voice from quivering, "today is our final session."

His smile slipped away. "Oh dear, I did too. Are you sure you won't reconsider? Maybe do a little freelance work on the side?"

"If I do, you'll be the first to know."

"Well then, how about staying for another cup of tea and a slice of fruitcake? I promise it's not one of those dreadful, petrified doorstops. This was made for me by a parishioner."

"Very tempting, but I have an appointment with a first-timer." She pulled both slouchy socks higher over her leggings, stalling as she waited for Graeme to leave the room. The moment he was out of sight, she unzipped her backpack and removed the Advent-purple cable knit mittens she'd specially made to fit his extra-large hands. After tucking the surprise beneath his pillow, she slung her bag over one shoulder and followed him out to the kitchen.

"But I thought you said you're no longer taking appointments. How did a first-timer manage to slip one past the goalie?"

"Um, that phrase doesn't mean quite what you think, Father." She flushed with embarrassment. "It's slang for impregnating someone while using birth control."

"Oh, I see." He chuckled to himself. "I've never heard that before. Might make a good set-up joke for my immaculate conception sermon." He refilled the tea kettle and moved it over the blue flame on the stove. "So, this first-timer's your last client, hmm?"

"He's paid for a full session and to be honest, I think he may need every minute of it." She shrugged. "It is Christmas Eve, after all."

"Ah, yes, the Super Bowl for priests and professional cuddlers. No one understands better than we do how triggering the holidays can be. You do holy work in bringing comfort to others, Joyce, and I speak from experience as a solitary fellow in an isolating profession."

"No matter the collar we wear, we all crave connection." She smiled reassuringly, pulling on her woolly hat with the wobbly pom-pom before lifting her coat off the back of a chair. "The agency will be in touch with the names of recommended cuddlers to take my place."

"No one can replace you in my books." Father Graeme handed her a chunk of fruitcake in wax paper, then wrapped his big bear arms around her. They embraced in the doorway. "If the spirit moves you, you're welcome to join us at Mass tonight. The children's choir will be singing carols, and we've wrangled two donkeys, a goat, and an alpaca for the live nativity scene."

"Thank you, Father, I'll keep that in mind. Merry Christmas."

"Merry Christmas, my dear Joyce. God bless."

As Joyce departed the church rectory at St. Bart's, she left a sliver of her heart behind. A symptom of a gentle soul doing tender work. Holding back tears as she trudged through the fresh snow, she thought about Father Graeme and the other regulars she would dearly miss. Like Evelyn, the fragile divorcee navigating life alone for the first time. There was also Pascal, the insomniac struggling to come to terms with his sexual identity, and Ajay, the gregarious and wildly imaginative adventurer confined by spina bifida. Each of them had brought something unique and wonderful to her life, and their connection ran deeper than mere client and cuddler. To Joyce, they were friends, and friends were worth giving her all, along with giving extra time off the clock, giving out her phone number, and yes, even giving hand-knit Christmas gifts.

"Forms unhealthy relationships," her supervisor jotted on her annual performance review, berating Joyce for bucking the agency's commandment to remain emotionally distant from her clients. "We have strict rules, and for everyone's sake, you must adhere to those set boundaries."

Things went downhill from there, with her supervisor implying that Joyce had only taken the job to fill a void.

"Perhaps you're lonely. Or maybe you're lacking in intimacy in other areas of your life," she said. "Have you tried dating? It might be helpful to divert some of your extra time and energy to a romantic relationship instead."

Joyce thought it was a joke, except that when she laughed, her supervisor remained stony, dug in her heels, and presented an ultimatum: either

Joyce detach from her clients, or she could find a new line of work after Christmas.

As much as it hurt to move on and allow her friends to move on without her, Joyce began to accept that she wasn't cut out for cuddling. Just like she wasn't fit to be a foster dog mom, since she could never surrender the furry charges that the mutt rescue service placed in her temporary care. Now she owned not one, not two, but three scrappy mongrels. Maybe her supervisor was right. Maybe she was lonely and guilty of being too invested in the lives of those she held in her arms. Maybe she didn't only wear her heart on her sleeve, but on her entire coat.

But if anyone honestly believed her worst fault was having too much love to give, then let them eat fruitcake.

Chapter Three

"Please? I promise I'll be as quiet as a fart at a funeral," Fiona pleaded. "You won't even know I'm here."

"Believe me, I'll know." Marcus flung a pillow on the bed, and it landed with a *whomp*. "Even when you're not here, you're here because you never go away. You're like herpes. Or Taylor Swift."

"Haters gonna hate!" She crossed her arms in a huff. "Why do I have to leave? I'm the one who gave you this gift."

"And I'm asking for some privacy to make the most of it. Surely there's something else you can do to keep busy. Maybe find a miserly old cuss you could teach the true meaning of Christmas to?"

"I'm looking at him." Fiona scowled. "All right, fine, I'll go. But I want to hear all the juicy details afterwards."

"It's not a date, Fee, it's a therapy session. There won't be any juicy details."

"That's what you think," she scoffed. "By the way, for someone who had to be pushed into doing this, you're awfully eager to make a good impression on this girl. You brushed your teeth in the middle of the day, washed the dishes, and you even made your bed, which happens about as often as a total solar eclip--"

BZZZZZT!

His head swiveled toward the door buzzer. "Great, now the cuddler is down there and you're still up here. Would you please get lost already?" Marcus limped to the door, pressing the call button and bowing to the speaker. "Hello?"

"Hey, it's me, Joyce."

"Hi, come on up." He buzzed her in, and by the time he turned around, Fiona was gone.

Joyce's shoulders and backpack were covered in snow, tiny flecks of ice stuck to her eyelashes and rosy cheeks.

"Guess what? It's still snowing," she laughed, grabbing her hat by its grapefruit-sized pom-pom and shaking off the outdoors before stepping inside. "Big, fat Charlie Brown flakes."

"So I see." He smiled as tufts of the white stuff fell around her feet. "Did you leave any of it outside?"

She bent down to unlace her hiking boots. "I only live a few blocks from here, so I walked over after I let my dogs out between appointments. Do you have any pets, Marcus?"

"Uh no. The only beast around here is my pesky roommate," he joked. Joyce shed her outerwear and it didn't occur to him to offer to take her coat until she asked where she could hang it. Rarely did he entertain, and his hosting manners suffered because of it.

She vigorously rubbed her hands over her arms to warm up as she admired the loft. "This is such a cool space. Could maybe use a Christmas tree, but otherwise, it's great."

"It was an abandoned warehouse," he said, draping her wet coat over a wall hook. "I moved in here just before..." He bit his tongue. No reason to let his sob story dampen the first stimulating conversation he'd had with a woman since 2018. Joyce's presence had already brought a warmth to the loft. And to him. He kinda liked it. And her. But it wasn't like this was a date or anything. After all, they were only climbing into bed together.

Joyce swiveled to face him. "...just before?"

"Before the market boomed and prices in this area went through the roof," Marcus rallied. "Got lucky, I guess."

"Very lucky, I'd say." She ran her hand along the back of the couch as she gazed out the floor-to-ceiling windows, the ledges catching the sticky snow piling up. "I could probably fit three of my studio apartments into one of yours."

"Can I offer you something to drink? You'll be disappointed to hear that I'm fresh out of mulled wine and eggnog, but I've got some India pale ale. I also have water and orange juice, or I could make us coffee."

"Actually I'd prefer tea if it's not too much trouble. Herbal, if you have."

He rummaged around for the ancient box of English Breakfast buried in the back of the cupboard where forgotten condiments went to die. Nope. Turned out it was Earl Grey, and he held it out for Joyce's inspection. "Will this do?"

Her lips puckered. "I brought some orange rooibos with me. It's soothing and it doesn't have the jittery effect of black tea. Want to give it a try?"

Marcus shrugged a *why not* and she went to retrieve her backpack.

"I like to carry a few provisions, should emergency relaxation be required," she called out. "Herbal tea, scented candles, peppermint oil, and extra t-shirts."

"Extra t-shirts?"

"I've learned from experience to carry a few spares in case a client cries on my shoulder," she explained. "It happens."

Geez, is that what the cuddling experience typically brought out in people? Would it reduce him to a puddly mess too? "Hopefully, you won't be needing those today."

She dug through her bag and produced the tea. "I've also downloaded a couple of chill playlists in case you're interested."

"One thing I definitely have covered is the music," he said, pointing out his massive vinyl collection along the back wall. Her eyes widened like a kid let loose in a 99-cent store with a crisp new twenty.

"Oh, wow." She dropped the tea on the counter and made a beeline for the stacks. "Marcus! You must have a couple thousand LPs here."

"Three thousand, four hundred and sixty-two to be precise," he answered proudly before turning his attention back to making tea. "Go ahead and put something on. Whatever you like."

While Joyce was deeply engrossed in perusing, Marcus couldn't resist covertly checking her out. A baby blue cardigan and a long t-shirt modestly covered most of her, but even multiple layers couldn't completely disguise her soft, feminine outline, nor the nicely-shaped legs her violet leggings revealed. The thick socks pooling at her ankles matched her sweater, an adorable ensemble that made her altogether huggable. He, on the other hand, looked like a rumpled hobo people would cross the street to avoid. At least he managed to put on clean sweatpants to go with his distressed Alice in Chains tee, a step up from his usual practice of picking something straight off the floor.

Marcus planted two mugs of tea on the coffee table. Between the couch and the bed, the couch seemed the safest option, and being a gentleman, he didn't dare presume Joyce would want to get horizontal right off the hop. Hell, he wasn't all that eager to get there either. As he got situated, his ears tuned in to the crackle of a turntable needle nestling into vinyl grooves. What did she choose? Bob Marley? Bon Iver? She did claim to know her music, but it remained to be seen if her taste lived up to the hy--

Wait a minute, was that... James Taylor?

"Nice," he marveled, "unexpectedly nice." She had over three thousand LPs to choose from but somehow managed the perfect mellow pick. *"Sweet Baby James."*

"It's a real mood, isn't it? You can't help but love JT's button-down denim, Americana sound."

"Not many people know this about me, but I've got a soft spot for old-school folk rock."

She beamed, shrugging off her sweater. "Me too. I love this laidback, early seventies groove. I've always said I was born in the wrong decade." She plopped on the couch and proceeded to peel back a layer of crinkly paper from the dark, boozy brick in her hand before holding it out to him. "Fruitcake?"

He grimaced. "Uh, no thanks, never been a fan. But you go ahead."

"I love fruitcake. It tastes like Christmas," she said. He had to agree, recalling past family gatherings soaked in alcohol and filled with nuts. Joyce popped a mummified morsel into her mouth before wrapping up the rest. "That should keep the tummy-rumbling at bay for a while."

"I can order up some food for us if you're hungry."

"Thank you, but I'm all right for now. Maybe later."

She sat back and they sipped their tea, listening to the album in silence for a bit. "How are you feeling, Marcus? Are you comfortable?" she asked softly. He nodded. "Good. Let me know when you're ready to begin."

"Uh, I guess we can start now," he said, resting his mug on the table. "What do you want me to do first?"

She placed her mug next to his and scooched closer. "Well, I find a hug is always a good place to start. Would that be okay?"

"Sure."

She opened her arms. He reciprocated and they leaned into one another to embrace. It was pretty nice. Well, okay, it was all right. Frankly, it was kinda awkward given they were both seated, forcing their elbows to pretzel and kneecaps to crunch together. He silently counted five Mississippis as if holding his breath underwater, barely making it to five before suffocating. He pulled back first.

She seemed to pick up on his uneasiness. "This might work better if we stood up," she suggested. "Let's try that instead."

Joyce was already upright by the time Marcus got to his feet. Even at her full height, the little thing barely reached his shoulder, so he didn't get how this position would be any better, until—oh.

Okay, that was new.

She wrapped her arms snugly around his midsection and molded herself to his body, filling the gaps between them to fit everywhere. His arms went around her shoulders, pulling her in closer. She nestled against his chest as naturally as if they'd been holding one another for years.

Marcus closed his eyes. A warm push of oxytocin flowed through his veins and contentment swept over him like a summer breeze. His nerves subsided. His mind stilled. Even his breathing slowed.

In their embrace, the slightest movement was reminiscent of swaying to music, dancing together until the record nearly reached the end of the first side. This time, he was reluctant to let go first, so he didn't, until Joyce looked up at him.

"How was that?"

"Good. Really good," he said, unable to stop from smiling. "It was amazing, actually."

"What say we give the couch another try but in a different position?"

He followed Joyce's lead, watching as she propped herself against the opposite arm of the couch, feet up and splayed apart.

"It's just like floating in a boat," she said, patting the cushions in invitation for him to recline in the void created between her bent knees. Marcus slid into place and lay back in her arms with his legs outstretched. "Deep breath in..." she whispered soothingly, "and slowly release." He closed his eyes, his head lolling back against her shoulder. "That's it. Just like we're floating in a boat."

Fully relaxed, he sailed away on a river of serenity. Floating, buoyant, weightless.

But then his imagination began drifting to other water bodies. Like being submerged naked in a milky bath between Joyce's lush thighs, his head resting on her sublime, champagne glass breasts bobbing just above the surface. And... oops! Up popped the weasel.

Marcus tugged his t-shirt down to cover the source of his embarrassment, immediately regretting the decision to wear loose sweatpants. "Shit, I'm sorry. I'm not finding this relaxing. Just the opposite, I'm afraid."

Her cheeks flared pink as she diplomatically danced around his dilemma. "Oh, hey, don't worry about it. It happens."

But he felt skeevy and sleazy. Skeezy. Here she was being so tender and sweet, and he could've pounded nails with the ball-peen protrusion in his pants. "I-I'm sorry, I haven't been this close to an attractive woman for a while, I guess."

"Don't feel bad. Arousal is a perfectly natural physiological response to intimacy," she said, reciting the words like they'd been memorized from the cuddler's guidebook. "We'll change positions and continue. Ignore it and it'll go away on its own."

Ignore it? She obviously had no idea how the little master had a mind of its own. "Um, sure, let's try something different."

Joyce sat up and put her arm around his back, inviting him to nestle his head in the crook of her neck. Bringing his arm around her waist, they snuggled deeper into the couch and propped their feet up on the table next to each other. Her fingers fluttered over his shoulder, her other hand tenderly stroking over his arm, up and down, before completing the circuit over again. Gradually relaxing, Marcus felt the tension leave his body and gave in to enjoying a wonderfully tender massage he didn't know he'd been missing.

"How's that feel?"

"That's nice," he said, yielding to the gently rippling sensations. "Where did you learn to do this?"

"I told you, I'm certified in the ways of the Cuddle Sutra," she kidded.

"You have magic hands, Joyce. Your boyfriend is a lucky guy, er... or your girlfriend. She'd be lucky too, of course. I mean, well, you know--"

"It's okay," she said, poking a hole in the ballooning awkwardness. "I'm a solo act. A table for one. A single occupant. There isn't anyone in my life right now except Barry, Robin, and Maurice."

Marcus chuckled. "The Bee Gees?"

"My dogs," she said, laughter rumbling in her chest. "What about you? No one special in the picture?"

"Uh, no, of course not. I wouldn't be doing this if I had a significant other."

"I've met a lot of clients who are in relationships, including married folks," she said, still stroking his arm. "The need for affection isn't always fulfilled by what we get from family and friends."

He knew that all too well. Growing up with an aloof mother and a neglectful business suit for a father, Marcus realized early on that his parents' affection was doled out only when earned or absolutely necessary, amounting to little more than a handshake or a pat on the head. As far back as he could remember, his only solace and source of comfort was music. And Fiona.

"Clients have told me this feels liberating because they're free to get what they need without judgement or having to give something in return. I think that's a universal truth regardless of relationship status."

Joyce was on to something. Being held close and caressed by her, Marcus felt a weight lifted. But there was more to it than that. It was a seismic shift, like the seal on his inner vault had been miraculously broken and was about to crack wide open.

"I haven't been in a serious relationship for a long time," he admitted. "My ex told me I have intimacy issues, but I think it's more like we weren't all that compatible. I don't know. They say there's a lid for every pot, but what if I'm not a pot? What if I'm an irregularly-shaped cast iron skillet without a lid?" He imagined his face flattened and round like a frying pan. "Ironic, because before she left, my ex called me the Tin Man. Cold, deflective, and heartless."

Joyce remained quiet, raking her fingertips up his arm. Marcus took her silence as encouragement to continue rambling.

"I know I'm standoffish. Fiona razzes me about coming off like an arrogant jerk, but I don't mean to. I don't want to. And it doesn't mean I don't want someone in my life again."

"Someday you'll find your lid, Marcus," she reassured him. "And by the way, the Tin Man happens to be my favorite *Oz* character. You know why? Because despite believing he's the most damaged, he's actually the one who feels and loves the deepest."

Marcus swallowed the lump clogging his throat and willed the swell of emotion from leaking out his tear ducts. *Dammit, man, you are not going to cry. You are not going to cry and make this woman change her shirt.* "That's very kind of you to say."

"Do you mind if I ask you a question?"

"Fire away," he replied, hoping that whatever it was, it veered away from weepy topics.

"Um... who's Fiona?"

Chapter Four

J oyce felt Marcus' pulse quicken.

"Wh-why do you ask?" he stammered.

"I'm sorry, I didn't mean to upset you. You mentioned someone named Fiona, so I thought... no, forget it. I promised that we wouldn't talk about anything you don't want to."

He moved away from her, clearly agitated. "If it's okay with you, I'd rather not."

"Of course." Joyce shifted to a new distraction and music seemed a safe default. "Why don't you put on a new record? It's your turn to pick. Maybe we can make a game out of it."

He nodded.

She went to the kitchen to refill their mugs while he pulled the next selection. "Don't make it easy. Or Nickelback."

"Ha!" he cackled from across the loft. "No, I have something in mind I think you'll enjoy."

"How'd you amass such a huge collection? Because you're a music critic?"

"The other way around. Music influenced my career choice," he called out. "I've been collecting LPs since I was a kid. Picked up a lot from vintage shops and hanging around radio stations when they were getting rid of records by the truckload. I can't tell you how many hours I've spent poring over bins of vinyls in record stores."

Joyce laughed. "I'm glad I'm not the only one who does that. I can't even walk by a yard sale without stopping in to browse through the records."

Marcus stopped his quest to glance her way. "Oh yeah? Just window shopping, or are you chasing a unicorn?"

"You're going to laugh."

"I won't, I promise," he said. "Tell me."

"I don't have a prayer of finding it, but I've been searching for the original 1957 pressing of Elvis' Christmas album on RCA Victor. It's limited edition with a ten-page booklet insert, but making it even more rare is the fact that it's--"

"...red vinyl!" Marcus chimed in at exactly the same time. Uncanny.

"You know it? Well, of course you do. Then you probably know that it's notoriously hard to find. In mint condition, it fetches more money than I make in a year."

"You never know. Someone might be sitting on a gold mine in their basement and it'll pop up at a flea market or something. It does happen."

"That's what I keep hoping," she said. "My grandfather... the one who was Tandy's department store Santa? He used to own a copy of it, believe it or not."

"Seriously?"

"He always played it around the holidays. I can still hear him crooning along with Elvis to 'Blue Christmas.'" The happy memory brought a smile to her face. "When I was little, he told me that the red vinyl was made out of cherry candy. Of course, I ate it up."

"Not literally, I hope."

She laughed. "No, although I did lick it once. Tasted like bitter disappointment."

"Sounds like your grandfather was quite a character."

"He was wise and funny and so generous. The sweetest man with the biggest heart. I miss him every day, but especially at this time of year."

"Okay, I'm ready to play the next record. Care to take a guess?"

"Hmm. Velvet Underground?"

He laughed. "No dice, but a great idea. Maybe later."

"Arcade Fire? Ray Lamontagne? Jamiroquai?"

"Wrong on all three counts. I'll give you one more."

Joyce drummed her fingers on her cheek and swung for the fences. "Elton John, *Captain Fantastic and the Brown Dirt Cowboy?*"

"No, but that's your closest guess yet. This is from the same era." Marcus focused on the turntable, gently lowering the stylus until it touched the record. A moment later, orchestral strings began to swell. "Figured it out yet?"

Clueless, she shrugged, so he showed her the album cover.

"The Carpenters' *Christmas Portrait*," he said. "'Tis the season, after all."

She was stunned as well as impressed. "Wow, Marcus... if I didn't know better, I'd think you might be coming around to liking the holidays."

"I still don't, but I know *you* do," he said.

He hobbled back to the couch, and she met him in front of it with the freshly-poured tea. "I'd like to try lying down in bed next to you while we listen to this," he said coyly, as if shy about even suggesting it. It was downright endearing. "If that would be all right?"

"It's more than all right," she affirmed, quite charmed by the lanky gent's soft-spoken request.

It might have been the crabby demeanor he used to hide his big ol' teddy bear heart that she found intriguing. Or maybe it was a combination of his intellect, his towering height, the scruffy shadow of his ginger-tinged beard, or his rather sexy crooked smile that was so alluring. Blame it on the music, the mood, or the magic of Christmas Eve, but she couldn't deny the spark. Their connection was quickly gaining momentum like a sled hurtling down the steep grade of attraction to desire.

No, no, no. It would be completely wrong to act on impulse. Marcus might have been the first man she'd strongly reacted to in recent memory, but she was still bound by a professional code of ethics until six o'clock. Better tamp those wayward feelings down. "I'd like that too," she said, trying to keep her tone appropriate.

They crossed the loft and climbed onto his bed. Side by side, they lay together, staring at the ceiling. She was careful not to make a sudden move that might cause him to change his mind. Instead, she inched her hand closer to his. When he didn't pull away, she gently nudged him into holding hands until he closed his fingers around hers and they were palm to palm. They both let out contented sighs as Karen Carpenter serenaded them.

"Her voice is so pure," Marcus said. "Angelic."

Joyce agreed. "I read that she had perfect pitch. She could record anything in one take without needing to re-dub."

He turned his head to look at her. "Can I just say how refreshing it is to meet someone who knows so much about music? Most of the women I've met don't realize there was anything decent to listen to before The Spice Girls."

"Hmph, *wannabes*," she teased.

He laughed and squeezed her hand. "You're really something, Joyce."

"You're really something too, Marcus. I'm glad I got a chance to meet you before..."

"Before...?"

"I wasn't going to mention it during our session, but you're the last client I have booked. Today's my final day at the agency."

"It is? But why? You're so good at this."

Her face flushed. "Thank you, that's sweet. I do love the work and I love the people I've met doing it, but I've been told I'm too much of a bleeding heart to be any good as a cuddler."

"I beg to differ. I find you genuinely caring and empathetic, and those qualities make you perfect for doing this," he said, squeezing her fingers again. "You made a believer out of me, and I'm made of hollow tin, remember?"

She smiled. "Just as well, I'll look for something new in January. It's the best time of year for a fresh start."

His chin pointed toward the ceiling again. "That's a shame, because I really think this is your calling. You have a way with people, Joyce. Even grumpy curmudgeons with a chip on their shoulder and an aversion to Christmas."

As much as she'd tried to push it away, something inside kept prodding and nudging her to invite Marcus out so that he wouldn't spend Christmas Eve alone. Yeah, it meant blurring the line between personal and professional once again, but what the heck. "Um, I'm getting together with some people in my block for a potluck tonight. Sort of a Friendsgiving meets The Island of Misfit Toys. The food's not fancy and the festivities aren't formal, but we do have a heck of a lot of fun. Anyway, I'd like to invite you to join us."

"While I appreciate the offer, that's not really my thin—"

He was interrupted by the record skipping during "Have Yourself a Merry Little Christmas." It got hung up on the line: "All our troubles will be out of sight... out of sight... out of sight... out of sight..."

"It sounds like she's singing 'outasight,' as in, all our troubles will be *outasight!*" Joyce giggled. "Everything's gonna be cool, baby. Groovy, dynamite, get down!"

Marcus laughed too, and suddenly the record righted itself from the rut. "I think I like your version better."

She continued. "If you change your mind about the potluck, the address is 505 Herald Street. It's easy to remember, like 'Hark the Herald Angels Sing.' Anyway, like I said, zero pressure or obligation, but I'd love it if you came. The more the merrier."

"I know you don't believe me, Joyce, but I swear, I'm not a Christmas person and I really don't enjoy making awkward small talk at parties. I would much rather just stay heee—"

The record skipped a second time. "If the fates al-low... al-low... al-low..."

He started to get up, but she wrapped her hand around his forearm. "Just give it a sec. It might fix itself again." And then it did, so he settled back down once more. "Why don't we try lying on our sides for a while?"

Marcus turned over and assumed the little spoon position. Joyce curled up behind him, arms wrapped around his body, knees tucked behind his knees, stomach pressed to his back. He intertwined their fingers and held her hand snugly against his heart. She caressed his feet with her toes, aware of his slowed breathing. It was the closest he'd allowed her to get and the most intimate they'd been, and she felt him melting into her embrace with every passing moment.

"Joyce? I... I want to tell you something," he finally said, "but it's not easy for me to talk about."

"Take your time," she said, resting her cheek on the back of his warm neck, their breaths falling into a slow, steady rhythm. "Whenever you're ready."

Another song and a half went by before he broke his silence.

"I suffered a hemorrhagic stroke. Doctors say that kind is uncommon for someone under forty-five, but I guess I was one of the lucky ones," he said, his voice shaky. "That's why I use the crutch. I never regained full mobility on one side."

She was grateful he felt safe enough to open up. "Thank you for sharing that with me."

"Um, wait, there's more." Emotion caused his voice to crack. "The day I had the stroke, it... I mean, I was... it happened just when..."

"It's okay, Marcus. Whatever it is, it's all right, I promise," she reassured him, trying to soothe away his anxiety. "Deep breath in, hold it for three seconds. Okay, now gradually let it out."

He exhaled, releasing a long, shuddery breath. "The stroke happened while I was driving, and I blacked out behind the wheel. My car, it... it went off the road and over an embankment. Somehow, I survived, b-but I wasn't alone when the accident happened." He gulped and she gripped him tighter. "My sister died in the car I was driving. I killed Fiona."

The grief spilled out of Marcus in sobs.

Joyce comforted him as best she could as tears rolled down her own cheeks. She tightened her hold around him, rocking his body. "I'm so sorry, Marcus," she whispered. Her heart ached for his. "If you feel up to it, I'd love to hear about your sister. What was she like?"

"Fiona?" He sniffed. "She was brilliant. Beautiful. My best friend. Total drama queen but wore that crown with pride. Always the best dressed one in the room. Liked animals more than people. She also loved banana milkshakes, anything that ended with a cliffhanger, reading tabloid headlines aloud while in line at the supermarket, and dating tortured artists. Not necessarily in that order," he said, laughter tickling his voice. "But above all, Fiona was, without a doubt, the biggest pain in the ass you'd ever meet."

A startling crash in the kitchen shattered the moment, bolting them both upright in bed. A plate had fallen off the counter, smashing to pieces.

"How did that happen?" Joyce gasped.

Marcus' expression changed from shock to dismay, before turning angry. "Seriously? That was a perfectly good plate!" he huffed, staring at the pile of porcelain. "What the hell's your problem now?!"

Chapter Five

"Apain in the ass? That's the thanks I get?" Fiona stomped on the broken shards.

"What are you doing back here?" Marcus barked. "I thought you vanished!"

"I lied. I've been in stealth mode. You think it's merely a coincidence that the record started skipping?"

"Marcus, w-who are you talking to?" Joyce's voice quivered. "Who's going to vanish?"

"Uh... um, no one," he said, doing a poor job of sounding calm and reassuring. "Sorry, I tend to talk out loud to myself sometimes. Bad habit."

Fiona leaned on the counter and, with the tip of her index finger, nudged a drinking glass to the edge and let it wobble precariously.

"Don't you dare!" Marcus fumed. "I mean it!"

With a mischievous wink and a quick tap, she sent it sailing over the side. *Smash!*

Joyce shrieked, leaping off the mattress. "Marcus! That glass jumped off the counter! Are we having an earthquake? Hurry! We have to get out NOW!"

Fiona cackled. "Earthquake? Ha! When was the last time a woman felt the earth move in your bed?"

As much as he wanted to tell Fiona off, he had to get Joyce to calm down first. "Please don't be scared. The ground's not shaking and the building's not about to collapse, I promise."

"Then how do you explain that?" She pointed a trembling finger at the shattered pile on the kitchen floor.

"I think I can, but you'd better sit down first," he said. "Please."

Warily, she perched on the edge of the bed. Her frightened face was both pale and flushed, likely a symptom of being torn between fight or flight. This was going to take some finesse.

"I know this will sound crazy, but that commotion was only Fiona."

"Fiona... you mean, your sister?"

"She's here, and she's pissed at me about something."

Joyce's eyes darted around the loft. "But I thought you said that she was..." Fiona chose that very moment to pick up a teaspoon and wiggle it loosely between her fingers.

Joyce screamed and fainted backwards with a flop.

Marcus scrambled to his feet. "Fee! Cripes, stop terrorizing her, will ya? She's done nothing to you!"

"What good is being a ghost if you can't be a little naughty now and then?"

He leaned over Joyce's limp body, patting her cheek to resuscitate her. "Joyce? Please wake up. It's okay."

Fiona shrugged. "Aren't you supposed to splash cold water on her or something?"

He went into the kitchen, sidestepping the broken glass. "You'd better clean that up," he barked, turning on the tap and filling a cup.

"Or what?" she taunted.

By the time he returned to her bedside, Joyce was starting to come around. "Uh... what happened?" she moaned, holding her head.

"You fainted." He held out the water. "Here, drink this."

She propped herself up on an elbow and slugged back a gulp. "I was hallucinating. I swear I saw a spoon floating by."

"You weren't hallucinating," Marcus said, taking a deep breath. "Remember I told you I had a roommate? Well, it's Fiona."

"B-but you said that Fiona died."

He nodded, cautiously gauging her reaction. "When I woke up from the coma after the accident, the nurses told me Fiona didn't make it. But I didn't believe them because I could plainly see her at the foot of my ICU bed. And she's been living with me every day since."

Joyce was still and expressionless. "Living with you? You mean, like, in spirit?"

"Well, yeah, but it's more than that. I can see and hear Fiona as clearly as I can see and hear you."

Joyce blinked slowly as she scanned the room. "Where is she? I don't see her."

"Fiona," Marcus commanded, "do something to show Joyce you're here with us."

Silence. Crickets.

An uncomfortable chuckle escaped him. "Cut it out, Fee. You're just trying to make me look bad, not to mention certifiably insane. Show yourself."

Fiona crossed her arms and shook her head. "No can do, bro. You said not to scare the poor girl."

"Come on, Fiona! We're waiting!"

"I'm not a trained circus poodle that dances when you snap your fingers!"

Embarrassed, he turned to Joyce. "I'm sorry, she's being a diva right now. Like I said, she's a real pain in the--"

Suddenly, the lights turned off and on. Fiona scowled as she fidgeted with the wall switch. "There, happy now?"

"Yes, thank you," Marcus said.

"That was your sister?" Joyce asked. He nodded. "But why is she haunting you?"

He shrugged. "I don't know. I've tried everything, but I can't get rid of her."

Fiona hopped up on the counter and crossed her arms. "Tell Joyce that I'm responsible for bringing her here."

Marcus relayed the message. "My sister just told me to tell you that she deserves the credit for bringing you here. She was the one who suggested I give cuddling a try."

"I did more than suggest it. I made it all happen, remember? I was the one who picked Joyce out to be your cuddle buddy."

"Okay, okay," he said on a gust of breath. "Fiona says she made it all happen and that she picked you out for me."

Fiona continued to prod him. "Now tell her why."

"No," he said.

"Tell her, Marcus! Or God help me, I'll break every single one of your soup bowls and you'll have to slurp chowder out of the palm of your hand."

He sighed. "Fine. Fiona thought hiring you would help me come out of the shell I've been living in since the accident."

"...and that you're a sad sack living a hollow existence because you're missing out on the joys of having a genuine connection with someone."

"She says I've been missing a conn—no, you know what, Fiona? This is too messed up." He grimaced. "I refuse to be the Whoopi Goldberg to your Patrick Swayze!"

Joyce sprang up from the bed and immediately started gathering her things. "I can't explain the broken dishes or the flickering lights, but to believe it was your sister's ghost? That's pretty out there, Marcus. Maybe we got a bad batch of rooibos infused with mind-altering herbs."

"Believe me, I wish it was the tea. I was convinced she was a side effect of the trauma or a psychosomatic condition, but no amount of brain scans or visits to a shrink can explain Fiona."

Joyce jammed her arms into her sweater and swung her backpack over her shoulder. "I'll tell the agency that I got sick and to refund your session in full."

"No, wait," Marcus called out, "please don't go..." He watched her yank on her unlaced boots, clomping to retrieve her coat before reaching for the door handle. "Dammit, Fiona! This is all your fault! Do something!"

"Tell Joyce that her grandfather's here!" Fiona panicked. "Quick! Tell her Boppa Joe has something he wants to say to his Doodlebug!"

As Joyce was on the verge of leaving, Marcus hollered the nonsensical phrase at her back. She froze in her tracks and slowly turned around.

"B-Boppa Joe?"

"Your grandfather, yes. He's here with Fiona."

Joyce's eyes narrowed. "Did I tell you I called him Boppa? Or that he used to call me...?"

"Doodlebug?" Marcus restated. "No, you didn't. I've never heard either of those words in my life."

Her glassy eyes welled up until a single tear spilled out. She sniffed the rest away and wiped her cheek. "I'm sorry Marcus, but this is beyond me. You need some real help."

An empty sadness burned the back of Marcus' throat as he helplessly watched the door close behind her. "You just had to come back and wreck everything, didn't you?" he croaked. "Things were going great with Joyce. We were connecting. We shared a real moment there."

"That's precisely why I needed to intervene," Fiona said, pointing to the door. "You were completely blowing it. That girl invited you to a party tonight. A par-tayy, for Pete's sake!"

"I hate parties."

"But you like Joyce, don't you? You said yourself that she's refreshing, and I saw you give her the once-over at least three or four times. So why wouldn't you jump at the chance to get to know her better?"

"I—I don't know."

"Listen, dork, I'm proud of the way you opened up to Joyce. You let yourself be vulnerable and spoke from the heart without sounding like a complete tool. But for the millionth time, you are not to blame for the accident, so stop punishing yourself by wallowing in your misery. It's a real downer during pillow talk."

"Geez, sorry if my personal anguish is such a turn off. But it doesn't matter anyway. Joyce's interest in me is purely professional, nothing more."

"Ugh, men! Why are you so dense?" Fiona rolled her eyes. "She likes you."

"She does?"

"There's no accounting for taste, but yeah, she likes you. If she didn't, why would she invite you out? It's not like she had to. She's not being paid to babysit you after six p.m."

He hadn't thought of it like that. "Maybe she was only being nice."

"Sound the alarm! Pull up the drawbridge! Man the fortress! A woman was being nice to you!" She scoffed. "Guess what? Joyce *is* nice.

She's also cute AF, not to mention sweet and affectionate. She gives you an intellectual boner when she talks music, and sees right through your grumpy-ass bullshit. Brother, I'd say you just met your match and let her walk out the door."

Marcus slumped on the couch and stared at the frosty scene outside the window, the snow still falling in hefty clumps. *Charlie Brown flakes*, Joyce called them. Even that was freakin' adorable. He pictured her standing at the door shivering and dusted in the white stuff, and yet there wasn't a hint of discomfort on her shiny face. Seriously, who does that? Who visits complete strangers in the middle of a snowstorm to deliver armfuls of comfort and stays to soothe them while they spill their guts? Who?

Fiona ran her fingers through his rumpled hair until his eyelids grew heavy and he began to drift off.

"What am I going to do with you, hmm? I threw you the easiest pass for a touchdown and you still fumbled the ball at the goal line." She sighed. "You're hopeless, darling. I love you to bits, but you're completely hopeless."

Chapter Six

"Slow down! Where are you taking me?" Father Graeme bellowed as Joyce hauled him down the street like a tugboat towing a barge. "You said this was a life-or-death situation. That's the only reason I agreed to leave the church with four hundred people coming to witness a live nativity scene in ninety minutes!" he wheezed. "For the love of Jude, tell me what's going on!"

Snow pelted her face, blinding her as they rounded the corner. "Forgive me, Father, for I have schemed. I didn't know who else to turn to." She yanked him into the entrance of the brick-faced building and hammered her mitten on the door buzzer.

No answer.

She smashed it repeatedly until Marcus finally responded.

"If this is carollers, you can shove off," he snarled.

"Marcus, wait! It's me! Joyce!" she shouted into the speaker. "I brought help!"

"...Joyce?" he echoed. "What do you mean? Help for what?"

"We're freezing down here, Marcus! Just let us in. Please!"

The buzzer sounded and seconds later, she was yanking Graeme through the vestibule and into the elevator.

"Joyce, you know I think the world of you, but I don't have time for shenanigans," he gasped, trying to catch his breath. "If you don't explain what's going on—"

"An exorcism!" she blurted as the doors closed them inside the elevator car. She jammed her finger on the fourth-floor button. "I need you to perform an exorcism tonight."

"B-but I don't... I mean, I've never..."

"Didn't they teach you in seminary college how to cast out spirits?"

"It's a little above my pay grade," he choked. "That kind of thing is usually reserved for an archbishop. Besides, I—I don't have the proper doctrine or even a Bible with me. One should never face an evil adversary unprepared."

"This one's not evil, she's just a pain in the ass. Pardon my French," she repented. "She's Marcus' dead sister and she refuses to leave his apartment!"

Graeme stared blankly. "Who's Marcus?"

"He's the first-timer I had booked after leaving your place," she explained. "He's a bit grumpy until you get to know him, but once you do, you'll see how sweet and funny and clever and kind-hearted he really is." The elevator doors slid apart, and Joyce jerked Graeme out by the sleeve to drag him down the corridor. "But he's got a big problem. And her name is Fiona."

Marcus stood waiting for them at the end of the hall, leaning on his crutch with a crooked smile. "You came back."

"With reinforcements." She nodded. "This is Father Graeme of Saint Bartholomew's. He's going to help with your Fiona problem."

Marcus looked horrified. "A priest? That's a tad extreme, don't you think? I mean, I'm not exactly possessed."

"You said you couldn't get rid of Fiona no matter what you did. Bet you haven't tried an exorcism." Joyce shouldered her way past him. "Now come on, we have to make this snappy. Father Graeme walked out on an altar filled with live animals."

"You're sacrificing live animals?" Marcus asked.

"Nativity scene," Graeme clarified, and both men nodded. "So, Joyce tells me you're having an issue with a, uh... supernatural entity? Can you see and hear her?"

"All the time, Padre. All. The. Time." Marcus told a shortened version of the story leading to Fiona's persistent appearance up to taunting Joyce with floating cutlery. "My sister's a prima donna, but otherwise, she's a harmless but stubborn houseguest who refuses to leave."

"Any bright ideas?" Joyce asked Graeme.

"If her intentions are pure, maybe she'll be willing to reason," he replied. "Marcus, I'd like to ask Fiona some questions if you don't mind relaying her responses."

Marcus looked toward the corner before answering. "She says she'll cooperate as long as you don't sprinkle her with holy water. She's wearing Armani."

Graeme asked Marcus to light a single candle and place it on the kitchen table, which he did. The priest silently blessed himself, blessed the table, and blessed the immediate space surrounding it, amen. He then pulled out a chair and invited Joyce and Marcus to do the same. The three of them sat together, eyes closed, heads bowed, hands tightly clasped together. It felt eerily like a séance, but Joyce was comforted knowing that an ordained man of the cloth was leading the ritual.

"Fiona, can you make your presence known to us in a gentle way?"

The leg of the empty fourth chair squeaked on the floor.

"What did she say?" Joyce whispered to Marcus.

"Nothing. She's just standing behind the chair with a smirk on her face," he whispered. "She thinks this is hilarious."

"Thank you, Fiona," Graeme spoke calmly. "Can you tell us why you're here?"

There was a lengthy pause before Marcus answered on Fiona's behalf. "She says it's because I needed her to stay after the accident. I was scared and alone and wished I was dead. She didn't give up on me so that I wouldn't give up on myself."

"But that was ages ago," Joyce said. "Why is she *still* here?"

He drew in a deep breath. "She'd like to move on, but she says something is holding her back." He closed his eyes, and his clenched jaw shifted as if he was concentrating hard. "It's me," he finally said. "Fiona says I'm the one who's keeping her around."

Joyce squeezed his hand, urging him to continue.

Marcus opened his eyes and met her gaze across the table. "She says I still rely on her too much. Apparently, my brace isn't the only crutch I've been leaning on since the accident."

A pang of sadness pierced Joyce's heart. Poor Marcus. She reached up and tenderly brushed his cheek with the backs of her fingers.

"Fiona says it's time I realized all the good things in front of me so I can let go of what needs to be left behind," he relayed. "When I let go, she'll let go too."

"Fiona," Father Graeme said, "I hate to rush this, but can you please tell your brother what he needs to do to set you free?"

The air around them was silent and stagnant as they waited. And waited.

Joyce studied Marcus' solemn face and then turned to Graeme, whose eyes were clenched in prayer.

Was Fiona being stubborn again? Surely it had to be easier than this to banish a ghost. Recite a few chants in Latin, burn some incense, and poof! But nope. Maybe speaking woman-to-woman was the kind of shake-up this séance needed.

"Hey Fiona, it's me, Joyce. I realize we don't know each other and that things kinda got off to a rocky start earlier, but I think you understand I'm only here because I care about Marcus. I agree that the time has come for him to move on without feeling guilty about being happy. But I'm not certain he can do that when you're always hanging around."

Marcus squeezed her hand. "Fiona says she's glad you came back. And that she thinks your pom-pom hat is bangin'."

Joyce beamed. "Thanks, I knit it myself."

"Ahem," Graeme interrupted. "Joyce, we really need to focus here. Tick tock?"

"Oh, right. Sorry." She closed her eyes and bowed her head again. "As I was saying Fiona, if there's anything I can do, or that we can do to help Marcus move on..."

She waited to hear Fiona's reply in Marcus' voice, but instead tuned into the faint sound of singing somewhere far in the distance. It gradually increased in volume and clarity until the crooning became utterly unmistakable. "I'll have a bluuuuuue Christmas, without youuuu..."

"Boppa Joe!" Joyce exclaimed giddily. "Is that really you? Or are you just a figment of my imagination?"

"It's really me, Doodlebug. My friend Fiona called on me because she needs some help. She's been worried about Marcus here like I've been worried about you."

"You're worried about me? Why?"

"You know how proud I am of you, Joyce. You've always brought joy and comfort to everyone you meet," the big man said. "But I worry that giving too much of yourself away to strangers and strays has taken a toll. You've been so busy caring for others that you've forgotten to make room in your life for someone who can care for you too."

She sighed. "Maybe that's true, but..."

"Please listen," he interrupted. "The greatest gift is to love and to be loved in return. That's all I want for you, and that's what... or rather, who, I'm giving to you this Christmas."

"Who? But how? Am I supposed to look for someone wearing a big red bow?"

"Oh, that's the best part. I don't need to gift wrap this present. He's already arrived."

"He has?"

"You think it's a coincidence that Marcus is your final client?" Boppa laughed heartily. "Fiona and I have been trying to get you two together for the past year and a half. Problem is, you keep missing each other. When you're strolling down the street, he's hailing a cab. When you're going into the pet store, he's leaving the barber shop next door. You go left, he goes right. You zig, he zags. It's been as farcical as it's been frustrating."

"Me and... and M-Marcus?"

"I think it's a brilliant idea if I do say so myself. You share similar values and interests, enjoy each other's sense of humor, and have so much to learn from each other. He's a good-hearted man who not only likes and trusts you, but he genuinely sees you. Appreciates you. You'll both bring out the best in one another. Plus," Boppa said, "I have a hunch that Marcus is just your brand of catnip. Tall, bearded, and brooding, am I right?"

"Nailed it," she laughed. "You must've read my wish list."

"I always did love playing Santa Claus for you, didn't I? Take good care of each other, and Merry Christmas, Doodlebug. Ho ho ho!"

Joyce's eyes snapped open. Across the table, Marcus was smiling at her. "Fiona told me that she and your grandfather have been in cahoots trying to get us to meet for over a year."

She gasped. "He just told me the exact same thing!"

Father Graeme was dumbfounded. "Joyce? You can hear your grandfather?"

She nodded. "Only in my head, but yes, he spoke to me. It's never happened before."

Marcus' eyes were starry as he grasped both her hands. "Go figure. My sister and your grandfather tag-teaming on the other side to bring us together."

She was floating on a dreamy, whipped cream cloud and couldn't keep from grinning ear to ear. "Boppa Joe said that you're my Christmas gift."

He chuckled. "All along, Fiona insisted she picked you out for me. I thought she meant for the cuddling session."

"This is wonderful." Father Graeme laughed as he placed his large hands squarely on each of their shoulders. "I believe my work is done without further sacramental intervention required. I'll leave you two to take things from here." He pushed his chair back from the table and stood up. "Now if you'll excuse me, I really must see a man about an alpaca."

Chapter Seven

Marcus adjusted his shirt collar in the mirror. Not bad. Spiffed up, spritzed, and groomed, he looked like a new man with a sparkle in his eye and—dare he say it?—a touch of holiday spirit. "I still can't get over you and Joyce's grandfather playing matchmaker for us."

"Boppa Joe is a real mensch. It was a pleasure doing business with him. But all we did was give you two the nudge you needed. You'll have to figure the rest out for yourselves, but you will." Fiona clucked her tongue as the door buzzer sounded. "There's your ride."

Marcus reached for his crutch, slipping his forearm into the cuff. Shifting his weight, he snapped to attention for her final inspection. "How do I look?"

She nodded her approval. "Like a nimrod ready to seal the deal. In other words, perfect."

He took one long last look at his sister, knowing she'd be gone for good once he left. "You may not believe this, but I'm really gonna miss you around here."

"Don't I know it," she tossed out light-heartedly. "I definitely added a certain *je ne sais quoi* to this dump."

"I mean it, Fee. Thank you. For everything. You got me through my darkest days and gave me something to live for again. For an angel, you're one hell of a wingman."

She dotted away a tear before it smudged her immaculate makeup. "Now look at what you've done, you big dope. I can't spend eternity with raccoon eyes, I have a date with Heath Ledger on New Year's Eve."

Marcus laughed along with her. "Then how about one more hug before I go?"

Fiona went to him, and they held one another tight. Their hearts said everything that needed to be said, and when they were done, they pulled back from their embrace. "Wow, I think that was the best hug you ever gave me," she marveled.

"I guess Joyce has already taught me a thing or two." He shrugged. "I'm going to get even better at it. I'm going to work hard to be the man she deserves."

"I know you will," Fiona said. "And you can start by putting more effort into Christmas. I don't ever want to hear about Joyce getting a pine-scented air freshener in her stocking."

"I will, promise."

"By the way, tell your driver to make a stop at the Asian deli. There's an order of shrimp rolls for you to bring to the potluck. I figured you'll be rusty at this whole social etiquette thing for a while, so I wanted to start you off on the right foot."

"Pun intended?"

"Pun definitely intended, ya gimp." The door buzzed again. "Go on now, you're running behind, and the snow has made traffic a nightmare."

Marcus pulled on his hat, swung his scarf around his neck, and then pointed himself toward the door. "I love you, Fiona. I'll see you when I see you."

"I'll see you when I see you," she called out. "Love you too, bro. Merry Christmas."

Half an hour later, the car slowed to a stop in front of the brownstone at 505 Herald Street. Marcus cheerily wished the driver happy holidays, then handed him an extra cash tip before climbing out. Clutching the bag of fresh-made shrimp rolls in his free hand, he leaned on his crutch, counted the eight snow-covered steps from sidewalk to stoop, and carefully started his slow ascent.

Halfway to the top, the entry door suddenly swung open, and a blast of festive music and a tantalizing mix of aromas escaped. Joyce popped out too, her face lighting up like a Christmas tree.

"Marcus! You're here!" Ignoring the snow, she bounded down the steps like a stunning yuletide vision, nearly bowling him over with her short, snug-fitting red velvet dress and pearl-like strands of festive lights around her neck. He was relieved she'd reached him before he toppled.

Joyce stood one step above to close their gap in height. Marcus' stare fell to her mouth, shapely and plush, with a luscious lower lip that looked to be a lovely place for a fellow to land. Where was a sprig of mistletoe when you needed one? "I told you I wouldn't miss it."

"I know, but I wasn't going to hold you to it. I mean, you hate Christmas. And meeting people. And parties. And you especially hate meeting people at Christmas parties."

"I've recently had reason to re-evaluate a few things I may have previously misjudged," he said with a smile. "Besides, two people worked very hard to make sure we were together tonight, and it wouldn't be right for us to let them down."

"I'm so happy you came. And I'm especially happy that you're not my client anymore," she said, dark eyes shimmering, "because now I can give you this."

She leaned in until they were a whisper apart and sweetly nuzzled his nose. Breathless with anticipation, he closed his eyes, heart pounding a deafening timpani in his ears, until she placed a kiss on him as soft and delicate as a perfect snowflake, fluttering, floating, free.

She pulled back and they both smiled. He put down the shrimp rolls, freeing his hand to cup her pink-flushed cheek and gently guided her mouth back to his again. Their lips sensually brushed and bumped, and he lightly caressed the velvety flesh of her bottom lip with the tip of his tongue, needing to feel her, taste her, savor her. This woman was definitely made to kiss him, he'd never been so sure of anything.

"Wow," she sighed. "Marcus. That was... wow."

"Yeah," he agreed, instantly missing her exquisite lips, his body aching in spots where it yearned for her expert touch. "Really wow."

In a surge of passion, she locked her arms around his neck, hungrily branding him with a searing kiss that made them both moan with pleasure. His arm circled her waist to hold this glorious creature tighter as he lost himself in their deepening kiss. Time and space suspended as the world blurred into a wonderful, magical snow globe, with only Joyce in the center of it.

She was his all-time favorite gift. She was a dream. She was... music.

"Ahem." A distant cough from outside their sphere of bliss startled Marcus, and their intense lip-lock unsealed abruptly. "Pardon the intrusion, lovebirds, but you're going to catch your death of cold snogging out here in the storm. Come now. The party's getting started."

Joyce pulled back, and, with a sly smile, dabbed at the corners of her beautiful mouth before turning around. "Uh, thank you, Bert. We were just saying hello."

Lightheaded, Marcus refocused his fuzzy eyes on the balding, bespectacled Brit guarding the entrance and gave him a friendly wave. "Nice to meet you, Bert. Merry Christmas."

"And a Merry Christmas to you, er..."

"This is Marcus," Joyce said. "He's the one I've been waiting for." With a smile, she retrieved the bag of shrimp rolls from the step and then reached for Marcus.

He smiled back as he tightly gripped her hand, and without hesitation, let her lead the way.

THE END

'Twas the Night Before

BY LEILA LOVE

When native Washingtonian Ava crosses paths with native New Yorker Sterling at an iconic hotel bar on Christmas Eve, they escape their tough choices and drop all pretenses on an enchanting city tour that could change everything–in one night.

About the Author

Leila Love is a girl from the city with roots in the South weaving happily-ever-afters. Her stories empower women to exist authentically and love unapologetically, alongside charming heroes who respect, cherish, and fight for these women who challenge and capture their hearts.

Instagram: @leilalovewrites
Facebook: Leila Love
Website: https://www.leilalovebooks.com

Chapter One

Ava

I f New York is the city that never sleeps, Washington, DC is the city
that sleeps with one eye open. But since it's Christmas Eve, I had
hoped that maybe, just maybe, Santa's gift to me would come early
and sleep would claim the masses early – leaving an empty seat at the
Round Robin Bar for a good-girl-gone-bad.

Let me explain.

I am a good girl—to a fault. I have a good government job. I live in a
good neighborhood. I went to good schools. I got good grades. I'm a good
cook. I'm a good daughter, sister, aunt, and friend. I come from a good
family. I'm good in bed—so I've been told. I volunteer on Saturdays and
go to church on Sundays. And my intentions are always good. In a
nutshell, I'm the good girl cliché found in books and movies all over the
world.

So, my goodness quotient is high. Or at least it was. Until my good
boyfriend proposed and I graciously declined. Turns out, he was more like
good enough and I couldn't settle.

Now, this good-girl-gone-bad just needs a gorgeous, warm, and sweet
Christmas cocktail to take the edge off before joining my family in

Middleburg, Virginia. I was supposed to already be there, but when work calls, I always answer for my good government job. Can't allow the good girl meter to fall too low all at once.

I'll just hit the road before sunrise to see my nieces and nephews tear through their Christmas gifts, delirious with anticipation. That, and the Christmas brunch my parents painstakingly plan and cook every year, will be the highlight of my day.

The sidewalks are less crowded, but a parade of cars still lines 14th Street—some escaping the city and others dashing through the snow for dinner reservations at the latest Michelin starred restaurants.

The temperature has dropped to just above freezing and small clouds of moisture form in front of me with every breath. I adjust my scarf to cover my nose and mouth and pick up my pace. I'm not wearing the most sensible shoes, but my destination is just a half-block away and my festive red bottoms are meant to be seen.

As I step under the iconic glass canopy of The Willard, I'm draped in the comfort of familiarity.

"Good evening, Miss Ava. Didn't expect to see you here tonight."

Mr. Paul greets me – dapper in his dark overcoat and hat – and I'm equally as surprised to see him. I don't know how old he is, and despite the looseness of his deep cocoa skin and the slight slope in his dark brown eyes, he's sprite, trim, quick-witted, and possessing just the right temperament to greet guests, move the tourists along, and keep the traffic flowing simultaneously at the entrance of The Willard.

"I could say the same to you." I pause to slip him a holiday tip with an extra hand squeeze and to give my feet a reprieve without looking too obvious. "Thought you would be with your daughter and grandchildren this evening."

"You young ladies sure have a talent for managing a man's schedule," he says, his warm Southern accent masking his sarcasm, while waving another sedan forward and smirking at me. "I'm leaving right after my shift. Even taking one of those Ubers to her house. She insisted. Waste of money if you ask me, but she didn't want me taking the Metro tonight."

"I like how your daughter thinks."

A couple with two small kids pours out of the dark sedan with suitcases, a stroller, and a car seat – and I'm in the way.

"Merry Christmas, Mr. Paul, if I don't see you before you leave tonight."

"Thanks, Miss Ava. You, too. And don't you stay at that bar too late, young lady," he admonishes without looking at me or missing a beat with his new guests.

I chuckle and promise to not shut the joint down.

I take the few steps up to the entrance, where the doorman ushers me in as I unravel my scarf and peel off my coat in one fluid motion. This hotel, this lobby, its bar, the cafe, and its afternoon tea service are my happy place, my home away from home, my decompression chamber in my city divided by more than political leanings. And when I'm greeted by the magnificence of the Christmas tree practically grazing the gilded high ceilings, I start to reclaim some of my Christmas spirit.

Inside my coat pocket, my cell phone vibrates. I dig it out and see that I've missed seven text messages in rapid succession, and one is in draft.

Anya: Where are you?

Anya: Are you on the road? If so, I can forgive you for not responding. NO TEXTING AND DRIVING!

Anya: What time are you arriving? Your nieces and nephews are looking for you.

DJ: What's up, Sis? You coming through or nah?

Anya: You better not still be working. Seriously, Ava. Get the hell out of DC!

DJ: You solo or is your boring Boo-Thang coming with you?

Anya: Okay...Mom and Dad are now officially worried but don't want to bug you. You better get here soon!

I watch the little text bubble with its three little dots and contemplate a response. Whatever I say will be a disappointment. *I had to work late. I'm not coming until morning. I broke up with my Boo-Thang.*

Since I'm already on a bad girl streak, I ignore the text messages, drop the phone in my bag, and head to the bar, where Christmas did come early.

There are only a few people seated around the circular bar, and the vibe is low-key festive with just enough decor to compliment the warm walnut interior and soft holiday jazz flowing through the space.

There are three consecutive seats on the left side of the bar and I plan to take the center one to avoid small talk – at least until I've had one cocktail to lift my spirits and ease my guilt.

As I saunter through, I'm careful not to make eye contact with any other patrons, needing a few minutes to wind down. I take my seat and immediately order my holiday favorite – the warm mulled wine laced with apple brandy and sweetened to perfection with a sugar and spice rim.

My phone vibrates again and I resist the urge to just shut it off. But when I pull it from my bag, I see it was a missed call from my bestie, Lena Vaughn—publicist to the East Coast glitterati. A few high-profile authors round out her elite clientele because she's a closeted book nerd and writer who loves having an excuse to speak at all the literary festivals across the country, making it about book publicity when really she just wants to hang out with authors. I'm pretty sure one day she's going to tackle that dream deferred, run away from home, and become a best-selling novelist.

I debate calling her back when the voicemail notification pops up on my screen. Lena left a message. I slip on my AirPods to listen.

"Hey, girl, hey! I'm just checking on you. And you better call me when you get to Middleburg. It's dark as hell on those country roads. And if you need backup with the fam when you break the news, I'm one helicopter ride away. Ciao!"

Leave it to Lena to be overprotective, super supportive, and a ride-or-die diva all at once. If you looked up multitasker in the dictionary, Lena's headshot would be there.

She's a gorgeous blend of her Cuban father and African-American mother, with long dark hair that she finally gave up trying to control, dark eyes, and full lips with a Beyoncé body that she doesn't even have to work for. She's an extrovert when she's working and a complete introvert all other times. She's glam on the surface and girl-next-door on the inside. She can't be trusted to boil water, but she has an awesome chef and can throw a party without flinching. We met in college on the first day of our freshman year, pledged the same sorority, and have been inseparable ever since.

But that chick hates driving. She owns a Maserati that barely leaves her garage and a Tesla Model X to pick up and drop off book donations for her literacy nonprofit—mostly driven by one of her volunteers. It's the privately owned helicopter that she gets the most mileage out of up and down the East Coast. And since there's a resort with a helipad near my family's home in Middleburg, Lena can be there in under an hour.

I decide to call her back when I leave the bar for a pep talk and a little advice about dealing with the fallout awaiting me with my family.

As I finally start to settle in, I glance around the bar at my fellow Christmas Eve revelers, and directly across from me is an unexpected but familiar face. His expression pensive, his demeanor reserved, his shirt and jacket impeccably tailored, and his facial features impeccable. S. J. Russell is cloaked in refinement, disguising his boy-from-the-hood origins. The bad-boy-gone-good.

"Another Macallan, please," he says to the bartender as his eyes meet mine.

I want to look away but can't. His eyes are a mix of sadness and mischief, the deepest brown swirling with bursts of hazel. His tie is loosened, and the two top buttons of his shirt are undone—an immaculate mess. He looks like I'm feeling.

"And add whatever she's having to my tab," he adds to the bartender with his eyes settled precisely on mine.

Chapter Two

Sterling

She'd slipped in, eyes lowered and footsteps measured, in a flawless black pantsuit and silk holiday-crimson blouse. She raised her hand to pull her dark hair behind her ear, parted down the middle and hung straight past her shoulders, surrounding flawless caramel skin and full lips tinted with deep red lipstick.

She was trying to fly under the radar, but who was she fooling? A woman like that – even on her worst day – couldn't hide that kind of unforced beauty. Some women just have a presence, an energy that invites adoration. They own whatever space they occupy, unless they choose otherwise. And for some reason, this gorgeous woman was alone on Christmas Eve and I couldn't look away.

But I knew I should. Now is not the time for dabbling in a one-night stand—not even for a woman so classy and modestly stunning. I'm having a shitty holiday, fighting with my best friend and seriously nervous that the damage can't be undone.

Lady in black and red sat directly across from me, scrolling on her phone and ordering her cocktail with barely a glance at the bartender, something I assume is frilly and sweet. And then she averted her gaze from him and our eyes locked.

A tilt of her head indicated curiosity and surprise, but she didn't look away. Not daring me to break the connection first, but more like studying me. Her eyes softened and then she lowered them back to her cell phone.

But I wasn't ready to disconnect just yet, so I ordered another drink and told the bartender to put her cocktail on my tab.

She peeped up without lifting her head. I had regained her attention.

She nodded and smiled, and I expected that to be the end of it. But this woman possesses a measure of Christmas magic.

"Thank you, Mr. Russell. But that's really not necessary. I have a running tab. But please let me take care of that Macallan for you. Merry Christmas."

She gestures to the bartender and returns to scanning her phone.

The bartender shrugs, types her request into the computer, and pours my drink. "She's a regular," he says to me. "And what Ava wants...you get it."

Did she just reject my holiday goodwill and then pay for my drink? I don't know whether to be offended or flattered. And how does she know who I am?

It's decision time. Sit here, wonder, and just accept the damn drink. Or take one of those available seats next to her and ask the right questions.

Since nothing else is going right today, I take the leap and stride over to where she's sitting.

"Thank you for the drink, Miss..."

"Ms. Jones. And you're welcome." She's polite but detached as she meets my gaze and quickly returns to whatever she was responding to on her phone. Probably a boyfriend, but if he isn't here with her, he's a fool and not worth her time. And now that I'm this close to her and I've caught a trace of Yves Saint Laurent perfume and I can see the exposed skin on her slender neck and the tiny diamond pendant dangling from a gold chain on her chest, there is no way I'm returning to my lonely side of the bar when Christmas literally just walked through the door and gifted me a drink.

I pull out the seat next to her and she doesn't flinch, barely acknowledging my existence. But once I'm settled in, I ask my first question.

Sipping my drink, I lean in, turn my head towards her, and keep the tone of my voice precise. "So, how do you know me?"

Without looking at me, she replies, "I don't know you. I just know your name and your face. And what I've read about you."

It's an answer – sort of. More elusive than direct.

"What have you read about me?"

She finishes typing on her phone, slides it in her designer bag, and leisurely leans back in her chair with her cocktail in hand.

"S. J. Russell...short for Sterling, Jr...high school basketball phenom... career-ending injury your freshman year in college...dropped out...got in a little trouble back in NYC...went back to college and got a dual degree in sports management and an MBA...now a top sports agent in the NBA, WNBA, NFL, tennis, women's soccer, and baseball." She took a sip of her cocktail and asked, "Does that cover it?"

To my surprise, she didn't mention any of the myriad of women I'd been attached to over the years, but she was probably being polite.

"I guess so." I lean back and hold my glass up for a toast, and she taps her cocktail glass against mine with a smirk. When she doesn't speak, I add, "I'm impressed."

"Why?" Her voice is provocative and her tone deep. I've struck a nerve.

"It's just..." I hesitate, not wanting to invite judgment. But I take the leap. "Most people only recognize me when I'm courtside, on the side-lines, or in some other sports capacity. And what most people read about me is more salacious than biographical."

This time she chuckles and tilts her head back. I walked right into it.

"If you stick around long enough, you'll learn that I'm not like most people and I definitely don't judge people for having a personal life. But I've followed your career since we were both in East Coast high schools, and I think your happily-ever-after is better than the one you had planned."

She's beautiful and intriguing and not just interested in talking to new-money me. To my stark surprise, she knew me when all my dreams were trapped in an inflated orange ball.

"You are a breath of fresh air." I feel the tension lifting and feel semi-comfortable with her, so I lean back in my chair and take a long sip of my drink before adding, "And for the record, I agree. This is a much better happily-ever-after."

Chapter Three

Ava

I can't tell if he's flirting with me or confused that a woman is not flirting with him. So, I decide to get an answer.

"So, why are you alone at a bar on Christmas Eve? Certainly, a man of your notoriety and success must have invitations for all manner of holiday shenanigans." I raise my eyebrows slightly and signal to the waiter for another round to give Mr. Russell a chance to formulate a response. I know it will be good and worth this pregnant pause.

"You're right." He nods without looking at me, both hands wrapped around his glass, monogrammed cuffs peeping through his jacket sleeve. "I have lots of invites, but most of them are more of the same. And I'm in DC visiting my best friend for the holidays. She's my homegirl – like, since kindergarten. So, when she invited me to join her and her family for Christmas, I couldn't resist. We don't get to see each other much these days, and I miss her."

Not at all what I was expecting, but it's a good look for him. He doesn't seem to be flirting and is handling my attempts to not flirt. Guess I shouldn't underestimate the substance of this man. But I should be careful. He does have a reputation.

I smile and watch as he downs the rest of his drink, that pensive look returning. Still without looking at me, he keeps talking.

"I'm alone tonight because she's upset with me. We're arguing, and honestly, I don't know if there is any way for us to come out of this one unscathed."

His shoulders drop and all that oozing, masculine confidence drains from him.

"Sounds deep."

I immediately hate myself for being so dismissive. He's clearly struggling with their disagreement, but I don't really know him – I just know of him.

I try to recover.

"Well, if it's any consolation, my entire family is waiting for me in Middleburg, Virginia, at my parents' new retirement horse farm, and I've been avoiding them. I just finally broke the news that I won't be there until morning and now I refuse to read another text message. And that's not even the worst of it."

He perks up and leans into me, his Tom Ford cologne haunting me. I steal a tiny inhale and fight back the urge to lick my lips. *What the hell is wrong with me?*

"I hope not, because that sounds pretty mild." His smile melts me, and I can't help but let my eyes wander over his perfectly lined up haircut and his dark, neatly trimmed facial hair against skin a shade lighter than mine. The corners of his eyes crinkle when he smiles, and one perfect dimple makes a surprise appearance.

But he's too perfect—the kind of perfect that screams for me to run fast and far. And yet, that doesn't stop me from spilling my guts. What harm could there be? I won't see this man again after tonight.

"My parents are expecting their good daughter to bring her boyfriend-turned-fiancé home for Christmas. Trouble is, he popped the question and I politely declined. So, the family fallout is inescapable and I'm in no hurry to have my choices dissected under a microscope."

S.J. sits back and massages his chin. Damn, I wish he wouldn't do that.

"That's tough. But why did you...?"

I cut him off before he could finish. "No more questions about that." I tap my phone and it lights up with the time. It's only 6:45 p.m.

"Am I keeping you from something else?"

There's hope in his voice, so who am I to disappoint him?

This time I lean in closer, one elbow keeping me perfectly perched on the bar. "Since we're both single, free, and disengaged, are you up for a little platonic Christmas Eve adventure?"

"Damn right, I am. But I'm from New York and you know how we do Christmas. Where to first? And don't disappoint me."

"Challenge accepted. Meet me in the lobby in a half-hour. And remember, I'm third-generation born and raised in DC. My city and I could never disappoint."

Chapter Four

Sterling

I rush up to my room to change into jeans and sneakers and to grab my coat, while Ava walks back to her office to swap suit pants and heels for jeans and boots from her overnight bag.

Back in my suite, I check my cell phone, but there are no messages from Cass. I hate how I left things with her. But what she was asking of me – from me – just felt like too much. I understand, in theory. But in practice, I just can't fathom it. However, I do know I can't let this disagreement fester and that we need to talk after we've both cooled down. Our conversation had been heated today, and I stormed out before we both said things we couldn't take back. Now I feel like shit. Like a selfish jerk not willing to make a sacrifice for a friend who rarely asked for anything. Guess she was calling in three decades of IOUs, saved up for the one moment she could ask for everything.

It literally makes my head throb just thinking about it, so I pop two aspirin and push the worry back into the recesses of my mind. I can't figure it out now. And hopefully, I can distract myself with Ms. Ava "Unengaged" Jones.

When I make it back down to the lobby, Ava in jeans and boots with a raspberry beret tilted to the side is equally as alluring as suited up Ava. She's snapping pics of the Christmas tree while two small kids wearing Santa hats count the gift-wrapped boxes beneath. This isn't New York, but I have to admit, the holiday decor in this hotel is tastefully extravagant with a traditional Christmas vibe, wrapped in deep red, shimmering gold, and emerald green. It shines without trying too hard, and yet it's warm and makes you want to sit by an open fire and read *'Twas the Night Before Christmas*. I've been here a week and I've seen so many people in and out of the hotel lobby, taking photos, listening to the evening Christmas carolers, or getting hot chocolate from the cafe. It was a whole mood that I willfully ignored.

"Playing tourist, Ms. Jones."

She looks over her shoulder at me and smirks.

"You dress down nicely," she says flippantly. But I watch her eyelashes flutter as she scans my gear, starting with my shoes until she meets my eyes. "Are you sure about those Jordans? It's cold out."

"I'm good. Trust me. But are you done with the tourist photo shoot? Or are you stalling?"

"I have no reason to stall. You're going to love my city at Christmas. These photos are for my nieces and nephews. They won't make it to DC to see the hotel this year, so I'm getting them a few shots."

"So, you're a good daughter and a good auntie."

"I'm good at most things." She pauses, refocuses her camera phone, and practically whispers, "Maybe a little too good."

There's something there, by the way her tone dropped and her words trailed off. But I don't want to pry.

I take a few steps closer to her to see what she was capturing through her phone lens, to see her perspective. She has a good eye. But then she does something weird: she angles the phone up to the ceiling, zooms in, and snaps a pic. Then she takes a few steps backwards and repeats the ceiling shot.

"Why the ceiling shots?" My neck is now craning up to figure out what is so interesting.

"Every state seal is represented on this ceiling. See..." she says, pointing out Virginia and then Maryland.

She's right. At the corner of every box, there is an ornate gold and silver depiction of every state's seal – not that I recognize them all. But it is impressive.

"I always bring my nieces and nephews here for Christmas and take their pictures under the states where they were born. I've done it since they were babies. So, since they aren't here, I'll AirPlay the pics on my parents' smart TV and let them stand next to it." Her eyes sparkle as she smiles through her words. "A break in Christmas traditions with the kiddos is a nonstarter."

"Cool." I am truly awestruck by the artistry. The detail is exquisite, and I'm sure the history is twice as fascinating. But also, Ava. It's really thoughtful to start and honor a tradition with the kids in her life.

Kids. People change their whole lives for them. Even take photos of ceilings in public to keep a promise.

I've never been bitten by that bug. But with Cass planning to start a family with her partner, it's inevitable. Maybe.

This time, Ava laughs out loud, a perfectly timed interruption. "*Cool?* How very understated of you."

"No offense," I assure her, tightening my scarf around my neck. "I'm just blown away that I've been walking through this lobby all week and never noticed these details."

"Pay attention, Mr. Russell. There's beauty hidden in the complicated history and culture of this city in the most unexpected places."

She lights up when she talks about the city. A DC girl to her core. This is the most she's smiled since we met, and I sense she's in her element.

"Then I guess I have the right tour guide for the evening."

"The best," she corrects. "And let's start right here in this lobby."

She spins around like she's choosing where to begin and just takes a few steps forward towards a sitting area.

"I like to imagine that this is the exact spot where Dr. King put the finishing touches on his *I Have A Dream* speech right here in this lobby. Most people know about all the Presidents that have visited and stayed here, but that piece of history means the most to me. It's why whenever I step through those doors, I walk like I'm Dr. King's wildest dream come true."

"You're making that up. No way Dr. King was here." I'm astonished and impressed and mortified that I really don't know anything about where I'm staying. Cass had recommended this hotel, but she neglected to school me on its history.

"Google it," Ava says playfully, putting her arm through mine and guiding me toward a staircase. At the top, the scent of gingerbread wafts through the air and I am a goner.

As we descend further, I peek ahead, eager to see where she's taking me.

"Since this is a really nice hotel, I'll calm my suspicions. But I hope something good is waiting at the bottom."

Ava grins. "Just disconnect from your New York State of Mind and you'll be fine."

Chapter Five

Ava

It takes all I have not to bounce down these stairs like Dorothy from *The Wizard of Oz*, with S.J. in the role of the Cowardly Lion. I know his type – control freak in all things and in all ways. I know it must be killing him to just be at my mercy.

And just as the staircase twists, sprawling before us is this year's gingerbread display – featuring a replica of my favorite DC monument, known affectionately by native Washingtonians as "The Big Chair."

I look at S.J., and his expression is equal parts amused and confused. I drop my head and seal my lips shut to force back a giggle.

"Is that...a big chair made from gingerbread?"

This time he pulls me forward, not breaking the connection.

The giggle that I've been suppressing finds its way free when I respond.

"It is not a big chair, it is *The* Big Chair. A true DC landmark in Anacostia – and my homegrown favorite. It's in a predominantly African-American community, and the chair was built on the property of a former furniture store as a marketing stunt but has become something so much more. And what's great about this display is that some high school kids built it."

It's his turn to smile. "A big, monument-sized chair...now that's something I'd like to see."

I squeeze his arm a little tighter while we both enjoy the scenery. "I can arrange that."

"I like this gingerbread twist on Christmas." He sounds genuinely impressed.

"What's even better is they feature a different historic DC landmark every year. A few years ago, they did Reagan National Airport and even had the live air traffic control radio playing."

"Damn. Who knew?"

"Yeah, I know. But we've got lots of stops to make on our Christmas Eve adventure, so let's grab some hot chocolate from the cafe and head to the next spot on our tour," I prompt, letting my arm drop casually away from his.

It isn't that I don't like it. I don't *want* to like it.

I place our orders with extra whipped cream and a couple macarons for the road. While we wait, I ask him about how long he's been in the city, when he's leaving, and what he's done to keep busy. I'm surprised at how mellow his trip sounds. I guess I just envisioned him living this sexy, fun, celebrity lifestyle all the time. And maybe he did. But that doesn't seem to be the case on this trip.

I don't push. Plus, I don't want to ask any questions I'm not willing to answer myself.

"So, which suite are you staying in? Because I know you're not in a basic room."

He smirks, and there's that damn dimple again.

"You're right. Nothing basic about me or for me. I'm in one of the Oval Suites—makes me feel presidential," he admits.

"Barack Obama or Fitzgerald Grant presidential?" I ask, expecting to trip him up with the real-versus-fictional Presidential comparison. But clearly, I need to manage my expectations better, because he counters with a self-assured smirk, "For this trip, I'm all Barack. But I've been known to invite *Scandal* into other hotel suites."

All I can do is chuckle and look towards the counter, robbing this tempting conversation of oxygen. Once I'm confident I've broken the connection, I turn back to him.

"The Oval Suites are nice, but my favorite is the Jenny Lind Suite. It's one of a kind, but that price tag is too steep for my government salary. So, it's on my bucket list."

"Ms. Jones, your order is ready." Gianna is working the cafe counter this evening, and I make sure to leave her a hefty holiday tip. She works part-time evenings and goes to Howard University during the day. My college experience was similar.

We grab our orders and exit the cafe out onto the sidewalk. The cold air hits us immediately, but neither of us flinches. Northern winters can be brutal, so the chill in the air is nothing either of us hasn't felt before.

"We're walking to the next spot?"

"We are," I say, gripping my hot chocolate between both gloved hands and taking a tentative sip. "You're used to this. And I think your Jordans will survive. We'll take Ubers the rest of the night."

"My Jordans are fine," he defends. "But I have a car service. We don't need Uber."

Of course, he has a car service. Duh. That will make getting around much easier.

"Great. You can give them our next location and they can pick us up from there."

We walk in silence, sipping hot chocolate and joining small clusters of people navigating vehicle and foot traffic. It's busier than I thought it would be, but there is a stillness—a calm not often felt in the city. Christmas has a way of exposing our commonalities and giving us permission to let our differences melt away, if only for a day or two.

The National Christmas Tree is just off in the distance—tall and glorious, symbolic of the kind of peace we hope can last always but rarely does. Blanketed in red, white, and blue lights, it's a festive beacon of hope that I visit as much as possible to restore my faith in mankind.

I need it tonight to restore my faith in myself.

I glance over at S.J., curiosity coloring his cheeks crimson. Or maybe that's the cold.

"Welcome to the National Christmas Tree," I say, slowing our pace to let him take it all in. "I know it's not Rockefeller Center, but its magnificence is not in its size or its lights or its decorations. Its real beauty is in the smaller trees surrounding it."

S.J. takes in the full measure of the tree, head lifted and nodding in admiration as he walks closer.

"And there's a train set!" His voice is enthusiastically boyish, his eyes a little wider and steps a little quicker.

"Yep. Now, that's something you won't see at Rockefeller Center." It's just a little dig.

His eyes follow the train until it disappears, and then he follows it. I stay a couple feet away while he walks the circumference of the tree before turning to the smaller Christmas trees.

He finally looks back at me and says, "Something else I missed that was so close to the hotel. Guess I'm not good at being a tourist."

"That's your New York bias, but that'll change after tonight."

Now standing near the tree identified as Alaska, he looks back at me again. "So, there's one for every state?"

"Indeed, there is."

"I want to see New York!"

"Go for it. They're in alphabetical order."

While he searches for his home state tree, I go to the souvenir booth and buy him a White House Christmas tree ornament—a small token to remember this trip. When I find him, he's kneeling down reading messages left on the ornaments.

"I got you something."

He looks up and smiles—a big, goofy, dimpled smile. "This tree has Christmas wishes from kids! All over it!"

I can't help but to meet his enthusiasm with my own silly smile, because this is so much better than just impressing him. I think he's enchanted. And for a man like S. J. Russell, that's a triumph.

It's a moment worth preserving, so I ask him to stand near the tree and I snap a photo of him. When I walk over to let him see, he turns to me with a smirk.

"So, am I like one of your little nieces and nephews now?"

"You'd be so lucky."

Shaking his head, he continues on the path, stopping at some of the trees and just glancing at others. I don't really know him, just mostly the stuff that I've read, but I know to have the kind of success he's made for himself, he must work nonstop. Watching him stroll through a few dozen Christmas trees with awe in his eyes is a gift I didn't know I needed.

I check the time and realize we need to move on to the next stop if we're going to do everything on my list. And I'm reminded of a call I need to make now to arrange for our entry at the fourth stop.

"You should call your car service and have them pick us up soon. And tell them we're headed to Georgetown."

Chapter Six

Sterling

J acob arrives fifteen minutes later, and I open the rear passenger door
to help Ava in first. The black Range Rover sits high off the ground,
at odds with its rugged name, but with a smooth ride and luxurious
interior. Once she's inside, I close her door and climb in on the opposite side—because one thing I've learned is women don't like sliding across
the seat.

After I'm settled, I peep over at Ava and see she's texting on her
phone. She's not smiling, so I assume it's family stuff and I don't want to
interrupt her.

That gives me a chance to check my own text messages. Still nothing
from Cass. But there are holiday messages from many of my clients, and
that gives me a fresh dose of holiday cheer.

I'm lucky to work with the athletes represented by my agency and I
never take it for granted. I'm accessible to them 24/7, and sometimes that
means holidays. I always have a few rookies on the roster, and trouble has a
tendency to find them—especially during the holidays. But this year it's
been quiet. Guess Santa knew I needed a reprieve as a gift this year to deal
with Cass.

We turn onto Constitution Avenue, passing the Washington Monument and green space and historic buildings blending with the mundane mechanics of city life.

When I slide my phone back in my pocket, Ava is slightly slumped and staring out her window, tapping her now empty hot chocolate cup on her bottom lip, transferring red lipstick to its rim. I have the urge to reach out and touch her, sensing she might need some comforting. She's doing a good job of shutting out her impending family drama, but I can tell it's bothering her. From what I can see, she's devoted to her family and she doesn't want to disappoint them.

I've been there, done that, and can confirm it also applies to friendships.

Yet despite whatever is happening with her, she's out with me on Christmas Eve trying to lift my holiday spirits. So yeah, I want to comfort her, but I don't want to overstep.

So, I use my words.

"Everything okay?"

I see Jacob peer at us through the rear-view mirror and quickly divert his eyes back on the road. I've gotten to know him over the week I've been in the city because there's lots of time to talk when there are no other passengers joining me.

Until tonight.

Ava adjusts her posture and turns to face me, a trace of sadness in her eyes but a polite smile on her lips.

"It will be. Once I get comfortable with not being my parents' good daughter, disappointing my family, and breaking the heart of a perfectly good guy."

So, not really okay.

After revealing the string of her perceived offenses, she fidgets with the armrest and pops open the cup holders to free her hands of the now empty hot chocolate cup. I sense she had been making a statement and it isn't up for discussion.

She opens the bag of macarons and chooses the eggnog-flavored, white decadent cookie, and I can smell the dusting of nutmeg on top. She passes the bag to me and I choose the peppermint flavor, hoping to cool down the warmth building towards a woman I only met a couple hours ago.

She takes the first bite and I watch her savor it, chewing slowly with her eyes closed. Then she looks directly at me and says, "Hey, but I'm a work in progress. I'll get used to my new normal."

I'm at a loss for how to respond when Donny Hathaway's "This Christmas" suddenly flows through the sound system. It's my chance to lighten the mood and cheer her up a little by embarrassing myself a lot.

I use my hot chocolate cup as a fake microphone and take my shot. I typically only pull out my secret weapon with family and my church congregation—but Ava deserves a Christmas treat. When I start to hum, the deep baritone of my voice barely present in harmony with Mr. Hathaway, she tilts her head to the side and looks in my direction, eyes squinting and lips twisted.

She's fighting back a smile and I am determined to pull it out of her.

I sing along to the second chorus, and she's quickly losing the battle.

When the song reaches the hook, I turn to sing directly at her, and she finally joins in. In the front seat, Jacob nods slightly to the beat while Ava and I turn the song into a duet. She can hold a tune, but she'd never make it in my church choir. And I'll never tell her that.

When the song ends, her giggle and approving smile are the evidence I need to know our version of Christmas Car Karaoke has worked – a distraction from the weight of her family drama.

We've gone around the edge of the Tidal Basin, past the Kennedy Center and the infamous Watergate, when Jacob slows the SUV beneath an overpass and near the Potomac River.

"This is the Georgetown waterfront," Ava tells me. "Let's get out here."

I hop out first and go open her door to help her out.

Once she's on solid ground, I expect her to let go so we can walk side by side, but she slides her arm through mine with a gentle grip. She explains the gesture, "It's cold out here."

I need no explanation. She initiated and I am happy to oblige if it means she can let go of her troubles and just enjoy the evening.

"That it is," I agree, not wanting to make it into a thing.

We walk in silence until we turn a corner and are hit with holiday music and a neon-lit tunnel curving in multiple directions.

"Wow." It comes out more like a whisper, my awe subdued but obvious.

"I know, right. And this is only the beginning," she says, clearly satisfied that she's giving me a true DC Christmas experience to rival what I've known my whole life in New York.

"The beginning of what?" I've picked up the pace, eager to stand beneath the tunnel and get the full experience.

"Georgetown Glow—light installations all throughout the neighborhood, all created by local artists. But I won't bore you with the details; you can Google it. Let's go!"

Before I can react, she slips her arm out of mine and runs towards the tunnel, disappearing inside. I follow, and when I get inside, she's holding up her camera phone.

"Strike a pose," she says playfully. "A GQ-pose for my private collection."

She's funny but truly mistaken if she thinks I'm about to be out in the cold posing like some cologne model.

"Nah. I'll pass."

She laughs and meets me halfway. Sliding her arm back through mine, she coyly suggests through fluttering eyelashes, "Then let's do a selfie."

Before I can refuse, her arm is outstretched, her head is tilted in closer to my chest, and I'm looking down at the outline of her face. Her little raspberry beret is cashmere-soft against my chin as she nuzzles closer to get us both in the frame.

The click interrupts my impulse to pull her closer, and then I look up.

"Another one, please. You weren't looking up. Pay attention, Mr. New York State of Mind," she quips.

This time, I'm looking up with a crooked smile when she snaps the photo.

"Now, do something silly!"

She crosses her eyes and sticks out her tongue, sliding it to the left. Like the idiot boy on a playground that does anything the girl he likes asks him to do, I surprise myself, stick out my tongue, and open my eyes wide.

Click, click, click—in rapid succession. And now she has all the evidence she'll ever need against me to have me at her mercy and forever doing her bidding.

But the quality of the pics is great. The green and blue and pink and yellow neon lights glow in the darkness of the hour, illuminating our backdrop. The intricately weaved pattern in between the black metal fencing is like a lightning strike in a dark sky: vibrant, electric, and beautiful.

And I have been completely bamboozled into taking selfies with a woman—in the real world, this never happens. Cass is not going to believe I allowed myself to get caught up like this. Just strung along like a helpless boy.

At the thought of Cass, I remember why I'm out with a stranger instead of celebrating with my best friend. This BS with her has me twisted up inside.

Looking at the photos she's just taken, Ava quietly decides they're good and moves me along. We walk the length of the tunnel and then climb a hill to a canal entrance, all while Ava schools me on DC's George-town history.

We descend a slender cobblestoned staircase leading to the walls surrounding the canal. The aged stone is dark and creviced, now invigorated with intermittent pink, purple, and blue floodlights the full height of the walls.

Ava stands in a funnel of pink light and hands me her phone.

"Can you get a pic of me here?"

I slide my leather glove off and angle the camera to get the full view. With one leg bent and both palms pressed against the wall, her head tilted right, she smiles and I snap the photo. Then I zoom in and tell her to lift her head just a little. She obeys and her smile softens. There's a twinkle in her eye that I could easily mistake as teasing. But I don't think it is. I think it's a release and relief. And a sign that she can get her groove back if she would only free herself.

I take another pic and study her smile, committing it to memory to call upon whenever I doubt the inherent goodness of people.

She steps away from the wall and I show her the photos.

"These look good, Mr. Russell. I saw you with the Drake angles."

I can't help but laugh at the reference, because while most people don't recognize me in public, when someone thinks they do, I'm mistaken for Drake. But thankfully, my eye color saves me. His is dark and mine is mostly light. But I really can't deny the other similarities.

With the impromptu photo session over, we continue our stroll along the canal, arm in arm. At the end of the walkway, we climb another set of stairs and land in an alleyway with glowing, oversized neon ornaments strung across and dangling and swaying overhead. And there's a full-size Steinway piano at the end with a musician dressed in all black and a top hat playing jazzy holiday tunes. Slim Christmas trees line the walls as kids race back and forth, pausing to pop their heads up occasionally.

Not typically a man that loses his words, but I am speechless. And Ava reads my mood and doesn't interrupt me as I absorb it all.

When we step out onto the sidewalk, I'm surprised at all the people out on Christmas Eve, mostly adults. It's probably the best time to avoid mobs of children during the holidays.

"Are you thirsty? Starbucks is across the street."

"I'm good. Would you like something?"

"Nope. Just being a good tour guide." She pauses and adds, "Speaking of...look across the street and up."

My head follows the direction of her hand. A bright neon-white figure appears on the rooftop in a running stance. And then another, and another, and it continues across the width of the building, giving the appearance of a person running and jumping across the edge of the roof.

"Now that's creative." I watch it three times and take a video while she takes photos of me before moving me along.

We walk through another walkway with what appears to be a garden of long lollipops in clusters of fluorescent colors. This time, I take her picture with her arms raised in the middle of the display and smiling like her greatest Christmas wish has come true.

"Okay, let's head back and get to the next stop." She slides her arm through mine again and I let her take the lead.

We stop at one more installation in a church courtyard adorned with neon string lights tightly strung across and through the tree limbs.

"It just keeps getting better," I say, legitimately impressed.

"Wow," she says sarcastically. "Mr. New York State of Mind likes what he sees. And we're not even close to done yet."

Her tone is light and easy, and she's obviously embracing the momentary reprieve from real life. As am I. We walk back to the SUV arm in arm.

I'm so grateful for this escapade, but I can't help but wonder how Cass is feeling and if she's okay. If *we're* okay.

Chapter Seven

Ava

B ack in the SUV, I ask Jacob to fire up that Christmas playlist. First up is the Jackson Five, "Santa Claus is Coming to Town." It's a classic that even Jacob can't resist, so he joins in. I take the lead like Fergie and the Black-Eyed Peas or Lauryn Hill and the Fugees. Sort of. But neither Jacob nor S.J. discourage me, so I must be doing okay.

We leave Georgetown and head to the upper Northwest.

"Where to next?"

"Be patient, Mr. Russell. Good things come to those who wait."

That came out a little flirtier than I intended, but he takes it in stride.

"You're enjoying this, aren't you? Having complete control over this night." He's leaning on the arm rest and looking right at me.

It makes me uncomfortable, but I also like it. Nervously, I pull off my beret and run my fingers through my hair and over my scalp to let it breathe.

"I am enjoying myself, but I don't know what you mean about enjoying control." I don't dare look at him and get caught up in those dazzling eyes. So, I check the time on the phone instead.

When I don't take the bait, he looks forward and sways slightly to the Alicia Keys version of "Little Drummer Boy."

"We can only spend about twenty minutes at the next stop because we have a reservation soon."

"A reservation? When did you do that?"

"I have connections in this city that you will benefit from tonight, Mr. Russell. You just sit back, relax, and be enchanted by Christmas, DC style."

"You've proven your Black Girl Magic superpowers just by commanding a bartender with a nod. But I still don't know what you do for a living."

This is easy. "I'm head of the agency responsible for sports and entertainment in the city. So, I'm part of the Mayor's cabinet, I am the liaison with some of the federal agencies, and I lead all related events throughout DC."

"Does that include events like NBA All-Star Weekend?"

"Exactly. And don't even start asking me for the hook-up," I tease, knowing I would actually have to ask him for a favor to access his noteworthy circle of associates, clients, and friends.

"I'm good. But I will give you the hook-up whenever you ask. It's the least I can do after tonight."

He is really making it hard for me to not like him as more than just a guy from the bar. But I'm sensible and I know this can't lead to anything real.

As we go further up Connecticut Avenue, S.J. comments. "This is the way to Cass's house. My best friend," he reminds me.

"She lives in Woodley Park?"

"Ah, maybe." He slides to the edge of the seat to ask Jacob. "Does Cass live in Woodley Park?"

"She does, Mr. Russell."

"Wow," I say. "Now I'm the one super impressed. That's some high-end real estate—the high rent district, as my friend Mr. Paul likes to call it. And I know because my parents still own a house in that neighborhood. It's been in our family for generations. We've survived gentrification, but we could never buy there now. Well, maybe my parents could, but I definitely can't on my government salary."

"Yeah. Sounds about right. Cass is a private practice plastic surgeon. She's doing well for herself. I'm proud of her."

When he talks about Cass, it's endearing. Makes me wonder if there's more to the friendship that he just isn't admitting to himself. One more reason for me to stay away.

We finally arrive at the entrance of the National Zoo, and Callie meets me at the opening.

"Hey, Ava," she says, speaking to me but looking at S.J., her eyes scanning him with intention, like she's taking his measure...or maybe undressing him. This must happen to him all the time.

I clear my throat. "Hey, Callie," I say, breaking the spell. "This is S. J. Russell." I turn to him and say, "S.J., meet Callie Thorn, the lead on this event."

She returns to her senses and they shake hands.

"Are we all set?" I ask, just in case his touch weakened her resolve.

"Oh, yeah–yeah, we are," she stammers. "Let's get you two inside."

I purposely don't grab his arm as we pass through the lit Zoo Lights sign. I don't want to give Callie the wrong impression—nor something to gossip about. Our tour starts with me guiding him through the winter wonderland of lit displays of all sorts of animals: lions, bears, flamingos, and even a scene from The Lion King, some of them animated. We don't have time to cover the full distance, but I make sure we walk through one of the open areas.

Just as we enter the opening, the volume of music grows louder and S.J. takes notice, searching for the speakers. Eventually, colorful lasers of light shoot across overhead, synced to the holiday tunes, and he twists his head to follow them. He wears a boyish grin as he watches, and I swell with pride. This is how I want everyone to feel when they visit my city.

I feel my phone vibrating in my pocket, more an alarm than a notification. I pray it isn't my sister or my mother, and the holiday is obviously conspiring in my favor because it's Lena.

Stepping a few feet away from S.J., I answer. "Hey, Lena. What's up?"

"Don't 'Hey, Lena' me. Where the hell are you? And don't say on your way to your parents', because I called there when your phone went to voicemail and your brother said you aren't arriving until morning. What the hell are you doing? Or is this your way of avoiding them until the last possible moment?"

She was speaking so fast she didn't give me a chance to answer or explain.

I say, "If you would stop talking and listen for a minute, I'll explain. I worked late and decided to drive early in the morning. Yes, I'm kind of avoiding the inevitable. But that's not all of it. You will never believe who I'm with right now."

"I am not in the mood for guessing games. I just know it better not be your ex."

"Not the ex. I'm with S.J. Russell."

She goes quiet.

Lena's never quiet.

"Hello. Did you hear me? Earth to Lena."

"Damn right I heard you. How did you end up with S. J. Russell on Christmas Eve? And what are you doing? I hope it's something nasty and worth you ditching your family."

"It's a long story. But we met at Round Robin and he thinks New York Christmas is better than DC Christmas, so I'm challenging his assumption and taking him on a little holiday tour."

"Are you a Hallmark Channel character right now? What kind of damn tour? You're with a man who is arguably New York's most eligible bachelor, fine as hell and even richer than that, and you're looking at Christmas lights. Do you have a fever? Love hangover? Do you need me to tell you what to do with a man like S. J. Russell?"

This is not helping. I know the answers to all of her questions, but I just don't have the energy to do anything more with this man than see some Christmas lights and drink some hot chocolate.

I say, "I know who he is, but I can't go there with him. Not right now. My wound is too fresh."

"What wound? You broke up with nice-but boring-as-navy-blue-shoes Geoff. He's the wounded party. You need a transition man to get you back in the game. And one has literally landed in your lap—that visual, by the way, is what you should be focusing on—and you're playing tour guide."

"Damn it, Lena!" My voice is a bit higher than I'd meant, and S.J. notices. Now he's walking in my direction.

"Hey," he says, his voice low and concerned. "You alright?"

I nod, anxious to get her off the phone and guilty about outing us spending time together.

"Okay, Lena. I'll call you when I get home. Bye."

I hit end, turn the phone off, and slip it back in my pocket. No more unwanted interruptions.

"Just my bestie, Lena. Calling to make sure I'm okay."

He nods with some skepticism and returns his attention to the light show while I force my heart to stop racing.

When the show is over, we start to head back to the entrance. There are a few other people inside, lots of young couples with babies and taking advantage of the thin crowds.

A couple passes by with a stroller that's partially covered and an infant bundled in blankets sleeping peacefully. S.J. watches them as they pass us, and his head follows them further into the zoo. It's very odd how he watches them, or maybe he's just caught up in the moment.

"Do you know them?"

He flinches, like he'd been caught opening his Christmas gifts early. When he looks at me, that sadness in his eyes is back.

"Nah. It's just nice to see young families."

He isn't convincing, but it's none of my business what he was thinking. And since we are obviously both on edge, no need for either of us to push the other.

"Cool. Let's get back so that we can get to the next stop. I have a *big* surprise for you!"

Chapter Eight

Sterling

The ride from the zoo to the next spot is the longest yet. Jacob keeps the holiday music in rotation, and we swap work stories and family expectations while finishing up the rest of the macarons. My takeaway from our conversation is we are both over-achieving, workaholic perfectionists equally benefiting from this impromptu break in our norm.

My other takeaway is she has been wearing her good girl armor so long that this one tiny dent threatened to break her to pieces. She is being too hard on herself and probably isn't giving her family enough credit. It's clear they love her and would understand her choice. And if they wouldn't, they'd get over it.

Along the route, Ava asks Jacob to go through the neighborhood with the baseball stadium. As we drive down smaller streets, there are even more people out at restaurants and going to what looks like another Christmas light display.

"Is that where we're headed next?"

"Nah," she says. "You've seen enough light displays tonight. Our next stop, ironically, just might be your favorite stop."

"What does that mean?" I ask.

"You'll see."

We cross a beautifully designed bridge and then enter an entirely different DC. We pass a church and a metro station, then turned onto Martin Luther King Jr. Avenue.

"The baseball stadium is in Southeast, but this is Southeast Anacostia. Affectionately known as East of the River. I live a few miles away, but on the Northeast side."

I take in the scenery and it feels like home. Small stores and restaurants. Fish fry joints and wired-money-transfer services. Churches, a community center, historic buildings, and even a Starbucks. The houses are smaller but well preserved. The streets are narrower and everything just feels closer—like community.

As we drive further down the Avenue, in the distance I see something that would not be familiar if Ava had not started our little tour at The Willard.

"Is that the...?"

"You know it," she says, cutting me off before I can even finish my question.

On the corner ahead is the biggest chair I've ever seen in my life. And beneath, a small cluster of Christmas carolers, all bundled in heavy coats and hats, holds sheet music and sings to a small crowd of people.

Before we get to the parking lot, we pass a street and Ava directs Jacob to turn right and slow down. Jacob is also from DC and knows exactly where we are headed.

"Roll down your window and look to your right," she instructs. "That's the home of Frederick Douglas."

Jacob pulls the car over and stops right in front of the house.

I ask, "How can this kind of history be tucked away in this little residential neighborhood? Do they get a lot of visitors?"

"Believe it or not, it's always busy. DC is known for the National Mall and its monuments, but it's this type of history that really makes it special."

Ava leans closer for a better view, her perfume and gentle breathing distracting me. But it's her sense of wonder, spreading and sucking me in, that makes me want more of her, to be closer to her.

I look over my shoulder at her and smile. "Thank you for tonight. This has been so much more than just a Christmas challenge." I twist a little more in the seat to get a better look at her and add, "And I can admit I don't know New York nearly as well as you know your city, and I admire that in you. And I'm humbled that you would share it with me."

She blushes and lowers her eyes. I take one of her hands in mine and squeeze until she looks up at me.

"Promise me you'll never lose this light, this sense of wonder and belonging. And that you'll share it with the world."

I've clearly caught her by surprise, because she has to look away and clear her throat before responding.

"Thanks for saying that. And it's really been my pleasure. I do this every year—make the time to just enjoy Christmas. But it's been a long time since I've seen it through someone else's eyes—someone that obviously enjoys it as much as I do. And I can admit you've surprised, Mr. Russell."

I want to know what she means by that, but I also want to just bask in it for a few minutes.

"Jacob, next stop: The Big Chair."

When we arrive and walk towards the carolers, a woman steps away to greet us. She hugs Ava first and then me, introducing herself as Miss Bailey. She's Ava's office manager.

"Come on, you two. Join in," she commands, wedging herself between us, arm in arm.

Ava shrugs and mouths, "You want to?"

And I nod.

We take our places just as the carolers transition to *O, Holy Night,* and my whole mood shifts—the lyrics remind me of the miracle of one life over so many other lives.

I am elevated out of my despair over Cass, and I land softly with a sense of peace and empathy. The answer has been here all along.

When we're done, I'm ready for the next song, but Ava squeezes my upper arm and whispers, "We have to go if we're going to make our reservation."

Chapter Nine

Ava

When we're back in the car, Jacob takes a different route and I put on my tour guide voice.

"I wanted you to see some of the other neighborhoods, since you've been existing between downtown and upper, upper Northwest."

We drive through a public housing area that had once served as military housing. Then we venture down Florida Avenue, where the row houses have been for over 200 years, still standing—some heavily renovated, others boarded up and others livable but in need of some attention.

"I like driving down Florida Avenue. It's like a thumb print of this city's history. The good. The bad. And indifferent."

When I look over at S.J., he's leaning on his door, taking it all in—the history, the culture, and the questionable.

"But next, I'm taking you to Black Broadway," I add, knowing this will get the New Yorker riled up.

He looks at me, incredulous. "Black Broadway? Ava, you know DC can't compete with Broadway in New York. You almost have me on Christmas, but I might have to take it back if you get too cocky."

I chuckle. "Haven't you learned anything on my little Christmas tour? Every place we've visited, I've given you a little slice of history. This next stop is no different."

He smirks, unconvinced. And I enjoy watching all the ways he smiles, smirks, laughs, and how he unconsciously moistens his lips with his tongue as protection against the cold.

I have no right to study him, watch his movements, or wonder about those movements in a different context. But it's happening, and I am trying to fight it.

I'm not doing a very good job, and Lena's rant didn't help.

"Okay. We'll see," he says, voice laced with fake outrage and over-exaggerated skepticism.

When we cross over U Street, I welcome him to Black Broadway and school him.

"When black people couldn't get a job on your New York Broadway, it didn't matter. Because they had their own version right here in DC."

Jacob meets my eyes in the rearview and grins. He knows. He's a native Washingtonian, too. He lowers the volume of the music and slows our pace.

I point out the Howard Theater, the statue of Duke Ellington, the Lincoln Theater, Lee's Flower and Card Shop, The Republic Gardens, and the first black-owned bank and YMCA, explaining how this U Street corridor became known as Black Broadway and a city within a city.

"Isn't Howard University near here?" he asks.

"It is. And it's the anchor of this neighborhood. Everything here was built up around it. And to satisfy your curiosity about why it was called Black Broadway, just consider all of the performers that graced these places. Pearl Bailey, Cab Calloway, Sarah Vaughn—and Duke Ellington grew up around the corner, and Langston Hughes worked as a busboy nearby at the Wardman Park Hotel. There's even a namesake restaurant for him on V Street: Busboys and Poets."

I pause for him to absorb it all, but also for myself. Revisiting this history is bittersweet because I love the cultural diversity of my city, but I also know what was sacrificed to get it.

"This place is special," I add. "Let's give it the respect it's owed."

S.J. is quiet. Watching the people in and out of the restaurants and lounges, the traffic congestion, the blended families, the homeless, the holiday street vendors—he's contemplative.

"Much respect," he finally says without looking at me. "I never knew how much black history was right here in DC. Guess I missed that class in high school."

All three of us chuckle at his last statement, and I use it to bring us back around to our final stop on the tour.

"So, many people don't know that DC used to be known as Chocolate City. And before you ask, there's a book about it and a ton of articles, so you know what to do."

"Google it," he says through a smile.

"But I want you to have a taste of that vibe, and I want to feed you after running you all over DC. I know you must be hungry."

Jacob stops us on the corner of 14th and U Streets, and we get out. I guide us through clusters of people to a dark metal door with its street number on the frame.

"This looks like somebody's apartment," S.J. suggests while looking left towards another restaurant entrance. "Maybe we should walk up to that door."

"Trust me," I say without looking at him. "We're at the right place."

Finally, the door opens, and my friend Caleb steps back to let us in.

"What's up, Ava? You all good?"

"All good. This is S.J., my new friend. S.J., this is Caleb."

They do that man-hand-grip thing, and we head inside.

The faint thrum of jazz pours from the speakers, setting the mood, and not too loud to be disruptive of the intimate conversations happening all throughout the space. It's dark and cavernous with lowlights and flickering candles atop tables. We walk past the bar where every stool is occupied and head to the back corner to an empty booth. I slide in first and pat the seat next to me. S.J. looks over his shoulder like he's searching for permission to sit next to me.

"Or you can sit across from me. Your choice."

I begin unraveling my scarf and peeling off my gloves and coat while he contemplates his options. I look up at him and can see the moment he chooses to let go.

I fold my coat neatly to my right and help him out of his. He's sitting upright and stiff like pasta noodles before they melt into hot water. I inch in closer.

"Relax yourself," I whisper, laying one hand on top of his hand resting on the table. Tension falls from his shoulders, and he eases back against the leather seating. He releases a deep breath he'd been holding and gazes around the bar.

"What is this place? I like the vibe."

"It's Gibson's. A speakeasy. My best friend Lena is a regular, therefore so am I. She likes it because the bartender/sommelier creates literary-inspired cocktails. Lena is a closet book nerd, so this place makes her feel like Zora Neale Hurston or F. Scott Fitzgerald or some such famous author. I just like it because if you don't know, you don't know. It's a secret hiding in plain sight."

He plants those dreamy, inquisitive, light brown eyes on me. "Is that why you brought me here? To keep me a secret from your friends?"

He smiles when he says it, but it's a naughty, teasing smile. Like he's dangling temptation in front of me to see if I'll reach out and grab it. And I want to...but I won't.

"No need for secrets with me. I'm an open book, and I am free to be out with whomever I choose."

He leans in and I get a whiff of his cologne. "Even though you just broke up with your boyfriend? Won't people talk?"

I know I shouldn't be this close to him, but I've melted into this seat.

"So what if they do? I'm a big girl. I can handle it."

There's false confidence in my statement, and by the glint in his eye, he knows it.

"So, why did you decline his proposal?"

His question is sincere, and I answer without looking at him. My words can hide some of my truth, but never my eyes.

"It just felt like settling. I love him, but I was never *in love* – just comfortable. I definitely never expected he would go to my parents for permission to propose without us having a serious conversation about it. I think he was just checking off his list of things he wanted to accomplish before 35. I made the list."

Saying it out loud reveals just how offensive it really is.

"I don't want to be an item on a to-do list. I want to be the love of someone's life."

He eases back, puts some distance between us, and asks about ordering. Guess I struck a nerve.

"I've already ordered a tasting menu for us. I wasn't sure if you're vegan or some other such thing, so we'll have a variety of options. You will, however, have to choose your own cocktail. I would never deny anyone that pleasure. You don't just drink them—you experience them."

I direct his attention to a chalk board over the bar with the specials, suggesting he choose from there because it's something different every day.

If this were a sugar and spice themed party, S.J. would definitely be the spice, choosing the Merry Traveler made with Scotch and Amaro and garnished with a flaming cinnamon stick. And I would be the sugar, opting for the champagne cocktail with peppermint schnapps, fresh muddled mint leaves, and a rim dipped in dark chocolate and crushed candy canes.

When our drinks arrive, S.J. raises his glass to toast. I sit up and lift my glass, eager to hear what we're toasting to.

"To new friends and new traditions."

We tap glasses and take our first sips.

"Damn, that's good," he remarks, his eyes squinted and tone appreciative.

"I told you," I say, easing back into the seat. "Doesn't get much better than this. I know a lot of places claim the 'speakeasy' vibe, but this place is the real deal." I take a long sip of the champagne, a fresh tingling sensation on my tongue as the effervescent bubbles go down easily.

"You've won me over, but I think you should let me do the same for you next year in New York. Maybe not on Christmas Eve—wouldn't want to keep you from your family. But you could come in early December and I could play holiday tour guide."

Is he opening the door for whatever this thing is between us to extend beyond tonight? Or does he think it's the polite thing to do? And which do I prefer?

I decide to go neutral.

"That could be fun. I've been to New York during Christmas, but it would be cool to experience it with a New Yorker. I'm sure there are some hidden gems I would never uncover on my own."

He sips his drink and licks his lips.

I wish he wouldn't do that.

"You're being modest," he teases. "I get the sense that you'll do your homework and probably bring your own list of spots to hit."

How he can know me so well after a few hours is beyond me. It's not an easy feat.

I chuckle. "You're probably right. But that would make it interesting, right?"

"True that," he says.

There's something that I've been wondering about him for years, and it's been nagging at me all night.

"So, can I ask you a personal question?"

"Go right ahead," he says, meeting my eyes.

"Why don't you use your first name—Sterling? It's such a solid name. It's actually kind of sexy," I add, the alcohol clearly taking over my sensibilities.

"Well, maybe I will use it now since I know you like it," he jokes.

Now I'm blushing, my mind trying to balance regret for the sexy comment and curiosity for wanting to see his response.

He stares down into his drink before continuing, and I hope I haven't opened some wound. He swallows hard and I watch his throat contract. There's a small mole beneath his right ear, and I now have a full view of the contour of his muscles through his perfectly fitted sweater. His shoulders are broad and his chest sculpted. Plus, I'm sure he has rippling abs and one of those V-shapes hiding beneath the waist of his jeans, because there is nothing loose about his skin. Just tight, lean muscles my fingertips yearn to touch.

Snap out of it, Ava!

"It's not a long story, but a sad one. I'm a junior and my father died when I was really young. I barely remember him. But my mother—who never said a negative thing about him—struggled after his death. I always thought it was because she really missed him, but I eventually learned that she was worried that I might be more like him than she could handle. He suffered from mental illness and ultimately gave up on life. She had given me his name, then once he was gone, she started calling me S.J. and it stuck. Just saying *Sterling* was a source of pain for her and so I only use it for government business. Most people don't even know my full name."

He looks up from his glass and at me.

"But you do. Guess you've technically known me a lot longer than I've known you. You've got me at a disadvantage."

"Not really. It was easy to know you. For a long time, this whole country practically knew you."

"So, you never played sports yourself? If you know all about my high school career, you had to be close to the game?"

He changes the subject, and I go with it, not wanting to drag him any further down this rabbit hole.

"I'm not really athletic, though I tried. When nothing worked out, I went to the numbers. I became a statistician for our middle school girls' basketball team and then in high school transitioned to boys' basketball. I kept it up in college and always made sure I knew all the best players. It helped me anticipate plays and capture shots and fouls with so much accuracy, the college coach I worked for demanded that I be able to travel with the team. So that's my story of how I know so much about your story."

"Life is so crazy," he says, finishing off his drink with one big swallow. "But in all seriousness," he adds, "I'm glad we met tonight. This has been the best Christmas Eve ever. Spontaneous, fun..."

"And don't forget informative," I interrupt.

"And that, too. I like you, Miss Ava Jones. And that's real talk. And if you want to call me Sterling, it would be my pleasure."

Our food arrives. We eat, laugh, talk, and have two more rounds of cocktails. A co-worker and her partner stop by our table to say hello, and we chat with them for a few minutes.

When they walk away, his phone vibrates on the table and he snatches it up.

Without looking at me, he stands and says, "I need to take this." And then he hurries away.

I assume it's a call from his friend Cass and hope that this will be the beginning of reconciling whatever is happening with them.

Sensing this is the end of the night, I order a to-go box for Jacob and pay the bill.

Then I sit alone for nearly ten minutes—just enough time for me to come to my good girl senses.

Chapter Ten

Sterling

Cass is calling me to apologize, but the ask is still the same. She says she just wants me to take a couple days and think it over. Not be so dismissive of the idea.

And she graciously accepts my apology for behaving like a neanderthal. I make her a promise to keep an open mind and to list out and weigh the pros and cons—this is her *get-shit-done* mantra. Then I spend the last few minutes of our call telling her about my evening with Ava, and she geeks out. I tell her to control herself because this is not a thing nor a fling. It's a platonic Christmas Eve challenge and nothing more.

I make one more call and go back to Ava.

We return to the car, but the spell is broken. We had clicked at Gibson's, but now it feels like we're back at the Round Robin feeling each other out.

The drive back is silent but for the holiday music Jacob continues streaming. Ava has her head back and eyes closed, blocking any chance of a conversation.

When we pull up to the entrance of The Willard, she asks me if Jacob can drive her back to her office to get her car.

"Of course, but I was hoping you'd join me for a nightcap. I have a surprise for you."

"What sort of a surprise?"

"Well, it wouldn't be a surprise if I told you, now, would it?"

She exchanges a glance with Jacob, and he nods.

"Okay. But not a nightcap in your room. At the bar."

"Fair enough," I say.

Inside, we find two seats at the bar, and once we've ordered, I step out to the check-in desk. When I return, I lay a key card on the bar in front of her.

"What is this? A one-night stand proposition?" I've unintentionally offended her.

"Absolutely not," I assure her. "You just spent the entire evening with me. Have I given you any indication that I would be so forward? So presumptuous?"

Ava stares at the key like it's poisonous mistletoe – intended to invoke passion, but dangerous all the same. Then she looks up at me. "No. So what is it for?"

"I booked you an overnight stay in the Jenny Lind Suite—as a surprise and a thank-you for your hospitality tonight. You did something truly remarkable for me today, and now I'd like to do the same for you. Not as repayment, but just as a kind gesture. Please accept it."

Her body language softens, and I can see she's considering my offer.

"It's all paid for, and it's just for you. No expectations at all. You don't even have to have a coffee with me in the morning, because I know you have to get to your family. Just have a luxurious night in your bucket list hotel room—my treat."

She taps her manicured fingernail on the key card and then looks at me again.

"I accept. Thank you."

"You're welcome."

"And I'm sorry for thinking the worst."

"No apologies necessary," I assure her. "I didn't think through how it might look just handing you a key card. That's on me."

She picks up the key card and rubs it between her fingers. And then, with the sweetest puppy dog eyes, she looks up at me.

"Can we skip the nightcap? I'd love to spend as much time as possible in that suite."

My heart sinks just a little. I don't want the night to end, but it wouldn't be right to offer her a gift and then dictate how she uses it. I swallow my ego and man up.

"Of course. It's your gift, your way."

We leave the bar and head to the elevators. One opens immediately, and all I can think is, *Damn, even the elevators are conspiring against me.*

Thankfully, our suites are on the same floor. But this is it. I may never see her again. As the elevator silently sails upward, I think about asking her to exchange numbers with me, but it seems awkward. So, we ride in silence while I twist my gloves in my hands and she toys with the key card—like two teenagers at the end of a movie date, both wondering if there would be a kiss.

When the doors open, my suite is to the left and Ava's is to the right.

"I'll escort you to your room," I say.

"How chivalrous of you, *Sterling*."

Her tone is sweet again, and gone is the disappointment I'd felt when I gave her the room key.

Her calling me Sterling has heat rushing from my face, through my chest, and right down to my manhood. I yearn to taste my name on her lips. But I have to control it. This isn't that kind of night.

We reach her door and she touches the key card against the pad. It unlocks, and she twists the handle. I stand back and watch as she slowly steps inside, sliding her beret off simultaneously. Her hand lingers on the door, and I think maybe she has forgotten I'm even standing there.

Then she turns and smiles at me.

"We could have a nightcap in here if you're still interested."

Ava

"I would love to have a nightcap with you," he says.

I hold the door open and let him step inside, watching him come through. He is such a deliciously handsome man. Tall, muscular, stylish, and without an ounce of toxic masculinity. Sure, he is obviously a bit of a player with the women, but it isn't in a disrespectful way—of that, I'm sure.

Once inside, I give him the tour. Even though it's my first time inside the suite, I've studied the photos of it for years on the website. I totally feel like I have just unwrapped the Christmas gift on every kid's list that was sold out everywhere. This is a one-of-a-kind suite, with a view of the monument and a canopy bed and a marble bathroom. My idea of perfect.

I flop my body down on the sofa and he dials room service for a bottle of champagne. Then he takes off his coat, and I take his full measure. Slim, dark denim jeans that fit just right. Classic Jordans, clean and unscuffed. A black cashmere crew neck sweater that was so soft, I want to lay my cheek against his chest just to feel it against my skin.

Well, that isn't the only reason I want to put my face to his chest. This man is my other idea of perfect.

We talk about our plans for the next day and replay our favorite moments from the night until the champagne arrives. He pops it open and pours, and I suggest another toast.

"To Christmas wishes coming true."

We touch glasses and sip, eyes connected and neither of us looking away. When he pulls his glass away first, he licks his lips, but I don't think it's because they're dry.

I pull my glass away and step closer to him–not touching him, just breathing him in. Looking up into his eyes, I want him to read my mind and pull me close. I want him to feel the heat surging through me and give me a reason to release it.

And S.J. does seem to understand–he slips his free hand to the small of my back and firmly brings my body closer to his. S.J. used his free hand and laid it on the small of my back, firmly bringing my body closer to his. His palm is warm, and I can feel the tips of his fingers tracing circles on my back, the thin silk of my blouse the only barrier between us. My heart begins to race, matching my desire to be touched, to be kissed, to be consumed by this man.

He lowers his face closer to mine, warm breath near my ear. I nearly gasp as he whispers, "May I kiss you, Ava?"

I wrap my free arm around his neck and exhale, "Please kiss me. Now, Sterling."

He pulls back from me to set his glass down and to take mine. Now with both our hands free, we're entering dangerous territory—passing the point of no return.

Then he gently cups my face with his hands and looks into my eyes, a grin creeping across his face.

"I've wanted to do this ever since you stepped into that bar tonight."

"So stop talking about it and do something about it," I dare him.

He leans in and I close my eyes, ready to feel his lips against mine.

But instead, he kisses my right cheek gently. Then my left cheek as he rubs his thumb across my bottom lip. He kisses the tip of my nose and up to my forehead and back around to my cheek and down the side of my neck. He nibbles at my collarbone, and a moan of desperation escapes from my mouth.

Sterling catches it just as he presses his lips against mine, and he slides his tongue across the opening of my mouth, seeking permission to enter. Our tongues touch, and I taste the champagne as we caress and explore.

When my breath catches, his kisses become more intentional, firmer, and I can feel him rising against my leg. I know we should stop, but I don't know how we can. And I don't want to. I run my hands down his back and then finally under his shirt, eager to feel his skin and hard muscles. I let my fingertips trace the dip in his spine and tickle the skin around the waist of his pants.

I can feel him growing thicker, harder, as he presses against me and grips my shoulders.

And then his grip loosens, and his pace slows.

He pulls back from me, desire coursing through his eyes. My breath catches again.

"I don't want to stop," I whisper to him.

"I don't either," he says. "But we can't keep going. This is not why we came to your room."

"I know. But I want you." I pause and take both of his hands in mine. "I need you."

I can see his body working against his mind - desire overtaking common sense.

"But we don't have protection," he finally acknowledges. Like that would be enough to stop this before it's too late.

"I do."

He squints at me, curious about why I would have condoms in my purse.

"A gift from Lena for my birthday. She calls it an emergency booty call kit. But never mind that. We're prepared."

He steps back, still unsure. "Okay. Let's cool down first and be sure we really want to take this step. Let's turn on a Christmas movie, finish our champagne, and then see if it's something we still want to do."

I'm shocked and impressed, and it makes me want him even more.

"Mind if I use your bathroom?" he asks.

"Of course. You know where it is."

I sit back on the sofa, down the rest of the champagne in my glass, and pour another full glass. While I'm sipping, I hear a phone vibrating on the table. I think it's mine, but then I realize my phone is in my bag. Sterling's phone is on the edge of the coffee table, and it tumbles off from the vibration.

When I reach down to pick it up, I see notifications from Cass.

The messages are coming in rapid succession, and the last one reads:

Cass: I really want to have this baby with you. Please just think about it. Love you, man.

I stare at the phone for a few seconds, then drop it like it's on fire.

A baby? Is that what they've been arguing about? Did he get her pregnant and now she wants to have the baby and he doesn't want her to? And what kind of game is he playing with me?

I feel dizzy and nauseous all at once.

But I have to keep it together. And I've got to get away from him.

When he returns from the bathroom, I fake a headache and tell him I just need to lie down. I promise to call him in his room in the morning before I check out, and I push him out the door.

Once he's gone, I lean my body against the door and fight back tears threatening to expose me.

I'm such an idiot. Trying to play the part of a bad girl when I am forever doomed to be the good girl in a big, bad world.

Chapter Eleven

Sterling

My cell phone alarm blares and a slice of sunshine cuts across my suite. It's 8:00 a.m. on Christmas morning, and I lift my head off the pillow, realizing that nothing in my space celebrates the holiday. The date on my phone screen is the only indication.

I call the front desk for any messages. There are none. I ask if Ms. Jones has checked out, and they confirm that she left the hotel at 5:00 a.m.

By now she's in Middleburg, probably watching her nieces and nephews rip open gifts. I press rewind on the last thirty minutes of our night together and can't figure out what happened to change her mood. Maybe she really did have a headache, but she practically pushed me out the door. Gone was the smile, the desire, the teasing, the fun. It had been replaced with angst in a matter of minutes.

Since it's Christmas, I'll be spending the day with Cass and her family —hopefully not talking about babies and sperm donations. I unplug my phone from the charger and unlock it.

I have six missed text messages from Cass.

When I read them, I realize exactly what has happened.

So, I do what any man in trouble with a woman would do. I call my best friend to help me undo the damage.

I tell Cass what I think happened, and she agrees that I'm probably correct and that if Ava read her messages, she probably thinks we're having a baby together through an unplanned pregnancy.

"What the hell am I supposed to do now? I don't even have her cell phone number. I know where she works, but she won't be back in the office until the New Year. Come on, Cass! Help me figure this out!"

Cass asks all the right questions: *Where does she live? Could she have shared her number with Jacob? Did she AirDrop you any photos?* I don't have any answers to help us. I just know that her parents have a home in Cass's neighborhood and a horse farm in Middleburg, Virginia.

Finally, Cass comes through. Her partner is a realtor specializing in high-end real estate in DC, Maryland, and Virginia. She searched her database and got an address in Middleburg for Ava's parents.

"What are you going to do now?" Cass asks.

"We're going to Middleburg."

"Who is we? I know you don't think I'm driving with you almost two hours to Middleburg on Christmas morning. Are you still tipsy from last night?"

"You are going because she'll only believe this if you tell her. And we're not driving. We're taking a private helicopter service out of Reagan National Airport. Pick me up in an hour."

Ava

I convinced Lena to drive to Middleburg with me. I needed backup, a sounding board, and my friend. Somebody on my side no matter what.

On the drive down, I gave her all the details about my time with Sterling. I even showed her all of the photos. But when I told her about the text messages, she thought that something was missing. She wasn't convinced that he would have gotten his best friend pregnant and then be out with me.

I didn't know what to believe, but I needed to talk through it and get it out of my system. Especially before dealing with my family.

When we arrive, everyone is asleep but my mom. She meets us on the front porch with two piping-hot cups of coffee and ushers us in. After we sit at the kitchen table, the inquisition begins.

"So, Ava, care to explain why Lena is your Christmas plus-one and not your fiancé?"

"Because I said no, Mom. I couldn't marry him. I wouldn't be happy and I wouldn't be able to make him happy."

"But he's a good man, Ava. Not every man checks all your boxes. What's most important is that you have a partner who respects you and is willing to grow with you. I thought that's what your father and I taught all you kids."

My mother's long hair is pulled up in a high ponytail with a bright red scarf protecting her edges. The kitchen gets hot and she has never liked a strand of hair out of place. Her smooth mahogany skin barely shows any signs of aging, except for a few wrinkles around her eyes when she smiles.

I set my coffee down but keep my hands wrapped around it.

"Mommy, you and Daddy did show us that. But you showed us so much more. You showed us what real love is like. Anya and DJ got the lesson, and look at how happy they are. Even when they have a little trouble in paradise, it doesn't stick because they found more than mutual respect—they found love. They didn't settle. And I don't want to settle either."

My mother sips from her coffee and looks at Lena, who tries to divert her eyes.

"I sense there's more to this story, Lena. Am I right?"

Lena takes a big swig of coffee, buying time before she answers. I stare at her, eyes pleading with her to keep my secret. But it's all for naught. She sings like a canary.

"She met someone last night and from all that she's told me, he might be the one."

"Last night? Be serious, Lena!" My mother is incredulous. She turns to me. "Is this true, Ava? You met a man last night and think he might be *the one*. In under twenty-four hours? You young people!"

She shakes her head, and Lena tells me to show her the photos on my phone and tell her about our Christmas Eve challenge.

My mom shakes her head again but says she'll listen. So, I start the story all over again. And the more I tell it, the more I know that Sterling had awakened something in me I never knew existed.

When I finish, my mother simply says, "Maybe. I guess it's possible. But you left him and now you'll never know."

She goes back to cooking, and three sets of small feet bound down the stairs, rushing into the kitchen. My nieces and nephews climb all over me while my mom and Lena laugh and snap pics.

We take the party to the family room and let them sort their gifts until their parents join. Once we're all together, the holiday paper hurricane begins, and I feel like myself again.

My parents go back into the kitchen to finish cooking brunch while I unload my unbelievable holiday story on my sister and brother, who are fascinated. My sister forgives me, and my brother wants to meet Sterling.

A couple hours have passed and brunch is nearly ready. I'm leading the kids in clean-up when the doorbell rings. My mother goes to the door, her etiquette antenna on high alert and visibly irritated about who might just drop by on Christmas morning.

And then I hear his voice.

I'm on my knees, clutching two fistfuls of wrapping paper and ribbon while strategically avoiding stray Lego pieces, when my mother walks him and a strange woman into the family room.

"What are you doing here, Sterling?" I ask weakly. "How did you even find me?"

The strange woman spoke first. "I can answer both those questions for you, if you'll give me just a few minutes of your time."

And then it registers for me. *Tall. Girl-next-door beautiful. Poised. Direct.* "You're Cass."

"I am. Sterling's best friend who is probably the reason you have the wrong idea about him. Please, just give me a few minutes. And if you don't believe me, we'll leave and you won't hear from him again."

Sterling stands quietly, hands folded in front of him, wearing a crooked smile and pleading eyes.

"I can't believe you would show up like this, Sterling." I'm a mix of anger and hurt, which is quickly being erased by the tiniest bit of happiness that he would go to these lengths to find me.

"I know," he says, lowering his head. "I'm sorry, but I can't just let you walk out of my life. At least not without the truth. And once you have the truth, if you never want to see me again, I'll leave you alone. I promise."

I push past him and tell Cass to follow me.

We go into my father's study and sit across from each other in two brown leather chairs, where she spills the whole complicated mess. Turns out, she and her partner want to start a family and they've asked Sterling to be their sperm donor because they don't want to have a baby with a stranger. They want a family made with love. In theory, Sterling understood and agreed. But in practice, It freaked him out, and they argued about it. Have been disagreeing for days.

"I'm so sorry for any hurt or confusion I may have caused for you. And I mean it." She leans in to cover my hand with her warm palm and lowers her voice to a whisper. "Because when he called me frantic this morning, I knew that you were something special. And now that I've met and seen you on your knees cleaning Christmas debris with your nieces and nephews, I can tell what kind of woman you are. The kind I've prayed he would find."

I have no words, just emotion bubbling up inside. He isn't having a baby with his best friend—well, not in the traditional sense. And he hasn't misled me. Plus, I guess he feels what I'm feeling if he came all this way to explain on Christmas morning.

Cass has been watching me cycle through a bevy of thoughts. I slide my chair back and stand, and she awkwardly joins me. Our eyes meet and I reach in to hug her. "Thank you for doing this for me. For us." I release my embrace and can feel her muscles relax. "Something happened between us last night that we both tried to fight. And it hurt to think that maybe only I was feeling it."

"You weren't. I might even argue that he's feeling it more. He chartered a private helicopter to get us here in under an hour!"

We both laugh, and I ask her to send Sterling back here.

I pull myself together, and when he enters the study, I think I know what I want to say. But then I just rush over, hug him tight, and kiss him deep. He pulls me closer and responds in kind.

When we come up for air, I say, "I thought I would never see you again," fighting back happy tears.

"I had the same thought and it scared me. I thought I had really messed up with you. Thank you for listening to Cass."

"Thank you for bringing her. And for the record, if it matters at all to you—I think you should do it. Be her sperm donor."

"You do?" I can tell he's really surprised.

"I do. She's your best friend, so you'll be a part of her child's life anyway. And you all can work out the details as you go. I know it seems like a big ask, but it also speaks to big love. The fact that she's not worried that you'd try to take the kid from her or something else foolish speaks volumes about your friendship. It's equal risk and double the joy."

Sterling stands close to me and wraps his arms around me. He doesn't kiss me, just holds me, and I can feel his heart beating through his shirt. It's slow and steady.

We stay like that for what feels like an eternity, detached from the real world and simply sharing air, space, and the magic of the moment. When he finally pulls away, he grips my hands in his and says, "Thanks to you, *'Twas the Night Before Christmas* has brand new meaning. And my Christmas wish is that last night 'twas the night before everything for us."

THE END

A Billionaire for Christmas

BY LISA M. MILLER

Patrick comes to the small town where his family has chosen to retire, to spend Christmas with his parents. What he didn't expect was falling for the local girl-next-door.

About the Author

Lisa M. Miller is a contemporary author from Manchester, UK. She's been writing stories since she was fifteen. In 2021 she re-released her first book - Missing (an office romance novella).
She loves all of her book boyfriends equally, but in particular she's drawn to her Billionaires (a girl can dream–right?).
In 2022 she started her first series: Billionaire Boss–which starts with Our Best Friends Wedding.
When she's not writing, you can usually find her reading or drinking tea/wine (depending on the time of day).

IG: @lmmillerbooks
Lisa M. Miller's Bossy Boys Facebook Group

Chapter One

Patrick

I've always loved the drive from Seattle to my parents. I've not been with the family for Christmas, for several years, always using work as an excuse. With Dad's health problems earlier this year, Mom wanted to make sure I'd be here this Christmas. Driving has forced me to not work the whole time. I laugh to myself, looking at my phone as another email pops onto my screen. Okay, I guess I'm not working as much.

I decided to leave in the middle of the night knowing the roads would be quieter that way and so far, the peace and quiet is relaxing, just what I need. It's a long drive, but I love nothing more. I've always found something eerily comforting about driving through the night.

After spending hours on the road and stopping every couple of hours for coffee, I see the snow on the mountains ahead of me. Mom and Dad retired here ten years ago or so. Well, I say retired; Dad is still a board member, but nothing hands on. We always used to come here for the holidays when I was younger, so it made the most sense that they'd want to retire here. I just wish it wasn't quite so far.

As I drive through town, it's now late afternoon and some of the shops are still open. This place is as small-town as you can imagine. It takes you all of about fifteen minutes to drive round the whole town. Maggie's Diner is the only place to serve a decent cup of coffee. You have the hardware store across the road that always seems to be open. The town hall is in the center of the community, along with the park. I swear this place was made just so everyone knows what everyone is doing. Everyone knows each other and is ready to help each other without a second thought.

My family holds a fundraiser every year since they moved here for the local children's charity, and if I know my mom at all, she's going to want me helping in some capacity. What she doesn't know is every year I give one of the highest donations. My dad gives the highest.

I pull up outside Maggie's Diner and walk towards the counter. Maggie is standing pouring a coffee but smiles at me as I walk towards her.

"Hey there, Patrick. You taking a seat, or are you on the go?"

"Hey Maggie, on the go. I still need to get to the cabin, then I'm having dinner with Dad."

"Your dad said you were going to be here for the holidays. He's still surprised you're staying the whole time."

Everyone in town loves my dad.

"Yeah. I think my mom might have had something to say about that if I didn't turn up." I know I have an edge to my voice, but I can't help it. I'm used to living in the city and not knowing who my neighbors are. This small-town life is not for me.

"They miss you, that's all."

I take a twenty dollar bill out of my wallet and hand it to Maggie, turning to leave.

"Patrick Jacobs, you know damn well that coffee is nowhere near this. You may be used to paying this for a black coffee, but not here you don't."

I smile to myself and walk out. Keep the mask in place, Patrick.

I get back in my Land Rover and pull out onto Main Street heading straight to the road that leads me up to where my cabin is.

· · ·

414

When I open the door, the smell of the fire pit instantly makes me smile. Mom must have hired someone to clean the place and get a fire going. This place is my sanctuary. It's the place that is mine. None of the women I've dated have ever seen this place. Hell, nobody except the family knows I own the place.

I pull my bags out of the doorway, close the door, and see straight away my mom has already been round.

The cabin has a tree and decorations up, and sitting on my coffee table in the living room is a box with a note with her handwriting on the folded piece of paper.

Patrick,
I hope you didn't drive too long without taking a break. Why you insisted on driving I don't know.
Anyway, your fridge is stocked with the things you'll need until tomorrow. In case your father forgets; you're having breakfast at the house tomorrow.
Sorry I can't be with you boys tonight but, with a week to go before the charity event I need to finish some of the arrangements.
Love You.
Mom.

I laugh and see she's left me with enough stuff to last me my whole stay. I walk to the big glass windows at the other side of the room and take in the view. It really is amazing here with the snow on the mountains around us. I throw a log on the fire and sit back and relax.

I hear my phone ping. I don't know what it is about this place, but I don't have any desire at all to answer the emails I know are waiting for me.

I'm not someone who has ever been comfortable living out of a suitcase. Even if I'm staying somewhere for one night, I have to unpack. Of course, I keep some stuff here, but Mom made a note on more than one occasion to remind me I needed formal wear too. I've never stayed at the cabin for as long as I am this stay. I needed some extra clothes.

Snow is lightly falling, and I sit back next to the fire and open the brown paper bag Maggie gave me with my coffee. That woman has not once forgotten my love of her apple pie. Of course, she's known me since I was old enough to cause trouble. Her son Joe and I were always getting into trouble... He made coming home for the holidays every year exciting though. He never once let me feel left out year-after-year. Of course, he's married with a couple of kids now, something my mom brings up in conversation at least a couple of times a week. I can't blame her though. I'm her only child, her baby. At least that's what she tells me.

I know she wants to see me happy. I'm just not ready to settle down. I enjoy my random hook-ups.

I walk into the restaurant where I'm meeting Dad. This small town in Montana has one fancy steak house at the edge of town. Dad loves this place. I'm sure he's what's keeping them in business.

The hostess at the entrance smiles at me and, holy crap, she's good-looking. The black dress she's wearing is hugging her in all the right places, and I'm suddenly wishing I wasn't here to have dinner with my dad.

"Are you ok?" she asks me.

I realize I've just been staring at her this whole time.

"Yeah. Sorry. I'm here to meet my dad. We should have a table booked for Jacobs?"

Now it's her turn to stare at me. She starts to get all flustered. "Oh. Wow. You're Kent's son?"

"Yeah."

"He's already here." She smiles and picks up a menu off the stand and walks deeper into the restaurant.

I see my dad straight away talking to a couple at the table next to him.

"Hey, Dad."

Chapter Two

Lilly

When Kent's son walked in a moment ago, I turned into an idiot. I should have recognized him from the photos Mallory has up in the house, but damn, he's better-looking in person. When Kent turned up twenty minutes ago, he asked to be seated before his son arrived. I think he likes to be surrounded by people. At least that's what Mallory thinks.

I take Kent's son over to the table, and sure enough, Kent is chatting away to the couple nearest him.

"Hi, Dad." He sits down after handing me his coat.

I hand him the menu and try not to say too breathlessly, "Someone will be here to take your orders in a minute."

I walk away, and I'm sure I can feel his eyes following me. Do I put a little extra spring in my step? Yes, I do.

The restaurant is busy tonight, especially for a Sunday. I turn to see the guys behind the bar laughing with Sammy, the waitress.

"Who's the hottie sitting with Kent?" Sammy says, fanning herself with her order pad, her eyes not leaving the men in question.

"His son."

The three of them look amongst themselves.

"I didn't know he had a son?"

"Yeah, he lives in Seattle. He's here for Christmas. He has stopped by a couple of times over the years, never staying this long though. I know Mallory is excited to have him around."

I walk over to the table of another one of our regulars and remind them that we're selling tickets to the annual Children's Christmas charity event. Everyone has been so great it looks like we're going to have more people turn up than we did last year.

I look over to Kent and his son while they laugh and are deep in conversation. I keep feeling his eyes on me though, as I move around the room.

I'm around until closing, and Kent leaves a very generous tip on the table, for the staff.

I smile at him from across the room.

His son is still sitting at the table, finishing his whiskey, typing away on his phone. The guy spent half the night on the thing.

I take the money off the table and walk over to my friends. Sammy and the guys are sitting round the bar; it's become our thing to do on a Sunday after closing.

When Kent's son stands, I walk over to him and hand him his coat.

"Hope to see you around," he says, his eyes roaming over my body.

I feel my skin blush and hear a murmur from my friends behind me.

He smiles at me as he leaves the restaurant. Locking the door behind him, I look over to see my friends staring at me. Sammy is smiling from ear to ear with a mischievous look on her face.

While we spend the next hour drinking and listening to Christmas songs over the sound system, I try to brush off her comments about any interest I might have from our town's handsome visitor.

I love walking through our small little town in the middle of nowhere. At night it's so quiet and I love it at this time of year, with the Christmas tree in the middle of the town square and Christmas lights all over the place. My AirPods are playing Christmas songs in my ear, and I love it.

One of the guys had offered to give me a ride home, but I don't live far from the restaurant, and I like the peace and quiet. Hopefully my best friend will be home. No doubt she'll be baking some kind of sweet goodies that I can dig into tomorrow. Abby has always loved to bake. The snow really came down while I was at work, it's the perfect Christmas postcard.

The house is dark and quiet when I get home, I'm a little disappointed, but also kinda glad of the peace. I switch on our little Christmas tree in the corner of our living room and ask my speaker to play my favorite Christmas playlist. I love this time of the year.

Working till closing time always leaves me super wide awake after, and I need time to chill out and decompress.

My best friend walks in and plonks herself down on the couch next to me. I'm enjoying a hot chocolate and eating one of the Christmas cookies she'd made earlier when I was leaving for work. She always bakes a batch for me and puts them in my favorite tin.

"You still okay helping at the children's charity event this coming week?" I ask.

"Yes, I can't wait. I spoke to my boss and he said he's going to call you or Mallory tomorrow to arrange some things for the big event."

"Wow. That's excellent. Thanks, Abby."

"No problem. See you tomorrow." She gives me a squeeze on the couch and leaves to go upstairs to her room.

I grab my folder and bag with all the things I need for my meeting with Mallory. When she asked me two years ago to help her with this event, I was so excited. Mallory is famous for her charity work and the Children's Christmas event is always so magical. I never in my wildest dreams thought I'd one day be able to help run the thing.

On the breakfast bar in the kitchen is a box with a note on the top.

For Mallory and Kent.

Don't sneak any. I'll make you another batch when I finish work.

I laugh to myself as I put the box in my bag with all my things. I grab my car keys out of the dish and head out of the house.

I love driving up to Mallory and Kent's cabin. It's huge and so fancy. When I was younger, I always dreamed I'd meet Prince Charming and we'd live in a luxury cabin like this. The thing is bigger than my house as well as a couple of other houses added together.

I notice the steps and path have already been swept and salted. Mallory must have got started early.

I knock on the door and hear Mallory shout for Patrick to get the door. I look at my hair in the reflection on the window to check I don't look like a mess. Nobody wants to look bad in front of a hot guy even if you know he's way out of your league.

I take a deep breath just as I'm about to knock again, but Patrick opens the door, and he looks even more attractive in jeans and a sweater than he did last night in his casual suit.

"Hi, I'm Lilly. We met last night. I'm here to help your mom with the charity event." I hold my hand out. What the hell am I doing? Lilly, you babbling idiot.

He shakes my hand with a bemused look on his face and moves out of the way so I can come into the house.

"Lilly, is that you?" says Kent walking down the stairs. I smile up at him, and he gives me a big hug.

"Patrick, this is Lilly. I know you met last night, but you're probably going to see a lot of her this week."

"Hi," he says, like I'm keeping him from something important.

We head towards the kitchen, where Mallory and I spend most of our time. We both have a serious coffee addiction and I need some close by when an important event is coming up. She gives me a big hug and puts a coffee in front of me just the way I like it.

Mallory looks over my shoulder, and I turn and notice Patrick is just standing in the doorway looking at us with a puzzled expression on his face.

Chapter Three

Patrick

I wasn't expecting to see a bundle of sunshine walk into my parents' house like it's a common thing. I certainly wasn't expecting my parents to hug the girl I spent way too much time thinking about last night. It seems that Lilly, that's her name, is close to my parents. Hell, my mom is acting like she's the daughter she never had.

I watch as she takes her coat off and hangs it on the hook in the mud room, totally at ease in the place. She seems more at ease in this place than I do.

I can't take my eyes off her though, as she laughs with my parents and makes herself at home.

"Abby sent these over," she says, giving my dad a wink, passing him a box.

"Yes, please tell me she's almost ready to open her own shop?"

"She sure is. She's hoping to be opening in the new year. She signed the lease yesterday. But I'm sure you already knew that."

If I didn't know better, I'd think she was flirting with my dad, but Mom just laughs at them.

She pulls out some pens while I help myself to coffee. When Dad told me I needed to help Lilly with some jobs around the town, I was expecting one of my mom's friends, not the hot maître-de from the restaurant.

Mom puts some pastries on the table while Lilly fires off a list to her.

I cross my legs at the ankle, leaning against the counter. It's not until I hear my dad's voice louder that I realize they've been trying to get my attention. I move my gaze away from Lilly, who's turned a lovely shade of pink, and look at my mom, who looks like she's fighting to hide a smile. Unsuccessfully, I might add.

"Lilly needs help collecting some things people have donated. I'd really appreciate it if you'd be able to help her with the decorations as well."

WTF! Doesn't the place we're using have staff for that?

As if reading my mind, Lilly says, "I'm sure Patrick has more important things to do." Her eyes looking over her list *again*!

"Yes..."

"No..." my dad says at the exact same time.

Lilly sits back in her chair and is fighting back a laugh, along with my mom, as Dad and I glare at each other from across the room. I avoid looking at my mother, since I know one look at her and I'd cave in an instant. I told myself I was going to take a real break this Christmas, not a half-assed one like I did last year. Hell, last year I didn't even make it home.

What am I thinking? This place has never been my home. A holiday home, yeah. I guess home is where your family is, and as the only child of Kent and Mallory Jacobs, I at least deserved to make this a happy one.

Mom and Lilly are talking amongst themselves in hushed tones, but I don't miss the feel of my mom's eyes looking my way every couple of minutes.

"Okay, I'll need to go back to my cabin first and change." I can hear the grumble in my tone, nobody needs to tell me.

Seeing Lilly biting her lips together, I can't help but laugh to myself.

"Be ready to leave in 15 minutes," I say in the tone I use with employees who are on my last nerve.

As I leave the room, I hear my dad laugh. "His bark is usually worse than his bite."

I drive around to the front of my parents' house and Lilly is waiting. Clipboard in hand, pen resting on her bottom lip, a lip I would like to bite, if my mind was to get its own way.

"Thanks, Patrick. I'll try to make this as painless as possible," she smirks.

"That's usually my line," I whisper.

She takes a moment to process what I've said, then turns bright red. Oh, this is going to be fun!

I take the clipboard off her and see all the places she needs us to go. "Is my mom joking? This is huge," I said.

"That's what he wants you to think," she whispers under her breath, going red again.

I'm sure she wasn't expecting me to hear her. God, she's cute when she gets annoyed and that blush spreads over her body. I'd love to see other parts of her body go that color too.

I laugh, handing back the clipboard.

We've been working our way through the list and only stopped at two places, and I'm already starting to get a headache. Lilly pats me on the back and smiles. She's always smiling, I've noticed. She screams 'people pleaser', she's just so happy all the time.

The more time I spend with her, the more relaxed I'm getting. This should have my bachelor alarm bells ringing, but for the first time in my life, that's not happening.

"Coffee?" she asks, giving me that megawatt smile again. I want to see that smile on her face every day. "My treat." She nods her head towards Maggie's Diner.

"Sure, why not."

I put the boxes in the car and I walk with her to Maggie's. When we open the door the place is busy; that's not surprising considering it's late morning. The smell of coffee and baked goods hits us as we walk in. Maggie has Christmas songs playing in the background of the chatter of the people.

"Patrick Jacobs!" a voice I know well shouts over from somewhere in the back of the diner. Everyone stops what they're doing to look at us.

I laugh, knowing that it's Maggie's son and one of my oldest friends. Well, friends in the sense that he's known me longest, ever since my parents first started vacationing here.

"Joe," I say, patting him on the back.

"Lilly, what are you doing with this one?"

"I'm helping her with some of the things for my mom," I answer for her.

Her body language changes, and I can tell I've just said something wrong.

"Yeah, your dad said you were coming home for Christmas."

"Hope you're working him hard," says Maggie, passing two cups of coffee over to Lilly.

"Oh, she is."

I hear her take a deep breath next to me. She smiles at Maggie, but it's not as bright as her usual smile. She hands her the money. "Bye, Maggie."

"Bye, sweetheart."

We both head towards the door and go for the handle at the same time. Our hands touch and, not for the first time today, a spark ignites between us. Joe stops us, and a couple of customers around us look at us, stifling laughs.

I look at Joe as he points his finger up. We both slowly look up. I know what it's going to be before I even catch my eyes on it. Mistletoe!

I don't know whether to hug Maggie or slap Joe at this point, because they've just given me an opportunity I've wanted all day with Lilly.

"Fuck," Lilly whispers next to me.

Chapter Four

Lilly

Patrick pushed my last nerve answering for me with Maggie. And how did I not see the mistletoe over the door before today? I'm here every day to get my caffeine fix!

I can feel everyone's eyes on us, and there is no way in hell the sex god in front of me is going to want to kiss me in front of all these people.

I try to move in front of him, but he's staring at me, and for the first time since we got ourselves into this predicament, I'm looking into his eyes. Those eyes have mischief in them and I'm worried he's going to do it.

He pulls me to him with my thick woolen coat and kisses me right in front of everyone.

One, two, three.

He deepens the kiss and I grab onto the opening of his coat and meet him kiss for kiss.

This is a man who knows how to kiss a girl. He's kissing me hard, and I know my lips are going to be red after. Being this close to him, I'm getting an even stronger smell of him. He's smelt expensive and manly ever since I got in his car. I deepen the kiss as he pulls me nearer to him. Hell, I didn't even think that was possible.

I'm on my tiptoes, and it's as if we're the only people in the room. A groan escapes both of us as we continue to kiss each other. It's then I feel how hard he is in his jeans.

I open my eyes. Fuck! I hadn't even noticed I'd closed them. I look to see Patrick smiling back. So, the guy *can* break into a smile.

We pull away from each other and I look out of the corner of my eye to see the whole diner has gone silent and slack-jawed. Maggie and Joe are smiling from ear to ear.

My body is vibrating all over and all I want to do is find somewhere quiet, where we can continue this in private.

"Happy now?" Patrick says, looking at Joe.

He laughs and goes back into the kitchen area, whistling as he goes.

How stupid was I to think he kissed me because he wanted to? There was a moment when we both were getting into it, I know we were, but I guess I was wrong.

I open the door and head towards his car, and I feel him behind me as he runs to catch up to me.

I feel so embarrassed. Not that he kissed me. No, because I thought for those seconds, that felt more like minutes, that he wanted me just as much as I wanted him. Seeing him again this morning in his parents' kitchen made me realize his hotness wasn't a fluke last night.

I pull open the car door and get inside. He keeps looking over to me while I smell my coffee and look out of the window.

"You cannot be pissed that I kissed you," he grumbles.

Is he fucking kidding me!

I take a deep breath and close my eyes. It works wonders at work.

"Oh, so you're happy for me to talk now?" I have a touch more anger in my voice than I wanted.

He stops the engine and turns to give me his full attention. Okay, not what I wanted. I continue to look out of the window, but he's just staring at me.

A glance shows me his jaw is clenching and I can tell he's annoyed or something, right now.

"I hate it when guys think they're the most important person in the room. I have been managing to talk to Maggie most of my life, think I could answer her and Joe's questions."

Sighing, he turns the engine on and starts to drive down the street.

"Since you asked, the kiss was okay."

Who the hell am I kidding? That kiss was possibly the best kiss I've ever had. I hear my phone ping, so I grab it out of my pocket.

Abby: Who's the hottie I heard you just kissed at Maggie's?

I left two minutes ago, and Abby wasn't even there. How did she already know?

I can't help looking across the room at Patrick as the ladies from the fundraising committee fuss all around him. I've checked inside this box a dozen times, but I can't stop thinking about that kiss. It's obviously been too long if I'm getting this distracted over a pretty boy and a kiss. I mean, it was like we were the only two people in the room, was the type of kiss you'd see on any movie or tv show. I could have stayed in that bubble for a long time.

Abby walks through the door holding a box of what I already know will be delicious treats. I can't wait for her to open her own cake shop in town next month. She's worked hard and I couldn't be happier for my best friend.

I see her giving him a slow once-over as she walks towards me.

"Please tell me you didn't come over because the gossip machine that is our town sent you here."

"Ha. Of course, it did. Once I heard some hot guy had breezed into town and was kissing my best friend for everyone to see, I had to see what all the fuss was about. It's all everyone was talking about when I went into Maggie's for this." She motions to the drink in her hand.

I peep in the box and see she's made my favorite chocolate chip cookies. All decorated with green, white, and red frosting; she's going to send me into a sugar coma one of these days.

"You going to go over there and save him?" she asks, sipping her coffee from her travel mug that seems to always be in her hand.

"Nope," I say, biting into the chocolaty goodness.

We both burst out laughing when we see that the ladies have him up a ladder and hanging stuff up. Every woman in the room is looking at his ass right now, I guarantee you. Me included!

"Fine. I'll go over there and help him."

Chapter Five

Patrick

The last couple of days have been pure torture. When Mom said she expected me to help with some Christmas stuff, I thought she meant getting her some last-minute presents or helping decorate a little. I was not expecting to spend most of the last few days helping Lilly get ready for the charity event.

I know it means everything to my mom. It's been a good distraction though; work keeps calling and I've no desire to answer any of the calls, except a couple of emails, because hell, I've not had a *total* body transplant the last couple of days.

From what I've managed to gather, Lilly is pretty much loved by everyone in town, so I'm not surprised Mom and Dad love her so much.

I put my iPad down on the coffee table and take my mug of coffee with me to get ready. I told Lilly I'd pick her up today. No point in her trekking all the way up here only for us to go back into town.

I pull up in front of a nice house. Like all the houses on the street, it's two-storey. Lilly's house, though, is the most decorated on the street. It has a lovely porch that looks like it goes round most of the house. With Christmas lights wrapped around the top.

Just as I'm about to walk up the steps to her house, a woman opens the door, and I stop in my tracks. It takes me a minute to remember I saw her talking to Lilly yesterday at the town hall.

She's holding a mug of coffee and it's so cold out you can see the steam coming up. "You want to come in for a coffee or are you guys heading to Maggie's?" she laughs.

See some things never change. I still have a couple of friends in town from my breaks coming back here, so I already know everyone in town was talking about our kiss yesterday. Seems this place really has nothing going on if this is what classifies as hot gossip. One kiss between two virtual strangers.

Is it a kiss I've thought about a lot? Yeah, probably more than I should have, if I'm being honest. Is it something I want to do again? Hell yes, it is. Lilly is hot. I knew it the first time I saw her, but I also know she's the type of girl who probably doesn't have flings; she has 'relationship girl' written all over her.

Starting something with her would certainly make my Christmas break here enjoyable. I also know not to shit where I eat. I would never hear the end of it from Mom and Dad. Hell, they have already been dropping not-so-subtle hints of what a lovely girl Lilly is. So, while they think that pushing her more and more towards me will make me like her more than I already do, it's actually having the opposite effect.

"Coffee sounds great."

The Christmas market stalls are lining the street, and I hate to admit it, but it really does look good. Everyone seems to know Lilly; everywhere we go, people want to stop and talk to her. We could have got most of the jobs done quicker if we'd split up, but I will not admit this to anyone... I'm kind of having fun. Seeing things through someone else's eyes is kind of nice, I guess.

My attraction to her is only getting stronger the more time I spend with her. I know she feels it too. There's no missing the lust in her eyes as she keeps looking over at me when she thinks I'm not paying attention. She's staying in my thoughts way more than she should be.

I take her bags off her.

"You don't need to do that," she whispers.

"What about if I want to?"

She takes a deep breath and I see her fighting a smile. I see an Italian bistro up ahead and the words are out of my mouth before I can stop them. "Let's grab something to eat. My treat."

I take a few more steps before I realize she's stopped walking next to me.

"What?" I ask.

"Why?"

"Why what? I'm hungry. I'm guessing you are too."

"Okay," she says slowly as she walks next to me.

I open the door for her as she goes in.

"Lilly!" A young Italian man, I'm guessing who's about the same age as her, walks over to her, then hugs her and kisses her cheeks.

I know the feeling that's coming over me, I just don't understand why it's happening here.

Lilly looks embarrassed as she looks over her shoulder to me.

"A table for two," I say as I snake my arm around her.

Yeah, that guy just made me jealous as hell. He laughs, raising his eyebrows, as he sees my blatant pissing contest in front of him.

"Lilly, it's been too long." He looks at my arm around her shoulders. It suddenly dawns on me that I don't know anything about Lilly. For all I know, this guy might be her boyfriend.

Though I guess not. I guess he wouldn't be smiling at some guy with his arm around his girl.

We take a seat near the window, and it's a really nice place for a small town.

I order us a bottle of expensive red wine, expensive for here I suppose. She sips the wine, her cheeks pinking when she notices I'm watching her. She's gorgeous and she doesn't even know it.

Spending time with Lilly is a lot more fun than I thought it would be, and I'm definitely getting more attracted to her the more time I spend with her.

I rub my thumb over her hand and watch her close her eyes and turn a slight change of pink. Good to see I'm not the only one fighting this obvious attraction. She already told me she enjoyed the kiss the other day, so why not have a little fun over the holidays?

"Why do you act all Mr. Broody with everyone, Patrick?"

I'm surprised she's being so bold. I guess the glass of wine gave her some courage.

"Because I'm not a great guy, Lilly. I work way too hard and push people away. You seem to have gotten under my skin though."

"You do realize that you've not once answered a single work call while we've been spending time together. I saw you looking at your phone and turning the ringer off." She smiles at me, I don't know if it's because she thinks she knows something about me or she just enjoys spending time with me.

I take a deep breath. She's right. "Okay, I guess you're right. It's the first Christmas I've taken off in five years and I guess I needed the break. I have a lot of very competent people working for me, at least I hope so. I pay them well enough. They should be capable of handling things without me for a couple of weeks." For the first time, I'm saying these words and really meaning them.

We enjoy the rest of the meal. We laugh and joke and it feels nice! It's reminding me of how she was earlier with her friend, all easy going. Of course nothing surprised me as much as when she threw the snowball at me. The look on her face. It wasn't until I laughed that she did as well.

I grab hold of her hand as we walk out of the restaurant, carrying her shopping in my other hand.

"Do you have to work again tonight?" I ask. I'm hoping she doesn't. It took all my willpower not to go to the restaurant she works at last night, and I'm not sure I could handle that again.

She has the biggest smile on her face, and I know the answer before she speaks. "Nope. I have the rest of the week off."

Chapter Six

Lilly

When Patrick dropped me off earlier, I really wanted to invite him inside, especially after the butterfly-inducing kiss he gave on my front porch. But I could hear Abby was home.

I wasn't expecting him to invite me round to his place later tonight though.

I walk out of my room in a skirt and Christmas sweater; I have hundreds of the things. I made the mistake one year of telling someone that one was cute, and ever since I've been gifted them for Christmas and birthdays (since my birthday is in January). I guess this is more of a winter sweater, but still.

My heart is pounding and my palms are sweating, I don't know why I'm feeling so nervous. I mean, we spent the last couple of days together just fine. When we went to Luca's family restaurant, I just about wanted to die. I hardly ever go in there since Luca and I broke up. Of course, that was over a year ago. But our town has two restaurants: Luca's family's restaurant, which is a more family-friendly place, and then the place where I work. I guess it was inevitable I was going to have to go in there eventually.

The kiss, though, and handholding from Patrick, I wasn't really expecting any of that.

Abby is sitting on the couch playing a game on her iPad when she looks up at me. Before I can tell her I'm on my way out, there's a knock at the door. She looks from the door to me, and a huge smile spreads across her face.

"Please tell me you and Mr. Sexy Ass are going out tonight?"

I give her a nervous laugh and grab my coat off the hook.

"You are *not* going out dressed like that!"

"Yes, I am. We're just hanging out."

"Hmmm. Okay, play it like that."

She opens the door and Patrick is standing there in jeans and a dark V-neck sweater. I'm so glad he went with casual too.

"Abby," I say, fastening my coat and hugging my best friend.

"Okay, you guys have fun. Don't do anything I wouldn't do."

I see Patrick hiding his smile, if only he knew.

I can't believe I'm sitting in Patrick Jacobs' cabin. This place is nice and way more modern than I would have expected. I shouldn't have expected anything else, really. I mean the guy is richer than sin, but he's just under 40 and trendy too. Yeah, I may have Googled him a couple of days ago. What! I'm only human.

There's a jug of what can only be home-made mulled wine on the coffee table. The fragrance strong in the air. I put my glass down and walk over to the floor-to-ceiling window. I can see the lights twinkling below. I bet this view is amazing in the daylight. The snow is really starting to fall outside; I officially love this view.

"Dinner will be ready soon," he says all huskily, creeping up behind me, he makes me jump a little, putting his arms around me, looking out at the view with me.

I turn around to see him smiling at me, his eyes roaming up my body. I took my boots off when I arrived, so I'm a lot shorter around him than I'm used to.

"It smells amazing."

He moves away from me, and I instantly miss his touch. He throws another log on the fire and moves it around with the poker.

I sit on the comfiest couch I've ever sat on and curl into it. He comes and sits next to me. My heart starts doing that galloping thing it did earlier, and I already know I'm going to miss him when he leaves in a couple of weeks.

He moves to kiss me and this time I don't tense up, because I'm expecting it. It feels nice as I grab hold of the back of his neck, encouraging him to kiss me harder.

I don't want this kiss to end. I forgot how good this man smelled in the couple of hours we've been apart. He pulls me towards him so my knees are straddling him as he deepens the kiss, and a low moan escapes me. I can't help it.

He's hard as a rock between my legs; it must be so uncomfortable pushing against his jeans. I grind against him, and he holds me tight.

The guy knows how to kiss. His hands are in my hair, holding me to him. I couldn't move away even if I wanted to. He puts just the right amount of pressure on my lips that I know they're going to be bruised when he pulls away.

I grind against him again. I know what I need. I need him.

"Grrrrrmmmmmm," he groans.

We both stop when we hear a small beeping noise coming from the kitchen.

He pulls away from my lips, keeping our faces attached at the forehead. "Fuck!" he whispers.

I smile at him, knowing how he feels. I bite my bottom lip and a low groan escapes him again before he rises from the couch, adjusting himself as he moves.

A small laugh escapes me. After I get my bearings a little, I take a deep breath and follow him into the kitchen, my glass of mulled wine in hand.

"Patrick, this looks amazing." I'm surprised to see he cooked some lovely steaks with veggies. I take a sip of my wine and take a seat at the breakfast bar, where he already had two places set out.

Dinner turns out to taste amazing too. I'm surprised at how comfortable I've gotten with him the last couple of days after our disastrous start at the beginning of the week.

I insist on washing up after the amazing food he made, he smiles over at me. I notice he's staring at me.

Just as I'm finishing up, he comes up behind me. I close my eyes, loving the feel of his hard body against me. He's hard *everywhere*. I drop the cloth in my hand as he kisses the crook of my neck, and a moan escapes me. I feel him smiling as he kisses me again in the same spot, drawing another moan out of me. He knows my body well.

He spins me around and I wrap my still-wet hands around his neck. He kisses me again, this time lifting me up by my ass and lowering me onto the counter.

"Please tell me you want this to go further," he whispers, need in his voice.

Hell yes, I want this to go further. I nod my head, looking down at him.

"Good," he says in complete control now. His hand snakes up my leg to find my thong soaked. A groan escapes him as he pushes his thumb under the elastic.

"I told you I wanted this," I whisper. I need more of this man. A *lot* more.

Chapter Seven

Patrick

She is so responsive to my every touch. I knew she was attracted to me; I just wasn't expecting her to be so open to this progressing this quickly.

I'm not complaining.

Usually, I wouldn't think twice about screwing a date on the kitchen counter, but for some reason that doesn't appeal to me with Lilly. I feel things for her. I want to treat her differently than I usually would someone I was gonna take to my bed. She deserves better than a quick fuck against my kitchen worktop.

I move between her open legs and keep the pressure I was already using with my thumb while I kiss her. She's clawing at my neck and I know she's feeling this need as much as I am. She kisses me down my neck, her hands feeling me all over. She attempts to pull up my sweater, but I stop her and lift her in a fireman's lift over my shoulder. I want to take my time with her and really cover every inch of this body. My bed is the perfect place to do that.

I climb the stairs and feel her laughing as I stroke the back of her thighs, loving the feeling of her squirming against me.

After walking her over to the bed, I put her down so she's standing near the foot of the bed, and I see the flushed look on her face. Her eyes are dilated; she needs me as much as I need her.

She pulls her sweater over her head and throws it on the floor next to the bed. I'm pulling my clothes off in an equally hurried manner and not having a care in the world where they're landing.

I stop a moment to take in her body. Her skin is flushing all over, everywhere my eyes seem to go. She reaches up on her tiptoes and wraps her arms around my neck again. I lift her and then lower her onto the bed, and she relaxes underneath me. I kiss my way down her body and stop to look up at her from her navel.

She's following me with her eyes, both hands grabbing onto the pillows surrounding her. She looks so hot.

"Stop teasing me, Patrick," she whispers. She's smiling up at me, but there is a hint of need still in her voice.

If I was an evil S.O.B. I'd stop and draw this out some more, but I need to be inside her as much as she needs me. Maybe more so if my dreams since I met her are anything to go by.

I pull away from her to walk to my bedside drawer and grab the unopened box of condoms. She doesn't need to know I only bought them this afternoon, hoping that tonight was going to go the way it has.

I rip the box open and notice Lilly has propped herself up on her elbows. I let the box and its contents fall onto the bed as I slowly draw her attention to my cock, which is currently painfully aware that he's seconds away from getting exactly what he wants.

I need to be inside her. I tear it open with my mouth. Her eyes only leave mine to watch me pull the condom on. Her eyes widened in excitement. Now I *really* need to be inside her.

I kiss Lilly, like I need my next breath, and slowly ease my way into her. She moans as I push my way through her soft opening.

I swallow her sounds of pleasure kissing them away and replacing them with a few of my own as I build up pace to push us both over the edge.

She's gasping and moaning, and I'm not going to lie, it's a real turn on to know I'm having this effect on her. She feels perfect in my arms too.

I move my hand to between her legs and, just as I thrust harder into her, I add pressure onto her clit. She moans louder this time, her ass almost lifting off the bed. She cums and I follow her right over the edge of the cliff in front of us.

When I crash next to her, we're both covered in sweat.

"You're staying the night. I'm not ready for this to end," I say, grabbing hold of her face so she looks at me. I kiss her before leaving the bedroom and heading towards my connecting bathroom.

I woke up an hour or so ago, and this is the only time I've given myself to work. I'm surprised to see Lilly walking down the stairs already dressed. She stops mid step and her eyes roam over my naked torso; if I was jackass, I'd let her know I'm noticing her checking me out. I put my laptop down on the coffee table in front of me.

"Hi," she says, looking flushed. "I didn't mean to spend all night."

She looks embarrassed, and it's cute, really. I don't know how she looks as fresh as she does. We both woke each other up a couple of times in the night. Tasting her and touching her and making her scream was music to my ears. I was hoping to head back to bed before she woke up. She must have been tiptoeing around as I didn't hear a peep from her.

"I meant what I said last night." I get up. "Do you want some coffee?" I say, motioning towards the kitchen.

"Yeah," she smiles, pulling at the end of her sweater.

She meets me in the kitchen, and I pull her in for a kiss. I'm hoping this will let her know I'm serious about wanting to spend more time with her. She stiffens in my arms at first, but she soon softens and melts into me. A low moan escapes her and I push her against the counter. The same counter I nearly took her on top of last night.

I offer her the glass bowl with the various coffee pods I have for the machine, and she picks one out.

"So, I need to do some last-minute Christmas shopping today for family and friends," Lilly says.

"Okay. Sounds like a plan."

Her eyes nearly bug out of her head. I guess she wasn't expecting me to want to tag along.

Yes, I am just going to insert myself into her life. What can I say? I enjoy spending time with her. There's something about her. Come new year I'm sure I'm going to miss her—something I wasn't expecting when I took a few weeks off to spend time with my parents. Not that I've really spent too much time with them, except in the evening.

"Of course, if you don't want me tagging along, I'm sure I can find something else to do."

She smiles at me, and I know in that moment that she wants to spend more time with me too.

Chapter Eight

Lilly

After spending a small amount of time getting some little bits of presents for Christmas, we decided it might be better to go to the next town over. Everyone seemed to be watching our every move and, to be honest, it felt a little weird. I mean, I'm used to everyone getting in everyone's business, but this is bad even for them. They've never been this invested in my social life before, so I'm guessing it has more to do with the guy I seem to be spending *all* my free time with.

My phone pings in my pocket.

Abby: I want all the details later.
Abby: I noticed your bedroom was still empty. Good for you girl.
Abby: People in Maggie's are putting bets on you guys.

For crying out loud, do these people not have anything better to do with their time?

Lilly: People need to get a life.
Abby: Why are you texting me when you should be screwing the hot billionaire?
Lilly: Going now!
Abby: Have fun. Tell Patrick I said hi.

I look up from my phone and see Patrick looking at me from his side of the car.

"I'm hoping that's your friend who's got you smiling like that. I'd hate to think I'm having to compete with some other guy."

What the...?

"I was joking," he genuinely sounds worried.

When we get out of the car, he pushes me against the door like he can't keep his hands off me. He keeps doing this and, I'm not going to lie, I'm loving every minute of it. I bend my knee and he finds the perfect opening between my legs and pushes against me even harder. I can feel the beginning of his erection pushing against me.

I'm going to miss Patrick when he leaves after Christmas.

That thought leaves me with a bad taste, and I can't help but groan, sounding my disappointment. Patrick pulls away from me and looks confused.

"What just went through your pretty little head then?"

I could lie. I should lie. But Patrick seems to understand me better than anyone ever has before.

I take a deep breath. "I was just thinking I'm going to miss being shoved against hard surfaces when you're gone."

He holds my head in both hands and moves it so I can look up at him.

"I didn't expect to feel things either," he says before kissing me way more gently than he usually does.

"Patrick!" a woman shouts, and it takes us both a moment to realize we both know that voice.

"Mom?" says Patrick, turning round.

We spend an amazing couple of days, almost, in our own little bubble. And I'm starting to feel real feelings for Patrick. I mean, who wouldn't? He's pretty great. I get the impression not many people know this side of him. He's known some of the guys in town for years, from what I've been able to gather, but even Joe says he's seen a different side to him since he's been back.

Abby brings me a mug of hot chocolate with enough whipped cream and marshmallows to give me a total sugar high. This should keep me hyper while I'm at work.

"Spill," she says, sitting next to me and resting her head on my shoulder.

"I'm getting feelings for Patrick."

"Well duh. Of course, you are. From what you tell me he's great in bed, you're both spending so much time with each other, and he's loaded too. What's not to fall for?"

"You know two of those don't really matter." I say holding back my smile.

She lifts her head off my shoulder to look at me, her eyebrows raised.

"Okay. *One* of those doesn't matter." I admit smiling at my best friend.

"I know."

I sit and I can't help thinking that for my own piece of mind, I need to cut Patrick off, like, right now.

My shift at work is my last one until after Christmas Day, and for mid-week we're pretty quiet. I'm surprised when, an hour before I need to lock up, Patrick walks in and heads straight for the bar. He's been coming in most nights that I've worked. Just yesterday I'd have been happy about that. But after my conversation with Abby, I'm feeling all kinds of emotions.

I watch him chat to the guys at the bar, and he seems like a completely different guy than the one who turned up here for dinner with Kent.

It's snowing when I lock up the restaurant, and Patrick takes my hand. I look around but don't see his car.

"I thought we could walk through the town to see the Christmas lights."

What has Patrick done to the moody guy I met his first night here?

He pulls me into him and he kisses my forehead.

I lean into him as we walk in the direction of my house.

Chapter Nine

Patrick

Christmas Eve-Eve

When my mom saw us the other day, I couldn't help noticing the panic in Lilly's eyes. Of course, my mom and dad had heard the rumors spreading through town about Lilly and I spending almost all of our spare time together. Still, it wasn't until my mom cornered me that I realized something. When our Christmas fling is over, Lilly will have to carry on living here with all the gossip that goes along with that.

It's the day before the charity event. We've just finished dropping things off at the town hall where some of the day's events are happening. Still, Lilly wants to check on the hotel on the far side of town, where the auction and other things are happening, to ensure everything is ready. I admit, when my mom told me I needed to bring my tux a few weeks ago, I didn't think I'd be so excited by the time the event was coming around.

I can't wait to see what Lilly is going to wear. She's kept pretty quiet about the whole thing. I wanted to surprise her with something, but I heard how excited she was talking to Abby about collecting the dress she's been saving up for over the last month. I could have waltzed in like Prince Charming, but I also know Lilly would hate that.

"You're quiet," I say to her as I sit next to her in the hotel lobby.

"Yeah. Just thinking about a few things."

"I can think of a way to get you out of your own head for a bit," I whisper, wiggling my eyebrows at her playfully. "I mean, we are in a hotel after all."

She turns away from me, but not before I see her roll her eyes.

I'm about to ask her again what's up when someone from the hotel calls her over, so we follow the woman up the stairs to the function room. Sensing Lilly's mood, she tells us to give her a shout if we want anything.

Lilly moves away from me as soon as we're alone, and I'm more than a little confused at what's changed her mood.

"I'm not a mind-reader," I say. I don't mean to sound so bitter.

"Patrick. Just leave me alone, okay?"

What the hell has gotten into her? She's been in a crappy mood since I picked her up, and honestly, I don't know what could be the matter. Everything was fine when I walked her home from work last night.

"This was all my fault, okay? Patrick, just back off and leave me alone." She takes a deep breath, closes her eyes, a look of frustration on her face. "You're leaving town in a week anyway, so maybe we need to stop this now." Her voice gets louder with each word.

"Lilly..."

"Patrick, I swear. Leave! I need you out of my space right now!"

I pull up in front of my parents' house and debate on whether to go inside. I guess I did come to spend some time with them—something I've not really been doing. All my employees are finishing today, so I don't expect any of them to contact me. Most have been quiet while I've been away. I'm dreading the work load I'm going to find on my desk when I return.

I receive a text from my friend and think about ignoring it. But maybe he can shed some light on why Lilly suddenly turned into a completely different person almost overnight.

Josh: How's things going with your parents? I can't believe you lasted as long as you have.
Patrick: Funny guy. I've met someone.

The three little dots appear and disappear nearly a dozen times before his next message comes through. Then another of our friends messages me.

Adrien: Who is she?
Patrick: How the...

Of course, Josh would message Adrien; not only are they good friends, but they're business partners too. This year they've managed to fall for their special people too. Mike and I, now being the only singles in the group.

Josh: He wanted to know what I was laughing so hard at.
Patrick: Why do I even tell you things?

I receive a message to join a different chat.

Request to join Twisted Brothers
Patrick: You guys can be a pain in the ass sometimes.
Mike: Patrick my man, what's this I hear about a girl?

Mike: You cannot leave me as the only single guy.

Josh: That doesn't have to be the case.

Mike: Shut up!!!!

Patrick: Guys.

Adrien: Guys, Patrick can't please his woman and wants all our help.

Patrick: For crying out loud.

I go on to tell them everything that went down and how things seemed so okay last night. As soon as the details are out, I realize I can't believe I told the guys. I'm already beginning to regret this.

Chapter Ten

Lilly

Christmas Eve - Event Day

I've not been here ten minutes and I already know today is going to be a day from hell. When Joe texted me this morning to tell me he couldn't be the Santa for the kids this afternoon, I almost had a heart attack. Mallory had left two things for me to be in charge of: one was sorting out the Santa for the kids coming to the family day we arranged for today, and the other was to make sure we had a good selection of auction items for the dinner tonight.

My phone rings and I get a sick feeling as I see Mallory's name flash up on my screen.

"Hi Mallory."

"Hey. I just heard about Joe."

"It's okay. I'm trying to sort out a replacement Santa right now."

"That's what I'm calling about. I've managed to find one. He should already be there. He collected the suit an hour ago."

I should have put Mallory on the case earlier. Nobody can say no to that woman.

We discuss meeting up at the dinner tonight. We're off the call before I think to ask her who the replacement Santa is going to be.

As I walk through the town, some of the family events are in full swing and, while it snowed a lot last night, I'm happy to see nothing had to be changed. We have some home-made craft stalls and some lovely Christmas decorations that the old ladies made. I swear every baby who's been born in town has had something made for them off these ladies. Abby and myself included. Abby has a stall selling cakes and cookies and stuff. I can't wait for her shop to open soon.

Abby stops me on the steps as I'm heading up to our town hall, turning me around.

"I need to show you something."

She drags me off in the direction that I know her stall is.

"What are you..." I stop mid-sentence when I see that the Santa has been moved to the outside and has a reindeer with him. Okay, that I hadn't organized.

"He needed to move the pictures with Santa to earlier, as the guy Mallory hired can only do it for a couple of hours," said Abby, bouncing up and down.

The children all around him are laughing and Santa is taking his time with all of them. Whoever this guy is, we're hiring him again next year.

I check on all the other people and finally make my way to Santa when I see he's not too busy. Every child that I saw coming away from him looked so happy. It made my day.

While I go, I keep looking around. I had hoped to see Patrick. He's helped so much with all this. I feel kind of guilty about the way I treated him yesterday. Made even worse when I told Abby and she winced.

I know I was wrong to push him away like that. I should have acted like the grown-up I pretend to be most of the time.

I take my phone out and take a video of all the things, as well as some photos that will be good to use as marketing for next year. Maybe I'll send them to Patrick too, as a peace-offering.

Lilly: I need to see you before tonight.
Lilly: VIDEO
Lilly: We did good together.

I'm about to put my phone back in my bag when I see Santa pulling his phone out of his pocket after checking none of the kids were about.

Patrick: Glad it was a success. You worked hard.

It's now I realize that Santa is Patrick.

Lilly: You should come down here and see our hard work.
Patrick: I was around earlier. It looked like it was a success.
Lilly: You look really good in that Santa suit by the way.

He looks around and then he sees me. He puts his phone in his pocket and I walk over to him.

"Who spilled?" he asks, stroking the reindeer.

"Abby dragged me out here."

"She was supposed to keep you away till I was finished. I know I've done something to upset you, I just don't know what I did. I didn't want to ruin your day."

"Come here," I say, reaching up to kiss him on the lips.

Patrick holds the car door open for me as I get out at the hotel where the dinner is being held. I've loved this event ever since I worked my first one as a waitress my last year in high school.

"I can't wait to get you out of this dress later," he whispers in my ear.

A moan escapes me, but my focus *needs* to be on the event. We walk up to where some photographers are taking everyone's picture. This event has gotten bigger every year and it's now one of the biggest events at Christmas.

The room looks amazing. As always, Mallory is standing with Kent, talking the ear off anyone that will listen while waiters carry around trays with champagne in flutes.

"I see you two look happier now," Kent says to me, giving his son a knowing smile.

"I don't know what you're talking about." Patrick says his arm tightening around me.

"Okay, son, play it like that. I saw Joe just before we were leaving. Funny how he managed to get better in a couple of hours."

I burst out laughing. Patrick and I had a long chat before I left this afternoon to get ready. It turns out he too wasn't ready to say goodbye at the end of the holidays and wasn't looking forward to going back to Seattle either. We made plans to see each other as often as possible. It looks like he and I are going to be spending a lot of weekends traveling.

I lean into Patrick as his arm scoops around my shoulders. I almost dragged him into my house when he turned up in a tux to pick me up.

"So does this mean we're going to start seeing a bit more of you?" Mallory asks her son, sounding hopeful.

I look up at Patrick and give him a huge smile.

"Yeah, you could say that. We're going to give it a try. Of course I'd be happier if Lilly moved to Seattle."

"I see a lot of flights in our future," I say, bumping my elbow into him. "In both directions."

I don't miss the smile that Patrick and his mom share.

Epilogue

Patrick

1 Year Later

I push Lilly up against the door and nudge her legs wider just where the slit of her dress opens. Yes, I had this exact moment in mind when I bought it for her. We've been together a whole year, and last night in my cabin I proposed to her. I could have made a big fuss, but I know my girl. She'd have hated a big fuss, so I cooked her the same meal I cooked her a year ago and we sat in front of my log fire. She'd already agreed to move in with me in the new year.

"Patrick, anyone could walk in at any minute," she says. She's telling me one thing, but the way she's rubbing against my leg, I know she needs this just as much as I do.

"I could just stop, and we could go back out to the party," I say.

"Don't you dare. You can't get me like this and then leave me hanging. I've not seen you for weeks. I need you. If this event wasn't so important to me and your mom, I'd have told you to blow it off."

Her hands move to the zip on my pants, and she slips her hand in and gives me a firm stroke. Now it's my turn to groan.

"I think we both know you need to be inside me just as much."

I kiss down the side of her neck, the opposite side to where her hair is falling down, and I want to take her dress off, but we both know we don't have the time.

I lift her dress and push inside her. She melts around me, grabbing hold of the back of my neck. I kiss her to stop her moans from getting any louder.

"I've missed you," I whisper.

I move her away from the door while still inside her, and she grabs hold of the coat railing while I fuck her against someone's coat. She feels amazing and I'm so greedy for her. I'd love nothing more than to be balls deep in her all night, but we need to show our faces at this thing.

I push into her firmly and hard, and I can tell by the way she is biting her lips closed that she is loving every minute. Her fingers are gripping hard on the clothes pegs making her knuckles white, and her heels are really starting to dig into my legs.

I lower my hand to stroke her clit. She cums around my cock in no time at all, and I follow her.

We walk out of the cloak room some time later, and I keep hold of her hand the rest of the night.

"Mallory," says Lilly, handing my mom a drink with her left hand. We decided to wait to tell my parents about the engagement till we were at the party.

Mom takes Lilly's hand, and we share a look. Before we know what's happening, my mom has Lilly in a hug and is smiling right at me.

"Well, it took you long enough," she says, holding my girlfriend— fiancée's—hand. "I've been waiting for this ever since you asked your dad for his mother's ring."

The bell rings, letting us know dinner is ready to be served, which means the auction is not far off. Then we can sneak out of here. We follow my parents into the big function room where everyone will be seated.

The room is full of tables. We make our way towards the front, which has always been our table.

I put both my arms around her and pull her against my body. "Merry Christmas," I whisper.

"Merry Christmas," she says, kissing me.

THE END

A Marine for Christmas

BY LAURA MOWERY

Two people searching for love. One honest mistake that could cost them everything. Will a Christmas miracle be enough to save their happily ever after?

About the Author

Interested in Luke and Liv's story and need more of Jackson and Brando in your life?
Check out The Infinitum Series, filled with super soldier romance and suspense.
Subscribe to my newsletter https://BookHip.com/HQKVSHA and you'll receive a free series prequel novella!

www.lauramowery.com
Laura is an air force brat who grew up on Edwards Air Force Base in Southern California. She recently relocated from San Diego, CA to San Antonio, TX with her husband, two cats, and a dog. Her husband is a former Marine and the inspiration for the hilarious moments between the military men in her books. If she's not writing, you'll find her adventuring her new city with her husband, eating tacos, drinking local craft beer, or curled up with a book.

Chapter One

Kristy

Brandon Myers is the sexiest man on the planet. His crooked grin, arm and neck tattoos, and take-no-shit attitude make him a prime candidate for magazine and romance novel covers. And that's not even mentioning his chiseled body, designed purely for sin. He moves around the dance floor with practiced ease, two-stepping to a Thomas Rhett song as the lucky woman in his arms laughs and eats him up with her eyes.

Unfortunately, that woman isn't me. Nor will it ever be. For that to happen, he'd have to know that I've had a crush—bordering on obsession —on him for the last three years. And he'd have to acknowledge my existence for that to be a possibility.

"Do you need a rag for that drool?" My best friend's voice forces my eyes away from the Adonis in jeans and a light blue Henley.

I glance at her with a nervous laugh and go back to stacking glasses while I wait for table three's order. I'm a bartender, but we're short a server tonight, so I'm pulling double duty, helping Austin and Greg at the bar while I serve tables. Of course, I volunteered. I always do.

"Nice try, but you're totally busted."

I shrug. "So what? He's hot. Everyone stares at Brando." Everyone calls him "Brando," and I've always been curious why he dropped the last letter, but it's not like I'd ever have the nerve to ask.

"I don't know why you don't just jiggle your tits at him. There's no way he'd deny them."

I roll my eyes at Natalie. She's by far the prettiest employee at The Lone Boot. With her dark brown skin, smoky gray eyes, and slamming body, she's often sought after by both men and women. She's not interested in any of them because she's in love with her equally gorgeous boyfriend. Greg winks at her as he passes, and she grins, pushing her black hair behind her ear. I glance between them and sigh. They're so adorable.

Chubby, curvy, pleasantly plump, and voluptuous are all words that people have used to describe me when they don't want to call me fat to my face. I prefer smart and beautiful, but nobody seems to care what I think. I'm comfortable in my skin. My Polish farm girl genetics didn't give me a choice, so I own it. I'm a catch, but Brandon Myers has never chased after my brand of beauty. I'd love to be the first, but I'd die of mortification if he rejected me.

The platinum blonde bombshell gazing into the eyes of the man of my dreams is Vera. She showed up out of nowhere a few months ago and did the impossible: she kept Brando's attention for more than one night. They come in here together often and as much as I'd like to make a voodoo doll with little straw hair, I can't hate her. She tips well and treats me like a friend. Plus, she's a total badass who could rip me to shreds with a look, so I prefer to stay on her good side.

I take the food to table three and make sure they're settled before I return to the bar. The song ends and Vera bounces over to me. "There's my favorite bartender! Another round, please."

I plaster on a smile and pour their shots. They'll be leaving soon now that they're at the proper amount of buzzing for their kinky sexual adventures. God, I'm so damn jealous it's not even funny.

They down their shots and make out right in front of me. I sigh and busy myself with the next customer.

My boss and the co-owner of this fine establishment, Jackson Waller, sits next to them and they pull their lips apart. Jackson and his best friend

Austin are the world's greatest bosses. It sounds like a line you put on a coffee mug, but it's true. They joke around with us, but they never flirt with their employees. They maintain a surprising level of professionalism, considering how much they get around with the patrons of The Lone Boot.

Jackson's billionaire best friend and the owner of Reilly Tech, Luke, joins them with his girlfriend, Liv, who is Vera's best friend. My coworkers were green with envy when Liv snagged Luke's attention. But I think they're perfect for each other. He looks at her with such love and devotion, you can't help but swoon.

Their friend Mark takes the stool in front of me. "Hey Kristy. How's your night?"

I smile for the man who I would be crushing on if Brando didn't exist. He always asks how I'm doing and gives off those genuine, caring vibes. Natalie says he checks me out all the time, but he's never made a move. It's for the best. He's too old for me and I'm way too hung up on his friend.

"Doing great now. Thanks, Mark." I slide his favorite beer to him, and he smiles and raises it in thanks before turning to face the crowd.

A new song plays, and Vera pulls on Brando's arm. "This is my favorite!" He chuckles and wraps his arm around her, kissing her temple as they make their way back to the dance floor.

Women glare at Vera as the couple passes, proving I'm only one of thousands of admirers. I've never been competitive, though, so I admire from afar and fantasize an alternate reality where I am that woman who has the audacity to jiggle her tits at him.

I grab another order and head to my next table, smiling at the customers and doing my best to put the happy couple out of my mind.

Natalie and Greg live three doors down from me, so we drive home together. I stare out the window from the backseat of Greg's truck and wonder if I'll ever not be sad. The image of Brando and Vera kissing plays in my mind and I sigh. Maybe it's time to move on.

"Hey, Nat?" I ask.

She turns her head to look at me. "Yeah?"

"Can you set me up on a date with that guy you mentioned?" She's been bugging me for weeks to go out with Greg's friend.

She grins. "Hell yes."

Greg smiles at me in the rearview mirror, and I settle into my seat and blow out the breath I was holding. Here goes nothing.

Chapter Two

Forrest

"Jackson Waller, as I live and breathe." I embrace my old friend in a long hug.

"Forrest, you son of a bitch," Jackson says before releasing me. It does my heart good to see the man who saved my life one cold and dreary night in Afghanistan in what seems like a lifetime ago.

"Nice place you got here." I motion to the massive neon Lone Boot sign hanging above the bar.

He grins. "Told you I'd make it happen."

"Never doubted you for a second."

He grins and we take our seats on the nearby bar stools. It's before the dinner rush, so we have the place almost to ourselves. "I never thought you'd leave the South," he says.

"Me neither. But life throws shit at you when you least expect it."

"Ain't that the truth?"

The bartender approaches, and when our gazes lock, the room narrows and time slows. I always assumed that was just a saying, but here I am with sweaty palms and a rapid heartbeat.

With a mind-numbing smile, the most gorgeous woman in existence speaks, but I'm too mesmerized by her face to catch her words.

Jackson nudges me and I blink away my stupor. "Get whatever you want. It's on the house."

"Oh, uh, thanks. I'll take your best pilsner."

She grins and grabs a glass. I sense Jackson's eyes on me. Being in the Marines together makes you have ESP. It's strange, but there's a comfort in knowing that your brothers will always get you. But nothing could pull my gaze away from the vision in front of me.

"Are you new to town?" she asks.

"Yes, ma'am. Just moved here last month."

"Do you like San Diego?" She sets my glass in front of me on the coaster and fills another.

"I love it, ma'am."

She scrunches her cute little nose. "I know it's polite and proper where you're from, but ma'am makes me feel old."

I shrug with a grin. "Sorry, ma'am."

She tilts her head back and laughs as she hands Jackson his beer. "You can take the country boy out of the South..." She winks, her eyes twinkling with joy.

We maintain eye contact as Jackson speaks. "Thanks, Kristy. This is my buddy, Forrest. He's a Marine, so he gets the house rules."

Kristy smiles, and it feels like it's meant just for me. "Of course. Thank you for your service, Forrest. Cool name, by the way."

Is she flirting or only being nice because I'm Jackson's friend? It's been ages since I've been this attracted to a woman. The divorce from my wife last year was brutal. Thank God we never had kids, so I never have to see her cheating, lying ass again.

"Thanks," I mutter, not sure what else to say.

She nods and returns to the customers who sit nearby. My eyes trail down her silky blond waves and stay glued to her curves as she walks away. Damn. I'd love to get a handful of that. Her tits jiggle when she laughs, and I can't help but imagine my face between them as I sink deep into her–

"Rule number one. No one-night stands with my employees. I don't need that kind of drama in my life. If you're going after her, you better buy a damn ring first."

I roll my eyes and yank my gaze to Jackson. "Can't a guy admire beauty when he sees it?"

He laughs and shakes his head. "I take it you haven't dated since Chelsea?"

My grin drops and I hide my sour face by taking a sip of beer. "Yeah."

"Plenty of fun to have here, if you're interested."

I shrug. One-nighters were never my thing. Sure, I partook when I was a young dumbass Marine. But when I met Chelsea, I thought I found the one. Turns out I was only a slightly older dumbass. I thought I could be the one to fix her, but people who only care about themselves never change. Lesson fucking learned.

"Not really my thing."

Jackson nods. "I figured. So, what brings you out here?"

I take another sip and sigh. "I sold the farm and gave Chelsea half. She got what she wanted, and I never have to see her again."

His face falls. "Shit. I'm sorry. I know how much it meant to you. How did your dad take it?"

I shrug. "He's been in Florida for years with his girlfriend. He didn't seem upset by it. But I was always more invested."

"That blows, man. I'm sorry to hear that."

I grunt and take another pull of my beer. Kristy passes by, carrying mixed drinks to the other patrons. I watch her graceful movements as Jackson speaks.

"What are you doing now?"

"I'm working for my aunt as a construction project manager in Del Mar. I'll be doing that while I figure out how to start my furniture business."

Jackson grins. "I knew it." He slaps the bar top he commissioned from me. "This thing will last longer than my grandkids."

I laugh. "It better. Took me forever to make."

Kristy bustles past us, and I catch her eye. She smiles and I can't help doing the same. Her cheeks turn pink, and she glances away, busying herself with her task. My hands twitch with the urge to touch. Jesus, she's breathtaking.

"Well, I'll be damned."

I spin to find Brando behind me and stand, giving him a back-slapping hug.

He grins and takes the empty stool next to me. "It's been years, man. Are you just visiting?"

"I'm a Californian again," I say.

"About damn time. I know a good gym that will help you with that dad bod too." His eyes sparkle and I roll mine.

"Sorry, we can't all look like the God of Thunder. You got an eight-pack yet?"

He laughs and the three of us fall right back into old times, giving each other shit and smiling because it's how we show our love.

"Where's Luke? I heard he was in San Diego now?"

The mood shifts and they share a glance. "He moved to LA last week. There were some... complications in his love life," Brando says.

"Complications?"

"He broke up with the perfect woman for him because he's a damn coward," Jackson all but snarls.

My eyes bounce between them, filled with questions, but I know they're going to be tight-lipped about Luke. I'm their friend, but I'm not in the billionaire's inner circle.

"He'll figure it out," Brando says.

"Well, I hope it works out for him."

Kristy appears, bringing sunshine to our rainy-day parade. She sets a beer in front of Brando, and he smiles politely before thanking her.

"You're welcome," she says, a bit too loud, and we all stare at her. Her cheeks turn a bright red. "Sorry, uhm..." She pushes her long wavy ponytail behind her shoulder.

"This beer is pretty good. Is it local?" I preen like an idiot under her attention. Contrary to Brando's statement, I don't have a dad bod. But I'm not a jacked motherfucker like the two gym rats I sit between.

"It is. Would you like another?" she asks.

"Yes, ma'am."

She rolls her eyes at me and blood rushes to places it shouldn't as I wonder how far her sass goes. She takes my glass and pours me another before refilling Jackson's. I watch her work as the guys start the chatter up again.

A few hours pass and the bar gets busy as they clear the tables from the dance floor. I say my goodbyes as they make fun of me for being an old man out past my bedtime, even though I'm younger than them by a couple of years. Once they're out of sight, I approach Kristy as she's wiping up the end of the bar. I pull out a twenty and hand it to her. "This is for you."

She shakes her head. "Thank you, but it's on the house. Jackson's rules."

"I insist. You work hard, you deserve the tip."

She takes it with a smile. "Thank you, Forrest. I hope we'll be seeing more of you."

I screwed things up with Chelsea. Marriage is a two-way street and I acknowledge my part in its failure, but I never should have married her. I tried to force a square peg into a round hole. The only time we weren't arguing was when we were fucking.

I've known Kristy for all of a few hours, and I can tell she's different. I'm probably going to screw this up too, but I have little to lose. If I'd only listened to my instincts when I met Chelsea, I would have avoided a helluva lot of heartache. Right now, those instincts are screaming at me to spend more time with Kristy, and I'll be damned if I make the same mistake again.

I lean closer and shoot her the crooked grin that always worked when I was younger. "You can count on it."

I take a few steps backwards, holding her gaze and memorizing the way her lips parted when I spoke. Then I turn and head towards the door. When I glance behind me, she's still watching me leave, but I lose sight of her as a group moves between us.

A woman at a small table calls out to me. "Are you interested in signing up for the Reilly Tech veteran's Christmas raffle?"

I pause and move over to her. "Sure."

"We will announce the winner the day after Christmas. You don't have to be present to win. It's ten dollars per ticket. The winner gets free drinks for a year and a thousand-dollar gift card for Reilly Tech equipment."

I pull my wallet out and hand her a fifty. She beams at me and hands me my stack of tickets.

"Just put your first name and your phone number on the back of each one."

Once I'm done, she grins. "Thank you for your donation. Are you a veteran?"

"Yes, ma'am. And I'm familiar with the charity. They do great work."

She grins again and takes the tickets from me, plopping them into a half full jug. "Have a great night, and thank you for your service."

I head to my truck and sigh. Thanksgiving is next week, but it's still a balmy 70 degrees tonight. Christmas is my favorite time of the year. I go all out with the decorations and gifts.

But this year will be different. I'll be alone.

With that bleak thought, Kristy's bright smile pops into my brain, and I start the truck with a grin. If I play my cards right, maybe this holiday season won't be so lonely after all.

Chapter Three

Kristy

I stare after Jackson's handsome friend as he leaves the bar, my mouth gaping open as the after-effects of his sultry gaze and deep voice finish making my insides mush. I saw him the second he walked in. He's not my usual type. I'm drawn to the pretty boys with six-packs, not bearded mountain men with smooth Southern drawls and deep green eyes I could get lost in.

"Holy shit. Did he invite you to his hotel room?" Natalie says, and I close my mouth.

"No, but it felt like it."

Natalie grins. "He was eye fucking the shit out of you all night. I bet he'll be back for more of that sweet ass." She smacks said ass, and I giggle.

The date with Greg's friend last month didn't go anywhere. He was nice, and I had fun, but that spark was missing. I only ever get hit on by drunken idiots at the bar, so I never take it seriously. Forrest only had the two beers hours ago. My brain runs through a thousand different ways I could have misinterpreted him. But the way he looked at me? I hope Natalie is right.

Another hour passes and my mind keeps wandering to Forrest. Goosebumps dot my skin and I bite my lip. I haven't been this excited about a man since I met Brando. When I made a fool of myself in front of him earlier, Forrest pulled me out of my embarrassment with his smile. If he asks me out, I'd be crazy not to say yes.

Natalie runs up to me with that glint in her eyes that means she has gossip. I swear she missed her calling as an FBI agent.

"You won't believe this," she says, rubbing her hands together and bouncing on her feet.

"Believe what?"

"Vera dumped Brando. She's dating someone else."

My eyebrows fly to the ceiling. "What?" I scan the dancefloor and find Brando chatting with Austin at the other end of the bar.

"Now's your chance. Go talk to him." She nudges my shoulder, but I stay rooted to the spot.

"I don't want to be his rebound." But that's one hundred percent a lie. One night with him will fulfill all my wildest fantasies, and a part of me hopes that once he sees the type of love I could give him, he won't let me go.

She sighs. "You're probably right. But don't wait too long." She wiggles her eyebrows before she heads off to serve more customers.

Should I even bother making a move? It's not like he's ever shown me any interest, even before Vera, but Jackson's stupid rule could be to blame.

Forrest's smile pops into my mind and I frown. He's shown interest, despite Jackson's rule. Brando is like a peacock, fluffing his feathers and strutting around being loud and cocky. Forrest is more like an eagle. Strong, sturdy, and intense. He knows what he has to offer and doesn't care if you like it or not.

Which bird do I want?

I laugh at my weird comparison.

I want the pretty peacock. Right?

The next week flies by and then it's Thanksgiving night. I volunteered to work because that's what I do. We're closed on Christmas Day, but that's the only day I wouldn't volunteer. It's my favorite holiday and my mom is visiting for the first time since I moved here. I can't wait to show her around, even though she's already complaining about not having snow for Christmas. She'll get over it when she's not freezing her ass off as we sing our carols.

We're working with a skeleton crew this evening. There's a handful of us doing twice the amount of work, so the time flies by. Around nine, I switch places with Jenna at the bar so she can take a break.

My pulse quickens when a familiar face sits down near me. He smiles and I plop a coaster in front of him, placing his pilsner on top. "Happy Thanksgiving, Forrest."

He's trimmed his beard, so it's not too long, but not short. He wears a deep green flannel button-up that matches his eyes and he's rolled his sleeves, exposing muscled forearms. A well-worn ball cap covers his dark hair, and I'd bet my tips tonight that his boots are legitimate work boots, scuffs and all. Nerves flutter in my gut, but instead of making me freeze up, it excites me. He excites me.

"Happy Thanksgiving, Kristy." He grins and raises his glass at me before he sips.

"Taking a break from the turkey?"

He chuckles. "I went to church with my aunt, and we had dinner, but she turned in early. I thought I'd come check out the nightlife."

"Well, you came to the right place. People love it here because it's owned by a true Texan. It's the only legitimate country bar in the area."

He throws his head back and laughs. "He's got them all fooled."

I gasp and lean closer, lowering my voice. "You mean he's not from Texas?"

He laughs again, and I decide it's my new favorite sound. "Oh, he's from Texas all right. But this place ain't authentic."

I laugh as I grab a glass for the refill I know the guy nearby is about to ask for. "What's missing?"

He grins. "It's too clean in here, for starters. Plus, you've got that hip hop crap playing every ten songs. And don't get me started on the beer." He waves his hand towards the wall lined with taps behind me.

I pass the guy next to Forrest his beer and he tips his Stetson. "Thank you, darlin'," he says in a terrible mimicry of a Southern accent before he leaves.

Forrest raises his eyebrow and shakes his head before taking a sip of his beer, and I laugh.

We spend the next few hours chatting while I serve other customers. He leaves me be when it gets busy and waits for me to talk to him again when the crowd at the bar thins. I work faster just so I can talk to him.

On my break, I take the seat next to him and he faces me, spreading his long legs to the outside of my knees and resting his hands on his thighs. His body heat warms my skin through my jeans, and an image of his calloused palm trailing up my inner thigh forces me to press my legs together.

"So, Virginia, huh? How did you end up out here?" he asks.

"West Coast dreaming, I suppose. I went to community college but dropped out after a year. The collegiate path wasn't right for me."

"I hear that. That's why I joined the Marines."

"What part of Texas are you from?"

He grins. "I'm from Tennessee, actually. I owned a cattle farm, but I had to sell it last year."

"Is that why you're out here?"

He nods. "I enjoyed my time on Camp Pendleton with the boys. So, I thought why not come back?"

"Please tell me you have stories about Jackson." I clasp my hands together in excitement, and he chuckles.

"I sure do. But none that I'll share."

I shove his shoulder and pout. "You're no fun."

He grins. "I'm plenty fun, but I ain't keen on getting my ass beat."

I throw my head back and laugh, resting my hand on his arm. His bicep twitches and I clear my throat as I take my hand back. Yep, solid muscle under that shirt.

"You could take him."

He smiles and sets his beer on the coaster. "I appreciate the vote of confidence."

There are shouts behind me and I turn towards the sound, but the crowd moves, and I'm shoved off my seat. I land on Forrest with a yelp. He wraps his arms around me, and I dangle between his legs, my hands gripping his firm shoulders.

He smells nice. Like sawdust and pine soap. Our noses are millimeters apart, my body flush against his, our eyes wide as the commotion behind us gets cleared up by the bouncers. Neither of us moves as my heart pounds in my chest and he holds my stare.

"Are you ok?" he whispers.

I swallow and nod.

He lowers me to my feet, dragging my body against his, but doesn't let go. His big hand moves from my hip to my face, and he pushes my hair behind my ear. "You're so beautiful."

I glance to my left at his unfinished beer. He's only had one. There's no way he's drunk.

Jenna catches my eye with a raised eyebrow, and I clear my throat. "I need to get back to work."

He gives me room to maneuver around the other stool. I already miss his hands on me as I make my way to the other side of the bar.

"Sorry if I made you uncomfortable. I'll get out of your hair," Forrest says.

His deep voice sends a warm tingle through me, and I close my eyes. When I open them, he's standing and tucking his wallet into his back pocket. A twenty sits next to his beer glass.

"Forrest, wait..." I call as he walks away.

He pauses and looks over his broad shoulder. "I had fun tonight. Thanks for the beer and company."

"I hope I'll be seeing more of you?"

He smiles. "You can count on it."

I grin, and he hesitates, then nods and strides away.

"You done yet?" Jenna calls, annoyance in her tone.

"Yeah, sorry. I'm back."

I finish out the next hour, thinking about Forrest as I go through the motions. He was so easy to laugh with. I've never even had a full conversation with Brando because I get so tongue-tied, which is pathetic now that I think about it.

"Here's the latest batch of raffle tickets," Natalie says as she enters Jackson's office. I'm borrowing his desk to work out the logistics of the Christmas raffle and the New Year's Eve party.

If all goes well, I'll get the management promotion of my dreams. I volunteered for the event, hoping to show my worth. Event planning is something I've always enjoyed. People have asked me to plan their birthday parties and bridal showers for years. This will be the biggest event I've ever coordinated, but I've been working hard for months, and I refuse for it to be anything less than spectacular.

"Thanks," I say, keeping my gaze on the screen as she dumps the contents of the jar into the bigger tub in the corner. It's almost full and people have been so generous with their donations. It warms my heart.

"You need help with anything else?"

"No, just finishing up."

"So, uh, how serious are you about Brando?" she asks, and I pause, turning to face her.

"Why do you ask?"

She sighs and crosses her arms. "Greg told me he hooked up with other girls when he was with Vera, and she knew about it. They had an open relationship type thing."

I frown and return my eyes to the screen. "Maybe it would be different with me."

"If he's got any smarts to go along with those good looks, it will be. But I don't want you to get hurt."

I save my work and close out of the program. "I know he's a player, but he hasn't met someone who appreciates him like I do."

She sighs and shrugs. "Maybe you're right. So, you're serious about giving it a shot then?"

"Yes." The word pops out, but it's only half true.

She glances at the clock. "Alright. I better get back out there, but we'll talk later."

She bends to put the lid on the raffle ticket bin, and I stand. "I'm gonna use the restroom. I'll meet you out there."

She nods and we leave the room.

A few minutes later, I find Natalie again and help her finish setting up the tables.

"Oh, you left your phone in the office. Here," she says, handing it to me, and I pocket it.

Hours go by fast on a busy Saturday night. When it's time for my break, I head to our small break room and slump into a chair at the table. I pull out my phone and frown when I see I have a text from an unknown number, and the frown deepens when it appears I texted them first.

Me: Hey. This is Kristy. I hope it's ok that I got your number. I know this is crazy, but I've had a crush on you from the moment we met.

Unknown: This is crazy, because I've also had a crush on you since we met.

My heart pounds in my chest as I re-read it a dozen times. My eyes widen and I storm back to the bar, zeroing in on my bestie. She looks at me and grins. "Did he respond?"

"What did you do?"

She shushes me. "What did he say?"

I narrow my eyes. "Who is he?"

She giggles and points to the end of the bar where Brando sits with Jackson. The walls cave in and my face turns the color of a tomato. Oh my God, Oh my God, Oh my God. He knows. *He knows!*

Natalie grabs my phone. "Holy shit! I didn't expect that!"

"Tell me what you did. Right now."

"I saw his name on one of the raffle tickets, so I used your phone to text him. You're welcome. You better name your kid after me."

I stare at the text. He sent it over an hour ago. Is this happening? Is this really freaking happening? I race back to the break room, Natalie hot on my heels.

"What do I say?"

"Tell him you want his babies."

I ignore her unhelpfulness and chew my lip as I type.

Me: I'm so happy to hear you say that.

I hit send and wait, but nothing happens. Minutes pass and the message sits unread.

"Back to work, ladies," Austin calls as he passes the room, and we both sigh and return to our stations. I put the vibration alert on high so I don't miss his reply. I scan the room for him, but he and Jackson have disappeared.

My heart races whenever I spot a tall blond guy, but Brando never reappears, and my message stays unread. When we're stacking chairs and the bouncers are clearing the building, I check my phone and gasp when the text bubbles appear and Natalie dashes over, rubbing her hands together with a Cheshire grin on her face.

A few minutes pass and Natalie smiles. "Aww, he's nervous."

I roll my eyes because Brando has never been nervous about anything a day in his life. Of that, I'm certain.

Unknown: Sorry I took so long to respond. Got held up at work, and I hope this doesn't wake you. I'm so glad I didn't scare you away.

"Ahhhh!" Natalie squeals, and I shush her.

I pause as I begin typing.

"What is it?" Natalie asks.

"How would he scare me away?"

Natalie smacks my arm. "Who cares? Don't overthink it."

I shake my head. She's right. "What do I say next?"

"Ask him when you can see him."

Me: When can I see you?

The bubbles appear, then disappear at least a half dozen times while I chew my thumbnail.

Unknown: I would love nothing more than to spend time with you, but this work thing just got intense. I don't want to commit to something and disappoint you if I have to cancel. I'm so sorry, this is just the worst timing. But if I find a free moment, I promise I'll stop by to see you.

What could possibly be intense at a gym? I glance at Natalie and find her eyes narrowed as she analyzes his words. I wait as she taps her finger on her chin. She sighs and shrugs. "I think he's telling the truth."

Me: I'm sorry to hear that. I hope it won't last too long.

Unknown: It should be over by Christmas. Then I'll have tons of free time to stare at your pretty face.

"Hope he plans on doing more than just staring," Natalie murmurs, and I chuckle while I try to contain my blush. *Brandon Myers thinks I'm pretty!*

Unknown: How about I take you out the day after Christmas? Will you be in town?

Me: Yes, but I'll be with my mom.

Unknown: Ok, well, just hit me up when you're free. I promise to make this up to you with a date you'll never forget.

Oh my God! My hips shake in a little happy dance.

"Ow ow! Hot mama's got a date!" Natalie shouts, dancing along with me. We giggle and laugh at our stupidity before I return his text.

Me: Sounds like a plan. I can't wait :)

Unknown: Me either :)

I stare at his message for a moment, then program his number into my phone under his name with a heart next to it. "Is this real life?" I ask Natalie, and she grins.

"Better believe it. Who loves ya?"

I tackle her in a hug and we both squeal in excitement as we make our way to the break room to get our things.

Chapter Four

Forrest

My boot covered feet dangle off the edge of the truck bed, my sandwich halfway to my mouth in my other hand while I stare at the text on my phone's screen.

Unknown: Hey. This is Kristy. I hope it's ok that I got your number. I know this is crazy, but I've had a crush on you from the moment we met.

My first instinct is that this is some kind of joke. But I don't think Jackson has time to mess with me right now. Brando is too busy sticking his dick into the next willing female. But what if it's her? She got nervous when I almost kissed her a few days ago, and I thought I had read all her signs wrong. But what if she felt the spark between us, too?

I type my response and continue to stare at the screen while I chew on my sandwich. The message sits unread for the rest of my lunch break, so I pack it up. It's probably just a prank.

"Hey boss, we got a suit out back," Rick, the Foreman, calls. I heave a sigh and hop off the tailgate, tucking my phone into my pocket.

Rick falls into step next to me. We make our way around the framework of the building, the whir of the power tools like a song to my soul.

Being around wood is something I've enjoyed since woodshop in high school. One day I'll build my home and everything in it. But for now, I have to deal with assholes like the one waiting for me.

The pain-in-the-ass assistant to our high-end client stands in his crisp burgundy suit with shoes that are way too pretty for a construction site. "Mr. Barthane. We weren't expecting you." I extend my hand to shake, and the pompous prick sneers at it before ignoring it altogether. He speaks and I drop my hand.

"I'd much rather be in Manhattan. I never understood the appeal of the West Coast." He looks around in disgust, like San Diego personally offends him. Who the hell doesn't like palm trees and warm weather?

"What can I do for you?"

"You're behind schedule and Mr. Angelo hates to be kept waiting. So, how do we fix this situation?"

I narrow my eyes at the weasel. "I don't understand. We're ahead of schedule."

His condescending chuckle makes me want to punch him into next week, where we'll still be ahead of schedule, but I refrain.

"Do you know who Victor Angelo is?" he asks for the fourth time since I met him last month.

"Of course. He's the owner of the second largest tech company in the world. Right behind Reilly Tech."

Mr. Barthane purses his lips. "He's also going to put your tiny little company on the map, so I suggest you get back on schedule."

"Like I said, we're ahead. If you care to clarify, we can get this sorted for you." I grit my teeth into what I hope is a smile.

"Mr. Angelo wants the boutique ready by Christmas Eve for his fiancèe."

My jaw drops and Rick tenses next to me. "We agreed on Valentine's Day, and like I said, we're ahead. It will be complete by the first week of February."

His sneer grows as I talk. "It's not my fault you misunderstood the holiday, Mr. Forrest." He waves a dismissive hand and I clench my fists. I'm not an idiot. He's the one who got the date wrong, and he's trying to pin it on us. I squeeze my eyes shut, then exhale.

"Alright. Christmas Eve."

Mr. Barthane grins and pats my shoulder. "Good lad. Carry on." He trots off to the waiting SUV, and it peels out of the parking lot.

"What the hell, Forrest?" Rick says.

I sigh and let my shoulders drop. "Gale needs this. We can't fuck it up or she'll go under."

Rick deflates and rubs the back of his neck. "Shit. I didn't realize it was that bad."

Gale is my mom's sister. She reached out to me when she heard I'd sold the farm and asked me to help with her failing business. She'd already agreed to the Angelo deal before I came onboard, otherwise I never would have let her sign the paperwork. Luke mentioned Victor Angelo in the past and that their feud was more than just a rivalry. I was going to ask Luke for advice, but it sounds like he's got a lot on his plate right now, so I'm on my own.

I spend the next several hours trying to come up with a miracle to get this project completed over a month early. My back aches from hunching over plans and paperwork, so I slam my pencil down and stretch. I rub my fingers over my tired eyes and stand, leaning my head back to get the crick out of my neck. My eyes land on the picture of me, Jackson, Jordy, Tank, and Steve from our first deployment that's pinned to the bulletin board above my desk. Steve never made it home. I adjust the metal bracelet around my wrist with his name on it and stop the memories from taking over.

I stand and pull my phone out of my pocket, and my eyes widen. Kristy responded hours ago. I type out a hurried response so she doesn't think I ghosted her.

I can't contain my grin when she asks to see me again, but it slips from my mouth when I glance at my messy desk. *Fuck.* I decide to go for honesty and hope she'll understand. My smile returns when she agrees to the date after Christmas.

Kristy: Sounds like a plan. I can't wait :)
Me: Me either :)

My stomach protests at the lack of food, and I glance at my watch. I skipped dinner. With a sigh, I shut off the light and head to the nearest fast-food joint that's still open. I should be in a pissy mood over the stunt

Barthane pulled today, but I catch the grin on my face in the side mirror and shake my head. It was my full intent to keep my head down and stay single when I came out here. I left the relationship drama behind.

But I can't ignore the pull towards Kristy, and it looks like I won't have to. I just need to be careful and keep my head on straight.

Chapter Five

Kristy

My head stays on a swivel the next few days, but Brando never shows. The weekend rolls around and I raise my eyebrows when I find Luke's ex-girlfriend, Liv, wearing The Lone Boot t-shirt and cut-off shorts behind the bar while Austin explains our stocking process.

"Hey, Kristy. This is Liv. She's our new barback."

"Welcome to the team. Let me know if you have questions."

She smiles, but her eyes are sad. The rumors are flying about the break-up, but I doubt it's anything she wants to talk about, so I make a point not to bring it up.

Natalie has the night off, which should be illegal. Working with your bestie is one of God's precious gifts. I say hi to my coworkers and tie my hair into a ponytail at my locker, glancing in the mirror and fixing my eyeliner. Austin checks in, and I head out to greet our thirsty patrons. It's slow for a Friday, but it's the typical pre-Christmas lull.

On my break, I grin from ear to ear when I find a text waiting from Brando.

Brando: Hey pretty lady. Hope your night is going well.

Me: Better now. How are you?

Brando: Super stressed but having our date to look forward to helps.

Me: I wish I could help you more.

Brando: Believe me. You're doing great.

I send the laughing emoji and throw in a heart because I'm in an adventurous mood.

Me: I still can't believe you have a crush on me.

Brando: Well, you better, because I do.

Me: We need to talk about something. This is a deal breaker for me, so no pressure. But what's your favorite holiday?

Brando: That's easy. Christmas. My dad and I used to go all out with decorating and gifts. Did I pass?

Me: With flying colors. Mine is Christmas too. My mom is coming out this year and I can't wait to show her what I'm doing at the bar.

Brando: Are you in charge of decorating?

Me: I am. Santa is about to sneeze wreaths and candy canes all up in this joint. I'm also in charge of the Christmas raffle and the New Year's Eve party. I'm hoping to impress Jackson and Austin enough to get promoted to events manager.

Brando: I'm sure they'll promote you. Jackson has an eye for talent. And I can't wait to see what you do with the bar. I'll bring a tissue for Santa ;) But I have a deal breaker too. What's your favorite Christmas song?

Me: Crap. Well, it's been fun.

Brando: Oh, come on. It can't be that bad.

Me: I'm a Swifty. So, I play Christmas Tree Farm on repeat.

Brando: Shut up. I love Taylor Swift!

Me: Oh, please. You're lying.

Brando: LOL. Only a little. I don't hate her.

I giggle as I type.

Me: Did I pass?

Brando: Nope, but I'll let you make it up to me if you hang mistletoe.

Me: Anyone in particular you'd like to meet under it?

Brando: Jackson. He's a looker.

I laugh out loud.

Me: We all saw that coming.

Brando: LOL. Or, better idea, how about you and I share our first kiss under the mistletoe?

Oh. My. God. You can probably see my smile from space.

Me: I would love that.

I won't tell him I've dreamt of kissing him under the mistletoe about a thousand times. He sends me a heart emoji, and I almost die right there at the table. Who knew Brando could be adorable?

This is why I've always been attracted to military men. To protect, you also have to care. I can't speak for all of them, but in my experience, there's something about the way they carry themselves that stays with them long after their active duty days are over. Maybe I'll get my wish and have my very own Marine for Christmas this year.

I float on cloud nine for the rest of my shift and stay up late texting Brando. I should call him, but I'm too nervous. This is the perfect way to ease me into reality, because a huge part of me still worries this is too good to be true.

Ten days pass and I spend every night giggling like an idiot while I lay sprawled on my bed in all different angles, my phone in my face. Talking to Brando is so easy. I'm kicking myself for not making a move sooner. Natalie gives me constant shit like any good best friend would, but she hugs me tight and tells me how happy she is for me.

"Look at you, you're all glowy," she says.

I roll my eyes but grin at my reflection. I am glowing. My dream is coming true. I shut my locker and follow her into the hall.

We both freeze as Brando walks towards us. My heart flutters out of my chest. Is he going to kiss me?

"Hi, handsome."

He does a double take and slows, quirking an eyebrow as he scans my body from head to toe and back again, sending a wave of heat that flushes my cheeks. His lip quirks up on the side like it does when he sees something he likes, and I have an out-of-body experience as he moves in front of me. "Hey, yourself."

His voice rolls over me and I press my thighs together. Oh. My. God. I can't do this right now.

He tilts his head. "Was there something you needed?"

I blink as the stupid grin falls from my face. "Oh, um. No. Just saying hi." Why does it have to come out in a squeak?

He narrows his eyes. "It's Kristy, right?"

I laugh and push his arm, trying not to gulp when he doesn't budge, and my palm meets hard muscle. "You're silly."

He smiles like I said something cute. "Right. Sorry to cut this short, but I need to talk to Jackson."

My face falls. He didn't come here to visit me? "Oh. Ok." I step out of his way, but his smile grows, and he moves closer.

"So, I'll see you around then, beautiful?"

My face heats again. Hearing him say it out loud is a whole other ball game. I swallow hard and nod. "You better."

His gaze lingers for a moment, then he winks as he makes his way to Jackson's office. He looks back at me with that panty-melting grin before he disappears through the door.

"Holy crap. You two are totally in love! Those sparks were off the chart!" Natalie whispers as she grabs my arm, snapping me out of my stupor. I follow her to the bar and start cleaning to get my mind working again.

An hour passes before Brando reappears, but I lose him in the crowd. I'm disappointed that he didn't say goodbye, but he did mention he was crazy busy with that deadline.

He surprised me a few nights ago when mentioned he was into making furniture and wanted to turn it into a business. Things got awkward when I asked why he got into the fitness industry instead, so I dropped it. I don't want to push him away.

"You have a visitor," Natalie says as she wiggles her eyebrows and hooks a thumb over her shoulder. Forrest grins at me, and my nerves settle. He says something in greeting, but I can't hear him over the music, so I just smile.

"How are you? It's been a while," I say.

He blinks for a second and tilts his head. "I had a break, so I came to say hi."

"Oh, that's great. Jackson is around here somewhere."

Forrest frowns. "I was just with him and Brando. I needed some advice."

"Everything ok?" I pour him a beer and he takes it. Our fingers brush and my body heats. Did someone mess with the thermostat again?

"Yep, nothing you need to worry about." He takes a sip. "I haven't told Jackson about us yet."

I narrow my eyes as I try to decipher what he means. The last time we spoke was weeks ago when I fell into his lap and we almost kissed. He must be talking about that. My eyes widen and I shake my head, but a customer flags me down and I jump at the opportunity.

I can't deny that I had hoped to see Forrest again after our fun night on Thanksgiving. But I'm getting my once in a lifetime chance with Brando, and I can't give it up. I'll have to tell Forrest that I'm off the market.

Easier said than done.

"Who's the lumbersnack?" Natalie asks as she fills a glass next to me at the taps.

I laugh at her and shake my head. "Jackson's friend, Forrest. Remember?"

"Damn, girl. When it rains, it pours!" she shouts as she returns to her customer.

The night is busy, so I don't have time to speak with Forrest. He keeps glancing at his watch, and it seems like he wants to tell me something, but I can't deal with the awkwardness at work.

When I glance up again a few minutes later, he's gone, and a sadness settles in my heart. Had our paths crossed at any other time, things would be different.

When my shift ends, I frown at the text waiting from Brando.

Brando: I'm sorry I showed up unannounced when you were busy. I hope I didn't upset you?

My fingers fly.

Me: OMG no. Why would I be upset?

Brando: You didn't seem excited to see me, but I might have read that wrong?

Me: Uh, yea. That was me being super nervous to see you in person. Like I said, I still can't believe you like me.

Brando: I know we just started talking, but you're special to me. I'd like to tell Jackson, so you don't have to worry about upsetting him. But if you're not ready, can we sneak away to the closet so I can kiss you? Not being able to touch you is driving me crazy.

Sweet baby Jesus, this can't be real. I debate telling him how many times I've fantasized about secret naughty rendezvous with him in the supply closet but decide to keep the crazy locked up for eternity instead. I have the urge to call him, but based on our earlier encounter, I'd probably blabber like a fool.

Me: You can tell Jackson, but we can also sneak off to the closet.

He sends the laugh emoji followed by the heart and kiss, and I swoon. Why does this man sending me emojis make me weak in the knees?

Brando: Text me when you get home, so I know you made it safe.

My cheeks hurt from smiling so much. Everything about him is surprising, which makes me wonder why he hides himself from the world behind the cocky playboy exterior.

An unwanted, nagging thought wiggles its way forward. He hasn't brought up Vera and their recent break-up. I've avoided it because I don't want to burst this happy bubble. But I would be devastated if this blew up in my face.

I hustle home and I'm texting him before the front door thuds shut behind me.

Me: I made it home. And I have an uncomfortable question I have to ask. Please don't hate me.

Brando: You can ask me anything.

I bite my lip, my foot tapping a beat before I type.

Me: Are you still hung up on your ex?

The bubbles reappear and disappear while my palms sweat.

Brando: I'm not sure what Jackson told you, but no. The divorce is final.

They got married? Natalie will never believe this.

Me: I didn't realize you were married.

Brando: Oh. Well, I hope it doesn't taint your opinion of me. We were young and dumb. That chapter of my life is over.

Wait... he can't be talking about Vera.

Me: No, of course not. How long ago was it?

Brando: We separated over two years ago, but the divorce finalized last year.

Yep, not Vera. I tap my lip, debating if I should even bring her up. I guess she wasn't that important to him after all.

Brando: What about you? Any past relationships you're still hung up on?

I blow raspberries even though he can't hear them.

Me: Nope. My ex grew tired of hiding his chubby girlfriend from his friends. Tale as old as time.

I regret it when I hit send. He makes me so comfortable I forget I'm not gabbing with a friend.

Brando: Jesus. What a moron. If you were my girlfriend, I'd pass out flyers at the grocery store and leave them on windshields to make sure the whole damn world knew you were mine. You're gorgeous, babe.

My eyes water as I laugh. It hurt like hell when my ex told me he couldn't be with me because I didn't match whatever made-up idealization he had in his head. I'm better off without him, but it took years of positive self-talk and a total perception change to get to where I am now. The memory still stings, though.

But wait, did he just talk about me being his girlfriend? Oh. My. God.

Me: You think I'm gorgeous?

Brando: Can I Facetime you?

My insides squeeze in panic.

Me: Um, sorry, I'm not decent.

Brando: That's fine. No pressure.

I sigh in relief. I love that he doesn't pressure me.

Brando: To answer your question, I can't wait to show you how gorgeous you are ;)

I squeeze the phone to my chest and wiggle in a happy dance. I can't wait for him to show me either.

Brando: Oh, by the way, I talked to Jackson tonight. He's cool with everything.

I blink at the words. A part of me thought he was joking about talking to Jackson. But the fact he did means he's serious. He wants this. He wants me. Is this really happening?

Me: That makes me so happy. I know how important Jackson is to you. It means a lot that you talked to him for me.

Brando: I don't want you to have to worry about anything. And plan on being happy a lot from now on ;)

I'm sure anyone watching me squeal like a toddler as I pound my feet against the couch cushions would worry about my sanity, but I don't care. My patience has paid off, and Brando was well worth the wait.

Chapter Six

Forrest

I stay up talking with Kristy way too late, but I have no regrets. I didn't think I could get to know someone over texting. It's inconvenient, but I'd communicate via smoke signals if that's what she needed to feel comfortable.

It seems like my phone alarm blares only five minutes after I close my eyes, but a few hours have passed. I silence the racket and grunt as my feet hit the floor. I'm eye to eye with my rock-hard erection. Looks like another Kristy-inspired morning wood salute. I shuffle to the bathroom and flip on the taps, squirting shampoo in my hand and fisting my cock, imagining her on her knees, her gorgeous eyes watching me as she worships me with her hot mouth. I come in a gasping grunt against the wall and take a moment to clear my vision before I finish my shower and get ready for the day.

Last night, I asked Jackson for advice about my Victor Angelo problem, knowing he's had to deal with him for Luke in the past. When he asked me to come see him at the bar, I jumped at the chance. Brando joined us and they both told me to not worry about it. If Angelo tried any shit, Luke would step in, no problem. I hope it won't come to that, but

I'm relieved knowing they have my back. When we finished, Brando took off, and I pulled Jackson aside.

"Hey, man. I wanted to talk to you about Kristy."

He raised his eyebrows. "What about her?"

"I don't have a ring, but I care about her. We've been texting for a bit, and I want to date her, but she's worried about losing her job."

He rolled his eyes. "I'd never fire her. This place would go to shit without her."

"So, you're ok with it?"

He grinned. "That rule is more for Brando. I'm not worried about you breaking her heart."

"Harsh."

He shrugged. "I accept him for who he is, but that doesn't mean I'll let him hurt my employees or anyone else I care about. Now go see your woman."

When I found Kristy, it took everything in me not to dip under the bar and pull her into my arms, but my fantasies came to a screeching halt when she only offered a polite smile. She kept glancing over at Jackson, and I tried to get her attention to tell her I'd already talked to him, but she avoided me. I left so I didn't agitate her even more. Something was off and I was at a loss as to what it was. She erased my fears quickly though, and the relief that it was only a misunderstanding confirmed how much I want her in my life.

I finish getting ready and pour my coffee into my thermos for the day. The nutty aroma brings me to life, and a scene of me sharing a cup of coffee with Kristy in the morning, her in my lap, hair tangled from my hands running through it, puts a smile on my face that I can't shake all day.

The workday greets me with another visit from Mr. Barthane. This time, my smile isn't fake, because I fucking did it. I might have had to pull money from my savings to make it happen, but I hired enough extra help to make sure this building is sparkling on Christmas Eve.

The pompous dipshit sneers at me as he looks around the lot. "Well, you've made progress. I'll give you that."

"Thank you, Mr. Barthane. It will be ready on Christmas Eve, as Mr. Angelo requested."

He looks behind me and raises an eyebrow. "But you're missing an entire section."

I don't know where I find it, but I have to dig deep to keep my hands at my sides. "What?"

"The cafe. Where is it?"

Rick moves towards him, but I put my hand on his arm to stop him. "There was no discussion of a cafe."

Barthane rolls his eyes and huffs. "Do I have to do your job for you? This is getting ridiculous. Maybe we should take our business elsewhere."

And there it is. That's what he's been trying to do this entire time. But now, I'm ready for him. "You wouldn't want Mr. Angelo involved in a lawsuit, would you?"

Barthane narrows his eyes. "Are you threatening us?"

"The contract states what you see before you."

Barthane eyes me for a full minute. "You can't afford to sue Mr. Angelo. He'll bury you so deep in legal fees, you'll never see daylight again."

"Don't you worry about my finances. My lawyer and I have it covered. Are you familiar with Andrews of Andrews and Lawson?"

He pales and I smirk. Fucking prick. Jackson gave me the name of Luke's lawyer and told me if his name didn't get the fucker off my back, then Luke would.

He stares at me for a long moment. "I suppose the cafe is secondary to the boutique."

"We'll need to add it to the contract. But we'd be happy to have it ready for you by Valentine's Day." I offer a bright smile and he sneers again.

"I'll have it sent over." With that, he turns on his heel and stomps towards the SUV, yelling at his driver as he slams the door shut behind him.

"Holy shit, boss. That was epic. Is Andrews really our lawyer?" Rick asks once the SUV leaves.

"Nope. We could never afford him."

Rick roars with laughter, and we get back to work.

Me: Good morning, beautiful. Only two days 'til Christmas. Are you excited?

Kristy: Ecstatic! My mom will be here on Christmas Eve and the festivities begin. Only...I don't suppose you'd want to come over for Christmas dinner?

My grin splits my face.

Me: You want me to meet your mom?

Kristy: Yeah, if you're ok with it. It's too soon, but you said you loved Christmas and you were going to be alone and it made me sad and I just... you shouldn't be alone on Christmas. But if it's too weird, I get it. No strings attached here, just offering some Christmas cheer.

Is it weird that I want those strings already? Fuck, I'm in it deep.

Me: I'd love to.

Kristy: Yay! I'm so excited!

I chuckle and type, but shouts ring through the air, followed by a thundering crash, and I sprint out the door. One of my guys is on the ground. He clutches his leg and screams in agony.

I dial 911, sliding to my knees next to him. "Don't move," I bark, and he stills but groans as Rick appears. The other guys give us space while I talk to the dispatcher. I hang up when I hear the sirens in the distance.

Time moves in a blur, and I stand with my arms crossed, frowning at the workers milling around. We can't continue until the insurance guy does his assessment, which could take all fucking day. A day I don't have.

"How is he?" I ask as Rick appears beside me.

"It was a clean break. He's lucky."

I sigh and drop my head into my hands. "We're fucked."

He grabs my shoulder. "We'll be fine. You've got Barthane by the balls."

I nod and drop my arms. "Tell the guys to take the rest of the day off and be back at oh-five-hundred."

Back in my office, my phone buzzes in my pocket and I scramble for it.

Kristy: I hope I didn't scare you off...

I glance at my watch. I haven't responded in six hours.

Me: I'm so sorry, there was an emergency at work. One of my guys got injured. He's going to be ok, but it means we won't make the deadline and I might lose everything.

Kristy: Oh my God, I'm so sorry! Anything I can do to help?

Me: Unless you have a team of construction workers on standby willing to work for free, probably not. But I appreciate the thought.

Kristy: Do you have to close the gym?

I sigh. Why does she think I work in a gym? I'm too tired to puzzle it out. All I want is to hold her in my arms.

Me: Are you working tonight?

Kristy: Yep :)

Me: Can I come see you?

Kristy: Of course

She sends the heart emoji and I smile.

Me: Did you hang that mistletoe we talked about?

Kristy: I did :)

My chair scrapes the floor, and I fly to my house. I shower in record time and throw on a flannel, thankful that it's getting cold here. I roll up the sleeves and comb my hair back, annoyed with how long it's getting, but at least it matches my growing beard, so I don't have to shave.

Not in the mood to deal with downtown traffic or fight for a parking space, I order a ride share. I have him drop me off at a grocery store near The Lone Boot and buy Kristy a Christmas colored bouquet and hustle to the bar, nodding to the bouncer who lets me cut the line. Being friends with Jackson has its perks.

I spot her behind the bar right away. She looks up as I approach and smiles, but it's that same damn polite smile from last time. I look around for Jackson, but I don't see him.

Her eyes light up when she sees the flowers. "Oh my God! Did Jackson call you? You're a lifesaver." She holds out her hand. Not sure what else to do, I give her the bouquet and she puts it in an empty red vase near the back wall.

"It's silly, but I hated having the one bare spot," she says, pulling out a glass and pouring a beer from the tap. She slides it to me on a coaster and moves on to the next customer.

I stare at her profile for a minute before I take the stool in front of me. What the fuck is going on?

It's not super busy, so she returns a few minutes later. "Thanks again. I kind of go crazy for Christmas decorations, so I appreciate the help."

I furrow my eyebrows again, and she tilts her head as she speaks.

"You ok? It's good to see you again. It's been a while."

Is she messing with me? She pushes her hair behind her ear and glances to the entrance behind me before she busies herself with cleaning the already clean bar top.

"The decorations look amazing. Santa sure sneezed it up in here pretty good," I say, trying to understand this odd feeling in my gut.

She laughs. "I thought I was the only one who said that. I love Christmas. Don't you?"

I frown at her again. "Yeah, but you already know that."

She blinks and glances behind me. "Right," she says with an awkward chuckle as she fills a glass for the guy who scooted in next to me.

"You seem nervous. Everything ok?" I ask.

She nods and glances behind me again before she sighs and sets her rag down. "I'm so sorry, Forrest. You're a great guy, but our timing is off. I've had a crush on someone for eons and he's finally interested in me. He's on his way here right now, and I'm freaking out."

Her smile is apologetic as I stare at her in disbelief. She's not joking. My stomach drops and my heart throbs. I stare at the countertop as I try to wrap my head around what's happening.

This whole time she thinks she's been talking to someone else? All I can do is stare at her with my mouth open as my heart crumbles. Her feelings for me aren't real. But mine sure as fuck are.

I swallow hard. "Kristy, I think there's been a misunderstanding."

She gasps, her eyes lighting up with excitement as she looks behind me. I frown when Jackson and Brando walk in.

"That's him. Sorry, I gotta go. We'll talk later." She doesn't even look at me as she speaks.

She rushes over to Natalie, and they put their heads together. Her friend watches with a shit-eating grin as Kristy approaches Brando, who waves at Jackson as he heads over to the broody guy in the corner of the bar. Brando does a double take, and his eyebrows raise. He smirks and looks her up and down, and my hackles rise. *Son of a bitch.*

I flag Natalie down and she comes over, her brows furrowed. "Hey, it's Forrest right? What can I do for you?"

Kristy confessed a while ago that Natalie got my number from the raffle ticket and sent her initial text. It's not Natalie's fault. It's not anybody's fault, but Kristy is about to get her heart broken if I don't do something.

"Forrest is my last name."

She tilts her head. "Oh?"

"My first name is Brandon."

She stares at me for a long moment and her eyes go wide. She fidgets and grabs the rag Kristy left. "Oh. That's cool. Yeah. Um, weird question, but did you put in for that raffle we're having?"

"Yes, and if you don't stop her, your friend is about to make a huge mistake."

She curses and bolts towards Jackson, and I chase after her.

Chapter Seven

Kristy

I try not to freak out when Brando stops texting me. He's been spoiling me with his attention, so I'm sure he's just busy. It doesn't help that I had a mind-blowing sex dream last night that required quality time with my vibrator when I woke up.

Only Brando wasn't the star of the show. It was Forrest.

I try to brush off the unsettling confusion all day, but the dream stays with me. Brando finally texts me back and my excitement skyrockets when he tells me he's on his way. But I'm thrown for a loop when Forrest shows up. I can't look him in the eye as the naughty things we did in my head play in the back of my mind like a permanent movie.

Brando walks in and the movie pauses, and everything else in the room disappears. Well, except for Forrest's shocked expression. I shouldn't have gushed to him about Brando, but I couldn't lie to him. I float to Natalie for a quick pep talk and stride towards my man, ready to have the first kiss I've been dreaming about for years.

Once Jackson leaves him, I make my move. "Hey, handsome. Are you ready for that kiss?"

Brando does a double take like he wasn't expecting me, and I laugh at how silly he is. Something about his cocky grin makes me falter.

He looks me over with curiosity and shrugs. "Sure."

I blink at his nonchalance. Why is he trying to play it cool? I thought we would be past that after our endless conversations. Before I can protest, he takes my hand and pulls me down the hall and into Jackson's office. He locks the door behind us and pushes me against it, caging me with his massive arms as he looks down at me like I'm his favorite snack.

"I didn't hang the mistletoe in here."

He smirks. "You're cute. Are you sure you're willing to do this? I have a few rules..."

He reaches up and toys with the end of my hair as I frown.

"Rules?"

He shrugs. "If Jackson finds out, I won't go to bat for you. You'll have to deal with the consequences. But I'll do my part to keep this discreet."

I stare at him, confusion dampening the raging desire in me. "What?"

"My friendship is more important than a quick fuck. But I'm down if you are."

"I know Jackson is important to you." Wait... did he call this a quick fuck?

He furrows his brow and shrugs. "Cool."

He leans down and presses his lips to mine. Our tongues tangle and I wait for the world to spin, but it stays put. There's nothing wrong with the kiss, it's just... underwhelming. We move over to the desk, and he sets me on top of it, yanking off my shirt. It happens so fast, the tiny voice screaming for me to stop is just as shocked as I am.

He kisses my neck and my eyes close as his cologne takes over my senses. He gropes my breast over the bra and leans back to stare. "Damn. Your tits are amazing." He bends down and yanks my bra off with the flick of his wrist, tossing it aside. His mouth covers my nipple and I freeze.

"Um..."

My heart thuds in my ears as I try to figure out why my brain wants me to stop when my body urges me to keep going.

He reaches down and unbuttons my shorts, sliding his fingers into my waistband, and my brain wins the battle. I grab his wrist to stop his descent and he pops my nipple out of his mouth to straighten. "Something wrong?"

My face heats from embarrassment. I'm ruining my moment with the man of my dreams. But he's ruining it, too. "Why are you acting like this?"

He removes his hand and sighs. "Do you want this or not? I promise you won't be nervous after I make you come." He grins and a tiny part of me considers it, but the part of me that's been talking to him every night for the past few weeks rebels against the idea.

A loud bang on the door is our only warning before the jangle of keys. Brando curses and pulls me against him as the door opens and Jackson and Natalie appear.

"God dammit, Brando!" Jackson bellows as his eyes widen and glue to the ceiling. Natalie's hand goes to her mouth, and she backs out of sight, revealing Forrest right behind her.

Our eyes lock and a heartbreaking sadness fills them before his face turns to stone, and he disappears. An overwhelming compulsion to follow him sends a wave of confusion through my already rattled brain.

"Get dressed," Jackson says, then backs out of the room, slamming the door shut so loud I flinch.

"Fuck," Brando mutters as he bends to collect my clothing. "Sorry, sweetheart. Fun's over."

With numb hands, I button my shorts, and Brando hands me my bra and shirt. My boss walked in on me half naked with his best friend. I'm so fired. What the hell was I thinking?

Once I'm dressed, Brando puts his finger under my chin and our gazes meet. "Don't look so glum. He won't fire you. We can finish this later."

When I only stare at him, he shrugs. "Or not."

He walks over to the door and yanks it open. A fuming Jackson barges in, slamming the door in Natalie's concerned face.

I expect Jackson to lay into me, but he glares at Brando. "She's Forrest's girl, you idiot."

What the hell?

Brando puts his hands up. "I didn't know. She started it."

Jackson narrows his eyes. "I don't give a shit."

Brando sighs. "This was inevitable. She's had the hots for me for years."

"Which is why I told you to stay the fuck away."

I stare at Brando, my mouth open. *Who is this man?*

"How could you do this to Forrest?" Jackson says, his glare now pinned on me.

I blink in confusion. "How is he involved?"

Jackson scrunches his eyebrows, and I turn to Brando as I struggle to hold back the tears.

"Why are you doing this?"

He frowns. "Don't pin this on me. Jackson will always have my back."

I should have listened to the voice telling me this was too good to be true. But why did he lie to me if he already knew I liked him? "Brando, we've been texting for weeks. I don't understand what's happening."

He frowns. "Kristy, I've talked to you maybe three times in my life. I don't even have your number. What the hell are you talking about?"

Jackson sighs and mutters a curse. "You weren't texting Brando."

I stare at him, my lips parted. "What?"

"Did he talk about construction and furniture? Did he mention he was divorced?"

I nod as I sink into the chair in front of his desk.

Brando scoffs. "Like I'd ever get married."

"You were texting Forrest," Jackson says.

His words slow as the realization slams into me. The hurt in Forrest's eyes when he saw me wrapped up in Brando's arms hits me next, and my heart lurches.

"How did this happen?" I ask as the tears fall.

"We have the same first name. Maybe that's how things got mixed up?" Brando says. His defensiveness has disappeared, and he rubs the back of his neck.

The raffle ticket. I squeeze my eyes shut. What a mess. I take a deep breath and let go of the fantasies that will never happen with Brando. Natalie was right. He's not the man I thought he was.

I should be heartbroken, or at least disappointed, but it never happens because everything I thought I felt for Brando belongs to someone else.

I jump to my feet and fly out of the door. Natalie yells my name as she chases after me. "I'm so sorry! The ticket said Brandon, and I thought—"

I spin to face her. "Did he leave?"

She scrunches her eyebrows. "Who?"

"Bran—Forrest. Where is he?"

She shrugs. I race around the bar, but there's no sign of him. An idea hits and I run to the break room, grabbing my phone from my purse. I type as fast as I can.

Me: Forrest, I'm so sorry. Can we meet up to talk? I know I screwed this up, but please let me make it right.

The message sits unread for a few minutes.

Me: Please. I'm sorry.

That also goes unread. I try calling, like I should have done in the beginning, but it goes to voicemail. "Forrest, I'm so sorry. This is a huge misunderstanding, but I... Just please talk to me?"

Jackson approaches me as I hang up, and I steel myself. I'm about to lose my job, too.

"I'm so sorry, Jackson. That was unprofessional and I understand–"

He shakes his head, and I stop talking. "It's not the first time I've caught Brando in my office with someone he shouldn't be with. But I never expected it to be you."

I drop my gaze to the ground, my face heating.

He sighs. "Kristy, you deserve so much better than Brando. That's why I told him to stay away from you. It's not my place, but I have my reasons. Give Forrest some time. Once he calms down, he'll listen to you. He cares about you a lot. He told me so himself."

I sniffle, and he pulls me in for a hug. "I'm such an idiot."

He rubs my back and squeezes me tighter. "It was an honest mistake," he says.

"So, I'm not fired?" I ask as he releases me.

He laughs. "No fucking way. Just try to keep your clothes on at work, yeah?"

I chuckle and he winks.

"Take the rest of the night off. I'll cover for you."

I sob and hug him again. "You're the best boss in the world."

"Don't you forget it."

Natalie grabs me as soon as Jackson leaves, and I reassure her I don't blame her for this mess. I head home and keep my phone glued to my hand.

After a few hours of Forrest not calling or texting back, I scroll through our messages, picturing him behind the words. The sobs continue even as I smile.

I fall in love with him all over again as I read through every detail we shared.

Sleep never comes, and I stroll into work Christmas Eve with dark circles decorating my puffy eyes. I have no idea how to fix this. The fake snow falling from the rafters and festive music does nothing to lighten my mood. I can't even find the energy to be embarrassed about the rumors I hear whispered about me being naked in Jackson's office.

Natalie gives me a hug, but even she's at a loss for how to cheer me up. On my break, I scroll through my texts with Forrest again and stop on ones about him needing a construction crew to work for free. My eyes widen as an idea forms, and I rush into Jackson's office. He looks up from his computer with a raised eyebrow.

"Forrest needs help. Did he tell you what was happening?"

He leans back in his chair and regards me for a moment. "Have a seat."

I do as he says.

"So, it's Forrest you want? Not Brando?"

"Brando was a fantasy. I want reality. I want Forrest."

"How can I help?" He grins and I smile. I scoot my chair closer and tell him everything.

A few hours later, our ragtag crew arrives at Forrest's construction site.

"Go on," Jackson urges when I hesitate. Their Marine buddies wait off to the side with Brando.

There are six in total, and I'm floored that they showed up last minute, so close to Christmas, no less. Jackson said he's not surprised at all. When a brother needs help, they only ask when and where.

I gather my courage and walk towards the sounds of power tools from the building where they're installing enormous bay windows. Forrest is with them, his muscled arms straining against his long-sleeve work shirt. He calls out instructions to someone who runs to do his bidding. He's in calm control, and damn if it isn't the sexiest thing I've ever seen. The words we exchanged make so much more sense coming from this man. A sense of relief rushes through me.

Turns out, the peacock was only a distraction from what I've wanted all along.

Chapter Eight

Forrest

For the first time in my life, I'm late to work. I spent hours last night scrolling through my texts with Kristy because I'm a glutton for punishment. I found all the signs I missed. They're so obvious in hindsight, maybe I didn't want to see them. I fell asleep somewhere around four in the morning and woke up with a start as sunlight filtered through the break in the curtains. My phone laid dead on the bed next to my face, so I missed my alarm.

I walk into our office trailer and Rick looks up from his desk. "You look like shit."

I laugh without humor and shake my head. "That tracks. Everything going ok?"

"Yeah, just glad you're not dead. I was about to drive to your house."

I sigh and sink into my chair. When I don't offer any explanation, he stands.

"I'll put on some coffee. You look like you need it."

"Bless you," I mumble.

I shouldn't have followed Jackson down that hall yesterday. I should have left, because the sight of Kristy's naked chest pressed up against

Brando instead of me brought me right back to the day I caught my ex cheating with a wrangler on the farm.

Even though it's not Kristy's fault, the devastation still smacks me in the gut. Her eyes locked onto mine, and I swear in that brief instant she felt my pain. I left then, just as Jackson slammed the door shut, trying to save me from what he thought was my girlfriend cheating on me because I didn't have time to explain. But it turns out she was never mine.

Kristy texted me, but I didn't read it. She called, but I ignored that too. I don't want her apology, and I can't face the fact that her words were meant for someone else. Jackson called too, but I silenced my phone. I promised myself I would stay away from the drama, and I've found myself smack dab in the middle of it yet again.

Rick hands me my coffee, and I take a sip and tell him everything. He sighs and squeezes my shoulder, offering sympathy and camaraderie that lifts my spirits enough to shift my focus to work. Barthane will be here tonight, so we have less than seven hours to pull off a miracle.

The guys keep a wide berth, sensing my foul mood. I do my best not to be short with them, but not only did I lose the woman I was falling for, I'm probably going to lose this contract and my aunt will lose her business. Merry fucking Christmas to me.

Hours pass and I shout some instructions to the guy about to fuck up the window installation. I do a double take when Kristy stops a few feet away with a tentative smile on her face. She fidgets with the hem of her shorts. She's only wearing a light sweater over her t-shirt. Her eyes are red and puffy, and she looks as sad as I feel. My instinct is to reach for her, but I keep my face neutral and my hands on my clipboard.

"Hey," she says.

I sigh and set the clipboard down. "Kristy, I can't do this right now. I'm on a deadline."

"I brought help." She hooks a thumb behind her, and I frown as Jackson appears in the doorway with a few guys I recognize from the Corps.

"What are they doing here?"

"You said you needed a construction crew that could work for free. I found one."

I search her pretty face for a moment. Why would she do that for me?

We've already established I'm not Brando. She shivers, and I grab my thick hoodie off the table and bunch it up, pulling it over her head. She pushes her arms into the sleeves, and I pull it down over her torso. "I was joking. You'd know that if you ever dialed my number and spoke to me." I regret my snark the instant it leaves my mouth, but my emotions are raw.

She frowns. "You never called me either."

"You asked me not to."

She sighs and pushes her hands into the front pocket of the hoodie. "I just want to help you."

"Why?"

She hesitates and Jackson's voice echoes through the space. "Where do you need us, boss?" He holds a power drill in one hand and pulls the trigger twice with it pointed towards the ceiling.

"You can't help me. There are rules. I won't risk this company's reputation by breaking them."

Brando steps around the corner and joins Jackson. "Raise your hand if you've worked construction before." Four of the guys in the back raise their hands.

None of this is Brando's fault, but I'm not ready to accept it yet. "Get off my lot."

"Make me." He flashes a cocky grin on purpose, giving me an outlet for the anger and disappointment I've bottled up since yesterday. I lunge for him, but Jackson jumps in front of me.

"Not here," he barks, and I clench my fists and turn around. Kristy is right behind me and my anger fizzles as she gazes up at me.

"Just go," I say and stalk out the door.

"And they call me the drama queen," Jackson mutters as I pass, but I ignore him.

I trudge toward the construction office and cringe when I turn the corner and find Barthane waiting for me. I stop in my tracks and do my best to gather my wits. Of course he'd show up early.

"Using company time to socialize with your friends?" Barthane says as he takes in the group that stops behind me.

"They thought they could help me meet your impossible deadline." I have to force the words through my gritted teeth as I approach him.

"Well, I have good news. Mr. Angelo's fiancèe has decided she'd rather spend Christmas in the Bahamas. They're boarding the jet as we speak, so you have more time. Let's say... Valentine's Day?" The man's slimy grin makes my lip curl.

My hand shakes against my restraint to punch this bastard. But Brando appears and does it for me. I can't hide my satisfaction at the piggy squeals that escape the asshole as his driver attempts to console him. Brando didn't even hit him that hard.

"You'll pay for this, Forrest! Losing your jobs will be the least of your problems," he seethes as he palms the left side of his face.

Jackson steps up to my other side. "We haven't been introduced. My name is Jackson Waller. This is Brando Myers. We're friends of Forrest's from the Marines."

Barthane glowers at him. "Thank you. Now I know whose business to destroy next."

Jackson chuckles and sets his hands on his hips. "You may be familiar with our other friend from the Marines. Luke Reilly?"

Barthane pales, and I can't help but grin. I didn't want to pull Luke into this, but maybe I should have sooner. "We're acquainted," Barthane spits.

"Good, good. He has investments in our businesses. So, if you try to go after us, be prepared for a fight, fuckwad." Jackson spits on the ground, some of it splattering on Barthane's shoes, and I've never loved my brother more.

Barthane glares at me but stomps off to his car, and they drive away. I sigh and turn to Brando. "Thanks, man."

He grins and takes my extended hand, pulling me in for a hug. "She wants you. Don't fuck it up," he whispers before he steps away so Jackson can hug me.

"You're an asshole and I love you," I say.

He laughs. "I love you too, sweetie." He pulls me closer so he can talk in my ear. "Give her a chance." I sigh as I meet his eyes and nod. He smacks my ass as I turn to the rest of the group.

"Let's pack it up! I better not see any of your faces until next year." Raucous cheer fills the air as guys pound on the building and use their power tools to celebrate. I can't help but smile as they race to sweep up messes and put their tools away.

I find Kristy not far away, watching me with concern. She looks so cute in my hoodie. Hope swells in my chest. I head her way, but Rick intercepts and I'm stuck helping him finish the paperwork and tying up loose ends.

Most of us end up at the Lone Boot a few hours later. Jackson buys everyone dinner and drinks, and I catch up with my old buddies. Kristy works behind the bar all night. I've sensed her eyes on me, and when my friends leave or head to the dance floor, I make my way through the crowd. She watches me approach and wipes her palms on her shorts.

"Do you have a minute?" I ask.

"She's got all night," Jackson says, hip bumping her aside so he can take over for her. He whispers something to her, and her eyes water as she squeezes his arm and makes her way to me.

She follows me and we settle on two empty stools at the end. "I'm so sorry, Forrest. I never meant to hurt you."

"You don't need to apologize. This isn't anyone's fault. But that doesn't make it any less shitty."

She sighs and nods.

"Was any of it real? Were your words meant for him? Or is there any part of you that knew it was me?" I ask.

She turns towards me, her knee touching mine, and I resist the urge to rest my palm on her thigh. "My words were meant for a man who thought my obsession with Christmas and Taylor Swift was endearing. A man who made me feel beautiful and seen. My words were always for you, Forrest, even if I didn't realize it."

"Do you wish I was him?" It comes out in a whisper, and I cringe at my vulnerability. I'm not used to this. But she takes my hand and holds it in her lap. It's the first time we've done this, and it's as natural as breathing.

"If there was a lie in this, it was Brando. Look at him." She motions with her hand, and I find Brando dancing with a blonde. "That's the real Brando. I don't want that. When we met and when you came to see me was real. I understand what I was sensing back then. You're my match, Forrest. Everything I felt for Brando was superficial. But with you it's so freaking real, it scares me. I can't tell you how happy I am that you're the man I was talking to. I'm falling for you, Forrest."

Tears slip down her cheeks and I can't stand it. I swipe them away and pull her against me. My mind whirls with her words, and I struggle for a response. I'm terrified that I'm going to make another mistake.

"Thank you for your honesty. I just need some time to process."

She smiles. "I understand. You know where to find me."

I struggle against the urge to turn around as I walk away from her. Jackson puts a hand on my shoulder as I pass.

"Before you do something you'll regret, you should know that Brando said she stopped him right before we barged in. She wasn't going through with it."

I pause, looking at Kristy over my shoulder. Natalie is attempting to console her. I stare at the ground and nod.

"What's holding you back?" he asks.

"What if this happened for a reason?"

Jackson smirks. "I'm the last person to be giving relationship advice, but love ain't supposed to be easy. Why do you think I avoid the hell out of it?"

I crack a smile. "And here I thought it was 'cause you hadn't found the right woman yet."

He shrugs. "Just ain't for me." My ESP tells me he's lying, but I don't push him. He's not ready. "So, what are you going to do?"

I glance at Kristy. "Can you do me a favor?"

He grins. "Anything, brother."

Chapter Nine

Kristy

Brandon Forrest is the sexiest man on the planet. I watch him all night, aching to be near him. I poured my heart out to him, but it wasn't enough. When he leaves, tears threaten, but I swallow the burn. He was ready to give me everything I've always wanted, and because I stayed in make-believe land like a fool, I let it slip through my fingers.

My mom calls and the tears fall when she says she got snowed in and they canceled her flight. I'll be alone for Christmas, which is just as well. Natalie holds me while I sob.

We close at midnight, and I finish cleaning up behind the bar with a sigh, bending to sweep the pile of debris into the dustpan. Natalie wanted to stay, but I sent her home with Greg when her shift ended an hour ago.

Taylor Swift's *Christmas Tree Farm* plays from the speakers, and I frown. The bouncers cleared the place already, so the DJ should be gone. I stand and look around, but the place is empty. Austin is always the last to leave, but even he's disappeared.

My eyes widen when Forrest appears on the dance floor under the spotlight. The snow machines whir to life, and the air fills with tiny little snow-mimicking bubbles.

"Don't leave him hanging," Austin says from the door to the kitchen. We grin at each other and I hand him the broom.

Forrest watches me approach and his gaze leaves a trail of heat behind as he scans my body. He takes my hand when I stop in front of him and runs his thumb over my knuckles.

"I'm falling for you, too," he says.

He glances up and I grin when I see the mistletoe hanging above us, glittering underneath the disco ball. His gaze drops to my lips, and he tilts his head. I pull his neck down and slam my lips to his.

We melt into each other as the world fades away. It's better than I could ever imagine. He deepens the kiss and I do everything I can to get closer to him.

We're interrupted by obnoxious whistles and catcalls, and I laugh at Brando and Jackson as they hoot and holler from the DJ booth.

"Do you want to get out of here?" Forrest asks.

"Absolutely."

He takes my hand and waves at the guys.

"Have a good fuck," Brando calls and Jackson smacks him upside the head, even as he laughs.

Forrest shakes his head, but I giggle and wave to them. Brando winks at me, and I smile and follow Forrest out of the bar.

Forrest pulls me into him as we reach his front porch. Oh. My. God. Kissing him is my new favorite activity. His lips are so soft.

The energy shifts, and he pushes me against the door and kisses my neck.

"Kristy, I need you," he says, his voice shaking.

I've never reduced a man to desperation before, and my desire flares to new heights.

"Then take me," I whisper.

He groans and whips open the door. I'm off my feet as he carries me down the hall, slamming the door shut behind us. His lips never leave mine until I'm on his bed. The soft comforter envelopes me like a cloud, and he stands over me, unbuttoning his flannel. I sit up and pull off my shirt as he shrugs out of his, and a soft "Oh" escapes me at the sight.

Muscles earned from hard manual labor fill his arms and chest. His stomach is flat and a trail of dark hair trails in a line into his jeans. His eyes are on fire as he drinks me in.

I take back everything I ever said about Brando. I was woefully misinformed because I didn't know this existed. This is sexy. He's real, and he wants me. The girl who's obsessed with Christmas and weighs a few extra pounds because she loves ice cream and cookies and wouldn't be caught dead in a gym. The naive girl who thought she was in love with a player but had the real deal in front of her all along.

He's all I want.

I unhook my bra and unbutton my jeans. He does the same, his gaze roaming over my naked body with something I can only describe as rapture. "Is this really happening?" he asks.

I giggle and nod. He yanks his pants down and his cock pops free. The head seeps with need for me, and I look up at him, unable to contain my blush.

"You're so fucking perfect," he says, moving over me. He settles between my legs and his erection presses against my stomach.

I run my hand through his thick, dark hair. "Funny, I was thinking the same thing." He grins and I chew my lip. "I had a sex dream about you."

He quirks an eyebrow. "Oh yeah? Was I any good?"

"It was the night before everything blew up. I was so confused, but deep down, I always wanted it to be you."

His silly grin drops, and he brings his hand up to cup my cheek. He swallows and presses a gentle kiss to my lips. "Let's get your pretty pussy ready for my cock."

Oh. My. God.

He winks, then drags his tongue between my breasts, taking his time as he sucks each nipple into his mouth, flicking his tongue and moaning when I arch my back. He moves down my stomach, stopping to place wet kisses around my belly button before he continues his delicious path. His eyes roll back as his tongue dives into my pussy, and I gasp and squirm under his firm grip on my thighs. In seconds, he's blown all previous experiences out of the water. Nobody has ever savored me like this.

My legs tense as he pushes me closer and closer to the edge. He flicks his tongue against my clit, and I shoot off like a rocket, clamping my thighs around his head and howling like a possessed woman.

When I relax, Forrest comes up for air with a huge grin, his beard coated with my slick. "That was incredible."

I laugh, delirious from the best orgasm of my life, and kiss him as he hovers over me, settling between my thighs again.

I brush the hair out of his eyes, and he brushes my lips with a soft kiss before he reaches for his nightstand, pulling out a condom. He moves to his knees and slides it on, then returns between my legs, but I stop him.

"I've never been on top."

His eyebrows lower. "Like never ever?"

I laugh and sit up, pushing on his shoulder until he lies on his back.

"Why not?" he asks.

"No one ever made me feel comfortable."

I lean down and kiss him, putting everything into it.

"But you do," I say, and his smile lights up my universe.

I grab his cock and bring it to my sopping wet entrance. This experience has been the highlight of my life, and it's about to get even better. I plant my hands on his chest, running my fingers through the soft hair as I lower myself onto him. He places his hands on my hips, guiding me. His stomach tenses as he enters me and his gaze fills with a sense of wonder.

I take a breath and sink fully over his cock. I hiss through my teeth as he groans. "Keep going," he says, and I move, rocking back and forth.

I ride him as he stretches me, watching him take in every moment with nothing but heat in his gaze.

He slaps my ass, and I move faster. "Yes, girl. Just like that. You're so fucking gorgeous."

He reaches a hand up and pulls on my nipple, sending electricity to my clit, and I groan.

"You feel so good," I say, and he grabs my hips as we move together, finding a perfect rhythm that hits every pleasure spot inside of me.

His calloused palms slide over my thighs, coaxing me to move faster. "Come for me," he whispers.

I let go and ride him until colorful dots explode behind my closed eyelids, and I scream my intense pleasure for the world to hear.

When awareness returns, my breath catches when I find him staring at me.

"You're stunning," he says.

Before I can react, he sits up and hooks his arms under my thighs. He stands and, like I weigh nothing more than a feather, he pushes me against the wall and pounds into me in a deep rhythm, setting the perfect pace like he already knows what I need. I grip his shoulders and arch my back.

Sweat beads on his forehead, but he shows no sign of slowing down. "Come on my cock, baby. Now."

Three more hard thrusts and I do as he commands. He takes me in several more positions before he finds his own release. It's the hottest thing I've ever seen as he grunts and gasps, his grip tightening on my calves as he holds them in the air and rests on his haunches.

He smiles at me with hooded eyes and pulls me against him.

"It's real," he whispers, then kisses my forehead.

This is what I've always wanted. It may not be from the man I thought it would, but it's better than anything I ever expected. "Merry Christmas," I say, and he chuckles.

"Merriest Christmas ever."

Chapter Ten

Forrest

"You need a rag for that drool?" Natalie asks as I watch my girlfriend serve customers at the other end of the bar. I laugh, and she grins before moving on to help another customer. I can't help but stare at my gorgeous girlfriend. She's so pretty, but when she smiles, it takes my breath away.

We spent Christmas Day together, wrapped in each other's arms. I'll never forget holding her on my lap while we watched the sunrise from my back porch. She fell asleep in the quiet. I stared out over the valley with my lips pressed to her head, thanking God for that moment as I held her close.

When her stomach grumbled, I tucked her hair behind her ear and kissed her forehead before I stood and carried her inside. She woke as I settled her onto the couch, and then we made breakfast together.

"I'm sorry I don't have a gift for you," I said.

She scoffed. "I got a Marine for Christmas. I'm not complaining."

She was wearing nothing but my flannel shirt from the night before, so I ripped it open and plopped her sweet ass on the counter.

"Again?" she chuckled.

"You're about to find out what having a Marine really means."

Her laughter turned to sweet moans as I bent to one knee and worshiped her in my kitchen. I lost count of how many times I made her come throughout the day. I was ready to send her into oblivion all night, but when her eyes drooped as we drank our mulled wine by the fireplace after dinner, we took a long hot shower, just kissing and talking and we fell asleep wrapped up in each other for ten hours straight.

The next day, I received a call from Luke. We caught up for a while, but then he told me if I was serious about starting my furniture business, he'd consider investing. He told me to send him my business plan when I was ready, and I'm giddy at the possibilities. Kristy is already going into planning mode and ordering a fancy letterhead. She has zero doubt that I'll win Luke over.

I glance around at the bustling crowd and can't help but grin. I'm so proud of Kristy for throwing an amazing New Year's Eve party. The bar is at capacity for the first time, and Jackson is living his best life. We're getting close to midnight, so I give up my stool and wind my way through the crowd. Brando nods at me, another woman hanging all over him. Jackson is with Luke's ex, Liv, giving her a hug while her broody body-guard hovers nearby.

I grab Kristy from behind, pressing my lips to her neck. She spins and grins up at me, wrapping her arms around me with another of those breathtaking smiles. "I got the job!" She bounces in my arms, and I laugh.

"Congrats, babe! I knew you would."

The MC starts the countdown, and we stare into each other's eyes as the year ends. I throw up a prayer of thanks that I found the woman of my dreams. We kiss as the new year begins, and I fade into her as joyful chaos erupts around us and we're smothered in confetti.

We've only been together for a week, but I already know what's in my heart. She giggles as I pepper kisses on her sweet mouth and cute little nose.

"I love you," I say, and she grins.

"I love you, too."

THE END

Kiss Me

BY CINDI PAGE

An ex-army officer has decided that the cute British TV star sitting next to her at the Christmas table is definitely NOT her type.

About the Author

If you enjoyed *Kiss Me* and want to know about the other Taylor Brothers and the women who turn their lives upside down and show them what love is, then visit www.cindipage.com and download *Love Me* when you sign up for Cindi Page's newsletter.

Cindi Page writes about second chance romance because she is the girl who fell in love with the same boy twice (and married him). She lives her happy ever after in Surrey, England with her husband, two sons, and their adopted Shih Tzu, Charlie.

Follow her on Instagram, TikTok, & Twitter as @cindirellawrites

Chapter One

Leo

I'm staring at the luminous green juice in my bottle: Swamp Juice.
Ugh. It's been two weeks of strict liquid lunches of Swamp,
Sunshine, and The Pink One smoothies with lean, white protein
and steamed broccoli for dinner. I dare not leave the house until premiere
night in case I gravitate towards a drive-through and consume my body
weight in greasy burgers, fries, and milkshakes.

My phone pings. I open the group chat channel I have with my
brothers called BFTSM (Brothers From The Same Mother).

ADAM: Evie says to come anytime on Friday. After lunch?
ROBBY: (thumbs up)
LEO: Can I bring anything?
ADAM: Negative. Evie has the whole Christmas Eve menu planned down
to the T.
LEO: Can't wait (licking lips).
ROBBY: Tired of your Shrek juice? (Sick face/ laughing)
LEO: FO
ADAM: When's the big night L?

LEO: Tomorrow.

ROBBY: Our brother, the star of *Farthington*. Why couldn't you get a part in a Marvel movie? That would have been cool. Now I'm forced to watch you in a top hat and tails!

LEO: If you think that will be the worst part of it to watch, I've got a surprise for you.

ROBBY: Please tell me there's no (aubergine) (peach)...

LEO: (flames)

ADAM: I'll be leaving the room to make tea at that part... Before I forget, got two more coming on Fri. Old pal from my Afghan days +1. Long story.

LEO: (thumbs up)

ROBBY: (thumbs up)

ADAM: You'll be great, L.

ROBBY: How many scenes are you shirtless in? Need to mentally prepare... Wait, who's your date for the premiere?

LEO: None of your business.

ROBBY: So, no one?

LEO: Stick to your video games, okay?

I close the chat and throw my mobile across the kitchen counter. Does it bother me I don't have a date for the premiere of the highly anticipated Season 2 of *Farthington*? Nope. Not at all. Not one little bit. I really could have had a date, but since the last woman I asked out tipped off the press and then sold photographs of us on our date to one of the trashiest gossip magazines in England, I'm happier in my own company for now.

I rake my fingers through my hair with more intensity than needed. Robby's teasing still echoes in my head. He can be such an arse, but he's my baby brother, and we've been best friends since the day Mum brought him home from the hospital and let me hold him.

It's been a year since Mum and Dad sat Rob and I down and told us their story. How they fell pregnant when Mum was barely sixteen. Their parents forced them to give the baby up for adoption. They had lost hope that he would come looking for them, but then thirty years later, Adam found them. When Adam got reunited with our family, I gained a big brother, and the three of us have been slowly getting to know each other.

524

Remembering some of those awkward first get-togethers makes me smile now. We've come a long way and now I can't imagine a world without my big brother, his wife Evie, and my sweet niece, Stella. Around them, I can let my guard down and just let it all hang out without fear of judgement.

It was Evie's subtle prodding that got Adam to suggest that we three spend Christmas Eve together before the old folk join us for lunch the next day.

I squeeze my eyes tight and drink my greens. Damn, I'm looking forward to Christmas lunch.

Katja

"Kat!"

I hear my English name before I glimpse Divya's bangled arms wave over her head like an airport traffic controller signalling an incoming plane. I smile when I see her shoulder her way to the front of the crowd, ignoring the looks of annoyance and disapproval of those nudged out of her way.

"You're here!" She's on her tiptoes, pulling me into a hug, and it honestly feels like I have landed. That this temporary stopover in the UK is just what I need before I sign on the dotted line for a very cushy contract job in Dubai.

"Just in time for Christmas!" I laugh.

Divya pulls out a selfie stick from her oversized on-trend handbag. She clips on her mobile phone within seconds. I look around and see a couple of eyerolls in our direction.

I shake my head in protest, but it's too late. My long-time friend, the now YouTube cooking star, posts to Instagram like her livelihood depends on it—which I guess it does.

"Just a sec," and I see she is now clipping a small ring light to the top of the contraption. "Say eighty-six thousand followers and counting!"

There's just no point in arguing, so I crouch a bit to better get into the photo and give her my best Insta-worthy smile.

"How is your skin so flawless with no makeup?" she moans as she shoves the stick and phone back into her bag and we make our way across Heathrow Airport to the car park.

"No makeup at work policy," I remind her.

"I'd die!"

As soon as the words are out, she stops and grabs hold of my arm.

"Oh, Kat, I'm so sorry. I didn't mean to..."

Even though I know she didn't mean to stab me, I still swallow hard and blink back the sting of tears. When the memory of Pete is locked safe in my mind, it's like he is still with me. Like I hear his commentary on everything I do and see. But as soon as anyone acknowledges his death, the spell is broken and the reality that my fiancé is gone squeezes the air right out of my lungs.

It's been almost exactly a year since Pete got shot and died in Afghanistan. Fifty-two weeks ago, he died, and fifty weeks ago, he choppered into Kamp Holland where I was based and proposed to me after a three-month whirlwind romance.

"I'm an idiot."

I shake my head. "No, it's okay. I'm okay." I'm not, but I really want to be. That's why I quit the Army and took Divya up on her offer to come to share her flat with her in London as a stopgap.

Divya nods slowly and gently pries one of the suitcases I'm steering out of my hand.

The wind cuts through my jeans as we walk in silence across the car park. I'm grateful that I'm wearing a sensible down-filled jacket. Divya leads the way to her candy-apple-red Mini Cooper.

"Sweet ride, Divi."

"It took me two years of working my behind off, filming and editing every episode of *With a Twist!* myself, but eventually the sponsorships came in, and then the ad money went from being a trickle to a steady stream and I saved enough to buy this beaut cash." She strokes the roof of the car lovingly. "She's not a J Lo, though. She's not got much of a backside, so we'll have to dump the suitcases on the backseat."

Turns out the backseat isn't that big either, but we get the luggage in.

When we get into the car, I turn to her. "Proud of you, Divi, you chased your passion and are living your dream."

Divya brushes off my praise and gets on with the business of driving: seat belt, key in the ignition.

"My dream, not Mum and Dad's. According to them, my primary goal in life should be to find a husband and get married... five years ago!"

"But you're only twenty-four!"

"That's sixty-five in Indian Bride Years, darling."

We both laugh.

"It gets worse. They're now paying a 'professional' matchmaker to find me a husband. Even I didn't think they'd go that far. Which is why I'm so grateful you got us invited for lunch with Adam and his family."

"Adam is an old friend, and he was happy I got in touch... But Divya, an arranged marriage?"

She nods. "I guess they figured it worked for them, so it can work for me."

"Wait. You're not upset with them?" But what I really want to ask is, "Don't you want more?"

She shrugs, eyes flicking from review to side mirror as we merge onto the congested motorway. "It's the way we do things, you know? We're not raised on Cinderella stories and fairytales. The most important part of marriage is the coming together of like-minded families. Joining forces for future prosperity. Sometimes, people get lucky and actually do fall in love with their match before the wedding, but it's more common to grow into love."

Her matter-of-fact attitude shouldn't really surprise me. You don't just land a lucrative YouTube channel by not making sacrifices and sprinkling fairy dust into the camera. The woman has grit and determination along with a very level head for business. But love?

"Grow into love...?" I'm still turning the concept over in my mind.

"Learning to love your husband or wife after the wedding, over the course of your marriage."

I'm struggling to wrap my head around learning to love someone after the ring is on the finger and the marriage license is signed. I don't expect to fall in love again, but marrying for anything except love seems insane to me.

When we pull up in front of a block of flats, Divya turns to me and says, "Welcome to your new home, Katja Janssen."

She puts an arm around my waist, and we stand on the pavement and stare up at the red brick building.

"What are you thinking?" she asks.

"That there's going to be so much delicious food in my future..." I take an exaggerated sniff of the air.

Divya shoulders me and laughs, "Hope you like biryani."

"With a Twist!" I give her a wink.

Divya Kumar, my friend the Indian cooking goddess, feigns exasperation as she dumps one suitcase on the pavement and threatens to charge me rent if I continue to make fun of her cooking channel.

She helps me lug the heavy bags up the four flights of stairs anyway. I'm welcomed by the spell of warm spices.

There's nowhere else I'd rather be.

Chapter Two

Leo

"Brother!" Adam pulls me into a great bear hug, even though I can't hug him back because I'm carrying armfuls of presents.

"Merry Christmas," I say, smiling. There was a time when, still new to the family, Adam had his guard up all the time and he greeted me with a cool, hard handshake.

"Geez, Leo, who called you up and made you Santa Claus?" Adam says, pointing at wrapped packages spilling from my arms.

I clear my throat. "Actually, there's more. In the car... I may have gone a little overboard with the online shopping."

Adam lets out a roar of laughter and I feel my cheeks flush.

"I haven't gone out much lately," I say under my breath.

"Ignore him," Evie says to me before instructing Adam to make himself useful and fetch the gifts in the car.

Stella, perched on her mother's hip, babbles and when her eyes lock with mine, she gives a little high-pitched squeal, which obviously means she is happy to see me.

"There she is!" I say in that voice all adults succumb to when they talk to cherub-faced babies.

I dump the gifts under the tree and make a direct beeline for my niece. If someone had tried to tell me a year ago that I could feel this much love for someone else's kid, I would have told them to sod off. But then Adam came into our lives like a missing puzzle piece and Stella was born, welding our family together.

Evie gives me a kiss on the cheek before she passes Stella to me.

"Santa," Stella says, her chubby hands pressed into my face.

I laugh. "Leee-o," I tell her.

"Nee-o," she tries to mimic me.

"You know what? I'll take it. I loved that movie."

"Nee-o, Nee-o, Nee-o," Stella chimes, still exploring my face with her hands, fascinated with the bit of stubble I've allowed over the holidays.

"I don't know how you get anything done," I say to Evie. "She's too cute a distraction!"

Evie busies herself with the chopping of an onion. She smiles, but the almost imperceptible sag of her shoulders hints at something more.

"She is a delight..." she assures me before wiping away tears from her eyes, and I'm not sure if she's crying or if it's just the onion at work.

"Are you okay?" I ask, bouncing little Stella on my hip like I've seen Evie do.

She nods but turns away to wipe her eyes with some kitchen towel.

Just then, Adam enters with the boxes from the car.

"Do I even want to know what this is?" he asks, shoving the biggest present under the tree.

"You really don't," I tell him and shoot a look in Evie's direction. Her back is still turned to us, but her shoulders are visibly shaking.

"Darling, what's the matter?" Adam is at her side in an instant and wraps her in his arms. Their intimacy, this display of deep understanding and love, makes me uncomfortable, and I pivot on my heel and head for the living room where I chat to Stella about a big present for a big, clever girl.

"It's a baby size Porsche," I whisper in her ear, and she giggles as if she knows what the hell I'm talking about.

A few minutes later, Evie and Adam reappear, and Stella immediately stretches her arms out towards her mum.

"Sorry, Leo. I don't know what's come over me. I'm so tired nowadays and my emotions are all over the place. Last night I cried during an Aldi ad on TV."

"That's alright, I almost shed a tear during that baking show a couple of days ago because I was craving Paul Hollywood's buns."

This makes Evie laugh.

"I'm so glad you came early," she tells me. "I can't wait to see you in *Farthington*. It airs tomorrow night, right?"

I nod. "We don't have to make a big deal of it," I tell her.

"Don't be ridiculous, Leo," Adam says, "it is a big deal. You're a bloody celebrity now!"

I run my fingers through my hair. What he says is true, but it's not the whole truth. I want to tell him there's more to me than the fame, but I don't.

"What can I do to help before the others arrive?" I ask Evie.

Adam's mobile rings, and he excuses himself as he walks away to take the call.

"Everything is just about done, it's just the gravy and Yorkies that need doing now. Do you want to help Adam set the table?"

"Of course."

"Who was that?" Evie asks Adam as he rejoins us.

"That was Janssen double checking we didn't need anything from the store. They are only a few minutes away."

"That's nice of her," Evie says.

"What do you mean, her?" I ask, trying to sound casual.

Adam and Evie both give me a very quizzical look.

"Lieutenant Katja Janssen is a woman?" Adam offers.

"Right... I just assumed..."

"Don't worry, mate, she's Army. Not your typical girly type. She won't have a cooking clue who you are, and even if she did, I doubt it would impress her. Plus, I'm pretty sure she is off the market."

"Gay?" My curiosity is properly piqued by the description of this elusive GI Jane.

Adam laughs so hard he nearly chokes. "No, not gay. Just... unattainable."

"We'll see," I say before I can stop myself.

Adam's face has gone serious. "Listen, Leo, not Katja, okay? She's been through a lot. Just stay away. Anyway, she's not your type."

"How the hell do you know what my type is?" I challenge him.

"Everyone knows what your type is: busty brunettes with Colgate smiles. What's the name of that actress we saw a picture of in *OK!* the other day?"

"For fuck's sake! We went on one date! And why the hell are you reading trashy paparazzi magazines?"

"It was my fault. I saw you on the cover and..." Evie chimes in sheepishly.

I let out a deep, long breath to calm myself. Adam steps up to me and puts a hand on my shoulder.

"You're right," he says. "I actually do not know what your type is, and I should know. I'm your brother."

I nod, but I'm annoyed as fuck. Assumptions. Everyone seems to have an opinion about me and my life nowadays.

"But listen, about Katja. That's a no-go zone. You'd be wasting your time anyway." Adam says.

"You wanna bet?" I say, only half-joking.

Adam considers me, and Evie protests from the kitchen that this is a terrible idea.

"Sure," Adam says, "I bet you your new car Katja won't fall for you this weekend."

I laugh out loud. "You want to bet my brand new electric Land Rover?"

Adam has a glint in his eye I want to poke right out.

I extend my hand. "Done."

On cue, the doorbell rings, and Adam grips my hand in a solid shake that seals the deal. I turn to face Evie, who shakes her head in disapproval before handing Stella back to me as she makes her way to greet the arrivals at the door.

"Leo, this is Katja—Lieutenant Janssen—and her friend Divya," Adam steps aside and introduces me.

"Nice to meet you," she says, stretching out a hand.

"Yes," I say, "a pleasure." My eyes are instantly locked in hers, and she holds me there for a long, mercurial second before she turns to her friend, whose reaction to me is somewhat different. She squeals and then slaps a hand over her own mouth.

I keep cool and say hello, aware of Katja's gaze bouncing between Divya and me as she tries to assess the situation.

"Does someone want to tell me what's going on?" she asks, glaring first at me, then at Adam and Divya.

"He's Leo Taylor!!!" Divya squeals again. "I'm your biggest fan," she tells me.

"Thanks," I say.

Katja is still confused, but she studies me more intently.

"I'm sorry, I'm not up to speed with..."

"No problem," I tell her, doing my best not to get lost in her cornflower blue eyes again. I turn my attention to Stella, who has a handful of my hair in her hands and is yanking it impressively hard for a one-year-old.

"Let me take her," Adam says, prying his daughter out of my arms.

"Something smells amazing," Divya says, following Evie and Adam to the kitchen, leaving me to have an awkward moment with the tall, blonde lieutenant.

Adam was right. She is all wrong for me. A plain Jane. Much too tall. Too... upright. And I've never had a thing for blondes. But those eyes? They're captivating.

She catches me checking her out and her right brow arches.

I clear my throat. "Drink?" I offer. "I'm sure there's some mulled wine somewhere."

"I brought beer. I've never understood the concept of hot wine."

She disarms me with her forthrightness, and we exchange a smile.

"I could go for a little shandy," I tell her.

She finds this hilarious and looks away to laugh at me. Definitely at me.

"Why is that funny?"

Katja steadies her gaze to mine, her eyes playful and cheeky. "Well, where I come from, in Holland, they serve diluted beer to children, so..."

"My drink of choice is childish?" I finish her sentence for her.

"No! I mean, yes... sorry, I shouldn't have laughed. I've just never met a guy who's asked for a shandy before. In Afghan, it was safer to drink the beer instead of water," she says, her eyes intent on mine, dispelling any notion of nastiness.

I make light of the situation and assure her I'm likely to give her plenty of reason to make fun of me over the weekend.

"Why is that?" she asks.

"All will be revealed tomorrow night," I say, leading the way to the cold beers and lemonade.

Katja

Divya pulls me aside into the passageway by the stairs.

"Holy guacamole! You could have warned me that your buddy's brother was Leo-freaking-Taylor!"

"I don't even know what you're saying right now," I tell her.

Divya glares at me, her eyes stretched wide in disbelief. She closes the gap between us and lowers her voice.

"That is Duke Harrington."

"He's not royalty. He's Adam's brother." I tell her, taking a big swig from my beer bottle.

"Look, I know you didn't have TV in Afghan," she says, and I try to correct her, but she raises a hand to shut me up. "But Leo-freaking-Taylor is *theeee*," she stresses, "star of the best TV drama to come to Flix since, since forever. He is the duke in *Farthington*, and every mother and child in Britain watched him–" She takes pause to look past me to the crowd in the kitchen, before dramatically mouthing the F-Word "–his wife in every position possible in regency England. And–" Divya grabs me by the shoulders and swings me round to see him leaning against the kitchen counter casually sipping from a tall glass of shandy, "–he is hot."

I turn back to face my friend. "If you say so."

"Seriously?"

I shrug. "He's really not my type. At. All."

"Katja, the man is basically eating you with his eyes. And, oh, did I mention he is Leo-freaking-Taylor! Grrrrr." She rolls her eyes at me.

"Well, if you like him that much, we'll make sure you get seated next to him at the table."

I leave her with that and head back to the kitchen where I offer to take over the setting of the table from Leo, who has baby Stella in his arms again. I give Divya a conspiratorial wink for good measure. She responds with an eyeroll before turning to Evie and offering to help pour batter into smoking hot pans.

"Thanks," he says, peeling one of Stella's hands off his face and giving it a kiss.

If he wasn't such a pretty boy, I would probably find a man doting over a baby quite irresistible.

He's an actor! My logical brain reminds me. He can make selling laundry detergent look sexy.

I know this and yet I catch my heart beating faster when he gives me a dimpled smile.

"No problem," I say, deliberately shifting my gaze back to the placing of the cutlery and folding of paper napkins.

I count the settings.

"Are we missing someone?" I ask him.

"That would be my baby brother. Always late. Here–" He passes Stella to me before I can protest.

Stella studies me. "Hello," I say shyly. I know I'm missing the maternal gene. I'm awkward with babies and they generally howl when they see me. It's like they just know I don't have what it takes to keep them alive.

Stella is regarding me with her wise baby eyes.

"I'm better with dogs," I whisper to her apologetically.

On cue, she lets out an earsplitting wail. Within seconds, Adam is there to take her from me.

"I'm not good with..." I start.

"Don't be silly," he assures me, "she's just overtired."

Just then, the doorbell rings. "Divya, do you mind getting that?" I hear Evie ask.

"That must be Robby," Adam says.

"Full house," I smile.

"It's the best way to celebrate Christmas," he says, planting a kiss on his daughter's cheek.

Looking around, the decorated tree, large wood-burning fire, smell of a roast dinner, and iconic "All I Want for Christmas is You" in the background unexpectedly clench my heart.

"You're a lucky man," I tell him before I head outside for some air.

Chapter Three

Leo

Robby arrives, juggling his Xbox and one of those Bags for Life shopping bags. He has traded his signature knitted beanie for a Christmas hat. With his black-rimmed glasses, he is one hundred percent a computer guy geek, but in a cute Clark Kent way. You'd never know he had biceps the size of small melons under his old university hoodie. For the past year, we've been meeting up at the boxing gym most weeks where he takes out the stress of his job on the punching bag... or me.

We greet each other with a hug and exchange the usual banter.

"You're supposed to bring boxes of presents, not gaming consoles," I say as I pull him into a hug.

"I know, but I have to play this game through one more time to check that I squashed all bugs. It's being released at midnight on the 31st."

"Bugs?" a small voice says behind us. It's Katja's tiny friend, Divya, my biggest fan. But when I turn around, she is looking right past me, eyes only for my baby brother. I look at Robby and see he has suddenly lost the ability to speak.

I introduce them. "He doesn't mean insects. Go on, explain yourself," I tell him.

"I write code? For games? When there are glitches, we call them bugs."

"Oh, cool. What game?" I'm not imagining it, Divya has gone completely doe-eyed.

"Halo," Robby says shyly.

"Oh my god! I used to play that with my older brother all the time. Do you need a Player 2?"

"Sure." My brother looks like he's walked into a bush of stinging nettles. Flushed pink and shuffling from one foot to the other.

"It's nice to meet you, by the way," Divya says, stroking the long, raven black ponytail hanging over her shoulder. I may as well be invisible, so I gingerly step away from whatever sparks are flying between those two.

I scan the dining room, but Katja is nowhere to be seen.

In the kitchen, I find Evie hacking at a butternut squash with a butcher's knife.

"Can I do that for you?" I offer.

She shakes her head. "This is the last bit. Dinner should be ready soon."

We are both looking out of the kitchen window. Katja is on the swing Adam made even before Evie moved in. He was right, the giant oak tree needed a swing.

"You should go check up on her," Evie says. I nod and grab two more beers before heading out into the clear, frosty night.

My boots crunch under the path of walnut shells Adam laid last summer with my and Robby's help. Back-breaking work, but fun too. Katja turns to see me coming but immediately turns away again and looks up at the sky. Now and then, she gives herself a little push with her feet and rocks gently in the swing.

I sidle up beside her and put a beer in her hand. We don't speak, but we chink the necks of the bottles together as if we are toasting to something.

"I see you've levelled up to real beer now," she teases, still preferring to look at the sky than me.

"You gotta give me some points for trying, eh?"

This makes her smile, and my chest expands with a sense of satisfaction that I could make her smile.

We sip our beers and I find myself strangely comfortable in the silence with her.

"So you're a semi-famous actor," she says in a way that comes across as verbal contemplation instead of a question.

"And you're a ranking Army chick," I retort.

"Ex-Army," she corrects me, "and that's still lieutenant to you, not *chick*."

We hold each other's gaze, and I find myself turned on by her forthright, don't-give-a-rat's-arse confidence. Adam was right. She will not fall for the duke or any other version of me. So, I do something I've never done with a potential hook-up before: I decide to just be myself.

"Want to hear something stupid?" I ask.

She shrugs and takes longer steps backwards to swing higher.

"I didn't have a date for my latest premiere a couple of days ago."

She brakes hard with her feet and stops to study my face. She squints her eyes slightly. Then she shrugs again and works up the momentum of her to-and-fro on the swing.

"Women probably think you're too cute to date."

I scoff. "Wait. You think I'm cute?" I can't wipe the smirk off my face.

"Not me," she assures me. "I'm not into..."

"Actors?" I finish her sentence.

"I was going to say pretty boys."

Ouch. I let out a low whistle. I've never experienced a woman so... unfazed by me, and I must say, it's refreshing. My blood is beating hard, my senses suddenly prickled, like I'm some kind of animal enjoying the challenge of the chase. Unfamiliar territory for me.

"Don't spare me your opinion of me," I say with a bit more sting than I intended.

Once again, she pauses in motion to look me over.

"My fiancé died last year. He was in Adam's unit. Our life together was over before it began... so being here with the only other person on earth who really knew him, as only your military friends can know you, is... hard."

I process what she is telling me, and now Adam's caution makes sense.

And I realise he was right. I am going to lose my new Land Rover because there is no way I can pursue Adam's best friend's widow without being a complete wanker.

I must stare in the vehicle's direction because Katja points to it. "Is that yours?"

"Yes," I say, and before I can tell how sorry I am for everything she has been through, she interrupts me.

"Nice," she says. "I like off-road cars best."

"It's not bad," I tell her, "but I doubt I'll be able to keep it."

"How so?" she asks just as I realise what a huge slip of the tongue that was.

I'm about to come up with a pathetically concocted story when there's a blood-curdling scream from inside the house.

We both drop our beers and sprint in that direction.

Katja

When we get to the house, Adam already has Evie's bloodied hand wrapped in tea towels and is heading towards the door.

"We have to go to A&E. She fainted and the knife–Stella!" Adam is speaking fast, his eyes darting from Evie to the staircase.

"Go. I've got this," I assure him and a look of understanding passes between us.

He nods.

"Let me drive you," Leo offers.

"No, you stay. Stella will need a familiar face," Adam says over his shoulder as he steers Evie out of the door. She is pale and mute, but tears are sliding down her cheeks.

"Keep her talking," I remind Adam of Army trauma protocol. Again, he nods, and then they are gone.

"Shit, that was a lot of blood," Leo says wide-eyed.

I nod. "I hope she didn't slice and damage anything that will be a permanent issue."

"Where's Robby and Divya?" he asks, looking around.

We walk through the house to the living room and find them sitting side by side on the oversized leather sofa, jostling controllers–headphones covering their ears.

Leo's strides become faster and longer, and when he block's Robby's view, he pulls the headphones from his head.

"Hey!" Robby tries to protest, but Leo's face is stone, his lips a thin line and his eyes blazing.

"Walk with me," he commands Robby, who throws down his controller in a huff but complies.

Divya slowly removes her headphones. "What's going on?"

I fill her in.

"We couldn't hear a thing with these noise-cancelling headphones. I feel terrible. Do you think she'll be okay?"

"I hope so. But I think we should see what still needs doing in the kitchen. Evie won't be in any state to cook when she gets back."

We're pulling burnt Yorkshire puddings out of the oven when Leo and Robby return. Robby immediately makes himself useful and helps Divya with the cremated puddings.

"Noise-cancelling headphones," I say to Leo. "You can't be too harsh on him. It wasn't his fault."

"Maybe. But he is forever lost in his gaming worlds. Oblivious to everyone around him. Mum's lucky if he remembers to call once in a while, and he would forget her birthday if it wasn't for the rest of us." He rakes his fingers through his hair before he turns to me. "We should probably check on Stella. These two can see to the food."

We tiptoe up the stairs and peek into Stella's room. In the soft glow of the night light, among the stars projected on the bedroom ceiling, she sleeps outstretched like a starfish.

Leo and I exchange a smile, and he holds my gaze. He whispers, "I wanted to say... when we were outside... I'm sorry about your fiancé."

His sincerity is a tiny, forgotten key, but it unlocks something in me and I have to blink back the sting of tears. He sees it and takes my hand. His grip is firm and comforting.

For a while, we remain that way in the doorway, my hand in his, occupied by our own thoughts, before Leo's phone buzzes. He lets go of my hand and digs it out of his jeans pocket.

"Adam," he whispers and opens the message so that I can read it next to him. I have to blink a few times to make sense of the message. I'm distracted by being this close to Leo. All I can think about is how good he smells.

I'm still staring at his phone screen when he gently nudges his arm against mine. My throat is dry, and I catch my tongue sliding over my bottom lip.

"It's good that they're keeping her overnight, right?"

I shake my head to break the crazy spell I'm clearly under.

"Yes... I mean, no, it must have been quite bad, but at least she is being taken care of."

He agrees and steps away, opening all the spaces our bodies filled, and I immediately wish he hadn't. The man radiates a magnetic heat I'm suddenly wanting.

Downstairs, Divya and Robby assure us that dinner is in hand, and Leo updates them about Evie's condition and the fact that she has to stay overnight.

"Adam insists we eat without them."

We all take turns looking at each other. No one wants to eat Christmas Eve dinner without Adam and Evie.

"Look," Divya says, "we can keep all of this for tomorrow, refrigerate what we can, and freeze other things. And I can rustle up something else for tonight. I'm sure Evie won't mind us foraging through her cupboards."

"If there was Pizza Hut out here in the sticks, I'd be on that like a bear," Robby says, patting his stomach.

Divya gives him her biggest smile. "Well, you're in luck. I'm an excellent pizza maker. And you can help me. I could use some brawn when working the dough. And if you're really good at it, I might film it and post it to my channel."

Robby's face flushes scarlet, and Leo and I both look away to hide our amused grins. Divya has always been flirty, but clearly, Robby is unaccustomed to female wiles. It makes for some fun viewing as a bystander.

When I catch Leo's eye again, he arches a brow and tilts his chin in the lounge's direction. I nod and follow him there.

The single leather sofa is substantial enough that when I take my place on one end, there's at least a couple of feet of distance between us. I kick off my Doc Martens and curl my feet close to me, but not before I knead the aches out of the soles of my feet with my hands.

"New shoes hurting you?" Leo asks, leaning back into the plump cushions. I can't help but register that when he stretches his arms across the back, his hand comes very close to me. And he has good, strong hands for a pretty boy.

"No, it's not the shoes. It's just years and years of wearing hard-soled army boots."

He pats his thigh. "I'll massage them for you."

"What? No. I'm not letting you touch my feet!"

"And why not?" He cocks his head, the small upturn at the corner of his mouth giving away his pleasure in making me squirm. And it infuriates me he has this effect on me, because I am suddenly restless in my seat.

"You can trust me. If you have feet like a troll, I won't tell a... sole."

"I do not–haha. Punny," I say.

"Then let me. Please."

Once again, he pats his thigh, which is visibly taut despite a layer of denim. This time, I yield.

His face breaks into a proper smile when he takes hold of my foot.

"Santa socks. I approve." His eyes twinkle, and I have to look away. "Do you mind?" he asks, tugging at the sock to remove it.

I have a lot of words flying around in my head, but none of them have found a voice. So, I shake my head and watch him peel the red and white striped sock from my foot. My breath hitches. No one has touched me in such a long time that I shudder.

"Don't worry, they won't be cold for long," he assures me as if that must be the reason I'm trembling.

I try to focus on the fresh pine tree on the other side of the room and the ornaments twinkling in the low light coming from the fireplace. But it's no use. His hands are kneading my feet in places I didn't know existed, causing heat to spike and pool between my thighs. I shift in my seat, and he grips my ankle to steady me.

"Try to relax," he says, his voice so low, so gruff that together with the delicious pressure he is administering, I hear myself moan as my toes literally curl.

A sharp cry from upstairs makes both of us jolt. Leo releases my foot and is upon his feet.

"Stella," he says, not quite meeting my eyes before turning on his heel and racing up the stairs two at a time.

I take a few moments to gather myself. What the hell just happened? I roll my shoulders to release the tension built up and shake off the pulsing desire that seems to have spread through me like wildfire.

Get a grip! I tell myself.

I hear Stella's cries intensify and steady my nerves before I make it my mission to calm the baby and not go ga-ga over a pretty boy actor with a talent for foot rubs.

Chapter Four

Leo

"Oh, baby. What's the matter? *Shh, shh.*"

I shift Stella into my other arm and bounce her on every *shh, shh*, but her wailing only gets more distressing–for the both of us. I rack my brain for techniques for soothing infants and come up with a song. It's worth a shot.

Since it's the season, I go straight for the classic "Silent Night." For the first two lines, Stella's tears persist, but then she quietens down, and by verse three, I'm making up the words I can't remember and she is resting her head on my shoulder, thumb in mouth. I dare not stop singing or swaying, just in case that's the thing that's working, so I immediately move to the next song in my school-nativity-play repertoire and sing "Away in a Manger."

"You should have started with that one, no?" a whisper floats in my direction from the doorway.

Still swaying to my tune, I turn to face Katja, who is leaning against the doorway in that girl-next-door kind of way, her jeans pinching her tiny waist in a way that reveals her hips and promises a backside worthy of a cheeky smack.

"Is she sleeping?" I mouth.

Katja nods.

As I step closer to the cot to lay Stella down, I hesitate. Will laying her down wake her? I turn to face Katja again; this time my face is all furrowed brow and question marks. She gestures for me to follow her. When we get to Adam and Evie's bed, she steps aside so that I can lay my sleeping niece down.

"We should stay with her for a bit," she whispers as she climbs on top of the covers on one side of the sleeping cherub. I follow suit and take my place on the opposite side.

For the longest time, we just lie here like human safety nets, lost in our own thoughts while watching over Stella.

"You're great with her," Katja whispers, her eyes soft and searching.

"I've always wanted kids, so... You?"

"I'm better with bombs than babies," she assures me with a sad smile.

"So you don't want kids?"

She shrugs, "Maybe? I don't know. After Pete died... I just don't see it in my future anymore?"

I nod. I don't really understand it, though. I look at my parents, and Adam and Evie, and I know that marriage and kids are the natural order of things. The secret sauce of a happy life.

"So, you're wife hunting?" she teases. Her voice is soft, her eyes amused.

I stifle a chuckle to avoid making any noise.

"Surely Leo Taylor can have any woman he wants?" she pokes fun at me.

"Not any woman," I say, recalling Adam's warning and our wager involving my car.

She arches a brow, and it's only semi-visible in the low light of the room.

"Well, I can't have you," I whisper with more confidence than I feel. Fuck it, I may as well throw my hat in the ring than give up without trying to get the woman, right?

It may be my imagination, but I'm sure I hear her breath catch.

"Correct," she tells me, matter-of-factly. "Not even your freakishly good foot rubs would land you me."

"Wow, you're a hard sell," I play along, enjoying our little game. "What about my fame? Lots of women find that... worth putting up with me for... for a while, at least."

At this, she scoffs. "Nope. Not interested."

"Let me kiss you," I blurt out.

"Excuse me?"

"I bet if you let me kiss you, you'd fall for me. Guarantee it."

"I'm not hating your confidence. I'll give you that." I'm tickled by the twinkle in her sapphire blue eyes.

"The kiss?" I tease.

"No! The confi–never mind!" she hisses in the dark.

Stella stirs and we both hold our breath until she settles again. Embarrassingly, my stomach makes its need for food known with a loud, very unsexy bubble-grumble.

"Sorry," I whisper.

"You should go get some of that pizza. I'll stay," Katja offers.

I don't want to go, but I also don't want to stay and have her listen to my body betray me.

"Are you sure?"

She nods.

"Thank you," I whisper into the semi-darkness before I slide off the bed in stealth mode.

I do not know what she's thinking, but I get the idea she is warming to me. Perhaps I'll keep my Land Rover after all.

The smell of melted cheese lures me into the kitchen, where I find my brother and Divya in very close quarters.

I exaggerate the clearing of my throat and watch them jump apart when they see me.

"Please tell me there isn't garlic on those pizzas," I say. Garlic would seriously derail my plan to kiss a certain Army chick tonight.

Katja

A gentle touch on my face stirs me from sleep. The caress is so light, so tender that I'm almost sinking back into...

My eyes fly open. Someone was touching me.

I lie still, every nerve ending on high alert. And then the soap and spice smell of him reassures me it's just Leo. I pretend to be fast asleep, and he draws a quilt from the foot of the bed over me before leaning across me to drop a kiss on Stella. He is so close I can hear his breath; I can feel it. He lingers, and with every passing second, I wait for him to shift a little more my way and put his mouth on mine.

But he doesn't. Instead, he settles back into his spot on the other side of his niece, and I listen to how his breathing becomes deep and slow as he drifts to sleep.

Unable to get back to sleep after Leo rejoins me on the bed, I end up lying awake for hours contemplating my future. The job offer in Dubai as a personal protection offer is still waiting for an answer. I should have just said yes right away, then I would not be overthinking it and the deal would be done. And I would be some rich kid's shadow 24/7. I roll onto my back and stare at the ceiling.

"You okay?" a groggy voice whispers from across the bed.

"Sorry I woke you. I should just get up. Go back to sleep." I leave the warmth of the bed and head downstairs to find coffee.

The cottage is quiet. Robby is asleep on the couch minus Divya, who I assume has taken up the bed in the spare room. Fosters, Adam's three-legged Army rescue dog, stirs on the rug close to Robby, but immediately dismisses me and puts her head down to go back to sleep. I flick on a light and move around the kitchen in my socks, readying a mug and opening cupboards in search of coffee.

I nearly jump out of my skin when I see Leo's athletic frame in the doorway.

"Sorry, I didn't mean to scare you."

"You didn't," I say, turning away from him.

"Right," he says under his breath.

And then he is behind me, so close the energy between us prickles my skin. It's as if he has dropped a match on dead grass. Does he not know he is risking a wildfire? I feel the heat ignite in the dormant parts of me and I suck in a breath.

"Here, let me." His arms encircle me from behind as he reaches for the coffee. I swallow hard, and I'm sure the sound of my heart beating wildly in my chest is apparent to him as well.

He isn't even technically touching me, but he has instigated an ache between my thighs. My body wants him, even if my brain isn't in agreement. I stand frozen, acutely aware of his limbs brushing against mine as he reaches for the coffee. Coffee jar set down; his arms trap me as he clutches the edge of the countertop. His breath tickles my ear, and oh my god, the scent of him is making me heady.

My turn is swift. My arms fly around his neck as I pull his face to mine.

I may have been the one to make the first move, but he takes ownership of kissing me. He pulls me closer. There is nothing remotely soft about this pretty boy. I shift to feel more of him, and he smiles through our kiss.

"Shit!" I say, pulling away.

"No... definitely not shit," he counters, giving me space.

I have to look away from his eyes. They are set on mine and there is lust there. Raw. Magnetic.

"I-I can't," I stammer.

"I think you just did," he breathes. He reaches for me, taking hold of my hand.

"You're not my type," I tell him, trying to regain some semblance of sanity. I still can't meet his eyes.

He chuckles, "So I've heard."

I'm about to protest some more, but he shuts me up with another kiss that turns my knees to pudding.

When his lips eventually leave mine, he gives my hand a squeeze. "How do you take your coffee? Let me guess: black, no sugar?"

I nod.

"I can do that," he smiles, flashing me his deep-set dimples.

That's the moment I know.

I'm in big, big trouble.

Chapter Five

Leo

That kiss is all I can think about, but for the rest of the morning, I keep my distance respectful because I do not want to freak her out even more. But there's something between us, a pull neither of us can deny.

We drink coffee. We talk. When Adam's message comes through about Evie being discharged, we wake the other two, who we almost forgot were even there.

"We should probably wake Stella?" Katja suggests.

I shake my head. "Never wake a sleeping baby. Evie taught me that in How to Be a Good Uncle 101."

This makes her smile. My chest swells. She is gorgeous when she allows herself to relax. I want to tell her this, but we're interrupted.

Divya enters the kitchen with a stretch and yawn but freshly dressed. "Reporting for duty!" she announces, and we make a list of all the tasks that need doing and delegate jobs.

"I can do something. But make sure it's basic, please," Robby moans. "We all know no one would want me to cook. I could burn a pot of water," he assures us.

"Fine." Divya beats me to a cheeky reply. "You can mop the floors and make sure we have enough settings for the table. Kat, you're with me on a fresh batch of Yorkshire puds and potatoes."

With no jobs left, I tell everyone I'll walk Fosters. Just then, Stella can be heard from upstairs.

"Sorry, girl," I say to the eager canine wagging her tail beside me, "there's a baby who needs a change which has to be dealt with first."

I catch Katja's wide-eyed expression.

"You think I can't change a baby?"

Stella's cries intensify, and I don't have the luxury of waiting for her rebuff but hear Robby tell her I'm the proper uncle who offers to babysit because I'm totally smitten with my brother's child. I can literally hear the points pile up in my corner as I rush upstairs.

Katja

All at once, the house is a noisy, messy, happy place. No one allows Evie to lift a finger, and Adam appears to shadow her whenever she moves, never letting her out of sight. Mr and Mrs Taylor Senior arrive, depositing more wrapped gifts under the tree, and there's a lot of fuss and family banter around the lunch table.

"I can't imagine what life in the military must be like for a woman," Mrs Taylor says to me as she passes the gravy.

"You get used to it, but it can be brutal, Mrs Taylor."

She waves a hand in the air between us. "You must call me Patty."

I smile, "Patty."

"Is that why you left?" Her bright blue eyes, the Taylor family trait, pierce mine.

"I..." I don't really want to have this conversation with her, or anybody really. I stall by taking a sip of Prosecco.

Leo leans into the conversation from his seat beside me and saves me from either having to explain or lie. Both are terrible options.

"She's decided to become a close protection officer. More money," he says, dropping a wink in my direction.

"Is that like a bodyguard? Yes, yes, that makes more sense. Leo should hire you; he is always being harassed by the press, aren't you darling?" Patty pivots the conversation into a new direction, and I drain my glass of bubbly with a sense of relief, but not before I almost choke on her suggestion.

Being Leo's protection? Fancy events and gorgeous women swarming him? No. Definitely not. I look over to Leo, who simply shrugs at his mother's suggestion, and the entire conversation is dropped right there, thank god.

"Thank you," I mouth the words to him, and he reaches under the table and gives my knee a squeeze.

This makes me sit a little more upright, and I catch a look from Adam and then a silent exchange between Adam and Leo. Heat flushes my cheeks. I reach for the jug of water, hoping more cold liquid will extinguish the flames lapping at my core.

Fortunately, the rest of the meal passes without incident. Leo keeps his hand on my thigh, and while it's a huge turn on, it's also a comfort. We settle into a conversation about how addictive gaming is with Robby and the perils of social media as another type of addiction. Every so often Leo leans into me, and our arms touch.

I'm regretting the Christmas jumper; it's nothing more than an unnecessary layer between us and, if I'm honest with myself, I don't want any layers between us.

When it's time to pull the crackers, we all joke and laugh, and Leo places the paper crown on my head. The urge to kiss him is overwhelming, and he leans in just as I run my tongue over my wanting lips. Adam breaks the spell when he taps on his wine glass with a spoon to get everyone's attention.

Leo runs his hand further up my thigh and I have to work hard to pay attention to what Adam is saying.

"So something wonderful came to light when we were at the hospital," he says, beaming a loving smile down at Evie. "Stella's going to have a sibling!"

A half-second of silent shock ripples through the room, but then everyone is on their feet giving them hugs and well wishes. I do the same, and yet I can't suppress the tears threatening to flow. They're joyful tears– I explain my uncharacteristic display of emotion to Divya before I rush to the bathroom to collect myself.

I'm just so happy for them, I tell myself in the mirror. My pale blue eyes are glassy and rimmed pink, and I splash my face with water again. My thoughts go back to Pete and I strolling through the streets of Paris, fantasising about living in a country cottage with a house full of kids. He came from an extensive family and dreamed of the same for us.

Motherhood. Another element intertwined with my grief. No one warns you that when you lose someone you love, you don't just grieve them, you also have to bury all the hopes and dreams you had for the future.

A gentle knock on the door and Divya's voice force me to take a deep breath. I let her in, and she immediately pulls me into a hug and holds me there.

"You're going to be okay," she tells me softly.

I nod.

"We can leave if you want to," she says, studying my face for my true feelings.

I shake my head and take the bunched-up loo roll she offers me. I blow my nose.

"No, I'll be alright," I say, giving her a small smile.

"Okay then. We better join the rest for the big *Farthington* Watch Party. Robby's been taking the piss out of Leo, so I suspect this should be good. Apparently, we'll see his naked butt!"

The visual image makes me giggle despite the cacophony of emotions I'm feeling.

"Ready?" she checks with me before we join the family.

"Just one thing," I ask. "Is something going on between you and Robby? You really seem to hit it off."

"Maybe," she says, curling her lips into a naughty smile. "I'll tell you on the drive home. Come, I have a naked duke butt to inspect. You can't tell me you aren't just a teeny bit curious?"

I don't answer, but I feel my cheeks flush.

"I knew it!" she says with an annoying amount of glee before she opens the door and leads us back into the fold.

"Just in time!" Robby announces. "I set up my projector so that we can watch the action in life-size."

"What action?" Patty asks with my mild confusion, "I thought it was a period piece?"

"It is, Mum. Robby is just being a–" Leo glares at his brother.

Mr Taylor Senior intervenes, "Come now, boys."

"Everyone ready?" Adam hollers from the far end of the sofa, with Stella in his arms sucking on a bottle and Evie resting her head on his shoulder.

We all quiet down and I brace myself for seeing another side, so to speak, of this pretty boy that has begun to unravel me.

Chapter Six

Leo

The childhood habit of biting my nails happens subconsciously while I try to decipher my family's reaction to the scene I know is about to unfold, and thanks to Rob, life-size, on screen. On TV, I've led Lady Harrington to the horses' stables, and I'm about to ravish her on a pile of (sanitised) hay.

When my shirt comes off, Katja pulls a blanket halfway over her face and eyes me gingerly. I try my best to seem nonchalant, but inside I'm squirming.

"Who wants tea?" Dad asks, jumping out of his seat with some haste before turning to Mum. "Patty, help me?"

Mum nods her head vigorously and follows him out of the room, which makes Robby and Divya laugh so hard they hold their sides.

"Don't be embarrassed," Evie says kindly. "You're an artist, and this is your job. You look bloody amazing, by the way."

"Thanks," I say, clearing my throat.

"Did you get a bonus for every item of clothing you stripped off?" Adam asks, which makes us all laugh.

I can barely watch myself in the choreographed lovemaking scene, but

I can say it looks very realistic. That last-minute spray tan on my arse was also worth every damn penny.

Katja excuses herself and leaves the room in a hurry. I wait until Robby calls for Mum and Dad to let them know it's safe to return before I go looking for her.

I find her outside, back on the swing. She is typing on her phone and doesn't look up as I approach.

"Was I that awful to watch?" I only half-joke. A slight tremor in my voice belies the fact that I do actually care what she thinks.

Her derisive laugh corrodes my ego.

"Okay then, I'll leave." I turn to walk away, praying she won't let me.

One. Two. Three. Four agonising steps before she clears her throat. I halt.

More seconds pass before she speaks.

"I'm sorry. It's not you... you were... incredible. It's me. I don't belong here."

I retrace my steps back to her and go down on one knee in front of her, stilling the rocking of the swing so that I can speak directly into those eyes I want to lose myself to.

"Why would you say that?" I ask.

Her head dips so low that her chin is nearly on her chest, and she shakes her head and wipes stray tears from her cheeks.

I reach to comfort her, but she swats me away.

"I don't fit in your world, Leo. I see you on TV and I realise that whatever this is," she waves a pointed finger between us, "would never work out of this Christmas bubble. We are too different."

I have things I want to say. I want to argue that it's too soon to disregard our connection. Because I have never met anyone who has made me feel the things she has in the last twenty-four hours. And I'm not ready for it to end.

But I don't get a chance to say any of it. Instead, my phone buzzes in my pocket.

"Shit!" I growl. "Look, I want to have to have this conversation, it's just that—"

"Hollywood is calling?"

Her snide remark slaps me in the face, and I turn my cheek. I grind my teeth.

"I'm going to take the job in Dubai. That's what I was doing. I was emailing the recruitment agency."

She drops that bomb at my feet, either oblivious or knowing that she's blowing us up before we've even begun.

I should walk away. Run. But I just can't.

I try. "Please wait. Don't. Just hold off on making your decision until we can talk. Please?"

She shakes her head. "No, I'm going back to London tonight."

"Jesus, Katja!" I swivel on my heel and rake my fingers through my hair. "You won't give me a couple of hours? Does our attraction scare you that much?"

I see how her eyes widen. I'm right. These magnetic pulls, these smouldering coals, frighten her.

"Look, why don't you come with me to do this thing I need to do? We can chat on the drive? It'll only take an hour or two, max."

She doesn't answer.

"Please?" I plead.

"Fine. But whatever it is, it will not work. I've made up my mind and I can be very stubborn."

"I can see that," I say, letting out a long breath. There's hope. I have not lost her yet.

"By the way, where are we going?" she asks as we walk to the car.

"Tesco," I tell her point-blank.

"You urgently need to go to a supermarket?" She wrinkles her nose in a way that I find so adorable I want to kiss her. I resist the urge.

"Uh-ha."

"On Christmas?" She is incredulous, and I'm enjoying her puzzling far more than I should.

"Yup!"

"What on earth for?" She climbs into the passenger seat in my car.

"I have a click-and-collect order I need to fetch."

"On Christmas?"

"Yes, we've established this. Tesco doesn't care about Jesus' birthday," I say, unable to suppress a grin.

She folds her arms across her chest. "Are you going to tell me what this is all about or not?"

"Definitely not," I tell her, driving in the store's direction.

Katja

He wasn't kidding. We drove to the chain grocery store, and he picked up a boot full of groceries and other things like school supplies, toiletries, and more tins of chocolates and biscuits than I've seen in my life. When everything was loaded, he thanked the Tesco guy for his help, signed an autograph, and posed for a selfie.

He climbed back into the car beside me and said, "One more stop."

I didn't bother asking him where we were going. We have a car full of food and stationery supplies. For all I knew, he could kidnap me for a weekend of arts and crafts.

That should have been a distressing thought, but it wasn't. Instead, the idea of being swept away by him made me fantasise about him and me on hay bales in a barn.

"Earth to Katja," he jolts me back to reality. "We're here."

I register my surroundings. It's dark outside, but we've pulled up in front of what looks like a community hall. There are lights burning inside, but outside, the parking lot is deserted.

"Where are we?" I turn to him.

"It's a shelter for women and children. Many of them are refugees that have had no choice but to flee their home countries in search of safety. They leave with the clothes on their back and what they can carry... I have so much... it doesn't seem... fair."

His voice rises and falls and falters.

"Leo, that's so kind," I utter.

"I've had insomnia. Turns out I shop when I should be sleeping." He makes light of this deeply generous gesture.

I want to lean in and kiss him, but I don't.

"Need a hand to carry those bags in?" I ask.

"You know, I was hoping you'd say that." He flashes me those insanely cute dimples.

"I know," I tell him. And then I can't help myself. I lean in and invite his mouth to find mine.

There's a bit of chaos when we enter the hall. Women and children line up for hugs and selfies with Duke Harrington. He is patient, always asking their name and saying something to make them laugh. From a distance, I admire his ability to be so personable. The ease with which he moves through the world with his guard down is foreign to me. He is one hundred percent himself, always surrendering to the moment fully.

A small girl, maybe four or five years old, comes to him, and he drops to a knee to listen to her. I can hear bits of their conversation.

"No, I don't know if Santa is going to find you here tonight, but I brought some presents. Do you want to see them?"

She nods eagerly.

"What are you hoping for?"

The little girl leans in and cups a tiny hand at his ear as she whispers to him.

Leo nods in understanding and then looks my way and calls me over.

"Maya, this is my friend Katja," he introduces me. I give a little wave, and the girl flashes me a smile, revealing a missing front tooth.

"She is here to help me with all the presents, and I'm sure she will find some paper and coloured pens in our bags. And maybe even some chocolate."

Maya nods and takes my hand.

"I can do that," I tell her. "Do you want to draw a picture?"

She shakes her head. "I need to write a letter."

"Oh. That's a very grown-up thing to do," I say.

"I'm seven," she points out.

It's my turn to nod. "May I ask who you are writing to?"

"The Queen."

"Right..." I say, leading the way to the stationery supplies. "Well, that sounds important, so let's get you what you need. I'm sure I saw some glitter pens somewhere."

I find paper and glitter pens and chocolate and hand it all to the girl, whose eyes have become serious.

"Thank you," she says. "I hope the Queen will like the glitter pens and read my letter and help me find my father and brother."

I gulp. A sizeable chunk of sadness lodges in my throat.

I give her a hug, blinking back the sting in my eyes.

Leo and I dish out treats and necessities in equal measure, and I follow his lead in taking a minute to talk to the women and make jokes with the kids.

By the end, I feel lighter. Lucky. Grateful.

When we both are back in the car, we sit in the dark. I reach for him, and we cling to each other. He kisses me without apology or restraint, and I respond by pressing against him, wanting to be even closer.

"Katja," he says, and I love the way my name rolls off his tongue and onto my neck, cheek, lips. He might not know it, but he is undoing me bit by bit.

When we return from the shelter, Adam raises a brow in our direction. "Where did you two disappear to?"

We stomp the mud and dirt off our shoes at the door of the kitchen. Everyone else seems to be in the living room or elsewhere. I look at Leo, unsure if his charity work is something he wants to share.

"None of your business," he says with a smirk, clearly enjoying keeping his brother in the dark.

Adam squares up slightly, and my eyes dart between the two brothers.

"I'd argue it is my business," Adam says evenly, and Leo's jaw twitches before he looks away and then back at Adam.

"We'll talk later, okay? Deal's off," Leo says.

"Deal? What deal?" I ask, not liking the tension in the room.

Adam's eyes land on mine. "He means bet."

"Adam!" Leo tries to stop him from saying more.

"Bet?" My question is for Leo.

"Please," Leo's voice has gone soft, desperate.

Adam holds us in silence. "If you don't tell her, I will. I warned you. This is a bad idea."

"What's a bad idea?" I ask, my own voice gone small.

"I'll let him come clean himself." Adam walks away, leaving us alone.

Leo curses, rakes his fingers through his hair before facing me again.

"I took a bet with Adam," he starts.

"Okay, what has that to do with me?" The penny drops before the question is fully formed.

He dips his chin to his chest.

"You bet him you could get into my pants?" I spit.

His head rolls from side to side. "Not exactly."

I cross my arms in front of my body and take a step back from him. Retreat! My brain cries out. Retreat!

"I bet him I could get you to fall for me... but I wanted to call it off, you know, after last night and tonight... I just didn't get the chance to. I swear."

My fragile heart is splintering, but the soldier in me squares up. My spine stiffens.

A tightly drawn silence grows heavy between us. When he tries to come closer to me, I step further back, resisting the urge to run and take cover.

"I'm sorry," he says.

I raise my hand to his face and block his meaningless apology.

"Say something?" he pleads.

"Okay, Leo, I'll say something," I hiss. "You have lived up to every expectation I had of you when I met you: a spoilt pretty boy who thinks he can have whatever he wants. Including me. Well, let me assure you, that is definitely not happening. Ever."

I wait for him to argue with me, but he doesn't. Instead, he nods, grabs his keys from the table, and slams the door as he leaves.

The next morning I'm at the kitchen table. The mug of coffee I've wrapped my hands around has gone cold.

"Morning, Lieutenant!" Adam's jovial as he fills the kettle with water.

"Do you want to tell me why you had a bet with Leo?" I keep my voice steady even though the words grate my throat.

Adam pauses before he swings around. He sits down opposite me and covers my hands with his.

"I'm sorry. It was stupid. My younger brother shows up here with a brand-new Land Rover, and let's face it, he is everyone's darling... good-looking and genuinely nice, it's fucking annoying."

Despite how raw I feel, I feel my lips loosen into a smile.

"When he heard you were coming, he seemed interested. Despite being able to date anyone he wants, he keeps to himself... Anyway, I told him you were out of bounds, and I should have known better. You can't tell any hot-blooded Taylor there's a woman he can't have. It's our nature to then pursue only that one."

Adam is shaking his head.

"I never wanted you to get hurt, and honestly, I didn't think you'd fall for him!"

I pull my hands away from his and use the back of my hand to wipe away the fat tears sliding down my face.

"I'm so sorry, Katja. It went too far. But for what it's worth, I think he genuinely likes you. He's a decent actor, but I can't imagine any man looking at a woman like he's been looking at you these last few days and it being just an act to win a bet."

Divya comes into the kitchen and immediately senses the mood in the room.

"What's going on?" she asks and then drops to her knees beside me when she sees I've been crying.

"Can we leave?" I ask her.

Divya's brows knit together and she shoots Adam an angry look.

"Of course. Now? You want to go now?"

I nod. More tears spill down my cheeks as I scramble to leave the room and pack my things.

Chapter Seven

Leo

The drive from the countryside of Herefordshire to London's Notting Hill does nothing to clear my head. I ignore the incessant buzzing of my phone and decide to switch it off completely when I walk into my apartment.

I used to love this space. The uncluttered minimalism of it. But today all the grey and white feels cold and disconnected. The fake ficus tree in the corner of the room (for that splash of colour, the decorator assured me) just reminds me I can't be trusted with caring for a plant, let alone another person.

Fuck. I really messed up. Katja is everything I've never known I needed in a woman. And I've totally blown it with a stupid bet.

I scan the letters that have come in the mail. Late Christmas cards from people I hardly know. I toss those straight in the bin and justify it with my minimalist values, but the truth is I'm struggling to care about anything.

But there's one envelope I don't open. The thick embossed paper sealed with a wax stamp, addressed to me in longhand calligraphy, and the accompanying signature scent smells more like money than lavender. I know what it is. It's the invite to Colin Firth's New Year's 'get-together', a black-tie ball at his country home in Winchester. It's not one of those things you have to RSVP to. You get the invitation and it's assumed you'll be there.

I met Colin on set with *Farthington*, where he played the cynical and meddling monarch. Turns out he fancies a round of golf now and again, and we got together for a few games. And now I'm on 'the list'.

I sigh, deflated. I'm not sure what's worse, not going at all or going alone. Both scenarios twist my guts into knots.

I try not to think of it. I change into my running gear and climb onto the treadmill. And then I run and run until I want to vomit.

I replace dinner with a bowl of popcorn and a bottle of water and lie on the sofa with my favourite comfort movie on in the background–*Notting Hill*. It's my secret indulgence: rom-coms. I turn on my phone and read through the messages. Every member of the family has texted to find out where I am, except my brothers. Robby demands to know what the hell I did to cause Divya to leave early with Katja. Adam leaves me a serious voice note instructing me to call him ASAP.

So Katja left? Of course, she would have. And she's probably taken that job in Dubai... and...

My phone rings. Adam.

"I don't really want to talk to you," I say to him when I answer.

"Too bad," he retorts. "You need to hear this. Katja is in love with you and if you feel anything for her... if you really have feelings, which I think you do, and this entire weekend wasn't just about the bloody bet, then I suggest you do something about it."

I don't answer, and the pause between us stretches.

"You still there?" Adam asks.

"I don't know how to fix it," I admit.

I hear my brother huff on the other end. The guy is not known for his patience unless it comes to Evie and Stella.

"Look," he says, "I know you watch those fluffy films. Take a leaf out of that book and go do the grand gesture if you have to. But win the woman back, Leo. Unless it was all just pretend?"

He provokes me and it gets me spitting mad. "Fuck off!" I shout as I hang up.

I'm on my feet. How dare he imply I was just acting? That is insane. I'm so damn smitten I can't help myself. It should be obvious to anyone with eyes.

And I don't want her to go to Dubai.

Adam is being a proper prick but is right about one thing. I do need to show her I'm serious.

My eyes have rested on the New Year's Eve invitation without me realising it. And I know now that she's the only person in the world I want to be at my side that night. Clocking in the new year with her would mean everything to me.

My phone buzzes. A message from Adam.

ADAM: Don't be an idiot. Go find her. This is her address and telephone number.
ME: Thank you, brother.
ADAM: I'll always have your back.
ME: I know.

Katja

"Yes, but are you sure you want to babysit some oil royalty kid?" Divya asks me for the umpteenth time in the last hour.

I've been telling her how great this job in Dubai will be, but she's not buying it. Exotic foreign country. More money than I could have earned in five years in the military. A brand-new car. Plenty of international travel.

It's New Year's Eve and tomorrow is the deadline for my answer to the recruiter. We should be getting ready for some party, but Divya insisted we keep things low key. She invited Robby over for dinner and movies on the sofa.

"What the job entails is also important," she stresses again.

"I know, but the perks won't hurt," I counter.

My friend stares at me, calling me out on my BS without saying the words.

"Fine," I admit, "I'm going to take this job because it means I can't run into You Know Who." I cross my arms over my chest.

"Leo," she says his name.

It slices me across the heart. My eyes itch.

"Oh, my friend..." She comes round to my side of the kitchen counter, pulls up a stool, and wraps her arms around me.

"It's so stupid. I wasn't supposed to fall for a bloody movie star!"

"But you did, and I must say, you made a spectacular choice," Divya says a bit too dreamily.

"Divya!"

"Sorry, but holy guacamole, he is dishy, isn't he?"

"Not the point!" I insist.

"Definitely not the point," she reassures me.

"And let's not forget what an arsehole he is," I add.

"The biggest," she agrees.

"I never want to see him again!"

"Except maybe on TV," she gives me a reality check.

I groan and drop my forehead onto my arms at the kitchen counter. Oh my god, she is right. I'm never going to escape the guy. It's enough to make me weep.

The doorbell rings, and a second later, Divya's smart speaker redundantly announces that there's someone at the door. It's a recent addition to her flat, a gift from Robby that had her smiling from ear to ear when it arrived.

What if it's him? The thought passes between us wordlessly.

"Probably just an online delivery." She pats my leg before she swings off the stool and goes to see who it is.

I tear a piece of kitchen towel off the roll and wipe my eyes. I hear the exchange of words, and then she yells for me to come to the door.

"I didn't order anything!" I tell her.

"Kat! Come now! Hurry!"

I rush over.

"Are you Katja Janssen?" A man in a dark suit, chauffeur's hat, and dark sunglasses asks me.

"I am."

"This is for you." He hands me a large, shallow rectangular box. It's white and tied with an elaborate red velvet ribbon.

"I didn't order anything," I repeat.

"It's for you," he says flatly.

"There's a note." Divya points to the envelope tucked under the ribbon.

She helps me hold the mystery box while I rip the note from its envelope.

I'm sorry I hurt you. I've fallen in love with you, Katja. Please be my date for tonight's party at Mr Firth's house?
-Leo
P.S. Look up.

I read the note over, and then Divya reads it aloud over my shoulder.

"Holy shit! The real life Mr Darcy! Look up? What does he mean?"

Divya is squealing, so I assume Mr Firth is also pretty famous. I step out and look to the sky. Overhead is a micro-plane zipping through the heavens.

It's written the words:

Katja... please... say... yes.

Chapter Eight

Leo

I'm waiting for her at the party, and the moment she steps into the room, I catch my breath.

She is exquisite. The red ball gown clings to her in all the right places, and my Army chick is rocking the high heels. Her natural beauty outshines every other cover model and movie star in the room.

"Who's that?" Sandra, my *Farthington* co-star, asks me.

"That's my date," I say, unable to wipe the goofiest grin from my face.

I make my way to her, grabbing two glasses of champagne from a passing waiter.

"You made it," I say, handing her a glass. "You look... breathtaking." Her blue eyes are wide, giving away her nerves, but she is smiling. I place a hand on the small of her back and steer her across the room. We glide together, or that's how it feels.

And Katja is turning heads. My chest swells. I'm the luckiest bugger in the room and I know it.

"That was some invitation, pretty boy," she murmurs, keeping her smile.

I chuckle. "It was Adam's idea–the grand gesture."

"Of course," she responds. "I'm glad he approves."

"I wouldn't care if he didn't," I tell her. And I mean it.

She nods and looks away, and I understand then that Adam's opinion matters to her because of their history. Not just Army history, but because Pete was Adam's best friend.

We join a group of well-known English actors, and I have to suppress a smile when I see how Katja disarms and thoroughly charms them by genuinely not knowing who they are.

I lean in and whisper in her ear, "I assume you do at least know who the host of the party is?" She follows my gaze across the ballroom.

"I do now," she says, leaning into me, "Divya made me watch *Bridget Jones's Diary* while I was getting ready... but I missed the end."

Her gaze breaks from mine and dips to my lips, and I have to swallow hard. Her mouth inches close to mine. Our little crowd has dispersed, doing their rounds, greeting more newcomers, and working the room. It's just us, standing close together.

I can feel the heat between us. Our fingertips touch. Sparks. She turns to me.

"Does he get the girl?" she asks.

"He gets the girl."

The errant twinkle in her eye flips every switch in my body. I'm alive and dying all at once.

I drain the flute of champagne and take her hand in no uncertain terms.

"Come, let's get out of here." I lead the way.

"But I haven't met Mr Firth yet!" she pretends to complain. "And this beautiful dress. I've hardly had it on!"

I stop and swing her into an embrace that leaves zero inches between us.

I growl, impatient. "Fine," I say. "Colin!" I call to our party host, and he obliges good-naturedly and walks towards us.

"This is my... Katja. She's a huge fan."

Katja blushes and extends a hand, and everyone's Mr Darcy takes her hand and kisses it.

"Nice to meet you," she says, clearly quite starstruck, and I won't lie, it irks me.

"Unfortunately, we have to leave. I'm not feeling well. But we'll set up a four-ball at the club?" I try to appease him.

"Sounds wonderful," he says, "Pity you can't stay."

We exchange pleasantries and goodbyes.

In front of the mansion, Maurice pulls up in a Bentley my agent rented for me for the night. I help Katja into the car. Her long, shapely legs should be criminal. The sight of them as the slit in her dress rides up her thigh holds me hostage. My blood is calescent. I tug at the black bowtie around my neck and loosen it at once.

A brazen smile dances on her lips, and I can't wait another second. I lean into the car and capture her mouth with my own. I drink from that sweet well, but it does nothing to sate my thirst for her. It just makes me hunger for her more.

My hand cups her face, and then my fingers find the thin straps over the shoulders. They fall away without resistance.

"I do love you in this dress," I rasp.

Is she trembling?

"Good," she breathes.

I work my fingers on the other strap and watch it fall over her shoulder in the same way. I kiss her again, harder.

Maurice clears his throat, reminding me I've still got my arse hanging out of the car.

I curse under my breath and rush to get in beside her, and when I do, she wraps her arms around my neck and pulls me to her.

I've kissed plenty of women on and off camera, but Katja seems to hypnotise me with her tongue. She tugs at my bottom lip with her teeth.

And then she pushes me away.

"Wait," she says, "there's something I have to say."

"Now?" I groan. Her eyes flit down to the straining bulge in my trousers, but she is adamant.

"Yes, now."

I inhale and try to gain composure.

"Okay. Of course," I say, trying hard to think of my grandmother's knickers on the washing line or anything equally disturbing to distract the throbbing in my pants.

"In your note, you said you were in love with me. Did you mean it?"

There's caution in her eyes, and I restrain the urge to make a joke about how obvious it is.

"Yes. I'm in love with you. Madly. Madly. In love."

She nods, relaxing into her seat.

"Good, because I'm in love with you too."

That's all I need to hear. I lean in and press my forehead against hers.

"Is this about Dubai?" I ask.

Her chin dips.

"Will you stay?" I ask.

She hesitates, and then she nods again.

I take her face in my hands and kiss her hard.

"Thank you. Thank you. Thank you," I say again and again as I kiss her all over her face, ears, neck.

She laughs and pulls my face back to hers.

"Where are you taking me, by the way?" she asks.

"Home."

Epilogue

THREE MONTHS LATER

Katja

T tiptoe from the bed to the kitchen for a drink of water. I'm parched.
I've lost count of how many times we've made love. My whole body
aches from the exertion. Even now, I can feel the imprint of his
fingers on my hips. Three months in and the man is still as insatiable as he
was on the first night.

The memory of it makes me smile to myself.

Life is good.

I say these words quietly to myself, too afraid to really feel it. In the
military, when everything seems too easy, it's usually a trap, and I'm
trained to be on high alert for danger. But I'm learning to lean into this
unprecedented feeling of joy without foreboding. Leo is teaching me.

We've settled into a kind of routine. I still have my room at Divya's,
and occasionally I'll go stay the night, but most nights, I'm here. And Leo
and I spend almost every day together.

He is preparing for a new role. I offered to help him with his condi-
tioning. Turns out Marvel heroes need a lot more bulk and definition
than the gentry of *Farthington*. Once we started seeing results, more actors
and actresses offered to hire me to help them do the same. And now my

no-nonsense boot camp programme is getting attention from some high paying clients. Who knew the rich and famous like being yelled at and being tortured to an inch of their lives?

"Babe?"

"I'm here." I fill a second glass of water and take it to him.

"You're a lifesaver," he tells me, pulling me in for a kiss before taking the glass.

"No, you saved me, remember?" I remind him.

"No way." He sets the glass down on the bedside table. "You definitely saved me. From myself."

This is a non-quarrel quarrel we have often: who saved who.

I curl up against him and breathe in the faint smell of soap and spice still lingering on his skin.

Two simple facts come to mind.

We saved each other.

And I'm home.

THE END

Let It Snow

BY NICOLE SHARP

Avery Dean is not enchanted at being snowed in on a last-minute job assignment in the small town of Eden, Colorado at Christmastime. But when she stumbles upon handsome Nick Hall and a secret turn-of-the-century love story, well…maybe things aren't all that bad. Let it snow!

About the Author

Nicole Sharp swigs cappuccinos the way a dehydrated sailor with scurvy would whiskey as she writes about love, coffee, and the quirky adventures of fearless women. She lives in the Pacific Northwest with no houseplants and three pink stovetop espresso makers.

www.nicolesharpwrites.com

Chapter One

A very rang the bell on the small, makeshift desk just inside the door of the Grand Rose Bed and Breakfast.

"Coming," a voice called from another room.

Avery stretched her fingers out in front of her, which were cramped from the white-knuckle drive through the snowstorm; thankfully the rental car had all-wheel drive.

"Oh." A matronly woman, early sixties, shoulder-length black hair with a fine dusting of gray, came around the corner and looked wide-eyed at Avery. "Miss Dean?" she asked.

Avery nodded. "Yep. I made it." She held out her arms in a floppy 'ta da'.

"Oh my...an avalanche was just reported."

Avery swallowed hard, "An avalanche?"

"South of here, about ten miles. You just missed it. And the road north of us was closed this afternoon."

"Does that happen a lot?" Avery's mouth went dry.

"In the middle of winter, in the Colorado mountains?" The woman nodded her head then waved her hands to erase the worry. "But we've got plenty of room for the next week."

"The next week?" Avery parroted and glanced at the foyer of the three-story Victorian B&B touted for its location "just off historic Main Street."

"Honey, the weather is calling for snow and then more snow." She laughed at her joke. "You're going to be with us for the duration."

"I'm snowed in?" Avery asked.

"Snowed in," the woman apologetically verified.

"Do you think they'll have the roads opened by next Tuesday?" Avery did a quick count; diligent crews could have snow cleared in four days, couldn't they?

"Miracles happen all the time."

"If the roads were cleared by then, I could still get home in time for Christmas." Avery hoped that whatever force made miracles happen at Christmastime would hear her.

"Well honey, let's not worry about that now. I think you'll find our little town of Eden a welcoming place to be stranded. I'm Maggie, by the way." The woman's reassuring smile was lost on Avery.

This was the very reason she had argued that she did *not* need to come on this trip. Even if she got her report in on Monday, which was the deadline, the office was running on a skeleton crew. Of course, the whole point of this trip was to get the paperwork filed before the end of the year...

"What if there's an emergency?" Avery asked, not that she was planning on having one.

"We have folks trained for such things and a small medical facility. Doctor Pine can handle about anything that comes up."

Avery nodded.

"I'll show you to your room so you can shake off your drive and then come have some dinner." Maggie produced a key and led the way.

Avery followed Maggie up the ornate staircase wrapped in thick holly and ivy garland. She glanced numbly at the careful refurbishing details of the Victorian building, her mind trying to grasp her snowed in situation.

"When you made the reservation, you mentioned assessing the Allen House?" Maggie asked.

"I'm an architectural historian."

"Are you with the forest service, then, or do you work for an agency?"

Avery was impressed. "I work for Smith and Dugan, and they report to the National Park Service."

"I figured. When you live in a small historic mining town, you get used to all the preservationists and assayers coming and going. It's a heck of a time of year to come for a visit though."

"Deadlines," Avery said. "We have to finalize the assessment before the end of the year."

"Ah, tax reasons." Maggie continued up a second flight of stairs to the top floor. "I put you in the blue room. It faces Palace Mountain and has the best view."

Great, the best view of the snow keeping me hostage.

"You know after Ace Barber robbed the First National Bank in Silver City, they say he hid out in the Allen House." Maggie waved a hand. "Of course, this town claims that Wyatt Earp, Billy the Kid and a whole list of famous gunslingers and gamblers came through. Even Lincoln."

Avery muttered, "They always do." She cleared her throat. "Lincoln. Everyone claims he visited their town."

Maggie opened the glossy mahogany door bearing the number 10 and stepped aside.

A detailed Victorian room preened. Dark wood floor in a parquet pattern was draped with an ornamental blue rug. Busy blue wallpaper and a navy-blue bedspread. A dark wood desk and armoire matched the headboard. There was a bathroom off of the room; a new addition Avery was happy about.

In the corner was a slender Christmas tree, decorated with strings of dried fruit, popcorn and wooden shapes. Very Victorian, except for the soft LED lights.

"Internet?" Avery asked, continuing to try and shake off her shock at the current situation.

"We have it, just know it'll be spotty. On the desk is the connection information. The phone lines work best, if you need to call anyone," Maggie offered. "I'll leave you to it. When you're ready, come on down. It's shepherd's pie tonight for dinner. My husband, Edwin, does the cooking. He's a fine chef. You'll see."

Avery thanked her and was grateful Maggie closed the door. She stood in the middle of the dimly lit room; the gray dusk of the evening illuminated the large sheets of snow falling beyond the blue-curtain-framed window.

"Snowed in." Her announcement gave a lonely echo.

Chapter Two

"Amy," Avery sighed her coworker's name, "I might have to spend Christmas here. Alone."

"Yes, and you were going to spend Christmas *alone* in Denver," Amy argued.

Avery snarled, "In Denver I'd be in my own home."

"I'm sorry. I didn't mean it that way. You said you didn't care about Christmas this year because your folks were in Switzerland and, I quote, Christmas can go fuck itself."

"Well..."

"Because fucked-up Todd broke up with you last Christmas."

"Yes, I remember."

Amy continued, "So snowed in, in a quaint old mining town or hunkered down in your own home..."

"I get it, I get it."

"I say have fun."

"Fun," Avery snorted.

"You get to study the details of a historical home, and while you're there, you can do a deep dive into its history. I know you: the idea of playing in the archives sounds fun. So, yes, have fun. Think of this as a paid vacation."

A slight weight tried to loosen itself from Avery's shoulders, but she wasn't ready to let it go yet. "Amy, just...email me those files so I can download them before I lose the internet connection again." It had already happened twice since she'd woken up. And that was just an hour ago.

"I will. You have fun."

Avery grudgingly agreed, then saved the files to her computer. With nothing left to do, she headed to breakfast. Maggie hadn't exaggerated when she said Edwin was a fine cook. 'Fine' didn't describe the delectable food she was treated to the previous evening.

She heard the conversational uproar before she turned the corner and was taken aback by the bustle of full tables in the dining area. The Rose only had ten rooms, but there were at least twenty tables.

Maggie caught sight of her and crossed the room. "Mornin', honey. I have your table ready."

"It's so busy."

"We open the restaurant to the public for breakfast," she explained as she led Avery to a small table in the corner by the wall of windows, "but we keep tables open for our guests."

"So...all these people live here?"

Maggie had been carrying a carafe; she turned over the waiting cup on the table and filled it. "Just because we're snowed in doesn't mean everything in town stops. Most restaurants are open, as well as the two coffee shops and the bars. Oh," Maggie pointed across the room toward a bright green flyer hung neatly on a corkboard, "we have our annual Christmas Dance Monday night too."

Avery licked her lips, "Well..."

Maggie patted her shoulder. "Just know you're invited and there's still plenty to explore. Even the shops will open a few hours a day, for last minute gifts. I can always contact someone for you if they aren't open."

"Like the archive?"

Maggie gave a thoughtful nod, "Elizabeth is in town, I'll call her and find out what hours work best. So, what would you like this morning?"

Avery glanced at the simple menu, "Eggs Benedict."

Maggie winked and was off.

Avery cradled her cup as she watched out the window. The snow continued, not in a sweet twirl of flakes, but a wall of white.

She didn't mind the snow. It was the shock of being trapped and the change of plans; she just needed to recalibrate her expectations and everything would be fine.

Amy was right, Avery had no plans this Christmas and there was no difference between being alone in Denver or alone here. And researching in a small-town archive *was* her idea of fun. Maybe she *would* think of this as a mini paid vacation. Who knew what she might find in Eden, Colorado?

Chapter Three

Maggie stood next to Avery on the covered sidewalk in front of The Rose. The snow had become a soft twirl, so Avery decided to keep her noon appointment with the owners of the Allen House. Only, when she walked out to her car, she found the town snowplow had buried her car. Maggie suggested snowshoes or cross-country skis.

Avery opted for the snowshoes and a borrowed pair of snow pants from Maggie.

"Snowshoes have changed since I was a kid." Avery clicked her feet into the bindings and tightened the straps with the ratchet, beaming at her success.

Maggie patted her on the shoulder, "There you are. Now, have fun."

Maggie showed Avery a tourist map of the town and pinpointed the house. The simple grid street plan of Eden made it impossible to get lost.

The crunch of snow under her feet made her smile. She tripped over her feet, steadied herself, then widened her stance a bit so the snowshoes wouldn't crowd each other. It was awkward at first, but then she looked up and let the purr of soft, snowy silence soothe her. "Okay, this is cool."

Low clouds and snow formed a soundless barrier. There was no hissing of power lines, no hum of traffic in the distance, no car alarms or honking or buzz of technology. It was just quiet. The last bits of worry about being snowed in slid off Avery's shoulders as she breathed in deep the peace and quiet.

As she walked, she studied the refurbished, turn-of-the-century Main Street buildings. Their bright colors fought the quiet, gray day. The homes several blocks over were just as alluring. And as the Allen House came into view, she thought that pictures hadn't done the three-story Victorian justice.

Draped in snow, the steep gabled roof and decorative woodwork looked more like an elegant gingerbread house. The railing on the wrap-around porch was decorated with pine garland. A matching wreath with a velvet red bow hung on the front door.

Avery walked up to the house across the path that had been cleared. She dislodged herself from the snowshoes and gloves, then rang the bell.

No answer.

She glanced behind her and saw that a gray Chevy Tahoe with a light dusting of snow was parked on the snowplowed section of the street. Someone must be home.

She peeked in the front bay window; the lights were on. Another knock, louder.

Still no answer. She tromped to the back door hoping the noise would announce her arrival.

No answer there either.

She surveyed the rest of the property. A truck was parked in the drive-way, bundled under snow, but behind it was the large detached two-story garage. The side door was open slightly, light streaming out.

"Hello?" She didn't expect an answer. She forwent putting the snow-shoes back on, it wasn't that far.

However, on the third step into the deep drifts, she regretted her deci-sion. Too late; she continued the Stairmaster from hell, crawling out of each divot her foot sank into.

When she arrived at the garage and flat land, she stomped her feet as she pushed open the door. "Hello?"

She was met by a woman whose hourglass figure had been painted into beige snow pants and a fuzzy white sweater, her brunette hair hanging in wild curls around her shoulders. She swayed slightly to the

Pearl Jam song that was playing while peeking under the hood of an old Ford, her rapt attention on the other side.

And Avery understood why: leaning over the engine was a lumberjack of a man. Disheveled, short brown hair, a five o'clock shadow darkening a strong jawline, with shoulders pressing against the confines of a flannel shirt that was being held together precariously by two buttons.

"Hello..." Avery tried again. The man turned his eyes toward her arrival, and dear Lord, she felt his gaze in her stomach.

He righted himself and smiled. Now *that* she felt a little lower.

"Hey there, darlin'," he called, then grabbed a rag and wiped his hands as he walked toward her.

Avery glanced behind her; had someone else walked in?

No, just her.

He looked to be mid-thirties, maybe. Taller than she'd realized, well over six feet. Gorgeous green eyes which she got a close-up view of as he pushed past her personal space and pulled her into his arms.

"Please," he whispered the plea as he hugged her, "pretend to be my girlfriend." She felt the heat of his breath against her ear and goosebumps formed on her arms.

He pulled away and she looked up into his leveled gaze; did she understand?

She understood he had amber flecks in those green eyes. This muscle hard man who smelled like sweat and coffee and grease and sex was still holding her hands, making all her senses erupt and spiral at once.

He raised an eyebrow in question and Avery gave a slight nod; she understood.

He turned his attention to the twenty-something pin-up girl leaning on his truck, his arm around Avery's waist. "Lexi, this is my girlfriend."

"A..." she cleared her throat, "Avery." She gave a lame wave.

Lexi righted herself with a frown and pressed her hands into her lower back, which jutted her impressive chest out - a practiced move. "I didn't know you had a girlfriend." She looked Avery up and down disapprovingly.

"Now you do." He tightened his grip and Avery thought he was holding on for dear life, as if she might run away and causeLexi to certainly come for his soul.

"It's pretty new," Avery offered, "the relationship."

"Where have you been?" Lexi asked suspiciously.

Avery held up the snowshoes. "Just wanted to take advantage of the snow."

Lexi gave a humph in reply.

"Well, Lex, it was good seeing you," the man tried to excuse her.

"When did you get to town?"

He answered that question, "She got in two days ago, just before the storm started."

"Flew in," Avery offered.

He gave another squeeze. Avery glanced sideways at him, which was a big mistake. From this angle and the way his shirt lay open, she could see the fine sprinkle of dark hair on his chest and the muscles beneath. Her fingers suddenly itched to trace some of the thick patterns.

"Why wasn't she with you last night at the Forester?"

Avery was glad for the interruption. "Headache."

Lexi raised an eyebrow. She wasn't buying it.

Avery cleared her throat and righted herself. "Hey babe," she said softly. He turned his attention to Avery as she reached up and traced his jawline with her hand, hoping Lexi didn't see the slight tremor. "I'm gonna go make some coffee. Come in soon?"

His eyes sparkled with interest at her action. Avery figured, since her hand was already there and she liked the feel so much, she might as well continue the momentum; she cupped the back of his head and gave a gentle tug.

The corner of his mouth turned up on a grin, and his eyes darted to her lips. Avery's shallow breathing was audible, she second-guessed her actions until he licked his lips a mere breath away from her. Oh, she wanted to taste those lips. And she *was* doing the guy a favor. What harm could one little kiss do?

Avery meant it to be a show for Lexi. A gentle, teasing kiss. Yet the moment his warm lips touched hers, something sparked primal, rushed like hot water through her veins and jolted through her body.

A light touch of lip against lip flamed something sensual. His lips were soft, demanding, and full of promise. He moved his hands into her hair and tilted her head, taking more of her. And she was intoxicated. Hell, even Eddie Vedder was singing about still being alive and Avery could attest to that.

Somewhere in another world, she heard a loud clearing of a throat. "Well..."

He pulled away first, a curious gleam in his eye, his hands still twisted in her hair. Avery's hands had curled around his neck. He moved ever so slightly toward her again.

"I suppose I'll just let myself out." Lexi's announcement was filled with rage.

"K..." he muttered.

Avery reached up and touched his hands, then gently removed herself from his proximity as Lexi slammed the garage door in frustration.

Avery cleared her throat. "So, that happened."

"Thanks." He took a step back and leaned against the workbench. "Lexi doesn't know how to take no for an answer."

Avery licked her lips, "Was she propositioning?"

He nodded. "And she does not get told no that often."

"Glad I could help."

An awkward silence stretched between them as he studied her from his relaxed stance.

"I'm Avery...Dean," she finally offered.

He returned the introduction, "Nick Allen."

Her attention was drawn to his shirt; one button held it together now. She glanced around the large garage. When had it gotten so hot? *Was* it hot in here or was that her reaction to his shirt?

"I was...looking for Gladys or Andrew."

"They aren't here," Nick said.

"I had an appointment..."

"They were in Cedar City, visiting friends when the road was closed."

"Oh." Avery shifted her weight. "I'm the architectural historian, doing the principal investigation for the National Park Service." She fought the urge to roll her eyes at how ridiculous the introduction sounded.

Nick smiled, "I'm the nephew. I came for the holidays." He righted himself and nodded toward the door. "I suppose we better go have that coffee after all and see how I can help."

He headed out, but Avery was frozen in place. Her imagination was suddenly taken up with stimulating ideas of how he could help her.

"Avery?" he called from the doorway.

She followed outside where he stepped to the right onto a cleared pathway. She did roll her eyes then. Nick glanced at the still-visible divots in the snow and looked back at Avery with a questioning look.

"Did they tell you I was coming?" she asked, instead of admitting to her folly.

Nick stopped and turned his full attention to her, causing her breath to catch. The wind took care of unhooking that last button. He was a temptation, a wild creature, and Avery wanted to be his prey.

"My aunt said something last night, but she was sure that if they were snowed out, you would be too."

She fought to keep her eyes on his, but his grin suggested he knew where her eyes continued to dart. "I just made it to town before the avalanche."

He continued to the house, then stomped his big boots on the porch. Avery followed suit. Nick held the door open and pointed to the coat rack in the mudroom. She put her shoes down and hung up her coat.

"This is for the historical plaque?" he asked as he walked into the kitchen, giving no indication she should follow other than a continuation of conversation.

"Well...yes, the denotation of historical status," she muttered.

"Well, my aunt and uncle have worked tirelessly the past two years refinishing the place." He had buttoned his shirt back up and was pulling out two delicate porcelain cups along with the coffee pot. Setting them on the table, he nodded to the sugar bowl and asked, "Cream?"

She shook her head. "Just black."

He sat down, placing the coffee pot on a trivet. "So, you decide which homes get to be historical?" he asked, doctoring his coffee with sugar.

Avery sat back and cuddled the cup in her hands, grateful for the distraction. Although, the way his large hands tenderly held the porcelain cup caused her mouth to run dry. What other kind of tender work could this man's hands do?

Avery, pull yourself together.

"I just do the paperwork."

"So, do you need my aunt and uncle here, or is it just photos and measurements or something?"

Avery smiled. "Well..." She took a drink.

"You have a nice smile," he interrupted.

The comment caught her unawares and she swallowed wrong, causing a very unladylike coughing fit.

"You okay?" He moved to rub her back.

She waved him away, squirming from his attention until she finally caught her breath.

"Swallowed wrong," she finally said, then took the cup of water he offered before sitting down again.

"Where were we?" he asked.

I have a nice smile.

"When I talked to Mrs. Dugan, she mentioned there was an interesting story she wanted to tell me; something found while they were working on the renovations." She wasn't sure how much Nick knew.

"Ace Barber," he sighed.

Avery nodded.

He was quiet for a moment and then asked, "Do you think this home can be granted historical status without the infamous outlaw Ace Barber?"

Avery nodded. "That was what we were filing for in the first place, for the historical preservation tax. And from the preliminary reports, not to mention the fact that the town itself already has historical status..." she shrugged, "...but Mrs. Dugan said what she found would change the type of historical marker."

"Go to dinner with me tonight."

"Dinner?" The invitation surprised her.

"A girl's gotta eat," he reasoned.

She licked her lips and tried to make light of the situation. "Do we need to be seen together so Lexi doesn't return?"

"Something like that."

In that moment, Avery was aware there was no reason to decline his invite. What was she going to say, that she had a previous engagement? Where? With whom? And she also felt his dinner invitation in her spine, the way his deep voice didn't necessarily ask and didn't necessarily demand to take her to dinner. And she could think of worse views to sit across from. She let her gaze drop to his lips before returning to her cup. Those were two very good reasons to agree.

"Maybe."

"We'll go to The Western. They have great Rocky Mountain oysters."

Avery rolled her eyes. "I'm from Denver, I know what they are and I'm not a fan of bull testicles."

He grinned. "They also have really good tortilla soup." He tapped the table with his hand, "Well how about a tour? Then I'll get in touch with Aunt G and let you know what she says."

"I...can you drive in this?" Obviously Lexi had; that must have been her car in front of the house.

"Snowmobile," Nick announced.

Yet again, Avery was glad she had packed for snow. "I'm at The Rose..."

"I know."

"You do?"

Nick shrugged. "Maggie and Edwin have great breakfast, most people go there. This morning I might've had the early bird special and heard about the girl who narrowly escaped the avalanche."

Avery's eyes widened.

Nick shrugged. "Darlin', it's a small town. Kinda like living in a fishbowl."

She ignored how that drawl of 'darlin' tucked itself inside her chest and looked for another avenue of conversation, "Did you grow up here?"

"No, I grew up in Montana. Though I did spend many summers here."

She wasn't really listening to his answer, "The girl who escaped the avalanche?" she repeated.

"Narrowly escaped," Nick corrected her.

She shook her head and sighed, "Show me the house."

Chapter Four

"Here it is," Elizabeth, the archivist, called out.

Avery wandered to the archive after she left Nick. She needed to do something to shake the meeting off.

The archive was a lovely structure, built to look like an early 1900s Victorian home. But inside, the front room was broken into two sides; one housed the archivist's workspace and the other had two twelve-foot tables for guests. The rest of the building was an impressive climate-controlled room with wall to wall shelving.

"I'm so glad you came by today. I just love this kind of research. I didn't have anything going on, other than the Widow Masterson wanting to drop off another box of her great grandfather's photos." Elizabeth shuddered. "She likes to insist it was *her* people who single handedly founded, ran, and rebuilt this town after all the mines failed. But everyone knows her people were thieves."

Avery raised an eyebrow. The young woman in her early thirties had given her credentials and life story in a matter of moments after Avery had arrived. Elizabeth was five-one and bouncy. Long blonde hair was twisted into a bun atop her head, her glasses pushed up on her forehead. She wore jeans, a Marilyn Monroe T-Shirt, a pink sweater and a grin.

Elizabeth met her husband, the famous Doctor Pine, when he was working on his PhD in Denver. After they married, they spent that summer in Eden. When the Historical Society caught wind of Elizabeth's history degree, they showed up on her doorstep with a loaf of fresh-baked bread and a job offer. She and her husband began to divide their lives between Denver and Eden; nine months in Denver, three months in Eden.

According to Elizabeth, the downfall of the 'lovely archive' was that the whole system was reliant on volunteer staff.

"Allen." Elizabeth pulled out an archival shoebox and peeked inside. "Each volunteer has a different idea of how things should be organized. Things aren't where you'd think they go."

"So, turn-of-the-century assayer photos?" Avery asked.

"I've been trying to arrange them by address. But folks who volunteer know the families that lived in the homes and think the photos should be placed under the family name. It gets messy."

"I suppose it's a good thing I'll be around for a while."

Elizabeth leaned against the shelves and bit her lower lip.

Avery rolled her eyes. "You heard?"

"About how you escaped the avalanche?"

"I didn't *escape*; I just...missed it," she mumbled.

Elizabeth smiled. "I married one of Eden's own, and I've been working here for five years, but I'm still considered an outsider. I get excited when I get to spend time with another 'outsider.'" She laughed and jerked her head toward the seating area in the front. "Let's see what information is in here." As she walked, she asked, "Did you see the house yet?"

"Yes. It's really quite lovely."

"So, you met Nick?"

"Yes." Avery tried to sound nonchalant.

Elizabeth smiled over her shoulder. "He's quite lovely too."

"This town *is* a fishbowl!"

"Gladys and Andrew are stuck in Cedar City," Elizabeth said by way of explanation. She handed a pair of white handling gloves to Avery, then took the lid off the box.

Avery glanced at Elizabeth, who was more interested in the box, and decided to take a chance on gaining more information. "When I went to the house this morning, a woman named Lexi was visiting Nick."

Elizabeth gave a grunt. "Of course she was. Nick is single, and Lexi is very..."

"Eligible?"

"To put it politely," Elizabeth laughed. She didn't look up as she pulled out the first segment of photographs from the box. "Nick and my husband are old friends, so we see him when he comes to visit."

Avery slowed her breathing. She was so interested in this unsolicited information, she feared any slight movement would distract Elizabeth.

"He was married once, but I'm not really sure what happened there."

In the half hour Avery had been here, Elizabeth proved that she was very social and very starved for company. This proved a helpful combination when a person was trying to find out all she could about a man who'd become quite intriguing after one cup of coffee and one hell of a kiss.

Avery touched a finger to her lips and a shiver ran down her spine.

Elizabeth saw the shiver and frowned. "Is it too cold in here? I can turn up the heat. The Society keeps it at 68."

"No, it's fine." Avery studied the first few pictures as Elizabeth lined them up. "There's the house. Is that around the 1920s?"

Elizabeth turned the photo over and nodded. "Yup, 1921. These are all from the Founder's Day parade. The Allens always had a float and had one of the first cars in town."

Avery looked through a few more photos, then blurted, "He asked me to dinner tonight."

"Who, Nick?"

"Yes."

"Oh, really..." Elizabeth drawled, turning her attention to Avery.

Avery's cheeks burned. "It's no big deal. We both have to eat. And he wanted to talk to his aunt. So, it's really a working dinner."

"I see."

Avery needed someone to talk to. It had been a handful of minutes since she left Nick and she wanted to pontificate about his lips, re-live each glimpse she caught of his chest and abs and tell someone what it felt like to be pressed against the heat of that tall, fine-ass man. She eyed Elizabeth. The young woman's eyes were alight with contagious energy. Avery decided, what the hell?

"I walked into the garage and found Lexi coming on to Nick. He asked me to pretend to be his girlfriend."

"Do you want a coffee? I convinced the Society to buy me a Nescafé machine."

Avery decoded the offer. "Yes, I need to talk."

"Come on." Elizabeth led the way to the far end of the room where two armchairs were set up near a stand with the coffee maker. "How did it happen?"

Avery explained how he hugged her and whispered the favor. She left out the part about how that first view of him affected her, how just the swagger as he walked toward her made her want to run away from him and, at the same time, crawl into his lap.

A new thought stopped Avery's explanation. "Elizabeth, exactly how fast does news travel in this town?"

"You mean, if you told someone like Lexi that you were Nick's girl-friend?" Elizabeth's eyes sparkled. Avery frowned, but the woman continued to confirm Avery's worries, "Fast enough that it's going to look really strange when people find out Nick Allen's girlfriend is staying at The Rose and not with him."

"Shit." Avery sat down in one of the armchairs.

Elizabeth handed over a coffee, then settled herself, smiling at Avery.

"I think I need an ally," Avery said from behind her cup.

"Oh me, pick me!" Elizabeth laughed.

"Lexi didn't seem to believe we were dating, so I figured I would try to convince her and...I might have kissed him..."

"And? How was it?"

"Stupid..." Avery muttered. "Good. Weird. Sexy as hell." *I want more of it.*

"Oh, I knew he had to be good." Elizabeth wiggled deeper into the chair.

"This isn't a big deal."

"No, it isn't," Elizabeth agreed.

"Who cares if she tells everyone I kissed him? It's the twenty-first century."

"Exactly."

"I mean, people kiss all the time."

"*All* the time." Elizabeth was eager with reason.

"So what if people think we're dating and we go to dinner and then I go back to The Rose?"

"You're being respectful to Mr. and Mrs. Dugan," Elizabeth helped.

"Exactly."

Elizabeth took another sip and then sat forward. "Was it a good kiss? Like, hot and manly, or was it all promising and soft...?"

Avery swallowed. "You won't tell anyone?" God, she sounded like a teenage girl with a crush.

"No. I really *do* understand what it's like to have your business plastered all over this town."

"But you're secretly happy the *business* is mine and not yours, huh?"

The sparkle returned. "Best. Christmas present. Ever."

Avery moaned.

"Hey, it's no big deal. You'll probably be out of here before Christmas. The crews work fast. Why not have dinner with a good-looking man?"

Another eruption of excitement bumped around Avery's stomach, and a tingle just further south agreed fully with this idea. But Avery felt the need to justify her actions: "It's really just a business dinner."

"Exactly. A girl's gotta eat." Elizabeth unknowingly repeated Nick's loose argument, and strangely, it helped her seal the lie into place.

Chapter Five

A very studied herself in the bathroom mirror. She'd been trying to get her makeup just right for the past thirty minutes. That soft and effortless effect. And it was working.

You have a nice smile.

The compliment echoed. She dropped the mascara and stood back.

She wore a long-sleeved white sweater and black slacks. Of course, she would put the ski pants and jacket over it. She left her hair down, allowing the shoulder-length brown locks to curl around her face. She had an oatmeal knit beanie, but she would put that on later. After Nick saw her.

Nick.

She couldn't stop reliving that little, insignificant, breathtaking kiss. She attributed her reminiscing to the *lack* of kissing the past year. And the lack of sex. And the lack of sexual tension with anyone, for that matter. Oh yeah, and the fact that Todd had *never* kissed her that way. And that kiss was just for show. Imagine what an intended kiss would be like. Those big strong hands digging into her hips, pulling her against that hard body. The heat-

A knock on her door shook her, and thoughts of a strong man's hands fell to the floor. She gathered herself and opened the door expecting Nick

—instead she found Maggie with a Cheshire grin. "Your young man is waiting."

"He's not my...man."

Maggie winked. "You look nice."

Avery grabbed her purse and the extra layers. "It's just dinner." But if it really was just dinner, what was with the impressive, anxious flutter wreaking havoc on her nervous system?

As they turned down the last flight of stairs, Maggie announced, "I've fetched your young woman."

Avery needed a moment before she made eye contact with the object of today's recurring fantasies, so she started at his feet. He wore snow boots, dark jeans and held his gloves loosely in his large, capable hands. She swallowed, realizing this approach wasn't any better. His jacket was thankfully bulky, so she could gather her wits before she made eye contact.

Big mistake.

Piercing green eyes sparkled in the glow of the twinkle-light-decorated foyer.

"Ready?" he asked.

"Do I need snow pants?" She lamely held the pants aloft.

"It's not snowing that badly, and we're only going two blocks. Up to you."

Maggie settled the issue. She took the pants and set them on the desk, then turned and helped Avery with her jacket. "You'll be fine with just your coat. Now, you two have a wonderful evening."

Avery muttered a "thanks" while Nick nodded and held the door.

She pulled on her gloves as she walked toward the snowmobile, but the glowing light display of Main Street stopped her progression.

"Oh, wow."

Wrought iron recreations of Victorian-era street lamps glowed a yellow hue, a spotlight for the airy snow that fell softly around them. White Christmas lights were strung over the street every fifty feet until they met in the middle in an intricate snowflake design.

Avery glanced down the length of Main Street, the whole of it a parade of Christmas magic. "It's beautiful."

"It is," Nick agreed. Only, when she glanced at him, his attention was on her.

Nick's gaze was mesmerizing; it radiated into Avery's stomach. She opened her mouth, but nothing came out. Finally, she pointed to the snowmobile. "So..."

He unhooked a helmet and explained, "It isn't far, but this will keep you from getting too cold."

Avery put her hat in her pocket and reached for the helmet. Nick ignored her outstretched hand and began to help her.

"I can do it," she muttered.

"But if I help, I have a reason to stand close to you."

As far as arguments went, that was a good one. She could feel the heat he radiated and smell his light aftershave in the cold, snowy evening. His eyes continued to flicker from his hands to her lips. When he clasped the buckle under her chin, he lingered.

Avery held her breath as Nick brushed his thumb across her neck, just a touch, just slightly, but she was well aware of the heat that simple touch ignited.

She was able to breathe once again when he turned his attention to putting on his goggles. He brushed the new snow off the snowmobile, climbed on, and then gestured for Avery to get on.

Moment gone.

"Jesus."

"What?"

She shook her head, not about to admit she just realized how intimate the seating would be. She used his body for leverage as she climbed on, thinking she'd try and keep some distance, but the tilt of the seat and her polyester slacks had other ideas of making sure she was fitted perfectly against his backside.

Avery tried to keep her hands on the side of the vehicle itself, only Nick turned and found her right arm, pulled it until it was wrapped around his waist, then gestured for the other, pulling her hands into a clasp around him, firmly pressing her against his back. He patted her hands—a gesture she figured meant 'stay'.

Those damned butterflies kicked again and Avery let loose the grin she'd been holding back. She looked up into the snow illuminated by the twinkle of street lights. The flakes fell on the clear shield of the helmet, and had it not been for the modern whir of the machine, she thought this must have been what it was like to be in an open sleigh during Christmastime at the turn of the century.

Chapter Six

T he Western was a large, dimly lit, high-ceiling room with worn
tables, a long, dark wooden bar that sat at least fifteen, and old
west paraphernalia nailed to each available surface.

A dusty, taxidermy black bear and cougar stood on either side of the
entrance, both wearing holiday wreaths around their necks as twangy
Christmas music echoed a greeting from hidden speakers.

Half the tables were filled, as well as half the bar stools. A few people
glanced up when Nick and Avery entered, but thankfully no one seemed
to give them much attention.

"Hiya, Nick, bar or table tonight?" A woman wearing a black T-shirt
with 'The Western' logo greeted them.

"Hey, Stacy, a table'd be great."

She grabbed two menus and waved them to follow. At the table, Avery
and Nick discarded their jackets. Avery was kind of disappointed to find
Nick wore a roomy black sweater.

"What would you like to drink?" Stacy asked Avery.

"Do you have an amber ale on tap?"

"Sure thing. Nick? Coors in the bottle?"

"Please."

Avery glanced up the wall closest to her, decorated with a turn-of-the-century tire, three old Colorado license plates, three sets of warped leather boots, and two bras. The awkward collage was framed by colored Christmas lights.

"That has to be an interesting story," she nodded to the bras.

"They have good food," Nick said, an attempt to defend the décor.

"So I've been told." She turned to the menu that boasted World Famous Wrangled Steak, Wild West Black Beans, Creek Caught Trout and Buckaroo Burgers. Avery read the descriptions; most of the dishes had green chilies added to them. "I forgot how much the southwestern part of this state loves its green chilies."

The drinks were delivered by a smiling Stacy,. "You need another minute?"

"I hear the tortilla soup is good." Avery smiled back. "And a Buckaroo Burger with cheese, please."

"You got it. Nick?"

"Stew with the cornbread."

"Sounds good." She left to put in their order.

Avery corrected Nick's order, "The Mountain Man Stew."

He winked at her in reply. Avery dismissed the action by taking a sip of her beer and turning her attention to the patrons. Across the room she saw a familiar hourglass figure at the bar, only this time it was poured into jeans and a black and white flannel.

As if Lexi knew she was being watched, she turned in her stool and glared.

Avery waved, but mid-wave, Nick gently took her hand in his. The shock of his warm touch brought her attention back to him with pinpoint precision.

"Hey," he smiled.

"Showtime?" she asked.

"Something like that." He brushed his lips across her knuckles, sending heat pulsating through her body.

What the hell was happening?

Avery had been in this man's presence for less than an hour. Total. And he continued to affect her in physical ways that made her think she was going through early menopause, had been exposed to a gas leak, or was losing her grip on reality.

She swallowed audibly. "How do you think she gets into her clothes? She's squeezed into them so tight I keep thinking it looks like they are painted on."

Nick laughed while his fingers caressed her hand. "Your skin is so soft," he whispered the compliment.

"I wish you'd worn a tighter sweater." She meant for it to sound like a joke, but the ragged confession betrayed her.

"Oh really."

Avery blushed. She tugged to release her hand while Nick tightened his grip.

"You also look really nice tonight," he said.

Avery laughed, "You are..."

Sexy as hell. Full of it. Dangerous.

"I'm what?" He released her hand and sat back comfortably in his seat.

Avery figured they were already so awkwardly past the usual steps of getting to know each other, it didn't matter what she admitted to now.

"You're handsome as hell and that kiss was supposed to be a joke, but..." She faltered and hid behind a sip of beer. Then she pressed the cold glass to her cheek.

"I've been thinking about you a lot today too." A grin turned up the corners of his mouth. "And that kiss."

"So, the happy couple comes to dinner," Lexi drawled, pressing her hip against the table. Her body turned toward Nick, cutting off Avery.

"Lexi," Nick cautiously greeted.

"I heard your girlfriend is staying at The Rose. And she drove in *yesterday*." She tsked.

"It's really none of your business," Avery shot back.

Lexi lazily twisted her head to gaze down her nose at Avery.

"Do you practice these poses?" Avery asked. 'If I didn't know any better, I'd think you spend as much time practicing your poses in a mirror as you do squeezing yourself into your clothes."

Nick hid a laugh behind a cough.

Lexi's eyes narrowed. "Fine," she waved a hand at Nick, "you can have him. I heard women leave him all the time anyway. He must be defective."

Avery saw a flash of anger and hurt cross Nick's face as Lexi sauntered away.

Avery waited a beat. "Excuse me." She caught up to Lexi and grabbed her upper arm.

"Stop it."

"That wasn't very nice," Avery started. Lexi tried to pull free, but Avery kept her in place. "You know, I think you're lonely. Living in this town, you've convinced yourself all you've got going for you is your looks. And I'll admit you look great."

"Leave me alone," Lexi hissed.

"I'm just saying, you're not going to find your self-worth in some guy's bed. It's okay to respect yourself."

Lexi narrowed her gaze at Avery. "Aren't you trying to find your worth in Nick's bed?"

Avery glanced at Nick.

"I'm not sure exactly what that is yet. But sweetheart, I know who I am. That's the difference." She let go and patted Lexi on the shoulder. "You're better than this."

Avery smiled at Nick, and instead of returning to her chair, she walked to his, placed her hands on his shoulders, and leaned down to place a quick kiss on his lips.

An eruption of heat waylaid her 'quick' intentions.

Nick's hands found her hips and instant yearning spread hot throughout her body; just kissing this man and being touched by him ignited a longing she didn't understand.

He turned his head for better access to her, and Avery appreciatively tasted him; heat, faded mouthwash, and desire. She wanted more, but when a glass shattered somewhere behind her, she realized where she was and pulled away.

It took a second to gather her wits, and Nick's hands stayed on her hips, steadying her. She glanced over her shoulder and found Lexi was gone.

"I don't like mean girls," she explained as she returned to her seat and took a long pull of her beer.

"I might encourage Lexi to stick around if it means you're gonna keep kissing me." His voice was thick and gruff.

Avery was finding it difficult to breathe again.

"Here we go, folks." Stacy's delivery of food was a welcome distraction. The conversation turned to condiments, napkins, and tastes; easing the attraction that was difficult to keep at bay.

Avery thought she'd shaken off the residue of the kiss when Nick reiterated, "You know how good you look, right?"

Avery finished her bite, feeling victorious she didn't choke. "*You* know you've given me a lot of compliments, right?"

He shrugged. "I thought that's what a man is supposed to do on a date."

"You said this was just dinner."

"It was, until you kissed me like that." His eyes narrowed on her lips. In a whispered voice he verified, "This is definitely a date."

Chapter Seven

The lights of The Western dimmed. The loud crooning of country Christmas music had gone from corny to smooth and dreamy. That could also be the beer that had rubberized Avery's bones, *or* the way the Christmas lights made Nick's eyes sparkle, *or* how his interest in their small talk made her feel good about herself.

Of course, it could also be the elevation and snow and Christmas spirit playing tricks on her senses.

Stacy stopped by the table. "Any dessert tonight? We've got a Christmas bread pudding that'll knock your socks off."

Nick glanced at Avery. "Split one?"

She nodded. "Do you have decaf coffee?"

"Make it two," Nick added.

Avery yawned and stretched.

Nick tilted his head in response. "Am I that boring?"

"No, I'm that relaxed," she admitted.

Nick opened his mouth to say something but stopped.

"What?" Avery asked.

He cleared his throat. "What do you know about Ace Barber?"

Avery had a sneaking suspicion that wasn't what he wanted to ask.

"Well, I know he robbed banks from Colorado to California and was eventually killed in New Mexico."

Nick nodded. "He was also a good card player. They say he played cards against Doc Holliday and won. It was Holliday who gave him the nickname Ace."

Avery smiled. "What's it like, living in an old mining town that keeps the old west alive for tourists?"

"I don't live here," he said with a shrug.

"I know...but you visit often, right?"

Nick tilted his head. "I do."

"So where do you live?"

"Boulder."

"Are you upset at the possibility of being alone for Christmas?"

"No. I kinda like the peace and quiet."

A litany of questions begged to be asked. Instead, Avery swallowed them. "So Ace Barber stayed at the Allen House once?"

"Something like that."

"He didn't?"

Nick took a deep breath and blew it out, "Aunt G has this romantic notion, based on a handful of letters..."

"Concerning Ace Barber?"

Nick laughed, "I don't know you."

Avery frowned. She didn't know him either. But what did that have to do with the house?

"In your job, are you required to divulge all the information you find?" Nick asked.

Avery felt like they were getting further away from whatever it was he was trying to spit out. "Like attorney-client privilege sort of thing?"

Nick started again, "Imogene Allen was my great-great-aunt."

"So, Gladys married a Dugan?"

"Yes, she's an Allen by birth. She found some letters this past year. That's what she wants to show you. The letters tell a story that would... shine a light on Imogene's misfortunes. But I don't think it's worth dragging her through the mud just so her descendants can claim..."

Avery was intrigued. This hunk of a sexy man, who looked as comfortable over an engine as he did holding a porcelain cup, was concerned about a long dead relative's good name. There was more to him and more of a story here. And damned if Avery didn't want to know all of it.

She thought she understood his hesitation. "One of the issues that comes up in archeology classes is the right to unearth tombs and the bodies that are housed in them. The Greeks thought it was highly disrespectful to bother the dead. I never gave it much thought because I went into architectural history." She smiled. "When I started working in the field, I began to really love the stories. Some people are so open and excited to tell their family histories. However, there is also this generation born between the 1920s and 1940s, sometimes referred to as the silent generation."

Avery continued, "The silent generation are those grandmothers that always said 'leave it alone' when asked about their childhoods." She leaned forward, excitement in her eyes. "So, now there is a new question: When those 'silent generation' members of our family pass away, will we 'leave it alone'? If we find the letters and the photos, then we take DNA tests and find out the secrets anyway, what do we do? Is it a version of uncovering the dead that had asked to remain buried?"

Nick sighed, "So you understand."

"I think so."

Stacy delivered the coffee and a heaping plate of bread pudding drizzled with cream sauce. Avery wondered what made it Christmassy.

"Milk or sugar?" Stacy asked.

"Sugar for me, she takes hers black," Nick answered.

What was it about a man who knows such an inconsequential thing as how you like your coffee?

Nick caught Avery's gaze. "You okay?"

Avery nodded and hid behind a bite of the gooey dessert. It melted in her mouth. The sauce was white chocolate and there were dried cranberries in the bread pudding. "How did cranberry and white chocolate become synonymous with Christmas?" she asked.

In answer, Nick took an appreciative bite and Avery knew what he'd taste like now. "Christmas." She sighed.

She hadn't meant to say the word aloud. She straightened and licked her lips.

"Ancestors," she said too loudly, "ancestors have different views on their family stories. Some are worried, still carrying the shame or judgment on their own shoulders, while others love to tell the seedy tales."

Nick reached into his coat pocket, retrieving a faded envelope. He turned it over in his hands several times before handing it to Avery.

Chapter Eight

DECEMBER 24, 1894

My dearest love,
Be at peace.
The paper was delivered this morning. Two weeks late due to the avalanche
that prohibited the train entrance to town. People said receiving the mail
and goods was a Christmas Miracle, but for me, it brought only heartache.
You wrote me of your regret, but I never wrote you of my joy.
I have relived each and every moment of our time together a thousand times.
Each tender word, each look of longing, each touch. I would brandish my love
for you, regardless of the ruinous whispers, time and time again.
Your letter and funds found me. My mother sent me away, but you didn't
know that. How could you? I never told you I was with child. But when I
received your letter, the heartbroken sentiments...I might have to live without
you, but I would not give up the part of you I could keep. I admit the money
allowed me courage to run to my own freedom.
My dearest, I gave birth to a girl. I named her Annabella.
I lived for a time in the town of Rayton in the hopes I would catch word of
you. I worked for a strong woman who ran her own laundry. She instilled in
me strength of character I was not aware I had.

My mother passed away several months ago. My father's entire estate is now mine. I came home, my love. I brought our daughter to the place we lived, even though it was only a few beautiful fleeting moments, it was where we loved each other. I will raise our daughter among the ghosts of our love. Annabella will be four this spring. She plays at my feet as I write this letter. The house is warm with Christmas promises and hope. I am content to live for the memory of how you loved me and to give the best life I can to our daughter.

There is nowhere to send this letter, so I write it for myself.

Be at peace, my love. I am forever yours,

Imogene

Chapter Nine

"It doesn't say who the father is." Avery held the faded love letter reverently.

Nick took it back, folded it, and put it back in his coat jacket.

"Ready?" he asked, his manner strained. He stood and placed several bills on the table.

Avery slipped on her coat, betting the sudden change in Nick's demeanor had to do with the letter. Because if the father of Imogene's child was Ace Barber, then that meant...

She stared wide-eyed at Nick as she walked past him and the door he held open for her. When they were alone by the snowmobile she said, "You're a descendant of Ace Barber. If he's the father..."

He didn't answer, just handed her the helmet and put on his goggles, a definitive end to the conversation.

This time, when Avery situated herself on the back of the snowmobile and held lightly to his waist, he didn't modify the situation.

Nick pulled to a stop in front of The Rose. The snow had stopped, and moonlight tried to peek through a momentary clearing in the clouds. The Main Street lights looked brighter now.

Avery climbed off the snowmobile and handed Nick the helmet. "Well, thank you for dinner." She nodded, unable to think of anything else to say.

"Avery." Her name on his lips was a soft whisper as he climbed off the snowmobile.

"Nick." She matched his tone.

"No goodnight kiss?" he asked.

Her legs wobbled. She most definitely wanted a goodnight kiss, and if she were being honest, she wanted a good morning kiss as well. And a bunch in between.

Nick took her gloved hands in his, guided her arms to his shoulders as he inched closer. He playfully bumped her nose with his, then tilted his head and brushed his lips against hers. He pulled back, pausing, waiting, allowing their breath to mingle with the cold winter and a lifetime of stories before he sealed them.

Avery's stomach tightened. The kiss burned and flamed, a continuation of the building need that tormented her all day.

The sound of a snowmobile on another street brought her back to reality. She pulled away.

"What?" Nick asked, not letting her go.

"You're nice...and attractive..."

"You're nice and attractive too." He nipped at her lower lip.

She laughed, "I should go in. Maggie's probably watching in the shadows."

"Can I see you tomorrow?"

"Hell yes."

He raised an eyebrow at the answer. She pressed herself against him and let her pent-up need radiate out of her body and into his.

He backed her up, pressed her against the stone building and, with the new leverage, they began to feed off of each other. She felt the intense urge to run her hands over his back and feel his hair slide through her fingers, but the abundance of clothing made her laugh mid-kiss.

Nick blinked down at her in question.

"We're pretty overdressed." She held up her gloved hands. "I..." she cleared her throat, "...I should go."

He kissed her on the forehead. "Tomorrow," he promised.

Avery slipped out of his grasp and unevenly walked to the door. She glanced once more at Nick before turning the handle.

Nothing happened.

Shit.

"What?" Nick asked.

She tried again. "I think it's locked."

"Sometimes these old doors stick." He tried to help, jiggling the handle. "Where's your key?"

"Maggie only gave me a key to my room." Oh no, had she locked Avery out? "What time is it?"

Nick looked at his watch. "It's 11:15."

She bit her lip and looked through the glass door into the dark hallway.

"You can stay with me."

Avery didn't want to wake Maggie up, but after the exchange between her and Nick and the sexy-ass way he whispered that offer, she probably *should* wake the woman up.

"Avery."

"I think I should call Maggie."

"I think you should stay with me."

She gave an unladylike grunt. "That's not a good idea." A harmless flirtation was one thing, but the undeniable building need for him made the idea of a sleepover an obvious minefield.

"I'll be a perfect gentleman."

That was a disappointing prospect too.

Avery glanced at the door; she could get in that hotel if she wanted. She looked at Nick, into those eyes sparkling. *Aw hell.* There was definitely another door she wanted to get into at the moment.

"Okay."

Chapter Ten

A *woman has needs. People meet every day and jump in bed together and scratch those itches. I mean, Nick flirted back. He's* the one *who kissed you all hot and heavy, so why the hell not rip that damn sweater off and get your hands on him?*

She talked herself into and out of Nick's bed a dozen times by the time they arrived at the house.

It had begun snowing. Again. The soft glow of the Christmas lights on the house made the large flakes glitter as they twirled down around them.

And Avery was back on the pro-jump-in-bed mood once again. She pushed off the snowmobile before Nick could help.

The motorized whir of several snowmobiles was heard before the lights and vehicles themselves came cruising around the corner.

Nick gave a frustrated grunt.

"Who's that?" Avery asked as she watched four snowmobiles do cookies in front of the house.

"It's Lexi and her friends."

Avery corrected the distance she had placed between her and Nick, linked her arm in his, and waved.

He chuckled. "C'mon. I'll show you your room and we can have a nightcap."

In the house, Nick pointed Avery to the guest room, then took her into his aunt and uncle's room. They both stood awkwardly in front of the dresser.

"I was at a friend's house when I was a kid, and we found his mom's vibrator in her drawer," Nick blushed. "I've been reluctant to go through people's drawers since then."

Avery laughed. "I would too."

"Aunt G would be okay with you borrowing her clothes."

Avery glanced sideways at Nick. She could ask him for one of his shirts. The idea dried her throat and quickened her breath. She quickly pulled open the top drawer, grateful to find it had yoga pants and T-shirts.

They both let out an audible sigh of relief.

Avery grabbed the first shirt and pair of yoga pants.

"I'll meet you downstairs." Nick left her.

She changed and realized she was a few inches taller than Aunt G. The clothes weren't tight, but the pants hugged Avery's calves and the bright pink shirt that said 'Come classy, leave trashy' barely touched the waistband of the pants.

"This shirt is not an omen," she told her reflection.

Her reflection winked in reply.

She placed her other clothes in the guest room and found Nick in the kitchen. He'd changed into a pair of red flannel pants and T-shirt. A tight shirt. The kind she wished he'd worn to dinner.

He looked up and broke into laughter when he saw her. "Aunt G loves Hawaii and shirts with bad puns."

She looked down. "I'm suddenly curious about the others."

"Would you like a drink?"

"Do you have mulled wine?"

He raised an eyebrow. "I don't think so. It's whiskey or Baileys."

"Baileys, please."

She yawned and was thankful for the bright florescent light of the warm kitchen, which released a valve on the evening's building tension.

"So, tomorrow everyone will know the *horrific* truth of our torrid affair," she joked.

"They will."

"Do you think Maggie locked me out on purpose?"

Nick nodded. "I wouldn't put it past her."

"This town..."

"Do you know they get about three thousand visitors a day during the summer months?"

"What? No."

He nodded, situating himself opposite Avery. "All tourists want to eat in an old-time saloon, have pictures taken in front of the cool old buildings, and hear the stories of the famous outlaws and soiled doves who once walked these streets."

"It's a need to physically touch history."

Nick tilted his head and smiled at Avery's statement, then continued, "There are no known descendants of Billy the Kid. Those who think they are want to dig up his remains and have DNA tests done."

"They aren't even sure it's Billy who's buried in that grave."

"Could you imagine, if someone had an irrefutable item of Billy the Kid? Like a lock of hair?" Nick gestured to the worn green shoe box he'd brought to the table.

A current of excitement radiated through Avery, "Can I...?"

Nick hesitated, then nodded.

Avery wiped her hands on her pants and gingerly pulled out three letters and a handkerchief. Nick pointed to the letter on top. "That one first."

Chapter Eleven

Dearest,

I can still taste your skin on my lips. Is it dishonorable of me to start a letter so boldly? I cannot help it. You took me in, you mended my wounds, but moreover, you mended my very soul and stole my heart. I am yours, always. I write a few lines from the muck of a hovel, but in my mind, I am in your parlor, holding you in my arms, dancing in the sliver of moonlight slipping through that front window.

Conditions being what they are, I'm glad you didn't come with me. Life on the trail isn't for the likes of a woman with your upbringing. You deserve better than me, yet I still love you with my whole heart and soul, and wish I could have you for myself.

I write you love letters that I can't send and I write you love letters in my sleep. This time, I will attempt to post this one. Authorities be damned. I just hope it doesn't bring you trouble.

Here is a locket of my hair. You gave me a locket of yours, and I keep it close to my heart. It sustains me through the dark nights. I thought you might want the favor returned.

Don't worry about me, my love. Whatever happens, I brought it on myself. Always, your loving servant,
Charles Edward Barber

DECEMBER 22, 1891

Chapter Twelve

Avery's eyes darted to the handkerchief, her throat dry. "Is that..."

"A locket of hair."

"His?"

"Gladys sent a sample of it, along with her DNA, to a lab in Denver." He cleared his throat. "Did you know, Wild Bill Hickock's love letter was auctioned for almost two hundred thousand dollars? Gladys told me."

Avery was curious about the concern in his voice, "What is it?"

"I was raised by a single mom, in a time when it wasn't a bad thing to be, but still..." He took a sip of his drink. "I just wonder, if this gets out, will Imogene be reduced to the woman knocked up by Ace Barber? Just so this house can have a plaque that says *Ace Barber slept here*?"

"Should the dead be left to rest?" Avery asked.

He nodded.

"What does your aunt think?"

"That it's romantic."

Avery ran a finger over the edge of the letter, "He robbed two trains and several banks."

Nick nodded. "Supposedly gave a lot of money to orphanages, but also killed two men."

"In barroom brawls?" Avery couldn't remember the circumstances.

"Does it matter why one man kills another?"

"I suppose it doesn't." She folded the letter and placed it back in the envelope.

"The next letter is to her mother, after she ran away from the convent. She admits Ace Barber is the child's father."

"And the other one?" She gestured to the largest envelope that looked the right size for sending money to someone.

Nick opened it and handed the short note to Avery.

My darling love,
I have failed you.
It turns out that sometimes, love isn't enough and difficult circumstances always prevail.
This will help you start a new life.
Your eternal loving servant,
Charles Edward Barber

The echo of the grandfather clock accompanied the finished drinks and the end of Imogene and Ace Barber's tragic love story.

Nick tapped the table. "I suppose that's enough history for one night." He carried the glasses to the sink.

Avery stood and eyed the stairs but called out for him instead: "Nick."

He glanced over his shoulder from the sink. "You okay?"

She shook her head.

Nick narrowed his gaze, took a few steps toward her, and Avery felt her knees wobble with relief when she saw her own want and need reflected in his eyes.

She gestured between them. "I don't know what this is, but..."

"But..." he repeated, taking another few steps toward her.

"I'm very...interested."

He raised an eyebrow. "Interested?"

Avery was losing her momentum. She swallowed. "Aren't you?"

"God, yes."

They collided against each other. Nick emitted a low growl as lips and hands took possession. Shockwaves of heat accompanied the full, open-mouth kiss. Avery was intoxicated by the taste of him; whiskey and want.

Nick guided her into the living room, which was dimly lit by tree lights. They agonizingly broke the kiss long enough to discard clothing, trying their best to keep connected through kisses and caresses until they'd rid themselves of all barriers. Avery stepped back to take in his naked form, salivating at the view, but she wasn't given much time; he wrapped a hand around her waist and pulled her against him and nipped at her lower lip. She pressed herself against his hardness and moaned at how his rough, warm chest felt like heaven. She couldn't get enough, so she seized his mouth once more. His arms multiplied, warm hands soothed her back, and reached between them to cup her breasts.

Nick grabbed a blanket off the sofa and tossed it on top of the rug before lowering Avery down. He began a trail of kisses down her neck, breasts, stomach. His hands lusciously following the trail he made.

Avery writhed beneath him. She needed more. She shamelessly wanted him, wanted his weight, his heat, "Nick."

He gazed up, his eyes glazed over with wanton yearning. She grinned and he resumed his exploration of her until his tongue, rich and velvet, found her center; she arched, a new fire of longing building.

Blood rose, pounding between her eardrums; ancient rhythms of unrestrained fervor. Her whole body lurched off the floor, her thighs squeezed, and she felt the fire in her center scream its height and release.

But it still wasn't enough; panting she cried out his name. Nick knew what she wanted and when he climbed back over her body, a carnal grin in place, she knew he'd give her what she craved. He kissed her possessively and she licked his lips, the heady sensation of tasting her own heat.

"One sec," he groaned and moved to his discarded jeans.

Avery blinked, confused, until she saw he'd retrieved a condom.

He returned, ran his hands up her calves to her thighs, placed a chaste kiss on her stomach, then cupped her breasts, kissed her neck, and finally found her lips once more.

She reached between them, her first opportunity to take him in her hands. He moaned and she guided him into her, unable to wait. He slipped into her and Avery's body radiated with relief of fullness.

They gazed wide-eyed at each other, a pause, a flash, a recognition. A breath separated them, a breath that became erratic and urgent. The desire fragmented and they became a tangle of fierce, animalistic moans and thrusts, both working inside a whirlwind of carnal, possessive heat toward a common end.

Another explosion of light and sound. Avery sobbed, shocked at the second orgasm Nick rode the wave of her fulfillment, quickening his pace until his release ended with her name spilling from his lips.

Chapter Thirteen

The gray dawn light was muted by sheer curtains hung over the window, but as Avery blinked away the sleep, she could still make out the snowfall.

She was suddenly feeling very positive about being snowed in. She stretched, her limbs feeling exhausted and lovely.

The bed they moved to at some point was empty, but how far could Nick have gone?

Throughout the night they fluctuated between exhausted naps and reignited passions. Accommodating each path until they were sated.

Avery ran her hands over her body, unable to keep a smile at bay; she still had 'it.' When Todd admitted he'd been cheating on her, Amy had demanded Avery jump into bed with someone else, to "get rid of Todd's residue."

Avery didn't, however. Todd stole her ability to see herself as sexy or worthy. Asshole.

But Amy had been right.

Avery felt sexy and wanted and satisfied in a way Todd had never accomplished.

She reached for the borrowed clothes and laughed. "You know I'm leaving trashy," she told the shirt.

Coffee was ready in the kitchen, but Nick wasn't there. She looked out the window, toward the barn. A path had been cleared through the new snow and the door was open.

Cup in hand, she wandered to the living room. Heat rose in her cheeks. She could still feel Nick's phantom caresses.

The Christmas tree centered in the bay window was fashionably decorated with gold, silver, and red, but upon closer inspection, Avery found many of the ornaments were Hawaiian themed.

She turned back toward the kitchen when Ace Barber's words returned. *I am in your parlor, holding you in my arms, dancing in the sliver of moonlight slipping through that front window.*

From the little that Avery could piece together, Imogene lived in this home with her mother. Her father had passed away. But why was she alone when Ace Barber found her? *You mended my wounds.* That would not have been an overnight visit.

But her own overnight desires took precedence, and she wanted more. The silent admission started a throbbing in her center.

She slipped on snow boots and a jacket and trudged the cleared path to the barn. It wasn't Pearl Jam this time but classical music. She stepped into the garage and into an oven.

Had it been this hot yesterday?

Yesterday. She just met Nick yesterday and she'd jumped into bed with him.

So what? It was worth it.

Nick was working on the engine of the old truck again, his hair mussed, his flannel shirt flapping open and a light sheen on his forehead. Avery's stomach tightened.

He stood up and the shirt hung open, revealing his taught, strong, sculpted chest. She sucked in a breath. "Geez."

Nick smiled. "Morning."

She had to clear her throat to find her voice. "It's so hot in here."

He nodded. "That's why I keep the door open, the heater has two settings. Off and fires of hell."

She tried to hold his gaze, but she couldn't help the sexy picture he made standing by that damn truck. She'd run her hands all over that body. And that body had felt so damn good under her caress.

"Breakfast?" she blurted the word with more force than intended.

He tilted his head. "What are you offering?"

Her cheeks burned. She was too aware of him when he was at a distance. Closer, when there was a physical connection, she was better, so she corrected the problem.

When she reached him, she placed a shaky hand on his chest; his breath caught. She pushed the shirt off his shoulders and splayed both hands across his broad chest.

This was exactly what she wanted.

She met his gaze. He was burning for her again, and she was afire for him. On her tiptoes she placed a chaste kiss on his neck, releasing their ever-present desire.

He slipped off her jacket and pushed his hands under her shirt. He claimed her lips just as the very loud ringing of a phone screamed through the garage.

Avery's whole body reacted to the air-raid siren-sound. "What the hell?!"

Another screaming ring.

Nick hurried toward the earsplitting distraction, explaining, "Uncle Andy's hearing is going. He had a supercharged ringer installed. Hello?"

Avery sighed at the silence and leaned her hip against the truck bumper.

"Hey, Aunt G." He began his one-sided conversation, "Yes, I met with her yesterday." He winked at Avery. "I did show her the letters."

After a few moments, he waved her over.

"Aunt G," he covered the receiver, "do you mind talking to her?" Avery glanced at the clock across the room: 9:30. That was a respectable time to be visiting, right? She nodded, so Nick said, "She's actually here right now. How about you talk to her?"

They traded places, only Nick moved behind Avery, brushing a kiss on her neck that was left in offering to him when she held the phone.

"Hello, Mrs. Dugan." She pushed Nick's attentions away. "Yes, Nick has shown me the house and the receipts. You've kept such pristine records and done a wonderful job with the restoration."

His hand snaked down her sides and teased the band of the pants, so she swatted him again.

"Yes, he showed me the letters. It's a very interesting story you have."

His hands stayed on the outside of her clothing, but he was running his fingers up the inside of her thighs. She turned and dislodged his hands and gave him a silent warning.

"Can't blame me," he whispered.

She narrowed her gaze as Gladys expressed how glad she was Avery hadn't died in the avalanche. "Oh, thank you. If I may, Nick told me that you've sent your DNA to be tested against the hair sample." That stilled Nick's attentions. "I think there is more research to be done on the Ace Barber story. I would suggest that for this tax year, we continue the paperwork to register the property in the State Register of Historic Places. That way, you'll be able to claim the Historic Property Tax Credit. Then you have time to hear back from the testing facility and we can do some more research before we attempt to designate the house with landmark status." She took a deep breath and aimed a questioning look at Nick. "What do you think?"

He placed a chaste kiss on her forehead. When his aunt marveled at the idea, Avery gave Nick a thumbs up.

"Yes, ma'am. I hope we can meet in person soon as well. I will file the paperwork by close of day tomorrow and we'll go from there." Avery hung up the phone and told Nick, "I had the idea this morning."

He slipped his hands around her waist and pulled her toward him. "What do you want for breakfast?"

She raised an eyebrow. "Isn't it obvious?"

Chapter Fourteen

Avery wanted to go to the archive before she headed back to The
Rose. Nick offered to take her, but the one-block snowmobile
drive was prolonged by his detour to the end of town and his
slow parade back up Main Street. Avery rolled her eyes when Nick waved
to the group coming out of a restaurant and slowed to wave at a group of
women coming out of a coffee shop.

When they arrived at the archive, she slipped off the snowmobile, took
off her helmet and asked, "Did you have fun?"

"Oh yeah."

"Well, I can now add 'snowmobile ride of shame' to my bucket list."
She handed the helmet to him, "I'll...see you later." She didn't know what
to say or how to leave him. But she had so much work to do, and if he
were hanging around, she wouldn't get any of it done.

He slipped the goggles on top of his head, fixed that intense green gaze
at her, and crooked a finger, enticing her closer; the whole action caused
her abdomen to quiver.

When she was close enough, he snaked his arm around her waist. She
melted into him. "What's goin' on, darlin'?"

She took a deep breath. "This...between us...it's too fast. But good...
but so different."

"Monumental?" he asked while brushing the back of his hand against her cheek.

"Does it scare you?" It took a lot to ask the question.

Nick nodded, "Though it's kind of exciting."

"That's one word for it." She anchored herself in his eyes.

His lips just a fraction from hers, he whispered, "Will I see you tonight?"

"If I get my work done."

"Then please, get your work done." He sealed the request with a kiss.

"Good morning," Elizabeth drawled the greeting. She wasn't waiting on the front porch, but she had the look of someone who had definitely been watching from the window.

"Thanks for agreeing to meet today."

"You called from the Allen House." Elizabeth's grin widened.

"Well, a lot's happened in the past twenty-four hours." *Talk about understatements.*

Elizabeth clapped. "Tell me *everything!*"

"No." Avery hung up her jacket and then peeked back. "He makes my damn spine tingle."

"Oh, yes." Elizabeth beamed.

Avery shook herself. "Do you have a picture of Ace Barber?"

Elizabeth raised an eyebrow.

"My legs feel like Jell-O."

"Is that Nick's fault or Ace Barber's?"

"It's the snow." Avery fell into an overstuffed chair. "I have no idea what's happening. Elizabeth, if I tell you a story, you're going to have to keep it to yourself for a while."

Elizabeth sat on the edge of the other chair. "I know I come across as excitable, but I swear, when it comes to the work, I can be discreet." She held up three fingers. "Girl Scout Promise. I won't say a word until you say I can. Now tell me everything that's happened in the past twenty-four hours."

"Actually, this might be Maggie's fault, since she locked me out." Avery scrubbed her face with her hands. "Do you believe in love at first sight?"

"Are we talking Ace Barber or Nick?"

"Both?"

Elizabeth nodded. "Well, yes. I do believe in love at first sight." She sat back. "I think it's lust and attraction first, like there is an acknowledgment of similarities, on an animalistic level."

"But that isn't always enough," Avery said.

"Not always." Elizabeth gave a dry laugh. "I can only speak from experience, and I know how good that first blush of passion can be." She winked. "But after that, life happens. There are circumstances and just the day in and day out of life that needs to be dealt with. And sometimes, something more can be created on top of that original passion."

"And other times?"

Elizabeth shrugged. "Sometimes it doesn't work. But *that's* where our growth and resilience come from."

Avery laughed. "Are you really a sage old woman disguised as...?" She waved toward Elizabeth's Ramones shirt and pink rimmed glasses.

Elizabeth grinned. "I am. But you know what the fun part is? When love finds a way."

Again, the words of Ace Barber echoed: *It turns out that sometimes, love isn't enough.*

"I don't think I'm going to be able to sleep tonight," Elizabeth said as she opened the *Book of Famous Colorado Outlaws* to the warped sepia photo of Ace Barber.

They had mapped out the dates of the letters and Ace Barber's known movements, which helped them to develop a direction of inquiry.

Avery tried to use the *Colorado Historic Newspaper* database, but the storm continued to interfere with a reliable connection, so she studied what poorly organized papers the archive had.

It was well past three when Avery reluctantly left Elizabeth. They were both hungry and had a mountain of work before them.

"Want me to call Nick to pick you up?"

Avery shook her head. "Do you mind dropping me off at The Rose?" She wanted to finish her work, take a shower, and get her clothes. If she saw Nick, she wasn't sure she would use her time diligently.

Chapter Fifteen

Avery fell asleep on the desk after fighting technology for the better part of the evening, all intentions of calling Nick gone.

She smoothed her hair as she made her way to breakfast. When she reached the bottom step, she found that the snow had stopped falling. That was something. She wanted to head over to Nick's, but she'd missed dinner and the home-cooked smells interrupted any other needs.

The clink of dishes and sounds of breakfast conversation caused an eruption of nerves. She held her breath as she turned the corner, worried that somehow everyone would know the girl who survived an avalanche had just had the best mind-blowing sex in the soon-to-be-historic Allen House.

"Good morning, honey," Maggie was nearby, "I believe your table is ready." She winked.

Avery followed the carafe she pointed with. Her table was set with a tall, broad-smiling, green-eyed man with dark hair.

He stood and Avery awkwardly blurted, "I fell asleep."

"I figured, I was worn out myself." He took her hands in his, pulled her close enough so he could brush a kiss on her cheek, lingering.

Avery leaned into him, then thought better of the fodder they were offering the gossips of Eden.

"What's for breakfast?" she asked as she sat down.

"I missed you last night," Nick replied just as Maggie walked up to the table and poured coffee and a refill.

"Will I see you two tonight at the dance?"

Nick sat back with a smile. "Well, Mags, you beat me to it, but that's why I came looking for Avery."

Maggie clapped. "Oh, I had a feeling about you two."

Avery hoped her blush wasn't too obvious.

"That's just wonderful. I'll go get your breakfast. This morning Edwin's just serving country potato scramble."

Once Maggie was gone, Avery said, "I don't think she'll ever admit to locking me out." She cradled her cup, studying Nick.

"Will you go with me tonight?"

"Probably." The idea of being in his arms again was one of the top ten reasons she would go. She licked her lips. "I missed you too."

"Good, because you've got me all tangled up."

"Well..." She hid her blush behind a sip of coffee.

"Did you find anything interesting at the archive?" He changed tactics.

"Yes." She sat forward. "Have you ever looked up Imogene's obituary?"

"I don't think Aunt G's gotten that far."

"Nick, her tombstone is engraved, 'Beloved wife, mother, and grand-mother.' Who did she marry?"

Nick frowned. "I guess we don't know the whole story."

"You know, we don't know each other's stories either," she pointed.

Nick shot that easy smile at her. "I live in Boulder. I'm a physical ther-apist. I tore my ACL sophomore year of college. My PT changed my life, and I loved how he helped so many people in pain. I switched majors and never looked back." He gestured to Avery. "You live in Denver. Work for..."

"A historical architecture firm that reports to the National Park Service."

"A.k.a, you love old buildings."

"I love old buildings," she agreed. "You care about others' feelings, even if they're almost 200 years old."

634

"And I love Christmas."

"Really?" That idea shocked Avery. "What do you like most?"

"The smells. Everywhere you go smells fresh baked. Don't you like Christmas?"

Avery shrugged. "Well...this year, I wasn't going to celebrate, much less *like* Christmas. Last Christmas Eve, my boyfriend...I found him in bed with another woman. It had been going on for months."

Nick cleared his throat. "But now?"

After a moment she said, "The idea of liking Christmas again is growing on me."

"Oh really?"

"It's the snow," she waved, "I like the snow. And the precarious situation it can put a person in."

Nick's voice was syrup smooth: "I cannot wait to get you into another precarious situation."

Avery imagined crawling over the table and climbing into his lap. Her heart slammed against her chest and she had difficulty drawing a full breath and she loved it.

"Here we are." Maggie arrived with two plates, the heat rising into the air matching the heat at the table.

"Thank you," Avery croaked.

It took a lot of deep breathing and another interruption of Maggie refilling coffee for the temperature to normalize.

"What do you need to do today?" Nick asked.

"I'm almost done with my work. I just need to get a signal long enough to send the final attachments. Make sure everything goes through. Then I suppose I need to get ready for a dance."

Nick nodded. "I'll pick you up at five?"

"Snowmobile?"

"No, we'll take the truck."

"Where is the dance held?"

"There's a large barn just as you come into town. It was refurbished as an all-purpose hall years ago." He continued, "It's a potluck, so we'll eat there as well."

Avery nodded. She couldn't think of anything else to say, because what she really wanted was action. Actionable moves that ended with her and Nick tangled up in sheets and sweat.

Chapter Sixteen

The large, refurbished old barn was warm and welcoming. White twinkle lights cascaded down the walls of the barn, and each exposed beam was wrapped with lights. Next to the stage, a majestic seven-foot Christmas tree twinkled. Round tables encircled the dance floor, covered with a mixture of red, white, and green tablecloths; all with evergreen centerpieces. A line of tables had been set up against the far-right wall, and people filling their plates blocked the view of the food. Christmas music was being played over an impressive sound system, and a handful of couples twirled around the dance floor.

Nick held a foil-covered casserole dish provided by his aunt's freezer as he directed Avery through the room. They'd already deposited their coats by the front door where a rack with hangers was set.

Maggie loaned Avery a flattering deep maroon, knee length, lace dress with cap sleeves. She knew just how flattering it was when Nick, once again waiting at the bottom of the stairs, couldn't find his voice for several moments when he first saw her.

Of course, his freshly shaved face and slicked brown hair set off the white button-down shirt visible under his unzipped jacket. The top button, tantalizingly open.

Nick steered Avery toward the food table. He nodded at a few people in greeting before they were met by a squeal.

Avery smiled at Elizabeth who exclaimed, "You look so nice," then she gestured to the tall lanky man grinning next to her. "This is my husband, Aidan. Aidan, this is Avery."

Avery shook the man's hand, followed by Nick, who greeted him, "Staying out of trouble, Big Aid?"

Avery raised an eyebrow. Aidan rolled his eyes. "Nick and I go way back, so when you want to hear all the good dirt, come sit by me."

Bing Crosby began crooning "White Christmas" and a few people applauded the song choice.

"If you'll excuse us?" Nick took Avery's hand and led her to the dimly lit dance floor. It was easy to blend into the crowd of couples.

She slid into his embrace, pressed against his body as they swayed together. Never had a Christmas song sounded so winsome or so damn sexy.

The dance floor stayed full all evening. As if the magic of the Christmas season and the snowy situation a group of people found themselves in was a blessing. Avery was truly feeling that way.

When the DJ played "Let It Snow," the crowd gave an uproar of agreement. Nick taught Avery how to foxtrot to the song.

"Who taught you how to dance?" she asked.

"When you continuously visit an old west town...you pick a few things up," he explained.

They broke to eat dinner, sitting with Elizabeth and Aidan. The conversation was stuttered, as people stopped by to shake hands with Nick, ask after his family, and be introduced to the woman who survived the avalanche.

"Should I start charging for autographs?" she muttered to Elizabeth.

Another slow song began, and Nick took Avery once more into his arms.

"You like to dance?" she said, more of an observation.

"I like the opportunity to get you in my arms," he whispered in her ear.

Avery liked feeling his full length pressed against her body, liked the smell of him. The evening was intoxicating; she even liked the laughter and conversation that mingled in the rafters, which added to the enchantment.

"Do you think they felt this way?" Avery asked.

"Who?"

"Imogene and Ace? That letter about holding each other in the moonlight..."

"Yeah, I think it was something like this." Nick kissed Avery's forehead, and she smiled up at him. "Stay for Christmas."

"I don't think I have a choice." Avery smiled.

"Pretend you do. Would you stay with me?"

She would.

It was as simple as that. She wanted to stay in the warm arms of hope and promise and this man. She wanted a Christmas that blurred the remnants of last year from her memory.

"Yes." The answer barely out, his lips were on hers, sealing the promise. Avery smiled into his mouth and let all the hours they'd been apart echo in that sultry kiss.

Nick pulled away. "C'mon."

"What?"

"I've got to get you out of here before I take you right here on the dance floor."

The confession coiled through Avery. She gripped Nick's arm to steady herself.

He snuck them along the dark edges of the crowd, hastily gathered their coats, and helped her into the cold truck. The moon preened, finally visible after so many days of snow.

Nick turned the key and reached for Avery's hand as the truck warmed up. Eagerness and lust became visible, shallow breaths in the faint moonlight.

"Nick." His name was a plea on her lips.

He smiled and drove as quickly and safely as he could.

After he slammed the truck into park, he jumped out and retrieved Avery, carrying her, laughing, through the snow to the front door. He took his time, allowing her body to slip down his own, slowly. He captured her mouth, but the urgency was too great. He unceremoniously propelled them inside and it became desperation and fervor. Speed was crucial—it had been too long since they'd been joined. Knowing how good they were together, knowing what was coming and wanting to tease it out and be teased were at odds.

Avery pushed clothing out of the way until there was nothing between them but exquisite urgency. Nick navigated furniture and stairs, hurried them onto his bed, donned a condom, and amid moans of desperation, they joined together, their cries of relief a chorus that echoed into the night.

Chapter Seventeen

Laughter from the kitchen woke Avery. She froze, listening as her eyes adjusted to the morning light.

More laughter.

Shit.

She clutched the sheet to her chest and recalled her dress was discarded somewhere downstairs.

"Morning, sexy." Nick stood with a coffee cup in hand.

"Who's here?"

"Aunt G and Uncle Andy are home. They opened the pass north of here early this morning."

"Nick, I don't have clothes," she whispered.

"I hid them when I saw the car drive up."

That didn't solve her problem. "Nick..."

He held up a finger, and Avery stared wide-eyed at the door he left open.

He returned with clothes just as his aunt called for him.

"They know you're here. Don't be embarrassed. Come down and have breakfast." A wink and he was gone.

She looked at the clothes he grabbed and barked out a laugh. "Don't be embarrassed?"

When Avery walked into the kitchen, the talking stopped. Nick's eyes widened as he read the T-shirt he picked out, a bouquet of plumeria flowers above large letters insisting the reader 'GET LEI'D.'

Everyone laughed, including Avery. She pulled at the hem of the shirt and curtsied. When she righted herself she said, "Mr. and Mrs. Dugan, it's lovely to meet you. This isn't how I imagined it would be."

Gladys had short, straight gray hair, fashionably slicked into place. She had a sparkle in her eye, reminiscent of Nick's. A family trait, it seemed. She pulled Avery in for a hug. "It's so nice to meet you."

Nick sat next to Avery at breakfast, his knee touching hers under the table. Gladys and Andrew talked about their unexpected visit with friends the past few days.

Naturally, conversation turned to the Ace Barber excitement.

"I was so excited to find the letters," Gladys explained. "They were tucked away in the attic. Andy and I found them when we were remodeling this year." She shook her head. "We knew we were going to have the house registered for the property taxes, but I just thought if the hair was tested and you saw the letters...I don't know why it didn't dawn on me to do more research." She laughed, "I've lived in this town long enough to know how things work."

"You found out you might be a descendant of the infamous Ace Barber, that is pretty exciting," Avery soothed.

"It is," Gladys sighed and then shook her head. "Avery, we're going to have a few guests tonight for Christmas Eve. Nick told us you are staying and we're thrilled to have you. I don't think we've seen him smile or laugh this much since Evelyn left."

"I haven't gotten around to my sob story just yet," he interjected.

Gladys' eyes darted to her nephew. "Nicky, I'm..."

"It's okay." He tapped the table with his hands and turned his attention to Avery. "How about we go get your things from The Rose?"

Nick parked in front of The Rose but didn't turn off the truck.

"Do you want me to run in and get my things?" Avery asked.

He licked his lips. "I was married for three years. To Evelyn. I found her cheating on me and we got divorced."

Avery nodded; she knew from personal experience the worst thing she could do was tilt her head and exclaim, 'Oh, no.' She hated when it happened to her, and she wasn't about to wax over Nick's pain with a paltry exclamation.

She waited for him to continue.

"As you know, it's not fun to get your heart broken. A few weeks after we separated, she found out she was pregnant. So, in the storm of angrily divvying up his and hers items, there was a paternity test to wait for. I was not the father." He said blandly, "She married the guy. It's been two years. I've had a few dates, but..." He shrugged.

"They're awful, aren't they?" Avery asked.

Nick gave a dry laugh. "Did your friends ever set you up?"

"Yes." Avery mocked, "He's soooo nice, you two are *perfect* for each other."

Nick nodded. "Do you wonder what your friends actually think of you? Based on the people they set you up with?"

"Yes! For some reason, I went on three awful blind dates, then decided eating ice cream and watching the History channel was a lot more fun."

Nick studied Avery. "It's hard to trust again."

"It is," she agreed.

"But...whatever this is between us..."

Avery let a smile slip. "You know, Boulder's only thirty minutes from Denver."

"Exactly." Nick took Avery's hand in his and placed a soft kiss on her palm. "Be my girlfriend?"

"For real this time?"

"Hell yes."

"Avery!" Elizabeth entered the Allen House excitedly. She handed over a plate of cookies and her coat, then waved a file folder triumphantly in the air. "I have something to show you. All of you. It's why we came early."

Aidan shook hands with Nick and his uncle as Elizabeth gave Gladys a side hug and ushered her to the kitchen table.

Elizabeth took a stabilizing breath before she pulled several copies of a newspaper article out of the folder.

In the photo was a couple and a young child, standing in a happy triad. Below the photo was the announcement: Miss Imogene Parke united in marriage to Mr. E. Allen of Eden, Colorado.

"May 20, 1895

It is with great pleasure that Mr. Edward Allen, a recent transplant to Eden as well as the owner and operator of the new Eden Barber Shop, announces his marriage to Miss Parke. The marriage took place at noon, Friday last, at the Eden Courthouse and was presided over by The Honorable J. M. Clay.

Miss Parke was attired in a simple gown of blue organdie over white satin. Best Man, William S. Lake, and Maid of Honor, Nellie Plume, stood as witnesses over the vows. Miss Imogene's daughter, Annabella, was also present and acted as ring bearer."

Gladys gave an excited cry and hurried from the room.

Elizabeth pulled out a copy of the photo of Ace Barber and laid it next to the wedding announcement. "It's him."

Avery leaned forward with Nick at her side. They studied the similarities of the two men, though it was difficult to determine based on the warped newspaper photo.

"He became a barber?" Nick laughed.

"Here!" Gladys yelled. "I have it!"

She was carefully unwrapping old paper to reveal the same photo as the one in the newspaper, only this one was pristine.

She tenderly placed it on the table. Avery moved the photo of Ace Barber next to the photo.

"Oh my God," Gladys gasped. "He was right here, under everyone's noses. And no one knew."

Avery turned to Nick, "He came back for her."

He reached out and cupped the side of her face, shaking his head in disbelief. She took his hand in hers and brushed a kiss against his knuckles.

Elizabeth elbowed Avery. "I told you, the most fun is when love finds a way."

THE END

A Gorgeous Cowboy Christmas

BY GRETA ROSE WEST

Romance author Juneau Moonlight moves to snowy Wisper, Wyoming looking for a fresh start, but instead she finds a mysterious stranger dressed in Wranglers, a flannel shirt, and a black-as-sin cowboy hat who's bound and determined to be her endgame. Join her, Max, and some of Wisper's warmhearted characters for a country Christmas to remember.

About the Author

If you liked *A Gorgeous Cowboy Christmas*, visit gretarosewest.com for more. You can read *Burned*, the first book in the bestselling Cade Ranch series, for free!
Or join Greta's newsletter to hear about new releases and all the hot cowboys you could want.

Greta Rose West was a floundering artsy flake until cowboy Jack Cade showed up, knocking on the door of her brain, and then pounding on it, and then he just plain kicked it down. She lives in NW Indiana with her husband and her two precocious kitties, Geoff Trouble and Sally Mae Midnight. When she's not writing, she's reading and devouring music. She enjoys indie films no one else likes, and her favorite food is Aver's Veggie Revival pizza.

Chapter One

Juneau

The man standing at my front door cleared his throat when I opened it. "You Ms. Moonlight?"

Bright Wyoming sun was blinding me at seven in the freaking morning, reflecting off the foot and a half of fresh snow on the ground, and I shielded my eyes with my hand. Someone had already cleared my sidewalk and driveway, but I had no clue who it could've been since I hadn't yet met my new neighbors.

"Juneau Moonlight?"

"Yes?"

"That really your name?"

"Uh... Who are you?"

He rubbed his bare hands together against the cold. "I'm Max. You requested a quote on some builds?"

"Huh?"

"You wanted a quote for some carpentry. Somethin' about a kitchen island?"

"Oh, right. Wait. You do know it's seven in the morning, don't you?"

"Sure do. I emailed you yesterday and you said it was fine."

I shook my head. "I thought you meant seven p.m." What normal human conducted business at seven a.m.? On a Saturday? The sun had literally just poked its annoying head over the Teton mountains in the distance. And wasn't there some kind of unwritten rule that when it snowed, business took a break? Okay, maybe not for the whole day, but half a day at least. Like a snow day but for adults?

"Nope." He stared at me.

I couldn't help staring back. He was *all* Wyoming—worn cowboy boots with the fancy-looking filigree etched into the leather, lived-in jeans with holes starting in the knees and edges of the pockets, a light-blue denim shirt with white pearl buttons under a thick canvas jacket, and a cowboy hat. Pitch black. It sat low over his eyes until he noticed me looking, then he tipped it up.

"I can come back another time, ma'am, but it ain't gonna be today. I'm a cowboy over at the Milson ranch, and we usually work sun-up to sun-down. I got time off to be here, but I'll have to reschedule if you can't do this now."

"You're a cowboy? Like, a real cowboy? That's a thing?" I didn't miss his slow perusal of my pink onesie pajamas. His eyes lingered on the zipper which was only zipped up to the top of my breasts. I zipped it to my neck and he popped a brow.

"What thing?"

"No, I just meant, I didn't know cowboys actually existed. I guess I thought it was just a Halloween costume." I laughed, but he didn't seem amused.

He stared harder. "Yes, ma'am. Cowboys *actually* exist. I run cows for Hoover Milson, but we get a break for the holidays. So, startin' next week, I can work on whatever you need done here. If you hire me, that is." Rubbing his hands together against the cold again, he added, "So, we doin' this or not?"

"Right. Come in."

As a very single, never-been-married, thirty-*something* woman, I'd already done my research, and Max Gordon was as highly reputable as construction guys came. In fact, even in this incredibly small town of Wisper, Wyoming, he had over 300 reviews on the Friendly Neighbor app.

All five stars and mostly all from women, I'd noticed, and the reason was perfectly clear —ahem, aside from his surely stellar building and handyman skills.

Max Gordon should change his name to Max Gorgeous.

He was beautiful in that rugged, manly, "doesn't say much but you just know he's thinking deep and ardent thoughts" way. Or maybe that was just my overactive writer's imagination, but his hair was a sinfully sexy dark blond, and it struggled to stay hidden under his hat. Waves of it flipped all around his neck in an unruly way that I would've bet money pissed him off.

He hadn't smiled at me yet, but I could already tell his dimples were deep grooves under his five o'clock shadow, and it was only seven in the morning! Under his Carhartt coat, chest hair—not too bushy, not too thin—peeked out from the open top two buttons of his shirt, which was tucked into his jeans. And those jeans! *Mama mia.*

When he walked into my new house, removing his hat and running his fingers through his hair as he stepped over the threshold, I shut the door and followed him in, and his jeans were all I could look at. His ass was tight. Muscled. It was the kind of ass any straight woman—or gay man—would love to sink their nails into while they rode that cowboy like—

"Ms. Moonlight?"

I'd never had cowboy fantasies before. Rural men were literally last on my list of sexy. I hadn't even read a cowboy romance, and that was saying something since I read every other romance genre I could get my hands on.

"Huh?" My eyes snapped up to where they should've been the whole time, and he smirked. I was right! Oh, this man had dimples for days.

He tapped his watch on his left wrist, and I tried to follow the light hair behind it underneath his coat sleeve. "I don't have a lotta time."

"Right."

"You know that's the third time you've said that?"

"Said what?"

"'Right.'"

"I'm sorry?"

He laughed under his breath. "Nothin'. Why don'tcha go ahead and show me what you'd like done?" His voice was a low, lazy western drawl. It wasn't the first time I'd heard a Wyoming accent since I'd moved to the state chasing a clean slate and, hopefully, a home, but paired with his appearance and the air about him—hard and guarded but soft somewhere underneath, deep, deep inside—it was a little overwhelming.

"Right," I said again. *Ohh, 'right.' Juni, you idiot.* I didn't know if it was the early morning wake-up call or the fact that a guy with tantalizing green eyes, straight off the set of some modern-day western movie, was dominating my living room just by standing in it, but I couldn't manage to say anything coherent.

Deciding instead just to keep my mouth shut so nothing else ridiculous would fall out, I led him to the kitchen to show him where I wanted an island built, waiting while he measured the space, and then I motioned for him to follow me to my bedroom. I'd seen these amazing free-floating wooden bookshelves on Instagram, and I just had to have them.

Now that my contemporary romance books were finally selling, I could afford to have the shelves custom made. Which was exactly why I'd contacted Max Gorgeous. My entire life was still packed in boxes all over my new house, but I really wanted my bookshelves. Hashtag priorities.

Leading him down my hallway, I pushed open my bedroom door and stepped in front of him. "So, I'd like some bookshelves built. In fact, I'd like to cover that whole south wall there with them. And I'm thinking I'd like some in my office too. I saved a picture to show you. Here," I said, grabbing my cell from my nightstand.

When I turned toward him and looked up, he dragged his eyes to mine from my unmade bed, and his cheeks were pink under his stubble. He was either shy or he was seeing something I wasn't. Something blush-worthy.

Except now I could see it, and I think I might've drooled a little bit. This man was sex walking—the way he held himself, like he was filled with confidence, up to the tops of his surprisingly sexy ears. Could ears be sexy?

His were.

I hadn't slept with anyone but B.O.B. in a very long time. I was overdue. Way overdue. Like, ten-thousand-dollars-in-overdue-fines kind of overdue.

But sex was just a body mechanic to me now. I wrote so many steamy scenes for my novels that all the magic had kind of disappeared. Plus, there was no hunky, alpha hottie for me to swoon over in real life anyway. Men were such a disappointment. My best friend Jenn was constantly trying to convince me that I'd conjured up unrealistic expectations for myself because the men in my stories always turned out to be perfect in every way, but she was wrong.

My expectations were on point. It was the men who never lived up, and not because I expected the impossible. It was because they never gave a crap. They did the bare minimum in the relationship, then expected me to be some pole-dancing contortionist in the bedroom. They expected blow jobs but wouldn't spend more than three seconds between my legs.

And that was just the sex.

Was it too much to expect honesty, loyalty, and thoughtfulness from a man? Was it too much to expect someone to want to spend time around me because he actually liked me as a person?

No. It wasn't too much, but all the men I'd dated in the past several years had most definitely not lived up, and I was over it. My finger or my battery-operated boyfriend did the same job in less time, and the cost was much lower.

The cost wasn't my heart.

Was I in love with the characters from my books? Well, duh, of course I was because they were real men, not little boys, and—

"You always this distracted?"

"What? Oh, I'm sorry." I shook my head, and at the same time I realized I hadn't yet brushed my teeth. From behind my hand, I said, "It's kind of your fault. You woke me up." Glancing back at my bed, I was suddenly embarrassed about my green and purple llama-covered bedspread.

"You're unprepared for our meetin' and now you're blamin' me?" The low rasp to his voice made him sound irritated, but when I looked in his eyes, I could've sworn I saw laughter in those sexy green pools.

He was amused at my idiocy, and that pissed *me* off. "Just look at the picture." I held out my phone, and he took it from my hand with his finger and thumb. "Can you make those or not?"

After a quick peek at the screen, he said, "Yep. It'll take me a few hours to cut the wood. Then another day to sand and stain it. If you want me to install 'em, that's another half day probably. We'll need to figure out exactly where you want 'em. You have a wood preference?"

"Um, no. Just whatever's sturdiest, I guess. I'd like them to look distressed. Is that possible?"

"Yep, sure is. I'll get some reclaimed barn wood. Should do the job, plus it'll already be distressed, and I can ding it up a little more if you like. I don't have stain samples, so we'll need to take a trip over to the hardware store so you can pick the color. What about the kitchen island? You want it to match your white cabinets?"

"No. We'll just do the same color as the bookshelves. I like things to look a bit mismatched."

He scrunched his nose at that. "Okay, whatever you say. What kinda stone you want for the surface?"

"I don't know. Something funky. We could even do steel."

"Steel?"

"Yeah, haven't you seen those online? I think they look cool."

"Yeah, I've seen 'em, but steel really wouldn't fit with the rest of the house. You ain't in the city anymore, ma'am."

"Ma'am?" I rolled my eyes. "I'm aware of that, trust me, and I'm not from a big city. I moved here from Cincinnati, Ohio."

"Sounds big to me."

"Okay, well, whatever. I like things to look a little eclectic. Will that offend your down-home decorating sensibilities, or can we go ahead?"

His eyebrow twitched a little, but he nodded. "You're payin', so whatever you want is fine by me. Text me that picture and see if you can find an example or two of an island you like. I need to know how many drawers you want and what kind. You want a lazy susan?"

"Huh? A lazy who?"

He sighed. "A lazy susan." He spoke the words slowly, like he didn't think I understood English. "It's a cabinet with a spinnin' shelf inside, for spices and such."

"Oh, right. Uh, no, I don't think so. I don't cook very much. The island is more for storage and somewhere to sit, so..."

His eyes dipped to my mouth, then back up to mine. He licked his lips. "Alright then, anything else?"

"No. I think that— Oh, wait. Could you fix my shower? The water pressure is abysmal, and it drips all night long."

"Yeah, probably could," was all he said as he followed me across the hall. If I thought he seemed big in my living room, it was nothing compared to the way he took up all the air in the bathroom. He smelled like sawdust and some kind of musky, manly scent. Maybe it was his soap, but this close, it was beguiling.

"See? Look." Leaning over the tub, I turned the knob and water basically trickled out of the showerhead, the one that probably hadn't been replaced since 1982.

"Yeah, that looks pretty inefficient." Looking all around, he drew in a slow, deep breath. "So, I reckon this'll take me about two or three weekends, maybe a little more, for the island, bookshelves, and the shower. But honestly, we won't need a lot of supplies, and I already have all the tools I'll need. So why don't I just quote you for the labor and then I'll send you links to the parts and supplies we do need, and you can buy those when we go to town for stain. Then you can make color choices and all that. How's that sound?"

"Okay, that sounds fine."

"You gonna be around here next week? Where do you work?"

"Here, I work from home. Yes, I'll be here next week."

"What do you do for a livin'?"

"Oh, I'm a writer. I write books." I laughed under my breath. I still felt a little bit of imposter syndrome. I'd only been writing for a few years, and I'd only self-published my first three books over the last year. Saying "I'm a writer" still felt a little like a lie if I was honest. I used to be a CPA. How I went from such an analytical and numbers-focused job to one of the most creative was beyond me. But I'd never been so happy or felt so free.

I'd gone all in, and my racy billionaire bad-boy romances were selling like hotcakes. It was how I'd afforded moving across the country, how I paid for the little cottage I'd bought in this itty-bitty town of Wisper, Wyoming, and how I was able to hire a sexy cowboy to build my shelves.

And dammit, impostor or not, I was proud of myself for what I'd accomplished.

"What kinda books?"

I bit my lip. *Here we go.* "Romance. I write romance books."

"So then, Juneau Moonlight is like a fake name for your books?"

"What? No, it's my real name."

"Hm."

"You're not going to laugh? Not going to make some misogynistic comment about romance being porn for women or something invalidating like that?"

"Wouldn't dream of it. You do you." He looked at his watch. "Okay, I gotta hit the road. So, how 'bout two hundred bucks a day, and then you buy the supplies we need? Deal?" He extended his hand for me to shake.

"That sounds low." Was he trying to pull the wool over my eyes? Why would he offer so little for such a big job?

"Well, I could charge you more, but this ain't a big job, and I think you're probably gonna need your cash to reno the rest of this bathroom here pretty soon. It's a fair price. You might find cheaper if you go with someone else, but you won't find better work. Promise you that."

Thinking back to all the glowing reviews and recommendations I'd read, not to mention the pictures of his beautiful woodwork, I thought, *Why not? Take a chance, Juni. You deserve it.*

"Okay," I said, and I held my hand up in front of my chest. "Deal."

He shook it, one quick, hard shake. His hands were warm but rough, and his shake was so strong, I felt it in my lady parts. I heard the sound of a slot machine paying out in my head; those overdue fines were coming due loudly.

"Last question," he said.

"Yeah?" I asked as he followed me back to the front door.

"You got somethin' against Christmas?"

"What?" I laughed, confused. "No."

"I ain't seen one decoration and Christmas is three weeks away. Are you Jewish or Buddhist or somethin'?"

"No. I—well, I'm not really religious at all. I just moved in. Everything's still packed. Besides, it's just me. What's the big deal? I usually put a wreath on the door."

"A wreath?"

"Yeah, you know, a round thingie made out of dead pine boughs? You put ornaments on them or candy canes or something. I don't know."

When he stepped onto the porch, he plopped his big hat back on his head and turned toward me. "I'll bring lights."

"What? No. You don't have to do that."

"It's no problem. You don't wanna be the only dark house on Christmas."

"No, really, you don't—"

"I got a few extra outside strands. I'll bring 'em. See you next week. I'll text you times when I send you the links. Don't forget to send me pictures of an island you like."

"O-okay."

"Have a nice day now, ma'am." He tipped his hat and walked down my porch steps, and I would've bet all the money in my savings account that there was a smirk in his eyes when he said it.

Chapter Two

Max

Hot damn. Juneau Moonlight was... Well, she was the finest woman ever to hit the streets of Wisper, Wyoming, that was for sure. She was beautiful.

I wasn't a plumber, so technically, I wasn't qualified to fix her shower, but I didn't reckon I'd say no to anything she asked of me when she leaned over her bathtub like she had. Plus, replacing a showerhead wasn't hard.

A romance writer? I laughed to myself in my Chevy on the way back to work. Yeah, I was pretty certain she was way out of my league.

But beautiful was an understatement when it came to Ms. Moonlight. Her sexy auburn waves made my mouth water when I imagined her snuggled up to me in that messy bed of hers, 'specially when I imagined running my fingers through the thick locks.

And she was spunky. I didn't usually go for women who talked a lot, or talked at all, really. Mostly they just wanted to talk about feelings. Why did all women assume men sat around thinking about how a conversation made them feel? C'mon, if it didn't make us angry, we probably didn't give it much thought at all.

Just to see what I was up against, I called my cousin Aubrey at her bookstore downtown, Your Local Bookie. What a name for a business, but I figured if anybody was to know about romance books, it'd be her.

"Hey, cuz," I said, and I turned down the old-time version of "Have Yourself a Merry Little Christmas" playing on my dash radio when she answered.

"'Sup, Maxie? How's your ol' mama doin'? Auntie Mabel said she saw her at the hairdresser the other day. Her arm feelin' better? I can't believe she broke it playin' ping pong of all things."

"Yeah, she was in a death match with Buster Hennessy. You know she visits the ol' coot twice a week, says she's tryin' to keep him young. Luckily, Doc Whitley happened to be at the old folks' home that day, but she's doin' better. The cast just about drives her nuts, but she'll be fine. How 'bout you? How're the twins?"

"Oh, you know, same ol', same ol'. Those stinkers are always in some kinda trouble, but nothin' too illegal lately. The store's doin' good, business is pretty steady. Wisper peeps gotta get their fiction fix."

My cousin's twin teenage boys were known around Wisper—the infamous George twins. I was pretty sure the sheriff had Aubrey's phone number on his speed dial. If they weren't breaking into peoples' houses when they were out of town or stealing cases of Coors from the Liquor Depot, they were lighting fires somewhere or other. They weren't bad kids, necessarily, just bored, I figured. Aubrey's husband had died fighting with the Army overseas three years ago, and I promised her I'd take the boys to the ranch with me to try to teach them a trade, or just work their asses off so they'd settle down, but I hadn't gotten around to it.

Hopefully, I wasn't too late and they hadn't killed or impregnated anybody yet.

"You still over at Milson's?"

"Yeah, but we're about to break for the holidays. I just took a side job this mornin', though, buildin' bookshelves and a kitchen island. That's why I called. You ever heard of a writer called Juneau Moonlight?"

Aubrey laughed. "Have I heard of Juneau Moonlight? Oh boy, have I ever. I just bought a bunch of her paperbacks to sell here in the shop. She's real popular right now. Why you askin' about her? You're the last guy on earth I woulda expected to ask about romance books."

"That's who hired me."

"Juneau Moonlight hired you? Wait, she lives here? In Wisper?"

"Yep. Now don't go spreadin' that around. I dunno if it's a secret or somethin'. I mean, if she's some big, fancy author like Stephen King, she probably likes her privacy."

"Well, I wouldn't say she's like Stephen King. Wrong genre, and she ain't that big yet. More like up and comin'. And you know I won't go spreadin' gossip, but look here, I run a tiny little indie bookstore. You better ask her if she'll do a readin' for me. Give her my number. If you do that, I'll keep your secret."

"Fine. Deal."

"So, what's she like?"

"I dunno. She's just a person."

"Uh huh. 'Cept you wouldn't be callin' me to ask after her if she was 'just a person.' I've seen her picture on the back of her books. She's pretty."

I didn't mean to, but I cleared my throat before I said, "I didn't notice."

Aubrey laughed again. "Hey, cousin?"

Taking the last turn off the highway that would lead me to Milson's ranch, I said, "Yeah?"

"Remember how I always beat you when we played poker at Granny's house?"

"I reckon I recall you beatin' me a time or two. What of it?"

"Try *every single time we played*, and you wanna know why?"

"No, but I bet you're gonna tell me."

"I beat you because, without fail, every time you try to lie or bluff, you cough. You make it too damn easy." She chortled.

"Alright, alright. Well, I suppose I'll let you have poker, but you ever remember beatin' me at chess?"

Nothing but silence on the line after that.

"Uh huh. I see your memory is indeed in tip-top shape."

"Fine. So, we're even then." She chuckled a little. "I gotta go, but don't forget to give Ms. Moonlight my number, okay?"

"I will, Aubrey, promise."

"Oh, and if you wanna read her books, stop by the shop. I'll set a few copies aside for you."

I scoffed. Like I'd read a romance novel. Never gonna happen. The guys at the ranch would never let me live it down, and that was the only place I'd ever have time to read.

So then, why was I already aiming my truck back toward the bookstore?

"Whatcha got there?"

"None of your business, asshat. You finish muckin' them stalls yet?"

My right-hand man, Buckey, punched my arm. "Yeah. They're so damn clean, they're sparklin' in the sunlight. Seriously, what's that book you got?"

"Horse stalls can't sparkle, Buckey, since they're made outta wood. And I said it's none of your business. If the stalls are clean, get to groomin'. Those horses need it after our run this mornin'." I raised a brow at him, but he knew I was only halfway scolding him. We'd been friends since grade school, and I was best man at his wedding.

"Yeah, yeah. I'm on it." He peeked over my shoulder before I could hide the book under my thigh on the chair at the supper table in the bunkhouse. Looked like the guys had already finished cleaning up after breakfast. Buckey chuckled. "Ohh, Carly has that book. She says it's good. Lotsa smut."

"Smut?"

"Yeah. You know—sex. In fact, she gets awful horny after she reads it. She likes all them sexy books, 'specially the ones about rich dudes. She jokes and says she likes to imagine we're the couple in the books since that's the only way she's ever gonna know what it feels like to be taken care of by a billionaire."

"I'm pretty sure she ain't jokin', man."

"Whatever. You never know. I could be a closet gazillionaire. Like I'd tell you."

He wandered off to start grooming the horses, and I pulled the book back out and opened it. I mean, it was probably a good idea for me to read it, just to get a good feel for my new client. It might give me insight into her style preferences.

Right. That was why I was about to crack open a book called *Brianna's Billionaire Bad Boy.*

Flipping through, I stopped somewhere in the middle of the book...

"Stone, please, I need you."

"Oh yeah, baby, I love it when you beg."

What was this now? Sitting up a little straighter in my chair, I turned the page, but I peeked around first to make sure the other cowboys weren't lurking in the bunkhouse. Occasionally, one would sneak in for a quick fifteen-minute nap, but I didn't see anybody today. They were all probably out back, making sure to get their daily twenty-four ounces of beer consumed before lunch break was over.

He pushed me down to my knees and threaded his fingers through my hair, then tilted my head up so I could watch him lick his lips. He rasped, "Open your mouth, Brianna."

I did what he ordered, and why did it turn me on so much that there was a little threat in his voice? I'd never been wetter.

Shit! I slammed the book closed. I'd only read four sentences, and already, I was itching to lock myself in the bathroom with my fist.

Seriously? I thought I was gonna read about hearts and flowers or some shit. I mean, it wasn't like guys didn't have *Playboy,* but I had no idea women liked to read about sex. Did they do the same thing we did with it? Well, dammit, now *that* was all I could picture—beautiful Juneau Moonlight, rubbing herself to ecstasy on her bed, her legs bent and wide open, tangled in her purple sheets, lips wet, *everywhere* wet and her face flushed, her eyes closed and her hair a wild, red mess on the pillow.

I could practically hear her moaning with that sexy low voice of hers.

Stop thinking about it, you asshole. She's your client.

What if she called my name when she came? Oh man, now that was all I could hear.

Goddammit, Max, cut it out!

After checking again to make sure I was alone, I peeked in the book again.

Chapter 18: "Suck me into that pretty mouth of yours and touch yourself while you do it." Stone pulled my hair and I reached up to grip his...

Nope. Couldn't do it. *Not doin' it.* If I read any more, I'd never be able to look Ms. Moonlight in the eyes again.

But...maybe just one more page? I mean, reading books was an intellectual pursuit, right? Nothing wrong with that.

Chapter Three

Juneau

"Seriously? Six in the morning this time?" I grumbled to myself when I peeked through the curtains I'd tacked above the front-room window. I bought the damn curtain rods, but I was a little terrified of ladders, so I hadn't hung them up.

When I opened the door, Max Gorgeous said, "Yes, ma'am, it is six in the mornin'. I'm on the clock at seven, but I'm not chargin' you for this, so, figured I'd better get an early start."

"You heard me? And you're not charging me for what? I don't need handouts, and you do know it's Sunday?"

"Yep, heard you loud and clear, and it ain't a handout."

He grunted, hopping onto my porch railing with strands of twinkle lights wrapped around his neck. They dangled down both sides of his body, and for the briefest second, I wondered what he'd look like naked with the lights illuminating his probably fabulously sculpted chest and abs in my bedroom.

"It's neighborly," he said. "I told you I'd bring Christmas lights, and since it was my idea, I figured I'd hang 'em up. You're kinda short, so, be a lot easier for me. And, FYI, everyone else around here gets up with the sun. Maybe they don't do it like that in O-hi-o, but best just to get the day on."

"Fine. I'm up now. Guess I'll make coffee. Want some?"

"Sure. Thank you, ma'am."

"Please, for the love of all that's holy, I'm not Betty White. Just call me Juni."

The corner of his mouth twitched. "Alright then, Juni."

I made my way to the kitchen for the one appliance I'd made sure to unpack—my blessed French press—mumbling, "That's better than ma'am, I guess."

Handing him his coffee and sitting on my porch steps, I said, "Thank you for the lights. You really didn't have to do that, but that was really nice of you. I'll give you a good tip when you're finished with my island and shelves."

He eyed me while he sipped the steaming black coffee. Seeing him holding my "I like to touch my shelf" coffee mug was almost too much. Bookish coffee mugs were an obsession of mine. Ooo, that reminded me.

"Could I add something else to my list of things I'd like you to do?"

"Depends on what it is, and a tip ain't necessary."

"I'll tip you," I said, cocking my head, trying not to let my stubborn streak show too much. Neighborly was one thing, but I wasn't some little old lady who couldn't do anything for herself. And I had the money. I would pay and tip, as was customary. "I was wondering if you could build me a coffee mug display in the kitchen."

"A coffee mug display?"

"Yeah, you could use some of that reclaimed wood." Nodding to the pile on my porch he'd already cut into one-by-twos for my shelves, I sipped my coffee, too, holding the mug between both hands, trying to soak in the heat, and I burrowed into my pink puffy coat. We had snow back in Ohio, but there was something different about the snow and cold weather here. It was somehow colder when you could see the mountains in the distance. But remembering him working his power saw when he was cutting the shelves the day before warmed me up too. Sexy.

"It's basically just a board on the wall with little pegs you can hang coffee mugs from."

"Alright. I should have enough wood left over."

"I really feel like I'm getting the better end of this deal. You don't want to charge me extra to make that? You're not a very good businessman."

"Thanks for that. Fine," he said, and he sat beside me but then scooted two feet away. "Two-thousand dollars for your fancy coffee board. That make you feel better?"

"Two-thou—?" I almost spit my coffee out.

"Just pullin' your leg. Look, the wood was free, and I got drawers stuffed fulla nails in my garage. You're buyin' the stain, so all we need are the pegs. I probably got somethin' we could use at my house, but if you're determined to spend more money, you can buy some, though you'd probably like it better if I recycled somethin'. You fancy city types go nuts over reusable junk. Vintage, I think y'all call it."

I snorted. He wasn't wrong.

"Okay. Thank you."

"Well, you wanna hit the hardware store? We can pick up the stain and look at countertop choices for your island."

"Sure. I'll drive."

Looking at me like he thought I was kidding with his eyebrows raised over his gorgeous green eyes, he said, "Uh, okay, but um, that little car of yours is awfully small. Not sure my legs'll fit."

My eyes did a slow inventory of those strong, and yes, long legs. He was probably right since I barely fit in my tiny Nissan LEAF, and I was only five-foot-four. But it was electric!

"Fine. You can drive then."

"Probably a better idea," he said, and he tipped his hat and headed to start his truck parked in my short driveway. He opened the passenger-side door and waited patiently while I ran inside for my wallet and phone.

When I climbed Mount Cowboy Truck and my butt finally plopped on the seat, he shut my door with a nod and I inhaled. Jeez. If a truck could smell like sexy man, this one did. Leather, sweat, and pure M.A.N. Did he spray the interior with pheromones?

"You alright there?" he asked when he closed his door and started the engine. His old truck rattled a little when he gave it some gas. "You look a little weird."

"I'm fine. Are all trucks this high off the ground, or did you do something to jack yours up higher?"

"Yeah. The truck's previous owner lifted it. Lotta guys around here do that. Makes 'em feel bigger or somethin'. Don't really matter much to me. As long as the truck runs good and can haul shit, I'm happy." He took his hat off and set it on the dash, then ran his fingers through his mop of thick, wavy blond hair. "Oh dammit, I'm sorry for cursin', ma'am."

Rolling my eyes, I sighed. "Again, Max, my name is Juneau. Or if you like, you can call me Juni. That's what my friends call me. But if you call me ma'am one more time, you're fired. I'm only— Well, anyway, I'm not seventy-six freaking years old."

Surprise colored his face, and then he laughed, a rich, warm baritone chuckle rumbling in his chest. It rumbled in mine too. "Sorry, Juni. Force of habit."

"That's better," I said, nodding to myself. I was having serious sexual fantasies about this guy already. It was a direct hit to my pride to think he might see me like some soccer mom, or worse, a soccer mom's mom. He couldn't be that much younger than me; in fact, my gut told me we might be around the same age.

His body looked lived in. Fine, it looked lived in, loved in, and definitely up to task. I wanted to run my fingers over the tanned skin on the back of his neck. That skin had most definitely seen its share of sun, and I imagined him sweaty in a white T-shirt and worn jeans with a rope in his hands, training horses or cows or something.

Trying to make conversation to distract myself from my inappropriate thoughts, I asked, "So, what exactly is a cowboy's job? I mean, do you just take care of your boss's cows and horses?"

Backing out of my driveway with his arm resting dangerously close to me on the back of the seat while he looked for traffic, he said, "Uh, well, a cowboy has lots of different jobs on a ranch. I'm the foreman at Milson's, so basically, I'm in charge of the other guys. We do all kinds of stuff. I dunno. Whatever needs doin'."

"But like what?"

He peeked at me and then fixed his eyes back on the road as he put the truck in drive, and his engine rumbled in appreciation when we surged forward. "Like, we move the herds from one pasture to the next, we brand, we do vaccinations."

"Do you ride? Horses, I mean," I asked, suddenly realizing just how strong my need to see him ride a horse was.

"Yep, since I was three feet tall. You?"

I laughed a little. "No. I mean, I've been trail riding. Spent a lot of time camping when I was a kid—my parents were hippies, if you couldn't tell by my name, so we did all kinds of outdoorsy things—but they were too flaky to stay in one place long enough for me to take riding lessons or have a pet."

"Hm. That's too bad." He peeked at me again and then looked back through the windshield. It felt like he wanted to say something or ask me something else, but his next words were only, "You hungry? I guess me showin' up so early on a Sunday probably put a kink in your mornin' routine. We could stop by the diner, then make our way over to the hardware store in Jackson."

"Oh." Looking at him, I couldn't figure him out. I thought he'd be the strong, silent type, but he was chatty enough. "Um. Sure. Yeah, I guess I am kind of hungry."

"What?"

"Nothing, it's just... Is this normal, to go out for breakfast with your contractor?"

"Oh, well, I dunno, but we gotta eat, right?"

"I suppose we do. I haven't been to José's Diner yet. Is that where we're going?"

"Yep. Only diner in town, and probably the best in the state."

It was silly, but I was kind of excited to go to the diner. Living in a small town, where everybody knew everybody else, had always been my dream. I wanted the kind of neighbors you saw on TV. People who checked on you if you were sick, who watered your flowers if you were on vacation or shoveled your sidewalks and driveway because they knew you were new in town and probably didn't even know to buy a snowblower. Men who brought you Christmas lights and then hung them up for you without asking.

You'd think growing up with parents who couldn't sit still and moved every time they sneezed, I would've been around a lot of people like that, but I wasn't. And after my parents passed and I settled in Cincinnati, I'd kept to myself. Being an only child living out of the back of my parents' van for half my life hadn't really prepared me for small-town suburbia, but it was also the reason I longed for it.

I'd seen a TV show about a small town in Montana, where neighbors checked in on each other and brought fresh-baked pies or homemade cookies when someone got a promotion at work or had a new baby, and somehow, my search for a similar place had led me to Wisper.

I'd always wanted to know what it felt like to be a part of a community like that.

"I read your book."

My stomach dropped into my ratty Ugg boots, and I squeaked, "What?" Whipping my head to stare at him in utter embarrassment, I hoped my mouth wasn't too wide open, but I couldn't seem to close it.

"Here we are," he said when he parked in front of José's Diner downtown. It was only a mile from my house. The little restaurant looked full, at least as far as I could tell from my peripheral vision since I couldn't stop staring at him.

My voice came out almost in a whisper when I asked, "Wait. I mean, why would you tell me that?"

He blushed and said, "C'mon. Looks like the diner's busy. Better hurry if we wanna get a booth."

Uh... Okay?

Chapter Four

Max

S hit. *Why would you tell her that?*

With a wave of my hand, I motioned for her to sit in a booth in the front window of the diner, and I watched as she slid her bubblegum-pink coat from her shoulders, letting it slip down to the bench when she sat.

I sat across from her and fingered the—damn. I *messed* with the bottle of hot sauce in the middle of the table while I tried not to stare at the flat, pearly buttons on her shirt above her breasts. They were full and round, and they filled out the fabric better than any I'd ever seen. They drew my eye, and then both my eyes couldn't stop their slow ascent up her neck. When they landed on her face, and then when my eyes met hers, she blushed a deep rose color.

She leaned forward, talking in a low voice so no one else would hear, "Why?"

I knew exactly what she meant, but I said, "Why what?"

"You know exactly what."

"Right," I said, chuckling when I realized that was her line. "Uh, I dunno. My cousin owns the bookstore here in town—by the way, she asked me to ask you if you'd read to her. I dunno why she'd ask that, but anyway, when I asked if she'd ever heard of you, she gave me a couple of your books. I checked 'em out." I shrugged. "I like mysteries, but never read a romance book before. I was curious."

I cleared my throat.

I was a little nervous, but I didn't look away when I said, "I didn't know y'all read books like that," and I realized I was leaning over the table, too, my body straining toward hers, like it couldn't help itself.

Squaring her shoulders a little, she sat back. "Who's 'y'all' in this scenario, and books like what? What does that mean?"

"You know, women. I didn't know women liked to read sex books."

"Oh my God. I knew it." She crossed her arms over her chest, which made the buttons look like they might pop right off, and my mouth watered. "You're just like every other man."

"Hey now, that ain't fair. I don't mean any offense. I truly had no idea. But Aubrey—that's my cousin—she said it's a gazillion-dollar-a-year business or somethin' crazy like that. I just, really, I didn't know."

"It is. Romance books sell more than any other genre. There are endless sub-genres, so there's something for every taste, and besides all of that, romance novels can be empowering for women. They can teach and be inclusive. They make me feel like I'm not alone. I've learned a lot about life from them, and yes, about sex."

My eyebrows raised on their own.

"What?" she demanded. I'd offended her, but I truly hadn't meant to.

"I mean, maybe it's inappropriate of me to say, but what could you learn from a book like that? I mean, the scenario in your book wouldn't really happen. You know that, right?"

"Excuse me?"

Ah, Max, you moron. Now you've done it.

She stiffened and tightened her arms over her chest. It was pure torture trying *not* to look.

"Mornin', Max. Who's your friend?" José asked, handing me two laminated menus.

I couldn't look away from the angry glint in Juneau's blue-gray eyes when I answered him and handed one to her. "This is Ms. Juneau Moonlight. She's new in town. Just moved here from Ohio."

"Well, welcome to Wisper, Ms. Moonlight. I'm José," he said with his usual smile, extending his hand toward her.

She shook it and, though she still seemed pretty mad at me, she looked away, smiling genuinely at José. "Nice to meet you, José. I love your diner. It's so small-town Americana. Adorable."

"Aw, thanks. That's real sweet. I oughta use that on our Instagram profile."

Finally, I looked up at José in disbelief. "*You* have an Instagram profile?"

"'Course we do. To be fair, Daisy usually does the postin', but yeah. Don't you? It's a great marketin' tool."

"Uh, no. I do not have Instagram."

"Really?" Juni asked, finally looking back at me completely baffled, like it was a crime to be Instagram illiterate.

What use did I have for Instagram or TikTok? Like I was gonna get new clients from posting pictures of the calluses on my hands? Please. And ain't no way anybody could convince me to dance around like an idiot and then post videos of that. Not in this lifetime, for damn sure.

I assured them both, "Really."

"Well, your loss," José said, and he winked at Juni. Her eyes lit up, and I wondered if she thought he was handsome. Kinda old for her, and he was married to Daisy, but still, my pride was dented a little when I realized Juni hadn't yet smiled at me like that. "Anyway, what would y'all like to order?"

"Do you have any specials?" she asked, and the lilt in her voice made me smile, but I tried to control my face muscles so she wouldn't see.

"Yes, ma'am, we do. Crêpes are the special today. You have your choice of apple and cinnamon or cranberry with candied ginger. Both have a sweet cream cheese fillin'. Very festive. You can look those up on Instagram. My wife posted 'em yesterday."

"I'll have the cranberry. Sounds delicious. And may I have scrambled eggs on the side and sausage links? Oh, and hash browns?"

"You sure can. Max?"

"Uh, yeah, sure, just double all that. And coffee," I said, looking at Juni again. She nodded at José.

I was impressed. The last time I'd taken a woman to a restaurant, she ordered a piece of lettuce sprinkled with salt. Juni ordering half the break-fast menu was so sexy, I couldn't stop the grin on my lips now.

"What?"

"Nothin'," I said, and I felt José's smirk when he turned back toward his kitchen.

"Do you have a problem with a woman eating real food?"

"No, ma'am, I do not," I said, and my voice involuntarily dropped at least an octave when I said, "Ain't *nothin'* wrong with that."

Juni blinked a few times, and she relaxed, dropping her hands into her lap. "What were we talking about?"

I knew I was taking a risk, reminding her of what I'd said, but I was captivated by this woman, and I wanted to know her thoughts. Also, I wanted to know because the crude asshole in the back of my head wanted to be able to imagine her writing her smut books.

"We were talkin' about your book."

"Really? You're bringing it up again? I thought you were smarter than that." She sighed when I raised my eyebrows, waiting for her to expound. "Fine. Of course the scenes from my books are possible. I've done a lot of research."

"Research?"

"Well, yeah. I'm not going to write about something if I don't know anything about it."

"Right, but you had to look that up?"

"What does 'that' mean? I have no idea which book of mine you've read or what sexual act you're referring to. And again, I'm going to ask, is this normal? Talking about this with my contractor?"

"What's normal?" I shrugged. I wanted her to keep talking, though, so I kept on. "I read *Brianna's Billionaire Bad Boy*."

Her cheeks pinked. "That's my first book. It's not my best."

"What's that mean? The writin' was fantastic, it's just the"—I lowered my voice and leaned in again—"the sex scenes. They aren't realistic."

"How would you know? Have you ever had sex with a billionaire bad boy, or with Brianna for that matter?"

"Uh..."

"So how would you know?"

She had me there. "I'm just sayin', I've never spoken to a woman like that durin' sex before. That ain't really how men act."

"That's not how *you* act. You can't speak for all men."

"S'pose you're right. I can't," I said, and I relaxed against the booth back. I could tell I was irking her, and I liked that. She was sexy when she was pissed. Her face got all flushed, but the glint in her eye was just about the most enticing thing I'd ever seen. "I'm just sayin', is all."

"What?" She scoffed. "What exactly are you trying to say? You know, I thought you were some quiet, reserved guy, but I think you talk too much." She cocked her head a little.

Shrugging, I flashed a smirk while José set our breakfast in front of us. Neither one of us looked away, and I heard José's laugh when he left.

"Darn it. Thank you, José," she called after him, and her feisty armor fell away in her attempt to be polite.

Focusing back on me, she swiped her fork from the table and stabbed a sausage link, then bit it in two and poked the other half in my direction.

Chewing, she said, "I bet I could teach you a thing or two, Mr. Alpha Cowboy."

"Well," I said, delicately cutting a piece of a cranberry crêpe with my knife and fork, and I ate the bite, "now who's bein' inappropriate?" Damn, that was a good crêpe. The thing practically melted in my mouth.

She squeaked a little in incredulity. "You know what? I think we should just eat our breakfast in silence and agree to disagree. I don't need your validation. I sell plenty of books with my 'unrealistic sex scenes,' thank you very much. Your input is unwarranted and unneeded."

"Noted," I said, but I couldn't stop smiling.

"Argh. Just shut up and eat, would you?"

So, we ate like that. The tension between us was thick enough to cut, and we rarely looked away from one another. Every small movement she made had my imagination running wild, and I would've given anything to show her exactly what was on my mind.

Everything about her was sexy, right down to her indignation. It was a little uncomfortable considering it was still early morning and we were in a crowded diner, but I was busting through my jeans beneath the table, and I noticed her body language was favorable toward me, too, if the hard points of her nipples under her shirt and the rosy flush of her cheeks were any indication.

Oh boy, did that ever make it worse. But despite the pain, I was having the time of my life. I wasn't usually one to be boastful, but I was pretty sure she was attracted to me—she looked like she wanted to leap across the table and strangle the air right out of me, but not in a murderous way, and I got the feeling that that might just turn her on.

Maybe she *could* teach me a "thing or two."

Chapter Five

Juneau

"So, tell me about cowboy country." My best friend and number one cheerleader, Jenn, yeehawed into her cell phone. She was also my social media advisor and my sometimes-PR rep. Being an independently published author meant wearing a lot of different hats, and sometimes my head got way too warm, so Jenn helped when she could.

"You're not kidding. They're everywhere around here."

"Really? I *was* kidding."

"Seriously. Speaking of that, have you ever read a cowboy romance?"

"Uh, yeah. You haven't? Cowboys are like the ultimate alphas 'cause they're quiet but they explode in the bedroom, like you're a naughty little filly and they're the reigning champ of the rodeo."

"Oh my God, Jenn, please stop talking."

"Why do you ask?"

"I was just wondering."

"Uh huh. Right. And *why* were you wondering? Rural is not something I'd use as a descriptor for your books. Are you thinking about switching genres?"

"Uh, no." I laughed. "It's just, I met this...guy."

"Ha! I knew it. He's a cowboy, right?"

"Yeah, I mean, like, a literal cowboy. He works on a cow ranch."

"You mean a cattle ranch? Does he wear a cowboy hat?"

"As a matter of fact."

"Oh my God, text me a pic."

"I don't have a picture, Jenn. Jeez." But I remembered Max's profile from the Friendly Neighbor app. "Hold on, I can find one."

After I screenshotted Max's unsmiling profile picture and sent it to Jenn, she whistled and drawled in her best cowgirl accent, "Whoowee, honey, if you ain't gonna climb that pole, I'll be right there."

"You sound just like him."

"He has an accent? Does he chew on a toothpick like Rip Wheeler?"

"Ew, no. Who?"

"You know, that guy from— Never mind. I forgot, you're too busy writing to understand popular TV show references."

"Whatever. Well, so, anyway, I hired him. He's making me an island for the kitchen and bookshelves for my bedroom and office."

"Hold on, I just licked my phone. There's spit everywhere."

"Jenn!"

"Kidding. But are his eyes really that green in person?"

"Greener," I said with a scoff.

"What's the deal? He's hot AF, but you sound like you don't like him."

"He said my sex scenes are unrealistic."

"He's read your books? Juni! Marry him."

"Did you hear what I said? He said 'unrealistic.' And then I opened my stupid mouth and argued. I told him they were realistic, and I would know since I researched it."

Jenn laughed at me. "You did not."

"I did. I'm so embarrassed." I hung my head, covering my eyes with my hands, which was handy because I couldn't see Max's Christmas lights through my living room windows anymore. Looking at them made my face hotter.

"What's wrong with you? He probably thinks you're some kind of buttoned-up virgin now."

"Well, I didn't think it was appropriate to inform him in the middle of a family diner that my research consisted of dom/sub and BDSM topics."

She snorted. "Oh, Juneau, foot in mouth much? But seriously, if he's read the books, then I think he can figure out you're not a prude. What else did he say?"

"He said my writing was fantastic," I admitted, and I couldn't help my smile. I'd had a lot of compliments since publishing my books, even one from another big-name romance author. I used it in one of my books' blurbs, but it hadn't made my heart flutter like Max's compliment had.

"Well, that's something."

"I mean, yeah, I guess, but I don't think he knows much about romance books."

"Why does that matter? He knows how to *read*. Why are you always so quick to dismiss your talent?"

"What? I am not," I said, but I groaned because she was right. "Sorry, bad habit. I'm trying, Jenn, but it still feels weird to think of myself as an actual author. I mean, before the books, I was just a lowly assistant CPA. Not glamorous. But I'll get used to it. I hope."

"Well, what else do you know about him?"

"Not much. He's a handyman, or maybe a carpenter, but on the side. His nine-to-five is foreman at the cattle ranch."

"So, he's good with his hands. That sounds promising."

"Ugh, hush. I'm not sleeping with my...whatever he is."

"Why not?"

"Because it's unprofessional."

"He's not your boss."

"Technically, I'm his boss."

"Oh please. You know, eventually, you are going to have to refill your sex-scene reservoir."

"My what?"

"You've published three books now, and you have three more in the works, so eventually, you'll run out of ideas. You need to experience more life so you have more inspiration to draw from. This carpenter-slash-cowboy sounds like just what you need." Jenn tried to disguise the change in the tone of her voice, but I heard it. Pity was headed my way.

She didn't mean to do it, but she got mushy when the topic of my failed love life was concerned.

"Seriously, you haven't dated anyone since what's-his-name, the lawyer jackoff. Try something new. Step out of your comfort zone. You deserve to have a good time. You owe it to yourself to be happy, and they're not all bad, Juni. Josh is a fantastic boyfriend. He brings me flowers for no reason at all, he listens, even when I'm rambling about absolutely nothing, and he calls my mother on her birthday."

"Yeah, well, you lucked out. You got the last good one."

Jenn sighed. "If you'd give someone the chance, they might prove you wrong. And besides, B.O.B is a machine, and batteries are expensive and they're bad for the environment."

"Hi, José. How are you today?" The café was a lot less busy for lunch during the week, but there were still only a few booths open. I smiled at José when I stepped up to the counter.

"Oh, well, hello, Juneau. It's nice to see you again." He craned his neck, looking for someone. "Honey, c'mere." José draped his arm around his wife's shoulder and kissed her cheek when she passed him holding an orange-lidded decaf coffee pot. "This is my wife, Daisy. Daze, this is Juneau Moonlight. She just moved to Wisper."

"Juneau Moonlight? The author?"

My mouth dropped open. "You know my books?" Oh my gosh, my first author-in-the-wild experience, and Jenn was missing it!

"Are you kidding? I loved them. I have them in eBook and paperback."

"You're a writer, Juneau? Well, ain't that somethin'?"

"Please call me Juni, José, and yes. I just published my first three books earlier this year. Daisy, nice to meet you and thank you so much for reading."

"Well, if Daisy's read your books, then I know what kind they are. You should see the impressive pile of romance novels linin' the wall in our den. I've been meanin' to buy her a couple bookshelves."

"I'm having some built. Trust me, I know needing bookshelves."

"Well," Daisy said, smiling at me and wiping her hands on the rag she'd slung over her shoulder, "this'll be the talk of the town. I don't think Wisper's ever had an author in residence before."

"That's nice, but I'm just small potatoes."

"You might be new on the scene, Juni, but don't forget, I know how good your books are. You're going places, sweetie."

"Thank you."

José nodded to a couple cowboys who walked in and took a seat at the other end of the counter. Their hats gave them away. "That why you were with Max the other day? He the one buildin' your shelves?"

"Yeah, and a kitchen island."

"Oh, Max Gordon?" Daisy smirked, looking over at the newcomers.

"Yep, that's the one," I said behind heated cheeks, thinking I liked the nickname I'd given him in my head better. I checked the guys out, too, but they weren't nearly as gorgeous as Max.

She tilted her head away from José and wiggled her eyebrows knowingly. "Well, Max'll do a good job for you. I've heard he's really talented."

"Daisy!"

She laughed. "I meant he's a talented carpenter," she said to José, and to me, "He rebuilt my son Kevin's back deck and it's really nice. We have cookouts out there all summer and fall."

"That's nice," I said, smiling at the images she'd planted in my mind of a small-town barbeque, where everyone knew each other and everybody brought their favorite dishes to contribute to the meal. I imagined kids running around in the grass, playing tag, and old men falling asleep in wicker chairs in the sun, and their wives busying about, serving everyone and then cleaning up after.

"His partner is one of the town vets, so everybody stops by and they all bring their pets. It's a zoo, I tell ya."

"That sounds fun. Kind of what I imagined a small town would be like."

"Well, first get-together we have next year, you'll be the first person I call."

"Thank you. I'd love that."

"What can we get you today, miss Juni?" José asked.

"A sandwich. Do you make BLTs?"

"Sure do," he said. "You want that with avocado or without? I make a tasty aioli mayo. You'll love it."

"With," I said. "Is a BLT really a BLT without avocado?"

"My kinda girl," he said, and he winked and disappeared in the kitchen.

"Oh, you know, it's funny we met today," Daisy said, motioning to a chair at the counter. I sat, draping my purse strap on the back of the seat next to me. "I was just talking to someone about starting a book club after the holidays. Would you be interested in joining us? We were thinking about getting together twice a month. Romance books, mostly, but we might pick up a thriller or a mystery once in a while. I've asked my daughters-in-law and a couple friends and customers."

"I would love that. Really? But you don't even know me."

"Well, honey, what better way to get to know you, hm?" She patted my arm. "Coffee then?"

Chapter Six

Max

"Mornin', Mama. How's your arm?" I asked Friday on my lunch break when I pushed into her house with my hip 'cause my hands were full of her groceries. I needed to clear the snow from her driveway again, but it would have to wait till the next day before the job at Juneau's house.

"Oh, Maxie. You didn't have to bring me flowers. It ain't my birthday."

Leaning over the back of the couch, I kissed my mama's cheek and waited for her to take the bouquet I'd picked up for her. "It's just a bunch from the grocery store. Don't get yourself all in a tizzy."

She smiled and I chuckled. After my dad died, I was the only one left to carry on his tradition of a bouquet of gerbera daisies every year on the twenty-second. He'd done it since the day they met, December 22nd, forty years ago. They married in June, but they always celebrated that first day. "Happy anniversary, Mama."

"Thank you, baby. I'm not sure I'll ever get used to celebratin' our anniversary without your daddy." She clicked her tongue. "I'm doin' fine.

Doesn't even hurt anymore. See?" She lifted her bulky cast in the air and shook her arm a little.

We both missed my ol' man something awful, but Mama was a strong woman, and she was soldiering on. "Glad to hear it," I said, walking to the kitchen. "Oh, talked to Aubrey. I'm s'posed to tell you hi."

"How's she doin'? The boys givin' her trouble still?"

"I expect they always will, but everybody's fine."

Mama focused back on her stories on the TV while I put her groceries away. When I was finished, I filled a glass with water from the tap for myself and made her favorite spearmint tea, then sat in my dad's old armchair next to the couch to chat for a minute before I needed to head back to work. I only lived half a mile away, but with my job at the ranch and working side jobs on the weekends, sometimes we'd go a week or two without seeing each other. We talked on the phone and texted through the week, though, and I always peeked my head in when I stopped by to shovel her driveway or in the summer when I mowed her lawn.

I didn't really need the extra money I earned from my side jobs—Milson paid his cowboys well—but building things with my hands made me feel good. The creative outlet and the smell of wood and metal was my therapy.

"So, anything new?" she asked with just a little too much curiosity in her voice to be usual.

"Nothin' much," I said slowly, suspicion making the back of my neck itchy. I figured I knew where she was headed, so I tried to change the subject. "Today's my last day out at Milson's till after the new year. Oh, hey, I picked up that eggnog you like, and Jerry at the deli said he put some extra ham in the bag for you." I caught her eyes with mine and lifted a brow. "Deli meats for Christmas gifts? Mama, there somethin' you ain't tellin' me about you and Jerry the butcher?"

"Ach. Watch it, young man. You know your daddy was the love of my life. I ain't lookin' to replace him."

"I know, Mama. I was just jokin' with you."

"Well, that's alright then. And so what if an extra smile here or there makes Jerry happy. I can't help it if he gives me free deli." She smirked.

Shaking my head in mock disgust, I said, "Scandalous."

She shrugged, sipping her tea, and she blew on it. "So, there's nothin' you wanna tell me? Nothin' about, say, maybe a new woman you met?"

Rolling my eyes, I sighed. *Small towns.* "Now don't go gettin' your knickers in a twist. I took a job buildin' a kitchen island for a..." Who was Juni Moonlight? I couldn't decide how to describe her. I'd never met anyone like her. "Well, she's a young woman." I crossed my arms over my chest, then released them. "Not young, young, but you know, I dunno, around my age. Early thirties, maybe. Anyway, she's new to Wisper." I cleared my throat. "That's it. That's all the gossip you're gettin' from me."

"Oh, I already got plenty from José, and Carly called me. She said Buckey found you readin' some love book in the bunkhouse. What's that all about?"

"Mama, don't believe everything you hear. Don't y'all have anything better to do than talkin' about me? My life ain't that interestin'."

"So, you *didn't* meet a beautiful woman, the one you *didn't* take to breakfast at the diner? The one who definitely doesn't write risqué romance books?"

"Ughhh. I gotta go." I stood and walked over to grab Mama's reusable grocery bags off her kitchen counter to keep in my truck for next week.

"Uh huh. That's what I thought. Don't worry, I'll get it outta you yet."

"Yeah, I know you will," I said, shoving my arms in my coat.

When I opened the door to leave, pulling on my gloves, Mama called, "Stop by Susan Masterson's. She made me a chicken pot pie! All I gotta do's pop it in the oven, and that's three or four days' supper."

"Yeah, yeah. I'll drop it off after work."

"What was that?"

"Yes, ma'am," I said, and I turned to give her a smile and a nod.

"Thank you, Maxie. Love you, baby boy. Have a good day."

Baby boy. Like I was still five. "Love you too, Mama."

"Alright, whatcha think about this?" I asked when Juni walked into her kitchen the next Saturday holding a gigantic, rounded, "All I want for Christmas is to make a dent in my TBR pile" mug full of coffee. I smiled at that. I had no clue what a TBR pile was, but at least the mug was red, green, and Christmassy.

A purple pencil held her messy hair in a pile on top of her head, and she was mumbling to herself while she scrolled through her cell phone.

When I'd arrived to finish her kitchen island at seven, she let me in, said a few words, then ducked into her office, and I hadn't seen or heard from her till now. I wasn't sure if she had any idea it was Christmas Eve. She seemed to be in some kind of zone, she was still dressed in green and red Grinch-themed pajamas at ten in the morning, and the whole distracted-author thing was adorable.

"Huh?" She blinked and focused on me, like she'd forgotten I was even in her house.

"Finished your island. Like it? Just need to wait for the wood glue to dry, stain it, then attach the top. I've got some old drawer pulls we can use. I think you'll approve. They're 'eclectic.'"

"Oh." She stepped next to me and cocked her head to the side, sipping her coffee and thinking for a minute. A wisp of her hair came loose from the mess, falling down the back of her neck, caressing her skin like a lover. I couldn't take my eyes off of it. "I hate it."

"Wha—? Are you kiddin' me?" My eyes flicked to hers, and I glared at her and crossed my arms over my chest. "It looks exactly like the one you texted—"

She snorted. "Just joking." She laughed again but turned to face me, and she smiled that smile. The one I'd been in search of since I met her. "But seriously, I love it. It's beautiful. Thank you. I can't believe you built that with just your two hands, and so quickly."

I chuckled. "Well, alright then. You're welcome. Ain't much to it. You just need a plan first, so you know what size boards you need to cut. Then it's just about gettin' it done." Draping my dust rag over the side of the island, I said, "You wanna show me where you want those shelves installed in your bedroom? Since you're workin' in your office this mornin', I'll go ahead and get those started. The walnut color you chose is gonna look real good in there."

Turning, she left the kitchen and I followed. "Oh really? You like my design choices now?" She threw a smile over her shoulder, but I barely saw it 'cause I was focused on the sway of her ample hips and what 'just my two hands' could do to them.

When she stepped into her bedroom, the bright morning sun coming in her window illuminated her from head to toe, and it knocked the breath clean outta my chest, and I couldn't even see her face.

She set her mug on the bedside table and turned to me, looking at me quizzically. "What?"

I shook my head once. "Nothin'." After I cleared my throat, I said, "So, tell me again where you want your weird shelves."

She swatted my arm playfully. "They're not weird."

"Are too." I smiled, and then we were quiet.

We stood three feet apart, staring at each other for at least a minute, and then all hell broke loose.

She practically jumped the space between us, threw her arms around my neck, and fused our mouths together, and I froze. She tasted like silky coffee and sweet dreams, and after an eternity (okay, fine, it was probably more like three seconds), I gave in.

I was already hard—that was pretty much the case anytime I was near her—but in the moment, I thought I'd burst. She tilted her head, slipping her hot tongue in my mouth, and the velvet glide of that tongue over mine caused a short circuit in my thinking abilities.

It felt like my whole body was shaking with need. I lifted her with my hands gripping her hips, and she clung to me while I wrapped her legs around my ass and pressed myself hard into the heat between them.

She moaned and rubbed herself against me, and I nearly came in my jeans.

"Stop." *Fuck.* We had to stop.

"What? What's wrong?"

She pulled her head back, looking in my eyes with her stormy blue ones, and I almost couldn't speak. She was that beautiful. Her nose scrunched and her eyebrows dented down in confusion, and she dropped her legs.

I let go of her hips. "I'm sorry. I shouldn't have done that."

"You didn't do that. I did. What's the problem? You don't want—"

"No, oh, I do want it. It ain't that. It's just...you're a client."

"Seriously?"

"Yeah. I mean, that's unprofessional of me." I didn't want to be that guy. The guy who took advantage.

"Oh. Of course. I crossed a line. I'm sorry," she said, and she turned, grabbed her coffee, walked around me, and left the bedroom.

When she was in her office, the door thudded shut, and after about a minute, a text came through on my phone, and I pulled it from my back pocket.

It was from Juni. *"Just make it look like this pic if you can. I need to run some errands, so please lock up when you leave."*

A picture came through three seconds later of a wall covered haphazardly with floating wooden bookshelves. Various books, candles, and knickknacks filled the shelves, and they really did look good.

I heard her front door slam shut, so I peeked out the window to see her escaping to her car. She was still in her Grinch pajamas with her clunky snow boots on her feet, and she hopped in and backed out of her driveway too fast, almost backing into Mayor Covey's RAM when she hit the street. He honked and swerved, and Juni pumped her brakes. Her eyes met mine through her windshield, and she shook her head a little, then took a deep breath and left.

Ah, dammit. I'd embarrassed her.

Chapter Seven

"You did what?"

"You said 'climb that pole,' so I tried!" I whimpered, and Jenn laughed while I turned off the road into the All Animals Veterinary Clinic's parking lot and pulled into an empty parking spot. They were all empty. The animal clinic was closed. "Don't you dare laugh at me! I'm embarrassed enough as it is. He rejected me. He told me to stop."

"Did he say anything else?"

"Something about me being his client."

"He was just being professional. That doesn't mean he's not attracted to you."

"He flirts with me! That's the vibe I was getting. Why else would I attack him?" I groaned. "I can't go back there, Jenn. I can't go back to my own house. What am I supposed to say to him?" I dropped my head into my freezing hands because I hadn't given my car enough time to warm up, and I ran out of my house so fast that I didn't have a coat or gloves. "This is a disaster."

"It's not a disaster. Just go back and talk to him. If you were in another frame of mind, you'd be appreciative of the professional boundary he's trying to keep."

"I know. But he's all I think about. It's not normal. I've even stopped working on my new book to write a freaking cowboy romance. My editor's gonna kill me, but I can't help it. I can't get this cowboy out of my head!"

"Juneau Moonlight, drive back to your house right this minute and tell him that. Maybe you can date him after he's done with your projects."

"I am *not* telling him that, Jenn. Are you off your rocker? He'll think I'm a stalker. We barely know each other." Taking a deep breath, trying to calm my racing pulse, I looked down at myself. "I'm still wearing pajamas! The most embarrassing moment of my life just happened while I was wearing freaking Grinch pajamas. I'm stuck. I'm stuck in my car till he leaves my house. I can't go anywhere dressed like this. Oh my God."

"Please, have you seen what people wear to Walmart? Grinch pajamas are practically couture compared to some of those outfits. At least they aren't see-through, skin-colored leggings. You just have to wear them with confidence. You can pull it off."

"Jenn," I said, almost begging her, "I need you to be serious right now and help me think about what to do. I can't go home, and I can't go out in public."

"Okay, do you know anyone who lives around there? Could you maybe just casually stop by for a visit? Oh, well, it's December 24th, so that's probably a no-go."

"It is? How did I not know that? And why is Max working on Christmas Eve? He didn't say anything." I laughed at my patheticness and the ridiculous situation I'd brought on myself, then jumped when someone knocked on my window. "Shit!"

Jenn recognized the startled sound of my voice. "Juni? What's wrong?"

"I'm okay. There's a female Sheriff's deputy standing next to my car looking at me. I'll call you back." I hung up with Jenn and rolled down my window. "Hi."

"It's Christmas Eve. The clinic ain't open today except for emergencies," she said while she looked in my back window. Her stringy white-blond hair was falling out of the nub of a ponytail she had it in beneath her brown hat. "Where's your pet?"

"Oh, sorry. No, I don't need a vet. I was on my phone, so I pulled over."

"Oh. Everything okay? What's your name? You new around here?"

"Yes. I moved here a few weeks ago. I'm Juneau. Juneau Moonlight." Extending my hand out the window, I smiled, and she shook it.

"Oh yeah, I've heard all about you. I'm Deputy Abey Lee. You're that writer, huh? You write those sexy stories?"

"Uh, yep." I chuckled nervously. Great. I was already infamous in Wisper. Every time I met someone new, they were going to bring it up. I just knew it.

"You ever write LGBTQ love stories?"

"Oh, no, I haven't written any, but I know a few authors who have. It's a really popular genre."

"Hm. I'll have to look into that. Alright, well, don't linger here too long, else somebody might think you're casin' the clinic."

I groaned. "I don't have anywhere to go."

"Whatcha mean? Don't you have a house over on Baker?"

"Yeah—wait. How do you know that?"

"This is Wisper, Ms. Moonlight." She shrugged. "Everybody knows everybody's business. In fact, I kinda pride myself on knowin' it. Helps on the job." She flicked the brim of her hat.

"Right. Well, I, um, I'm kind of in a bit of a sticky situation right now with my, um...my handyman? Max Gorg— I mean, Max Gordon. I can't go home. But I ran out of my house in my pajamas, so I can't go anywhere else either."

She nodded, then walked around to my front passenger-side door, opened it, and slid into the seat. When she shut the door, she said, "G'head. Tell Officer Abey *all* about it."

I assumed she just wanted the gossip, but I couldn't stop the slew of embarrassing words from falling out of my mouth.

When I finished and was even more embarrassed for spilling my life story to Officer Lee, she said, "Phew. That's a conundrum, for sure. But you know, Max Gorgeous"—she winked and I winced—"is a good guy.

He was just bein' respectful. People gotta be careful about those kinds of situations in this day and age. You can't fault him for that."

"You're absolutely right, but it doesn't stop me from being mortified."

"You could fire him and then kiss him again."

Surprised at her train of thought, I laughed. "Huh, I hadn't thought of that. But I'm not sure he'd appreciate being fired."

"You're probably right about that. Men can be pretty prideful." She took a deep breath and opened the car door. "Okay then, my advice is to swallow your own pride and go talk to Max. Whatcha got to lose, besides some bookshelves?"

"Right."

"See ya later. Nice to meet you and all that."

I waved limply when she slammed my door shut, and she took off in her SUV.

Weird. But she wasn't wrong.

What did I have to lose?

Half an hour later, after two failed attempts at meditation to relax my seriously overactive brain, I snuck home. I felt like a bank robber breaking back into the bank she just robbed. But when I pulled into my driveway, Max's truck was gone.

He hadn't texted back when I sent the bookshelf picture, and when I looked in my bedroom, his supplies were still lined up along my wall, the shelves themselves stacked in four rows in the corner. Oh man, this didn't look good. Maybe he wouldn't come back.

Maybe he would quit.

Oh no. *Juni, you freaking jerk.* Now, not only had I accosted a perfect stranger, but I'd cost him his income. Well, I'd just pay him the full amount even though he hadn't finished the job. It was my fault. But wait, would that offend him? Officer Lee was right that some men could be really proud, and insulting him was the last thing I wanted to do.

But his work was beautiful, and he'd already spent hours on my island and shelves. I could definitely live without a coffee mug rack. And I could hire someone else to fix my shower. Someone older. Someone *not* sexy. A seventy-year-old guy with slouchy work pants and his hairy ass crack showing.

Okay, so then, I wouldn't pay Max anything other than what I owed for the hours he'd already worked, but I'd give him a good tip.

Except, how much was "good"?

Juni, you neurotic butthead. Get over yourself. You're an adult.

I tried to work for the rest of the day, my mind going round and round in circles about the tip—or should I not tip him? *Ughhh.*

I'd only cried once about being alone on Christmas, which I considered a win since every time I walked past my living room, Max's lights twinkled through my windows, and now it reminded me of all the Christmases I'd spent wishing for someone to share it with. Jenn had called back twice already to try to cheer me up, so I was finally laughing at her stupid antics and jokes when my doorbell rang.

My heart fell into my road-salt-crusted suede boots when I realized it was probably Max. Who else did I know in Wisper, unless it was carolers?

Stiffening my spine and inhaling a deep breath, I walked to the door, blew that breath out steadily, and opened it. Oh, it was snowing, and the snow fell in dreamy, lazy, fat flakes, landing on the layer of snow already covering my small front yard.

"Merry Christmas, Juni," Daisy said. She was smiling and holding something rectangular out in front of her, wrapped in a thin white-and-red striped towel. "José makes fabulous fruitcake every year for Christmas. It's actually more of a fruit and nut rum cake-slash-bread thing, but it's delicious. You're not allergic to walnuts, are you?"

"Uh, no, I like walnuts. Merry Christmas to you too."

"Oh, good. Here." She held the bread out to me, and I took it from her hands.

"Would you like to come in?" My laughing mood had disappeared, and the loneliness came back with a vengeance. It was so nice of her to think of me, but it made me miss my mom and dad, even if they were the worst about Christmas. They insisted that Christmas was just a capitalistic holiday, made worse every year by the advertisements and movies that came earlier and earlier every season. They weren't religious, but I never believed you needed to be devout to celebrate.

The holidays were about family and community and hope. And that was something to believe in and act upon no matter your religion or if you believed in God or not.

"Sure. I can only stay for a minute. I need to finish my deliveries before we head over to my sons' ranch. I have Christmas grandbabies to snuggle."

"Oh, that sounds really great," I said, and I stepped back and fell onto my couch. I tried so hard not to let them, but a few tears leaked out of my eyes.

"Juni, what's wrong?" Daisy sat next to me carefully, concern and kindness all over her face. It was lined and weathered a bit, like she'd lived a full life, and through my melancholy, I wondered what her story was. The curse of a fiction writer—I was always on the hunt for inspiration.

"It's nothing. I'm sorry. I'm a mess." I tried to smile, but she saw right through me.

"Honey, what's wrong? C'mon. Tell me."

She was such a mom, and I wanted to hug her and tell her everything. This was the second time in one day—on Christmas Eve, no less—that a virtual stranger had taken the time to listen to my problems. Wisper really was the small town of my dreams, and I was so grateful for the inclusion, but I didn't want to take her away from her family on the biggest holiday of the year.

"I'm fine." I wiped the tears away with my sleeve. "I'm just feeling a little... You know. The holidays can be hard sometimes." Sitting straight, I patted her hand on my knee. "Really, I'm okay. Thank you for thinking of me. I can't wait to try the fruitcake."

She studied my face for a few seconds. "You're alone for the holidays, aren't you?"

"Yes, but I'll be fine. I have plenty of work to keep me busy. Please, don't worry about me."

"Work? No." She clicked her tongue. "Why don't you come out to the ranch tonight? There'll be plenty of food and lots of neighbors to meet."

"Oh, thank you, but I couldn't intrude like that. That's your family."

"It is my family, but it's also a bunch of other people too. There are a lot of misfits here in Wisper. People whose families have passed, people who never really had a family, and we all kind of make up a big, new family. You're more than welcome, and I'd love to introduce you to my sons and their families. They're a funky bunch. I bet you'll fit right in. Plus, some of the book club ladies will be there."

"Really?"

"Really. I insist."

"Okay, I'll think about it. Thank you."

She nodded and stood. "Good. And you know, Max'll be there."

"Oh?" I squeaked. "Maybe it's better if I just stay home then. You know, he's my employee..."

"Don't be ridiculous. He's your handyman, not your cutthroat corporate underling. He's bringin' his mama. It's not like it's a set up or somethin' like that."

"Oh, okay." But I wasn't sure.

She dipped her head to catch my eye when I looked at the floor. "You know he likes you, right? He's not known for an overabundance of conversational skills, but José says it seems like he has no trouble talkin' to you." She chuckled. "I'll see you tonight. It's Cade Ranch on Route 20. Just go south till you see a ridiculous amount of multi-colored Christmas lights strung over a big wrought-iron sign. About 15 miles south of town. Six tonight."

"Thank you, Daisy," I said when she opened the front door and stepped onto the porch.

"Merry Christmas, sweetie," she said, and she winked and smiled when Max appeared at the bottom of my porch steps. "See? Told ya. Merry Christmas, Max. We'll see you and your mama tonight at Cade Ranch, right?"

"Yes, ma'am," he told her. "Merry Christmas."

"Bye, kids," Daisy said, and she disappeared. Well, disappeared from my view anyway, because all I could see was Max.

Chapter Eight

Max

I stood in front of Juni in her doorway, holding bags from the grocery store and more from a big supercenter store. "May I come in? I've got some stuff to drop off."

"Um, sure." She stepped back, allowing me to pass, giggling a little. She seemed nervous. "No cowboy hat?"

"No," I said, transferring all my bags to one hand so I could take my beanie off. "It's freezin' out there. You want my ears to fall off?"

"No. Of course not." She laughed incredulously at my question and stepped behind me to shut the door. "Um, Max. I'm sorry about—"

Whirling around, I dropped my bags to the floor. "I quit."

"Huh?" She turned to face me, eyes wide.

"First off, Merry Christmas. I figured you'd forgotten this mornin'. You seemed like you were really into whatever you were workin' on. Second, I brought you some things." I nodded down to my bags. "Plus, there's a jug of my buddy Buckey's homemade mulled wine gettin' cold next to your fancy coffee mug board on your porch. And third, I quit."

"Um, okay. I know I've made this uncomfortable between us. I didn't mean to—"

I took a step toward her. We were a foot apart, and I smelled her shampoo. She smelled like Christmas oranges, and it was intoxicating.

"I didn't mean to offend you," she whispered, smiling with uncertainty in her eyes. They were a little more gray than blue today.

Man, I swore my knees were about to buckle. She was the most beautiful woman in the world when her lips tipped up like that.

I was fixing to take a huge risk. We barely knew each other, but I was dying to know more about her, and what was the alternative? Walking away?

No. I wasn't doing that. I wanted her too much.

"I quit 'cause if workin' for you means I can't kiss you, then I don't want the job. Now, look here. I know I'm leavin' you high and dry, but I might know a guy who can finish your shelves. He'll even work for free in his spare time." I winked, hoping she was catching on. "Whatcha think about that?"

"Really?"

I cocked my head a little, smirking at her. "You know, for a writer, your conversational vocabulary's pretty lackin'."

"What do you mean?" The confusion on her face made me think she wasn't sure if she should be offended or not. She was still trying to figure me out.

"I mean tell me what you think. Tell me to kiss your ass and blow smoke. Tell me somethin'. Tell me how you feel. I know we don't know each other real well, but there's somethin' here, right? I mean, it's not just me?" It didn't escape my attention that I was the one droning on about feelings.

I was practically gazing into her eyes. I couldn't seem to help myself. It was hard waiting for her to respond, but I had nothing to lose and everything to gain. Maybe this amazing woman in front of me was the one I'd been waiting for my whole life.

If I didn't take the chance now, I might never get another one.

I raised my eyebrows. "Well?"

She squared her shoulders, took a deep breath, and planted her feet, and I watched as confidence spread throughout her whole body. "I think if you hadn't quit, I would've fired you. I want to kiss you too, and other things. Like, right now."

"Yeah?"

"Oh yeah."

Growling like a damn grizzly, I closed the distance between us, quick as I could, lifted her into my arms, and carried her to her bedroom. Her hands were almost frantic. They were all over me, in my hair, clawing and clutching my arms and shoulders while I kissed her like I'd never kissed anybody before.

My mouth was hot on hers, my tongue demanding her attention. She gave it, moaning, and her eyes were backlit with fire when I tossed her on the bed, dropped my coat to the floor, and tore my T-shirt over my head. I touched my fingers to my fly, ready to rip right out of my jeans too.

I lifted a brow in question.

"Yes," she said. "Now."

We were both breathless, both trying hard to control the need we'd felt since the first day we'd met.

"Wait. What's in the bags?"

"Oh." Thank the baby Jesus. I was worried she'd stop our momentum. "Just some Christmas decorations for your house and some champagne for New Year's."

"You bought me Christmas decorations?"

"I did. But don't you go thinkin' it's 'cause I like you or somethin'. I have a reputation to uphold. What would the neighbors say if my girlfriend's house was the only dark one on Christmas?"

"But you already put lights up outside."

"Well, yeah, but you need lights in your windows, and I brought a blow-up reindeer for your front lawn." Unbuttoning my jeans, I pushed them down to my hips, wrapping my hand around my hard-as-wood cock. I was so hard, it hurt.

Her eyes fell from my face to that hand, and she was having a hard time looking away. "Um, thank you, I think."

"You're welcome. You done interrogatin' me now?"

She sat up, her eyes finally meeting mine. "Interrogating you? Excuse me, I was just—"

Leaning down, I stopped her lips with mine. "Shush."

She grabbed my belt loop and pulled, and I twisted and fell to the bed on my back.

"Did you just shush me?" she demanded, climbing over me. Her legs straddled my hips, and I lifted them up, seeking any friction I could get. She moaned when I pressed my hard body to hers.

But she was still dressed in her Grinch pajamas pants, so I rolled her onto her back, lifted up onto my knees, and dragged those ridiculous things down her legs.

"Oh, Max. Hurry."

And with that, all the teasing was gone between us. Removing her T-shirt, she bit her lip, looking at me from beneath her dark eyelashes, and her auburn hair fell down all around her face. It was messy and wild, and the lust in her eyes was enough to do me in. I practically jumped out of my jeans and work boots, kicking them free of my feet, and one hit the wall, denting it.

"I'll fix that."

"Oh, God, I don't care," she said when I covered her body with mine.

I wanted all of her in my hands, and I touched every single inch of her body I could reach, and her breaths turned to quiet gasps the closer I got to where she wanted me, where she was already pumping her hips against me, begging for me.

"Max."

"Slow down, Juneau," I said, lifting up. "You keep goin' like that and this ain't gonna last very long."

"I don't care."

"I do," I said, locking my eyes on hers while I slid down her body. Lowering myself to my knees on the floor at the end of the bed, I gripped her thighs and pulled her closer to me, then spread them apart.

My mouth was inches from what I wanted, and I licked my lips. She smelled so damn good, and I could barely wait to taste her.

She yelped, then moaned low in her chest when my tongue lapped a slow path between her wet lips. She was soaked in need, and it was ambrosia in my mouth.

I got busy then, working her up till she was pulling my hair too hard for me to concentrate on the task at hand. Then I'd bring her back down, sliding a finger, then two inside her. I was slow and gentle, not using enough pressure to make her come, but enough to make her wetter, enough to make her writhe and beg me.

Finally, she lifted up on her elbows. "Please, Max. I can't take it anymore. Come inside me."

"Not yet. Watchin' you lost in pleasure is the sexiest damn thing I've ever seen. I *need* to see you come."

Her eyes grew darker, and she dipped her chin, watching and waiting.

With my fingers still inside her, I dipped down and sucked my thumb in my mouth, wetting it with saliva, and I pressed it to her clit, making fast circles while I slid my fingers in and out, faster and faster, till she fell back to the bed with a husky groan.

Her face was flushed, and she clamped her eyes closed, reaching for the bedsheets for something to hold onto while she fucked my hand. I was right—there was nothing more beautiful in the world than this woman, ready to come.

"Come, Juni. Please. Come on my fingers so you're wet and warm when I'm inside you."

"Oh my God. You really did read my book, didn't you?"

She was right there, her inner muscles trying to squeeze my fingers between them.

"Yes, ma'am, I did, and I've been turned on ever since." She moaned, thrusting harder. "That's it, Juni. Lemme see you. Open your eyes."

When she did, I leaned back down, and not looking away, I licked and flicked her clit with the tip of my tongue, still pushing my fingers in and out. I sucked it between my teeth, and her whole body arched up off the bed when she came. She cried out and reached with her hands for my face.

I let her pull me up, and she attacked my mouth, shoving her tongue inside when she kissed me. Through heaving breaths, she commanded, "Inside me. Now, Max."

"Yes, ma'am," I said again 'cause I knew it drove her nuts, and I obliged.

It might've been a little presumptuous, but I was glad just then for remembering to bring a condom. Grabbing it from her bedside table, I brought it up to my mouth and ripped the packet open with my teeth, and she took the condom and reached between us.

Breath rushed from my body when she rolled it on me, and I buried my head in her neck, licking and kissing her warm, soft skin.

I meant to say her name when I pushed inside her, but all that came out was "J... J..." and a lot of heavy breaths.

"No dirty words now?" she breathed in my ear.

"Juni, you feel so good. I can't think to talk."

She moaned, and I got busy.

I was slow at first, making sure we fit together and that it felt good for her, but oh, it did. Her eyes rolled back in her head, and she licked her bottom lip slow, like she was savoring the taste of herself I'd put there with my mouth.

It was the single most sexy action a mouth had ever made, and I needed to taste it too.

"Gimme your mouth, Juneau."

Her eyes flicked open, and pure sex spilled out when she licked those lips again while she dug her nails into my ass cheeks, pushing me harder inside her.

I thought about her books, and I wanted to be her hero. Maybe she'd write about me if I made her feel good enough. "Tell me what you want. Tell me like you say it in your books."

"I-I...can't."

"Why not?" I thrusted hard. Just once, but it was enough to make her want it again. She wrapped her legs around my ass, pressing with her heels, trying to make me fuck her harder.

"It's not real. I-I've never experienced anything like in my books."

"Make it real, Juni. Tell me what you want." Leaning down, I made sure to touch every inch of her full breast with my tongue, and I flicked her nipple, then sucked it in my mouth and tugged. Her breast jerked and bounced beneath my lips when I rolled my hips again, this time not stopping. Every push forward took me deeper inside her, and every snap back slid me out, and the motion almost made me dizzy. It was so damn good. "Make me want it too."

She was panting hard now, shaking her head on the pillow.

"Tell me."

"I want you to take me like you can't get enough of me. Like I'm the most beautiful woman you've ever seen, and you're addicted to me. I want it fast and hard, and I want your mouth on mine when I come again. Make me come again, Max. Please? Do it because I'm worth it."

"Oh, Juni, you are, and I'm gonna worship you."

I flipped us, settling on my back beneath her while I pushed her down on my cock, and when her body was wrapped firmly around me again, she gasped in a breath. Her head fell back and her eyes fell shut when I wrapped my hands around her waist, pushing her up and down.

When I smeared her cum on her clit with my finger, rubbing fast circles around it again, she whimpered, and I throbbed inside her.

"I want these in my mouth," I said, cupping her breast in my hand, and it looked small there.

"Yeah," she breathed. "Please?"

Sitting up, we were face to face. I rubbed harder, and her body gripped mine like a vice while she rode me. My tongue was everywhere, like she was candy. She tasted so good, and I bucked up into her like it was my mission.

"Yes!" She dug her nails in my thighs behind her, and the motion, with her arms behind her, popped her breast further in my mouth. I bit down gently with her nipple between my front teeth, and she called out, and I was done.

A strangled sound escaped my throat when I came, eyes wide open, watching her find ecstasy on my body.

Wrapping my arms around her back and threading my fingers in her messy red hair, I punched up inside her one more time as she looked down at me, and I kissed and worshipped that woman with my cock and my eyes and my mouth, just like I'd promised.

When we were spent, breathing hard side by side on the bed, her leg thrown over both of mine, she sat straight up and turned to me.

"Did you say you made me a coffee mug display, and did you call me your girlfriend earlier?"

"Oh yeah, will you go on a date with me?" I smiled, wrapping my hand around her waist.

"Y-yes...?"

"Was that a question or an answer?"

"Yes," she said when she lay back down, her fingers skimming circles over my stomach. "I'd very much like to go on a date with you." Her hair tickled the side of my face, but I didn't swipe it away. I liked feeling the waves lap at my skin.

"Good, then technically, you're my girlfriend. How 'bout tonight?"

"Tonight?"

"I figure, since we already slept together—three times in two hours, which is definitely a record for me, by the way—it ain't too soon."

She laughed and the sound was breathy and sexy.

"Good." I nodded. "Then we got a party to go to tonight."

I lifted my phone from her bedside table, searching for my favorite Christmas song. When I found the one I wanted, I hit play, and music filled the room while she relaxed back against my side, kissing my arms and chest. I had a feeling we'd be late for our party.

"Is that Dolly Parton?"

"Yep. You in the country now, girl."

"I like it. Speaking of country—guess what I've been working on?"

Rolling my head to study her, I guessed, "A new book?"

She nodded, and I tucked a strand of her hair that had fallen loose behind her ear.

"It's a...a cowboy romance."

"Oh, really now?" I chuckled and couldn't stop my smile. "Wonder where you came up with that idea." *Yes!* My pride pumped his fist in the air, and I swore I was hard again.

"You know where." She blushed, but she said, "And my cowboy talks dirtier than Brianna's bad boy."

"I would like to officially rescind my 'unrealistic' comment. You brought it outta me, and there is nothin' unrealistic about you, Juneau Moonlight. Not one thing a'tall."

"That's what I thought." She laughed, and her hand ran a lazy trail down my abdomen, stopping just shy of the best Christmas present I'd ever get.

"Merry Christmas, Juni," I whispered into her mouth when she leaned over and kissed me deep.

"Merry Christmas, Max Gorgeous. I think I'm gonna like it here."

THE END

Acknowledgments

CONTRIBUTING AUTHORS

Piper Lee Burns
M. K. Condry
K. L. Cottrell
Elle Fielding
Lili Grouse
Barbara Kellyn
Leila Love
Lisa M. Miller
Laura Mowery
Cindi Page
Nicole Sharp
Greta Rose West

COVER DESIGN

Tallulah Habib with input from everyone.

TITLE & BLURB COPY

Barbara Kellyn

PROOF READING

J. Grutzner

K. L. Cottrell

SOCIAL MEDIA GRAPHICS & GENERAL AWESOMENESS

Lili Grouse

MARKETING

All authors, but special mention to Greta Rose West for her invaluable input.

INSIDE JOKE

Piper Lee Burns